Praise for *Piece of My Heart*

"Robinson so perfectly recreates the '60s world of long-haired freaks and hippies, psychedelic drugs and mind-blowing rock 'n' roll.... Once again, Robinson here elevates the crime novel to its highest form."   — *Calgary Herald*

"MASTERFUL.... Robinson has penned a twisting, well-crafted story of two crimes that is both suspenseful and satisfying."
                — *Edmonton Journal*

"A FASCINATING and atmospheric exploration of the way the past intrudes on the present, *Piece of My Heart* is rather BRILLIANT."   — *Globe and Mail*

"Robinson has for too long, and unfairly, been in the shadow of Ian Rankin; perhaps *Piece of My Heart*, the latest in the Chief Inspector Banks series, will give him the status he deserves, near, perhaps even at the top of, the British crime writers' league."   — *Times* (London)

"*Piece of My Heart* is Robinson at his best.... It's clever, very well written, and A KILLER OF A BOOK."
                — *Hamilton Spectator*

"If Elmore Leonard is the 'Dickens of Detroit,' ... then Peter Robinson is, undeniably, the 'Tennyson of Toronto.' Who else but this Canadian crime writer can, like a literary shaman, pull tragedy from a bag and transform it into a good thing – with haunting, REMARKABLE murder stories as complex as they are redemptive, as profound as poetic?"   — *Ottawa Citizen*

Piece of My Heart

OTHER INSPECTOR BANKS NOVELS
BY PETER ROBINSON

ALSO BY PETER ROBINSON

PETER ROBINSON

Piece of My Heart

McCLELLAND & STEWART

Library and Archives Canada Cataloguing in Publication

Robinson, Peter, 1950-
Piece of my heart : an Inspector Banks novel / Peter Robinson.

ISBN 978-0-7710-7615-2

I. Title.

PS8585.035176P52 2007   c813'.54   c2006-904331-0

We acknowledge the financial support of the Government of
Canada through the Book Publishing Industry Development
Program and that of the Government of Ontario through the
Ontario Media Development Corporation's Ontario Book
Initiative. We further acknowledge the support of the Canada
Council for the Arts and the Ontario Arts Council for our
publishing program.

Typeset in Minion by M&S, Toronto
Printed and bound in Canada

McClelland & Stewart Ltd.
75 Sherbourne Street
Toronto, Ontario
M5A 2P9
www.mcclelland.com

3 4 5   11 10 09 08 07

For Sheila

Imagination abandoned by reason produces impossible monsters; united with it, she is the mother of the arts and the source of its marvels.

— Francisco Goya, 1799

Sooner murder an infant in its cradle than nurse unacted desires.

— William Blake, *The Marriage of Heaven and Hell*, 1790–1793

1

Monday, September 8, 1969

To an observer looking down from the peak of Brimleigh Beacon early that Monday morning, the scene below might have resembled the aftermath of a battle. It had rained briefly during the night, and the pale sun coaxed tendrils of mist from the damp earth. They swirled over fields dotted with motionless shapes, mingling here and there with the darker smoke of smouldering embers. Human scavengers picked their way through the carnage as if collecting discarded weapons, occasionally bending to extract an object of value from a dead man's pocket. Others appeared to be shovelling soil or quicklime into large open graves. The light wind carried a whiff of rotting flesh.

And over the whole scene a terrible stillness reigned.

But to Dave Sampson, down on the field, there had been no battle, only a peaceful gathering, and Dave had the worm's-eye view. It was just after eight in the morning, and he had been up half the night along with everyone else, listening to Pink Floyd, Fleetwood Mac and Led Zeppelin. Now, the crowd had gone home, and he was moving among the motionless shapes, litter left behind by the vanished hordes, helping to clean up after the very first Brimleigh Festival. Here he was, bent over, back aching like hell, eyes burning with tiredness, plodding across the muddy field picking up rubbish. The eerie sounds of Jimmy Page playing his electric guitar with a violin bow still echoed in his mind as he shoved cellophane wrappers and half-eaten Mars bars into his plastic bag.

Ants and beetles crawled over the remains of sandwiches and half-empty tins of cold baked beans. Flies buzzed around the feces and wasps hovered about the necks of empty pop bottles. More than once, Dave had to manoeuvre sharply to avoid being stung. He couldn't believe some of the stuff people left behind. Food wrappers, soggy newspapers and magazines, used Durex, tampons, cigarette ends, knickers, empty beer cans and roaches you'd expect, but what on earth had the person who left the Underwood typewriter been thinking of? Or the wooden crutch? Had a cripple, suddenly healed by the music, run off and left it behind?

There were other things, too, things best avoided. The makeshift toilets set over the open cesspit had been uninviting, as well as few and far between, and the queues had been long, encouraging more than one desperate person to find a quiet spot elsewhere in the field. Dave glanced towards the craters and felt glad that he wasn't one of the volunteers assigned to fill them up with earth.

In an otherwise isolated spot at the southern edge of the field, where the land rose gently towards the fringes of Brimleigh Woods, Dave noticed an abandoned sleeping bag. The closer he got, the more it looked to be occupied. Had someone passed out or simply gone to sleep? More likely, Dave thought, it was drugs. All night the medical tent had been open to people suffering hallucinations from bad acid, and there had been enough Mandrax and opiated hash around to knock out an army.

Dave prodded the bag with his foot. It felt soft and heavy. He prodded it again, harder this time. Still nothing. It definitely *felt* as if someone were inside. Finally, he bent and pulled the zip, and when he saw what was there, he wished he hadn't.

Detective Inspector Stanley Chadwick was at his desk in Brotherton House before eight o'clock Monday morning, as usual, with every intention of finishing off the paperwork that had piled up during his two weeks' annual leave at the end of August. The caravan at Primrose Valley, with Janet and Yvonne, had made a nice haven for a while, but Yvonne was obviously restless, as only a sixteen-year-old on holiday with her parents can be, and crime didn't stop while he was away from Leeds. Nor, apparently, did the paperwork.

It had been a good weekend. Yorkshire beat Derbyshire in the Gillette Cup Final, and if Leeds United, coming off a season as league champions, hadn't managed to beat Manchester United at home, at least they had come out of it with a 2–2 draw, and Billy Bremner had scored.

The only blot on the landscape was that Yvonne had stayed out most of the night on Sunday, and it wasn't the first time. Chadwick had lain awake until he heard her come in at about half past six, and by then it was time for him to get up and get ready for work. Yvonne had gone straight to her room and closed her door, so he had put off the inevitable confrontation until later, and now it was gnawing at him. He didn't know what was happening to his daughter, what she was up to, but whatever it was, it frightened him. It seemed that the younger generation had been getting stranger and stranger over the past few years, more out of control, and Chadwick seemed unable to find any point of connection with them anymore. Most of them seemed like members of another species to him now. Especially his own daughter.

Chadwick tried to shake off his worries about Yvonne and glanced over the crime sheets: trouble with squatters in a Leeds city-centre office building; a big drugs bust in Chapeltown; an assault on a woman with a stone in a sock in Bradford. Manningham Lane, he noticed, and everyone knew what kind of women you found on Manningham Lane. Still, poor cow, nobody deserved to be hit with a stone in a sock. Just over the county border, in the North Riding, the Brimleigh Festival had gone off peacefully enough, with only a few arrests for drunkenness and drug dealing – only to be expected at such an event – and a bit of bother with some skinheads at one of the fences.

At about half past nine, Chadwick reached for the next file, and he had just opened it when Karen popped her head around his door and told him Detective Chief Superintendent McCullen wanted to see him. Chadwick put the folder back on the pile. If McCullen wanted to see him, it had to be something pretty big. Whatever it was, it was bound to be a lot more interesting than paperwork.

McCullen sat in his spacious office puffing on his pipe and enjoying the panoramic view. Brotherton House perched at the western edge of the city centre, adjacent to the university and Leeds General Infirmary buildings, and it looked out west over the new Inner Ringroad towards Park Lane College. All the old mills and factories in the area, blackened by a century or more of soot, had been demolished over the last two or three years, and it seemed that a whole new city was rising from the ruins of its Victorian past: the International Swimming Pool, Leeds Playhouse, Leeds Polytechnic, the Yorkshire Post

Building. Cranes criss-crossed on the horizon and the sound of pneumatic drills filled the air. Was it just Chadwick's imagination, or was there a building site no matter where you looked in the city these days?

He wasn't sure that the future was better than the past it was replacing any more than he was sure the emerging world order was better than the old one. There seemed a monotonous sterility to many of the new buildings, concrete and glass tower blocks for the most part, along with terraces of red-brick council houses. Their Victorian predecessors, like Benjamin Gott's Bean Ing Mills, might have looked a bit more grimy and shabby, but at least they had character. Or perhaps, Chadwick thought, he was just becoming an old fogey about architecture, the same way he was about young people. And at forty-eight, he was too young for that. He made a mental note to try to be more tolerant of hippies and architects.

"Stan, sit down," said McCullen, gesturing to the seat opposite his desk. He was a hard, compact man, one of the old school, and fast nearing retirement. Grey hair in a severe crew cut, sharp, square features, an intimidating gleam in his narrowed eyes. People said he had no sense of humour, but Chadwick thought it was just so dark and buried so deep that nobody could recognize it, or wanted to find it. McCullen had served as a commando during the war, and Chadwick had seen more than enough active duty himself. He liked to think it created a bond between them, something in common that they never spoke about. They also shared a Scottish background. Chadwick's mother was a Scot, and his father had worked in the Clydebank shipyards. Chadwick had grown up in Glasgow, drifting down to Yorkshire only after the war.

Chadwick sat.

"I won't beat about the bush," McCullen began, knocking his pipe on the heavy glass ashtray, "but there's been a body discovered at Brimleigh Glen, the big field where they held the festival this weekend. I don't have many details yet. The report has just this minute come in. All we know is that the victim is a young woman."

"Oh," said Chadwick, aware of that cold, sinking feeling deep in his belly. "I thought Brimleigh was the North Riding?"

McCullen refilled his pipe. "Strictly speaking, it is," he said finally, releasing clouds of aromatic blue smoke. "Just over the border. But they're country coppers. They don't get many murders, just a bit of sheep-shagging now and then. They've certainly got no one capable of handling an investigation of this magnitude, given how many people must have been attending that festival, and they're asking for our help. I thought, perhaps, with your recent successes . . ."

"The locals still won't like it," Chadwick said. "Perhaps it's not as bad as having Scotland Yard tramping all over your provincial toes, but –"

"It's already cleared," said McCullen, turning his gaze back to the window. "There's a local detective sergeant, name of Keith Enderby. You'll be working with him. He's already at the scene." McCullen glanced at his wristwatch. "Better get out there, Stan. DC Bradley's waiting with the car. The doc'll be there soon wanting to get the body back to the mortuary for the post-mortem."

Chadwick knew when he was being dismissed. Solve two murders so far this year and you get lumbered with a case like this. Bloody hippies. Paperwork suddenly didn't look so bad, after all. *Tolerance*, he told himself. He stood up and headed for the door.

There was no easy access to the body in the field, not without getting his shoes muddy. Chadwick cursed under his breath as he saw his lovingly polished black brogues and the bottoms of his suit trousers daubed with brown mud. If he'd been a rural copper, he'd have kept a pair of wellies in the boot of his car, but you don't expect mud when you're used to working the streets of Leeds. If anything, DC Bradley complained even more.

Brimleigh Glen looked like a vast tip. A natural amphitheatre cupped between low hills to the east and north and Brimleigh Woods to the west and south, it was a popular spot for picnics and brass band concerts in summer. Not this weekend, though. A stage had been erected at the western end of the field, abutting the woods, and the audience had sprawled as far back as the hillsides on the eastern and northern sides, to a distance where, Chadwick guessed, nobody would have been able to see very much at all except little dots.

The small knot of people surrounding the body stood at the southern edge of the field, about a hundred yards back from the stage, near the edge of the woods. When Chadwick and Bradley arrived, a man with long, greasy hair, bell-bottomed jeans and an Afghan waistcoat turned and said with far more aggression than Chadwick would have expected of someone who was supposed to embrace peace and love, "Who the fuck are you?"

Chadwick feigned a surprised expression and looked around, then pointed his thumb at his own chest. "Who, me?"

"Yes, you."

A clearly embarrassed young man hurried over to them. "Er . . . I think that's probably the detective inspector from Leeds. Am I right, sir?"

Chadwick nodded.

"How d'you do, sir? I'm Detective Sergeant Enderby, North Yorkshire Constabulary. This is Rick Hayes, the festival promoter."

"You must have been up all night," said Chadwick. "I'd have thought you'd be long tucked up in bed by now."

"There's still a lot to see to," Hayes said, gesturing behind him. "That scaffolding, for a start. It's rented and it all has to be accounted for. I'm sorry, by the way." He glanced in the direction of the sleeping bag. "This has all been very upsetting."

"I'm sure," said Chadwick, making his way forward. There were four people besides himself and DC Bradley at the scene, only one of them a uniformed policeman, and most of them were standing far too close to the body. They were also very casually dressed. Even DS Enderby's hair, Chadwick noticed, was dangerously close to touching the collar of his jacket, and his sideboards needed trimming. His black winkle-pickers looked as if they had been dirty even before he crossed the field. "Were you the first officer to arrive at the scene?" Chadwick asked the young police constable, trying to move people back and clear a little space around the sleeping bag.

"Yes, sir. PC Jacobs. I was on patrol when the call came in."

"Who called it in?"

One of the others stepped forward. "I did. Steve Naylor. I was working on the scaffolding when Dave here shouted me over. There's a phone box on the road on the other side of the hill."

"Did you find the body?" Chadwick asked Dave Sampson. "Yes."

Sampson looked pale, as well he might, Chadwick thought. His own war service and eighteen years on the force had hardened him to the sight of violent death, but he hadn't forgotten his first time, and he never forgot how devastating it could appear to someone who had never witnessed it before. He looked around. "Any chance someone might rustle up a pot of tea?"

Everyone stared at him, dumbfounded, then Naylor, the stage worker, said, "We've got a Primus and a billycan back there. I'll see what I can do."

"Good lad."

Naylor headed for the stage.

Chadwick turned back to Sampson. "Touch anything?" he asked.

"Only the zip. I mean, I didn't know . . . I thought . . ."

"What did you think?"

"It felt like there was someone inside. I thought they might be asleep or . . ."

"On drugs?"

"Possibly. Yes."

"After you opened the zip and saw what it was, what did you do then?"

"I called over to the stage."

Chadwick looked at the speckled mess on the grass about a yard away. "Before or after you were sick?"

Sampson swallowed. "After."

"Did you touch the body at all?"

"No."

"Good. Now go over and give your statement to Detective Sergeant Enderby. We'll probably want to talk to you again, so stick around."

Sampson nodded.

Chadwick crouched by the blue sleeping bag, keeping his hands in his pockets so that he didn't touch anything, even by accident. Only the upper half of the girl's body was exposed, but it was enough. She was wearing a smocked white dress with a scooped neck, and the area under the left breast was a mess – knife work, by the looks of it. Also, her dress was bunched up around her waist, as if she hadn't had time to smooth it down when she got into the bag – or as if someone had shoved her in quickly *after* he'd killed her. The long dress could also have been raised for sexual purposes, if she had been sharing the sleeping bag with her boyfriend, Chadwick realized, but he would have to wait for the pathologist to find out any more about that.

She was a very pretty girl, with long blonde hair, an oval face and full lips. She looked so innocent. Not unlike Yvonne, he thought, with a sudden shudder, and Yvonne had been out all last night, too. But she had come home. Not this girl. She was perhaps a year or two older than Yvonne, and her eyeshadow emphasized the colour of her big blue eyes. Her mascara stood out in stark contrast to the paleness of her skin. She wore several strings of cheap coloured beads around her neck, and she had a cornflower painted on her right cheek.

There was nothing more Chadwick could do until the Home Office pathologist arrived, which should be very soon, McCullen had given him to understand. Standing, he scanned the ground nearby but saw only rubbish: KitKat wrappers, a soggy *International Times*, an empty pouch of Old Holborn rolling tobacco, an orange pack of Rizla cigarette papers. It would all have to be bagged and checked out, of course. He sniffed the air – moist but warm enough for the time of year – and glanced at his watch. Half past eleven. It looked like being another fine day, and a long one.

He turned his gaze back to the others. "Anybody recognize her?"

They all shook their heads. Chadwick thought he noticed a little hesitation in Rick Hayes's reaction.

"Mr. Hayes?"

"No," said Hayes. "Never seen her before."

Chadwick thought he was lying about not recognizing the girl, but it would keep. He noticed a movement by the stage and looked to see Naylor coming back with a tray and, following shortly behind him, a nattily dressed man who seemed to be about as happy to find himself walking across a muddy field as Chadwick had been. But this man was carrying a black bag. The pathologist had arrived at last.

October 2005

Detective Chief Inspector Alan Banks hit the play button, and after the heartbeats, the glorious sound of "Breathe" from Pink Floyd's *Dark Side of the Moon* filled the room. He still hadn't got the hang of the new equipment yet, but he was finding his way around it slowly. He had inherited a state-of-the-art sound system along with a DVD player, forty-two-inch plasma TV, forty-gigabyte iPod and a Porsche 911 from his brother Roy. The estate had gone to Banks's parents, but they were set in their ways and had no use for a Porsche or a large-screen TV. The first wouldn't last five minutes parked outside their Peterborough council house, and the second wouldn't fit in their living room. They had sold Roy's London house, setting them both up nicely for the rest of their lives, and passed on the things they couldn't use to Banks.

As for Roy's iPod, Banks's father had taken one look at it and been about to drop it in the waste bin before Banks rescued it. Now it had become as essential to him when he went out as his wallet and his mobile. He had been able to download the software and buy new chargers and cables, along with an adapter that allowed him to play it through his car radio, and while he had kept a great deal of his brother's music library on it, he had managed to clear a good fifteen hours' worth of space by deleting the complete *Ring* cycle, and that was more than enough to accommodate his meagre collection at the moment.

Banks headed into the kitchen to see how dinner was getting along. All he'd had to do was remove the packaging and put the foil tray in the oven, but he didn't want to burn it. It was Friday evening, and Annie Cabbot was coming over for dinner tonight – just as a friend – and the evening was to be a sort of unofficial housewarming, though that was a term Banks hesitated to use these days. He had been back in the restored cottage for less than a month, and tonight would be Annie's first visit.

It was a wild October night outside. Banks could hear the wind screaming and moaning and see the dark shadows of tree branches tossing and thrashing beyond the kitchen window. He hoped Annie would make the drive all right, that there were no trees down. There was a spare bed if she wanted to stay, but he doubted that she would. Too much history for that to be comfortable for either of them, although there had been moments over the summer when he had thought it wouldn't take much to brush all the objections aside. Best not think about that, he told himself.

Banks poured himself the last of the Amarone. His parents had inherited Roy's wine cellar, and they had passed this on to him, too. As far as Arthur Banks was concerned, white wine was for sissies and red wine tasted like vinegar. His mother preferred sweet sherry. Their loss was Banks's gain, and while it lasted, he got to enjoy the high life of first-growth Bordeaux and Sauternes, white and red Burgundies from major growers, Chianti Classico, Barolo and Amarone. When it was gone, of course, he would be back to boxes of Simply Chilean and Big Aussie Red, but for the moment he was enjoying himself.

Whenever he opened a bottle, though, he missed Roy, which was strange because they had never been close, and Banks felt he had only got to know his brother after his death. He would just have to learn to live with it. It was the same with the other things – the TV, stereo, car, music – they all made him think of the brother he had never really known.

Part of the way through "Us and Them" he heard the doorbell ring. Annie, half past seven, right on time. He walked through and opened the front door, flinching at the gust of wind that almost blew her into his arms. She edged back, giggling, trying to hold down her hair as Banks pushed the door shut, but even in the short trip from her car to his front door it had become a tangled mess.

"Quite the night out there," Banks said. "I hope you didn't have any problems getting here."

Annie smiled. "Nothing I couldn't handle." She handed Banks a bottle of wine – Tesco's Chilean Merlot, he noticed – and took out a hairbrush. As she attacked her hair, she wandered around the front room. "This is certainly different from what I expected," she said. "It looks really cozy. I see you did go for the dark wood, after all."

The wood for the desk had been one of the things they had talked about, and Annie had advised the darker colour, as opposed to light pine. What had been Banks's main living room was now a small study complete with bookcases, a reproduction Georgian writing table for the laptop computer under the window and a couple of comfortable brown leather armchairs arranged around the fire, perfect for reading. A door by the side of the fireplace led into the new entertainment room, which ran the length of the house. Annie walked up and down and admired it, though she did tell Banks she thought it was a bit of a bloke's den.

The TV hung on the wall at the front and the speakers were spread about in strategic positions around the deep plum sofa and armchairs. Storage racks on the side walls held CDs and DVDs, mostly Roy's, apart from the few Banks had bought over the past couple of months. At the back, French windows led through to the new conservatory.

They wandered into the kitchen, which had been completely remodelled. Banks had tried to make sure it was as close to the original as possible, with the pine cupboards, copper-bottomed pans on wall hooks and the breakfast nook, where bench and table matched the cupboards, but that strange, benign presence he had felt there before had gone for good, or so it seemed. Now it was a fine kitchen, but only a kitchen. The builders had run the conservatory along the entire back of the house, and there was also a door leading to it from the kitchen.

"Impressive," Annie said. "All this and a Porsche parked outside, too. You'll be pulling the birds like nobody's business."

"Some hope," said Banks. "I might even sell the Porsche."

"Why?"

"It just feels so strange, having all Roy's stuff. I mean, the TV and the movies and CDs are okay, I suppose, not quite as personal, but the car . . . I don't know. Roy loved that car."

"Give it a chance. You might get to love it, too."

"I like it well enough. It's just . . . oh, never mind."

"Mmm, it smells good in here. What's for dinner?"

"Roast beef and Yorkshire pudding."

Annie gave him a look.

"Vegetarian lasagna," he said. "Marks and Spencer's best."

"That'll do fine."

Banks threw a simple salad together with an oil and vinegar dressing while Annie sat on the bench and opened the wine. Pink Floyd finished, so he went and put some Mozart wind quintets on the stereo. He'd had speakers wired into the kitchen, and the sound was good. When everything was ready, they sat opposite one another and Banks served the food. Annie was looking good, he thought. Her flowing chestnut hair still fell about her shoulders in disarray, but that only heightened her attraction for him. As for the rest, she was dressed in her usual casual style, just a touch of makeup, lightweight linen jacket, a green T-shirt and close-fitting black jeans, bead necklace and several thin silver bracelets that jingled when she moved her hand.

They had hardly got beyond the first mouthful when Banks's telephone rang. He muttered an apology to Annie and went to answer it.

"Sir?"

It was DC Winsome Jackman. "Yes, Winsome," Banks said. "This had better be important. I've been slaving over a hot oven all day."

"Sir?"

"Never mind. Go on."

"There's been a murder, sir."

"Are you certain?"

"I wouldn't be disturbing you if I wasn't, sir," Winsome said. "I'm at the scene right now. Moorview Cottage in Fordham, just outside Lyndgarth. I'm standing about six feet away from him, and the back of his head's caved in. Looks like someone bashed him with the poker. Kev's here, too, and he agrees. Sorry, Detective Sergeant Templeton. The local bobby called it in."

Banks knew Fordham. It was nothing but a hamlet, really, a cluster of cottages, a pub and a church. "Christ," he said. "Okay, Winsome, I'll get there as soon as I can. In the meantime, you can call in the SOCOs and Dr. Glendenning, if he's available."

"Right you are, sir. Should I ring DI Cabbot?"

"I'll deal with that. Keep the scene clear. We'll be there. Half an hour at the most."

Banks hung up and went back into the kitchen. "Sorry to spoil your dinner, Annie, but we've got to go out. Suspicious death. Winsome's certain it's murder."

"Your car or mine?"

"Yours, I think. The Porsche is a bit pretentious for a crime scene, don't you think?"

Monday, September 8, 1969

As the day progressed, the scene around Brimleigh Glen became busy with the arrival of various medical and scientific experts and the incident van, a temporary operational head-quarters with telephone communications and, more importantly, tea-making facilities. The immediate crime scene was taped off and a constable posted at the entrance to log the names of those who came and went. All work on rubbish disposal, stage dismantling and cesspit filling was suspended until further notice, much to the chagrin of Rick Hayes, who complained that every minute more spent at the field was costing him money.

Chadwick hadn't forgotten Hayes's possible lie earlier about not recognizing the victim, and he looked forward to the pleasure of a more in-depth interview. In fact, Hayes was high on his list of priorities. For the moment, though, it was important to get the investigation organized, get the mechanics in place and the right men appointed to the right jobs.

Detective Sergeant Enderby seemed capable enough on first impression, despite the length of his hair, and Chadwick already knew that Simon Bradley, his driver, was a bright young copper with a good future ahead of him. He also demonstrated the same sort of military neatness and precision in his demeanour that Chadwick appreciated. As for the rest of the team, they would come mostly from the North Riding, people he didn't know, and he would have to learn their strengths and weaknesses on the hoof. He preferred to enter into an investigation on more certain ground, but it couldn't be helped. Officially, this was North Yorkshire's case, and he was simply helping out.

The doctor had pronounced the victim dead and turned the body over to the coroner's officer, in this case a local constable specially appointed to the task, who arranged for its transportation to the mortuary in Leeds. During his brief examination at the scene, Dr. O'Neill had been able to tell Chadwick only that the wounds almost certainly had been caused by a thin-bladed knife and that she had been dead less than ten hours and more than six before the time of his examination, which meant she had been killed sometime between half past one and half past five in the morning. Her body had been moved after death, he added, and she had not been in the sleeping bag when she died. Though stab wounds, even to the heart, often don't bleed a great deal, the doctor said, he would have expected more blood on the inside of the sleeping bag had she been stabbed there.

How long she had lain elsewhere before she had been moved, or where she had lain, he couldn't say, only that the post-mortem lividity indicated that she had been on her back for some hours. From an external examination, it didn't look as if she had been raped – she was still, in fact, wearing her white cotton knickers, and they looked clean – but only a complete post-mortem would reveal details of any sexual activity prior to death. There were no defensive wounds on her hands, which most likely meant that she had been taken by surprise, and that the first stab had pierced her heart and incapacitated her immediately. There was light bruising on the front left side of her neck, which Dr. O'Neill said could be an indication that someone, the killer probably, had restrained her from behind.

So, Chadwick thought, the killer had made a clumsy attempt to make it look as if the girl had been killed in the bag on the field, and clumsy attempts to mislead often yield clues. Before doing anything else, Chadwick commissioned Enderby to get a team with a police dog together to comb Brimleigh Woods.

The photographer did his stuff and the specialists searched the scene, then bagged everything for scientific analysis. They got some partial footprints, but there was no guarantee that any of these were the killer's. Even so, they patiently made plaster of Paris casts. There was no weapon in the immediate vicinity, hardly surprising as the victim hadn't died there, nor was there anything in the sleeping bag or near her body to indicate who she was. A lack of drag marks indicated that she might have been moved there before it rained. The beads she wore were common enough, though Chadwick imagined it might be possible to track down a supplier.

Some poor mother and father would no doubt be wringing their hands with worry about now, the same way he had been wringing his about Yvonne. Had she been at the festival? he wondered. It would be just like her, the kind of music she listened to, her rebellious spirit, the clothes she wore. He remembered the fuss she had made when he and Janet wouldn't let her go to the Isle of Wight Festival the weekend before. The *Isle of Wight*, for crying out loud. It was three hundred miles away. Anything could happen. What on earth had she been thinking?

For the time being, the best course of action was to check all missing persons reports for someone matching the victim's description. Failing any luck there, they would have to get a decent enough photograph of her to put in the papers and show on television, along with a plea for information from anyone in the crowd who might have seen or heard anything. However they did it, they needed to know who she was as soon as possible. Only then could they attempt to fathom who had done this to her, and why.

The darkness deepened the closer Banks and Annie got to Lyndgarth. It looked as if the wind had taken down an electricity cable somewhere and caused a power cut. The silhouettes of branches jerked in the beam of the car's headlights, while all around was darkness, not even the light of a distant farmhouse to guide them. In Lyndgarth, houses, pubs, church and village green were all in the dark. Annie drove slowly as the road curved out of town, over the narrow stone bridge and around the bend another half a mile or so to Fordham. Even in the surrounding darkness it was easy to see where all the fuss was as they came over the second bridge shortly after half past eight.

The main road veered sharply left at the pub, opposite the church, towards Eastvale, but straight ahead, on a rough track that continued up the hill past the youth hostel and over the wild moorland, a police patrol car blocked the way, along with Winsome's unmarked Vectra. Annie pulled up behind the cars, and wind whipped at her clothes as she got out of the car. The trouble was in the last cottage on the left. Opposite Moorview Cottage, a narrow lane ran west between the side of the church and a row of cottages until it was swallowed up in the dark countryside.

"Not much of a place, is it?" said Banks.

"Depends on what you want," said Annie. "It's quiet enough, I suppose."

"And there is a pub." Looking back across the main road, Banks fancied he could see the glow of candlelight through the pub windows and hear the muffled tones of conversation from inside. A little thing like a power cut clearly wasn't going to deprive the locals of their hand-pumped ale.

The light of a torch dazzled them, and Banks heard Winsome's voice. "Sir? DI Cabbot? This way. I took the liberty of asking the SOCOs to bring some lighting with them, but for the moment this is all we've got."

They followed the trail the torch lit up through a high wooden gate and a conservatory. The local PC was waiting inside the door, talking to newly promoted Detective Sergeant Kevin Templeton, and the light from his torch improved visibility quite a bit. Even so, they were limited to what they could see within the beams; the rest of the place was shrouded in darkness.

Treading carefully across the stone flags, Banks and Annie followed the lights to the edge of the living room. They weren't wearing protective clothing, so they had to keep their distance until the experts had finished. There, sprawled on the floor near the fireplace, lay the body of a man. He was lying on his face, so Banks couldn't tell how old he was, but his clothing, jeans and a dark green sweatshirt, suggested he was youngish. And Winsome was right; there was no doubt about this one. He could see even from a few feet away that the back of his head was a bloody mess, and a long trail of dark, coagulating blood gleamed in the torchlight, ending in a puddle that was soaking into the rug. Winsome moved her torch beam around and Banks could see a poker lying on the floor not far from the victim, and a pair of glasses with one lens broken.

"Do you notice any signs of a struggle?" Banks asked.

"No," said Annie.

The beam picked out a packet of Dunhill and a cheap disposable lighter on the table beside the armchair, towards which the victim's head was pointing. "Say he was going for his cigarettes," Banks said.

"And someone took him by surprise?"

"Yes. But someone he had no reason to think would kill him." Banks pointed to the rack by the fireplace. "The poker would most likely have been there on the hearth with the other implements."

"Blood-spatter analysis should give us a better idea of how it happened," Annie said.

Banks nodded and turned to Winsome. "First thing we do is seal off this room completely," he said. "It's out of bounds to anyone who doesn't need to be in it."

"Right, sir," said Winsome.

"And organize a house to house as soon as possible. Ask for reinforcements, if necessary."

"Sir."

"Do we know who he is?"

"We don't know anything yet," Winsome said. "PC Travers here lives down the road and tells me he doesn't know him. Apparently it's a holiday cottage."

"Then presumably there's an owner somewhere."

"She's in here, sir." It was the PC who spoke, and he pointed his torch into the dining room, where a woman sat in the dark on a hard-backed chair staring into space. "I didn't know what else to do with her, sir," he went on. "I mean, I couldn't let her go until she'd spoken with you, and she needed to sit down. She was feeling a bit faint."

"You did the right thing," said Banks.

"Anyway, it's Mrs. Tanner. She's the owner."

"No, I'm not," said Mrs. Tanner. "I just look after it for them. They live in London."

"Okay," said Banks, sitting down opposite her. "We'll get those details later."

PC Travers shone his torch along the table between them, so that neither was dazzled and each could at least see the other. From what Banks could tell, she was a stout woman in her early fifties with short greying hair and a double chin.

"Are you all right, Mrs. Tanner?" he asked.

She put a hand to her breast. "I'm better now, thank you. It was just a shock. In the dark and all . . . It's not that I've never seen a dead body before. Just family, like, you know, but this . . ." She took a sip from the steaming mug in front of her. It looked as if Travers had had the good sense to make some tea, which meant there must be a gas cooker.

"Are you up to answering a few questions?" Banks asked her.

"I don't know that I can tell you anything."

"Leave that to me to decide. How did you come to find the body?"

"He was just lying there, like he is now. I didn't touch anything."

"Good. But what I meant was: why did you come here?"

"It was the power cut. I live just down the road, see, the other side of the pub, and I wanted to show him where the emergency candles were. There's a big torch, too."

"What time was this?"

"Just before eight o'clock."

"Did you see or hear anything unusual?"

"No."

"See anyone?"

"Not a soul."

"No cars?"

"No."

"Was the door open?"

"No. It was shut."

"So what did you do?"

"First, I knocked."

"And then?"

"Well, there was no answer, see, and it was all dark inside."

"Didn't you think he might be out?"

"His car's still there. Who'd go out walking on a night like this?"

"What about the pub?"

"I looked in, but he wasn't there, and nobody had seen him, so I came back here. I've got the keys. I thought maybe he'd had an accident or something, fallen down the stairs in the dark, and all because I'd forgotten to show him where the candles and the torch were."

"Where are they?" Banks asked.

"In a box on the shelf under the stairs." She shook her head slowly. "Sorry. As soon as I saw him just . . . lying there . . . it went out of my head completely, why I'd come."

"That's all right."

Banks sent PC Travers to find the candles. He came back a few moments later. "There were matches in the kitchen by the cooker, sir," he said, and proceeded to set candles in saucers and place them on the dining table.

"That's better," said Banks. He turned back to Mrs. Tanner. "Do you know who your guest was? His name?"

"Nick."

"That's all?"

"When he came by when he arrived last Saturday and introduced himself, he just said his name was Nick."

"He didn't give you a cheque with his full name on it?"

"He paid cash."

"Is that normal?"

"Some people prefer it that way."

"How long was he staying?"

"He paid for two weeks."

Two weeks in the Yorkshire Dales in late October seemed like an odd holiday choice to Banks, but there was no accounting for taste. Maybe this Nick was a keen rambler. "How did he find the place?"

"The owners have a website, but don't ask me owt about that. I only see to the cleaning and general maintenance."

"I understand," said Banks. "Any idea where Nick came from?"

"No. He didn't have any sort of foreign accent, but he wasn't from around here. Down south, I'd say."

"Is there anything else you can tell me about him?"

"I only ever saw him the once," Mrs. Tanner said. "He seemed like a nice enough lad."

"How old would you say he was?"

"Not old. Mid-thirties, maybe. I'm not very good at ages."

Car headlights shone through the window and soon the small house was filled with SOCOs. Peter Darby, the photographer, and Dr. Glendenning, the Home Office pathologist, arrived at about the same time, Glendenning complaining that Banks thought he had nothing better to do than hang around dead bodies on a Friday evening. Banks asked PC Travers to take Mrs. Tanner home and stay with her. Her husband was out at a darts match in Eastvale, she said, but he would soon be back, and she assured Banks she would be fine on her own. The SOCOs quickly set up lights in the living room, and while Peter Darby photographed the cottage with his Pentax and digital camcorder, Banks watched Dr. Glendenning examine the body, turning it slightly to examine the eyes.

"Anything you can tell us, doc?" Banks asked after a few minutes.

Dr. Glendenning got to his feet and sighed theatrically. "I've told you about that before, Banks. Don't call me doc. It's disrespectful."

"Sorry," said Banks. He peered at the corpse. "Anyway, he spoiled my Friday evening, too, so anything you can tell me would help."

"Well, for a start, he's dead. You can write that down in your little notebook."

"I suspected as much," said Banks.

"And don't be so bloody sarcastic. You realize I was supposed to be at the Lord Mayor's banquet by now drinking Country Manor and munching vol-au-vents?"

"Sounds bad for your health," Banks said. "You're better off here."

Glendenning favoured him with a sly smile. "Maybe you're right at that, laddie." He smoothed down his silvery hair. "Anyway, it was almost certainly the blow to the back of the head that killed him. I'll know better when I get him on the table, of course, but that'll have to do for now."

"Time of death?"

"Not more than two or three hours. Rigor hasn't started yet."

Banks looked at his watch. Five past nine. Mrs. Tanner had probably been there about an hour or so, which narrowed it down even more, between six and eight, say. She couldn't have missed the killer by long, which made her a very lucky woman. "Any chance he got drunk, fell and hit his head?" Banks knew it was unlikely, but he had to ask. You didn't go off wasting valuable police time and resources on a domestic accident.

"Almost certainly not," said Glendenning, glancing over at the poker. "For a start, if it had happened that way, he would most likely be lying on his back, and secondly, judging by the shape of the wound and the blood and hair on that poker over there, I'd say your murder weapon's pretty obvious this time. Maybe you'll find a nice clean set of fingerprints and be home by bedtime."

"Some hope," said Banks, seeing yet another weekend slip away. Why couldn't murderers commit their crimes on Mondays? It wasn't only the prospect of working all weekend that made Friday murders such a pain in the arse, but that people tended to make themselves scarce. Offices closed, workers visited relatives, everything slowed down. And the first forty hours were crucial in any investigation. "Anyway," he said, "the poker was close to hand, which probably means that whoever did it didn't come prepared to kill. Or wanted to make it look that way."

"I'll leave the speculation to you. As far as I'm concerned, he belongs to the coroner now. You can remove the body whenever Cartier-Bresson here has finished."

Banks smiled. He noticed Peter Darby stick his tongue out at Glendenning behind the doctor's back. They always seemed to be getting in one another's way at crime scenes, which were the only places they ever met.

By now it was impossible to ignore the activity in the rest of the house, which was swarming with SOCOs. Thick cables snaked through the conservatory, attached to bright lights that cast shadows of men in protective clothing on the walls. The place resembled a film set. Feeling very much in the way, Banks edged out towards the conservatory. The wind was still raging, and at times it felt strong enough to blow the whole frail structure away. It didn't help that they had to leave the door open to let the cables in.

Detective Sergeant Stefan Nowak, the crime scene coordinator, arrived next, and after a brief hello to Banks and Annie, he set to work. It was his job to liaise between the scientists and the detectives, if necessary translating the jargon into comprehensible English, and he did it very well. His degrees in physics and chemistry certainly helped.

There are people who will stand for hours watching others work, Banks had noticed. You see them at building sites, eyes against the knotholes in the high wooden fences as the mechanical diggers claw at the earth and men in hard hats yell orders over the din. Or standing in the street looking up as someone on scaffolding sandblasts the front of an old building. Banks wasn't one of them. That kind of thing was a perverse form of voyeurism, as far as he was concerned. Besides, there was nothing much more he could do at the house now until the team had finished, and his thoughts moved pleasantly to the candlelit pub not more than thirty yards away. The people in there would have to be interviewed. Someone might have seen or heard something. One of them might even have done it. Best talk to them now, while they were still in there and their memories were fresh. He told Winsome and Templeton to stay with Stefan and the SOCOs and to come and get him if anything important came up, then called out to Annie, and they headed for the gate.

2

Monday, September 8, 1969

When Chadwick was satisfied that things were running smoothly, he called Rick Hayes over and suggested they talk in the van. It was set up so that one end was a self-contained cubicle, just about big enough for an interview, though at six foot two, Chadwick felt more than a little claustrophobic. Still, he could put up with it, and a bit of discomfort never did any harm when someone had something to hide.

Close up, Hayes looked older than Chadwick would have expected. Perhaps it was the stress of the weekend, but he had lines around his eyes and his jaw was tense. Chadwick put him in his late thirties, but with the hairstyle and the clothes, he could probably pass for ten years younger. He had about three or four days' stubble on his face, his fingernails were bitten down to the quicks, and the first two fingers of his left hand were stained yellow with nicotine.

"Mr. Hayes," Chadwick began. "Maybe you can help me. I need some background here. How many people attended the festival?"

"About 25,000."

"Quite a lot."

"Not really. There were 150,000 at the Isle of Wight the weekend before. Mind you, they had Dylan and the Who. And we had competition. Crosby, Stills and Nash and Jefferson Airplane were playing in Hyde Park on Saturday."

"And you had?"

"Biggest draws? Pink Floyd. Led Zeppelin."

Chadwick, who had never heard of either, dutifully made a note of the names after checking the spelling with Hayes. "Who else?"

"A couple of local groups. Jan Dukes de Grey. The Mad Hatters. The Hatters especially have been getting really big these past few months. Their first LP is already in the charts."

"What do you mean 'local'?" Chadwick asked, making a note of the names.

"Leeds. General area, at any rate."

"How many groups in all?"

"Thirty. I can give you a full list, if you like."

"Much appreciated." Chadwick wasn't sure where that information would get him, but every little bit helped. "Something like that must require a lot of organization."

"You're telling me. Not only do you have to book the groups well in advance and arrange for concessions, parking, camping and toilet facilities, you've also got to supply generators, transport and a fair bit of sound equipment. Then there's security."

"Who did you use?"

"My own people."

"You've done this sort of thing before?"

"On a smaller scale. It's what I do. I'm a promoter."

Chadwick scribbled something on his pad, shielding it from Hayes in the curve of his hand. Not that it meant anything; he just wanted Hayes to think it did. Hayes lit a cigarette.

Chadwick opened the window. "The festival lasted three days, is that correct?"

"Yes. We started late Friday afternoon and wrapped up today in the wee hours."

"What time?"

"Led Zeppelin played last. They came on shortly after one o'clock this morning, and they must have finished about three. We were supposed to wind up earlier, but there were the inevitable delays – equipment malfunctions, that sort of thing."

"What happened at three?"

"People started drifting home."

"In the middle of the night?"

"There was nothing to keep them here. The ones who had pitched tents probably went back to the campground to grab a few hours' sleep, but the rest left. The field was pretty much empty for the cleanup crew to start by dawn. The rain helped."

"What time did it start to rain?"

"Must have been about half two in the morning. Just a brief shower, like."

"So it was mostly dry while this Led Zeppelin was playing?"

"Mostly. Yes."

Yvonne had arrived home at six-thirty, Chadwick thought, which gave her more than enough time to get back from Brimleigh, if she had been there. What had she been doing between three and six-thirty? Chadwick decided he had better leave that well alone until he had established whether she had been there or not.

Given a time of death between one-thirty and five-thirty, the victim might have been killed while the band was playing, or while everyone was heading home. Most likely the former, he decided, as there would have been less chance of witnesses. And possibly before the rain, as there was no obvious trail.

"Are there any other gates," he asked, "in addition to where I came in?"

"No. Only to the north. But there are plenty of exits."

"I assume there's fencing all around the site?"

"Yes. It wasn't a free concert, you know."

"But no one would have had any real reason to go through the woods?"

"No. There are no exits on that side. It doesn't lead anywhere. The parking, camping and gates are all on the north side, and that's where the nearest road is, too."

"I understand you had a bit of trouble with skinheads?"

"Nothing my men couldn't handle. A gang of them tried to break through the fence and we saw them off."

"North or south?"

"East, actually."

"When was this?"

"Saturday night."

"Did they come back?"

"Not as far as I know. If they did, they were quiet about it."

"Did people actually sleep in the field over the weekend?"

"Some did. Like I said, we had a couple of fields for parking and camping just over the hill there. A lot of people pitched tents and came back and forth. Others just brought sleeping bags. Look, why does all this matter? I'd have thought it was obvious what happened."

Chadwick raised his eyebrows. "Oh? I must be missing something. Tell me."

"Well, she must have got into an argument with her boyfriend or something, and he killed her. She was a bit away from the crowds, there by the edge of the woods, and if everyone was listening to Led Zeppelin, they probably wouldn't notice if the world ended."

"Loud, are they, this Led Zeppelin?"

"You could say that. You should have a listen."

"Maybe I will. Anyway, it's a good point you've raised. I'm sure the music might have helped the killer. But why assume it was her boyfriend? Do boyfriends usually stab their girlfriends?"

"I don't know. It's just . . . I mean . . . who else?"

"Could have been a homicidal maniac, perhaps?"

"You'd know more about that than I do."

"Or a passing tramp?"

"Now you're taking the piss."

"I assure you, Mr. Hayes, I am taking this very seriously indeed. But in order to find out who might have done this, boyfriend or whatever, we need to know who she is." He made a note, then looked directly at Hayes. "Maybe you can help me there?"

"I've never seen her before in my life."

"Oh, come off it, laddie." Chadwick stared at him.

"I don't know who she is."

"Ah, but you *did* see her somewhere?"

Hayes looked down at his clasped hands. "Maybe."

"And where, perhaps, might you have seen her?"

"She may have been backstage at some point."

"*Now* we're getting somewhere. How does a person get to go backstage?"

"Well, usually, you need a pass."

"And who hands those out?"

"Security."

"But?"

Hayes wriggled in his chair. "Well, you know, sometimes . . . a good-looking girl. What can I say?"

"How many people were backstage?"

"Dozens. It was chaos back there. We had a VIP area roped

off with a beer tent and lounges, then there were the performers' caravans, dressing rooms, toilets. We also had a press enclosure in front of the stage. Some of the performers hung around to listen to other bands, you know, then maybe they'd jam backstage and . . . you know . . ."

"Who were the last groups to play on Sunday?"

"We kicked off the evening session with the Mad Hatters just after dark, then Fleetwood Mac, Pink Floyd and Led Zeppelin."

"Were they all backstage?"

"At one time or another, if they weren't onstage, yes."

"With guests?"

"There were a lot of people."

"How many?"

"I don't know . . . maybe fifty or so. More. That's including roadies, managers, publicists, disc jockeys, record company people, agents, friends of the bands, hangers-on and what have you."

"Did you keep guest lists?"

"You must be joking."

"Lists of those who were given passes?"

"No."

"Anyone keep track of comings and goings?"

"Someone checked passes at the entrance to the backstage area. That's all."

"And let in beautiful girls without passes?"

"Only if they were with someone who did have a pass."

"Ah, I see. So our victim might not have been issued a pass for herself. In addition to beer, were there any other substances contributing to that general sense of well-being backstage?"

"I wouldn't know about that. I was too busy. Most of the time I was running around like a blue-arsed fly making sure everything was running smoothly, keeping everyone happy."

"Were they?"

"For the most part. You got the occasional pillock complaining his caravan was too small, but on the whole it was okay."

Chadwick jotted something down. He could tell that Hayes was craning his neck trying to read it, so he rested his hand over the words when he had finished. "Perhaps if we were to narrow down the time of death, do you think you'd be able to give us a better idea of who might have been backstage?"

"Maybe. I dunno. Like I said, it was a bit of a zoo back there."

"I can imagine. Did you see her with anyone in particular?"

"No. It might have been her or it might not have. I only got a fleeting glance. There were a lot of people. A lot of good-looking birds." His expression brightened. "Maybe it wasn't even her."

"Let's remain optimistic, shall we, and assume that it was? Did the girl you saw have a flower painted on her right cheek?"

"I don't know. Like I said, I'm not even sure it *was* her. Lots of girls had painted flowers."

"Perhaps your security team might be able to help us?"

"Maybe. If they remember."

"Was the press around?"

"On and off."

"What do you mean?"

"It's a matter of give and take, isn't it? I mean, the publicity's always useful and you don't want to piss off the press, but at the same time you don't want someone filming your every move or writing about you every time you go to the toilet, do you? We tried to strike a balance."

"How did that work?"

"A big press conference before the event, scheduled interviews with specific artists at specific times."

"Where?"

"In the press enclosure."

"So the press weren't allowed backstage?"

"You must be joking."

"Photographers?"

"Only in the press enclosure."

"Can you give me their names?"

"I can't remember them all. You can ask Mick Lawton. He was press liaison officer for the event. I'll give you his number."

"What about television?"

"They were here on Saturday and Sunday."

"Let me guess, press enclosure?"

"For the most part, they filmed crowd scenes and the bands performing, within strict copyright guidelines, with permission and everything."

"I'll need the names of television companies involved."

"Sure. The usual suspects." Hayes named them. It wasn't as if there were that many to choose from, and Yorkshire Television and BBC North would have been Chadwick's first guesses anyway. Chadwick stood up, stooping so he didn't bang his head on the ceiling. "We'll have a chat with them later, see if we can have a look at their footage. And we'll be talking with your security people, too. Thanks for your time."

Hayes shuffled to his feet, looking surprised. "That's it?"

Chadwick smiled. "For now."

It was like a scene out of Dickens painted with Rembrandt's sense of light and shade. There were two distinct groups in the low-beamed lounge, one playing cards, the other in the midst of an animated conversation: gnarled, weather-beaten faces with lined cheeks and potato noses lit by candles and the wood fire that crackled in the hearth. The two people behind the bar were younger. One was a local girl Banks was sure he had seen before, a pale, willowy blonde of nineteen or twenty. The other was a young man about ten years older, with curly hair and a wispy goatee.

Everyone stopped what they were doing and looked towards the door when Banks and Annie walked in, then the card players resumed their game and the other group muttered quietly.

"Nasty night out there," said the young man behind the bar. "What can I get for you?"

"I'll have a pint of Black Sheep," said Banks, showing his warrant card, "and DI Cabbot here will have a Slimline bitter lemon, no ice."

Annie raised an eyebrow at Banks but accepted the drink when it came, and took out her notebook.

"Thought it wouldn't be long before you lot came sniffing around, all that activity going on out there," said the young man. His biceps bulged as he pulled Banks's pint.

"And you'll be?"

"Cameron Clarke. Landlord. Everyone calls me CC."

Banks paid for the drinks, against CC's protests, and took a sip of his beer. "Well, Cameron," he said, "this is a nice pint you keep, I must say."

"Thanks."

Banks turned to the girl. "And you are?"

"Kelly," she said, shifting from foot to foot and twirling her hair. "Kelly Soames. I just work here."

Like CC, Kelly wore a white T-shirt with "The Cross Keys Inn" emblazoned across her chest. There was enough candle-light behind the bar to see that the thin material came to a stop about three inches above her low-rise jeans and broad studded belt began, exposing a flat strip of pale white skin and a belly button from which hung a short silver chain. As far as Banks was concerned, the bare midriff trend had turned every male over forty into a dirty old man.

He glanced around. A middle-aged couple he hadn't noticed when he came in sat on the bench below the bay window, tourists by the look of them, anoraks and an expensive camera bag on the seat beside them. Several of the people were smoking, and Banks suppressed a sudden urge for a cigarette. He addressed the whole pub. "Does anyone know what's happened up the road?"

They all shook their heads and muttered no.

"Anyone leave here during the last couple of hours?"

"One or two," CC answered.

"I'll need their names."

CC told him.

"When did the electricity go off?"

"About two hours ago. There's a line down on the Eastvale road. It could take an hour or two more, or so they said."

It was half past nine now, Banks noted, so the power cut had occurred at half past seven. It would be easy enough to check the exact time with Yorkshire Electricity, but that would do to be going on with. If Nick, the victim, had been killed between six and eight, then, had the killer seized the opportunity of the cover of extra darkness, or had he acted sooner, between six and half past seven? It probably didn't matter, except that the power cut had brought Mrs. Tanner to check on her tenant, and the body had been discovered perhaps quite a bit sooner than the killer had hoped.

"Anyone arrive *after* the electricity went off?"

"We arrived at about a quarter to eight," said the man in the bay window seat. "Isn't that right, darling?"

The woman beside him nodded.

"We were on our way to Eastvale, back to the hotel," he went on, "and this is the first place we saw that was open. I don't like driving after dark at the best of times."

"I don't blame you," Banks said. "Did you see anyone else on the road?"

"No. I mean, there might have been a car or two earlier, but we didn't see anyone after the power went out."

"Where were you coming from?"

"Swainshead."

"Did you see anyone when you parked here?"

"No. I mean, I don't think so. The wind was so loud and the branches . . ."

"You might have seen someone?"

"I thought I saw the taillights of a car," the woman said.

"Where?"

"Heading up the hill. Straight on. I don't know where the road goes. But I can't be certain. As my husband says, it was a bit like a hurricane out there. It could have been something else flashing in the dark, a lantern or a torch or something."

"You didn't see or hear anything else?"

They both shook their heads.

A possible sighting of a car heading up the unfenced road over the moors, then; that was the sum of it. They would make inquiries at the youth hostel, of course, but it was hardly likely their murderer was conveniently staying there. Still, someone might have seen something.

Banks turned back to CC. "We'll need statements from everyone in here. Names and addresses, when they arrived, that sort of thing. I'll send someone over. For the moment, though, did anyone leave and come back between six and eight?"

"I did," said one of the card players.

"What time would that be?"

"About seven o'clock."

"How long were you gone?"

"About fifteen minutes. As long as it takes to drive to Lyndgarth and back."

"Why did you drive to Lyndgarth and back?"

"I live there," he said. "I thought I might have forgotten to turn the gas ring off after I had my tea, so I went back to check."

"And had you?"

"What?"

"Turned the gas ring off?"

"Oh, aye."

"Wasted journey, then."

"Not if I *hadn't* turned it off."

That raised a titter from his cronies. Banks didn't want to get mired any deeper in Yorkshire logic.

"You still haven't told us what's happened," another of the card players piped up. "Why are you asking all these questions?" A candle guttered on the table and went out, leaving his gnarled face in shadow.

"This is just the beginning," said Banks, thinking he might as well tell them. They would find out soon enough. "It looks very much as if we have a murder on our hands."

A collective gasp rose from the drinkers, followed by more muted muttering. "Who was it, if I might ask?" said CC.

"I wish I knew," said Banks. "Maybe you can help me there. All I know is that his name was Nick and he was staying at Moorview Cottage."

"Mrs. Tanner's young lad, then?" said CC. "She was in here looking for him not so long ago."

"I know," said Banks. "She found him."

"Poor woman. Tell her there's a drink on the house waiting for her, whatever she wants."

"Have you seen her husband tonight?" Banks asked, remembering that Mrs. Tanner had told him her husband was at a darts match.

"Jack Tanner? No. He's not welcome here."

"Why's that?"

"I'm sorry to say it, but he's a troublemaker. Ask anyone. Soon as he's got three or four pints into him he's picking on someone."

"I see," said Banks. "That's interesting to know."

"Now, wait a minute," protested CC. "I'm not saying he's capable of owt like that."

"Like what?"

"You know. What you said. Murdering someone."

"Do you know anything about the young man?" Annie asked. CC was so distracted by her breaking her silence that he stopped spluttering. "He came in a couple of times," he said.

"Did he talk to anyone?"

"Only to ask for a drink, like. And food. He had a bar snack here once, didn't he, Kelly?"

Kelly was on the verge of tears, Banks noticed. "Anything to add?" he asked her.

Even in the candlelight, Banks could see that she blushed. "No," she said. "Why should I?"

"Just asking."

"Look, he was just a normal bloke," CC said. "You know, said hello, smiled, put his glass back on the bar when he left. Not like some."

"Did he smoke?"

CC seemed puzzled by the question, then he said, "Yes. Yes, he did."

"Did he stand at the bar and chat?" Annie asked.

"He wasn't the chatty sort," said CC. "He'd take his drink and go sit over there with the newspaper." He gestured towards the hearth.

"Which newspaper?" Banks asked.

CC frowned. "*The Independent*," he said. "I think he liked to do the crossword. Too hard for me, that one. I can barely manage the *Daily Mirror*. Why? Does it matter?"

Banks favoured him with a tight smile. "Maybe it doesn't," he said, "but I like to know these things. It tells me he was intelligent, at any rate."

"If you call doing crossword puzzles intelligent, I suppose it does. I think they're a bit of a waste of time, myself."

"Ah, but you can't do them, can you?"

"Does either of you have any idea what he did for a living?" Annie asked, glancing from CC to Kelly and back.

"I told you," said CC. "He wasn't chatty, and I'm not especially the nosy type. Man wants to come in here and have a quiet drink, he's more than welcome, as far as I'm concerned."

"So it never came up?" Annie asked.

"No. Maybe he was a writer or a reviewer or something."

"Why do you say that?"

"Well, if he didn't have the newspaper, he always had a book with him." He glanced towards Banks. "And don't ask me what book he was reading, because I didn't spot the title."

"Any idea what he was doing here, this time of year?" Banks asked.

"None. Look, we often get people staying at Moorview Cottage dropping by for a pint or a meal, and we don't know any more or less about them than we did about him. You don't get to know people that quickly, especially if they're the quiet type."

"Point taken," said Banks. He knew quite well how long it took the locals to accept newcomers in a place like Fordham, and no holidaying cottager could ever stay long enough. "That just about wraps it up for now." He looked at Annie. "Anything else you can think of?"

"No," said Annie, putting away her notebook.

Banks drained his pint. "Right, then, we'll be off, and someone will be over to take your statements."

Kelly Soames was chewing on her plump, pink lower lip, Banks noticed, glancing back as he followed Annie out of the pub.

Monday, September 8, 1969

The newshounds had sniffed out a crime at about the same time that the incident van arrived, and the first on the scene was a *Yorkshire Evening Post* reporter, followed shortly by local radio and television journalists, the same people who had no doubt been reporting on the festival. Chadwick knew that his relationship with them was held in a delicate balance. They were after a sensational story, one that would make people buy their newspapers or tune in to their channel, and Chadwick needed them on his side. They could be of invaluable help in identifying a victim, for example, or even in staging a reconstruction. In this case, there wasn't much he could tell them. He didn't go into details about the wounds, nor did he mention the flower painted on the victim's cheek, though he knew that that was the sort of sensationalist information they wanted. The more he could keep out of the public domain, the better when it came to court. He did, however, get them to agree to let police look at the weekend's footage. It would probably be a waste of time, but it had to be done.

When Chadwick was done at the field, it was afternoon and he realized he was hungry. He had DC Bradley drive him to the nearest village, Denleigh, about a mile to the northeast. It had turned into a fine day, and only a thin gauze of cloud hung in the sky to filter a little of the sun's heat. The village had a sort of stunned appearance about it, and Chadwick noticed that it was unusually messy, the streets littered with waste paper and empty cigarette packets.

At first it seemed there was nobody about, but then they saw a man walking by the village green and pulled up beside him. He was a tweedy sort with a stiff-brush moustache and a pipe. He looked to Chadwick like a retired military officer, reminded him of a colonel he'd had in Burma during the war.

"Anywhere to eat around here?" Chadwick asked, winding the window down.

"Fish and chip shop, just round the corner," the man said. "Should be still open." Then he peered more closely at Chadwick. "Do I know you?"

"I don't think so," Chadwick said. "I'm from West Yorkshire police."

"Huh. We could have done with a few more of your lot around this weekend," the man went on. "By the way, Forbes is the name. Archie Forbes."

They shook hands through the window. "Unfortunately, we can't be everywhere, Mr. Forbes," said Chadwick. "Was there any damage?"

"One of them broke the newsagent's window when Ted told them he'd run out of cigarette papers. Some of them even slept in Mrs. Wrigley's back garden. Scared her half to death. I suppose you're here about that girl they found dead in a sleeping bag?"

"News travels fast."

"It does around these parts. Communism. You mark my words. That's what's behind it. Communism."

"Probably," said Chadwick, moving to wind up the window.

Forbes kept talking. "I still have one or two contacts in the intelligence services, if you catch my drift," he said, putting a crooked finger to the side of his nose, "and there's no doubt in my mind, and in the minds of many other right-thinking people, I might add, that this is a lot more than just youthful high spirits. Behind it all you'll find those French and German student anarchist groups, and behind them you'll find communism. Need I spell it out, sir? The Russians." He took a puff on his pipe. "There's no doubt in my mind that there are some very unscrupulous people directing events behind the scenes, unscrupulous *foreigners*, for the most part, and their goal is the overthrow of democratic government everywhere. Drugs are only a part of their master plan. These are frightening times we live in."

"Yes," said Chadwick. "Well, thanks very much, Mr. Forbes. We'll be off for those fish and chips now." He signalled for Bradley to drive off as he wound up the window, leaving Forbes staring after them. They had a laugh about him, though Chadwick believed there might be something in what he'd said about foreign students fomenting dissent, then found the fish and chip shop and sat in the car eating.

When Chadwick had finished, he screwed up the newspaper, then excused himself, got out of the car and put it in the rubbish bin. Next he went into the telephone booth beside the fish and chip shop and dialed home. Janet answered on the third ring. "Hello, darling," she said. "Is anything wrong?"

"No, nothing's wrong," said Chadwick. "I was wondering about Yvonne. How is she today?"

"Back to normal, it seems."

"Did she say anything about last night?"

"No. We didn't talk. She left for school at the usual time and gave me a quick peck on the cheek on her way out. Look, let's just leave it at that for the time being, darling, can't we?"

"If she's sleeping with someone, I want to know who it is."

"And what good would that do you? What would you do if you knew? Go over and beat him up? Arrest him? Be sensible, Stan. She'll tell us in her own time."

"Or when it's too late."

"What do you mean?"

"Oh, never mind," said Chadwick. "Look, I have to go. Don't bother keeping dinner warm tonight. I'll probably be late."

"How late?"

"I don't know. Don't wait up."

"What is it?"

"Murder. A nasty one. You'll hear all about it on the evening news."

"Be careful, Stan."

"Don't worry, I'll be fine."

Chadwick hung up and went back to the car.

"Everything all right, sir?" Bradley asked, window rolled down, halfway through his post-fish-and-chips cigarette. The car's interior smelled of lard, vinegar and warm newsprint.

"Yes," said Chadwick. "Right now, I think we'd better head back to Brimleigh Glen and see what's been happening there, don't you?"

The search team had fastened tape to the four trees that sur-rounded the little grove deep in Brimleigh Woods, about two hundred yards from where the body had been found. The woods were dense enough that from there you couldn't see as far as the field, and any noise would certainly have been drowned out by the music.

The police dog had found the spot easily enough by fol-lowing the smell of the victim's blood. Officers had also marked off the route the dog had taken and painted little crosses on the trees. Every inch of the path would have to be searched. For the moment, though, Chadwick, Enderby and Bradley stood behind the tape gazing down at the bloodstained ground.

"This where it happened?" Chadwick asked.

"So the experts tell me," said Enderby, pointing to blood-stains on the leaves and undergrowth. "There's some blood here, consistent with the wounds the victim received."

"Wouldn't the killer have been covered in blood?" Bradley asked.

"Not necessarily," said Enderby. "Peculiar things, stab wounds. Certainly with a slashed neck artery or vein, or a head wound, there's quite a lot of spatter, but with the heart, oddly enough, the edges of the wound close and most of the bleeding is internal; it doesn't spurt the way many people think it does. There's quite a bit of seepage, of course – that's what you're seeing here and in the sleeping bag – and I doubt he'd have got away with his hands completely clean. After all, it looks as if he stabbed her five or six times and twisted the blade." He gestured to the edge of the copse. "If you look over there, though, by the stream, you can see that little pile of leaves. They've got traces of blood on them, too. I reckon that he tried to wipe it off with the leaves first, then he washed his hands in the running water."

"Get it all collected and sent to the lab," said Chadwick, turning away. He wasn't usually sentimental about victims, but he couldn't get the image of the innocent-looking girl in the bloodstained white dress out of his mind, and he couldn't help but think of his own daughter. "When did the doctor say he'd get around to the post-mortem?"

"He said he'd try for later this afternoon, sir," said Enderby.

"Good."

"We've interviewed most of the people on security duty," Enderby added.

"And?"

"Nothing, I'm afraid, sir. They all agree there was so much coming and going, so much pandemonium, that nobody knows who was where when. I've a good suspicion most of them were partaking of the same substances as the musicians and guests, too, which doesn't help their memories much. Lots of people were wandering around in a daze."

"Hmm," said Chadwick. "I didn't think we could expect too much from them. What about the girl?"

"No one admits definitely to seeing her, but we've got a couple of cautious maybes."

"Push a bit harder."

"Will do, sir."

Chadwick sighed. "I suppose we'd better arrange to talk to the groups who were backstage at the time, get statements, for what they're worth."

"Sir?" said Enderby.

"What?"

"You might find that a bit difficult, sir. I mean . . . they'll have all gone home now, and these people . . . well, they're not readily accessible."

"They're no different from you and me, are they, Enderby? Not royalty or anything?"

"No, sir, more like film stars. But —"

"Well, then? I'll deal with the two local groups, but as far as the rest are concerned, arrange to have them interviewed. Get someone to help you."

"Yes, sir," Enderby replied tightly, and turned away.

"And Enderby."

"Sir?"

"I don't know what the standards are in North Yorkshire, but while you're working for me I'd prefer it if you got your hair cut."

Enderby reddened. "Yes, sir."

"Bit hard on him, weren't you, sir?" said Bradley, when Enderby had gone.

"He's a scruff."

"No, sir. I mean about questioning the groups. He's right, you know. Some of these pop stars are a bit high and mighty."

"What would you have me do, Simon? Ignore the fifty or so people who might have seen the victim with her killer because they're some sort of gods?"

"No, sir."

"Come on. Let's head back home. I should be in time for Dr. O'Neill's post-mortem if I'm lucky, and I want you to go to Yorkshire Television and the BBC and have a look at the footage they shot of the festival."

"What am I looking for, sir?"

"Right now, anything. The girl, anyone she might have been with. Any odd or unusual behaviour." Chadwick paused. "On second thought, don't worry about that last bit. It's all bound to be odd and unusual, given the people we're dealing with."

Bradley laughed. "Yes, sir."

"Just use your initiative, laddie. At least you won't have to watch the doctor open the poor girl up."

Before they walked away, Chadwick turned back to the bloodstained ground.

"What is it, sir?" Bradley asked.

"Something that's been bothering me all morning. The sleeping bag."

"Sleeping bag?"

"Aye. Who did it belong to?"

"Her, I suppose," said Bradley.

"Perhaps," Chadwick said. "But why would she carry it into the woods with her? It just seems odd, that's all."

3

It was after midnight when the lights came back on, and the wind was still raging, now lashing torrents of rain against the windows and lichen-stained roofs of Fordham. The coroner's van had taken the body away, and Dr. Glendenning had said he would try to get the post-mortem done the following day, even though it was a Saturday. The SOCOs worked on in the new light just as they had done before, collecting samples, labelling and storing everything carefully. So far, they had discovered nothing of immediate importance. One or two members of the local media had arrived, and the police press officer, David Whitney, was on the scene keeping them back and feeding them titbits of information.

Banks used the newly restored electric light to have a good look around the rest of the cottage, and it didn't take him very long to realize that any personal items Nick might have had with him were gone except for his clothes, toiletries and a few books. There was no wallet, for example, no mobile, nothing with his name on it. The clothes didn't tell him much. Nothing fancy, just casual Gap-style shirts, a grey pinstripe jacket, cargos and Levis for the most part. All the toiletries told him was that Nick suffered from, or worried that he might suffer from, heartburn and indigestion, judging by the variety of antacids he had brought with him. Winsome reported that his car was a Renault Mégane, and to open it you needed a card, not a key. There wasn't one in sight, so she had phoned the police garage in Eastvale, who said they would send someone out as soon as possible.

There was nothing relating to the car on the Police National Computer, Winsome added, so she would have to get the details from the Driver and Vehicle Licensing Agency in Swansea as soon as she could raise someone, which wouldn't be easy on a weekend. If necessary, they could check the National DNA Database, which held samples of the DNA not only of convicted criminals but of anyone who had been arrested, even if they had been acquitted. The public railed about its attacks on freedom, but the database had come in useful more than once for identifying a body, among other things.

They would find out who Nick was soon enough, but someone was making it difficult for them, and Banks wondered why. Would knowing the victim's identity point the police quickly in the direction of the killer? Did he need time to make his escape?

It was clear that only one of the two bedrooms had been used. The beds weren't even made up in the other. From what Banks could see at a cursory glance, it looked as if both sides of the double bed had been slept on, but Nick might have been a restless sleeper. Peter Darby had already photographed the room, and the SOCOs would bag the sheets for testing. There was no sign of condoms in any of the bedside drawers, or anywhere else, for that matter, and nothing at all to show who, or what, the mysterious Nick had been, except for the paperback copy of Ian McEwan's *Atonement* on the bedside table.

According to the Waterstone's bookmark, Nick had got to page sixty-eight. Banks picked up the book and flipped through it. On the back endpaper, someone had written in faint pencil six uneven rows of figures, some of them circled. He turned to the front and saw the price of the book, £3.50, also in pencil, but in a different hand, at the top right of the first inside page. A second-hand book, then. Which meant that any number of people might have owned it and written the figures in the back. Still, it might mean something. Banks called up a SOCO to bag it and told him to be sure to make a photocopy of the page in question.

Frustrated by this early lack of knowledge of the victim, Banks went back downstairs. Usually he had a person's books or CD collection to go on, not to mention the opinions of others, but this time all he knew was that Nick did the *Independent* crossword, was reading *Atonement*, was polite but not particularly chatty, favoured casual clothing, perhaps suffered from indigestion, smoked Dunhills and wore glasses. It wasn't anywhere near enough to help start figuring out who might have wanted him dead and why. *Patience*, he told himself, *early days yet*, but he didn't feel patient.

By half past twelve, he'd had enough. Time to go home. Just as he was about to get PC Travers to fix up a lift for him, Annie edged over and said, "There's not a lot more we can achieve hanging around here, is there?"

"Nothing," said Banks. "The mechanics are all in motion and Stefan will get in touch with us if anything important comes up, but I doubt we'll get any further tonight. Why?"

Annie smiled at him. "Well, I don't know about you, but I'm starving and, as I remember, Marks and Spencer's vegetarian lasagna heats up a treat. You know what they say about an army marching on its stomach and all that."

Monday, September 8, 1969

Yvonne Chadwick accepted the joint that Steve passed to her and drew deeply. She liked getting high. Not the hard stuff, no pills or needles, only dope. Sex was all right, too; she liked that well enough with Steve, but most of all she liked getting high, and the two usually went together really well. Music, too. They were listening to Hendrix's *Electric Ladyland*, and it sounded out of this world.

Take now. She was supposed to be at school, but she had taken the afternoon off. It was only games and free periods, anyway; the new term hadn't really got underway yet. There was a house just up the road from her school, on Springfield Mount, where a group of hippies lived: Steve, Todd, Jacqui, American Charlie and others who came and went. She had become friendly with them after she met Steve upstairs at the Peel, on Boar Lane, one night in April when she went there with her friend Lorraine from school. She had just turned sixteen the month before, but she could pass for eighteen easily enough with a bit of makeup and high heels. Steve was the handsome, sensitive sort of boy, and she had fancied him straight away. He'd read her some of his poetry, and while she didn't really understand it, she could tell that it sounded important.

There were other houses she visited where people were into the same things, too – one on Carberry Place and another on Bayswater Terrace. Yvonne felt that she could turn up at any one of them at any time and feel as if she really belonged there. Everyone accepted her just as she was. Someone was always around to welcome her, maybe with a joint and a pot of jasmine tea. They all liked the same music, too, and agreed about society and the evils of the war and stuff. But Springfield Mount was the closest, and Steve lived there.

The air smelled of sandalwood incense, and there were posters on the walls: Jimi Hendrix, Janis Joplin, a creepy Salvador Dali print and, even creepier, Goya's etching *The Sleep of Reason Brings Forth Monsters*. Sometimes, when she was smoking really good dope, Yvonne would lose herself in that one, the sleeping artist surrounded by creatures of the night.

Mostly, they all just sat around and talked about the terrible shape the world was in and how they hoped to change it, end the war in Vietnam, free the universities from the establishment and their professor lackeys, put a stop to imperialism and capitalist oppression. Yvonne couldn't wait to go to university; as far as she was concerned, that was where life got really exciting, not like boring old school, where they still treated you like a kid and weren't interested in what you thought about the world. At university you were a *student*, and you went to demos and things. Steve was a second-year English student, but the term wasn't due to start for a couple of weeks yet. He'd told her he would get her into all the great concerts at the university refectory next term, and she could hardly wait. The Moody Blues were coming, and Family and Tyrannosaurus Rex. There were even rumours of the Who coming to record a live concert.

They had already seen a lot of great local gigs together that summer: Thunderclap Newman at the Town Hall; Pink Floyd, Colosseum and Eire Apparent at Selby Abbey. She regretted missing the Isle of Wight – *Dylan* had been there, after all – but her parents wouldn't let her go that far. She had two years to wait to go to university, *and* she had to get good A levels. Right now, that didn't look like a strong possibility, but she'd worry about that later; she had just started in the lower sixth, so there was plenty of time yet to catch up. After all, she had managed to get seven very good O levels.

She had to admit, as she grinned through the haze of smoke, that things were looking pretty good. Sunday had been great. They had gone to the Brimleigh Festival – she, Steve, Todd, Charlie and Jacqui – and they had stayed up all night on the field sharing joints, food and drink with their fellow revellers. Steve had dropped acid, but Yvonne hadn't wanted to because there were too many people around and she worried about getting paranoid. But Steve had seemed okay, though she'd got worried at one time when he disappeared for more than an hour. When it was all over, they went to Springfield Mount for a while to come down with a couple of joints, and then she went home to get ready for school, narrowly avoiding bumping into her father.

She hadn't dared tell her parents where she was going. Christ, why did she have to have a father who was a *pig*, for crying out loud? It just wasn't fair. If she told her new friends what her old man did for a living, they'd drop her like a hot coal. And if it wasn't for her parents she could have gone to Brimleigh on Saturday, too. Steve and the others had been there both nights. But if she'd done that, she realized, they wouldn't let her out on Sunday.

They were sitting on the living-room floor propped up against the sofa. Just her and Steve this time; the others were all out. Some of the people who came and went she wasn't too sure about at all. One of them, Magic Jack, was scary with his beard and wild eyes, although she had never seen him behave in any other way than gently, but the most frightening of all – and thank God he didn't turn up very often – was McGarrity, the mad poet.

There was something about McGarrity that really worried Yvonne. Older than the rest, he had a thin, lined parchment face and black eyes. He always wore a black hat and a matching cape, and he had a flick knife with a tortoiseshell handle. He never really talked to anyone, never joined in the discussions. Sometimes he would pace up and down, tapping the blade against his palm, muttering to himself, reciting poetry. T.S. Eliot mostly, *The Waste Land*. Yvonne only recognized it because Steve had lent her a copy to read not so long ago, and he had explained its meaning to her.

Some people found McGarrity okay, but he gave Yvonne the creeps. She had asked Steve once why they let him hang around, but all Steve had said was that McGarrity was harmless really; it was just that his mind had been damaged a bit by the electric shock treatment they'd given him at the mental home when he deserted the army. Besides, if they wanted a free and open society, how could they justify excluding people? There wasn't much to say after that, though Yvonne thought there were probably a few people they wouldn't like to have in the house: her dad, for example. McGarrity had been at Brimleigh, too, but luckily he'd wandered off and left them alone.

Yvonne could feel Steve's hand on her thigh, gently stroking, and she turned to smile at him. It was all right, really it was all right. Her parents didn't know it, but she was on the pill, had been since she had turned sixteen. It wasn't easy to get, and there was no way she would have asked old Cuthbertson, the family doctor. But her friend Maggie had told her about a new family planning clinic on Woodhouse Lane where they were very concerned about teenage pregnancies and very obliging if you said you were over the age of consent.

Steve kissed her and put his hand on her breast. The dope they were smoking wasn't especially strong, but it heightened her sense of touch, as it did her hearing, and she felt herself responding to his caresses, getting wet. He undid the buttons on her school blouse and then she felt his hand moving up over her bare thighs. Jimi Hendrix was singing "1983" when Steve and Yvonne toppled onto the floor, pulling at one another's clothing

Chadwick leaned back against the cool tiles of the mortuary wall and watched Dr. O'Neill and his assistant at work under the bright light. Post-mortems had never bothered him, and this one was no exception, even though the victim had reminded him earlier of Yvonne. Now she was just an unfortunate dead girl on the porcelain slab. Her life was gone, drained out of her, and all that remained were flesh, muscle, blood, bone and organs. And, possibly, clues.

The painted cornflower blooming on her dead cheek looked even more incongruous in this harsh steel and porcelain environment. Chadwick found himself wondering, not for the first time, whether it had been painted by the girl herself, by a friend or by her killer. And if the latter, what was its significance?

Dr. O'Neill had carefully removed the bloody dress, after matching the holes in the material to the wounds, and set it aside with the sleeping bag for further forensic testing. So far they had discovered that the sleeping bag was a cheap, popular brand sold mainly through Woolworths.

The doctor bent over the pale, naked body to examine the stab wounds. There were five in all, he noted, and one had been so hard and gone so deep that it had bruised the surrounding skin. If the hilt of the knife had caused the bruising, as Dr. O'Neill believed it had, they were dealing with a single-edged, four-inch blade. A very thin, stiletto-type blade, too, allowing that it was a bit bigger than the actual wounds, owing to the elasticity of the skin. One strong possibility, he suggested, was a flick knife. They were illegal in Britain but easy enough to pick up on the continent.

Judging by the angles of the wounds, Dr. O'Neill concluded that the victim had been stabbed by a strong, left-handed person standing behind her. The complete lack of defence wounds on her hands indicated that she had been so taken by surprise that she had either died or gone into shock before she knew what was happening.

"She may not have seen her killer, then," said Chadwick, "unless it was someone she knew well enough to let that close?"

"I can't speculate on that. You can see as well as I can, though, that there appear to be no other injuries to the surface of the body apart from that light bruising on the neck, which tells me someone held her in a stranglehold with his right arm while he stabbed her with his left. We'll be testing for drugs, too, of course – it's possible she was slipped something that immobilized her: Nembutal, Iuinol, something like that. But she was standing when she was stabbed – the angles tell us that much – so she must have been conscious."

Chadwick looked down at the body. Dr. O'Neill was right. Apart from the faint discoloration on her neck and the mess around her left breast, she was in almost pristine condition: no cuts, no rope burns, nothing.

"Was he taller than her?" Chadwick asked.

"Yes, judging by the shape and position of the bruises and the angle of the cuts, I'd estimate by a good six inches. She was five foot four, which makes him at least five foot ten."

"Would you say the bruising indicates a struggle?"

"Not necessarily. As you can see, it's fairly mild. He could simply have had his arm loosely around her neck, then tightened it when he stabbed her. It probably all happened so quickly he didn't need to restrain her. We already know there are no defensive wounds to the hands, which indicates she was taken by surprise. If that's the case, she would have slumped as she died, and his arm could have caused the bruising then."

"I thought bodies didn't bruise after death."

"This would have been the moment before death, or at the moment of death." Dr. O'Neill turned his attention to the golden hair between the girl's legs, and Chadwick felt himself tense. So like Yvonne's when he had seen her naked that time by accident at the caravan. How embarrassed they had both felt.

"Again," said Dr. O'Neill, "we'll have to do swabs and further tests, but there doesn't appear to be any sign of sexual activity. There's no bruising around the vaginal areas or the anus."

"So you're saying she wasn't raped, she didn't have sex?"

"I'm not committing myself to anything yet," said Dr. O'Neill sharply. "Not until I've done an internal examination and the samples have been analyzed. All I'm saying is there are no obvious, superficial signs of forced or rough sexual activity. One thing we did find was a tampon. It looks as if our victim was menstruating at the time of the murder."

"Which still doesn't rule out sexual activity altogether?"

"Not at all. But if she did have sex, she had time to put another tampon in before she was killed."

Chadwick thought for a moment. If sex had been the reason for her death, then surely there would have been more signs of violence, unless they had been lovers to begin with. Had they made love first, then dressed, and while she was leaning back on him in the afterglow, he killed her? But why, if sex had been consensual? Had she, perhaps, refused, said she was having her period, and had that somehow angered her attacker? Were they really dealing with a nutcase?

As often as not, Chadwick knew, investigations, including the medical kind, threw up more questions than answers, and it was only through answering them that you made progress.

Chadwick watched as O'Neill and his assistant made the Y incision and peeled back the skin, muscle and soft tissues from the chest wall before pulling the chest flap up over her face and cutting through the rib cage with an electric saw. The smell was overwhelming. Raw meat. Lamb, mostly, Chadwick thought.

"Hmm, it's as I suspected," said Dr. O'Neill. "The chest cavity is filled with blood, as are all the other cavities. Massive internal bleeding."

"Would she have died quickly?"

Dr. O'Neill probed around and remained silent a few minutes, then said, "From the state of her, seconds at most. Look here. He twisted the knife so sharply he actually cut off a piece of her heart."

Chadwick looked. As usual, he wished he could see what Dr. O'Neill did, but all he saw was a mass of glistening, bloody organ tissue. "I'll take your word for it," he said.

Dr. O'Neill's assistant carefully started removing the inner organs for sectioning, further testing and examination. Barring any glaring anomalies, Chadwick knew it would be a few days before he received the results of all this. There was no real reason to stick around, and he had more than enough things to do. He left just as Dr. O'Neill started up the saw to cut through the victim's skull and remove her brain.

Saturday morning dawned fresh and clear, and Helmthorpe had that rinsed and scoured look: the streets, limestone buildings and flagstone roofs still dark with rain, but the sun out, the sky blue and a cool wind to rattle the bare branches.

Banks fiddled with the attachment that let him play the iPod through the car stereo and was rewarded by Judy Collins singing "Who Knows Where the Time Goes?" in a voice of such aching beauty and clarity that it made him want to laugh and cry at the same time. Sandy Denny's lyrics had never seemed so doom-laden; they made him think about his brother Roy. Almost as a rebuke, it seemed, the Porsche coursed smoothly and powerfully through the late autumn landscape.

After she had eaten the lasagna and drunk one small glass of wine, Annie had driven off to Harkside and left Banks to his own devices. It was after two in the morning, but he had poured himself a glass of Amarone and listened to Fischer-Dieskau's 1962 *Winterreise* in the dark before heading for bed with a head full of gloomy thoughts. Even then he hadn't been able to sleep. It was partly heartburn from eating so late – he wished he had taken one of Nick's antacids, as he had none in the house – and partly disturbing dreams during those brief moments when he did nod off. Several times he awoke abruptly with his heart pounding and a vague, terrifying image skittering away down the slippery slopes of his subconscious. He had lain there taking slow, deep breaths until he had fallen asleep, about an hour before the alarm went off.

The team gathered in the boardroom, crime scene photos pinned to the corkboard, but the whiteboard was conspicuously empty apart from the name Nick. An incident van had been dispatched to Fordham earlier in the morning, fitted out with phones and computers. Information collected there would be collated and passed on to headquarters. Banks was officially the senior investigating officer, appointed by Assistant Chief Constable Ron McLaughlin, and Annie was his deputy. Other tasks would be assigned to various officers according to their skills.

Since Detective Superintendent Gristhorpe had retired two months ago, they had been given a temporary replacement in Catherine Gervaise. There were those who muttered that

Banks should have got the job, but he knew it had never been on the cards. He had got on well enough with ACC McLaughlin, "Red Ron," and with the chief constable himself on those rare occasions when they met, but he was too much of a loose cannon. If nothing else, running off to London to look for his brother, and getting involved in all that followed from that, had put several nails in the coffin of his career. Besides, he didn't want the responsibility, or the paperwork. Gristhorpe had always left him alone to work cases the way he wanted, which meant he ended up doing a lot of the legwork and streetwork himself, because that was the way he liked it.

Catherine Gervaise was cool and distant, not a mentor and friend the way Gristhorpe had been, and under her rule he found that he had to fight harder for his privileges. She was an administrator, through and through, an ambitious woman who had risen quickly through the ranks via accelerated-promotion schemes, management and computer courses and, some said, by affirmative action. This would be her first major investigation at Western Area Headquarters, so it would be interesting to see how she handled it. At least she wasn't stupid, Banks thought, and she should know how best to use her resources.

Some were put off by her posh accent and Cheltenham Ladies' College background, but Banks was inclined to give her the benefit of the doubt, as long as she left him alone. The one thing they had in common, he discovered, was that she also had season tickets to Opera North, and he had seen her at a performance of *Lucia di Lammermoor* with her husband. He didn't think she had noticed him. At least, she hadn't let on. In appearance, she wore little makeup and was rather severe, with short blonde hair, rather unexpected Cupid's-bow lips and a trim figure. In dress she was conservative, favouring navy suits and white blouses, and in manner she was no-nonsense, remaining aloof and either not getting the squad-room humour, or not wishing to show that she did.

The superintendent asked for a summary of what they had so far, which wasn't much. The blood-spatter analysis was consistent with the theory that Nick had been bashed over the back of the head with a poker as he had been turning away from his killer, perhaps walking towards his cigarettes. After that, he had been hit once or twice more – they wouldn't know until Dr. Glendenning performed the post-mortem – no doubt to make sure he was dead.

"Have we got any further identifying the victim?" Superintendent Gervaise asked next.

"A little, ma'am," said Winsome. "At least the local memory tag on his licence plate number indicates the car was registered in London."

"It's not hired?"

"No. We finally got a look inside with the help of the garage. Unfortunately, there was nothing inside to indicate who he was, either."

"So someone really wanted to throw sand in our eyes."

"Well, ma'am, it's a fairly new car, and he might not have been the kind of person who lives out of it, but it certainly looks that way. Whoever did it must have known he could only have slowed the investigation down, though." Winsome looked at Banks, who nodded for her to go on. "Which probably means that he wanted to give himself a bit of time to get far enough away and arrange an alibi."

"Interesting theory, DC Jackman," said Gervaise. "But that's all it is, isn't it, a theory?"

"Yes, ma'am. For the moment."

"And we need facts."

That was pretty much self-evident in any investigation, Banks thought. Of course you wanted facts, but until you got them you played around with theories, you used what you did have, then you applied a bit of imagination, and as often as not you came up with an approximation of the truth, which was what he thought Winsome was doing. So Ms. Gervaise wanted to establish herself as a just-the-facts, no-fancy-theories kind of superintendent. Well, so be it. The squad would soon learn to keep their theories to themselves, but Banks hoped her attitude wouldn't completely crush their creativity and wouldn't stop them confiding their theories in him. It was all very well to come in with an attitude, but it was another thing if that attitude destroyed the delicate balance that had already been achieved over time.

They were drastically short of DCs, having recently lost Gavin Rickerd, their best office manager, to the new Neighbourhood Policing Initiative, where he was working with community support officers and specials to tackle the anti-social behaviour that was becoming increasingly the norm all over the country, especially on a Saturday night in Eastvale. Gavin hadn't been replaced yet, and in his absence the job this time had gone to one of the uniformed constables, hardly the ideal choice, but the best they could do right now.

Banks wanted Winsome Jackman and Kev Templeton doing what they did best – tracking down information and following leads – and when it came to that, Detective Sergeant Hatchley had always been a bit slow and lazy. His physical presence used to help intimidate the odd suspect or two, but these days the ex–rugby player's muscle had gone mostly to fat, and the police weren't allowed to intimidate villains anymore. Villains' Rights had put paid to that, or so it sometimes seemed, especially since a burglar had fallen off the roof of a warehouse he had broken into last summer, then sued the owner for damages and won.

"I'm trying to get in touch with the DVLA in Swansea," Winsome said, "but it's Saturday. They're closed and I can't seem to track down my contact."

"Keep trying," said Superintendent Gervaise. "Is there anything else?"

Winsome consulted her notes. "DS Templeton and I interviewed the people in the Cross Keys and took statements. Nothing new there. And when the lights came on we made a quick check of their outer clothing for signs of blood. There were none."

"What's your take on this?" Gervaise asked Banks.

"I don't have enough facts yet to form an opinion," Banks said.

The irony wasn't lost on Superintendent Gervaise, who pursed her lips. She looked as if she had just bitten into a particularly vinegary pickle. Banks noticed Annie look away and smile to herself, pen against her lips, shaking her head slowly.

"I understand you entered a licensed premises during the early stages of the investigation yesterday evening," Gervaise said.

"That's right." Banks wondered who had been talking, and why.

"I suppose you know there are regulations governing drinking whilst on duty?"

"With all due respect," Banks said, "I didn't go there for a drink. I went to question possible witnesses."

"But you did have a drink?"

"While I was there, yes. I find it puts people at ease. They see you as more like they are, not as the enemy."

"Duly noted," said Gervaise dryly. "And did you find any co-operative witnesses?"

"Nobody seemed to know very much about the victim," Banks said. "He was renting a cottage. He wasn't a local."

"On holiday at this time of year?"

"That's what I wondered about."

"Find out what he was doing there. That might help us get to the bottom of this."

Quite the one for dishing out obvious orders, was Super-intendent Gervaise, Banks thought. He'd had bosses like that before: state the obvious, the things your team would do anyway, without even being asked, and take the credit for the results. "Of course," he said. "We're working on it. One of the staff might know a bit more than she's letting on."

"What makes you think that?"

"Her manner, body language."

"All right. Question her. Bring her in, if necessary."

Banks could tell by Superintendent Gervaise's clipped tone and the way her hand strayed to her short, layered locks that she was getting bored with the meeting and anxious to get away, no doubt to send out a memo on drinking while on duty, or the ten most obvious courses to pursue during a murder inquiry.

"If that's all for now, ladies and gentlemen," she went on, stuffing her papers into her briefcase, "then I suggest we all get down to work."

To a chorus of muttered "Yes, ma'ams," she left the room, heels clicking against the hardwood floor. Only after she'd gone did Banks realize that he had forgotten to tell her about the figures in the book.

Monday, September 8, 1969
Janet was watching the *News at Ten* when Chadwick got home that evening, and Reginald Bosanquet was talking about ITA's

exciting new UHF colour transmissions from the Crystal Palace transmitter, which was all very well, Chadwick thought, if you happened to own a colour TV. He didn't. Not on a DI's pay of a little over two thousand pounds per year. Janet walked towards him.

"Hard day?" she asked.

Chadwick nodded, kissed her and sat down in his favourite armchair.

"Drink?"

"A small whisky would go down nicely. Yvonne not home yet?" He glanced at the clock. Twenty past ten.

"Not yet."

"Know where she is?"

Janet turned from pouring the whisky. "Out with friends was all she said."

"She shouldn't go out so often on school nights. She knows that."

Janet handed him the drink. "She's sixteen. We can't expect her to do everything the way we'd like it. Things are different these days. Teenagers have a lot more freedom."

"Freedom? As long as she's under this roof we've a right to expect some degree of honesty and respect from her, haven't we?" Chadwick argued. "The next thing you know she'll be dropping out and running off to live in a hippie commune. *Freedom.*"

"Oh, give it a rest, Stan. She's going through a stage, that's all." Janet softened her tone. "She'll get over it. Weren't you just a little bit rebellious when you were sixteen?"

Chadwick tried to remember. He didn't think so. It was 1937 when he was sixteen, before "teenagers" had been invented, when youth was simply an unfortunate period one had to pass through on the route from childhood to maturity.

Another world. George VI was crowned king that year, Neville Chamberlain became prime minister and looked likely to get along well with Hitler and the Spanish Civil War was at its bloodiest. But Chadwick had paid only scant attention to world affairs. He was at grammar school then, on a scholarship, playing rugby with the first fifteen, and all set for a university career that was interrupted by the war and somehow never got resurrected.

He had volunteered for the Green Howards in 1940 because his father had served with them in the first war, and spent the next five years killing first Japanese, then Germans, while trying to stay alive himself. After it was all over and he was back on civvy street in his demob suit, it took him six years to get over it. Six years of dead-end jobs, bouts of depression, loneliness and hunger. He nearly died of cold in the bitter winter of 1947. Then it was as if the weight suddenly lifted, the lights came on. He joined the West Riding Constabulary in 1951. The following year he met Janet at a dance. They were married only three months later, and a year after that, in March 1953, Yvonne was born.

Rebellious? He didn't think so. It seemed to be a young person's lot in life to go off to war back then, just like the generation before him, and in the army you obeyed orders. He'd got into minor mischief like all the other kids, smoking before he was old enough, the odd bit of shoplifting, sneaking drinks from his father's whisky bottle, replacing what he'd drunk with water. He also got into the occasional scrap. But one thing he didn't dare do was disobey his parents. If he had stayed out all night without permission, his father would have beaten him black and blue.

Chadwick grunted. He didn't suppose Janet really wanted an answer; she was just trying to ease the way for Yvonne's arrival home, which he hoped would be soon.

The news finished at ten-forty-five and the late night "X" film came on. Normally Chadwick wouldn't bother watching such rubbish, but this week it was *Saturday Night and Sunday Morning*, which he and Janet had seen at the Lyric about eight years ago, and he didn't mind watching it again. At least it was the sort of life he could understand, *real life*, not long-haired kids listening to loud music and taking drugs.

It was about quarter past eleven when he heard the front door open and shut. By that time, his anger had edged over into concern, but in a parent the two are often so intermingled as to be indistinguishable.

"Where have you been?" he asked Yvonne when she walked into the living room in her pale blue bell-bottomed jeans and red cheesecloth top with white and blue embroidery down the gathered front. Her eyes looked a little bleary, but other than that she seemed all right.

"That's a nice welcome," she said.

"Are you going to answer me?"

"If you must know, I've been to the Grove."

"Where's that?"

"Down past the station, by the canal."

"And what goes on there?"

"Nothing goes on. It's folk night on Mondays. People sing folk songs and read poetry."

"You know you're not old enough to drink."

"I wasn't drinking. Not alcohol, anyway."

"You smell of smoke."

"It's a pub, Dad. People were smoking. Look, if all you're going to do is go on at me like this, I'm off to bed. It's a school day tomorrow, or didn't you know?"

"Enough of your cheek! You're too young to be hanging around pubs in town. God knows who –"

"If it was up to you I wouldn't have any friends at all, would I? And I'd never go anywhere. You make me sick!"

And with that Yvonne stomped upstairs to her room.

Chadwick made to follow her, but Janet grabbed his arm. "No, Stan. Not now. Let's not have another flaming row. Not tonight."

Furious as he felt, Chadwick realized she was right. Besides, he was exhausted. Not the best time to get into a long argument with his daughter. But he'd have it out with her tomorrow. Find out what she was up to, where she had been all Sunday night, exactly what crowd she was hanging around with. Even if he had to follow her.

He could hear her banging about upstairs, using the toilet and the bathroom, slamming her bedroom door, making a point of it. It was impossible to get back into the film now. Impossible to go to sleep, too, no matter how tired he felt. If he'd had a dog he would have taken it for a walk. Instead he poured himself another small whisky, and while Janet pretended to read her *Woman's Weekly* he pretended to watch *Saturday Night and Sunday Morning* until all was silent upstairs and it was safe to go to bed.

4

Annie took a chance that Kelly Soames would be turning up for work on Saturday morning, so she parked behind the incident van in Fordham and adjusted her rear-view mirror so that she could see the pub and the road behind her. Banks had told her he thought Kelly didn't want to talk last night because there were people around and she might have a personal secret; therefore, it would be a good idea to get her alone, take her somewhere. He also thought a woman might have more chance of getting whatever it was out of her, hence Annie.

Just before eleven o'clock, Annie saw Kelly get out of a car. She recognized the driver; he was one of the men who had been in the pub the previous evening, one of the card players. As soon as he had driven off and turned the bend, Annie backed up and intercepted Kelly. "A word with you, please," she said.

Kelly made towards the pub door. "I can't. I'll be late for work."

Annie opened her passenger door. "You'll be a lot later if you don't come with me now."

Kelly chewed her lip, then muttered something under her breath and got in the old purple Astra. It was long past time for a new car, Annie realized, but she'd had neither the time nor the money lately. Banks had offered her his Renault when he got the Porsche, but she had declined. It wasn't her kind of car, for a start, and there was something rather shabby in her mind about taking Banks's castoffs. She'd buy something new soon, but for now, the Astra still got her where she wanted to go.

Annie set off up the hill, past the youth hostel, where a couple of uniforms were still making inquiries, on to the wild moorland beyond. She pulled over into a lay-by next to a stile. It was the start of a walk to an old lead mine, Annie knew, as Banks had taken her there to show her where someone had once found a body in the flue. That morning, there was no one around and wind raged, whistling around the car, plucking at the purple heather and rough sere grass. Kelly took a packet of Embassy Regal out of her handbag, but Annie pushed her hand down and said, "No. Not in here. I don't like the smell of smoke, and I'm not opening the windows. It's too cold."

Kelly put the cigarettes away and pouted.

"Last night, when we were talking in the pub," Annie said, "you reacted in a rather extreme way about what happened."

"Well, someone got killed. I mean, it might be normal for you, but not round here. It was a shock, that's all."

"It seemed like a personal shock."

"What do you mean?"

"Do I have to spell it out, Kelly?"

"I'm not thick."

"Then stop playing games. What was your relationship with the deceased?"

"I didn't have a relationship. He came to the pub, that's all. He had a nice smile, said have one for yourself. Isn't that enough?"

"Enough for what?"

"Enough to be upset that he's dead."

"Look, I'm sorry if this is hard for you," Annie went on, "but we're only doing this because we care, too."

Kelly shot her a glance. "You never even saw him when he was alive. You didn't even know he existed."

True, it was one of the things about Annie's job that she more often than not found herself investigating the deaths of strangers. But Banks had taught her that during the course of such investigations they don't remain strangers. You get to know the dead, become their voice, in a way, because they can no longer speak for themselves. She couldn't explain this to Kelly, though.

"He'd been in the cottage a week," said Annie, "and you're telling me you only saw him when he came into the pub and said hello."

"So?"

"You seem more upset than I think you would be if that was all."

Kelly folded her arms. "I don't know what you're talking about."

Annie turned to face her. "I think you do, Kelly."

They sat silently cocooned in the car, Kelly stiff, facing the front, Annie turned sideways in her seat, looking at her profile. A few spots of acne stood out on the girl's right cheek, and she had a little white scar at the outer edge of one eyebrow. Outside, the wind continued to rage through the moorland grass and to rock the car a little with unexpected gusts and buffets. The sky was a vast expanse of blue with small, high, fast-moving white clouds casting brief shadows on the moor. It must have been three, maybe four minutes, an awful long time in that sort of situation, anyway, before Kelly started to shiver a little, and before long she was shaking like a leaf in Annie's arms, tears streaming down her face. "You mustn't tell my father," she kept saying through the tears. "You mustn't tell my father."

Tuesday, September 9, 1969

On Tuesday evening, Yvonne was in her room after teatime reading Mark Knopfler's column in the *Yorkshire Evening Post*. He wrote about the music scene and sometimes jammed with local bands at the Peel and the Guildford, and she thought he might have something to say about Brimleigh, but this week's column was about a series of forthcoming concerts at the Harrogate Theatre – The Nice, the Who, Yes, Fairport Convention. It sounded great, *if* her father would let her go to Harrogate.

She heard a knock at her door and was surprised to see her father standing there. Even more surprised to see that he didn't appear angry with her. Her mother must have put in a good word for her. Even so, she braced herself for the worst: accusations, the cutting of pocket money and limitation of freedom, but they didn't come. Instead, they came to a compromise. She would be allowed to go to the Grove on Mondays but had to be home by eleven o'clock and must under no circumstances drink any alcohol. And she had to stop in and do her homework every other school night. She could also go out Friday and Saturday. But *not* all night. He tried to get her to tell him where she'd been on Sunday, but all she said was that she'd spent the night listening to music with friends and had lost track of the time. Somehow, she got the impression that he didn't believe her, but instead of pushing it, he asked, "Have you got anything by Led Zeppelin?"

"Led Zeppelin? Yes. Why?" They had only released one LP so far, and Yvonne had bought it with the record token her

Aunt Moira had given her for her sixteenth birthday back in March. It said in *Melody Maker* that they had a new album coming out next month, and Robert Plant had mentioned it at Brimleigh, when they had played songs from it, like "Heartbreaker." Yvonne could hardly wait. Robert Plant was so sexy.

"Would you say they're loud?"

Yvonne laughed. "Pretty loud, yes."

"Mind if I give them a listen?"

Still confused, Yvonne said, "No, not at all. Go ahead." She picked it out of her pile and handed it to him, the LP with the big Zeppelin touching the edge of the Eiffel Tower and bursting into flames.

The Dansette record player that her father had got for five thousand Embassy coupons before he stopped smoking was downstairs, in the living room. It was a bone of contention, as Yvonne maintained that she was the only one who bought records and really cared about music, apart from the occasional Johnny Mathis and Jim Reeves her mother put on, and her father's few big-band LPs. She thought it should be in her room, but her father insisted that it was the *family* record player.

At least he had bought her, for her birthday, an extra speaker unit that you could plug in to create a real stereo effect, and she had the little transistor radio she kept on her bedside table, but she still had to wait until her parents were out before she could listen to her own records properly, at the right volume.

She went down with him and turned it on. He didn't even seem to know how to operate the thing, so Yvonne took over. Soon, "Good Times, Bad Times" was blasting out loudly enough to bring Janet dashing in from the kitchen to see what was going on.

After listening to less than half of the song, Chadwick turned down the volume and asked, "Are they all like that?"

"You'd probably think so," Yvonne said, "but every song is different. Why?"

"Nothing, really. Just something I was wondering about." He rejected the LP and switched off the record player. "Thanks, you can have it back now."

Still puzzled, Yvonne put the LP back in its sleeve and went up to her room.

Banks looked out of his office window. It was market day, and the wooden stalls spread out over the cobbled square, canvas covers flapping in the wind, selling everything from cheap shirts and flat caps to used books, bootleg CDs and DVDs. The monthly farmers' market extended farther across the square, selling locally grown vegetables, Wensleydale and Swaledale cheese and organic beef and pork. Banks had thought all beef and pork – not to mention wine, fruit and vegetables – was organic, but someone had told him it really meant organically raised, without pesticides or chemicals. Why didn't they say that, then? he wondered.

Locals and tourists alike mingled and sampled the wares. When they had finished there, Banks knew, many of them would be moving on to the big car-boot sale at Catterick, where they would agonize over buying dodgy mobile phones for a couple of quid and dubious 50p ink-jet refills.

It was half past twelve. Banks had spent the rest of the morning after the meeting going over the SOCO exhibits lists and talking with Stefan and Vic Manson about fingerprints and possible DNA samples from the bedding at Moorview Cottage. What they would prove, he didn't know, but he needed everything he could get. And these were probably the kind of "facts" over which Superintendent Gervaise salivated. That wasn't fair, he realized, especially as he had decided to give her the benefit of the doubt, but that remark about going to the pub had stung. He had felt like a schoolboy on the headmaster's carpet again.

Martha Argerich was playing a Beethoven piano concerto on Radio 3 in the background. It was a live recording, and in the quiet bits Banks could hear people in the audience coughing. He thought again about seeing Catherine Gervaise and her husband at Opera North. They had much better seats than he had, closer to the front. They'd have been able to see the sweat and spittle at close hand. Rumour had it that Superintendent Gervaise was after a commander's job at Scotland Yard, but until something came up, they were stuck with her in Eastvale.

Banks sat down and picked up the book again. It looked well thumbed. He had never read any Ian McEwan, but the name was on his list. One day. He liked the opening well enough.

The book gave no clue as to where it had been bought. Some second-hand bookshops, Banks knew, had little stamps on the inside cover with their name and address, but not this one. He would check the local shops to see if the victim had bought it in Eastvale, where there were two possible suppliers and a number of charity shops that sold used books.

Nick hadn't even written his name on the inside, the way some people do. All it said was £3.50. There was a sticker on the back, and Banks realized it was from Borders; he'd seen it before. There looked to be enough coded information on there to locate the branch, but he very much doubted that that would lead him to the actual customer who had bought it originally. And who knew how many people had owned it since then?

Once again he turned to the neat pencilled figures in the back:

6, 8, 9, 21, 22, 25
1, 2, 3, 16, 17, 18, 22, 23
10, ⑫, 13
8, 9, 10, 11, 12, 15, 16, 17, 19, 22, 23, 25, 26, 30
17, 18, ⑲
2, 5, 6, 7, 8, 11, 13, 14, 16, 18, ⑲, 21, 22, 23

They meant nothing to him, but then he had never been any good at codes, if that was what it was supposed to be, or anything to do with numbers, really. He couldn't even tackle sudokus. It might be the most obvious sequence of prime negative ordinals or whatever in the world, and he wouldn't know it from a betting slip. He wracked his brains to think of someone who was good at stuff like that. Not Annie or Kev Templeton, that was for sure. Winsome was good with computers, so maybe she had a strong mathematical brain. Then it came to him. Of course! How could he have forgotten so soon? He grabbed his internal telephone directory, but before he could find the number he wanted, the phone rang. It was Winsome.

"Sir?"

"Yes, Winsome."

"We've got him. I mean, we know who he is. The victim."

"That's great."

"Sorry it took so long, but my contact at the DVLA was at a wedding this morning. That's why I couldn't get in touch with her. She had her mobile turned off."

"Who is he?"

"His name is Nicholas Barber, and he lived in Chiswick." Winsome gave Banks an address.

"Bloody hell," said Banks. "That's the second Londoner killed up here this year. If they get wind of that down south, the tourists will all think there's a conspiracy and stop coming."

"A lot of people might think that wouldn't be such a bad idea, sir," said Winsome. "Maybe then some of the locals would be able to afford to live here."

"Don't you believe it. Estate agents would find some other way to gouge the buyers. Anyway, now we know who he is, we can see about checking his phone records. I can't believe he didn't have a mobile."

"Even if he had, he couldn't have used it in Fordham. No coverage."

"Yes, but he might have gone to Eastvale or somewhere to make calls."

"But what network?"

"Check with all the majors."

"But, sir —"

"I know. It's Saturday. Just do the best you can, Winsome. If you have to wait until Monday morning, so be it. Nick Barber's not going anywhere, and his killer's already long gone."

"Will do, sir."

Banks thought for a moment – *Nick Barber*, there was something familiar about that name, but he couldn't for the life of him remember what it was – then he reached for the directory again and carried on with what he had been doing.

Annie let Kelly Soames collect herself and dry her eyes, trying to minimize the embarrassment the young girl obviously felt at her outburst of emotion.

"I'm sorry," Kelly said finally. "I'm not usually like this. It's just the shock."

"You knew him well?"

Kelly blushed. "No, not at all. We only . . . I mean, it was just a shag, that's all."

"Still . . ." said Annie, thinking that shagging was pretty intimate, even if there was no love involved, and that by speaking of it that way, Kelly was trying to diminish what had happened so she wouldn't feel it so painfully. If someone was naked with you one minute, caressing you, entering you and giving you pleasure, then lying on the floor with his head bashed in the next, it didn't make you a softie if you shed a tear or two. "Care to tell me about it?"

"You mustn't tell my dad. He'll go spare. Promise?"

"Kelly, I'm after information about the . . . about Nick. Unless you were involved in some way with his murder, you've got nothing to worry about."

"I won't have to go to court or anything?"

"I can't imagine why."

Kelly thought for a moment. "There wasn't much to it, really," she said finally. Then she looked at Annie. "Its not something I do all the time, you know. I'm not a slag."

"Nobody's saying you are."

"My dad would if he found out."

"What about your mother?"

"She died when I was sixteen. Dad's never remarried. She . . . they weren't very happy together."

"I'm sorry," said Annie. "But there's no reason for your father to find out."

"As long as you promise."

Annie hadn't promised, and she wasn't going to. The way things stood, she could see no reason why Kelly's secret should come out, and she would do her best to protect it, but the situation could change. "How did it happen?" she asked.

"Like I said, he was nice. In the pub, you know. Lots of people just treat you like dirt because you're a barmaid, but not Nick."

"Did you know his second name?"

"No, sorry. I just called him Nick."

The wind moaned and rocked the car. Kelly hugged herself. She wasn't wearing much more than she had been the previous evening. "Cold?" Annie asked. "I'll turn the heater on." She started the car and turned the heat on. Soon the windows misted over with condensation. "That's better. Go on. You got chatting in the pub."

"No. That's just it. My dad's always there, isn't he? He was there last night. That's why I . . . anyway, he watches me like a hawk at work. He's like the rest, thinks a barmaid's no better than a whore. You should have heard the arguments we had about me taking the job."

"Why did he let you take it, then?"

"Money. He was sick of me living at home and not having a job."

"That'll do it. So you didn't meet Nick in the pub?"

"Well, we did meet there. I mean, that's where we first saw each other, but he was just like any other customer. He was a fit-looking lad. I'll admit I fancied him, and I think maybe he could see that."

"But he wasn't a lad, Kelly. He was much older than you."

Kelly stiffened. "He was only thirty-eight. That's not old. And I'm twenty one. Besides, I like older men. They're not always pawing you like kids my own age. They understand. They listen. And they know about things. All the kids my age talk about is football and beer, but Nick knew everything about music, all the bands, everything. The stories he told me. He was sophisticated."

Annie made a mental note of that, while wondering just how long it took this Nick to start "pawing" Kelly. "How *did* you meet him, then?" she asked.

"In town. Eastvale. Wednesday's my day off, see, and I was out shopping. He was just coming out of that second-hand bookshop down by the side of the church, and I almost bumped into him. Talk about blush. Anyway, he recognized me, and we got chatting, went for a drink in the Queen's Arms. He was funny."

"What happened?"

"He gave me a lift back – I'd come on the bus – and we arranged to meet later."

"Where?"

"At the cottage. He invited me for a meal. I told my dad I was going out with some girlfriends."

"And what happened?"

"What do you think? He made a meal – a curry – he wasn't a bad cook, and we listened to some music and . . . you know . . ."

"You went to bed together."

"Yes."

"Only that once?"

Kelly looked away.

"Kelly?"

"We did it again on Friday, all right? I got two hours off in the afternoon to go to the dentist, but I rearranged my appointment for next Wednesday."

"What time on Friday?"

"Between two and four."

That was the afternoon of the murder. Only two or three hours after Kelly had left, in all likelihood, Nick had been killed. "And those were the only occasions you spent with him? Wednesday night and Friday afternoon?"

"We didn't spend the night together. Not that I wouldn't have, mind you. Just the evening. Had to be home by eleven.

As you might have gathered, my father's a bit of a Victorian when it comes to matters of freedom and discipline."

Yes, and you were off shagging some older bloke you'd just laid eyes on for the first time, Annie thought. Maybe Kelly's father had a point. Anyway, it was none of her business. She was surprised at herself for being so judgmental. "What does he do for a living?"

"He's a farmer. Can you imagine anything more naff?"

"Plenty of things."

"Huh. Well, I can't."

"Do you know someone called Jack Tanner?"

Kelly seemed surprised at the question. "Yes," she said. "He lives just down the road from the pub."

"What do you think of him?"

"I can't say I do very much. Think of him, that is. He always seems a bit of a miserable sod, to me. And he's a total lech as well."

"What do you mean?"

"He's always looking at my tits. He doesn't think I know, but it's well obvious. He does it with all us young girls."

"Have you ever seen him in the pub?"

"No. CC barred him before I started working there. He can't hold his drink. He's always picking fights."

Annie made a note to look into Jack Tanner further and went on. "What do you remember about the cottage?"

"It just looked like a cottage. You know, old furniture and stuff, a creaky bed, toilet with a wonky seat."

"What about Nick's personal things?"

"You must know. You were in there."

"Everything's gone, Kelly."

Kelly gave her a startled look. "Somebody stole it? Is that why they killed him? But there was hardly anything there, unless he was hiding money under the mattress, and I don't think he was. You could have felt a pea under that thing."

"What did he have?"

"Just a few books, a portable CD player with a couple of those small speakers you can set up. Not great sound, but okay. Mostly he liked old stuff, but he had some more modern bands: Doves, Franz Ferdinand, Kaiser Chiefs. And he had a computer."

"Laptop?"

"Yes. A little one. Toshiba, I think. He said he used it mostly for watching DVDs, but he did do some work on it, too."

"What kind of work?"

"He was a writer."

"What sort of writer?"

"I don't know. He never told me about it and I never asked. None of my business, was it? Maybe he was writing his auto-biography."

That would be a bit presumptuous at thirty-eight, Annie thought, but people had written autobiographies at earlier ages than that. "But he definitely said he was a writer?"

"I asked him what he was doing up here at such a miser-able time of year, and he said he wanted a bit of peace and quiet to do some writing. I could tell he was being a bit shy and secre-tive about it, so I didn't push. I wasn't after his life story, anyway."

"Did he ever show you anything he'd written?"

"No. I mean, all we did was have a curry, a chat and a shag. I didn't go searching through his stuff or anything. What do you think I am?"

"All right, Kelly, don't get your knickers in a twist."

Kelly managed a brief smile. "Bit late for that, isn't it?"

"What did you use for contraception?"

"Condoms. What do you think?"

"We didn't find any in the house."

"We used them all. On Friday, like, he wanted to, you know, do it again, but we couldn't. There weren't any left, and it was too late to go into Eastvale. I had to be at work. And there's no way I was going to do it without. I'm not totally stupid."

"Okay," said Annie. Once she had got Kelly talking, she had proved to be far less shy and reticent than she appeared in public. So that explained the rumpled bed and lack of condoms. But robbery hardly seemed like a motive. Obviously, if Nick had had something of great value there, he wouldn't have told some local scrubber he'd picked up in a pub, but why cart anything of value up here in the first place? Unless he was blackmailing somebody. Or making a payoff.

"Did he have a mobile?"

"He did. A fancy Nokia. Fat lot of good it did him, though. They don't work around here. You have to go to Eastvale or Helmthorpe. It's a real drag."

That was a problem in the Dales, Annie knew. They'd put up some new towers, but coverage was still patchy in places because of the hills. There wasn't a land line at the cottage – most rental places don't include one for obvious reasons – and both Mrs. Tanner and Winsome had used the telephone box across the road, by the church. "How did he seem when you were with him?" she asked.

"He was fine."

"He didn't seem upset, depressed or worried about anything?"

"No, not at all."

"What about drugs?"

Kelly paused. "We smoked a couple of joints, that's all. I'd never do anything harder than that."

"Did he have a lot of gear?"

"No, just enough for himself. At least that's all I saw. Look, he wasn't a drug dealer, if that's what you're getting at."

"I'm not getting at anything," said Annie. "I just want to establish some idea of Nick's state of mind. Was he any different on Friday afternoon?"

"No, not so's I noticed."

"He wasn't nervous or edgy, as if he was expecting someone?"

"No."

"Did you make any plans for the future?"

"Well, he didn't ask me to marry him, if that's what you're thinking."

Annie laughed. "I don't suppose he did, but were you going to see one another again?"

"Sure. He was up here for another week, and I said I could get away a few times – if he got some more condoms. He said I could come and see him in London, too, if I wanted. He gets lots of free tickets and he said he'd take me to concerts." She pouted. "My dad would never let me go, though. He thinks London's some sort of den of iniquity."

"Did Nick give you his address?"

"We didn't get that far. We thought ... you know ... we'd see one another again up here. Oh, shit! Sorry." She dabbed at her face again. Crying had made her skin blotchy. Other than that, she was a beautiful young woman, and Annie could see why any man would be attracted to her. She wasn't stupid, either, as she had pointed out, and there was a forthrightness about her attitude to sex that many might envy. But now she was just an upset and confused kid, and her skin was breaking out.

When she'd pulled herself together, she laughed and said, "You must think I'm well daft, crying over some bloke I just met."

"No, I don't," said Annie. "You felt close to him, and now he's dead. That must be terrible. It must hurt."

Kelly looked at her. "You understand, don't you? You're not like the rest. Not like that sourpuss you had with you last night."

Annie smiled at the description of Banks, not one she would have used herself. "Oh, he's all right," she said. "He's just been going through a rough time lately, too."

"No, I mean it. You're all right, you are. What's it like being a copper?"

"It has its moments," Annie said.

"Do you think they'd have me, if I applied, like?"

"I'm sure it would be worth a try," Annie said. "We're always looking for bright, motivated people."

"That's me," Kelly said with a crooked smile. "Bright and motivated. I'm sure my dad would approve."

"I wouldn't be too sure about that," Annie said, thinking of what Banks had told her about the way his parents reacted to his chosen profession. "But don't let it stop you."

Kelly frowned, then said, "Look, I've got to get to work. I'm already late. CC'll go spare."

"Okay," said Annie. "I think I'm just about done for now."

"Can you give me a minute before we go?" said Kelly, pulling down the mirror and taking a small pink container from her handbag. "I've got to put my face on."

"Of course." Annie watched with amusement while Kelly applied eyeshadow and mascara and various powders and potions to hide the acne and blotchiness, then drove down the hill to drop the girl at the Cross Keys before heading back up to see what was happening at the youth hostel.

5

September 10–12, 1969

Over the next few days, Chadwick's investigation proceeded with a frustrating lack of progress. The two essential questions – who was the victim, and who was with her at the time of her death – remained unanswered. Surely, Chadwick thought, someone, somewhere, must be missing her? Unless she was a runaway.

Things had been quiet on the home front since he and Yvonne had come to their compromise. He was convinced now that she *had* been at the Brimleigh Festival on Sunday night – she really wasn't a very good liar – but there seemed little point in pursuing the issue now. It was over. The important thing was to try to head off anything along the same lines in the future, and Janet was right: he wouldn't achieve that by ranting at her.

On Wednesday, though, Chadwick had paid a quick visit to the Grove, just to see the kind of place where his daughter was spending her time. It was a small, scruffy, old-fashioned pub by the canal, with one dingy room set aside for the young crowd. He checked with his friend Geoff Broome on the drugs squad and found it didn't have a particularly bad reputation, which was good news. God only knew what Yvonne saw in the dump.

Dr. O'Neill – whose full post-mortem report had yielded nothing to dispute the cause of death – had estimated the victim's age at between seventeen and twenty-one, so it was conceivable that she had left home and was living by herself at the time of her murder. In which case, what about her friends, boyfriends, colleagues at work? Either they didn't know what had happened, or they hadn't missed her yet. Did she even have a job? Hippies didn't like work, Chadwick knew that. Perhaps she was a student, or on holiday. One interesting point that Dr. O'Neill had included in his report was that there was a parturition scar on the pelvic bone, which meant that she had given birth to a baby.

DC Bradley had viewed all the television footage of the festival and spoken with newspaper reporters who had attended the event. He had learned precisely nothing. The victim was nowhere to be seen on the film, which more often than not panned over a sea of young, idealistic faces, and cut back and forth from the gymnastic displays of the bands on stage to close-shot interviews with individual musicians and revellers. Perhaps it might all be of some use in the future, when they had a suspect or needed to pick someone out of the crowd, but for the moment it was useless.

Bradley had also contacted the festival's press officer, Mick Lawton, and made a start phoning the photographers. Most were co-operative, had no objection to the police looking at their photographs and would be happy to send prints. After all, they had been taken for public consumption in the first place. What a difference it was from asking reporters to name sources.

The experts were still combing the area where the victim had been killed and the spot she had been moved to, collecting all the trace evidence for later analysis. If nothing else, it might provide useful forensic evidence in a trial. The lab had already reported back on the painted cornflower on the victim's cheek, informing Chadwick that it was simple greasepaint, available in any number of outlets. The flower was still one small detail the police had not yet made public.

When it came to questioning the stars themselves, Enderby's original doubts proved to be remarkably prophetic. It got done, mostly, but in a perfunctory and unsatisfactory way, as far as Chadwick was concerned, usually by the local forces, who had only minimal briefing in the case. There was more than one provincial DI just dying to have a crack at his local rock star, to bring in the dogs and the drugs search team, despite the fiasco of the Rolling Stones bust a couple of years ago, but asking a few questions about a poxy festival up north hardly excited anyone's interest. These long-haired idiots might be stoned and anarchic, the thinking mostly went, but they're hardly likely to be bloody murderers, are they?

Chadwick preferred to keep an open mind on the subject. He thought of the murders in Los Angeles, a story he had been following in the newspapers and on television, just like everyone else. According to the reports, someone had broken into a house in Benedict Canyon, cut the telephone wires and murdered five people, including the actress Sharon Tate, who had been eight and a half months pregnant at the time she was stabbed to death. Later that night, another house had been broken into and a wealthy couple had been killed in a similar way. There was much speculation about drug orgies, as the male victims had been wearing hippie-type clothing and drugs were found in one of their cars. There was also talk about a "ritualistic" aspect to the murders: the word PIG had been written in blood on the front door of Sharon Tate's house, and DEATH TO PIGS had been written on the living-room wall of the other house, also in blood, and HEALTHER SKELTER inside the fridge door, which the authorities took to be a misspelling of "Helter Skelter," a Beatles song from the *White Album*. What little inside knowledge Chadwick had been able to pick up on the grapevine indicated that the police were looking for members of some obscure hippie cult.

It had not occurred to Chadwick that the crimes had anything in common with the Brimleigh Festival murder. Los Angeles was a long way from Yorkshire. Still, if people who listened to Beatles songs and called the police pigs could do something like that in Los Angeles, then why not in England?

Chadwick would have interviewed the musicians himself, but they lived as far afield as London, Buckinghamshire, Sussex, Ireland and Glasgow, some of them in small flats and bedsits, but a surprising number of them owned country estates with swimming pools, or large detached houses in nice areas. He would have spent half his life on the motorway and the rest on country roads.

He had hoped that one of the interviewers might at least have sniffed out a half-truth or a full-blown lie; then he would have conducted a follow-up interview himself, however far he had to travel, but everything came back routine: no further action.

A lot of the bands whose names he had seen in connection with Brimleigh were playing at another festival, in Rugby, that weekend: Pink Floyd, The Nice, Roy Harper, the Edgar Broughton Band and the Third Ear Band. He sent Enderby down to Rugby to see if he could come up with anything. Enderby seemed in his element at the prospect of meeting such heroes.

Two of the bands at Brimleigh had been local. Chadwick had already spoken briefly with Jan Dukes de Grey in Leeds during the week. Derek and Mick seemed pleasant enough young lads beneath the long hair and unusual clothes, and both of them had left the festival well before the time of the murder. The Mad Hatters were in London at the moment but were expected back up north early in the following week, to stay at Swainsview Lodge, Lord Jessop's residence near Eastvale, where they were to rehearse for a forthcoming tour and album. He would talk to them then.

It was half past two in the afternoon by the time DC Gavin Rickerd managed to make it over to Western Area Headquarters in Eastvale. Banks was due to sit in on the Nicholas Barber post-mortem at three, but he wanted to get this out of the way first. He had rung Annie at Fordham, and they had given one another a quick update, agreeing to meet in the Queen's Arms at six o'clock.

"Come in, Gavin," said Banks. "How are things going in Neighbourhood Policing? Teething troubles?"

"Busy. You know how things are with a new job, sir. But it's fine, really. I like it." Rickerd adjusted his glasses. He was still wearing old-fashioned National Health specs held together at the bridge with sticking plaster. It had to be a fashion statement of some sort, Banks thought, as even a poor DC could certainly afford new ones. The words *fashion statement* and Gavin Rickerd hardly seemed a match made in heaven, so maybe it was an anti–fashion statement. He wore a bottle-green corduroy jacket with leather elbow patches and brown corduroy trousers a bit worse for wear. His tie was awkwardly fastened and his shirt collar bent up on the left side. From the top pocket of his jacket poked an array of pens and pencils. His face had the pasty look of someone who didn't get outside very much. Banks remembered the way Kev Templeton used to take the piss out of him mercilessly. He had a cruel streak, did Templeton.

"Miss the thrust and parry of policing on the edge?" Banks asked.

"Not really, sir. I'm quite happy where I am."

"Ah, right." Banks had never really known how to talk to Rickerd. Rumour had it that he was a bona fide trainspotter, that he actually stood out at the end of cold station platforms in Darlington, Leeds or York, come rain or shine, scanning the horizon for the Royal Scotsman, the Mallard, or whatever they called it these days. Nobody had actually seen him, but the rumour persisted. He also had a bachelor's degree in mathematics and was reputed to be a whiz at puzzles and computer games. Banks thought he was probably wasted in Eastvale and should have been recruited by MI5 years ago, but at the moment their loss was his gain.

One thing Banks did know for certain was that Gavin Rickerd was a fanatical cricket fan, so he chatted briefly about England's recent Ashes victory, then said, "Got a little job for you, Gavin."

"But, sir, you know I'm Neighbourhood Policing now, not CID or Major Crimes."

"I know," said Banks. "But what's in a name?"

"It's not just the name, sir, it's a serious job."

"I'm sure it is. That's not in dispute."

"The superintendent won't like it, sir." Rickerd was starting to look decidedly nervous, glancing over his shoulder at the door.

"Been warned off, have you?"

Rickerd adjusted his glasses again.

"Okay," Banks said. "I understand. I wouldn't want to get you into trouble. You can go. It's just that I've got this puzzle I thought you might be interested in. At least, I think it could be a puzzle. Whatever it is, though, we need to know."

"Puzzle?" said Rickerd, licking his lips. "What sort of puzzle?"

"Well, I was thinking maybe you could have a look at it in your spare time, you know. That way the super can't complain, can she?"

"I don't know, sir."

"Like a little peek?"

"Well, maybe I could just have a quick look."

"Good lad." Banks handed him a photocopy of the page from Nick Barber's copy of *Atonement* he had got from the SOCOs.

Rickerd squinted at it, turned it this way and that and put it down on the desk. "Interesting," he said.

"I was thinking you like mathematical puzzles and things, know a bit about them. Maybe you could take it away with you and play around with it?"

"I can take it away?"

"Of course. It's only a photocopy."

"All right, then," said Rickerd, evidently charged with a new sense of importance. He folded the piece of paper carefully into a square and slipped it in the inside pocket of his corduroy jacket.

"You'll get back to me?" said Banks.

"Soon as I've got something. I can't promise, mind you. It might just be some random gibberish."

"I understand," said Banks. "Do your best."

Rickerd left the office, pausing to glance both ways down

the corridor before he dashed off towards the Neighbourhood Policing offices. Banks glanced at his watch and pulled a face. Time to go to the post-mortem.

Saturday, September 13, 1969

Chadwick was hoping to get away early as he and Geoff Broome had tickets for Leeds United's away game with Sheffield Wednesday. At about ten o'clock, though, a woman who said she lived on the Raynville estate rang to say she thought she recognized the victim. She didn't want to commit herself, saying the sketch in the paper wasn't a very good likeness, but she thought she knew who it was. Out of respect for the victim, the newspapers hadn't published a photograph of the dead girl, only an artist's impression, but Chadwick had a photo in his briefcase.

This wasn't the kind of interview he could delegate to an underling like the inexperienced Simon Bradley, let alone the scruffy Keith Enderby, so before he left he rang Geoff Broome with his apologies. There would be no problem getting rid of the ticket somewhere in Brotherton House, Geoff told him. After that, Chadwick went down to his aging Vauxhall Victor and drove out to Armley, rain streaking his windscreen.

The Raynville estate was not among the best of the newer Leeds council estates, and it looked even worse in the rain. Built only a few years ago, it had quickly gone to seed, and those who could afford to, avoided it. Chadwick and Janet had lived nearby, on the Astons, until they had managed to save up and buy their semi just off Church Road, in the shadow of St. Bartholomew's, Armley, when Chadwick was promoted to detective inspector four years ago.

The caller, who had given her name as Carol Wilkinson, lived in a second-storey maisonette on Raynville Walk. The stairs smelled of urine and the walls were covered with filthy graffiti, a phenomenon that was starting to spring up in places like this. It was just another sign of the degeneracy of modern youth, as far as Chadwick was concerned: no respect for property. When he knocked on the faded green door, a young woman holding a baby in one arm opened it for him, the chain still on.

"Are you the policeman?"

"Detective Inspector Chadwick." He showed his warrant card.

She glanced at it, then looked Chadwick up and down before unfastening the chain. "Come in. You'll have to excuse the mess."

And he did. She deposited the baby in a wooden playpen in a living room untidy with toys, discarded clothing and magazines. It – he couldn't tell whether it was a girl or a boy – stood and gawped at him for a moment, then started rattling the bars and crying. The cream carpet was stained with only God knew what, and the room smelled of unwashed nappies and warm milk. A television set stood in one corner, and a radio was playing somewhere: Kenny Everett. Chadwick only knew who it was because Yvonne liked to listen to him, and he recognized the inane patter and the clumsy attempts at humour. When it came to radio, Chadwick preferred quiz programs and news.

He took the chair the woman offered, giving it a quick once-over first to make sure it was clean, and plucking at the crease in his trousers before he sat. The maisonette had a small balcony, but there were no chairs outside. Chadwick imagined the woman had to be careful because of her baby. More than once a young child had crawled onto a balcony and fallen off, despite the guardrail.

Trying to distance himself from the noise, the smell and the mess, Chadwick focused on the woman as she sat down opposite him and lit a cigarette. She was pale and careworn, wearing a baggy fawn cardigan and shapeless checked slacks. Dirty blonde hair hung down to her shoulders. She might have been fifteen or thirty.

"You said on the phone that you think you know the woman whose picture was in the paper?"

"I think so," she said. "I just wasn't sure. That's why I took so long to ring you. I had to think about it."

"Are you sure now?"

"Well, no, not really. I mean, her hair was different and everything. It's just . . ."

"What?"

"Something about her, that's all."

Chadwick opened his briefcase and took out the photograph of the dead girl, head and shoulders. He warned Carol what to expect, and she seemed to brace herself, drawing an exceptionally deep lungful of smoke. When she looked at the photo, she put her hand to her chest. Slowly, she let the smoke out. "I've never seen a dead person before," she said.

"Do you recognize her?"

She passed the photo back and nodded. "Funnily enough, this looks more like her than the drawing, even though she is dead."

"Do you know who she is?"

"Yes. I think it's Linda. Linda Lofthouse."

"How did you know her?"

"We went to school together." She jerked her head in a generally northern direction. "Sandford Girls'. She was in the same class as me." At least the victim was local, then, which made the investigation a lot easier. Still, it made perfect sense. While many young people would have made the pilgrimage from all parts of the country to the Brimleigh Festival, Chadwick guessed that the majority of those attending would have been from a bit closer to home – Leeds, Bradford, York, Harrogate and the surrounding areas – as the event was practically on their doorstep.

"When was this?"

"I left school two years ago last July, when I was sixteen. Linda left the same year. We were almost the same age."

Eighteen and one kid already. Chadwick wondered if she had a husband. She wasn't wearing a wedding ring, which didn't mean much in itself, but there didn't seem to be any evidence of male presence, as far as he could see. Anyway, the age was about right for the victim. "Were you friends?"

Carol paused. "I thought so," she said, "but after we'd left school we didn't see much of one another."

"Why not?"

"Linda got pregnant after Christmas in her final year, just before she turned sixteen." She looked at her own child and gave a harsh laugh. "At least I waited until I'd left school and got married."

"The father?"

"He's at work. Tom's not a bad bloke, really."

So she was married. In a way, Chadwick felt relieved. "I meant the father of Linda's child."

"Oh, him. She was going out with Donald Hughes at the time. I just assumed, you know, like . . ."

"Did they marry, live together?"

"Not that I know of. Linda . . . well, she was getting a bit weird that last year at school, if you must know."

"In what way?"

"The way she dressed, like she didn't care anymore. And she was more in her own world, wherever that was. She kept getting into trouble for not paying attention in class, but it wasn't as if she was stupid or anything, she even did okay in her O levels, despite being pregnant. She was just . . ."

"In her own world?"

"Yes. The teachers didn't know what to do with her. If they said anything, she'd give them a right clever answer. She had some nerve. And that last year she sort of stopped hanging around with us – you know, there were a few of us, me, Linda, Julie and Anita used to go down the Locarno on a Saturday night, have a good dance and see if there were any decent lads around." She blushed. "Sometimes we'd go to Le Phonograph later if we could get in. Most of us could pass for eighteen, but sometimes they got a bit picky at the door. You know what it's like."

"So Linda became a bit of a loner?"

"Yes. And this was before she got pregnant, like. Quiet. Liked to read. Not schoolbooks. Poetry and stuff. And she loved Bob Dylan."

"Didn't the rest of you?"

"He's all right, I suppose, but you can't dance to him, can you? And I can't understand a word he's singing about, if you can call it singing."

Chadwick didn't know whether he had ever heard Bob Dylan, though he did know the name, so he was thankful the question was rhetorical. Dancing had never been a skill he possessed in any great measure, though he had met Janet at a dance and that had seemed to go well enough. "Did she have any enemies, anyone who really disliked her?"

"No, nothing like that. I mean, you couldn't *hate* Linda. You'd know what I mean if you'd met her."

"Did she ever get into any fights or serious disagreements with anyone?"

"No, never."

"Do you know if she was taking drugs?"

"She never said so, and I never saw her do anything like that. Not that I'd have known, I suppose."

"Where did she live?"

"On the Sandford estate with her mum and dad. Though I heard her dad died a short while ago. In the spring. Sudden, like. Heart attack."

"Can you give me her mother's address?"

Carol told him.

"Do you know if she had the child?"

"About two years ago."

"That would be September 1967?"

"Around that time, yes. But I never saw her after school broke up that July. I got married and Tom and me set up house here and all. Then little Andy came along."

"Have you ever bumped into her since then?"

"No. I heard that she'd moved away down south after the baby was born. London."

Maybe she had, Chadwick thought. That would explain why she hadn't been immediately missed. As Carol had said, the likeness in the newspaper wasn't a particularly good one, and a lot of people don't pay attention to the papers anyway. "Have you any idea what happened to the baby, or the father?"

"I've seen Don around. He's been going out with Pamela Davis for about a year now. I think they might be engaged. He works in a garage on Kirkstall Road, near the viaduct. I remember Linda talking about having the baby adopted. I don't think she planned on keeping it."

The mother would probably know, not that it mattered.

Whoever had killed Linda Lofthouse, it wasn't a two-year-old. "Is there anything else you can tell me about Linda?" he asked.

"Not really," said Carol. "I mean, I don't know what you want to hear. We *were* best friends, but we sort of drifted apart, as you do. I don't know what she got up to the last two years. I'm sorry to hear that she was killed, though. That's terrible. Why would somebody do a thing like that?"

"That's what we're trying to find out," said Chadwick, trying to sound as reassuring as he could. He didn't think it came over very well. He stood up. "Thanks for your time, and for the information."

"You'll let me know? When you find out."

"I'll let you know," said Chadwick, standing up. "Please, stay here with the baby. I'll let myself out."

"What's up with you, then?" asked Cyril, the landlord of the Queen's Arms, as Banks ordered a bitter lemon and ice late that afternoon. "Doctor's orders?"

"More like boss's orders," Banks grumbled. "We've got a new super. She's dead keen and seems to have eyes in the back of her bloody head."

"She'll get nowt out of me," said Cyril. "My lips are sealed."

Banks laughed. "Cheers, mate. Maybe another time."

"Bad for business, this new boss of yours."

"Give us time," said Banks, with a wink. "We'll get her trained."

He took his glass over to a dimpled, copper-topped table over by the window and contemplated its unappetizing contents gloomily. The ashtray was half-full of crushed filters and ash. Banks pushed it as far away as he could. Now that he no longer smoked, he'd come to loathe the smell of cigarettes. He'd never noticed it before, as a smoker, but when he got home from the pub his clothes stank and he had to put them straight in the laundry basket. Which would be fine if he got around to doing his laundry more often.

Annie turned up at six o'clock, as arranged. She'd been at Fordham earlier, Banks knew, and had talked to Kelly Soames. She got herself a Britvic orange and joined him. "Christ," she said, when she saw Banks's drink. "They'll be thinking we're all on the wagon."

"Too true. Good day?"

"Not bad, I suppose. You?"

Banks swirled the liquid in his glass. Ice clinked against the sides. "I've had better," he said. "Just come from the post-mortem."

"Ah."

"No picnic. Never is. Even after all these years, you never get quite used to it."

"I know," said Annie.

"Anyway," Banks went on, "we weren't far wrong in our original suspicions. Nick Barber was in generally good health apart from being bashed on the back of the head with a poker. It fits the wound, and Dr. Glendenning says he was hit four times, once when he was standing up, which accounts for most of the blood spatter, and three times when he was on the floor."

Annie raised an eyebrow. "Overkill?"

"Not necessarily. The doc said it needn't have been a frenzied attack, just that whoever did it wanted to make sure his victim was dead. In all likelihood he'd have got a bit of blood on him, too, so that might give us something we can use in court if we ever catch the bastard. Anyway, there were no prints on the poker, so our killer obviously wiped it clean."

"What do you make of it all?"

"I don't know," said Banks, sipping bitter lemon and pulling a face. "It certainly doesn't look professional, and it wasn't frenzied enough to look like a lover's quarrel, not that we can rule that out."

"I doubt if the motive was robbery, either." Annie told Banks more detail than she had given him over the phone about her conversation with Kelly Soames and what little she had discovered about Barber from her.

"And the timing is interesting," Banks added.

"What do you mean?"

"Was he killed before or after the power cut? All the doc can tell us is that it probably happened between six and eight. One bloke left the pub at seven and came back around quarter past. The others bear this out, but nobody saw him in Lyndgarth. Banks consulted his notes. Name of Calvin Soames."

"Soames?" said Annie. "That's the barmaid's name. Kelly Soames. He must be her father. I recognized him when he dropped her off."

"That's right," said Banks.

"She said he's always in the pub when she's working. I know she was terrified of him finding out about her and Nick."

"I'll have a talk with him tomorrow."

"Go carefully, Alan. He didn't know about her and Nick Barber. Apparently he's a very strict father."

"That's not such a terrible thing, is it? Anyway, I'll do my best. But if he really *did* know . . ."

"I understand," said Annie.

"And don't forget Jack Tanner," said Banks. "We don't know what motive he might have had, but he had a connection with the victim, through his wife. We'd better check his alibi thoroughly."

"It's being done," said Annie. "Ought to be easy enough to check with his darts cronies. And I've got Kev following up on all the blokes who left the pub between the relevant times."

"Good. Now the tourist couple, the Browns, say they arrived at about a quarter to eight and thought they saw a car heading up the hill, right?"

Annie consulted the notes she had taken in the incident van. "Someone from the youth hostel, a New Zealander called Vanessa Napier, told PC Travers that she saw a car going by at about half past seven or a quarter to eight on Friday evening, shortly after the lights went off. She was looking out of her window at the storm."

"Did she get any details?"

"No. It was dark, and she doesn't know a Honda from a Fiat."

"Doesn't help us much, does it?"

"It's all we've got. They questioned everyone in the hostel and Vanessa's the only one who saw anything."

"She's not another one been shagging our Nick, too, has she?"

Annie laughed. "I shouldn't think so."

"Hmm," Banks said. "There seem to have been more comings and goings between half past seven and eight than there were earlier."

"Yorkshire Electricity confirms the power went out at 7:28 p.m."

"The problem is," Banks went on, "that if the killer came from some distance away and timed his arrival for half seven or a quarter to eight, he can't have known there would be a power cut, so it's not a factor."

"Maybe it gave him an opportunity," Annie said. "They're arguing, the lights go out, Nick turns to reach for his cigarette lighter and the killer seizes the moment and lashes out."

"Possibly," said Banks. "Though the darkness would have

made it a bit harder for him to search the cottage and be certain he took away everything he needed to. Also, your eyes need time to adjust. Look at the timing. Mrs. Tanner showed up at eight. That didn't give him much time to search in the dark and check Barber's car."

"He might have had a torch in his own car."

"He'd still have had to go and get it. There would've been no reason for him to be carrying one if he arrived *before* the power cut."

"Does the electricity failure really matter, then?"

"I think we can assume that the killer would have done what he came to do anyway, and if the lights went out, that just gave him a better opportunity."

"What about the Browns? Their timing is interesting."

"Yes," said Banks. "But do they strike you as the types to kill someone and then drop by the local pub for a pint?"

"It was dark. There was no electricity. Maybe the local was as good a place to hide as any."

"What about blood?"

"Winsome checked after the lights came back on," Annie said. "She didn't see any signs, but they'd hardly have hung around till the lights came back on if they were hiding bloodstains. We could hardly strip-search everyone."

"True," said Banks. "Look, we've still got a long way to go. You mentioned that Nick Barber was a writer?"

"That's what Kelly said he told her."

"Who'd want to kill a writer?"

"There were plenty I wanted to kill when I was at school doing English," said Annie, "but they were all dead already."

Banks laughed. "But seriously."

"Well, it depends what kind of writer he was, doesn't it?" Annie argued. "I mean, if he was an investigative journalist onto something big, then someone might have had a reason to get rid of him."

"But what was he doing up here?"

"There are plenty of cupboards full of skeletons in North Yorkshire," countered Annie.

"Yes, but where to begin? That's the problem."

"Google?" suggested Annie.

"That's a start."

"And shouldn't we be going to London?"

"Monday morning," said Banks. "Then we'll be able to talk to his employer, if we can find out who it is. You know how useless Sundays are for finding anything out. I've asked the locals to keep an eye on the place until then to make sure no one tries to get in."

"What about next of kin?"

"Winsome sorted that, too. They live just outside Sheffield. They've already been informed. I thought you and Winsome could go and talk to them tomorrow."

"Fine," said Annie. "I was only going to wash my hair, anyway. Oh, there's one more thing. About that book."

"Yes?"

"It looks as if he might have bought it just over the road here. Kelly said she met him coming out of the second-hand bookshop."

Banks consulted his watch. "Damn, it'll be closed now."

"Is it important?"

"Could be. It didn't look as if the figures were written in the same hand as the price, but you never know."

"We can ring the owner at home, I suppose."

"Good idea," said Banks.

"From the way you're still sitting there, I assume you're expecting me to do it?"

"If you would. Look, I'm sick of this bloody bitter lemon. As far as I'm concerned, we're off duty, working on our own time, and if Lady Gervaise wants to make something of it, then good luck to her. I'm having a pint. You?"

Annie smiled. "Spoken like a true rebel. I'll have the same. And while you're getting them in . . ." She took her mobile phone from her briefcase and waved it in the air.

Banks had to wait until a party of six tourists, who couldn't make up their minds what they wanted to drink, had been served, and when he got back with two foaming pints of Black Sheep, Annie had finished. "Well, he certainly didn't do it," she said. "Fair bristled at the idea of anyone writing anything but the price in books, even the blank pages at the back. Sacrilege, he said. Anyway, he remembers the book. It only came in the day before Nick Barber bought it last Wednesday, and he checks them all thoroughly. There was nothing written in the back then."

"Interesting," said Banks. "Very interesting indeed. We'll just have to wait and see what young Gavin makes of it, won't we?"

Saturday, September 13, 1969
Yvonne sat upstairs at the front of a number sixteen bus heading for the city centre, chewing on her fingernails and wondering what to do. Some clever sod had taken a marker to the NO SPITTING sign and altered it to read NO SHITTING. Yvonne lit a cigarette and pondered her dilemma. If she was right, it could be serious.

It had happened the previous evening, when her father came home late from work, as usual. He'd been taking something out of his briefcase when a photograph had slipped to the floor. He'd put it back quickly and obviously thought she hadn't seen it, but she had. It was a picture of the dead girl, the one who had been stabbed on Sunday at the Brimleigh Festival, and with a shock, Yvonne had realized she recognized her: *Linda*.

She didn't know Linda well, had only met her once and hadn't really talked with her much. But the local hippie community was small enough that if you hung around the right places for long enough, you'd come across pretty much everyone in the scene eventually, whether at the Grove, the Adelphi, the Peel or one of the student pubs on Woodhouse Lane, in Hyde Park or Headingley. Even as far away as the Farmer's Inn, where they had blues bands like Savoy Brown, Chicken Shack, Free and Jethro Tull on a Sunday night. You could also be damn sure that they'd all beg, borrow or steal to get to an event with a lineup like the Brimleigh Festival. So, when you thought about it, Linda being there wasn't quite so much a coincidence as it appeared on the surface. The thing was, you didn't expect to get killed there; it was supposed to be a peaceful event, a gathering of the tribes and a celebration of unity.

The bus lumbered down Tong Road, past the Lyric, which was advertising a double bill of last year's *Carry On up the Khyber* and *Carry On Camping*. What crap, Yvonne thought. It was a grey day, and light rain pattered against the windows. Rows of grim back-to-back terraces sloped up the hill towards Hall Lane, all dark slate roofs and dirty red brick. A couple of kids got on at the junction with Wellington Road, behind the Crown, by the flats, and took the other front seat.

They'd filmed part of *Billy Liar* there a few years ago, Yvonne remembered, while it was a wasteland of demolished houses, before the flats were built. Yvonne had been about eight, and her father had brought her down to watch. She had ended up in one of the crowd scenes waving a little flag as Tom

Courtenay drove through in his tank, but when she had watched the film, she couldn't see herself anywhere.

The kids lit cigarettes, kept looking over at her and making cheeky remarks. Yvonne ignored them.

She had met Linda at Bayswater Terrace one evening during the summer holidays. She had got the impression that it was just a flying visit, that Linda used to live there for a while but had moved to London. Linda was really fantastic, she remembered. She actually knew some of the bands and hung around with lots of rock stars at clubs and other "in" places. She wasn't a groupie – she made that clear – she just liked the music and the guys who played it. Yvonne remembered someone saying that one of the members of the Mad Hatters was Linda's cousin, but she couldn't remember which one.

Linda even played a bit of guitar herself. She had sat down that evening with an acoustic and played "As Tears Go By" and "Both Sides Now." Not a bad voice, either, Yvonne had thought, a little in awe of her and that sort of luminous haze her long blonde hair and the long white dress she wore created around her pale features. The guys were all in love with her, you could tell, but she wasn't interested in any of them. Linda didn't belong to anyone. She was her own person. She also had a great throaty laugh, which surprised Yvonne, coming from one who looked so demure, like Marianne Faithfull.

McGarrity had been there that night, Yvonne remembered, and even he had seemed subdued, keeping his knife in his pocket for once and refraining from muttering T.S. Eliot all evening. The guy they said was organizing the Brimleigh Festival, Rick Hayes, had also been present, which was how they managed to score some free tickets. He knew Linda from down in London and seemed to know Dennis, too, whose house it was. Yvonne hadn't liked Hayes. He had tried to get her to go upstairs with him and got a bit stroppy when she wouldn't.

That was the only time Yvonne and Linda had met, and they hadn't talked much, but Linda had made an impression. Yvonne was waiting for her O level results, and Linda had said something about exams not proving anything and the real truth of what you were was inside you. That made sense to Yvonne. Now Linda was dead. Stabbed. Yvonne felt tears prick her eyes. She could hardly believe it. One of her own. She hadn't seen her during the festival, but that wasn't surprising.

The bus carried on past the gasworks, over the canal and river and past the huge building site where they were putting up the new Yorkshire Post building at the corner of Wellington Street, then past the dark, high Victorian buildings to City Square, where Yvonne got off. There were a couple of new boutiques she wanted to visit and that little record shop down the ginnel off Albion Street might still have a copy of the Blind Faith LP. Her parents hadn't let her go to the free concert in London's Hyde Park last June, but at least she could enjoy the music on record. Later she was going over to Carberry Place to meet up with Steve and have a few tokes. A bunch of them were going to the Peel that night to see Jan Dukes de Grey. Derek and Mick were quite the local celebrities and they were like real people; they'd talk to you and sign their first LP cover, *Sorcerers*, not hide away backstage like rock stars.

Yvonne's problem persisted, though: whether to tell her father about Linda or not. If she did, the police would be at Bayswater Terrace like a shot. Maybe Dennis and Martin and Julie and the others would get busted. And it would be *her* fault. If they found out, they'd never speak to her again. She was sure that none of them could have had anything to do with what happened to Linda, so why bring grief on them? Rick Hayes was a creep and McGarrity was weird, but neither of them would kill one of their own. How could knowing about Linda being at Bayswater Terrace in July possibly help the police investigation? Her father would find out who Linda was eventually – he was good at finding things out – but it wouldn't be from her, and nobody would be able to blame her for what happened.

That was what she decided in the end, turning the corner into the wet cobbled ginnel: she would keep it to herself. There was no way she was going to the pigs, even if the chief pig was her father.

6

There were some advantages to being a DCI, Banks thought on Sunday morning as he lingered over a second cup of coffee in the conservatory and read his way through the Sunday papers. Outside, the wind had dropped over the past couple of hours, the sun was shining and the weather had turned a little milder, though there was an unmistakable edge of autumn in the air, the smell of the musty leaves and a whiff of acrid smoke from a distant peat fire.

He was still senior investigating officer, of course, and in a short while he would go to interview Calvin Soames. At some point he would also drop by at the station and the incident van to make his presence felt and get up to date with developments, if there were any. In an investigation like this, he could never be far away from the action for any length of time, but the team had enough to occupy itself for the moment, and the SOCOs had plenty of trace evidence to sift through. He was always only a phone call away, so barring a major breakthrough, there was no reason for him to appear at the office at the crack of dawn every day; he would only get lumbered with paperwork. First thing tomorrow morning, he and Annie would be on the train to London, and perhaps there they would find out more about Nick Barber. All Annie had been able to find out on Google was that he had written for *Mojo* magazine and had penned a couple of quickie rock star biographies. It was interesting, and Banks thought he recognized the name now that he saw it in context, but it still wasn't much to go on.

Just as Banks thought it was time to tidy up and set off for Soames's farm, he heard a knock at the door. It couldn't be Annie, he thought, because she had gone to see Nick Barber's parents near Sheffield. Puzzled, he ambled through to the front room and answered it. He was stunned to see his son, Brian, standing there.

"Oh, great, Dad, you're in."

"So it would appear," said Banks. "You didn't ring."

"Battery's dead and the car charger's fucked. Sorry. It *is* okay, isn't it?"

"Of course," Banks said, smiling, putting his hand on Brian's shoulder and stepping back. "Come on in. It's always good to see you."

Banks heard rather than saw a movement behind Brian, then a young woman came into view. "This is Emilia," said Brian. "Emilia, my dad."

"Hi, Mr. Banks," said Emilia, holding out a soft hand with long, tapered fingers and a bangled wrist. "It's really nice to meet you."

"Can we bring the stuff in from the car?" Brian asked.

Still puzzled by it all, Banks just said okay and stood there while Brian and Emilia pulled a couple of holdalls from the boot of a red Honda that looked as if it had seen better days, then walked back to the cottage.

"We're going to stay for a few days, if that's okay with you," Brian said, as Banks gestured them into the cottage. "Only I've got some time off before rehearsals for the next tour, and Emilia's never been to the Dales before. I thought I'd show her around. We'll do a bit of walking, you know, country stuff."

Brian and Emilia put their bags down, then Brian took his mobile phone from his pocket and searched for the lead in the side pouch of his holdall. "Okay if I charge up the phone?" he asked.

"Of course," said Banks, pointing to the nearest plug socket. "Can I get you something?" He looked at his watch. "I have to go out soon, but we could have some coffee first."

"Great. Coffee's fine," said Brian.

Emilia nodded in agreement. She looked terribly familiar, Banks thought.

"Come through to the conservatory, then," said Banks.

"Conservatory. La-di-da," said Brian.

"Enough of your lip," Banks joked. "There's something very relaxing about conservatories. They're a sort of escape from the real world."

But Brian was already poking his nose into the entertainment room. "Jesus Christ!" he said. "Look at this stuff. Is this what you got from Uncle Roy?"

"Yes," said Banks. "Your grandparents didn't want it, so . . ."

"Fantastic," said Brian. "I mean, it's sad about Uncle Roy and all, but look at that plasma screen, all those movies. That Porsche out there is yours, too, isn't it?"

"It was Roy's, yes," said Banks, feeling a bit guilty about it all now. He left Brian and Emilia nosing around the growing CD collection and headed for the kitchen, where he put the coffee maker on. Then he picked up the scattered newspapers in the conservatory and set them aside on a spare chair. Brian and Emilia came through via the doors from the entertainment room. "I wouldn't have had you down for a Streets fan, Dad," he said.

"Just shows how little you know me," said Banks.

"Yeah, but hip hop?"

"Research," said Banks. "Have to get to know the criminal mind, don't I? Besides, it's not really hip hop, is it? And the kid tells a great story. Sit down, both of you. I'll fetch the coffee. Milk? Sugar?"

They both said yes. Banks brought the coffee and sat on his usual white wicker chair opposite Brian and Emilia. He knew it was unlikely – Brian was in his twenties, after all – but his son seemed to have grown another couple of inches since he had last seen him. He was about six foot two and skinny, wearing a green T-shirt with the band logo the Blue Lamps and cream cargos. He had also had his hair cut really short and gelled. Banks thought it made him look older, which in turn made Banks *feel* older.

Emilia looked like a model. Only a couple of inches shorter than Brian, slender as a reed, wearing tight blue low-rise jeans and a skimpy belly top, with the requisite wide gap between the two, and a green jewel gracing her navel, she moved with languorous grace and economy. Her streaky brown-blonde hair hung over her shoulders and halfway down her back, framing and almost obscuring an oval face with an exquisite complexion, full lips, small nose and high cheekbones. Her violet eyes were unnaturally bright, but Banks suspected contact lenses rather than drugs. He'd seen her somewhere before; he knew it. "It really is good to see you again," he said to Brian, "and nice to meet you, Emilia. I'm sorry you caught me unawares."

"Don't tell me there's no food in the house?" Brian said. "Or worse, no booze?"

"There's wine, and a few cans of beer. But that's about it. Oh, there's also some leftover vegetarian lasagna."

"You've gone veggie?"

"No. Annie was over the other evening."

"Aha," said Brian. "You two an item again?"

Banks felt himself redden. "Don't be cheeky. And no, we're not. Can't a couple of colleagues have a quiet dinner together?"

Brian held his hands up, grinning. "Okay. Okay."

"Why don't we eat out later? Pub lunch, if I can make it. If not, dinner. On me."

"Okay," said Brian. "That all right with you, Emmy?"

"Of course," said Emilia. "I can hardly wait to try some of this famous Yorkshire pudding."

"You've never had Yorkshire pudding before?" said Banks.

Emilia blushed. "I've led a sheltered life."

"Well, I think that can be arranged," said Banks. He glanced at his watch. "Right now, I'd better be off. I'll phone."

"Cool," said Brian. "Can you tell us which room we can have and we'll take our stuff up while you're out?"

Saturday, September 13, 1969

The Sandford estate was older than the Raynville, and it hadn't improved with age. Mrs. Lofthouse lived right at the heart of things in a semi-detached house with a postage-stamp garden and a privet hedge. Across the street, a rusty Hillman Minx without tires was parked on a neighbour's overgrown lawn, and three windows were boarded up in the house next door. It was that kind of estate.

Mrs. Lofthouse, though, had done as much as she could to brighten the place up with a vase of chrysanthemums on the windowsill and a colourful painting of a Cornish fishing village over the mantelpiece. She was a small, slight woman in her early forties, her dyed brown hair recently permed. Chadwick could still read the grief in the lines around her eyes and mouth. She had just lost her husband and now he was here to burden her with the death of her daughter.

"It's a nice house you have," said Chadwick, sitting on the flower-patterned armchair with lace antimacassars.

"Thank you," said Mrs. Lofthouse. "It's a rough estate, but I do my best. And there are some good people here. Anyway, now Jim's gone I don't need all this room. I've put my name down for a bungalow out Sherbourne-in-Elmet way."

"That should be a bit quieter."

"It's about Linda, isn't it?"

"You know?"

Mrs. Lofthouse bit her lip. "I saw the sketch in the paper. Ever since then I just . . . I've been denying it, convincing myself it's not her, it's a mistake, but it *is* her, isn't it?" Her accent was noticeably Yorkshire, but not as broad as Carol Wilkinson's.

"We think so." Chadwick slipped the photograph from his briefcase. "I'm afraid this won't be very pleasant," he said, "but it is important." He showed her the photograph. "Is this Linda?"

After a sharp intake of breath, Mrs. Lofthouse said, "Yes."

"You'll have to make a formal identification down at the mortuary."

"I will?"

"I'm afraid so. We'll make it as easy for you as we can, though. Please don't worry."

"When can I . . . you know, the funeral?"

"Soon," said Chadwick. "As soon as the coroner releases the body for burial. I'll let you know. I'm very sorry, Mrs. Lofthouse, but I do have to ask you some questions. The sooner the better."

"Of course. I'll be all right. And it's Margaret, please. Look, shall I make some tea. Would that be okay?"

"I could do with a cuppa right now," said Chadwick with a smile.

"Won't be a moment."

Margaret Lofthouse disappeared into the kitchen, no doubt to give private expression to her grief as she boiled the kettle and filled the teapot in the time-honoured, comforting ritual. A clock ticked on the mantel beside a framed photograph. Twenty-five to one. Broome and his pal would be well on their way to Sheffield by now, if they weren't there already. Chadwick got up to examine the photograph. It showed a younger Margaret Lofthouse, and the man beside her with his arm around her waist was no doubt her husband. Also in the picture, which looked as if it had been taken outside in the country, was a young girl with short blonde hair staring into the camera.

Margaret Lofthouse came back with a tray and caught him looking. "That was taken at Garstang Farm, near Hawes, in Wensleydale," she said. "We used to go for summer holidays up there a few years ago, when Linda was little. My uncle owned the place. He's dead now and strangers have bought it, but I have some wonderful memories. Linda was such a beautiful child."

Chadwick watched the tears well up in her eyes. She dabbed at them with a tissue. "Sorry," she said. "I just get all choked up when I remember how things were, when we were a happy family."

"I understand," said Chadwick. "What happened?"

Margaret Lofthouse didn't seem surprised at the question. "What always seems to happen these days," she said, with a sniffle. "She grew up into a teenager. They expect the world at the age of sixteen these days, don't they? Well, what she got was a baby."

"What did she do with the child?"

"Put him up for adoption – it's a boy – what else could she do? She couldn't look after him, and Jim and I were too old to start caring for another child. I'm sure he's gone to a good home."

"I'm sure," agreed Chadwick, "but it's not the baby I'm here to talk about, it's Linda."

"Yes, of course. Milk and sugar?"

"Please."

She poured tea from a Royal Doulton teapot into fragile-looking cups with gold-painted rims and handles. "This was my grandmother's tea set," she said. "It's the only real thing of value I own. There's nobody left to pass it on to now. Linda was an only child."

"When did she leave home?"

"Shortly after the baby was born. The winter of 1967."

"Where did she go?"

"London. At least that's what she told me."

"Where in London?"

"I don't know. She never said."

"You didn't have her address?"

"No."

"Did she know people down there?"

"She must have done, mustn't she? But I never met or heard of any of them."

"Did she never come back and visit you?"

"Yes. Several times. We were quite friendly, but in a distant sort of way. She never talked about her life down there, just assured me she was all right and not to worry, and I must say, she always *looked* all right. I mean, she was clean and sober and nicely dressed, if you can call them sort of clothes nice, and she looked well fed."

"Hippie-style clothing?"

"Yes. Long, flowing dresses. Bell-bottomed jeans with flowers embroidered on them. That sort of thing. But as I said, they was always clean and they always looked good quality."

"Do you know how she earned a living?"

"I have no idea."

"What *did* you talk about?"

"She told me about London, the parks, the buildings, the art galleries – I've never been there, you see. She was interested in art and music and poetry. She said all she wanted was peace in the world and for people to just be happy." She reached for the tissues again.

"So you got along okay?"

"Fine, I suppose. On the surface. She knew I disapproved of her life, even though I didn't know much about it. She talked about Buddhism and Hindus and Sufis and goodness knows what, but she never once mentioned our true Lord Jesus Christ, and I brought her up to be a good Christian." She gave a little shake of her head. "I don't know. Maybe I could have tried harder to understand. She just seemed so far away from me and anything I've ever believed in."

"What did you talk to her about?"

"Just local gossip, what her old school friends were up to, that sort of thing. She never stopped long."

"Did you know any of her friends?"

"I knew all the kids she played with around the estate, and her friends from school, but I don't know who she spent her time with after she left home."

"She never mentioned any names?"

"Well, she might have done, but I don't remember any."

"Did she ever tell you if anything or anyone was bothering her?"

"No. She always seemed happy, as if she hadn't really a care in the world."

"You don't know of any enemies she might have had?"

"No. I can't imagine her having any."

"When did you last see her?"

"In the summer. July, it would be, not long after Jim . . ."

"Was she at the funeral?"

"Oh, yes. She came home for that in May. She loved her father. She was a great support. I don't want to give you the impression that we'd fallen out or anything, Mr. Chadwick. I still loved Linda and I know that she still loved me. It was just that we couldn't really talk anymore, not about anything important. She'd got secretive. In the end I gave up trying. But this was a couple of months after Jim's death, just a flying visit to see how I was getting along."

"What *did* she talk about on that visit?"

"We watched that man walk on the moon. Neil Armstrong. Linda was all excited about it, said it marked the beginning of a new age, but I don't know. We stayed up watching till after three in the morning."

"Anything else?"

"I'm sorry. Nothing else really stood out, except the moon landing. Some pop star she liked had died and she'd been to see the Rolling Stones play a free concert for him in Hyde Park. London, that is. And I remember her talking about the war. Vietnam. About how immoral it was. She always talked about the war. I tried to tell her that sometimes wars just have to be fought, but she'd have none of it. To her all war was evil. You should have heard it when Linda and her dad went at it – he was in the navy in the last war, just towards the end, like."

"But you say Linda loved her father?"

"Oh, yes. Don't get me wrong. I didn't say they saw eye to eye about everything. I mean, he tried to discipline her, got on at her for staying out till all hours, but she was a handful. They fought like cat and dog sometimes, but they still loved one another."

It all sounded so familiar to Chadwick that the thought depressed him. Surely all children weren't like this, didn't cause their parents such grief? Was he taking the wrong approach with Yvonne? Was there another way? He felt like such a failure as a parent, but short of locking her in her room, what could he do? When Yvonne went on about the evils of war, he always felt himself tense up inside; he could never even enter into a rational argument about it for fear he would lose his temper, lash out and say something he would regret. What did she know about war? Evil? Yes. Necessary? Well, how else were you going to stop someone like Hitler? He didn't know much about Vietnam, but he assumed the Americans were there for a good reason, and the sight of all these unruly, long-haired youngsters burning the flag and chanting anti-war slogans made his blood boil.

"What about the boyfriend, Donald Hughes?"

"What about him?"

"Is he the father?"

"I assume so. I mean, that's what Linda said, and I think I know her well enough to know she wasn't . . . you know . . . some sort of trollop."

"What did you think of him?"

"He's all right, I suppose. Not much gumption, mind you. The Hugheses aren't exactly one of the best families on the estate, but they're not one of the worst, either. And you can't blame poor Eileen Hughes. She's had six kids to bring up, mostly on her own. She tries hard."

"Do you know if Donald kept in touch after Linda left?"

"I doubt it. He made himself scarce after he found out our Linda was pregnant, then just after the baby was born he became all concerned for a while, said they should get married and keep it, that it wouldn't be right to give his child up for adoption. That's how he put it. *His child.*"

"What did Linda say?"

"She gave him his marching orders, then not long after that she was gone herself."

"Do you know if he ever bothered her at all?"

"I don't think so. She never said, never even mentioned him or the baby again."

"Did he ever come here after that, asking about her?"

"Just once, about three weeks after she'd left. Wanted to know her address."

"What did you tell him?"

"That I didn't know. Of course, he didn't believe me, and he made a bit of a fuss on the doorstep."

"What did you do?"

"I sent him packing. Told him I'd set Jim on him if he came back again and shut the door in his face. He left us alone after that. Surely you don't think Donald could have . . . ?"

"We don't know what to think yet, Mrs. Lofthouse. We have to look at all possibilities."

"He's a bit of a hothead, anyone will tell you that, but I very much doubt that he's a murderer." She dabbed at her eyes again. "I'm sorry," she said. "I still can't seem to take it in."

"I understand," said Chadwick. "Is there anyone you'd like me to get to stay with you? Relative? Neighbour?"

"Mrs. Bennett next door. She's always been a good friend. She's a widow, like me. She understands what it feels like."

Chadwick stood up to leave. "I'll let her know you want her to come over. Look, before I go, do you have a recent photograph of Linda I could borrow?"

"I might have," she said. "Just a minute." She went over to the sideboard and started rummaging through one of the drawers. "This was taken last year, when she came home for her birthday. Her father was a bit of an amateur photographer."

She handed Chadwick the colour photograph. It was the girl in the sleeping bag, only she was alive, a half-smile on her lips, a faraway look in her big blue eyes, wavy blonde hair tumbling over her shoulders. "Thank you," he said. "I'll let you have it back."

"And you'll keep in touch, won't you? About the arrangements."

"Of course. I'll also send someone to drive you to the hospital and back to make the formal identification."

"Thank you," she said, and stood with him at the door, holding a damp tissue to her eyes. "How can something like this happen to me, Mr. Chadwick?" she said. "I've been a devout Christian woman all my life. I've never hurt a soul and I've always served the Lord to the best of my ability. How can He do this to me? A husband *and* a daughter, both in the same year?"

All Chadwick could do was shake his head. "I don't know," he said. "I wish I knew the answer."

"Just outside Sheffield" turned out to be a quaint village on the edge of the Peak District National Park, and the house was a detached limestone cottage with a fair-sized and well-tended garden, central door, symmetrical up-and-down mullioned windows, garage and outbuildings. In the Dales, Annie guessed, it would be valued at about five hundred thousand pounds these days, but she had no idea what prices were like in the Peak District. Probably not much different. There were many similarities between the two areas, with their limestone hills and valleys, and both drew hordes of tourists, ramblers and climbers almost year-round.

Winsome parked by the gate and they made their way down the garden path. A few birds twittered in the nearby trees, completing the rural idyll. The woman who opened the door to them had clearly been crying. Annie felt grateful she hadn't been the one to break the news. She hated that. The last time she had told someone about the death of a friend, the woman had actually fainted.

"Annie Cabbot and Winsome Jackman from North Yorkshire Major Crimes," she said.

"Yes, come in," said the woman. "We've been expecting you." If the sight of a six-foot black woman surprised her at all, she didn't show it. Like many others, she no doubt watched crime programs on TV and had got used to the idea of a multiracial police force, even in such a "white" enclave as the Peaks.

She led them through a dim hallway where coats hung on pegs and boots and shoes were neatly aligned on a low slatted rack, then into an airy living room with French windows that led to the back garden, a neatly manicured lawn with stone bird bath, white plastic table and chairs and herbaceous borders. Plane trees framed a magnificent view over the fields to the limestone peaks beyond. The sky was mostly light grey, with a hint of sun hiding behind clouds somewhere in the north.

"We've just got back from church," the woman said. "We go every week, and it seemed especially important today."

"Of course," said Annie, whose religious background had been agnostic, and whose own spiritual dabbling in yoga and meditation had never led her to any sort of organized religion. "We're very sorry about your son, Mrs. Barber."

"Please," she said. "Call me Louise. My husband, Ross, is making some tea. I hope that will be all right?"

"That'll be perfect," said Annie.

"You'd better sit down."

The chintz-covered armchairs all had spotless lace antimacassars, and Annie sat carefully, not quite daring to let the back of her head touch the material. In a few moments a tall, rangy man with unruly white hair, wearing a grey V-neck pullover and baggy cords, brought in a tray and placed it on the low glass table between the chairs and the fireplace. He looked a bit like a sort of mad scientist character who could do complex equations in his head but had trouble fastening his shoelaces. Annie admired the framed print of Seurat's *Sunday Afternoon on the Island of La Grande Jatte* over the mantelpiece.

Once tea had been served in tiny rose-patterned, gold-rimmed cups, and everyone was settled, Winsome took out her notebook and Annie began. "I know this is a difficult time for you, but anything you can tell us about your son would be helpful right now."

"Do you have any suspects?" Mr. Barber asked.

"I'm afraid not. It's early days yet. We're just trying to piece together what happened."

"I can't imagine why anyone would want to harm our Nicholas. He was harmless. He wouldn't have hurt a fly."

"It's often the innocent who suffer," said Annie.

"But Nicholas . . ." He let the sentence trail off.

"Did he have any enemies?"

Ross and Louise Barber looked at one another. "No," Louise said. "I mean, he never mentioned anyone. And like Ross says, he was a gentle person. He loved his music and his books and his films. And his writing, of course."

"He wasn't married, was he?" They had been able to find no record of a wife, but Annie thought it best to make sure. If a jealous wife had caught wind of what Barber was up to with Kelly Soames, she might easily have lost it.

"No. He was engaged once, ten years ago," said Ross Barber. "Nice girl. Local. But they drifted apart when he moved to London. More tea?"

Annie and Winsome said yes, please. Barber topped up their cups.

"We understand that your son was a music journalist?" Annie went on.

"Yes," said Louise. "It was what he always wanted. Even when he was at school, he was editor of the magazine, and he wrote most of the articles himself."

"We found out from the Internet that he's done some articles for *Mojo* magazine and written a couple of biographies. Can you tell us anything else about his work? Did he write for anyone in particular, for example?"

"No. He was a freelancer," Ross Barber answered. "He did some writing for the newspapers, reviews and such, and feature pieces for that magazine sometimes, as you said. I'm afraid that sort of music isn't exactly to my taste." He smiled indulgently. "But he loved it, and apparently he made a decent living."

Annie liked pop music, but she hadn't heard of *Mojo*, though she knew she must have seen it in W.H. Smith when she was picking up *Now*, *Star* or *Heat*, the trashy celebrity gossip magazines she liked to read in the bath, her one secret vice. "You didn't approve of your son's interest in rock music?" she asked.

"It's not that we're against it or anything, you understand," said Ross Barber. "We've just always been a bit more inclined towards classical – Louise sings with the local operatic society – but we're happy that Nicholas seemed to pick up a love of music at a very early age, along with the writing. He loved classical music, too, of course, but writing about rock was how he made his living."

"He was lucky, then," said Annie. "Being able to combine his two loves."

"Yes," Louise agreed, wiping away a tear with a lacy hand-kerchief.

"Do you have any copies of his articles? You must be proud of him. A scrapbook, perhaps?"

"I'm afraid not," said Louise. "It never really entered our heads, did it, darling?"

Her husband agreed. "It wouldn't mean anything to us, you see, what he was writing about. The names. The records. We would never have heard of any of them."

Annie wanted to tell them that wasn't the point, but it would clearly do no good. "How long had he been doing this for a living?" she asked.

"About eight years now," Ross answered.

"And before that?"

"He got a B.A. in English at Nottingham, then he did an M.A. in film studies, I think, at Leicester. After that he did a bit of teaching and wrote reviews, then he got a feature accepted, and after that . . ."

"He never studied journalism?"

"No. I suppose you might say he got in through the back door."

"What's your profession, if you don't mind my asking?"

"I was a university professor," said Ross Barber. "Classics and ancient history. Rather dull, I'm afraid. I'm retired now, mind you."

Annie was trying frantically to puzzle out why anyone would want to kill a music journalist, but she couldn't come up with anything. Except drugs. Kelly Soames had said that she and Nick smoked a joint, but that meant nothing. Annie had smoked a few joints in her time, even while she was a copper. Even Banks had smoked joints. She wondered about Winsome and Kev Templeton. Kev's drug of choice was probably E washed down with liberal amounts of Red Bull, but she didn't know about Winsome. She seemed a clean-living girl, with her passion for the outdoors, and for potholing, but surely there had to be something. Anyway, it didn't help very much knowing that Nick Barber smoked marijuana occasionally. She imagined it was par for the course in the rock business, whichever end of it you were in.

"Can you tell us anything about Nick's life?" she asked. "We have so little to go on."

"I can't see how any of it would help you," said Louise, "but we'll do our best."

"Did you see him often?"

"You know what it's like when they leave home," Louise said. "They phone and visit when they can. Our Nick was no better or worse than anyone else in that regard, I shouldn't think."

"So he was in touch regularly?"

"He phoned us once a week and tried to drop by whenever he could."

"When was the last time you saw him?"

Her eyes filled with tears again. "Just the week before last. Friday. He was on his way up to Yorkshire, and he stopped over for the night. We always keep his old room ready for him, just in case."

"Was there anything different about him?"

"Different? What do you mean?"

"Did he seem fearful in any way?"

"No, not at all."

"Was he depressed about anything?"

The Barbers looked at one another, then Louise replied. "No. Maybe a little preoccupied, but certainly not depressed. He seemed quite cheerful, as a matter of fact. Nick was never the most demonstrative of children, but he was generally even-tempered. He was no different this time from any other time he called by."

"He wasn't anxious about anything?"

"Not as far as we could tell. If anything, he was a bit more excited than usual."

"Excited? About what?"

"He didn't say. I think it might have been a story he was working on."

"What was it about?"

"He never told us details like that. Not that we weren't interested in his work, but I think he realized it would mean nothing to us. Besides, it was probably a 'scoop.' He'd learned to become secretive in his business."

"Even from you?"

"The walls have ears. He'd developed an instinct. I don't think it really mattered to whom he was talking."

"So he didn't mention any names?"

"No. I'm sorry."

"Did he tell you why he was going to Yorkshire?"

"He said he'd found what sounded like a quiet place to write, and I think there was someone he wanted to see who lives up there."

"Who?"

Mrs. Barber spread her hands. "I'm sorry. But I got the impression it was to do with what he was working on."

Annie cursed under her breath. If only Nick had named names. If he'd thought his parents had the least interest in his passion, then he probably would have, despite his journalistic instinct to protect his scoop. "Is that what he was excited about?"

"I think so."

"Can you add anything, Mr. Barber?"

Ross Barber shook his head. "No. As Louise said, the names of these groups and singers mean nothing to us. I think he'd learned there was no point in mentioning them. I'm afraid I glaze over in discussions like that. No doubt members of his own generation would be very impressed, but they went right over our heads."

"I can understand that," said Annie. "What do you know about Nick's life in London?"

"He had a nice flat," said Louise. "Didn't he, Ross? Just off the Great West Road. We stayed there not so long ago on our way to Heathrow. He slept on the sofa and let us have his bedroom. Spotless, it was."

"He didn't live or share with anyone?"

"No. It was all his own."

"Did you meet a girlfriend or a close friend? Anyone?"

"No. He took us out for dinner somewhere in the West End. The next day we flew to New York. Ross and I have old friends there, and they invited us for our fortieth wedding anniversary."

"That's nice," said Annie. "So you don't really know much at all about Nick's life in London?"

"I think he worked all the hours God sent. He didn't have time for girlfriends and relationships and that sort of thing. I'm sure he would have settled down eventually."

In Annie's admittedly limited experience, if someone had reached the age of thirty-eight without "settling down," you were a fool if you held your breath and waited for him to do so, but she also knew that many more people were holding off committing to relationships for much longer these days, herself included. "I know this is a rather delicate question," Annie asked, "and I don't want to upset you, but did Nick ever have anything to do with drugs?"

"Well," said Ross, "we assumed he experimented, of course, like so many young people today, but we never saw him under the influence of anything more than a couple of pints of bitter, or perhaps a small whisky. We're fairly liberal about things like that. I mean, you can't teach in a university for as long as I did and not have some knowledge of marijuana. But if he did use drugs at all, they didn't interfere with his job or his health, and we certainly never noticed any signs, did we?"

"No," Louise agreed.

It was a fair answer, if not entirely what Annie had expected. She sensed that Ross Barber was being as honest as he could be. The Barbers clearly loved their son and were distraught over his death, but there seemed to have been some sort of communication gap between them. They were proud of his achievements, but not interested in the actual achievements themselves. Nick might well have interviewed Coldplay or Oasis, but Annie could just imagine Ross Barber saying, "That's very nice, son," as he pored over his ancient tomes. She couldn't think of anything else to ask and glanced over at Winsome, who shrugged. Perhaps Banks would have done better; perhaps she wasn't asking the right questions, but she couldn't think of any more. They would have a quick look in Nick's room, just in case he had left anything of interest, then maybe catch a pub lunch somewhere on the way back. After that, Annie would check in at the incident van and give Banks a ring. He'd want to know what she had found out, no matter how little it was.

Saturday, September 13, 1969

The young man in the greasy overalls was standing with a spanner in his hand surrounded by pieces of a dismantled motorbike when Chadwick arrived at the garage later that afternoon. According to the car radio, Leeds were one–nil up.

"Vincent Black Lightning, 1952," the young man said. "Lovely machine. How can I help you?"

Chadwick showed his warrant card. "Are you Donald Hughes?"

Hughes immediately looked cagey, put down the spanner and wiped his hands on his greasy overalls. "Maybe," he said. "Depends why you want to know."

Chadwick's immediate inclination was to tell the kid to stop messing about and come up with some answers, but he realized that Hughes might not know yet about Linda's murder, and that his reaction to the news could reveal a lot. Perhaps a softer approach would be best, then, at least to start with.

"Maybe you'd better sit down, laddie," he said.

"Why?"

There were two fold-up chairs in the garage. Instead of answering, Chadwick sat on one. A little dazed, Hughes followed suit. The dim garage smelled of oil, petrol and warm metal. It was still raining outside, and he could hear the steady dripping of water from the gutters.

"What is it?" Hughes asked. "Has something happened to mum?"

"Not as far as I know," said Chadwick. "Read the papers much?"

"Nah. Nothing but bad news."

"Hear about the festival up at Brimleigh Glen last weekend?"

"Hard not to."

"Were you there?"

"Nah. Not my cup of tea. Look, why are you asking all these questions?"

"A young girl was killed there," he said. "Stabbed." When Hughes said nothing, he continued, "We've good reason to believe that she was Linda Lofthouse."

"Linda? But . . . she . . . bloody hell . . ." Hughes turned pale.

"She what?"

"She went off to live in London."

"She was at Brimleigh for the festival."

"I should have known. Look," he said, "I'm really sorry to hear about what happened. It was a long time ago, though, me and Linda. Another lifetime, it seems."

"Two years isn't very long. People have held grudges longer."

"What do you mean?"

"Revenge is a dish that's best eaten cold."

"I don't know what you're on about."

"Let's suppose we start at the beginning," said Chadwick. "You and Linda."

"We went out together for a couple of years when we were fifteen and sixteen, that's all."

"And she had your baby."

Hughes looked down at his oily hands in his lap. "Yeah, well . . . I tried to make it right, asked her to marry me and all."

"That's not the way I hear it."

"Look, all right. At first I was scared. Wouldn't you be? I was only sixteen, I didn't have no job, nothing. We left school. Linda stayed at home with her mum and dad that summer and had the baby, and I . . . I don't know, I suppose I brooded about it. Anyway, I decided in the end we should make a go of it. I had a job here at the garage by then and I thought . . . you know . . . that we might have had a chance, after all."

"But?"

"She didn't want to know, did she? By then she'd got her head full of this hippie rubbish. Bob bloody Dylan and his stupid songs and all the rest of it."

"When did this start?"

"Before we split up. Just little things. Always correcting me when I said something wrong, like she was a bloody grammar expert. Talking about poets and singers I'd never heard of, reincarnation and karma and I don't know what else. Always arguing. It was like she wasn't interested in a normal life."

"What about her new friends?"

"Long-haired pillocks and poxy birds. I hadn't time for any of them."

"Did she chuck you?"

"You could say that."

"And when you came back, cap in hand, she wanted nothing more to do with you?"

"I suppose so. Then she buggered off to London soon as she'd had the kid. Put him up for adoption. *My* son."

"Did you follow her down there?"

"I'd had enough by then. Let her go with her poncy new friends and take all the drugs she wanted."

"Did she take drugs when she was with you?"

"No, not that I knew of. I wouldn't have stood for it. But that's what they do, isn't it?"

"So they stole her from you, did they? The hippies?"

He looked away. "I suppose you could say that."

"Made you angry enough to do her harm?"

Hughes stood so violently that his chair tipped over. "What are you getting at? Are you trying to say I killed her?"

"Calm down, laddie. I have to ask these questions. It's a murder investigation."

"Yeah. Well, I'm not your murderer."

"Got a bit of a quick temper, though, haven't you?"

Hughes said nothing. He picked up the chair and sat again, folding his arms across his chest.

"Did you ever meet any of Linda's new friends?"

Hughes rubbed the back of his hand across his upper lip and nose. "She took me to this house once," he said. "I think she wanted me to be like her, and she thought maybe she'd convince me by introducing me to her new friends."

"When was this?"

"Just after she left school. That summer."

"1967? When she was pregnant?"

"Yes."

"Go on."

"We weren't getting along well at all. Like I said before, she was weird, into all sorts of weird stuff I didn't understand, like tarot cards and astrology and all that crap. This one time she was going to see some friends and I didn't want her to go – I wanted her to come to the pictures with me to see *You Only Live Twice* – but she said she didn't want to see some stupid James Bond film, and if I wanted to be with her I could come along. If I didn't . . . well . . . she made it clear I didn't have much choice. So I thought, What the hell, let's see what's going on here."

"Do you remember *where* she took you?"

"I dunno. It was off Roundhay Road, near that big pub at the junction with Spenser Place."

"The Gaiety?"

"That's the one."

Chadwick knew it. There weren't many coppers in Leeds, plainclothes or uniformed, who didn't. "Do you remember the name of the street?"

"No, but it was just over Roundhay Road."

"One of the Bayswaters?" Chadwick knew the area, a densely packed triangle of streets full of small terraced houses between Roundhay Road, Bayswater Road and Harehills Road. It didn't have a particularly bad reputation, but quite a few of the houses had been rented to students, and where there were students there were probably drugs.

"That's the place."

"Do you know which one?"

"I can't say for sure, but I think it was the terrace. Or maybe the crescent."

"Remember where the house was?"

"About halfway."

"Which side of the street?"

"Don't remember."

"Was there anything odd about the place from the outside?"

"No. It looked just like all the others."

"What colour was the door?"

"I don't remember."

"Okay. Thanks," said Chadwick. Maybe he could find it. It was frustrating to be so close but still so far. Even so, it was probably a cold lead. The students who had been there two years ago might have graduated and left town by now. If they *were* students.

"What happened?"

"Nothing, really. There were these people, about five of them, hippies, like, in funny clothes. Freaks."

"Were they students?"

"Maybe some of them were. I don't know. They didn't say. The place smelled like a tart's window box."

"That bad?"

"Some sort of perfume smell, anyway. I think it was something they were smoking. One or two of them were definitely on *something*. You could tell by their eyes and the rubbish they were spouting."

"Like what?"

"I don't remember, but it was all 'cosmic' this and 'cosmic' that, and there was this awful droning music in the background, like someone rubbing a hacksaw on a metal railing."

"Do you remember any names?"

"I think one of them was called Dennis. It seemed to be his place. And a girl called Julie. She was blowing bubbles and giggling, like a little kid. Linda had been there before, I could tell. She knew her way around and didn't have to ask anyone, you know, like where the kettle or the toilet was or anything."

"What happened?"

"I wanted to go. I mean, I knew they were taking the mickey because I didn't talk the same language or like the same music. Even Linda. In the end I said we should leave, but she wouldn't."

"So what did you do?"

"I left. I couldn't stick any more of it. I went to see *You Only Live Twice* by myself."

There couldn't have been that many hippies in Leeds during the summer of 1967. It might have been the "Summer of Love" in San Francisco, but Leeds was still a northern provincial backwater in many ways, always a little behind the times, and it was only over the past two years or so that their numbers had grown everywhere. The Leeds drugs squad hadn't even been formed until 1967. Anyway, if there was a Dennis still living on Bayswater Terrace, it shouldn't be too hard to find him.

"How often did you see her after that?"

"A couple of times, then after the baby was born, you know, when I tried to make things up between us. Then she went down south and her bloody mother wouldn't even give me an address."

"And finally?"

"I got over her. I've been going out with someone else for a while now. Might get engaged at Christmas."

"Congratulations," said Chadwick, standing up.

"I'm really sorry about Linda," Hughes said, "But it was nothing to do with me. Honest. I was here working all last weekend. Ask the boss. He'll tell you."

Chadwick said he would, then left. When he turned on the car radio he found that Leeds had beaten Sheffield Wednesday 2–1, Allan Clarke and Eddie Grey scoring. Still, he hadn't missed the game for nothing; he now knew who the victim was and had a lead on some of the people she'd knocked around with in Leeds, if only he could find them.

7

The Soames farm was about half a mile up a narrow walled lane off the main Lyndgarth to Eastvale road, and it boasted the usual collection of ramshackle outbuildings, built from local limestone, a muddy yard and a barking dog straining at its chain. It also presented the unmistakable bouquet of barnyard smells. Calvin Soames answered the door and with a rather grudging good afternoon let Banks in. The inside was dim with dark, low beams and gloomy hallways. The smell of roast beef still lurked somewhere in the depths.

"Our Kelly's in the kitchen," he said, pointing with his thumb.

"That's all right," said Banks. "It's you I came to talk to, really."

"Me? I told you everything I know the other night."

"I'm sure you did," said Banks, "but sometimes, after a bit of time, things come back, little things you'd forgotten. May I sit down?"

"Aye, go on, then."

Banks sat in a deep armchair with a sagging seat. The whole place, once he could see it a bit better, was in some disrepair and lacked what they used to call a woman's touch. "Is there a Mrs. Soames?" he asked.

"The wife died five years ago. Complications of surgery." Soames spat out these last words, making it clear that he blamed the doctors, the health system, or both, for his wife's untimely death.

"I'm sorry," said Banks.

Soames grunted. He was a short, squat man, almost as broad as he was tall, but muscular and fit, Banks judged, wearing a tight waistcoat over his shirt, and a pair of baggy brown trousers. He probably wasn't more than about forty-five, but farming had aged him, and it showed in the deep lines and rough texture of his ruddy face.

"Look," Banks went on, "I just want to go over what you told us in the pub on Friday."

"It were the truth."

"Nobody doubts that. You said you left the Cross Keys at about seven o'clock because you thought you might have left the gas ring on."

"That's right."

"Have you done that before?"

"He has," said a voice from the doorway. "Twice he nearly burned the place down."

Banks turned. Kelly Soames stood there, arms folded, one blue-jeaned hip cocked against the door jamb in a graceful curve, flat stomach exposed. She certainly was a lovely girl, Banks thought again; she was fit, and she knew it, as the Streets would say. He'd been spoiled for lovely girls this morning, what with Brian's Emilia turning up, too.

Should he have said something? Brian and Emilia obviously just assumed they were going to sleep together under his roof, but he wasn't sure how he felt about that. His own son. What if he *heard* them? But what else could he have done? Made an issue of it? His parents, of course, would never have stood for such a thing. But attitudes changed. When he was young, he had left home and got a flat in London so he could sleep with girls, stay out late and drink too much. These days, parents allowed their kids to do all that at home, so they never left, had no reason to; they could have all the sex they wanted, come home drunk and still get fed and get their washing done. But Brian was only visiting. Surely it would be best just to let him and Emilia do what they usually did? Banks could imagine the kind of atmosphere it would create if he came on all disciplinarian and said, "Not under my roof, you don't!" But the whole thing, the assumption, the reality, still made him feel uneasy.

Despite her cocky stance, Kelly Soames seemed nervous, Banks thought. After what Annie had told him about her exploits, he wasn't surprised. She must be worried that he was going to spill the beans to her father.

"Kelly," said Mr. Soames, "make a cup of tea for Mr. Banks here. He might be a copper, but we still owe him our hospitality."

"No, that's all right, thank you," said Banks. "I've already had far too much coffee this morning."

"Please yourself. I'll have a cuppa myself, though, lass."

Kelly slouched off to make the tea, and Banks could imagine her straining her ears to hear what they were talking about. Calvin Soames took out a pipe and began puffing at some vile-smelling tobacco. Outside, the dog barked from time to time when a group of ramblers passed on the footpath that skirted the farm property.

"What did you think of Nick Barber?" Banks asked.

"Was that his name, poor sod?"

"Yes."

"I can't say as I thought much, really. I didn't know him."

"But he was a regular in your local."

Soames laughed. "Dropping by the Cross Keys for a pint every day or so for a week doesn't make anyone a regular around these parts. Tha should know that."

"Even so," said Banks, "it was long enough at least to be on greeting terms, wasn't it?"

"I suppose so. But I can't say as I have much to do with visitors myself."

"Why not?"

"Do you need it spelling out? Bloody Londoners come up here buying properties, pushing prices up, and what do they do? They sit in the poncy flats in Kensington and just pull in the cash, that's what they do."

"It brings tourism to the Dales, Mr. Soames," said Banks. "They spend money."

"Aye. Well, maybe it's all right for the shopkeepers," Soames went on, "but it doesn't do us farmers a lot of good, does it? People tramping over our land morning, noon and night, ruining good grazing pasture."

As far as Banks had heard, absolutely nothing ever benefited the farmers. He knew they had a hard life, but he also felt that people might respect them more if they didn't whine so much. If it wasn't EU regulations or footpath access, it was something else. Of course, foot-and-mouth disease had taken a terrible toll on the Dales farms only a few years ago, but the effects hadn't been limited to farmers, many of whom had been compensated handsomely. The pinch had also been felt by local businesses, particularly bed and breakfast establishments, cafés and tea rooms, pubs, walking-gear shops and market stallholders. And they hadn't been compensated. Banks also knew that the outbreak had driven more than one ruined local businessman to suicide. It wasn't that he had no sympathy for the farmers; it was that they often seemed to assume they were the only ones with any rights, or any serious grievances, and they had more than enough sympathy for themselves to make any from other sources seem quite superfluous. But Banks knew he had to tread carefully; this was marshy ground.

"I understand there's a problem," he said, "but it won't be solved by killing off tourists."

"Do you think that's what happened?"

"I don't know what happened," said Banks.

Kelly came back with the tea, and after she had handed it to her father, she lingered by the door again, biting her fingernail.

"Nobody around here would have murdered that lad, you can take it from me," said Soames.

"How do you know?"

"Because most know you're right. CC benefits from the holidaymakers, and so do most of the others. Oh, people talk a tough game, that's Dalesmen for you. We've got our pride, if nowt else. But nobody'd go so far as to kill a bloke who's minding his own business and not doing anyone any harm."

"Is that your impression of Nick Barber?"

"I didn't see much of him, like I said, but from what I did see, he seemed like a harmless lad. Not mouthy, or full of himself, like some of them. And we didn't even murder them."

"When you came home on Friday to check on the gas ring, did you notice anything out of the ordinary?"

"No," said Soames. "There were one or two cars on the road – this was before the power cut, remember – but not a lot. It was a nasty evening even by then, and most folks, given the choice, were stopping indoors."

"Did you see anyone near the cottage where Nick Barber was staying?"

"No, but I live the other way, so I wouldn't have."

"What about you, Kelly?" Banks asked.

"I was in the pub all the time, working," said Kelly. "I never left the place. You can ask CC."

"But what did you think about Nick Barber?"

This was clearly dangerous ground, and Kelly seemed to become even more nervous. She wouldn't look him in the eye. But Banks wasn't worried about her. She didn't know how far he was going to go, but without giving Kelly's secret away, he wanted to keep his eyes on Calvin to see if there was any hint that he had known what was going on between his nubile daughter and Nick Barber.

"Don't know, really," said Kelly. "He seemed a pleasant enough lad, like Dad says. He never really said much." She examined her fingernails.

"So neither of you knew why he was here?"

"Holiday, I suppose," said Calvin. "Though why anyone would want to come up here at this time of year is beyond me."

"Would it surprise you to hear that he was a writer of some sort?"

"Can't say as I ever really thought about it," said Calvin.

"I think he was mostly just looking for a secluded place to work," said Banks, "but there might also be another reason why he was up here rather than, say, in Cornwall or Norfolk, for example." Banks noticed Kelly tense up. "I don't know if he was writing fiction or history, but it's possible that, either way, he might have been doing some research, and there might have been someone he wanted to see, someone he'd been looking for with some connection to the area, maybe to the past. Any ideas who that might be?"

Calvin shook his head, and Kelly followed suit. Banks studied them. He thought himself a reasonable judge, and he was satisfied from the reactions and body language he had seen that Calvin Soames did not know about his daughter shagging Nick Barber, which gave him no real motive for the murder. No more than anyone else, anyway. Whether Kelly had a motive, he didn't know. True, she had been working at the time of the murder, but she admitted to seeing Barber in the afternoon, and if the doctor was at all wrong about the time of death, he could have been dead when she left him. But why? They'd only known one another a few days, according to Annie, and they'd both had a bit of fun without any expectation of a future.

It would be good to keep an open mind, as ever, Banks thought, but for now his thoughts moved towards London and what they might find out from Nick's flat.

Monday, September 15, 1969

One thing that disappointed Chadwick as he rifled through the stack of Brimleigh Festival photographs on Monday morning was that they had all, except for a few obviously posed ones, been taken in daylight. He should have expected that. Flash doesn't carry a great distance, and it would have been useless for shots of the crowd at night, or of the bands performing.

One photographer did seem to have got backstage, though; at least several of his photographs were taken there, candids. Linda Lofthouse showed up in three of them; the flowing white dress with the delicate embroidery was easy to spot. In one she was standing, chatting casually with a mixed group of long-haired people; in another she was with two men he didn't recognize; and in the third she was sitting alone, staring into the distance. It was an exquisite photograph, head and shoulders in profile, perhaps taken with a telephoto lens. She looked beautiful and fragile, and there was *no* flower painted on her cheek.

"Someone to see you downstairs, sir," said Karen, popping her head around his door and breaking the spell.

"Who?" Chadwick asked.

"Young couple. They just asked to see the man in charge of the Brimleigh Festival murder."

"Did they, indeed? Better have them sent up."

Chadwick glanced out of his window as he waited, sipping his tepid coffee. He was high up at the back and looked out over British Insulated Callender's Cables Ltd. up Westgate towards the majestic dome of the town hall, blackened like the other buildings by a century of industry. A steady flow of traffic headed west towards the Inner Ring Road.

Finally, there was a knock at his door and Karen showed in the young couple. They looked a bit sheepish, the way most people would in the inner sanctum of police headquarters. Chadwick introduced himself and asked them to sit down. Both were in their early twenties, the young man with neatly cut short hair and a dark suit, and the girl in a white blouse and a black miniskirt, blonde hair pulled back and tied behind her neck with a red ribbon. Dressed for work. They introduced themselves as Ian Tilbrook and June Betts.

"You said it was about the Brimleigh Festival murder," Chadwick began.

Ian Tilbrook's eyes looked anywhere but at Chadwick, and June fidgeted with her handbag on her lap. But it was she who spoke first. "Yes," she said, giving Tilbrook a sideways glance. "I know we should have come forward sooner," she said, "but we were there."

"At the festival?"

"Yes."

"So were thousands of others. Did you see something?"

"No, it's not that," June went on. She glanced at Tilbrook again, who was staring out of the window, took a deep breath and went on. "Someone stole our sleeping bag."

"I see," said Chadwick, suddenly interested.

"Well, the newspapers said to report anything odd, and it was odd, wasn't it?"

"Why didn't you come forward earlier?"

June looked at Tilbrook again. "He didn't want to get involved," she said. "He's up for promotion at the Copper Works, and he thinks it'll spoil his chances if they find out he's been going to pop festivals. They'll think he's a drug-taking hippie. *And* a murder suspect."

"That's not fair!" said Tilbrook. "I said it was probably nothing, it was just a sleeping bag, but you kept going on about it." He looked at his watch. "And now I'm going to be late for work."

"Never mind about that, laddie," said Chadwick. "Just tell me about it."

Tilbrook sulked, but June took up the story again. "Well, the papers said she was found in a blue Woolworths sleeping bag, and ours was blue and from Woolworths. I just thought . . . you know."

"Can you identify it?"

"I'm not sure. I don't think so. They're all the same, aren't they?"

"I suppose you both . . . er . . . it was big enough for the two of you . . . you spent some time in it over the weekend?"

June blushed. "Yes."

"There'll be evidence we can match. You'll still have to look at it."

June cringed. "I don't think I could. Is there . . . ? I mean, did she . . . ?"

"There's not a lot of blood, no, and you won't have to see it."

"All right. I suppose."

"But first give me a few details. Let's start with the time."

"We weren't really paying attention to time," said Tilbrook, "but it was late Sunday night."

"How do you know?"

"Led Zeppelin were on," said June. "They were the last band to play, and we went to see if we could get anywhere closer to the stage. We left our stuff, thinking if we did find somewhere, one of us could go back and get it while the other remained, but we couldn't find anywhere, it was so crowded near the front. When we got back it was gone."

"Just the sleeping bag?"

"Yes."

"What else did you have?"

"Just a rucksack with some extra clothes, a bottle of pop and sandwiches."

"And that remained untouched?"

"Yes."

"Where were you sitting?"

"Right at the edge of the woods, about halfway down the field."

It was close, Chadwick thought with a surge of excitement, very close. So the killer had walked two hundred yards through the dense woods to the edge of the field and found a sleeping bag. Had that been what he was looking for? He would certainly have known that plenty of people there had one. It would have been dark by then. The crowd would, for the most part, be entranced by the music, all their attention focused on the stage, and it would have been easy enough for a dark figure to pick up a sleeping bag, even if the owners had been sitting nearby, and slip back into the woods.

Putting it back on the field with a body in it would have been more difficult, of course, and Chadwick was willing to bet that someone had seen something, a figure dragging a bag of some sort, or carrying it over his shoulder. Why had no one come forward? Clearly they hadn't found what they saw suspicious, or they simply wanted to avoid any sort of contact with the police. Drugs might have played a part, too. Perhaps whoever saw it was too far gone to comprehend what he or she was seeing. On the other hand, the killer might have waited until Led Zeppelin had finished playing and people started wandering home. Then it would have been easy to plant the sleeping bag. However it happened, the best thing the killer had in his favour was that not one of the twenty-five thousand people present would expect to see someone dragging a body in a sleeping bag over the grass.

There were risks, of course; there always are. Someone might also have seen him steal the bag, for example, and raised a hue and cry. But it was so dark that they wouldn't have been able to describe him, and those hippies, in Chadwick's experience, had a very cavalier attitude towards private property. Also, someone might have found the body while he was away. Even then, all he would have lost was the opportunity to try to disguise the crime, to make it look as if the girl had been killed in the sleeping bag on the field.

It was clear they weren't dealing with a criminal genius here, but he had had luck on his side. Even if he hadn't disguised the crime scene and someone had found the body in the woods, there was still no evidence to link it to him, and the police would be exactly where they were now. Or at least where they had been before June Betts and Ian Tilbrook had come forward. It hadn't taken long to debunk the misleading evidence about where the victim was killed, and now, just as Chadwick had hoped, the attempt to mislead had yielded a clue. They now had a much better idea of the time of the murder, if nothing else, but they still didn't know what had happened to the knife.

"Can you be a bit more specific about the time?" he asked. "How long had the group been playing?"

"It's hard to say," said June, looking at Tilbrook. "They hadn't been on long."

"They were playing 'I Can't Quit You, Baby' when we set off to see if we could find somewhere nearer the stage," said Tilbrook, "and they were still playing it when we got back. I think it was their second number of the set, and the first was pretty short."

Chadwick had no idea how long these songs lasted, but he realized he could probably get a set list from Rick Hayes, to whom he wanted to speak again anyway. For now, this would have to do. "Say between five past one and half past, then?"

"We didn't have watches," said June, "but if you say they started at one, then yes, it would have been about twenty minutes into the show, something like that."

That would put the time at about one-twenty, which meant that Linda must have been killed between about one, when the band started, and then. He showed them her photograph. "Did you see this girl at any time?"

"No," they said.

Then Chadwick showed them the pictures of Linda with others. "Recognize anyone?"

"Isn't that . . . ?" June said.

"It could be, I suppose," said Ian.

"Who?" Chadwick asked.

"They're from the Mad Hatters," Ian explained. "Terry Watson and Robin Merchant."

Chadwick looked at the photograph again. He would be talking to the Mad Hatters that afternoon. "Okay," he said, standing up. "Now, if you'd like to come to the evidence room with me, you can have a look at that sleeping bag."

Reluctantly, they followed him down.

"I know you have a train to catch," said Superintendent Catherine Gervaise early on Monday morning, "but I wanted to have a quick word with you before you left."

Banks sat across the desk from her in what used to be Gristhorpe's office. It was a lot more sparsely decorated now, and the bookcases held only books on law, criminology and management technique. Gone were the leather-bound volumes of Dickens, Hardy and Austen with which Gristhorpe had surrounded himself, and the books about fly-fishing and drystone-wall building. One shelf displayed a few of the super-intendent's archery awards, alongside a framed photograph of her aiming a bow. The only true decorative effect was a poster for an old Covent Garden production of *Tosca* on the wall.

"As you probably know," Superintendent Gervaise went on, "this is my first murder investigation at this level, and I'm sure the boys and girls in the squad room have been having a good laugh at my expense."

"Not at —"

She waved him down. "It doesn't matter. That's not what this is about." She shuffled some papers on her desk. "I know a lot about you, DCI Banks. I make a point of knowing as much as I can about the officers under my command."

"A very wise move," said Banks, wondering if he was in for even more of the obvious.

She gave him a sharp glance. "Including your penchant for cheap sarcasm," she said. "But that's not why we're here, either." She leaned back in her executive chair and smiled, her Cupid's-bow lips turning up at the edges as if she was ready to fire an arrow. "I'd like, if I may, to be completely frank with you, DCI Banks, on the understanding that nothing that's said in here this morning goes beyond you, me and these four walls. Is that clear?"

"Yes," said Banks, now wondering what the hell was coming next.

"I'm aware that you recently lost your brother under appalling circumstances, and you have my sincere commiserations. I am also aware that you lost your home, and almost your life, not too long ago. All in all, it's been quite an eventful year for you, hasn't it?"

"It has, but I hope none of that has affected my job."

"Oh, but I think we can be quite sure that it has, don't you?" She was wearing oval glasses with silver frames, which she adjusted as she looked at the papers on her desk. "Withholding information in a major investigation, assault on a suspect with an iron bar. Need I go on. But you don't need much encouragement to go a little bit over the top, do you, DCI Banks? You never did. Your record is a patchwork quilt of questionable decisions and downright insubordination. *Res ipsa loquitur*, as the lawyers are fond of saying."

So you can quote Latin, Banks thought to himself. Big deal. "Look," he said, "I've cut a few corners, I admit it. You have to in this job if you're to keep ahead of the villains. But I've never perjured myself, I've never faked the evidence and I've never used force to get a confession. I admit I lost it in London last summer, but, like you said, a personal tragedy. You're the new broom, I understand that. You want to make a clean sweep.

Fair enough. If I'm a transfer waiting to happen, then let's get on with it."

"What on earth makes you think that?"

"Maybe something you said?"

She regarded him through narrowed eyes. "You got on very well with my predecessor, Detective Superintendent Gristhorpe, didn't you?"

"He was a good copper."

"What's that supposed to mean?"

"What I said. Mr. Gristhorpe was an experienced officer."

"And he gave you free rein."

"He knew how to get the job done."

"Right." Superintendent Gervaise leaned forward and clasped her hands on the desk. "Well, let me tell you something that may surprise you. I don't want you to change. I want you to get the job done, too."

"What?" said Banks.

"I thought that might surprise you. Let me tell you something. I'm a woman in a man's world. Do you think I don't know that? Do you think I don't know how many people resent me because of it, how many are waiting in the wings just to see me fail? But I'm also ambitious. I see no reason why I shouldn't make chief constable in a few years. Not here, necessarily, but somewhere. Maybe they'll give me the position *because* I'm a woman. I don't care. I've got nothing against positive discrimination. We've had it coming for centuries. It's well overdue. My predecessor wasn't ambitious. He didn't care. He was close to retirement. But I'm not, and I still see a career ahead of me, a long career, and a *great* one."

"And my role in all this is?"

"You know as well as I do that we're judged by results, and one thing I've noticed as I've studied your checkered career is that you do get results. Maybe not in the traditional ways, maybe not always in the legally prescribed ways, but you get them. And it may also interest you to know that there are relatively few black marks against you. That means you get away with it. Most of the time." She sat back and smiled again. "When the doctor asks you how much you drink, what do you tell him?"

"Pardon?"

"Come on. This isn't about drinking. What do you tell him?"

"You know, a couple of drinks a day, something like that."

"And do you know what your doctor does?"

"Tell me."

"He immediately doubles that figure." She leaned forward again. "My point is that we all lie about things like that, and this," she tapped the folders in front of her, "simply tells me that the number of times you got caught out in something not exactly kosher is the tip of the iceberg. And that's good."

"It is?"

"Yes. I want someone who gets away with it. I don't want black marks against you, because they'll reflect on me, but I do want results. And, as I said, you get results. It looks good on me, and when I leave this godforsaken wasteland of sheep shaggers and Saturday-night pub brawlers, I want to take a shining record with me. And that might be sooner than we think if the Home Office has its way. I assume you've been reading the newspapers?"

"Yes, ma'am," said Banks. Many of the smaller county forces, such as North Yorkshire, had recently been deemed by the Home Office as not up to the task of policing the modern world. Consequently, there was talk of them being merged with larger neighbouring forces, which meant that the North Yorkshire Constabulary might be swallowed up by West

Yorkshire. Nobody was saying what would happen to the present personnel if such a shakeup actually went ahead.

"You can give me that shining record," Superintendent Gervaise went on, "and in return I can give you enough rope. Drink on duty, follow leads on your own, disappear for days without reporting in. I don't care. But all the while you're doing those things, they'd damn well better be for the sake of solving the case, and you'd damn well better solve it quick, and I'd damn well better get all the reflected glory. No slacking. Am I still making myself clear?"

"You are, ma'am," said Banks, struck with admiration and awe for the spectacle of naked ambition unfolding before him, and working in his favour.

"And if you do anything over the top, make damn sure you don't get caught or you'll be out on your arse," she said. Then she straightened the collar of her white silk blouse and leaned back in her chair. "Now," she said, "don't you have a train to catch?"

Banks got up and walked to the door.

"DCI Banks?"

"Yes?"

"That Opera North production of *Lucia di Lammermoor*. Don't you think it was just a little lacklustre? And wasn't Lucia just a little too shrill?"

Monday, September 15, 1969

After a meeting with Bradley, Enderby and Detective Chief Superintendent McCullen later on Monday morning, Chadwick invited Geoff Broome for a lunchtime sandwich and pint at the pub across from Park Lane College. Most of the students hung out in the slightly more posh lounge, but the public bar was Chadwick's domain, and that of a few old-age pensioners who sat quietly playing dominoes over their halves of mild. With a couple of pints of Webster's Pennine Bitter beside them, and a plate of roast beef sandwiches each, Chadwick brought Broome up to date on the Linda Lofthouse murder.

"I don't know why you're telling me all this, Stan," said Broome, finishing his sandwich and taking out a packet of ten Kensitas, tapping one on the table and lighting it. "It doesn't sound like a drugs-related killing to me."

Chadwick watched Broome inhale and exhale and felt the familiar urge he thought he'd vanquished six years ago, when the doctor found a shadow on his lung that turned out to be tuberculosis and cost him six months in a sanitarium.

"Smoke bothering you?" Broome asked.

"No, it's all right." Chadwick sipped some beer. "I'm not saying it's a drugs-related murder, but drugs might play a part in it, that's all. I was just wondering whether you might be able to help me find out who the girl's contacts in Leeds were. You know that scene far better than I do."

"Of course, if I can," said Broome. As usual, his hair looked dishevelled and his suit looked as if it had been slept in. All of which might have masked the fact that he was one of the best detectives in the county. Perhaps not good enough to detect that his wife had been having it off with a vacuum cleaner salesman behind his back, but good enough to reduce significantly the amount of illegal drugs entering into the city. He also ran one of the most efficient networks of undercover officers, and his many paid informants within the drugs community knew they could depend on absolute anonymity.

Chadwick told him what Donald Hughes had said about visiting the house in one of the Bayswaters.

"I can't say anything springs immediately to mind," said Broome, "but we've had call to visit that neighbourhood once in a while. Let me do a bit of fishing."

"Bloke called Dennis," said Chadwick. "And it's maybe Terrace or Crescent. That's all I know."

Broome jotted the name and streets down. "You really think it's not just some random nutcase?" he asked.

"I don't know," Chadwick answered. "If you look at the crime, what we know of it, that's certainly a possibility. Until we know more about the girl's background and movements and whether she was drugged or not, for example, we can't really say much more. She was stabbed five times, so hard that the knife hilt bruised her chest and the blade cut off a piece of her heart. But there were no signs of any sort of struggle in the surrounding grass, and the bruising around her neck is minimal."

"Maybe it was a lover's quarrel? Lovers kill each other all the time, Stan. You know that."

"Yes, but they're usually a bit more obvious about it. Like I said, this has more deliberate elements. The killer stood behind her, for a start."

"So she's leaning back on him. She felt safe. What about her boyfriend?"

"Didn't have one, so far as we know. She had an ex, Donald Hughes, but his alibi checks out. He was working most of the night on a rush job at the garage where he works, and he wouldn't have had time to go anywhere near Brimleigh."

"Someone else close to her, then?"

"I suppose there's a chance she knew her killer," Chadwick admitted, "that it was someone she felt familiar with, felt comfortable with. Why he did it is another matter entirely. But to find out any more we need to track down her friends."

"Well, I can't promise anything, but I'll see what I can do," said Broome. "Good Lord, is that the time? Must dash. I have to see a man about a shipment of Dexedrine."

"All go, isn't it?"

"You can say that again. What's next on your agenda. Why so gloomy?"

"I've got an appointment with their Royal Majesties the Mad Hatters this afternoon," Chadwick said.

"Lucky you. Maybe they'll give you a free LP."

"They know what they can do with it."

"Think of Yvonne, though, Stan. You'd be golden in her eyes, you met the Mad Hatters and got a signed LP."

"Get away with you."

"I'll come back to you about the house," Broome said, then left.

Broome's cigarette butt still smouldered in the ashtray. Chadwick put it out. That made his fingers smell of smoke, so he went to the toilet and washed them before sitting down to finish his drink. He could hear a group of students in the lounge laughing over Stevie Wonder's "My Cherie Amour" on the jukebox, a song Chadwick actually quite liked when he heard it on the radio. Maybe it wouldn't be such a bad idea to get a signed LP for Yvonne, he thought, then immediately dismissed the idea. A lot of good that would do for his authority, begging a bunch of drug-addled layabouts for their autographs.

Chadwick tried to picture the twenty-five thousand kids at the Brimleigh Festival all sitting in the dark listening to a loud band on a distant lit-up stage. He knew he could narrow his range of suspects if he tried hard enough, especially now that he had a more accurate idea of the *time* of the murder. For a start, Rick Hayes was still holding something back, he was certain of it. The candid photographs proved that Linda

Lofthouse had been in the backstage area, and that she had talked with two members of the Mad Hatters, among others. Hayes must have known this, but he didn't say anything. Why? Was he protecting someone? On the other hand, Chadwick remembered that Hayes himself was left-handed, like the killer, so if he knew more than he was telling . . .

Still, he admonished himself, no point in too much theorizing ahead of the facts. Imagination had never been his forte, and he had seen enough to know that the details of the murder did not necessarily give any clues as to the killer's state of mind, or to his relationship with the victim. People were capable of strange and wondrous behaviour, and some of it was murderous. He finished his pint and went back to the station. He would get DC Bradley to give the boffins a gentle nudge while he went out to Swainsview Lodge with young Enderby.

8

Banks hadn't been to London since Roy's death, or since the terrible tube and bus suicide bombings that summer, and he was surprised, getting off the GNER InterCity at King's Cross that lunchtime, at how just being there brought a lump to his throat. It was partly Roy, of course, and partly some deep-rooted sense of outrage at what the place had suffered.

King's Cross station was the usual throng of travellers standing gazing up at the boards like people looking for alien spacecraft. There was nowhere to sit; that was the problem. The station authorities didn't want to encourage people to hang around the station; they had enough problems with terrorists, teenage prostitution and drugs as it was. So they let the poor buggers stand while they waited for their trains.

A uniformed constable met Banks and Annie at the side exit, as arranged, and whisked them in a patrol car through the streets of central London to Cromwell Road and along the Great West Road, past the roadside graffiti-scored concrete and glass towers of Hammersmith to Nick Barber's Chiswick flat, not far from Fuller's Brewery. It was a modern brick low-rise building, three storeys in all, and Barber had lived at the top in one of the corner units. The police locksmith was waiting for them.

When the paperwork had been completed and handed over, the lock yielded so quickly to the smith's ministrations that Banks wondered whether he had once used his skills to less legitimate ends.

Banks and Annie found themselves standing in a room with purple walls, on which hung a number of prints of famous psychedelic poster art: Jimi Hendrix and John Mayall at Winterland, February 1, 1968; Buffalo Springfield at the Fillmore Auditorium, December 21, 1967; the Mad Hatters at the Roundhouse on Chalk Farm, October 6, 1968. Mixed with these were a number of framed sixties album covers: *Cheap Thrills*, *Disraeli Gears*, *Blind Faith*, *Forever Changes* and Sir Peter Blake's infamous *Sgt. Pepper's Lonely Hearts Club Band*. Custom shelving held a formidable collection of CDs and LPs, and the stereo equipment was top-of-the-line Bang & Olufsen, as were the Bose headphones resting by the leather armchair.

There were far too many CDs to browse through, but on a cursory glance Banks noticed a prevalence of late sixties to early seventies rock, stopping around Bowie and Roxy Music, and including some bands he hadn't thought of in years, like Atomic Rooster, Quintessence, Dr. Strangely Strange and Amazing Blondel. There was also a smattering of jazz, mostly Miles, 'Trane and Mingus, along with a fair collection of J.S. Bach, Vivaldi and Mozart.

One shelf was devoted to magazines and newspapers in which Nick Barber had published reviews or features, and quickie rock bios. Some recent correspondence, mostly bills and junk mail, sat on a small worktable under the window. There was no desktop computer, Banks noticed, which probably meant Barber did all his work on the fly on his laptop, which had been taken.

The bedroom was tidy and functional, with a neatly made double bed and a wardrobe full of clothes, much the same as the ones he'd had with him in Yorkshire: casual and not too expensive. There was nothing to indicate any interests other than music, apart from the bookshelves, which reflected fairly catholic tastes in modern fiction, from Amis to Wodehouse, with a few popular science fiction, horror and crime novels mixed in – Philip K. Dick, Ramsey Campbell, Derek Raymond, James Herbert, Ursula K. Le Guin, James Ellroy and George Pelecanos. The rest were books about rock and roll: Greil Marcus, Lester Bangs, Peter Guralnik.

A filing cabinet in a corner of the bedroom held copies of contracts, lists and reviews of concerts attended, expense sheets and drafts of articles, all of which would have to be taken away and examined in detail. For the moment, though, Banks found what he needed to know in a brief note in the "Current" file referring to "the matter we discussed" and urging Barber to go ahead and get started. It also reminded him that they didn't pay expenses up front. The notepaper was headed with the *Mojo* logo and an address at Mappin House, on Winsley Street. It was dated October 1, just a couple of weeks before Nick Barber left for Yorkshire.

There were several messages on Nick's answering machine: two from an anxious girlfriend, who left him her work number, said she hadn't seen him for a while and wanted to get together for a drink, another from a mate about tickets to a Kasabian concert and one offering the deal of the century on double-glazing. As far as Banks could see, Nick Barber had kept his life clean and tidy and taken most of it with him on the road. Now it had disappeared.

"We'd better split up," he said to Annie. "I'll try the *Mojo* offices and you see if you can get any luck with the girl who left her work number. See if there's anything else you can find around the flat that might tell us anything about him, too, and arrange to have the files and stuff taken up to Eastvale. I'll take the tube and leave you the driver."

"Okay," said Annie. "Where shall we meet up?"

Banks named an Italian restaurant in Soho, one he was sure they hadn't been to together before, so it held no memories for them. They'd have to take a taxi or the tube back to their hotel, which was some distance away, just off Cromwell Road, not too far from the magnificent Natural History Museum. It was clean, they had been assured, and unlikely to break the tight police budget. As Annie busied herself listening to Barber's phone messages again, Banks left the flat and headed for the underground.

Melanie Wright dabbed at her cheeks and apologized to Annie for the second time. They were sitting in a Starbucks near the Embankment, not far from where Melanie worked as an estate agent. She said she could take a break when Annie called, but when she found out about Nick Barber's murder, she got upset and her boss told her she could take the rest of the afternoon off. If Nick had a "type," Annie was at a loss to know what it was. Kelly Soames was gamine, pale and rather naive, whereas Melanie was shapely, tanned and sophisticated. Perhaps the only similarities were that both were a few years younger than him, and both were blondes.

"Nick never let anyone get really close to him," Melanie said over a Frappuccino, "but that was okay. I mean, I'm only twenty-four. I'm not ready to get married yet. Or even to live with someone, for that matter. I've got a nice flat in Chelsea I share with a girlfriend, and we get on really well and give each other lots of space."

"But you did go out with Nick?"

"Yes. We'd been seeing one another for a year or so now, on and off. I mean, we weren't exclusive or anything. We weren't even what you'd call a couple, really. But we had fun. Nick was fun to be with, most of the time."

"What do you mean, most of the time?"

"Oh, he could be a bit of a bore when he got on his hobby horse. That's all. I mean, I wasn't even born when the bloody sixties happened. It wasn't my fault. Can't stand the music, either."

"So you didn't share his enthusiasm?"

"Nobody could. It was more than an enthusiasm with him. I mean, I know this sounds weird, because he was really cool and I got to meet all sorts of bands and stuff – I mean, we even had a drink with Jimmy Page once at some awards do. Can you believe it? Jimmy Page! Even I know who he is. But even though it all sounds really cool and everything, being a rock writer and meeting famous people, when you get right down to it, it's a bit like having any kind of all-consuming hobby, isn't it. I mean, it could have been trainspotting, or computers or something."

"Are you saying Nick was a bit of a nerd?"

"In some ways. Of course, there was more to him than that, or I wouldn't have hung around. Nerds aren't my type."

"It wasn't just for the bands, then?"

She shot Annie a sharp, disapproving glance. "No. I'm not like that, either. We really had fun, me and Nick. I can't believe he's gone. I'll miss him so much." She dabbed at her eyes.

"I'm sorry, Melanie," said Annie. "I don't mean to be insensitive or anything, but in this job you tend to get a bit cynical. When was the last time you saw Nick?"

"It must have been about two weeks ago, a bit over."

"What did you do?"

She gave Annie a look. "What do you think we did?"

"Before that."

"We had dinner."

"At his place?"

"Yeah. He was a fair chef. Liked watching all those cooking programs on TV. Can't stand them myself. You ask me what I can make, and I say reservations."

Annie had heard it before, but she laughed anyway. "Was there anything different about him?"

Melanie thought for a moment, frowning, then said, "It was just a feeling I got, really. I mean, I'd been around him before when he was pitching for a feature. It always mattered to him – I mean, he loved it – but this time, he was sort of anxious. I don't think he'd got the green light yet."

"Why do you think he was anxious? That he wouldn't get the assignment?"

"Maybe it was partly that, but I think it was more that it was personal."

"Personal?"

"Yeah. Don't ask me why. I mean, Nick was fanatical about all his projects, and secretive about the details, but I got the sense that this one was a little more personal for him."

"Did he tell you what, or who, he was working on?"

"No. But he never did. I don't know if he thought I'd tell someone else who'd get to it first, but, like I said, he was always secretive until he'd finished. Used to disappear for weeks on end. Never told me where he was going. Not that he had any obligation to, mind you. I mean, it's not like we were joined at the hip or anything."

"Did he say anything at all about it?"

"Just once, that last night." She gave a little laugh. "It was a funny sort of thing to say. He said it was a very juicy story and it had everything, including murder."

"Murder? He actually said that?"

Melanie started crying again. "Yes," she said. "But I didn't think he meant his own."

Monday, September 15, 1969

The Mad Hatters, Enderby explained as he negotiated the winding country roads with seeming ease, consisted of five members: Terry Watson on rhythm guitar and vocals, Vic Greaves on keyboards and backup vocals, Reg Cooper on lead guitar, Robin Merchant on bass and vocals and Adrian Pritchard on drums. They had formed about three years ago after they met at the University of Leeds, and so were considered a local band, though only two of them – Greaves and Cooper – actually came from Yorkshire. For the first year or so they played only gigs around the West Riding, then a London promoter happened to catch one of their shows at a Bradford pub and decided they'd fill a niche in the London scene with their unique blend of psychedelic pastoral.

"Hold on a minute," said a frustrated Chadwick. "What on earth is 'psychedelic pastoral' when it's at home?"

Enderby smiled indulgently. "Think of *Alice in Wonderland* or *Winnie the Pooh* set to rock music."

Chadwick winced. "I'd rather not. Go on."

"That's about all, sir. They caught on, got bigger and bigger, and now they've got a bestselling LP out, and they're hobnobbing with rock's elite. They're tipped for even bigger things.

Roger Waters from Pink Floyd was telling me just yesterday in Rugby that he thought they'd go far."

Chadwick was already getting tired of Enderby's name-dropping since the weekend, and he wondered if it had been a mistake to send him down to interview the Brimleigh Festival groups who were appearing in Rugby. He hadn't even found out anything of interest in two days, and reported that there had only been about three hundred people there. And he still hadn't got a haircut. "What the hell does Lord Jessop have to do with this?" he asked, changing the subject. "This place does belong to him, doesn't it?"

"Yes. He's young, rich, a bit of a longhair himself. He likes the music, and he likes to be associated with that world. Bit of a swinger, you might say. Actually, he's away a lot of the time, and he lets them use his house and grounds for rest and rehearsals."

"Simple as that?"

"Yes, sir."

Chadwick gazed out at the landscape, the valley bottom to his left where the River Swain meandered between wooded banks, and the rising slope of the daleside opposite, a haphazard pattern of drystone walls and green fields until about halfway up, where the grass turned brown and the rise ended in grey limestone outcrops along the top, marking the start of the gorse-and-heather moorland.

It was a fine day, with only a few high white clouds in the sky. Even so, Chadwick felt out of his element. It wasn't as if he had never visited the Dales before. He and Janet had had many rides out there when Yvonne was younger and he got his first car, a Reliant three-wheeler that rocked dangerously in even the slightest crosswind. He wasn't untouched by the beauty of nature, but he was still a city boy at heart. After a short while, the open country did nothing for him except make him miss the damp pavements, the noise and bustle and crowds even more.

If he had his way, they would spend their holidays exploring new cities, but Janet liked the caravan. Yvonne wouldn't be coming with them for very much longer, he thought, so he might just be able to persuade Janet to take a trip to Paris or Amsterdam, if they could afford it, and broaden her horizons. Janet had never been abroad, and Chadwick himself had only been on the continent during wartime. It would be interesting to revisit some of his old haunts. Not the beaches, battlefields or cemeteries – he had no interest in them – but the bars, cafés and homes, where people had opened their doors and hearts and shown their gratitude after liberation.

"Here we are, sir."

Chadwick snapped out of his reverie as Enderby pulled off the narrow track onto the grass. "Is this it?" he asked. "It doesn't look like much of a place."

What he could see of the house beyond its high stone wall and wooden gate was an unremarkable building of limestone with a flagstone roof and three chimneys. It was long and low with very few windows; all in all, a gloomy-looking place.

"This is just the back," said Enderby as they approached the gate. It opened into a flagged yard, and the path led to a heavy red door with a large brass knocker in the shape of a lion's head. "Tradesman's entrance."

Enderby knocked on the door, and they waited. The silence was oppressive, Chadwick thought. No birds singing. Even the sound of a rock band rehearsing would have been preferable. Well, on second thought . . .

The door opened and a young man of about thirty in a paisley shirt and flared black denim jeans greeted them. His chestnut hair wasn't as long as Chadwick would have expected, but it did hang over his collar. "You must be the police," he said. "I'm Chris Adams, the band's manager. I don't see how we can help you, but please come in."

Enderby and Chadwick followed him into a broad panelled hallway with doors leading off to the left and right. The dark wood gleamed, and Chadwick caught a whiff of lemon-scented polish. At the far end, a set of French windows framed a stunning view of the opposite daleside, an asymmetrical jumble of fields and drystone walls, and below them, at the bottom of the slope, was the river. The doors, Chadwick noticed as he got closer, led out to a terrace with stone balustrades. A table, complete with umbrella, and six chairs stood in front of the doors.

"Impressive," said Chadwick.

"It's nice when the weather's good," said Adams. "Which I can't say is all that often in this part of the world."

"Local?"

"I grew up in Leeds. Went to school with Vic, the keyboards player. It's down here."

He led them down a flight of stone steps, and Chadwick realized then that they had entered the house on its highest level and there was a whole other floor beneath. At least half of it, he noticed as they walked in through the door, was taken up by one large room, at the moment full of guitars, drums, keyboard instruments, microphones, consoles, amplifiers, speakers and thick, snaking electrical cords: the rehearsal studio, mercifully silent, except for the all-pervading hum of electricity. More French windows, these ones open, led out to a patio area in the shadow of the terrace above. Just beyond that, across a short stretch of overgrown lawn, was a granite and marble swimming pool. Why anyone would want an outdoor swimming pool in their backyard in Yorkshire was beyond Chadwick, but the rich had their own tastes, and the wherewithal to indulge them. Perhaps it was heated. Sunlight reflecting from the surface told him the pool was full of water.

Four young men sat around in the large room smoking cigarettes and chatting and laughing with three girls, and one lay on a sofa reading. On a table by one wall stood a variety of bottles – Coca-Cola, gin, vodka, whisky, brandy, beer and wine. Some of the others seemed to have drinks already, and Adams offered refreshments, but Chadwick declined. He didn't like to feel beholden in any way towards people who might very well be, or might soon become, suspects. Everyone was wearing casual clothes, mostly jeans and T-shirts, some tie-dyed in the most outrageous patterns and colours. Very long hair was the norm for both men and women, except for Adams, who seemed a shade more conservative than the rest. Chadwick was wearing a dark suit and muted tie.

Now that he was here, Chadwick didn't know exactly where to start. Adams introduced the band members, who all said hello politely, and the girls, who giggled and retreated to one of the other rooms.

Fortunately, one of the group members stepped forward and said, "How can we help you, Mr. Chadwick? We heard about what happened at Brimleigh. It's terrible."

It was Robin Merchant, bass and vocals, and clearly the spokesman. He was tall and thin and wore jeans and a jacket made of some satiny blue material with zodiac signs embroidered on it.

"I don't know that you can," said Chadwick, sitting down on a folding chair. "It's just that we have information the girl was in the backstage area at some point on Sunday evening, and we're trying to find out if anyone saw her there or talked to her."

"There were a lot of people around," said Merchant.

"I know that. And I also know that things might have been, shall we say, a wee bit chaotic back there."

One of the others – Adrian Pritchard, the drummer, Chadwick thought – laughed. "You can say that again. It was anarchy, man."

They all laughed.

"Even so," Chadwick said, "one of you might have seen or heard something important. You might not know it, what it is, but it's possible."

"Does the tree fall in the woods if no one is there to hear it?" chimed in the one on the sofa. Vic Greaves, keyboards player.

"Come again?" said Chadwick.

Greaves stared off into space. "It's a matter of philosophy, isn't it? How can I know something if I don't know it? How can I know that something happens if I don't experience it?"

"What Vic means," said Merchant, jumping to the rescue, "is that we were all pretty much focused on what we were doing."

"Which was?"

"Pardon?"

"What were you doing?"

"Well, you know," said Merchant, "just relaxing in the caravan, practising a few chord changes, or maybe having a drink or something, talking to guys in the other bands. Depends what time it was."

Chadwick doubted it. Most likely, he thought, they were taking drugs and having sex with groupies, but none of them was going to admit that. "What time did you perform?"

Merchant looked to the others for confirmation. "We went on about eight, just after, right, and we played an hour set, so we were off again just after nine. After the roadies moved the equipment around and set up the light show, Pink Floyd came on after us, about ten, then Fleetwood Mac, then Led Zep."

"And after your set? What did you do?"

Merchant shrugged. "We just hung around, you know. We were pretty wired, the adrenaline from performing and everything – I mean, it went *really* well, a great gig, and a big one for us – so we needed a couple of drinks to come down. I don't know, we just listened to the other bands, that sort of thing. I spent a bit of time in the caravan reading."

"Reading what?"

"You wouldn't have heard of it."

"Try me."

"Aleister Crowley, *Magick in Theory and Practice*."

"Never heard of it," said Chadwick, with a smile.

Merchant gave him a sharp, penetrating glance. "As I said, I didn't think you would have done."

"Did you stay until the end?"

"Yeah. Jesse said we could stay here for the night, so we didn't have too far to go."

"Jesse?"

"Sorry. Lord Jessop. Everyone calls him Jesse."

"I see. Is he here now?"

"No, he's in France. Spends quite a bit of his time there, down in Antibes. We saw him last month when we did a tour there."

"In France?"

"Yeah. The album's selling really well there."

"Congratulations."

"Thanks."

"Was Lord Jessop at Brimleigh?"

"Sure. He went down to Antibes maybe last Tuesday or Wednesday."

All of a sudden a loud, violent buzzing noise cut like a chainsaw through Chadwick's head.

"Sorry." A sheepish Reg Cooper, lead guitarist, apologized. "Feedback." He put his guitar down carefully. The noise ebbed slowly away.

"Boring you, am I, laddie?" said Chadwick.

"No," Cooper muttered. "Not at all. I said I was sorry. Accident."

Chadwick held Cooper's gaze for a moment, then turned his attention back to Robin Merchant. "Let's get back to the eighth of September," he said. "We think the girl was killed between about one o'clock and twenty past one in the morning, while Led Zeppelin were playing a song called 'I Can't Quit You, Baby.'" Such language came only with difficulty from Chadwick's mouth, and he noticed some of the others smirk as he spoke the words. "I understand that they're very loud," he went on, ignoring them, "so it's unlikely anybody heard anything, if there was anything to hear, but were any of you in Brimleigh Woods at that time?"

"The woods?" said Merchant. "No, we didn't go there at all. We were backstage, up front in the press enclosure or in the caravan."

"All of you? All the time?" Chadwick scanned the others' faces.

They all nodded.

"'If you go down to the woods today . . .'" Vic Greaves intoned in the background.

"Why would we go to the woods, man?" said Adrian Pritchard. "All the action was backstage."

"What action?"

"You know, man . . . the birds . . . the . . ."

"Shut up, Adrian," said Merchant. He turned back to

Chadwick and folded his arms. "Look, I know what preconceptions you coppers have of us, but we're clean. You can search the place if you like. Go on."

"I'm sure you are," said Chadwick. "You knew we were coming. But I'm not interested in drugs. Not at the moment, anyway. I'm more interested in what you were doing when this girl died, and in whether any of you saw her or talked to her."

"Well, I told you," said Merchant. "We never went near the woods, and how do we know if we saw her or not when none of us knows her name or what she looked like."

"You didn't see the papers?"

"We never bother with them. Full of establishment lies."

"Anyway," Chadwick said, reaching for his briefcase. "I was getting to that. As it happens I now have a fairly recent photograph. It should interest you." He took out the photograph of Linda with the members of the Mad Hatters and passed it to Merchant, who gasped and stared, open-mouthed. "Is that . . . Vic?" He passed it to Vic Greaves, who still lay sprawled on a sofa smoking and looking, to Chadwick, quite out of it. Greaves stirred and took the photo. "Fuck," he said. "Fucking hell." The photo slipped out of his hands.

Chadwick went over and picked it up, standing over Greaves. "Who is it?" he asked. "You know her?"

"Sort of," said Greaves. "Look, I don't feel too good, Rob. My head, it's . . . like snakes and things coming back, you know, man . . . like I need . . ." He turned away.

Merchant stepped forward. "Vic's not too well," he said. "The doctor says he's suffering from fatigue, and his emotional state is pretty fragile right now. This must be a hell of a shock for him."

"Why?" asked Chadwick, sitting down again.

He gestured towards the photo. "That girl. It's Linda. Linda Lofthouse. She's Vic's cousin."

Cousin. Mrs. Lofthouse had never mentioned that. But why should she? He hadn't asked her about the Mad Hatters, and she had probably been in shock. Still, this was a new development worth following. Chadwick looked at Vic Greaves with more interest. By far the scruffiest of the bunch, he looked as if he hadn't shaved in four or five days, and his skin was deathly pale, as if he never saw the sun, his face dotted with angry red spots. His dark hair stuck out in tufts as if he had slept on it and not washed or combed it for a week. His clothes looked rumpled, slept-in, too. There was a well-thumbed paperback on the sofa beside him called *Meetings with Remarkable Men.*

"Were they particularly close?" Chadwick asked Robin Merchant.

"No, not really, I don't think, just cousins. She grew up in west Leeds, and Vic's family lived in Seacroft."

"But we understand she lived in London," Chadwick said. "Isn't that where you all live now?"

"It's a big place."

Chadwick took a deep breath. "Mr. Merchant," he said, "I appreciate that you lads are busy, not to mention famous, and no doubt wealthy. But a young girl has been brutally murdered at a festival in which you were taking part. She was seen backstage talking to two of you, and now it appears that one of you is also her cousin. Is there any particular reason Mr. Greaves over there is suffering from fatigue, that his emotional state is distressed? That's exactly the kind of thing that killing someone might do to you."

A stunned silence followed Chadwick's controlled tirade. Greaves tossed on the sofa and his book fell to the floor. He put his head in his hands and groaned. "Talk to him, Rob, talk to him," he said. "You tell him. I can't handle this."

"Look," said Merchant. "Why don't we take a walk outside, Inspector. I'll answer all your questions as best I can. But can't you see it's upsetting Vic?"

Upsetting Vic Greaves was not Chadwick's main concern, but he thought he might be able to get a bit more information out of Robin Merchant, who seemed the most level-headed of the lot, if he did as requested. He gestured to Enderby to stay with the others and accompanied Merchant out to the flagged patio down the slope towards the swimming pool.

"Ever use it?" Chadwick asked.

"Sometimes," Merchant answered with a smile. "For midnight orgies on the two days in August when it's warm enough. Jesse tries to keep it cleaned up, but it's difficult."

"Lord Jessop isn't a relation, too, is he?"

"Jesse? Good Lord, no. He's a patron of the arts. A friend."

They stood by the side of the pool looking out across the dale. Chadwick could see a red tractor making its way across one of the opposite fields towards a tiny farmhouse. The hillside was dotted with sheep. He glanced down at the swimming pool. A few early autumn leaves floated on the water's scummy surface, along with a dead sparrow.

"All right, Mr. Merchant," said Chadwick. "Am I to I take it you're the leader of the group?"

"Spokesman. We don't believe in leaders."

"Very well. *Spokesman.* That means you can speak for the others?"

"To some extent. Yes. It's not that they can't speak for themselves. But Vic, as you can see, is not exactly a social charmer, though he's a great creative force. Adrian and Reg are okay, but they're not especially articulate, and Terry is way too hip to talk to the fuzz."

"You sound educated."

"I've got a degree, if that's what you mean. English literature."

"I'm impressed."

"You're not meant to be. It's just a piece of paper." Merchant kicked a couple of loose pebbles with his foot. They plopped into the swimming pool. "Can we get this over with? I don't mean to be rude or anything, but we do have a tour to rehearse for. Contrary to what a lot of people think, rock bands aren't just a random collection of layabouts with minimal musical ability and loud amplifiers. We take our music seriously, and we work hard at it."

"I'm sure you do. I think if I ask you direct, simple questions and you answer them straightforwardly, we'll soon be done here. How about that?"

"Fine. Ask away." Merchant lit a cigarette.

"Was it Mr. Greaves who got the backstage pass for Linda Lofthouse?"

"It was me," said Merchant.

"Why you?"

"Vic's not . . . I mean, as you can see, he doesn't deal well with rules, people in authority, stuff like that. It intimidates him. It was his cousin, but he asked me to do it for him."

"So you did?"

"Yes."

"She would have picked this up where?"

"At the entrance to the backstage area."

"From security, I assume?"

"Yes."

That meant either they'd missed out on questioning the guard who had given Linda the pass, or he had forgotten or lied about it. Well, Chadwick thought, people lie often enough to the police. They don't want to get involved. And there's always that little bit of guilt everybody carries around with them.

"Could she could come and go as she pleased?"

"Yes."

"What were you talking about when you were photographed with her?"

"Just asking if she was having a good time, that sort of thing. It was very casual. We only chatted for a couple of minutes. I didn't even know that someone had taken a photo of us."

"Was she having a good time?"

"So she said."

"Was anything bothering her?"

"Not as far as I could tell."

"What was her state of mind?"

"Fine. Just, you know, normal."

"Was she worried about anything, frightened by anything?"

"No."

"Did you talk to her again after the photo was taken, later in the evening?"

"No."

"See her?"

"Only around, you know, from a distance."

"Did she have a flower painted on her cheek later?"

Merchant paused for a moment, then said, "As a matter of fact, she did. At least, I think it was her. There was some bird doing body art in the enclosure."

Well, Chadwick thought, there went one theory. Still, it would be useful to track down the "bird," if possible, and establish for certain whether she had painted the flower on Linda's cheek. "How well did you know Linda?"

"Not well at all. I'd met her in London a couple of times. Once when we were doing the album she got in touch with Vic through his parents and asked if she could sit in on the studio sessions with a friend. She's interested in music – as a matter of fact, we let her play a little acoustic guitar on one track, and her and her friend did some harmonies. They weren't bad at all."

"What friend?"

"Just another bird. I didn't really talk to her."

"Did Linda ever go out with anyone in the group?"

"No."

"Come off it, Mr. Merchant. Linda Lofthouse was an exceptionally attractive girl, or hadn't you noticed?"

"There's no shortage of attractive girls in our business. Anyway, she didn't strike me as the sort to take up with a rock musician."

"What do you mean?"

"I mean that she seemed like a decent, well-brought-up girl, just a little brighter than most and with broader interests than her friends."

"She had a baby."

"So?"

"You have to sleep with someone to get pregnant. She did it when she was fifteen, so how can you tell me that on the strength of two meetings she wasn't 'that' sort of girl?"

"Call it gut instinct. I don't know. Maybe I'm wrong. She just seemed a nice girl, that's all. Didn't give off that kind of vibe. You get to recognize it, especially in this business. Take those three you saw when you came in."

"So Linda wasn't going out with anyone in the group?"

"No."

"What about the other groups at the festival?"

"She might have talked to people, but I didn't see her hanging around with anyone in particular for very long."

"What about Rick Hayes?"

"The promoter? Yeah, I saw her with him. She said she knew him in London."

"Was he her boyfriend?"

"I doubt it. I mean, Rick's a good guy, don't get me wrong, but he's a bit of a loser in that department, and they weren't acting that way towards one another."

Chadwick made a mental note. Losers in love often found interesting and violent ways to express their dissatisfaction. "Do you know if she had a boyfriend? Did she ever mention anyone?"

"Not that I recall. Look, have you ever thought that it was something else?"

"What do you mean?"

"They might have thought that it was something other than murder."

"They?"

"Figure of speech. Whoever did it."

"You've lost me."

"So I see. I don't know. I'm just speculating. Not everyone sees the world the same way as you do."

"I'm coming to realize that."

"Well . . . you know . . . I mean, murder is just a word."

"I can assure you it's more than that to me."

"Sorry. Sorry. I didn't mean to be offensive. But that's you. I'm just trying to show you that other people think differently."

Chadwick was beginning to think he had wandered into a *Wednesday Play*. Desperate to get back to more tenable ground, he asked, "Do you know where she lived?"

Merchant seemed to come back from a long way off and gather his thoughts before answering in a tired voice. "She had a room on Powis Terrace. Notting Hill Gate. That's what she said that time she came down to the studio, anyway."

"You don't know the number?"

"No. I wouldn't even know the street except when she said Notting Hill I asked her about it, because it's a great neighbourhood. Everyone knows Notting Hill, Portobello Road, Powis Square and all that."

Chadwick remembered Portobello Road from some leave he had spent in London during the war. "Expensive?"

"Bloody hell, no. Not for London, at any rate. It's all cheap bedsits."

"You said you met her a couple of times in London. When was the other time?"

"A gig at the Roundhouse last year. October, I think it was. One of the ones Rick Hayes promoted. Again, she asked Vic to get her and a friend backstage passes and he delegated it to me."

"The same friend who sat in on the recording session with her?"

"Yeah. Sorry, but, like I said, I didn't talk to her. I can't remember her name."

Chadwick stared out across the dale again. The tractor had disappeared. Cloud shadows raced across the fields and limestone outcrops as the breeze picked up. "Not much of a memory, have you, laddie?" he said.

"Look, I'm sorry if I'm not sounding helpful," said Merchant, "but it's the truth. Linda was never part of the entourage, and she wasn't a groupie. She got in touch with Vic exactly three times over the past two years, just to ask for little favours. We didn't mind. It was no problem. She was family, after all. But that's all there was to it. None of us went out with her and none of us really knew her."

"And that's it?"

"Yes."

"Back to last Sunday. Where were you all between one and twenty past one that night?"

Merchant flicked his cigarette end into the swimming pool. "I don't really remember."

"Were you with the others listening to Led Zeppelin?"

"Some of the time, yeah, but they're not really my thing. I might have been in the caravan reading, or in the beer tent."

"That's not much of an alibi, is it?"

"I wasn't aware I'd need one."

"What about the others?"

"They were around."

"Your manager, Mr. Adams. Was he there?"

"Chris? Yeah, he was somewhere around."

"But you didn't see him?"

"I don't really remember seeing him at any particular time, no, but I did see him now and then in passing."

"So any one of you could have gone out to the woods with Linda Lofthouse and stabbed her?"

"But nobody had any reason to," Merchant said. "We didn't hang out with her, didn't really know her. I just got the passes for her, that's all."

"Passes?"

"Yeah, two."

"You didn't say this before."

"You didn't ask."

"Who was the other pass for?"

"Her friend, the girl she was with."

"The same one you saw her with at the Roundhouse and the recording session? The one whose name you can't remember?"

"That's the one."

"Why didn't you say so earlier?"

Merchant shrugged.

"If you got her a pass, you must know her name."

"I didn't *look* at it."

"Did you see her later, at the festival?"

"Once or twice."

"Were they together?"

"The first time I saw them, yes. Later on they weren't."

"What do you know about this girl?"

"Nothing. She was a friend of Linda's and they sang together in clubs. I think they shared a pad or were neighbours or something."

"What does she look like?"

"About the same age as Linda. Long dark hair, olive complexion. Nice figure."

"What time did you last see her?"

"I don't know. When Pink Floyd were on. It must have been close to midnight."

"And were the two of them together?"

"I didn't see Linda then, no."

"What was this other girl doing?"

"Just standing around with a group of people drinking and chatting."

"Who?"

"Just people. Nobody in particular."

So who was she? Chadwick wondered. And why hadn't she reported her friend missing? Not for the first time, he began to wonder about the mental faculties of the world he was dealing with. Didn't these people care if someone stole their sleeping bag, or worse, if someone close to them simply disappeared? He didn't expect them to see the world as he did, with danger at every turn, but surely it was simple common sense to worry? Unless something had happened to her friend, too. He wouldn't find that out by hanging around Swainsview Lodge, he decided, and the thought of trying to talk to any of the others again brought on a headache.

Chadwick thanked Robin Merchant for his time, said he would have to talk to Vic Greaves at some point, when he was feeling better, then they went back inside. Enderby, looking pleased with himself, held out a copy of the Mad Hatters LP and asked Merchant if he would sign it. He did. The others were slouching in their chairs smoking and sipping drinks, Reg Cooper picking a quiet tune on his guitar, Vic Greaves apparently asleep on his sofa, tranquilized to the gills. The sound system was buzzing in the background. Chris Adams showed them out, apologizing for Greaves and promising that if there was anything else they needed, they should just get in touch with him; then he gave them his phone number and left them at the door.

"Where did you get that?" Chadwick said in the car, pointing to the LP.

"He gave it to me. The manager. I got them all to sign it."

"Better hand it over," said Chadwick. "You wouldn't want anyone to think you'd been accepting bribes, would you?"

"But, sir!"

Chadwick held his hand out. "Come on, laddie. Give."

Reluctantly, Enderby handed over the signed LP. Chadwick slipped it into his briefcase, suppressing a little smile as Enderby practically stripped the gears getting back to the road.

9

The *Mojo* office was a square, open-plan area on the same floor as *Q* and *Kerrang!* magazines, accommodating about twenty or so people. There were two fairly large windows at one end, and two long desks equipped with Mac computers in various colours and stacked with CDs, reference books and file folders. Cluttered, but appealingly so. Filing cabinets fitted under the desks. Posters covered the walls, mostly blow-ups of old *Mojo* covers. The people Banks could see working there ran the whole gamut: short hair, long hair, grey hair, shaved heads. Dress was mostly casual, but there were even some ties in evidence.

Nobody paid Banks any attention as John Butler, the editor he had come to see, led him to a section of desk close to the window. An empty Pret A Manger bag sat among the papers on his desk, and a whiff of bacon hung in the air, reminding Banks that it was mid-afternoon and he was starving. He could feel his stomach growling as he sat down.

John Butler looked to be in his late thirties and was one of the more casually dressed people in the office, wearing jeans and an old Hawkwind T-shirt. His shaved head gleamed under the strip lighting. There was music playing, some sixtiesish

PIECE OF MY HEART • 187

piece with jangling guitars and harmonies. Banks didn't recognize it, but he liked it. He could also hear the thumping bass of a dance mix coming from round the corner. He thought it must be hard to concentrate on writing with all that noise going on.

"It's about Nick Barber," said Banks. "I understand he was working on an assignment for you?"

"Yes, that's right. Poor Nick." Butler's brow crinkled. "One of the best. Nobody, and I mean nobody, knew more about late-sixties and early-seventies music than Nick, especially the Mad Hatters. He's a great loss to the entire music community."

"It's my job to find out who killed him," said Banks.

"I understand. Any help I can give, of course . . . though I don't see how."

"What was Nick Barber's assignment?"

"He was doing a big feature on the Mad Hatters," said Butler. "More specifically on Vic Greaves, the keyboards player. Next year is the fortieth anniversary of when the band was formed, and they're re-forming for a big concert tour."

Banks had heard of the Mad Hatters. Not many people hadn't. They had rebuilt themselves from the ashes of the sixties in a way that few other bands had, except perhaps Fleetwood Mac after Peter Green left and Pink Floyd after Syd Barrett had. But not without tremendous cost, as Banks recalled. "Where are they now?" he asked.

"All over the place. Most of them live in L.A."

"Vic Greaves disappeared years ago, didn't he?" Banks said.

"That's right. Nick had found him."

"How did he manage that?"

"He protected his sources pretty well, but I'd say most likely through a rental agency or an estate agent. He had his contacts. Vic Greaves doesn't go to extraordinary lengths to stay anonymous; he's just a recluse and he doesn't advertise his presence. I mean, he's been found before. The problem is that no one can ever seem to get much out of him, so they give up, except maybe some of the weirdos who see him as a sort of cult figure, which is why he guards his privacy to the extent that he does, or Chris Adams does. Anyway, however Nick did it, you can guarantee it wouldn't be through Adams, the manager."

"Why not?"

"Adams is very protective of Greaves. Has been ever since the breakdown. They're old friends, apparently, go back to school days."

"Where did Nick find Greaves?"

"In North Yorkshire. The Hatters always had a strong connection with Yorkshire through Lord Jessop and Swainsview Lodge. Besides, Vic and Reg Cooper, the lead guitarist, were both local lads. Met the others at the University of Leeds."

"North Yorkshire? How long has he been living there?"

"Dunno," said Butler. "Nick didn't say."

So the object of Nick Barber's pilgrimage had been right under his nose all the time, and he had never guessed. Well, why would he? If you wanted to live as a hermit in the Dales, it could be done. Now Banks had a glimmer of a memory. Something that he might have guessed brought Nick Barber to Swainsdale. "Help me here," he said. "I didn't grow up in the area, and I wasn't there at the time, but as far as I can remember, there was some other connection with the group, wasn't there?"

"Robin Merchant, the bass player."

"He drowned, didn't he?"

"Indeed he did. Drowned in a swimming pool about a year after Brian Jones did exactly the same thing. June 1970. Tragic business."

"And that swimming pool was at Swainsview Lodge," said

Banks. "Now I remember." He was surprised at himself for not getting the connection earlier, but when it came down to it, although he knew that Brian Jones had also died in a swimming pool, he didn't know where that pool was, either. To him, a swimming pool was a swimming pool. But Nick Barber would know things like that, just the way sports fans knew their team's scores, statistics and greatest players going back years.

"Swainsview Lodge has been empty for a few years now," Banks said. "Ever since Lord Jessop died of AIDS in 1997. There were no heirs." And nobody wanted the old pile of stone, Banks remembered. It cost too much to keep up, for a start, and it needed a lot of work. A couple of hotel chains had showed a brief interest, but the foot-and-mouth business had soon scared them off, and there was at one time talk of the lodge being converted into a convention centre, but nothing had come of it. "Tell me more about Nick Barber," he said.

"Not much to tell, really," said Butler.

"How did he get into the business? According to his parents, he had no training in journalism."

"This might sound a bit odd to you, but journalistic training is rarely encouraged in this line of work. Too many bad habits. Naturally, we require writing ability, but we judge that for ourselves. What counts most is love of the music."

That would suit Banks right down to the ground, he thought, if only he could write. "And Nick Barber had that?"

"In spades. And he had in-depth knowledge on all sorts of genres, too, including jazz and some classical. Like I said, a remarkable mind, and a tragic loss."

"How long had he been writing for you?"

"About seven or eight years, on and off."

"And his interest in the Mad Hatters?"

"The last five years or so."

"He seemed to live quite frugally, from what I've seen."

"Nobody said music journalism pays well, but there are a lot of fringe benefits."

"Drugs?"

"I didn't mean that. Backstage passes to concerts, rubbing shoulders with the rock aristocracy, a bit of cachet with the girls, that sort of thing."

"I think I'd rather have an extra hundred quid a week," said Banks.

"Well, I suppose that's one reason why this business isn't for you."

"Fair enough. Why didn't he have a job on staff?"

"Didn't want one. We'd have taken him on like a shot, as would the competition, but Nick wanted to keep his independence; he *liked* being a freelancer. To be quite frank, some people just don't function at their best in an office environment, and I think Nick was one of them. He liked the freedom to roam, but he always delivered on deadline."

Banks understood what Butler was talking about. Wasn't that pretty much what Superintendent Gervaise had said about him that very morning? Stay out of the office, but bring me results.

"How did he get the assignment?"

"He pitched for it. Funnily enough, we'd just had our monthly meeting and decided we wanted to do something on the Hatters. Anniversaries, reunion tours and things like that are usually a good excuse for a reappraisal, or a new revelation."

"So he rang you?"

"Yes. Just when we were about to ring him. He'd written about them before, only brief pieces and reviews, but insightful. Look, I can give you a few back copies, if you'd like, so you can see the kind of thing he did?"

"I'd appreciate that," said Banks, who knew that he had probably read some of Barber's pieces in the past. But he didn't keep his back issues of *Mojo*. The pile just got too high. "What was the next step?"

"We had a couple of meetings to sharpen things up and came up with a tight brief, a focus for the piece."

"Which was to be Vic Greaves?"

"Yes. He's always been the key figure, the mystery man. Troubled genius and all that. And the timing of his leaving couldn't have been worse for the band. Robin Merchant had just drowned, and they were falling apart. If it hadn't been for Chris Adams, they might have done. Nick was hoping to get an exclusive interview. That would have been a real scoop, if he could have got Greaves to talk. He also wanted to do something on their early gigs, before Merchant died and Greaves left, contrast their style with the later works."

"How long would it take Barber to write a feature like that?"

"Anything from two to five months. There's a lot of background research, for a start, a lot of history to sift through, a lot of people to talk to, and it's not always easy. You also have to sort out the truth from the apocrypha, and that can be really difficult. You know what they say about the sixties and memory? What they don't say is that if people can't remember it, they make it up. But Nick was nothing if not thorough. He was a fine writer. He checked all his facts and his sources. Twice. There's not a Mad Hatters gig he'd leave unexamined, not a university newspaper review he wouldn't dig up, not an obscure B-side he wouldn't listen to a hundred times."

"How far had he got?"

"Hardly begun. He'd spent a week or two driving around, making phone calls, checking out old venues, that sort of thing. I mean, a lot of the places the original Hatters played don't even exist anymore. And he might have done a bit of general background, you know, browsed over a few old reviews in the newspaper archives at the British Library. But he planned to get started on the main story up in Yorkshire. He'd only been there a week when . . . well, you know what happened."

"Had he sent in any reports?"

"No. I'd spoken to him on the phone a couple of times, that's all. Apparently he had to go into a public telephone box over the road to ring when he was in Yorkshire. He didn't have any mobile signal up there."

"I know," said Banks. "How did he sound?"

"He was excited, but he was also very cagey. A story like this – I mean, if Nick could really get Vic Greaves to open up about the past – well, if someone else got wind of it . . . you can imagine what that would mean. Ours can be a bit of a cut-throat business."

"We really need to know where Vic Greaves lives," said Banks.

"I understand that, and if I knew his address, I'd tell you. Nick mentioned a village called Lyndgarth in North Yorkshire. I've never heard of it, but apparently it's near Eastvale, if that's any help. That's all I know."

Banks knew that he ought to be able to find Vic Greaves in Lyndgarth easily enough. "I know it," he said. "It's very close to where Nick was staying. Walking distance, in fact. Do you happen to know if he had already spoken to Greaves?"

"Once."

"And?"

"It didn't go well. According to Nick, Greaves freaked out, refused to talk, as usual, sent him packing. To be honest, I very much doubt you'll get any sense out of him."

"What's wrong with him?"

"Nobody knows. He just went strange, that's all. Has been for years."

"When did Nick talk to him?"

"He didn't say. Sometime last week."

"What day did he phone you?"

"Friday, Friday morning."

"What was he going to do?"

"Talk to Greaves again. Work out a different approach. Nick was good. He'd simply tested the waters. He'd have found something to catch Greaves's interest, some common ground, and he'd have taken it from there."

"Have you any idea," Banks asked, "why this story should have cost Nick Barber his life?"

"None at all," said Butler, spreading his hands. "I still can't really believe that it did. I mean, maybe what happened was nothing to do with the Hatters. Have you considered that? Maybe it was an irate husband. Bit of a swordsman, was our Nick."

"Any husband in particular who might have wanted him dead recently?"

"Not that I know of. He never seemed to stick with anyone for long, especially if they started to get clingy. He liked his independence. And the music always got in the way. Most of our guys live alone in flats, when you get right down to it. They'd rather be ferreting out old vinyl on Berwick Street than go out with a girl. They're loners, obsessed."

"So Nick Barber would love 'em and leave 'em?"

"Something like that."

"Maybe it was an irate girlfriend, then?"

Butler laughed uneasily.

Banks thought of Kelly Soames again, but he didn't think she had killed Nick Barber, and not only because of the discrepancy in timing. There was still her father, though, Calvin Soames. He had disappeared from the pub for fifteen minutes, and nobody had seen him return to his farm in Lyndgarth to check the gas ring. Admittedly, it was a bad night, and the farm was off the beaten track, but it was still worth further consideration. The question was, had Soames been hiding the fact that he knew about Barber and Kelly? Banks couldn't tell. And if he had done it, why take all Barber's stuff?

When it came right down to it, though, Banks had a gut feeling that it was the Mad Hatters story that got Barber killed. He had no idea why. Unless you were a soul or a rap artist, music was generally a murder-free profession, and it was a bit of a stretch to imagine aging hippies going around bashing people over the head with pokers. But there it was. Nick Barber had headed to Yorkshire in search of a reclusive ex–rock star, had found him, and within days he had turned up dead, all his notes, mobile phone and laptop computer missing.

Banks thanked Butler for his time and said he might be back with more questions. Butler accompanied him back to the lift, stopping to pick out some back issues for him on the way. Banks walked out onto busy Oxford Street a little more enlightened than when he had entered Mappin House. He noticed that he was standing right outside HMV, so he went inside.

Monday, September 15, 1969
The mood in the Grove was subdued that Monday evening. Somebody had turned out all the electric lights and put candles on every table. Yvonne sat at the back of the small room, near the door, with Steve, Julie and a bunch of others. McGarrity was there, though thankfully not sitting with them. At one point he took the stage and recited a T.S. Eliot poem. That was typical of him, Yvonne thought. He dismissed everybody else's poetry,

but didn't even have the creativity to make up his own. There was a bit of talk about a concert in Toronto that Saturday, where John Lennon and Yoko had turned up to play with some legendary rock 'n' roll stars, and some desultory conversation about the Los Angeles murders, but mostly people seemed to have turned in on themselves. They had known the previous Monday that something had happened at Brimleigh, of course, but now it was all over the place – and the victim's name had been in that morning's paper and on the evening news. Many people had known her, at least by name or by sight.

Yvonne was still stunned by the signed Mad Hatters LP her father had given her before she went out that evening. She couldn't imagine him even being in the same room as such a fantastic band, let alone asking them to sign a copy of their LP. But he was full of surprises these days. Maybe there was hope for him yet.

McGarrity's Eliot travesty aside, most of the evening was given over to local folksingers. A plump, short-haired girl in jeans and a T-shirt sang "She Walks through the Fair" and "Farewell, Farewell." A curly-haired troubadour with a gap between his front teeth sang "The Trees They Do Grow High" and "Needle of Death," followed by a clutch of early Bob Dylan songs.

There was a sombre tone to it all, and Yvonne knew, although it was never said, that this was a farewell concert for Linda. Other people in the place had known her far better than Yvonne had; in fact, she had sung there on more than one occasion when she visited her friends in Leeds. Everybody had looked forward to her visits. Yvonne wished she could be like that, the kind of person who had such a radiant, spiritual quality that people were drawn to her. But she also couldn't forget that someone had been drawn to kill her.

She remembered the photograph that had slipped out of her father's briefcase: Linda with an expressionless face and eyes. The pathetic little cornflower on her cheek; Linda not at home; dead Linda, just a shell, her spirit soared off into the light. She felt herself well up with tears as she thought her thoughts and listened to the sad songs of long ago, ballads of murder and betrayal, of supernatural lovers, metamorphoses, disasters at sea and wasted youth. She wasn't supposed to drink, but she could easily pass for eighteen in the Grove, and Steve brought her drinks like Babycham, Pony and Cherry B. After a while she started to feel light-headed and sick.

She made her way to the toilet and forced her finger down her throat. That helped. When she had finished, she rinsed her mouth out, washed her face and lit a cigarette. She didn't look too bad. On her way out she had to squeeze past McGarrity in the narrow corridor, and the look of cruel amusement on his face at her obvious discomfort frightened her. He paused, pressed up against her breasts, ran one dirty, nail-bitten finger down her cheek and whispered her name. It made her shiver.

When she got back to Steve and the others it was intermission. She hadn't brought up the subject of Linda with Steve yet, partly because she was afraid that he might have slept with her, and that would make Yvonne jealous. It shouldn't. Jealousy was a negative emotion, Steve always said, to be cast aside, but she couldn't help it. Linda was so perfect, and beside her Yvonne felt like a naive, awkward schoolgirl. Finally, she made herself do it.

"Did you know Linda well?" she asked him, as casually as possible.

Steve rolled a cigarette from his Old Holborn tin before answering. "Not really," he said. "She'd gone before I came on the scene. I only saw her a couple of times when she came up from London and stayed at Dennis's."

"Bayswater Terrace? Is that where she lived?"

"Yeah. Before she went to London."

"With Dennis?"

"No, not *with* him, just at his pad, man." Steve gave her a puzzled look. "What does it matter, anyway? She's dead now. We have to let go."

Yvonne felt flustered. "It doesn't. It ... I mean ... I only met her once myself, and I liked her, that's all."

"Everybody loved Linda."

"Not everybody, obviously."

"What do you mean?"

"Well, somebody murdered her."

"That doesn't mean he didn't love her."

"I don't understand."

Steve stroked her arm. "It's a complicated world, Von, and people do things for many reasons, often reasons we don't understand, reasons they don't even understand themselves. All I'm saying is that whoever did it didn't necessarily do it from hatred or jealousy or envy or one of those other negative emotions. It might have been from love. Or an act of kindness. Sometimes you have to destroy the thing you love the most. It's not for us to question."

Yvonne hated it when he talked down to her like that, as if she were indeed a silly schoolgirl who just didn't get it. But she didn't get it. To her, Linda had been murdered. No amount of talk about killing for love or kindness made any sense. Perhaps it was because she was a policeman's daughter, she thought. In which case she had better stop sounding like one, or they would be on to her in a flash.

"You're right," she said. "It's not for us to question."

And the second half of the evening started. She could see McGarrity through the crowds, a dark shadow hunched in the candlelight, just to the right of the stage area, and she thought he was staring at her. Then a young man with long blonde hair climbed on the tiny stage and began to sing "Polly on the Shore."

In a booth in a noisy and smoky Italian restaurant on Frith Street, Banks and Annie shared fizzy water and a bottle of the house red, as Banks tucked into his veal marsala and Annie her pasta primavera. Outside, darkness had fallen and the streets and pubs and restaurants of Soho were filling up as people finished work, or arrived in the West End for an evening out. Red and purple lights reflected in the sheen of rain on the pavements and road.

"You've got a lot of explaining to do," Annie said, fixing her hair behind her ears so it didn't get in her mouth while she ate.

"About what?" said Banks.

"This Mad Hatters business. I hardly understood a word of what you were talking about before dinner."

"It's not my fault if your cultural education is severely lacking," said Banks.

"Put it down to my callow youth and explain in words of one syllable."

"You've never heard of the Mad Hatters?"

"Of course I have. I've even seen them on Jonathan Ross. That's not the point. I just don't happen to know their entire bloody history, that's all."

"They got big in the late sixties, around the same time as Led Zeppelin, a bit after Pink Floyd and the Who. Their music was different. It had elements of folk-rock, Byrds and Fairport Convention, but they gave a sort of psychedelic twist to it, at first, anyway. Think 'Eight Miles High' meets 'Sir Patrick Spens.'"

Annie made a face. "I would if I knew what either of those sounded like."

"I give up," said Banks. "Anyway, a lot of their sound and style was down to the keyboards player, Vic Greaves, the bloke we were talking about, who now lives in Lyndgarth, and the lead guitarist, Reg Cooper, another Yorkshire lad."

"Vic Greaves was the keyboards player?"

"Yeah. He was a bit of a Keith Emerson, got amazing sounds out of his organ."

Annie raised her eyebrows. "The mind boggles."

"They had light shows, did long guitar solos, wore funny floppy hats and purple velvet trousers, gold kaftans, and they did all that other sixties psychedelic stuff. Anyway, in June 1970, not long after their second album hit the charts, the bass player, Robin Merchant, drowned in Lord Jessop's swimming pool at Swainsview Lodge."

"*Our* Swainsview Lodge?"

"The one and only."

"Was there an investigation?"

"I should imagine so," said Banks. "That's something we'll have to dig up when we get back to Eastvale. There should be files in the basement somewhere."

"Wonderful," said Annie. "Last time I went down there I was sneezing for a week."

"Don't worry, we'll send Kev."

Annie smiled. She could imagine Templeton's reaction to that, especially since he had become puffed up to an almost unbearable level since his promotion. "Maybe your folksinger friend will know something?" she asked.

"Penny Cartwright?" said Banks, remembering his last, unsatisfactory encounter with Penny on the banks of the River

Swain one summer evening. "It was all long before her time. Besides, she's gone away again. America this time."

"What happened to the Mad Hatters?"

"They got another bass player."

"And what about Vic Greaves?"

"He'd been a problem for a long time. He was unpredictable. Sometimes he didn't show up for gigs. He'd walk off stage. He got violent with other band members, with his girlfriends. They say there were times he just sat there staring into space too stoned to play. Naturally, there were stories about the huge quantities of LSD he consumed, not to mention other drugs. He wrote a lot of their early songs and some of the lyrics are very . . . well, drug-induced, trippy, I suppose you'd say. The rest of the band were a bit more practical and ambitious, and they didn't know what to do about him, but in the end they didn't have to worry. He disappeared for a month late in 1970 – September, I think – and when they found him again, he was living rough in the countryside like a tramp. He wanted nothing more to do with the music business, been a hermit ever since."

"Did nobody do anything for him?"

"Like what?"

"Help him get psychiatric help, for a start."

"Different times, Annie. There was a lot of distrust of conventional psychiatry at the time. You had weirdos like R.D. Laing running around talking about the politics of insanity and quoting William Blake."

"Blake was a visionary," said Annie. "A poet and an artist. He didn't take drugs."

"I know that. I'm just trying to explain the prevalent attitudes as I understand them. Look, when everyone is weird, just how weird do you have to be to get noticed?"

"I'd say staring into space when you're supposed to be playing keyboards is a pretty good place to start, not to mention beating up your girlfriend."

"I agree there's no excuse for violence, but people still turn a blind eye, even the victims themselves, sometimes. And there was a lot of tolerance within the community for drug consumption, bad trips and suchlike. As for the rest, odd behaviour, especially onstage, might just have been regarded as nonconformist or avant-garde theatrics. They say that Syd Barrett from Pink Floyd once put a whole jar of Brylcreem on his head before a performance, and during the show it melted and dripped down his face. People thought it was some sort of artistic statement, not a symptom of insanity. Don't forget, there were so many weird influences at play. Dadaism, surrealism, nihilism. If John Cage could write four minutes and thirty-three seconds of silence, who's to say Greaves wasn't doing something similar by not playing? You ought to know this, given your bohemian background. Did nobody at your dad's place ever paint a blank canvas?"

"I was just a kid," said Annie, "but I do remember we had more than our fair share of freaks around. My dad always used to protect me from them, though. You'd be surprised in some ways how conservative my upbringing was. They went out of their way to instill 'normal' values in me. It was as if they didn't want me to be too different, like them."

"They probably didn't want you to be singled out and picked on at school."

"Ha! Then it didn't help. The other kids still thought I was a freak. How did the Mad Hatters survive all this?"

"Their manager, Chris Adams, pulled it all together. He brought a replacement in, fiddled with the band's sound and image a bit and, wham, they were off."

"How did he change them?"

"Instead of another keyboards player, he brought in a female vocalist. Their sound became a bit more commercial, more pop, without losing its sixties edge entirely. They just got rid of that juvenile psychedelia. That's probably the way you remember them, the nice harmonies. Anyway, the rest is history. They conquered America, became a big stadium band, youth anthems and all that. By the time they released their fourth album in 1973 they were megastars. Not all their new fans were aware of their early roots, but then not everyone knows that Fleetwood Mac was a decent blues band before Stevie Nicks and 'Rhiannon' and all that crap."

"Hey, watch what you're calling crap! I happen to like 'Rhiannon.'"

Banks smiled. "Sorry," he said. "I should have known."

"Snob."

"Anyway, that's the Mad Hatters' story. And you say the girlfriend —"

"Melanie Wright."

"Melanie Wright said that Nick thought he'd got his teeth into a juicy story and that she felt it was somehow personal to him."

"Yes. And he mentioned murder. Don't forget that."

"I haven't," said Banks. "Whose murder did he mean?"

"At a guess, from what you've just told me, I'd say Robin Merchant's, wouldn't you?"

Tuesday, September 16, 1969

"I want to apologize to you about that Mad Hatters LP," Chadwick said to DS Enderby over a late breakfast in the canteen on Tuesday morning. Geoff Broome had come up with an address on Bayswater Terrace, Enderby had driven down from Brimleigh, and they were fortifying themselves with bacon and eggs before the visit.

"It's all right, sir," said Enderby. "I got Pink Floyd to sign my copy of *More* last weekend. As a matter of fact, the Mad Hatters and even Floyd aren't really my cup of tea. I'm actually more of a blues man myself."

"Blues?"

"Howlin' Wolf, Muddy Waters, Chicken Shack, John Mayall."

"Right," said Chadwick, still no wiser. "Anyway, I am sorry. It was wrong of me."

"You were probably right, though, about not being seen accepting gifts."

"Well, I'd feel a bit better about saying that if I hadn't gone and given it to my daughter."

"You did what, sir?"

Chadwick looked away. "I gave it to my daughter. A few bridges to build, you know."

Enderby burst out laughing. "I'm sorry, sir," he said. "What did she say?"

"She seemed a bit shocked, but she was very grateful."

"I hope she enjoys it."

"She will. She likes them. And again . . . you know . . ."

"Don't worry about it, sir. Probably the best use for it. I'm only glad I didn't get them to sign it to me."

"Look, Enderby, about these young people. You seem to take them in your stride, but they stick in my craw."

"I'd noticed that, sir. It's just a matter of perspective."

"But I don't understand them at all."

"They're just kids, mostly, having a good time. Some of them are political, and that can become violent if they mix with the wrong types, and now that unscrupulous dealers have moved in on the drugs trade, that can be dangerous, too. A lot of them are confused by the world, and they're looking for answers. Maybe we think they're looking in all the wrong places, but they're looking. What's so wrong with wanting peace in the world?"

"Nothing. But most of them come from decent homes, have parents who love them. Why on earth do they want to run off and live in filthy squats and squalid bedsits?"

"You really don't get it, do you, sir?"

"That's why I'm asking you, dammit."

"Freedom. You know yourself how parents often disapprove of what their kids do and prevent them from doing it. These kids don't mind a bit of dirt and mess as long as they can come and go as they please."

"But what about the drugs, the sex?"

"That's what they want! I mean, they couldn't smoke pot and have sex if they lived with their parents, could they?"

Chadwick shook his head.

"It's more than that, though," Enderby went on. "Especially in the north. A lot of kids, girls like Linda Lofthouse, for example, they see a pretty bleak future waiting for them. Marriage, babies, dirty nappies, washing, cooking, a life of drudgery, slavery even. It can look a lot like a prison, if you've got a bit of imagination and intelligence, as it seems she had. And for the blokes it's not that much different. Same boring job at the factory, day in day out, down at the same old pub with your same old cronies night after night. Footie on Saturdays, telly most nights. If they catch a glimpse of something else, if they've got a bit about them, you can see how it might appeal. An escape, perhaps? Something new. Something different."

"But marriage and family are the cornerstones of our civilization."

"I know that, sir. I'm just trying to answer your question. Put myself in their shoes. Marriage and family are our traditional values. A lot of kids today argue against them, say that's why the world's in the trouble it's in. War. Famine. Greed. And girls these days think there ought to be more for them in life. They want to work, for example, and get paid as much as men for doing the same job."

"They'll be after our jobs before long."

"I wouldn't be too surprised, sir."

"Freedom, eh?" said Chadwick. "Is that what it's all about?"

"I think so, sir. A lot of it, at any rate. Freedom to think what you want and do what you want. The rest is just trappings, icing on the cake."

"But what about responsibility? What about consequences?"

"They're young, sir. Indestructible and immortal. They don't worry too much about those sorts of things."

"I thought freedom was what I was fighting for in the war."

"It was, sir. And we won."

"And this is the result?"

Enderby shrugged.

"All right," said Chadwick. "I take your point. We'll just have to live with it, then, won't we? Another fried slice?"

"Don't mind if I do, sir."

10

Tuesday, September 16, 1969

It was raining when Chadwick and Enderby paid their visit to Bayswater Terrace, and the rows of slate-roofed, red-brick houses looked suitably gloomy. DI Broome had found the number of the house they wanted easily enough. It wasn't known as a drug house especially, though Broome had no doubt that drugs were consumed there, but the police had been looking for a dealer who had slipped through their net a few months ago, and they had visited all his possible known haunts, including this house, rented by a Dennis Nokes since early 1967. According to their information, the occupancy turnover was pretty high and included students, hippies and general layabouts. Nokes described himself as a student and a musician, but as far as anyone knew, he was on the dole.

After the previous day's exhausting session with the Mad Hatters, Chadwick wasn't looking forward to the interview. He also hadn't been certain when was the best time to call to find somebody home. In the end he decided it didn't matter, so they went around lunchtime. Either these people didn't work or they were students, and the university term hadn't started yet, so the odds were that someone would be there at almost any time of the day or night.

Chadwick could hear the sound of a solo acoustic guitar coming from inside the house, which was encouraging. It stopped when Enderby knocked on the door, and they could hear someone shuffling down the hall. It turned out to be a young girl, surely no older than Yvonne, wearing only a long, grubby white T-shirt with a target on the front, which hardly covered her bare thighs. The top did nothing much to hide her breasts, either, as she clearly wasn't wearing a bra.

"Police," Enderby said. They showed their warrant cards and introduced themselves.

She didn't look scared or nervous, merely puzzled. "Police? Yeah. Right. Okay. Come in, then." She stood aside. When they were all inside the hall, she reached her arms in the air, pulling the T-shirt up even higher, and yawned. As he averted his gaze, Chadwick could see that Enderby made no effort to do likewise, that he was gazing with open admiration at her exposed thighs and pubic hair.

"You woke me up," the girl said. "I was having a nice dream."

"Who is it, Julie?" came a voice from upstairs, followed by a young man peering down from the landing, a guitar in his hand.

"Police," said Julie.

"Okay, right, just a minute." There was a short pause while the young man disappeared back into his room, then visited the toilet. Chadwick thought he could hear the sound of a few quid's worth of marijuana flushing down the bowl. If he'd been drugs squad, the young lad wouldn't have stood a chance. When he came down he was without his guitar. "What can I do for you?" he asked.

"Are you Dennis Nokes?"

"Yes."

"We'd like to talk to you. Is there somewhere we can go?"

Nokes gestured towards the rear. "Kitchen. Julie's crashing in the front room. Go back to bed, Julie. It's okay. I'll take care of it."

Chadwick could just about make out a sleeping bag, or a pile of blankets, on the floor before the door closed.

The kitchen was cleaner than Chadwick would have expected, but Janet would definitely have turned her nose up and gone at it with the Ajax and Domestos. The chairs were covered with some sort of red plastic material that had cracked and lined like parchment over time, and the table with a red and white checked oilcloth, and on it lay a magazine called *Oz* with a photograph of a white man embracing a naked black man on the cover. Beside that stood an open jar of orange marmalade, rim encrusted with dried syrup, a half-wrapped slab of Lurpak butter and some breadcrumbs. Nearby were a bottle of Camp coffee, salt and pepper shakers, a packet of Coco Krispies and a half-empty bottle of milk. Not to mention the overflowing ashtray to which Dennis Nokes, by the looks of it, was soon to add.

They sat down and Enderby took out his notebook and pen.

"It's only tobacco," Nokes said as he rolled a cigarette. He had a tangle of curly dark hair and finely chiselled, almost pixieish, features, and he wore an open-necked blue shirt with jeans and sandals. A necklace of tiny different-coloured beads hung around his neck, and a silver bracelet engraved with various occult symbols encircled his left wrist.

"It had better be," Chadwick said. "Pity you had to flush everything you had down the toilet when that's not what I came about."

It only lasted a moment, but Chadwick noticed the look of annoyance that flashed across Nokes's features before the practised shrug. "I've got nothing to hide from the fuzz."

"While we're talking," said Chadwick, "let's agree on a few ground rules. It's not fuzz, or pigs, it's DI Chadwick and DS Enderby. Okay?"

"Whatever you want," Nokes agreed, lighting the cigarette.

"Right. I'm glad we've got that out of the way. Now let's get to the real subject of our visit: Linda Lofthouse."

"Linda?"

"Yes. I assume you've heard the news?"

"Bummer, man," said Nokes. "I was trying to write a song for her when you guys arrived. It's okay, I mean, I'm not blaming you for interrupting me or anything. It wasn't going very well."

"Sorry to hear that," said Chadwick. "I don't suppose you thought for a moment to come forward with information?"

"Why, man? I haven't seen Linda in a while."

"When was the last time?"

"Summer. July, I think. Same time Rick was up."

"Rick?"

"Rick Hayes, man. He put on the festival."

"Was he with Linda Lofthouse in July?"

"Not *with* her, just here at the same time."

"Did they know one another well?"

"They'd met, I think. Linda's cousin's Vic Greaves, you know, the keyboards player in the Mad Hatters, and Rick promoted some of their gigs in London."

"Were they going out together?"

"No way, man." Nokes laughed. "Linda and Rick? You must be joking. She was way out of his league."

"I thought he made plenty of money from the concerts."

"It's not about money, man. Is that all you people ever think of?"

"So what was it about?"

"It was a spiritual thing. Linda was an old soul. Spiritually she was lifetimes ahead of Rick."

"I see," said Chadwick. "But they *were* here at the same time?"

"Yes. That time. Linda crashed here but Rick was staying in some hotel in town. Didn't stop him trying to pick up some bird to take back with him, but he ended up going alone."

"Why was he here?"

"I used to know him a few years ago when I lived in London. We're sort of old mates, I suppose. Anyway, he'd come up to check out something at Brimleigh Glen for the festival, so he dropped by to see me."

Chadwick filed all that information away for his next talk with Rick Hayes, who was proving to be even more of a liar than he had first appeared to be. "You say Linda hasn't been here since July?"

"That's right."

"Have you seen her since then?"

"No."

"Were you at Brimleigh?"

"Of course. Rick scored us some free tickets."

"Did you see her there?"

"No."

"Where were you between one and one-twenty on Sunday night?"

"How do you expect me to remember that?"

"Led Zeppelin had just started, if that refreshes your memory."

"Yeah, right. I sat through the whole set in the same place.

We were in the middle, quite near the front. We got there early on Friday and staked out a good space."

"Who was with you?"

Nokes nodded towards the front room. "Julie there, and the others from the house. There were five of us in all."

"I'll need names."

"Sure. There was me, Julie, Martin, Rob and Cathy."

"Full names, please, sir," DS Enderby interrupted. Nokes gave him a pitying look and told him.

"Are any of the others at home now?" Chadwick asked.

"Only Julie."

"We'll send someone over later to take statements. Now, about Linda. Did she stay here around the time of the festival?"

"No. She knows she's welcome here any time she wants, man. She doesn't have to ask, just turn up. But I don't know where she was staying. Maybe in a tent or out on the field or something. Maybe she was with someone. Maybe they had a car. I don't know, man. All I know is this is freaking me out."

"Stay calm, Mr. Nokes. Try a few deep breaths. I hear it works wonders."

Nokes glared at him. "You're taking the piss."

"Not at all."

"This is *very* upsetting."

"What? That Linda was murdered or that you're being questioned?"

Nokes ran the end of his index finger over some grains of salt on the tablecloth. "All of it, man. It's just so heavy. You're laying a real trip on us, and you're way off course. We're into making love, not killing."

His whiny voice was starting to grate on Chadwick. "Tell me about Linda."

"What about her?"

"When did you first meet?"

"Couple of years ago. Not long after I moved here, May, June 1967, around then."

"And you came up from London?"

"Yeah. I was living down there until early '67. I'd seen the sort of stuff that was happening, and thought I could make some of it happen up here. Those were really exciting times – great music, poetry readings, lightshows, happenings. Revolution was in the air, man."

"Back to Linda. How did you meet?"

"In town, in a record shop. We were both looking through the folk section, and we just got talking. She was so alone. I mean, she was changing, but she didn't know it, trying to find herself, didn't know how to go about it. Like a caterpillar turning into a butterfly. Know what I mean?"

"So you helped her to find herself?"

"I invited her around here from time to time. I gave her a few books – Leary, Gurdjieff, Alan Watts. Played music for her. We talked a lot."

"Did you sleep with her?"

"No way. She was six months pregnant."

"Drugs."

"Of course not."

"How long did she stay here?"

"Not very long. After she'd had the baby, she came here for a while, maybe a month or two the winter of '67, then she went to London early in '68. After that she'd crash here when she was up visiting."

"What did she do?"

"What do you mean?"

"Work? Earn a living? Did she have a job?"

"Oh, that shit. Well, she didn't when I first met her, of course. She was still living with her parents. Then the baby ... Anyway, she made really beautiful jewellery, but I don't think she got much money for it. Gave most of it away. Clothes, too. She could fix anything, and make a shirt from any old scraps of material. She was into fashion, too, did some of her own designs."

"So how did she make money?"

"She worked in a shop. Biba. It's pretty well known. They just moved to Kensington High Street. Do a lot of thirties nostalgia stuff. You know the sort of thing: all floppy hats, ostrich feathers and long satin dresses in plum and pink."

"Do you happen to know her address in London?"

Nokes gave him an address in Notting Hill.

"Did she live alone or share?"

"Alone. But she had a good friend living in the same house, across the hall. Came up here with Linda once or twice. American girl. Her name's Tania Hutchison."

"What does she look like?"

"Like a dream. I mean, she's like a negative image of Linda, man, but just as beautiful in her own way. She's got long dark hair, really long, you know. And she has a dark complexion, like she's half-Mexican or something. And white teeth. But all Americans have white teeth, don't they?"

It sounded like the girl Robin Merchant had described. So what, if anything, did this Tania Hutchison have to do with Linda Lofthouse's murder?

There was nothing more to be got from Dennis Nokes, so Chadwick gave Enderby the signal to wrap up the interview. He would send someone to talk to the others later. He didn't really think that Nokes and his pals had had anything to do with Linda Lofthouse's murder, but now he at least knew where she had been living, and this Tania woman might be able to tell him something about Linda's recent life. And death.

Before heading to interview Vic Greaves the following day, Banks first called at Swainsview Lodge out of curiosity, to soak up the atmosphere. He got the keys from the estate agent, who told him they had kept the place locked up tight since there had been reports from local farmers of someone breaking in. She thought it was probably just kids, but the last thing they needed, she said, was squatters or travellers taking occupation of the place.

Entering the cold and draughty hallway, Banks felt as if he were entering one of those creepy mansions from the old Roger Corman films of Poe stories, *The Fall of the House of Usher*, or something. The long wainscotted hallway had panelled doors opening off each side, and there were obvious spaces on the walls where paintings had once hung. Banks tried some of the doors and found they opened to empty rooms in varied states of disrepair. Bits of ceiling had crumbled, and a veneer of plaster dust lay over everything. Banks kicked clouds of it up as he walked, and it made him cough, made his mouth dry.

At the end of the hall, a moth-eaten, dusty old curtain covered French windows. Banks fiddled for the key and opened them. They led out to a broad, empty balcony. Banks walked out and leaned against the cool stone of the balustrade to admire the view. Below him lay the empty granite and marble swimming pool, its dark bottom clogged with weeds, lichen and rubbish. Lower down the hillside, the trees on the banks of the River Swain were red and brown and yellow. Some of the leaves blew off and swirled in the wind as Banks watched.

Sheep grazed in the fields of the opposite daleside, dots of white on green among the irregular patterns of drystone walls. The clouds were so low they grazed the limestone outcrops along the top and shrouded the upper moorland in mist.

Wrapping his arms around himself against the autumn chill, Banks went back inside the building and headed downstairs to the lower level, where he found himself in a cavernous room that he guessed must have been used as the recording studio. So this was where the Mad Hatters had recorded their breakthrough second album during the winter of 1969–1970, and several others over the years. There was no equipment left, of course, but there were still a few strips of wire lying around, along with a broken drumstick and what looked like a guitar string. Banks strained but could hear no echoes of events or of music long past.

He unlocked the doors and walked out to the edge of the swimming pool. There was broken glass on the courtyard and bottles and cans at the bottom of the pool, where it sloped down to the deep end. Banks saw what the estate agent meant, and guessed that local kids must have climbed the wall and had a party. He wondered if they knew the house's history. Maybe they were celebrating Robin Merchant the way the kids flocked to Jim Morrison's tomb in the Père-Lachaise cemetery in Paris. Banks doubted it. He thought he heard a sound behind him, in the abandoned recording studio, and turned in time to see a mouse skitter through the dust.

He tried to imagine the scene on that summer night thirty-five years ago. There would have been music, and probably lights strung up outside, around the pool. Incense. Drugs, of course, and alcohol, too. By the early seventies booze was coming back in fashion among the younger generation. There would also have been girls, half undressed or more, perhaps, laughing, dancing, making love. And when everyone was sated, Robin Merchant had . . . well, what *had* happened? Banks didn't know yet. Kev Templeton was still in the basement of Western Area Headquarters going through the archives.

A gust of wind rattled the open door and Banks went back inside. There was nothing for him here except ghosts. Lord Jessop was dead of AIDS, poor sod, and Robin Merchant had drowned in the swimming pool. The rest of the Mad Hatters were still very much alive, though, and Vic Greaves was around somewhere. If he would talk. If he *could* talk. Banks didn't know exactly what the official diagnosis was, only that everyone claimed he'd taken too much acid and gone over the top. Well, in a short while, with a little skill and a little luck, he would find out.

Wednesday, September 17, 1969
It had been a long time since Chadwick had walked along Portobello Road. Wartime, in fact, one of the times he had been back on leave between assignments. He was sure the street had been narrower then. And there had been sandbags, blackout curtains, empty shop windows, rubble from bomb damage, the smell of ash, fractured gas lines and sewage pipes. Now the biggest mess was caused by construction on the Westway, an overhead motorway that was almost completed, and most of the smells were exotic spices that took him back to his days in India and Burma.

Chadwick had taken the afternoon train down to King's Cross, a journey of about five hours. Now it was early evening. The market had closed for the day; the stallholders had packed up their wares and gone to one of the many local pubs. Outside the Duke of Wellington, a fire-eater entertained a small crowd. The atmosphere was lively, the people young and colourful in brightly printed fabrics, flared jeans with flowers embroidered on them, or gold lamé kaftans. Some of the girls were wearing old-fashioned, wide-brimmed hats and long dresses trailing around their ankles. There were quite a few West Indians wandering the street, too, some also in bright clothes, with beards and fuzzy hairdos. Chadwick was sure he could smell marijuana in the air. He was also sure he looked quite out of place in his navy-blue suit, although there were one or two business types mingling with the crowds.

According to his map, there were quicker ways of getting to Powis Terrace than from the Notting Hill Underground station, but out of interest he had wanted to wander up and down Portobello Road. He had heard so much about it, from the Notting Hill race riots of over ten years ago to the notorious slum landlord Peter Rachman, connected to both the Kray twins and the Profumo affair of 1963. The area had history.

Now the street was full of chic boutiques, hairdressers and antique shops with brightly painted facades. There was even a local fleapit called the Electric Cinema, showing a double bill of *Easy Rider* and *Girl on a Motorcycle*. One shop, Alice's Antiques, sold Edwardian policemen's capes, and for a moment Chadwick was tempted to buy one. But he knew he wouldn't wear it; it would just hang at the back of his wardrobe until the moths got at it.

Chadwick turned down Colville Terrace and finally found the street he was looking for. At the end of the block someone had drawn graffiti depicting Che Guevara, and underneath the bearded face and beret were the words LONG LIVE THE REVOLUTION in red paint, imitating dripping blood. The terraced houses, once majestic four-storey Georgian-style stucco, were now dirty white, with stained and graffiti-covered facades

– THE ROAD TO EXCESS LEADS TO THE PALACE OF WISDOM

and CRIME IS THE HIGHEST FORM OF SENSUALITY. Rubbish littered the street. Each house had a low black metal railing and gate, which led down murky stone steps to the basement flat. The broad stairs leading up to the front door were flanked by two columns supporting a portico. Most of the doors looked badly in need of a paint job. Chadwick had heard that the houses were all divided into a warren of bedsits.

There were several names listed beside the intercom at the house he wanted. Chadwick had timed his visit for early evening, thinking that might be the best time to find Tania Hutchison at home. The problem was that he didn't want her to be warned of his visit. If she had had anything to do with Linda's murder, then there was a chance she would scarper the minute she heard his voice. He needed another way in.

Tania's flat, he noted, was number eight. He wondered how security-conscious the other tenants were. If drugs were involved, probably very, though if someone was under the influence . . . He decided to start with the ground floor and after getting no answer went on up the list. Finally he was rewarded by a bad connection with an incomprehensible young man in flat five, who actually buzzed the door open.

The smell of cats' piss and onions was almost overwhelming, the floor was covered with drab, cracked lino and the carpet on the stairs was threadbare. If it had had a pattern once, it was indiscernible from the dull grey background now. The walls were also bare, apart from a few telephone numbers scribbled around the shared pay phone. Out of habit, Chadwick made a note of them.

Now he just had to find number eight. It wasn't on the ground floor, nor the first, but on the second floor, facing the front. That landing had another shared pay phone, and again Chadwick copied down the numbers. It smelled a little better up here, mostly due to the burning incense coming from one of the rooms, but the bulb was bare and cast a thankfully weak light on the shabby decor. Chadwick could hear soft music coming from inside number eight, guitars and flutes and some sort of oriental percussion. A good sign.

He tapped on the door. A few moments later, it opened on the chain. He wasn't in yet, but he was close. "Are you Tania Hutchison?" he asked.

"I'm Tania," she said. "Who wants to know?"

Chadwick thought he detected an American accent. Only a thin strip of her face showed, but he could see what Dennis Nokes had meant about her good looks. "I'm Detective Inspector Chadwick," he said, holding up his warrant card. "It's about Linda Lofthouse."

"Linda? Of course."

"Do you mind if I come in?"

She looked at him for a moment – he could see only one eye – and he sensed she was calculating what her best option was. In the end the door shut, and when it opened again it opened all the way. "All right," she said.

Chadwick followed her into an L-shaped room, the smaller part of which was taken up by a tiny kitchen. The rest was sparsely furnished, perhaps because there was so little space. There was no carpet on the floor, only old wood. A mattress covered in red cheesecloth and scattered with cushions sat against one wall, and in front of that stood a low glass table holding a vase of flowers, a copy of the *Evening Standard*, an ashtray and a book called *The Glass Bead Game* by Hermann Hesse. Chadwick had never heard of Hermann Hesse, but he had the feeling he would be safer sticking to Dick Francis, Alistair MacLean and Desmond Bagley. An acoustic guitar leaned against one wall.

Tania stretched out on the mattress, leaning against the wall, and Chadwick grabbed one of the hard-backed kitchen chairs. The room seemed clean and bright, with a colourful abstract painting on the wall and a little light coming in through the sash window, but there was no disguising the essential decrepitude of the house and neighbourhood.

The woman was as Dennis Nokes and Robin Merchant had described her, petite, attractive, with white teeth and glossy dark hair down to her waist. She was wearing flared jeans and a thin cotton blouse that left little to the imagination. She reached for a packet of Pall Mall filter-tipped and lit one. "I just found out yesterday," she said, blowing out smoke. "About Linda."

"How?"

"The newspaper. I've been away."

"How long?"

"Nine days."

It made sense. Chadwick had only discovered Linda Lofthouse's identity from Carol Wilkinson on Saturday, so it hadn't really hit the papers and other news media until Monday, and now it was Wednesday, ten days since the Brimleigh Festival had ended and the body was discovered. Looking at Tania, he could see that she had been crying; the tears had dried and crusted on her flawless olive skin, and her big green eyes were glassy.

"Where were you?" Chadwick asked.

"In France, with my boyfriend. He's studying in Paris. The Sorbonne. I just got back yesterday."

"I assume we could check that?"

"Go ahead." She gave him a name and a telephone number in Paris. It wasn't much use to Chadwick. The guy was her boyfriend, after all, and he would probably swear black was white for her. But he had to go through the motions.

"You *were* at Brimleigh, though?"

"Sure."

"That's what I want to talk about."

Tania blew out some smoke and reached for the ashtray on the table, cradling it on her lap between her crossed legs.

"What happened there?" Chadwick went on.

"What do you mean, 'What happened there?' Lots of things happened there. It was a festival, a celebration."

"Of what?"

"Youth. Music. Life. Love. Peace. Things you wouldn't understand."

"Oh, I don't know," said Chadwick. "I was young once." He was getting used to being criticized by these people for being old and square, and as it didn't bother him in the least, it seemed easier just to brush it aside with a glib comment, like water off a duck's back. What he still didn't understand, though, despite Enderby's explanation, was why intelligent young people from good homes wanted to come to places like this and live in squalor, probably hardly eating a healthy meal from one day to the next. Were all the sex and drugs you wanted worth such a miserable existence?

Tania managed a little smile. "It was different then."

"You can say that again. Swing. Jitterbug. Glenn Miller. Tommy Dorsey. Henry Hall. Harry Roy. Nat Gonella. Al Bowlly. Real music. And the war, of course."

"We choose not to fight in wars."

"It must be nice to believe that you have a choice," said Chadwick, feeling the anger rise the way it did when he heard such pat comments. He was keen to steer back to the topic at hand. They'd sidetrack you, these people, put you on the defensive, and before you knew it you'd be arguing about war and revolution. "Look, I'd just like to know the story of you and Linda, how you came to be at Brimleigh, why you didn't leave together, what happened. Is that so difficult?"

"Not at all. We drove up on Sunday morning. I've got an old Mini."

"Just the two of you?"

"That's about all you can fit in a Mini if you want to be comfortable."

"And you were only there for the one day?"

"Yes. The Mad Hatters said they could get backstage passes for us, but only for the day they were there. That was Sunday. To be honest, we didn't really feel like sitting around in a muddy field in Yorkshire for three days."

That was about the first sensible thing Chadwick had heard a young person say in a long time. "When did you arrive?"

"Early afternoon."

"Were the Mad Hatters there already?"

"They were around."

"What did you do?"

"Well, it was great, really. We got to park where the bands parked, and we could just come and go as we pleased."

"What was going on back there?"

"Music, mostly, believe it or not. When the bands were playing you could get around the front, in the press enclosure, if there was room. That was where you got the best view in the entire place."

"The rest of the time?"

"It's sort of like a garden party round the back. You know, a beer tent, food, tables and chairs, someone plucking on a guitar, conversation, jamming, dancing. Like a big club and a restaurant rolled into one. It got a bit chaotic at times, especially between bands, when the roadies were running back and forth, but mostly it was great fun."

"I understand there were caravans for some of the stars."

"People need privacy. And, you know, if you wanted somewhere to go and . . . Well, I don't have to spell it out, do I?"

"Did you go to a caravan with anyone?"

Her eyes widened and her skin flushed. "That's hardly a question a gentleman would ask of a lady. And I can't see as it has any bearing on what happened to Linda."

"So nobody needed to go into the woods for privacy?"

"No. It was like we had our own little community, and there was no one there to lay down the law, to tell us what to do. A perfect anarchist state."

Chadwick thought that was something of a contradiction in terms, but he didn't bother pointing it out. He didn't want to get sidetracked again. "Who did you spend your time with?" he asked.

"Lots of people. I suppose I was with Chris Adams a fair bit. He's the Hatters' manager. A nice guy. Smart *and* sensitive." She smiled. "And not too stoned to have a decent conversation with."

Interesting, Chadwick thought, that Adams hadn't mentioned this. But why would he? It would only connect him with events from which he wanted to distance himself and his group. "Were you with him during Led Zeppelin's performance?"

Tania frowned. "No. I was out front, in the press enclosure. I suppose he might have been there, but it was really crowded and dark. I don't remember seeing him."

"You're American, I understand," Chadwick said.

"Canadian, actually. But a lot of people make that mistake. And don't worry, I'm here legally, work permit and all. My parents were born here. Scotland. Strathclyde. My father was a professor at the university there."

A professor's daughter, no less. And no doubt they had moved to Canada because he was better paid over there. Even less reason, then, for Tania to be spending her days in a tiny, shabby bedsit in Notting Hill. "So what about Linda?" he asked. "Did she disappear into any caravans?"

"Not that I saw. Look, Linda got a bit claustrophobic, developed a headache, and when Led Zeppelin came on, she told me she was going for a walk in the woods. I told her I'd probably be heading back home as soon as they finished because I wanted to catch a bit of sleep before taking the ferry over to see my boyfriend, Jeff. She told me not to worry about her, she had friends she could stay with. I knew that. I'd been up with her before and met them. It was a place in Leeds, where she used to live before she moved to London."

"Bayswater Terrace?"

"That sounds right."

"So she told you she would stay there?"

"Not in so many words. Only that she wasn't planning on heading back to London with me that night."

"Any reason?"

"I guess there were just people she wanted to see. I mean, it was where she came from. Home, I guess."

"Did you see any of these people from the house with her at the festival?"

"No. Like I said, we had backstage passes. We were in with the bands. We didn't know anybody there apart from Vic, Robin, Chris and the rest. Didn't even know them very well. Look, as you can imagine, it got a bit wild at times, like all parties do. Linda slipped away. I didn't see her again."

"Did she have a flower painted on her face when she left you?"

Tania looked puzzled. "Flower? I don't think so. I don't know. It was dark. I don't remember."

"Would you have noticed?"

"Maybe. I don't know. Lots of girls had flowers painted on their faces. Is it important?"

"It could be." Chadwick remembered Robin Merchant saying that Linda *did* have the flower on her face when he last saw her. "How was she going to get to Leeds? It was the middle of the night."

"Hitch a ride. There were plenty of people heading that way. Most of the crowd came from Leeds or Bradford. Stands to reason."

"Was this your original plan? For her to stay in Leeds, hitch a ride?"

"Plan? We didn't have a plan. It was all pretty spontaneous. I mean, she knew I was going to Paris on Monday and I had to drive back Sunday night, but she also knew she could come back down to London with me in the Mini if she wanted."

"And what did you do?"

"After Zeppelin finished, I went round the back again, hung around a while and waited for her. There was still a party going on backstage, but people were leaving fast. I didn't see her, so I assumed she'd headed off to Bayswater Terrace. I got in my car and drove back down here. It was about four in the morning by the time I left, and I got home about nine. I slept till two, then drove to Dover and took the ferry to Calais."

"You must have been tired."

"Not really."

"Don't you have a job?"

"I'm between jobs. I'm a temp. I happened to be good at typing at school. I can choose my own hours now."

"But what about education? You said your father was a professor. Surely he would want you to go to university?"

She gave him a curious, almost pitying look. "What my father wants doesn't come into it," she said. "It's my life. I might go to university one day, but it'll be when I want to, not when someone else decides for me." Tania shook her hair back and lit another cigarette.

Chadwick thought he saw a mouse scurry across the kitchen floor. He gave a little shudder. It wasn't that mice scared him, but the idea of living with them held no appeal. "I'd like to know more about Linda," he said. "I understand she was a shopgirl?"

Tania laughed. "'Shopgirl.' How very quaint and English. I suppose you could say that. She worked at Biba, but she wanted to be a designer. She was good, too."

"Wouldn't they be worried about her not coming back?"

"She took the week off."

"So there was a plan?"

"There were possibilities, that's all. There were some people in St. Ives she wanted to see. Maybe she was going to stay in Leeds a few days, see her friends and her mother and then go down there. I don't know. She also had a friend living on Anglesey she wanted to visit. What can I say? Linda was a spontaneous sort of person. She just did things. That's why I wasn't worried about her. Besides, you don't think . . . I mean, we were with people who are into love and peace and all that, and you just don't expect . . ." Tears ran down her cheek. "I'm sorry," she said. "This is all too much."

Chadwick gave her a few minutes to compose herself and

wipe away the tears, then said, "When Linda left the enclosure for the woods, did you see anyone follow her?"

Tania thought for a moment, sucked at her cigarette and flicked some ash. "No," she said.

"Did you see anyone else go out around that time?"

"Not that I remember. Most of us were excited about Led Zeppelin, getting ready to go round the front and get our minds blown."

"Could she have arranged to meet someone? Could the headache have been an excuse?"

Tania gave him a blank look. "Why would she? If she'd been going to meet someone, she'd have said so. It wasn't Linda's way to be sly and sneaky."

Christ, Chadwick thought, it was a lot easier when you were dealing with ordinary folk, most of whom lied and cheated as easily as they breathed, rather than this lot with their fancy ideals and high-handed attitudes. "Did you notice anyone paying her undue attention?" he asked.

"Linda's a beautiful girl. Of course there were people talking to her, maybe trying to make an impression, pick her up."

"But nobody succeeded?"

Tania paused. "Linda wasn't seeing anyone this past while," she answered. "Look, I've seen what the newspapers say about us. The *News of the World*, the *People*, trash like that. They paint us as being some sort of drug-addled and sex-crazed subculture, nothing but orgies and excess. Well, some people might be like that, but Linda was a very spiritual person. She was into Buddhism, the Kabbalah, yoga, astrology, tarot, all sorts of spiritual stuff, and sometimes she just . . . you know . . . sex wasn't always a part of it for her."

"And drugs?"

"Out of the picture, too. I'm not saying she'd never smoked a joint or dropped a tab of acid, but not for a while. She was moving on, evolving."

"I understand the two of you performed musical duets together?"

Tania looked at him as if she didn't understand, then managed a brief smile. "*Performed musical duets?* We sang together sometimes, if that's what you mean, just in folk clubs and such."

"Can I have a look at Linda's flat?"

Tania bit her lip. "I don't know. I shouldn't. I mean . . ."

"You can come with me, keep an eye on me. It'll have to be done eventually. Officially."

Finally, Tania said, "Okay. I've got a key. Come on."

She led him across the hall. Linda's room was the same shape as Tania's, but like a mirror image. It was more luxuriously furnished, with a couple of patterned rugs on the floor and a stylized painting of a man sitting cross-legged under a tree, surrounded by strange symbols, on the wall. Chadwick recognized the signs of the zodiac from the newspaper horoscopes Janet read. There was also a small bookcase full of volumes on mysticism and the spiritual life and packs of variously scented joss sticks. An acoustic guitar, similar to the one in Tania's room, leaned against the wall.

Linda also had a small record player, and beside it stood a stack of LPs similar to those Yvonne had. There was nothing really personal in the room, at least not that Chadwick could find. One drawer held a couple of letters from her mother and some old photographs taken with her father. There were no diaries or notebooks – whatever she had been carrying with her at Brimleigh had disappeared – and very little else apart from her birth certificate and post-office book showing that she had £123 13s. 5d. in her account, which seemed rather a lot to Chadwick. She had also set up a sewing machine at a make-shift table, and there were a few bolts of printed fabric lying around. In her small wardrobe hung many long dresses and skirts of bright print fabrics and other materials.

He searched under the drawers and tried the cupboards and wardrobes for false bottoms but found nowhere that might have provided a good hiding place for drugs. If Tania knew this was what he was doing, she didn't say anything. She just leaned against the door jamb with her arms folded.

As far as food was concerned, the pickings were slim. Linda had no oven, only a gas burner beside the little sink, and the contents of her cupboard consisted of brown rice, chickpeas, muesli, tahini, mung beans and various herbs and spices. There was no refrigerator, either, and no sign of meat, vegeta-bles or dairy products, except for a bottle of sterilized milk on the table. Frugal living indeed.

Frustrated, Chadwick stood by the door and gave one last look around. Still nothing.

"What will happen to it now?" Tania asked.

"I suppose it'll be relet eventually," he said. "For the moment I'll get the local police to come in and seal it off until we've done a thorough search. What do you know about Rick Hayes?"

Tania locked Linda's door and led Chadwick back to her room, where they resumed their previous positions.

"Rick Hayes, the promoter?"

"That's the one."

"Nothing much. I chatted with him a couple of times. He's a bit of a creep. If you must know, he tried to pick me up, sug-gested we go to his caravan."

"And?"

"I told him to get lost."

"How did he react?"

"He laughed and said he liked a girl who spoke her mind. Look, Hayes is one of those men who asks every girl he meets to sleep with him. He thinks the odds are pretty good. If nine out of ten tell him what they think of him, or slap his face, there's always the tenth who might say yes."

"He knew Linda, is that right?"

"They'd met before, yes. Once we went backstage at a Mad Hatters concert at the Roundhouse and Rick was there. He's harmless enough, really. To be honest, he's far too taken with himself to really give much thought to anyone else."

"But if someone he wanted turned him down, do you think he could get violent?"

Tania gave him a sharp look. "I . . . I don't know," she said. "I've never really thought about it. He's got a bit of a temper. I saw him laying into one of the security guards, but that was just . . . I don't know, some sort of a power trip, I thought. You're not suggesting he might have killed Linda because she wouldn't let him fuck her?"

If the word was meant to shock Chadwick, it did. He wasn't used to such language coming from the mouths of such lovely young women. He was damned if he was going to give her the satisfaction of a reaction, though. "Did you see him leave the enclosure during the time you were there?"

"No. Mostly he was coordinating with the performers and roadies, making sure the equipment got set up right and everything went smoothly. There were a few problems with the PA system and so on that he also had to deal with. And he acted as emcee, introducing the bands. He was really pretty busy all the time. I don't think he'd have had a chance to slip away even if he'd wanted to."

"So he was always in sight?"

"Pretty much. Not always, but most of the time you'd see him out the corner of your eye here and there, running around. There was always somebody wanting him for something."

"Where was he while Linda was in the woods?"

"I don't know. Like I told you, I went round to the front to get a good view."

"Was he there?"

"No. He introduced the band, then he left the stage."

"Did you see him after that?"

"Come to think of it, no. But I don't believe it. I don't believe he could have had anything to do with what happened."

"Probably not," said Chadwick, standing to leave. "It just pays to cover all the angles, that's all." He lingered at the door. "Before I leave, tell me how Linda was behaving these past few weeks."

"What do you mean?"

"Did anything out of the ordinary happen?"

"No."

"Was she upset, depressed or worried about anything?"

"No, she was her usual self. She was saving up to go to India. She was really excited about that."

Chadwick, who had spent time in India before seeing action in Burma during the war, didn't understand what there was to get excited about. As far as he was concerned, the place was filthy, hot and unsanitary. Still, it explained the reason for the £123 13s. 5d. in her post-office account. "Is that all?"

"As far as I know."

"Had she fought or argued with anyone recently?"

"Not that I know. I doubt it, anyway."

"Why's that?"

"Linda didn't like scenes or arguments. She was a peaceful person, easygoing."

"Did anyone threaten her in any way?"

"Good Lord, no."

"Was anybody bothering her?"

"No. The only thing that was at all upsetting her was Vic
Greaves. They weren't close or anything, but they *were* family,
and on the two or three occasions we saw the Mad Hatters, he
seemed to be getting worse. She thought he ought to be getting
treatment, but whenever she mentioned it to Chris, he just said
shrinks were government brainwashers and mental hospitals
were prisons for the true visionaries. I suppose he had a point."

"Did either you or Linda try to do anything about Greaves?"

"What do you mean?"

"Persuade him to get treatment."

"Linda did once, but he refused point-blank."

"Did you try to change Chris Adams's mind?"

"It wasn't his decision," Tania said. "Look, nobody was going
to be party to getting Vic Greaves certified. Simple as that."

"I see," said Chadwick. The decision didn't surprise him
after the time he had spent with the Mad Hatters. He would
be talking to them again soon anyway. He opened the door and
went into the hall. "Many thanks, Miss Hutchison."

"No problem."

"I must say you seem to be one of the most sensible people
I've talked to since all this began."

Tania gave him an enigmatic smile. "Don't count on it," she
said. "Appearances can be deceptive."

Thursday, September 18, 1969

Perhaps it was the spices he had smelled in Portobello Road
that sparked it – they say smell is closest to memory – or maybe
it was even going to see *Battle of Britain* after his visit to Tania
Hutchison that brought it all back, but Chadwick awoke in his

hotel bed at three in the morning in a cold sweat. He couldn't say that it was a dream, because it had actually happened, but he had buried it so deeply in his subconscious that when it rose up, as it did from time to time, it did so in a jumble of images so vivid they were almost surreal.

Buried under two bodies, mouth and nose full of sand on Gold Beach, the air all smoke and fire, bullets cracking and thudding into the sand nearby, blood seeping through his uniform, the man on top of him whimpering as he died, crying for his mother. Charging the bunkers with Taffy in Burma. Taffy wounded, his guts poking out, stumbling forward into the gunfire, diving into the bunker of Japanese soldiers, knowing he was going to die and pulling the pin on his hand grenade. Bits of people raining down on Chadwick: an eyeball, pieces of brain, blood and tissue.

And so it went on, a series of fragmented nightmare images from the Burmese jungle and the Normandy beaches. He not only saw and heard but *smelled* it all again in his dream: the gunfire, smoke, heat, tasted the sand in his mouth.

He feared that there would be no more sleep tonight, so he sat up, took the glass of water he had left on his bedside table and drank it down, then went to refill it. Still hours to go until dawn. And these were the worst hours, the hours when his fears got the better of him. The only solution was to get up and do something to take his mind off it all. He wasn't going to go walking around King's Cross at this hour in the morning, so he turned on the bedside light, took Alistair MacLean's *Force Ten from Navarone* out of his overnight bag and settled back on the pillows to read. By the time the pale glow of sunrise started spreading over the city from the east, his book had fallen on his chest and he was snoring quietly in a dreamless sleep.

11

In a village like Lyndgarth, Banks knew, the best way to find out about any resident was to ask at the local pub or at the post office. In the case of Vic Greaves, it was Jean Murray, in the post office-cum-newsagents, who directed him towards the last cottage on the left on Darlington Road, telling him that "Mr. Jones" had been there for a few years now, was definitely a bit strange, not quite right in the head, but that he seemed harmless enough, and he always paid his newspaper bill on time. He was a bit of a recluse, she added, and he didn't like visitors. She had no idea what he did with his time, but there had been no complaints about him. Her daughter, Susan, added that he had few visitors, but she had seen a couple of cars come and go. She couldn't describe them.

Banks left his car parked on the cobbles by the village green. It was another miserable day, with wind and rain from the east, for a change, and the flagstone roofs of the houses looked as dark green as moss pools. Bare tree branches waved beyond the TV aerials, and beyond them lay the washed-out backdrop of a dishwater-grey sky.

At the top right of the village green between the old Burgundy Hotel and the dark, squat Methodist chapel, a narrow lane led down towards a wooded beck. On each side was a terrace of small, one-up one-down limestone cottages, once used to house farm labourers. Banks stood for a moment in front of the end one on the left and listened. He could hear no signs of life, see no lights. The downstairs curtains were closed, but the upstairs ones were open, as were the windows.

Finally, he knocked on the door.

Nothing happened, so he knocked again, harder this time.

When it seemed that no one was going to answer, the door opened and a figure stood there, looking anxious. It was hard to say whether it was Vic Greaves or not, as Banks only had the old group photographs to go by, when Greaves had been a promising twenty-something rock star. Now he must be in his late fifties, Banks thought, but he looked much older. Round-shouldered with a sagging stomach the size of a football, he wore a black T-shirt with a silver Harley Davidson on the front, baggy jeans and no shoes or socks. His eyes were bruised and hollow, his dry skin pale and lined. He was either bald or shaved his head regularly, and that accentuated the boniness of his cheeks and the caverns of his eyes. He looked ill to Banks, and light years from the pretty young boy all the girls adored, who had set the Mad Hatters' career in motion.

"I'm looking for Vic Greaves," Banks said.

"He's not here today," the man said, his expression unchanging.

"Are you sure?" Banks asked.

This seemed to puzzle the man and cause him some distress. "He might have been. He might have been, if he hadn't been trying to go home. But his car's broken down. The wheels won't work."

"Pardon?"

Suddenly, the man smiled, revealing a mouthful of stained and crooked teeth, with the odd gap here and there, and said, "He's nothing to do with me." Then he turned and walked back inside the house, leaving the door wide open. Puzzled, Banks followed him. The door led straight into the front room, the same as it did in Banks's own cottage. Because the curtains were closed, the downstairs was in semi-darkness, but even in the poor light Banks could see that the room was cluttered with piles of books, newspapers and magazines. There was a slight odour of sour milk about the place, and of cheese that has been left out of the fridge too long, but a better smell mingled with it: olive oil, garlic and herbs.

Banks followed the man through to the back, which was the kitchen, where a bit more light filtered in through the grimy windows and past half-open floral curtains. Inside, the place was spotlessly clean and neat, all the pots and pans gleaming on their wall hooks, dishes and cups sparkling in their glass-fronted cupboards. Whatever Greaves's problem was – and Banks believed he was Greaves – it didn't stop him from taking care of his home better than most bachelors Banks had known. The man stood with his back to Banks, stirring a pot on the gas range.

"Are you Vic Greaves?" Banks asked.

No answer.

"Look," said Banks, "I'm a police officer. DCI Banks. Alan, my name is Alan. I need to talk to you. Are you Vic Greaves?"

The man half turned. "Alan?" he said, peering curiously at Banks. "I don't know who you are. I don't know any Alans. I *don't* know you, do I?"

"I just told you. I'm a police officer. No, you don't know me."

"They weren't really meant to grow so high, you know," the

man said, turning back to his pot. "Sometimes the rain does good things."

"What?"

"The hillsides drink it."

Banks tried to position himself so that he could see the man's face. When the man half turned again and saw him, he looked surprised. "What are you doing here?" he asked, as if he had genuinely forgotten Banks's presence.

"I told you. I'm a policeman. I want to ask you some questions about Nick Barber. He did come and talk to you, didn't he? Do you remember?"

The man shook his head, and his face turned sad for a moment. "Vic's gone down to the woods today," he said.

"Vic Greaves is in the woods?" Banks asked. "Who are you?"

"No," he said. "He had to get some stuff, you know, he needed it for the stew."

"You went to the woods earlier?"

"He sometimes walks there on nice days. It's peaceful. He likes to listen to the birds and look at the leaves and the mushrooms."

"Do you live here alone?"

He sighed. "I'm just passing through."

"Tell me about Nick Barber."

He stopped stirring and faced Banks, his expression still blank, unreadable. "Someone came here."

"That's right. His name was Nick Barber. When did he come? Do you remember?"

The man said nothing, just stared at Banks in a disturbing way. Banks was beginning to feel thoroughly unnerved by the entire experience. Was Greaves off his face on drugs or something? Was he likely to turn violent at any moment? If so, there was a handy rack of kitchen knives within his reach. "Look," he said, "Nick Barber is dead. Somebody killed him. Can you remember anything about what he said?"

"Vic's gone down to the woods today," he said again.

"Yes, but this man, Nick Barber. What did he ask you about? Was it about Robin Merchant's death? Was it about Swainsview Lodge?"

The man put his hands over his ears and hung his head. "Vic can't hear this," he said. "Vic *won't* hear this."

"Think. Surely you can remember? Do you remember Swainsview Lodge?"

But Greaves was just counting now. "One, two, three, four, five . . ."

Banks tried to talk, but the counting got louder. In the end, he gave up, turned away and left. He would have to come back. There had to be a way of getting some answers from Vic Greaves.

On his way out of the village, Banks passed a sleek silver Merc, but thought nothing of it. All the way back to the station he thought about the strange experience he had just had, and even Pink Floyd's "I Remember a Day" on the stereo could not dispel his gloom.

"Kev. What have you dug up?" Annie Cabbot asked, when a dusty and clearly disgruntled DS Templeton trudged over to her desk and flopped down on the visitor's chair early that afternoon.

Templeton sighed. "We ought to do something about that basement," he said. "It's a bloody health hazard." He brushed some dust off his sixty-quid Topman distressed jeans and plonked a collection of files on the desk. "It's all here, ma'am," he said. "What there is of it, anyway."

"Kev, I've told you before not to call me ma'am. I know that Superintendent Gervaise insists on it, but that's her prerogative. A simple 'Guv' will suffice, if you must."

"Right, Guv."

"Give me a quick rundown."

"Top and bottom of it is," said Templeton, "that there was no full investigation, as such. The coroner returned a verdict of accidental death, and that was the end of it."

"No reservations?"

"Not so far as I can tell, Guv."

"Who was in the house at the time?"

"It's all in that file, there." Templeton tapped a thick buff folder. "For what it's worth. Statements and everything. Basically, there were the band members, their manager, Lord Jessop, and various assorted girlfriends, groupies and hangers-on. They're all named on the list, and they were all questioned."

Annie scanned the list quickly and put it aside. No one she hadn't expected, though most of the names meant nothing to her.

"It happened after a private party to celebrate the success of their second album, which was called – get this – *He Whose Face Gives No Light Shall Never Become a Star*."

"That's Blake," Annie said. "William Blake. My dad used to quote him all the time."

"Sounds like a right load of bollocks to me," Templeton said. "Anyway, the album was recorded at Swainsview Lodge over the winter of 1969–1970. Lord Jessop had let them convert an old banquet room he didn't use, first into a rehearsal space and then into a private recording studio. Quite a lot of bands used it over the next few years."

"So what happened on the night of the party?"

"Everybody swore Merchant was fine when things wound up around two or three o'clock, but the next morning the gardener found him floating on his back, naked in the pool. The post-mortem found a drug called Mandrax in his system."

"What's that?"

"Search me. Some kind of tranquilizer?"

"Was there enough to kill him?"

"Not according to the pathologist. But he'd been drinking, too, and that enhances the effects, and the dangers. Probably been smoking dope and dropping acid, as well, but they didn't have toxicology tests for them back then."

"So what was the cause of death?"

"Officially, he slipped on the side of the swimming pool, fell in the shallow end, smashed his head on the bottom and drowned. The Mandrax might have slowed down his reactions. There was water in his lungs."

"What about the blow to the head? Any way it could have been blunt-object trauma?"

"Showed impact with a large flat area rather than a blunt object."

"Like the bottom of a swimming pool?"

"Exactly, Guv."

"What did the party guests say?"

"What you'd expect. Everyone swore they were asleep at the time, and nobody heard anything. To be honest, they probably wouldn't have even noticed if they were all full of drugs and he just fell in the pool. Not much to hear. He was already unconscious from hitting his head."

"Any speculation as to why he was naked?"

"No," said Templeton. "But it was par for the course back then, wasn't it? Hippies and all that stuff. Free love. Orgies and whatnot. Any excuse to get their kit off."

"Who carried out the investigation?"

"Detective Chief Inspector Cecil Grant was SIO – he's dead now – but a DS Keith Enderby did most of the legwork and digging around."

"Summer, 1970," said Annie. "He'll be retired by now, most likely, but he might still be around somewhere."

"I'll check with Human Resources."

"Kev, did you ever get the impression, reading through the stuff, that anyone put the kibosh on the investigation because a famous rock band and a peer of the realm were involved?"

Templeton scratched his brow. "Well, now you come to mention it, it did cross my mind. But if you look at the facts, there was no evidence to say that it happened any other way. DS Enderby seems to have done a decent enough job under the circumstances. On the other hand, they all closed ranks and presented a united front. I don't believe for a minute that everyone went to sleep at two or three in the morning and heard nothing more. I'll bet you there were people up and about, on the prowl, though perhaps they were in no state to distinguish reality from fantasy. Someone could easily have been lying to protect someone else. Or two or more of them could have been in it together. Conspiracy theory. The other thing, of course, is that there was no motive."

"No strife within the band?"

"Not that anyone was able to put their finger on at the time. Again, though, they weren't likely to tell the investigating officers about it if there was, were they?"

"No, but there might have been rumours in the music press. These people lived a great deal of their lives in the public eye."

"Well, if there was anything, it was a well-kept secret," said Templeton. "I've checked some of the stuff online, and at that time they were a successful group, definitely going places.

Maybe if someone dug around a bit now, asked the right questions . . . I don't know . . . it might be different."

"Why don't you see if you can track down this Enderby, and I'll have a chat with DCI Banks."

"Yes, Guv," said Templeton, standing up. "Want me to leave the files?"

"Might as well," said Annie. "I'll have a look at them."

Thursday, September 18, 1969
Rick Hayes's Soho office was located above a trattoria in Frith Street, not too far from Ronnie Scott's and any number of sleazy sex shops and strip clubs. Refreshed by an espresso from the Bar Italia across the street, Chadwick climbed the shabby staircase and knocked at the glass pane on the door labelled HAYES CONCERT PROMOTIONS. A voice called out for him to come in, and he entered to see Hayes sitting behind a littered desk, hand over the mouthpiece of his telephone.

"Inspector. What a surprise," Hayes said. "Sit down. Can you just hang on a moment? I've been trying to get hold of this bloke forever."

Chadwick waited, but instead of sitting, he wandered around the office, a practice that he found usually made people nervous. Framed signed photos of Hayes with various famous rock stars hung on the walls, unfamiliar names, for the most part: Jimi Hendrix, Pete Townsend, Eric Clapton. Filing cabinets stuffed with folders. He was opening drawers in a cabinet near the window when his snooping obviously made Hayes worried enough to end his phone call prematurely.

"What are you doing?" Hayes asked.

"Just having a look around."

"Those are private files."

"Yes?" Chadwick sat down. "Well, I'm a great believer in not wasting time sitting around doing nothing, so I thought I'd just use a bit of initiative."

"Have you got a search warrant?"

"Not yet. Why? Do I need one?"

"To look at those files you do."

"Oh, I shouldn't think there's anything there of interest to me. The reason I'm here is that you've been lying to me since the moment we met, and I want to know why. I also want to know what you have to do with the murder of Linda Lofthouse."

"Linda Lofthouse?"

"Don't play games with me, laddie," Chadwick snarled, his Glaswegian accent getting stronger the more angry he became. "You'll only lose. That's the victim's name."

"How was I to know?"

"It's been in the papers."

"Don't read them."

"I know, they're all full of establishment lies. I don't care whether you read the papers or not. You saw the body at Brimleigh. You were there at the scene even before I arrived."

"So?"

"You were in a perfect position to mislead us all, to tamper with evidence. She was right there, lying dead at your feet, and you told me you hadn't seen her before."

"I told you later that I might have seen her backstage. There were a lot of people around and I was very busy."

"So you said. Later."

"Well?"

"There were two important things I didn't know then, things you could have told me but didn't."

"You've lost me. What are you talking about?"

Chadwick counted them off on his fingers. "First, that the victim's name was Linda Lofthouse, and second, that you knew her a lot better than you let on."

Hayes picked up a rubber band from his desk and started wrapping it around his nicotine-stained fingers. He hadn't shaved in a couple of days, and his lank hair needed a wash. He was wearing jeans and a red collarless shirt made of some flimsy material. "I've told you everything I know," he said.

"Bollocks. You've told me bugger all. I've had to piece it all together from conversations with other people. You could have saved me a lot of trouble."

"It's not my job to save the fuzz trouble."

"Enough of that phony hippie nonsense. It doesn't suit you. You're a businessman, a filthy capitalist lackey, just like the rest, no matter how you dress and how infrequently you wash. You knew Linda Lofthouse through Dennis Nokes, the house on Bayswater Terrace, Leeds, and through her cousin Vic Greaves of the Mad Hatters. You also knew Linda's friend Tania Hutchison, the girl she was with at Brimleigh, but you didn't bother to tell us that, either, did you?"

Hayes's jaw dropped. "Who told you all this?"

"That doesn't matter. Is it true?"

"What if it is?"

"Then you've been withholding important information in a murder investigation, and that, laddie, is a crime."

"I didn't think we were living in a police state yet."

"Believe me, if we were, you'd know the difference. When did you first meet Linda Lofthouse?"

Hayes glowered at Chadwick, still playing with the rubber band. "At Dennis's place," he said.

"When?"

"I don't know, man. A while back."

"Weeks? Months? Years?"

"Look, Dennis is an old mate. Whenever I'm in the area I drop by and see him."

"And one time you did this, you met Linda?"

"That's right. She was staying at Dennis's."

"*With* Dennis?"

"No way. Linda was untouchable."

So it looked as if Nokes was telling the truth about that, at least. "This would have been the winter of 1967, early 1968, right?"

"If you say so."

"How often have you seen her since?"

"Just a couple of times, you know."

"No, I don't. Enlighten me."

"I've done some concerts with the Hatters, and she was at one of them. I met her up at Dennis's again, too, but I didn't, like, *know* her or anything. I mean, we weren't close. We were just around the same scene sometimes, like lots of other people were."

"So why did you lie about knowing her if it was all so innocent?"

"I don't know, man. I didn't want to get involved. You guys would probably take one look at me and think I did it. Besides, every minute I was standing around in that field I was losing money. You don't know what this business is like, how hard it is just to break even sometimes."

"So you lied because you thought that if you told the truth I'd keep you from your work and you'd lose money?"

"That's right. Surely you can understand that?"

"Oh, I can understand it well enough," said Chadwick. "You're speaking my language now. Concern over money is a lot more common than you think."

"Then . . . ?"

"What were you doing after you introduced Led Zeppelin on Sunday night?"

"Listening to their set whenever I had a moment. They were incredible. Blew me away."

"Where were you listening?"

"Around. I still had things to do. We were looking to pack up and get out of there as soon as possible after the show, so I couldn't waste time. As it turned out . . ."

"But where did you go to listen to them? The press enclosure was roped off in front of the stage. Apparently that was the best place to watch from. Did you go there?"

"No. Like I said, I didn't have time to just stand there and watch. I had other things to do. It was pandemonium around there, man. We had people falling off the stage stoned and people trying to sneak in the front and back. Managers wanted paying, there were cars blocking other cars, limos turning up for people, pieces of equipment to be accounted for. I tell you, man, I didn't have time to kill anyone, even if I wanted to. Which I didn't. I mean, what possible motive could I have for killing Linda? She was a great bird. I liked her." He lit a cigarette.

"I notice you're left-handed," Chadwick said.

"Yeah. So?"

"The killer was left-handed."

"Lots of people are."

"Do you own a flick knife?"

"No way, man. They're illegal."

"Well, I'm glad to see you know the law."

"Look, are we finished? Because I've got a lot of phone calls to make."

"We're finished when I say we are."

Hayes bristled but said nothing.

"I hope you realize the extent of the trouble you're in," Chadwick went on.

"Look, I did what anybody would do. You've got to be crazy these days to give the fuzz an inch, especially if you're a bit different."

"In your case, it didn't work, did it? I've found out anyway. All we need now is one person, just one person who saw you leaving the backstage area for the woods while Led Zeppelin were playing. Are you so sure that no one saw you? After all, we've discovered all your other little lies. Why not this one?"

"I did not leave the enclosure, and I didn't see Linda leave, either."

"We're reinterviewing all the security personnel and everyone else we can think of who was there. Are you certain that's the story you want to stick to?"

"I did not leave the enclosure. I did not go into those woods."

"What did you do with the knife?"

"I can't believe this! I never had a knife."

Chadwick spread his hands on the table, the gesture of a reasonable man laying out his cards. "Look, Mr. Hayes, I'm not persecuting you because you're different. In fact, I don't believe you're that much different from most of the petty villains I come into contact with. You just wear a different uniform, that's all. Why don't you make it easy on us all and tell me how it happened?"

"I want my solicitor."

"What about Tania Hutchison? Did you try it on with her, too?"

"I'm not saying another word."

"But it was Linda you really wanted, wasn't it? Linda, who seemed so unattainable. 'Untouchable.' Isn't that the word you used? She was so beautiful. Thought you weren't good enough for her, did she? Even your money and your famous contacts didn't impress her, did they? So how did it happen? She wandered off into the woods. You did your emcee duties, and when everyone was enthralled and deafened by Led Zeppelin, you followed Linda into the woods. She rejected you again, and this time was once too many. She was having her period. Did she tell you that? Did you think it was just an excuse? Well, you were wrong. It was true. Maybe you were high? Maybe you'd been taking drugs? You could probably plead that you weren't responsible for your actions. But she turned her back on you for the last time. You grabbed her from behind and stabbed her. Then, when you realized what you'd done, you knew you had to throw us off the scent. It was a clumsy attempt, but the best you could come up with under pressure. You walked to the edge of the field, were lucky enough to steal a sleeping bag without being seen, and the body was still undiscovered when you got back to it. You shoved her in the sleeping bag – very carelessly, I might add, and that was my first indication she hadn't been killed in it – and you carried her to the field. While everyone's attention was riveted on the stage, in the dark, you set the sleeping bag down at the very edge of the crowd and hurried back to your duties. I don't suppose it took long. Was there a lot of blood to wash off your hands? I don't think so. You rubbed them on the leaves, then you rinsed them off in the beck. Did you get any on your clothes? Well, we can always check. Where did you hide the knife?"

As Chadwick talked, Hayes turned pale. "It's one thing accusing me of all this," he said finally, "but it will be quite another proving it."

"All we need is one witness who saw you leave the enclosure at the relevant time."

"And the non-existent knife."

That was clever of him, Chadwick thought. The knife would help a lot, especially if it had Hayes's fingerprints and Linda Lofthouse's blood on it. But cases had proceeded on less, and been won on less. Hayes might get a haircut and wear a suit for the jury, but people could still see through him.

Chadwick leaned forward and picked up Hayes's telephone. "I'm going to call a contact at West End Central," he said, "and in no time we'll have search warrants for your office, your house and anywhere else you've spent more than ten minutes over the past two weeks. If there are any traces of Linda's blood, believe me, we'll find them."

"Go ahead," said Hayes, with less confidence than he was aiming for. "And as soon as you've done that, I'll have my solicitor down here and sue you for wrongful arrest."

"I haven't arrested you," said Chadwick, dialing. "Not yet."

"Yes, I know what Mandrax is. Or was," Banks said to Annie over an off-duty pint in the Queen's Arms early that evening.

It was dark outside, and the pub was noisy with the after-work crowd, along with those who never worked and had been there all day, mostly loud kids with foul mouths telling fart jokes over the pool table in the back. A big mistake that table was, Banks had told Cyril, the landlord, but he had replied that he had to move with the times, or the younger crowd would all go to the Duck and Drake or the Red Lion. Good riddance, Banks thought. Still, it wasn't *his* livelihood.

The mix of accents said a lot about the changing Dales; Banks could discern London, Newcastle and Belfast mixed in with the locals. The yob factor was getting stronger in Eastvale, too. Everyone had noticed, and it had become a matter of concern, written up in the newspaper, argued over by members of the council and local MPs. That was why Neighbourhood Policing had been set up and Gavin Rickerd transferred, to keep tabs on known troublemakers and share that intelligence with other communities.

Even the police station's location right on the edge of the market square didn't seem to make any difference to the drunken louts who ran wild after closing time every Saturday night, leaving a trail of detritus and destruction in their wake on the ancient cobbles, not to mention the occasional bleeding human being. Town-centre shopkeepers and pub landlords scrubbing away the vomit and sweeping up broken glass on a Sunday morning was a common sight for the Eastvale churchgoers.

"Mandrax was a powerful sedative," Banks said. "A sleeping tablet, known affectionately as 'mandies.' Been off the market since the seventies."

"If they were sleeping pills," Annie asked, "why didn't they just put people to sleep?"

Banks took a swig of Black Sheep, the only pint he was allowing himself before the drive home to Gratly. "That's what they were supposed to do. The thing was, if you mixed them with booze and rode out the first waves of tiredness, they gave you a nice, mellow buzz. They were also especially good for sex. I expect that was why Robin Merchant was naked."

"Were they?"

"What?"

"Good for sex?"

"I don't know. I only took two once and I didn't have a girlfriend at the time. I fell asleep."

Annie patted his arm. "Poor Alan. So, was Merchant on his

way towards an assignation or was he just taking a post-coital stroll?"

"What did the files say?" Banks asked.

"They were remarkably silent on the subject. No one admitted to sleeping with him. Of course, if he'd been in the water all night, it would have been difficult for the pathologist to tell whether he'd had sex or not."

"Who was his girlfriend at the time?"

"No one in particular," said Annie. "No information on Robin Merchant's sexual habits or preferences made it to the official case notes."

"This Enderby character might remember something, if and when Templeton tracks him down."

"Maybe he was gay?" Annie suggested. "Him and Lord Jessop in the sack together? I could see why they might want to suppress that."

"There's no evidence to suggest that Lord Jessop was gay," said Banks. "Apparently he liked the ladies. For a while, at any rate."

"What happened?"

"He became a heroin addict, though he functioned well enough for years. Many addicts do, if they can get a regular and reliable supply. But heroin doesn't do a lot for your sex drive. In the end he got AIDS from an infected needle."

"You'd think he could afford clean needles, wouldn't you, him being a lord and all?"

"He was broke by then," Banks said. "Apparently he was rather a tragic figure towards the end. He died alone. All his friends had deserted him, including his rock star pals. He'd spent his inheritance, sold off most of his land. Nobody wanted to buy Swainsview Lodge, and he had no heirs. He'd sold everything else he had."

"Is that where he died, Swainsview?"

"Ironically enough, yes," said Banks. "That place has a sad history."

They both paused to take in the implications of that, then Annie said, "So they caused disorientation and tiredness, these mandies?"

"Yes. I mean, if Robin Merchant had been taking mandies and drinking, he could easily have lost his footing. I suppose when he hit his head on the bottom of the shallow end he'd already be feeling the effects of the drug and might have drowned. It's like Jimi Hendrix, in a way, you know, choking on his own vomit because he had so much Vesperax in his system that he couldn't wake up and stop it happening. Usually the body's pretty good at self-preservation, gag reflexes and such, but certain drugs can inhibit or depress those functions."

Across the room, a white ball cracked into a triangle of reds, breaking the frame and launching a new game. Someone started arguing loudly and drunkenly about the rules.

"So what happened to Mandrax?" Annie asked.

"I don't know the exact details, but they took it off the market in the late seventies. People soon replaced it with Mogadon, which they called 'moggies.' Same sort of thing, but a tranquilizer, not a sedative, and probably not as harmful."

Annie sipped some beer. "But someone *could* have pushed him, couldn't they?"

"Of course they could. Even if we could find a motive, though, we might have a devil of a job proving it after all this time. And strictly speaking, it's not our job."

"It is if it's linked to Nick Barber's murder."

"True enough. Anyway, I can't see Vic Greaves being much help."

"That really upset you, didn't it, talking to him?"

"I suppose it did," said Banks, toying with his beer mat. "I mean, it's not as if he was one of my idols or anything, but just to see him in that state, to see that emptiness in his eyes up close." Banks gave an involuntary shudder.

"Was it drugs? Was he really an acid casualty?"

"That's what everyone said at the time. You know, there was even a kind of heroic stature about it. He was put on a pedestal for being mad. People thought there was something cool about it. He attracted a cult following, a lot of weirdos. They still hound him." Banks shook his head. "What a time. The way they used to glorify tramps and call madmen visionaries."

"You think there was something else to it?"

"I don't know how much LSD he took. Probably buckets full of the stuff. I've heard he's done a few stints in various psychiatric establishments over the years, along with group therapy and any other kinds of therapy that happened to be fashionable at the time, but as far as I know there's still no official diagnosis. None of them seemed to know exactly what his problem was, let alone cure him. Acid casualty, psychotic, schizophrenic, paranoid schizophrenic. Take your pick. None of it really matters in the long run. He's Vic Greaves and his head's fucked. It must be hell inside there."

Brian and Emilia were in the entertainment room watching *La Dolce Vita* on the plasma screen when Banks got home. They were on the sofa, Brian sitting up with his feet on the pouffe, his arm around Emilia, who leaned against him, head on his chest, face hidden by a cascade of hair. She was wearing what looked like one of Brian's shirts. It wasn't tucked in at the waist because she wasn't wearing anything to tuck it into. They certainly looked as if they had made themselves at home during the couple of days they'd been around, and Banks realized sadly that he had been so busy he had hardly seen them. A tantalizing smell drifted from the kitchen.

"Oh, hi, Dad," said Brian, putting the DVD on pause. "Got your note. We were out walking around Relton way."

"Not a very nice day for it, I'm afraid," said Banks, flopping onto one of the armchairs.

"We got soaked," said Emilia.

"It happens," said Banks. "Hope it didn't put you off?"

"Oh, no, Mr. Banks. It's beautiful up here. I mean, even when it's grey and rainy it's got a sort of romantic, primitive beauty, hasn't it? Like *Wuthering Heights*."

"I suppose it has," said Banks. He gestured towards the screen. "And call me Alan, please. Didn't know you were Fellini fans. It's one of your Uncle Roy's. I've been trying to watch them all. Bergman. Truffaut. Chabrol. Kurosawa. I'm getting quite used to the subtitles now, but I still have a bit of trouble following what's going on half the time."

Brian laughed. "I heard someone talking about *La Dolce Vita* a while ago, how great it was, and there it was, right in front of me. Emmy here's an actress."

"I thought I'd seen you somewhere before," Banks said. "You've done TV, right?"

Emilia blushed. "A little. I've had small parts in *Spooks*, *Hustle* and *Bad Girls*, and I've done quite a bit of theatre, too. No movies yet." She stood up. "Please excuse me a moment."

"Of course."

"What's that smell?" Banks asked Brian when she had left the room.

"Emilia's making us dinner."

"I thought we'd get take-away tonight."

"This'll be better, Dad, believe me. You took us out on Sunday. Emilia wants to repay you. She's a gourmet cook. Leg of lamb with garlic and rosemary. Potatoes dauphinoise." He put his fingers to his lips and made a kissing sound. "Fantastic."

"Well," said Banks. "I've never been one to turn down a gourmet meal, but she doesn't have to feel obliged."

"She *likes* doing it."

"Then I'd better open a nice bottle of wine."

Banks walked to the kitchen and opened a bottle of Peter Lehmann Australian Shiraz, which he thought would go well with the lamb. When Emilia came in, she was wearing jeans, with the shirt tucked in at the waist and her long hair tied back in a simple ponytail. She smiled at him, cheeks glowing, and bent to open the oven. The smell was even stronger.

"Wonderful," said Banks.

"It won't be long now," said Emilia. "The lamb and potatoes are almost done. I'm just going to make a salad. Pear and blue cheese. That's okay, isn't it? Brian said you like blue cheese."

"It's fine," said Banks. "Sounds delicious, in fact. Thank you."

Emilia flashed him a shy smile, and he guessed she was a little embarrassed because he'd caught her with her trousers down, so to speak.

Banks poured himself a glass of Shiraz, offered one to Emilia, who said she'd wait until later, then went back to sit with Brian, who had now turned off the DVD and was playing the first Mad Hatters CD, which Banks had bought at the HMV on Oxford Street, along with their second and third albums.

"What do you think of it?" he asked Brian.

"It must have been quite something in its time," Brian said. "I like the guitar and keyboards mix they've got. That sounds quite original. Really spacey. It's good. Especially for a debut. Better than I remember. I mean, I haven't listened to them in years."

"Me neither," said Banks. "I met Vic Greaves today. At least, I think I did."

"Vic Greaves? Jesus, Dad. He's a legend. What was he like?"

"Strange. He spoke in non sequiturs. Referred to himself in the third person a lot." Banks shrugged. "I don't know. Everyone says he took too much LSD."

Brian seemed deep in thought for a few moments, then he said, "Acid casualties. Makes it sound like war, doesn't it? But things like that happened. It's not as if he was the only one."

"I know that," said Banks, finding himself starting to wonder about Brian. He was living the rock star life, too, as Vic Greaves had. What did he get up to? How much did he know about drugs?

"Dinner's ready!" Emilia called out.

Banks and Brian got up and went into the kitchen, where Emilia had lit candles and presented the salad beautifully. They talked about Brian's music and Emilia's acting ambitions as they ate, a pleasant relief for Banks after his distressing encounter with Vic Greaves. This time, Banks actually got as far as dessert – raspberry brulée – before the phone rang. Cursing, he excused himself.

"Sir?"

"Yes."

"Winsome here. Sorry to bother you, Guv, but it's Jean Murray. You know, from the post office in Lyndgarth. She rang about five minutes ago about Vic Greaves. Said she was out walking her dog and heard all sorts of shenanigans up at the house. Lights going on and off, people shouting and running around and breaking things. I thought I should tell you."

"You did right," said Banks. "Did you send a car?"

"Not yet."

"Good. Don't. Is there more than one person involved?"

"Sounds like it to me."

"Thanks, Winsome," said Banks. "I'll be there as soon as I can."

He thanked Emilia for a wonderful dinner, made his apologies and left, saying he wasn't sure how late he would be back. He didn't think Brian minded too much, the way he was looking at Emilia and holding her hand in the candlelight.

12

———————

Friday, September 19, 1969

Detective Chief Superintendent McCullen called a meeting
for Friday afternoon in the incident room at Brotherton
House. The town-hall dome looked dark and forbidding
against the iron grey sky, and only a few shoppers were walking
up the Headrow towards Lewis's and Schofield's, struggling
with their umbrellas. Chadwick was feeling a little better after
a decent and nightmare-free sleep in his own bed, helped along
considerably by the news that Leeds United beat SK Lyn Oslo
10–0 in the first round of the European Cup.

Photos were pinned to the boards at the front of the room
– the victim, the scene – and those present sat in chairs at the
various scattered desks. Occasionally a telephone rang and a
telex machine clattered in the distance. Present were McCullen,
Chadwick, Enderby, Bradley, Dr. O'Neill and Charlie Green, a
civilian liaison from the forensic laboratory in Wetherby,
along with a number of uniformed and plainclothes constables who had been involved in the Lofthouse case. McCullen
hosted the proceedings, calling first on Dr. O'Neill to summarize the pathology findings, which he did most succinctly.
Next came Charlie Green.

"I've been in meetings with our various departments this morning," he said, "so I think I can give you a reasonable précis of what we've discovered so far. Which isn't very much. Blood analysis determines that the victim's blood is group A, a characteristic she shares with about 43 per cent of the population. As far as toxicology has been able to gather so far, there is no evidence to suggest the presence of illegal substances. I must inform you at this point, though, that we have no test for LSD, a fairly common drug among ... well, the type of people we're dealing with. It disappears from the system very quickly.

"As you all know, the areas around where the body was found, and where the victim was stabbed, have both been searched exhaustively by our search teams and by specially trained police dogs. They turned up a small amount of blood at the scene, some on the ground and more on some nearby leaves. The blood matches the victim's group and we submit that the killer used the leaves to wipe her blood from his hands and perhaps from the murder weapon, a narrow, single-edged blade, the kind you often find on a flick knife. There are no footprints in the woods, and the footprints found near the sleeping bag were so muddled as to be useless.

"Upon examination, the sleeping bag yielded traces of the victim's blood, along with hair and ... er ... bodily fluids that contain the respective blood types of Ian Tilbrook and June Betts, neither group A, by the way, who claimed the sleeping bag was stolen from them while they sought out a better viewing position on the field."

"In all this, then," said McCullen, "there are no traces of the killer? No blood? No hair?"

"We still have unidentified hairs, some taken from the tree trunk near which the girl was killed," said Green. "As you know, hair comparison is weak, to say the least, and it often doesn't stand up in court."

"But you do have hairs, and they might belong to the killer?"

"Yes. We also have some fibres, again some from the tree and some from the victim's dress, but they're common blue denim, which I'm sure just about everyone was wearing, and black cotton, which is also common. There's a chance we might be able to make a match if we had the clothes, but I'm afraid these fibres aren't going to lead us to anything you can't get at Lewis's or Marks and Spencer's."

"Is there anything else?"

"Just one more thing, really."

McCullen raised his eyebrows. "Do tell."

"We found stains on the back of the girl's dress," Green said, hardly able to stop the smile spreading across his large mouth. "They turned out to be semen, a secretor, type A blood, same as the victim. Hardly conclusive, of course, but certainly interesting."

McCullen turned back to Dr. O'Neill. "Doctor," he said, "do we have any evidence of recent sexual activity on the part of the girl?"

"As I said to DI Chadwick at the post-mortem, the victim was menstruating at the time she was killed. Now, that doesn't rule out sexual activity, of course, but vaginal and anal swabs reveal absolutely no signs of it, and the tissue shows no signs of tearing or bruising."

"Was she on the pill?" McCullen asked.

"We did find evidence of oral contraception, yes."

"So perhaps," Chadwick said, "our killer got his pleasure by ejaculating *on* the victim, not in her."

"Or perhaps he couldn't help himself, and it happened as he was stabbing her. Was there a great deal of semen, Mr. Green?"

"No," said Green. "Minute traces. As much as might have seeped through a person's underpants and jeans, say."

"So what do we know about our killer in total, Mr. Green?" he asked.

"That he's between five foot ten and six feet tall, left-handed, wore blue denim jeans and a black cotton shirt or T-shirt, he's a secretor, and his blood type is A."

"Thank you." McCullen turned to Enderby. "I understand you've got something for us, sergeant?"

"It's not much, sir," said Enderby, "but DI Chadwick asked me to track down the girl who was doing the body painting backstage at Brimleigh. It seems there's some question about the flower painted on the victim's face, whether it was pre- or post-mortem."

"And?"

"Robin Merchant, one of the members of the Mad Hatters, told DI Chadwick that he saw her with a painted flower on her face late that evening. Her friend Tania Hutchison can't remember. Hayes was also uncertain. If she did have one, we were wondering if the killer did it for some reason."

"Did he?"

"I'm afraid we still don't know for certain. The body painter was a bit . . . well, not so much stupid as sort of lost in her own world. She couldn't remember who she painted and who she didn't. I showed her the victim's photograph, and she thought she recognized her. Then I showed her the design, and she said it could have been one of hers, but she didn't usually paint cornflowers."

"Wonderful," said McCullen. "Do any of these people have the brains they were born with, I wonder?"

"I know, sir," said Enderby, with a grin. "It's very frustrating. Should I continue my inquiries?"

McCullen looked at Chadwick. "Stan? You're in charge."

"I'm not sure if it's relevant at all," Chadwick said. "I simply thought that the drawing of such a flower by the killer indicated a certain type of mentality."

"A nutcase, you mean?" said McCullen.

"To put it bluntly, yes," said Chadwick. "And while I'm not saying our killer didn't do it, I'm beginning to think that if he did, it's simply another clumsy attempt at sleight of hand, like moving the body."

"Explain."

Chadwick took Green's place at the front by the boards. "Yesterday in London, with the permission of the local police at West End Central, I questioned Rick Hayes, the festival promoter. He's lied to me on a couple of occasions, and when I confronted him with this, he admitted to knowing the victim previous to the festival. He denies any sexual involvement – and I must add that a couple of other people I have spoken with regard this as highly unlikely, too – but he did know her. He's also the kind of man who asks just about every girl he meets to hop into bed with him, so I'm thinking there's a chance that if he was attracted to Linda and she rejected him . . . well, I think you can see where I'm going."

"What about his alibi?" McCullen asked.

"Shaky, to say the least. He was definitely onstage at one o'clock to introduce the last group. After that, who knows? He claims he was in the backstage enclosure paying people – I gather a lot of this sort of thing operates on a cash-in-hand basis, probably to avoid income tax – and seeing to various problems that came up. We can reinterview everyone who was there, but I don't think that'll get us anywhere. The point is that things were so chaotic back there when Led Zeppelin were playing that Hayes could easily have followed Linda out of the compound, stayed away for long enough to kill her and get back without really being missed. Don't forget, it was dark as well as noisy, and most people were at the front of the stage watching the band. The drugs they take also make them rather narcissistic and inward-looking. Not a very observant lot, by and large."

"Have we enough to hold him?"

"I'm not sure," said Chadwick. "With West End Central's help we searched his Soho office and his flat in Kensington and turned up nothing."

"Is he left-handed?"

"Yes."

"The right height?"

"Five foot eleven."

"So it's all circumstantial?"

"We've had worse cases, but there's nothing to directly link him to the murder, without the weapon, except that he knew the victim, he fancied her, he had a bit of a temper, he's left-handed and his alibi's weak. He's not a nutcase, so if he did paint the flower on her cheek, he did so to make us *think* it was the work of a nutcase."

"I see your point," said McCullen. "He still sounds like the best bet we've got so far. He could have ditched the knife anywhere. Talk to the kid who found the body again, ask him at what point Hayes turned up and what sort of state he was in. And organize another search of the woods."

"Yes, sir," said Chadwick. "What do we do about him in the meantime?"

"We've got enough to hold him, haven't we. Let's bring him back up here and treat him to a bit of Yorkshire hospitality.

Arrange it with West End Central. I'm sure there must be someone down there looking for a chance to come up and watch tomorrow's game."

"Which game would that be, sir?"

McCullen looked at him as if were mad and said, "Which game? There is only one game, as far as I know."

Chadwick knew he meant the Yorkshire Challenge Cup at Headingley, knew McCullen was a rugby man, so he was teasing. The others knew it, too, and they were grinning behind cupped hands.

"Sorry, sir," said Chadwick. "I thought you meant Leeds and Chelsea."

McCullen grunted. "Football?" he said with scorn. "Nothing but a bunch of sissies. Now enough of your cheek and get on with it."

"Yes, sir," said Chadwick.

The end cottage was quiet when Banks walked up to the door at around nine o'clock. He had called on Jean and Susan Murray, who shared the flat above the post office, just to let them know that he was there and they weren't to worry. Jean Murray's account of events in person was no more coherent than what Winsome had repeated on the phone. Noise. Lights. Things breaking. A domestic tiff, Banks would have guessed, except that he was certain Vic Greaves had been alone when he left, and he wasn't in any kind of shape to argue coherently with anyone. Banks had also considered calling in Annie, but there was no point dragging her in all the way from Harkside for what might turn out to be nothing.

He had parked his car by the green again, next to a silver Merc, because it wouldn't fit up the lane. He looked at the Merc again and remembered it was the same one he had seen when he left Lyndgarth in the late afternoon. Wind thrashed the bare branches in the streetlights, casting eerie shadows over the cottage and the road. The air smelled of rain that hadn't started falling yet.

The front curtains were closed, but Banks could see a faint light shining inside. He walked down the path and knocked on the door. This time, it was answered quickly. The man who stood there, framed by the light, had a red complexion, and his thinning grey hair was pulled back in a ponytail, which gave the effect of his having a bulbous, belligerent face, as if Banks were seeing it through a fish-eye lens. He was wearing a leather jacket and jeans.

"What the fuck do you want?" he said. "Are you the bastard who came round earlier upsetting Vic? Can't you sick bastards just leave him alone? Can't you see he's ill?"

"He did look rather ill to me," said Banks, reaching inside his pocket for his warrant card. He handed it over, and the man examined it before passing it back.

"I'm sorry," he said, running his hand over the top of his head. "Excuse me. Come in. I'm just used to being so protective. Vic's in a hell of a state."

Banks followed him in. "You're right, though," he said. "It was me who was here earlier, and he did get upset. I'm sorry if I'm to blame."

"You weren't to know."

"Who are you, by the way?"

The man stuck out his hand. "Name's Chris. Chris Adams."

Banks shook. Adams had a firm grasp, although his palm was slightly sweaty.

"The Mad Hatters' manager?"

"For my sins. You understand the situation, then? Sit down, sit down."

Banks sat on a cracked vinyl armchair of some indeterminate yellow-brown colour. Adams sat at an angle to him. All around them were stacks of papers and magazines. The room was dimly lit by two table lamps, with pink and green shades. There didn't seem to be any heat, and it was chilly in the cottage. Banks kept his coat on. "I wouldn't say I understand the situation," he said. "I know Vic Greaves is living here, and that's just about all I know."

"He's resting at the moment. Don't worry, he'll be okay," said Adams.

"You take care of him?"

"I try to drop by as often as I can when I'm not away in London or L.A. I live just outside Newcastle, near Alnwick, so it's not too long a journey."

"I thought you were all living in America?"

"That's just the band, most of them, anyway. I wouldn't live there if you paid me a fortune in gold bullion. Right now, there's plenty to do at this end, organizing the forthcoming tour. But you don't want to know about my problems. What exactly can Vic do for you?"

Now that he was here, Banks wasn't entirely sure. He hadn't had time to plan an interview, hadn't even expected to see Chris Adams this evening; he had come in response to Jean Murray's call. Perhaps that was the best place to start.

"I'm sorry I upset Mr. Greaves earlier," he began, "but I had a phone call a short while ago from someone in the village complaining about shouting and things breaking."

Adams nodded. "That would have been Vic. When I got here it must have been shortly after you left. I found him rolled up in a ball on the floor counting. He does that when he feels threatened. I suppose it's sort of like sheep turning their backs on danger and hoping it will go away."

"I thought maybe he was on drugs or something."

Adams shook his head. "Vic hasn't touched drugs – at least non-prescription drugs – in over thirty years or more."

"And the noise, the breakages?"

"I got him to sleep for a while, then, when he woke after dark, he got disoriented and frightened. He remembered your visit, and he got hysterical, had one of his tantrums and smashed a couple of plates. It happens from time to time. Nothing serious. I managed to calm him down eventually, and he's sleeping again now. Small village. Word gets around."

"Indeed," said Banks. "I've heard stories, of course, but I had no idea he was so fragile."

Adams rubbed at his lined forehead, as if scratching an itch. "He can function well enough on his own," he said, "as you've no doubt seen. But he finds interaction difficult, especially with strangers and people he doesn't trust. He tends to get angry, or to just shut down. It can be very distressing, not just for him, but for whoever is trying to talk to him, as you no doubt found out, too."

"Has he been getting any professional help?"

"Doctors? Oh, yes, he's seen many doctors over the years. None of them have been able to do much except prescribe more and more drugs, and Vic doesn't like to take them. He says they make him feel dead inside."

"How does he get in touch with you?"

"Pardon?"

"If he needs you or wants to see you. Has he got a phone?"

"No. Having a telephone would only upset him." Adams shrugged. "People would find out his number. Crazy fans. That's what I thought you were, at first. He gets enough letters as it is. Like I said, I just drop by whenever I can. And he knows he can always get in touch with me. I mean, he knows how to use a phone, he's not an idiot, and sometimes he'll phone from the box by the green."

"Can he get around?"

"He doesn't drive, if that's what you mean. He does have a bicycle."

A bicycle wasn't much good for many of these steep country roads, Banks thought, unless you were especially fit, and Greaves didn't look that healthy. But Fordham, he reminded himself, was only about a mile away, and you didn't need a car, or even a bicycle, to cover that sort of distance.

"Look, what's going on?" Adams asked. "I don't even know what you're doing here. Why do you want to know about Vic?"

"I'm investigating a murder," said Banks, eyes on Adams to judge his reaction. There wasn't one, which was odd in itself. "Ever heard of a man called Nicholas Barber?"

"Nick Barber? Sure. If it's the same man, he's a freelance music journalist. Been writing about the Hatters on and off for the past five years or so. Nice bloke."

"That's the one."

"Is he dead, then?"

"He was murdered in a cottage a little over a mile from here."

"When was this?"

"Just last week."

"And you think . . . ?"

"I happen to know that Barber was working on a feature about the Mad Hatters for *Mojo* magazine. He found Greaves up here and came to talk to him, but Greaves freaked out and sent him packing. He was planning on coming back, but before he could, he was killed and all his work notes were stolen."

"Of course he'd get nothing out of Vic. He doesn't like

talking about the old days. They're painful for him to remember, if indeed he *can* remember much about them."

"Makes him angry, does it? Gives him a tantrum?"

Adams leaned forward, face thrust out aggressively. "Now, wait a minute. You surely can't be thinking..." Then he leaned back. "You've got it all wrong. Vic's a gentle soul. He's got his problems, sure, but he wouldn't harm a fly. He's no more capable of –"

"Your confidence in him is admirable, but he certainly strikes me as being capable of irrational or violent behaviour."

"But why would he hurt Nick Barber?"

"You've just said it yourself. He's not good at interaction, especially with strangers or people he doesn't trust, people he perceives as a threat. Maybe Barber was after information that was painful for Vic to remember, something he'd buried long ago."

Adams relaxed and sat back in his chair. The vinyl squeaked. "That's a bit fanciful, if you don't mind my saying so. Why would Vic perceive Nick Barber as a threat? He was just another fucking music journalist, for crying out loud."

"That's what I'm trying to find out," said Banks.

"Well, good luck to you, but I honestly can't see you getting anywhere. I think you're barking up the wrong tree on this one. And besides, I'd guess there were plenty of heavy people more interested in Nick Barber than Vic."

"What do you mean?"

Adams gave a twisted smile, put his finger to one nostril and sniffed through the other one. "Had quite a habit, so I heard. They can be very unforgiving, some of those coke dealers."

Banks made a note to check into that area of Barber's life, but he wasn't going to be deflected so easily. "Did he talk to you?"

"Who?"

"Nick Barber. He was doing a feature on the Hatters reunion, after all. It would only have been natural."

"No, he didn't."

"I suppose he just hadn't got round to it," Banks said. "Early days. Were you present when Robin Merchant drowned in the swimming pool at Swainsview Lodge?"

Adams looked surprised at the change of direction. He took a packet of Benson and Hedges from his jacket pocket and lit one, not offering the packet to Banks. Banks was grateful; he might have accepted one. Adams inhaled noisily, and the smoke curled in the dim, chilly light of the pink-and-green shaded table lamps. "I wasn't present at the drowning, but I was in the lodge, yeah, asleep, like everybody else."

"Like everybody else said they were."

"And like the police and the coroner believed."

"We've had a lot of success lately with cold cases."

"It's not a cold case. It's an over-and-done-with case, dead and buried. History."

"I'm not too sure about that," said Banks. "Did you drop by to see Vic last week at all?"

"I was in London most of last week for meetings with promoters. I called in to see him on my way back up north."

"What day would that be?"

"I'd have to check my calendar. Why is it important?"

"Would you check, please?"

Adams paused a moment, obviously not used to being given orders, then pulled a PDA from his inside pocket. "Isn't it wonderful, modern technology?" he said, tapping it with the stylus.

"Indeed," said Banks. "It's one of the reasons we've had such a high success rate with cold cases. New technology.

Computers. DNA. Magic." Banks wasn't too sure about it himself, though. He was still trying to master a laptop computer and an iPod; he hadn't got around to PDAs yet.

Adams shot him an angry glance. "Are we talking about last week?" he asked.

"Yes."

"Then I would have seen him on Wednesday, on my way back from London. I'd been down there since the previous weekend."

"Wednesday. Was there anything odd or different about his behaviour, anything he said?"

"No, not that I noticed. He was quite docile. He was reading a book when I arrived. He reads a lot, mostly non-fiction." Adams gestured to the magazines, books and papers. "As you can see, he doesn't like to throw anything away."

"He didn't tell about anything unusual or frightening happening, about Nick Barber or anyone else coming to see him?"

"No."

According to John Butler at *Mojo*, Nick Barber had tracked down Vic Greaves to this cottage and paid him a visit, but Butler hadn't known the actual day this had happened. Vic had freaked out, refused to talk, become angry and upset, and Barber had said he was going to try again. The phone call to Butler had been made on Friday morning, probably from the telephone box by the church.

If Vic Greaves *hadn't* told Adams about his meeting with Barber, then it must have happened as late in the week as Thursday, perhaps, and Barber might have tried again on Friday, the day of his murder. Kelly Soames said he had been in bed with her between two and four, but that still left him virtually all day. Unless, of course, either Kelly Soames or Chris Adams was lying, in which case all bets were off. And of the two, Banks felt that while Kelly Soames would lie to protect herself from her father, Adams might have any number of less forgivable reasons for doing it.

"Where were you on Friday?" Banks asked.

"Home. All weekend."

"Any witnesses?"

"Sorry. I'm afraid my wife was away, visiting her mother."

"Can you give me the names and addresses of some of the people you met with in London, and the hotel you were staying at?" Banks asked.

"Am I hearing you right? Are you asking me for an alibi now?"

"Process of elimination," said Banks. "The more people we can rule out straightaway, the easier our job is."

"Bollocks," said Adams. "You don't believe me. Why don't you just come right out and admit it?"

"Look," said Banks, "I'm not in the business of believing the first thing I'm told. Not by anybody. I'd be a bloody useless detective if I were. It's a job, nothing personal. I want to get the facts straight before I come to any conclusions."

"Yeah, yeah," said Adams, tapping his way through the PalmPilot and giving Banks some names and numbers. "And I was staying at the Montcalm. They'll remember me. I always stay there when I'm in town. I've got a suite. Okay?"

"Appreciate it," said Banks.

They heard a bang from upstairs. Adams cursed and headed out. While he was gone, Banks took as good a look as he could around the room. Some of the newspapers were ten years old or more, the same with the magazines, which meant Greaves must have brought them with him when he moved in. The books were mostly biography or history. One thing he did find of interest, on the table half-hidden under the lamp, was a business card that had Nick Barber's Chiswick address printed on it and his Fordham address scribbled on the other side. Had Barber left this for Vic Greaves when he paid his visit? It should be possible to check it against a sample of his handwriting.

Adams came back. "Nothing," he said. "His book slipped off the bed to the floor. He's still out."

"Are you staying here overnight?" Banks asked.

"No. Vic'll sleep right through till morning now, and by then he'll have forgotten whatever upset him today. One of the marvels of his condition. Every day is a new adventure. Besides, it won't take me too long to drive home, and I have a lovely young wife waiting for me there."

Banks wished he had someone living with him, but even if he had, he realized, it wouldn't be possible with Brian and Emilia around. How ironic, he thought. They could do whatever they wanted, but he didn't feel he could spend the night with a woman in his own house while they were there. Chance would be a fine thing. Banks felt nervous about going home, fearing what he might disturb. He'd phone them on his way, when he got within mobile range, just to warn them, give them time to get dressed, or whatever.

He showed Adams the card. "I found this pushed under the lamp over there," he said. "Only the edge was showing. Did you put it there?"

"Never seen it before," said Adams.

"It's Nick Barber's card."

"So what? That doesn't prove anything."

"It proves he was here at least once."

"But you already know that."

"It also has his Fordham address written on it, so anyone who saw it here would know where he was staying when he was killed. Nice meeting you, Mr. Adams. Have a safe drive home. I'm sure we'll be talking again soon."

Saturday, September 20, 1969
While Chadwick was cheering on Leeds United to a 2–0 victory over Chelsea at Elland Road that Saturday afternoon, Yvonne walked over to Springfield Mount to meet Steve and the others. Judy was going to make a macrobiotic meal, then they'd smoke a joint or two and take the bus into town. There was a bunch of stuff happening at the Adelphi that night: poets, a blues band, a jazz trio.

She was surprised, and more than a little put out, when McGarrity opened the door, but she asked for Steve, and he stood aside to let her in. The place was unusually quiet. No music or conversation. Yvonne went into the front room, sat on the sofa and lit a cigarette, glancing at the Goya print, which always seemed to mesmerize her. A moment later, McGarrity strolled through the door with a joint in his hand and said, "He's not here. Will I do?"

"What?"

McGarrity put a record on and sat in the armchair opposite her. He had that sort of fixed, crooked smile on his face, cynical and mocking, that always made her feel nervous and ill at ease in his presence. His pale skin was pockmarked, as if he'd scratched it when he had chicken pox as a child, the way her mother said would happen to her, and his dark hair was greasy and matted, flopping over his forehead and almost covering one dark brown eye. "Steve. He's out. They're all out."

"Where are they?"

"Town Street, shopping."

"When will they be back?"

"I don't know."

"Maybe I should come back later."

"No. Don't go so soon. Here." He handed her the joint.

Yvonne hesitated, then put her cigarette in the ashtray, accepted it and took a couple of drags. A joint was a joint, after all. It tasted good. Quality stuff. She recognized the music now: the Grateful Dead, "China Cat Sunflower." Nice. She still felt uncomfortable with the way he was looking at her, though, and she remembered the other night at the Grove, when he'd touched her and whispered her name. At least he didn't have his knife in his hand today. He seemed normal enough. Still, she felt edgy. She shifted on the sofa and said, "Thank you. I should go now."

"Why are you being so rude? You'll share a joint with me, but why don't you want to stay and talk to me?" He handed her the joint again and she took another couple of drags, hoping it would set her at ease, calm her down. What was it about him that disturbed her so? The smile? The sense that behind it lay only darkness?

"What do you want to talk about?" she said, handing the joint back to him and picking up her cigarette again.

"That's better. I don't know. Let's talk about that girl who got killed last week."

Yvonne remembered McGarrity's knife, and that he had been wandering the crowds at Brimleigh during the festival. A terrible thought leapt into her mind. Surely he couldn't have . . . ? She began to feel real fear now, a physical sensation like insects crawling all over her skin. She looked at *The Sleep of Reason* and thought she could see the bats flying around the sleeping man's head, biting at his neck with vampire teeth. The cat at his feet licked its lips. Yvonne felt an electric tingling in her arms and in the backs of her legs. Insects and ee-lek-triss-attee. God, that hash was strong. And the song had changed.

It wasn't "China Cat" anymore, but "What's Become of the Baby?", a creepy sound collage of disembodied voices and electronic effects. Yvonne shuddered. "Linda?" she heard herself saying in a strange, distant voice that could have been someone else's. "What about her?"

"You met her. I know you did. Wasn't she pretty? Sad, isn't it? But it's an absurd and arbitrary world," he said. "That sort of thing could happen to anyone. Anywhere. Any time. The pretty and the plain alike. As flies to wanton boys are we to the gods. They kill us for their sport. Not with a bang but a whimper. One day you'll understand. Have you read about those people in Los Angeles? The rich people who got butchered? One of them was pregnant, you know. They cut her baby out of her womb. The newspapers are saying they were killed by people like us because they were rich piggies. Wouldn't you like to do something like that, little Von? Kill the piggies?"

"No. I don't want to hurt anyone," Yvonne blurted out. "I believe in love."

"His scythe cuts down the innocent and the guilty alike. And the dead shall rise incorruptible."

Yvonne put her hands over her ears. Her head was spinning. "Stop it!"

"Why?"

"Because you're making me nervous."

"Why do I make you nervous?"

"I don't know, but you do."

"Is it exciting?"

"What?"

He leaned forward. She could see the decay on his front teeth, bared in that arrogant, superior smile. "Being nervous. Does it make you excited?"

"No, it makes me nervous and you excited."

McGarrity laughed. "You're not as stupid as you look, are you, little Von? Even when you're stoned. And here was me thinking the only reason Steve wanted you was for your cunt. But it is a pretty little cunt, isn't it?"

Yvonne felt herself flushing to the roots of her being with anger and embarrassment. McGarrity was looking at her curiously, as if she were some unusual specimen of plant life. The owls in the Goya print seemed to be whispering in the sleeper's ear, just as the song's eerie voices were whispering in her head.

"You don't need to show me it," he said. "I've already seen it."

"What do you mean?"

"I've watched you. With Steve."

Yvonne's jaw dropped. She stubbed out her cigarette so hard the sparks burned her fingers, and tried to stand up. It wasn't easy. Somehow or other, she couldn't believe how, she found herself sitting down again, and McGarrity was beside her, grasping her arm. Hard. His face was so close to hers she could smell smoke and stale cheese on his breath. He let go of her arm and started rolling a cigarette. She thought she should make a run for it, but she felt too heavy to move. The joint, she thought. Opiated hash. It always did that to her, gave her a heavy, drifting, dreamy feeling. But this time the dream was turning into a nightmare.

He reached forward and touched her cheek with his finger just as he had done at the Grove. It felt like a slug. "Yvonne," he whispered. "What harm can it do? We believe in free love, don't we? After all, it's not as if you're the only one, you know."

Her chest tightened. "What do you mean?"

"Steve. Do you think you're the only pretty girl who comes around here to take her clothes off for him?"

Yvonne desperately wanted to get away from McGarrity's cloying and overbearing presence, but even more desperately, she wanted to know if he was telling the truth. "I don't believe you," she said.

"Yvonne: Fridays and Saturdays. You're just his weekend hippie. Tuesdays and Wednesdays it's the lovely Denise. Let me see now, who's Monday, Thursday and Sunday? Is it the same one all three days, or is it three different ones?"

He was looking at her with that mocking smile on his face again.

"Stop it!" she said. "I won't believe you. I want to go home." She tried to rise again and proved a little more successful this time. She was still dizzy, though, and soon fell back.

McGarrity stood up and started pacing up and down, muttering to himself. She didn't know if it was T.S. Eliot or the Book of Revelation. She could see the bulge at the front of his jeans, and she knew he was getting more excited every second. She didn't trust him, knew he had that knife somewhere. Unless . . . Christ, he had probably had his way with Linda and killed her and got rid of the knife. That was why he didn't have it. Yvonne's mind was spinning. Why didn't Steve and the others come home? What were they doing? Had he killed them all? Was that it? Were they all lying upstairs in their rooms in pools of blood with flies buzzing around? The ideas flashed and cracked electrically in her brain, bouncing around her mind like the thunderstorm in the painting.

Yvonne sensed that now was the time, while he was distracted. She went through it quickly in her head first, visualizing herself do it. She would have to be fast, and that would be the hardest part. She was still disoriented because of the hash he had drugged her with. She would have only one chance. Get to the door. Get outside fast. How did it open? Yale lock. In or out? In. So twist to the left, pull and run. There would be people out there, in the street, in the park. It was still light outside. She could make it. Twist to the left, pull and run.

When McGarrity was at the far end of the room, by the window, his back turned to her, Yvonne summoned up all her energy and made a dash for the door. She didn't know if he was after her or not. She bounced off the walls down the hallway, reached the door, twisted the Yale and pulled. It opened. Daylight flooded her like warm honey. She stumbled a bit on the top step but ran down the garden path and out of the gate as fast as she could. She didn't look round, didn't even listen for his footsteps following her. She didn't know where she was running. All she knew was that she had to run, run, run for her life.

13

Superintendent Gervaise had called another progress meeting in the incident room, as the boardroom had now become known, for early Wednesday morning. The team lounged around the polished table sipping coffee from Styrofoam cups and chatting about last night's television, or Boro's prospects for the weekend's football. The corkboards had acquired more crime scene photographs, and the names and details of various people connected with the victim were scrawled across the whiteboard.

Annie Cabbot sat next to Winsome and DC Galway, on loan from Harrogate CID, and tried to digest what Banks had told her over an early breakfast in the Golden Grill. The presence in the area of two people connected with the Mad Hatters, the band on whom Nick Barber had been writing a major feature, seemed too much of a coincidence for her, too. She knew far less about the group and its history than Banks did, but even she could see there were a few skeletons in those closets worth shaking up a bit.

Superintendent Gervaise clicked in on her shiny black heels, smoothed her navy pinstripe skirt and sat down at the head of the table, gracing everyone with a warm smile. A chorus of "Good morning, ma'am" rose up from the assembled officers.

She turned first to Stefan Nowak and asked if there was anything more from forensics.

"Not really," said Stefan. "Naturally, there are numerous fibres and hairs remaining to be analyzed. The place was supposed to be thoroughly cleaned after each set of guests, but nobody's that thorough. We've got a list of the last ten renters from the owner, so we'll check against their samples first. It was a busy summer. Some of them live as far afield as Germany and Norway. It could take a long time."

"Prints?"

"The poker was wiped clean, and there are nothing but blurs around the door and conservatory entrance. Naturally, we've found almost as many fingerprints as we have other trace evidence, and it'll all have to be sifted, compared to existing records. As I said, it will take time."

"What about DNA?"

"Well, we did find traces of semen on the bedsheets, but the DNA matches that of the victim. We're trying to separate out any traces of female secretion, but no luck so far. Apparently he used condoms and flushed them down the toilet." He glanced towards Annie for confirmation. She nodded.

"We know who this . . . companion . . . was, don't we, DI Cabbot?"

"Yes," said Annie. "Unless there was someone else, which I'd say he hardly had time for, Kelly Soames admits to sleeping with the victim on two occasions: Wednesday evening, which was her night off, and Friday afternoon, between the hours of two and four, when she rearranged a dental appointment so she could visit his cottage."

282 • PETER ROBINSON

"Resourceful girl," Superintendent Gervaise reflected. "And Dr. Glendenning estimates time of death between six and eight on Friday?"

"He says he can't be any more precise than that," replied Stefan.

"Not earlier?"

"No, ma'am."

"All right," said Superintendent Gervaise. "Let's move on. Anything from the house to house?"

"Nothing positive, ma'am," said Winsome. "It was a miserable night even before the power cut, and most people shut their curtains tight and stayed in."

"Except the killer."

"Yes, ma'am. In addition to the couple in the Cross Keys and the New Zealander in the youth hostel, who thought she saw a light-coloured car heading up the hill away from Moorview Cottage between seven-thirty and seven-forty-five, we have one sighting of a dark-coloured four-by-four going up the same lane at about six-twenty, before the power cut, and a white van at about eight o'clock, while the electricity was off. According to our witnesses, though, neither of these stopped by the cottage."

"Not very promising, is it?" said Gervaise.

"Well, one of them could have stopped farther up the lane and walked back. There are plenty of passing places."

"I suppose so," Superintendent Gervaise conceded, but it was clear her heart wasn't in it.

"Oh," Winsome added, "someone says he saw a figure running across a field just after dark, before the lights went out."

"Any description?"

"No, ma'am. He was closing his curtains, and he thought

he saw this dark figure. He assumed it was someone jogging and ignored it."

"Fat, thin, tall, short, child, man, woman?"

"Sorry, ma'am. Just a dark figure."

"Which direction was the figure running?" Banks asked.

Winsome turned to face him. "The shortcut from Fordham to Lyndgarth, sir, across the fields and by the river. It's a popular jogging route."

"Yes, but probably not after dark. Not in that sort of weather."

"You'd be surprised, DCI Banks," said Superintendent Gervaise. "Some people take their exercise very seriously indeed. Do you know how many calories there are in a pint of beer?"

Everyone laughed. Banks wasn't convinced. Vic Greaves didn't drive, so Adams had said, but it wasn't very far from his cottage to Fordham, and that would have been the best route to take. It cut the journey almost in half. He made a note to get Winsome to talk to this witness again, or to do it himself.

"What about this Jack Tanner character?" Gervaise asked. "He sounded like a possible."

"His alibi holds water," said Templeton. "We've talked to six members of his darts team and every one of them swears he was in the King's Head playing darts from about six o'clock until ten."

"And I don't suppose he was drinking Britvic orange, either," said Gervaise. "Maybe we ought to get Traffic to keep an eye on Mr. Tanner."

Everyone laughed.

"So do we have *any* promising lines of inquiry yet?" Gervaise asked.

"Chris Adams suggested that Nick Barber had a cocaine problem," Banks said. "I'm not convinced, but I've put in a request for the Met drugs squad to look into it. But there's something else." Banks told her about Vic Greaves's breakdown and the drowning death of Robin Merchant at Swainsview Lodge thirty-five years ago, and the feature Nick Barber had been writing for *Mojo*.

"It's a bit far-fetched, isn't it?" said Gervaise, when he had finished. "I've always been a bit suspicious of events from so far in the past reaching forward into the present. Sounds like the stuff of television. I'm more inclined towards the most obvious solution – someone closer to hand, a jilted lover, cheated business partner, whatever. In this case, perhaps some disgruntled drug dealer. Besides, I take it this Merchant business was settled at the time?"

"After a fashion," said Banks.

"What are you suggesting?"

"DS Templeton dug up the paperwork, and it looks to have been a rather cursory investigation," Banks said. "After all, a major rock star and a peer of the realm were involved."

"Meaning?"

Christ, Banks thought, do I have to spell it out for you? "Ma'am, I should imagine nobody wanted a scandal that might in any way touch the establishment and make it to the House," he said. "There'd been enough of that sort of thing over the previous few years with Profumo, Kim Philby and the rest. As it was, the tabloids no doubt had a field day. Sex and drug orgies at Lord Jessop's country manor. A deeper investigation might have unearthed things nobody wanted brought to the surface."

"Oh, for heaven's sake, Banks, this is paranoid conspiracy rubbish," said Superintendent Gervaise. "Honestly, I'd have thought better of you."

"Well," Banks went on, unfazed, "the victim's personal belongings are all missing, including his laptop and mobile, and he was definitely silenced for good."

"We do know that he had a laptop and mobile?"

"The girl, Kelly Soames, says she saw them when she visited him, ma'am," said Annie.

Gervaise frowned as if she had a bad taste in her mouth and tapped her pen on the blank pad in front of her. "People have been killed or beaten up for a mobile phone or less. I'm still not convinced about this girl, DI Cabbot. She could be lying. Talk to her again, see if her story's consistent."

"Surely you don't really believe that she might have killed him?" Annie asked.

"All I'm saying is that it's possible."

"But she was working in the pub at the time. There are plenty of witnesses to vouch for her."

"Except when she was supposed to be going to the dentist's on Friday afternoon, but was in actuality in bed with a man she'd only just met, a man who was found dead not long after. The girl can obviously lie with the best of them. All I'm saying is it's suspicious, DI Cabbot. And the MO fits. Crime of passion. Maybe he slighted her, asked her to do something she found repugnant? Perhaps she found out he had another girlfriend. Maybe she left the pub for a few moments later on, in the dark. It wouldn't have taken long."

"That would involve some premeditation, not a crime of passion, ma'am," said Annie, "and the odds are that she would have also got some blood on her."

"Perhaps this sense of being wronged built up in her until she snapped when the lights went out and seized her opportunity before they got organized with candles? I don't know. All I'm saying is that it's possible, and that it makes a good deal more sense than any conspiracy rooted deep in the past. Either way, push her a bit harder, DI Cabbot. Do I make myself clear? And DS Nowak?"

"Yes, ma'am?"

"Have a word with the pathologist, Dr. Glendenning. See if you can push him a bit on time of death, find out if there's any possibility that the victim could have been killed around four rather than between six and eight."

"Yes, ma'am." Stefan gave Annie a quick glance. They both knew Dr. Glendenning could not be pushed on anything.

"And let's have the girl's father in," Superintendent Gervaise went on. "He disappeared for long enough around the time of the murder. If he found out that this Barber character was having casual sex with his daughter, he might have taken the law into his own hands."

"Ma'am?" said Annie.

"What, DI Cabbot?"

"It's just that I sort of promised. I mean, I indicated to the girl, to Kelly, that is, that we had no need to tell her father about what happened. Apparently he's a bit of a disciplinarian, and it could go badly for her."

"All the more reason to have a close look at him. It might already have gone badly for Nicholas Barber. Have you thought of that?"

"No, ma'am, you don't understand. It's her I'm worried about. Kelly. He'll hit the roof."

Superintendent Gervaise regarded Annie coldly. "I understand perfectly well what you're saying, DI Cabbot. It serves her right for jumping into bed with every man she sees, then, doesn't it?"

"With all due respect, there's no evidence to suggest that

she does anything of the kind. She just happened to like Nick Barber."

Superintendent Gervaise glared at Annie. "I'm not going to argue sexual mores, especially with you, DI Cabbot. Ask around. Find out. The girl must have had other partners. Find them. And find out if anyone's ever paid her for it."

"But, ma'am," Annie protested. "That's an insult. Kelly Soames isn't a prostitute, and this case isn't about her sex life."

"It is if I say it is."

"I talked to Calvin Soames," Banks cut in.

Superintendent Gervaise looked over at him. "And?"

"In my opinion, he didn't know what was going on between the victim and his daughter."

"In your opinion?"

"Yes," said Banks.

"He couldn't have been hiding it?"

"He could, I suppose," Banks admitted, "but if we're assuming that he did it out of anger or righteous indignation, I think he would have been far more likely to be wearing his heart on his sleeve. He would have been angry when I was questioning his daughter about Barber, but he wasn't."

"Did you suggest they had slept together?"

"No," said Banks. "I merely asked her about her dealings with Barber as a customer in the Cross Keys. While her father was watching us, I was watching him, and I believe that if he'd known there was more to it than that, it would have shown in his expression, his behaviour or in something he said. In my opinion, he's not the sort of man accustomed to being sly."

"And it didn't?"

"No."

"Very well. I'd be more convinced, however, if I could witness his reaction to being told what his daughter had been up to."

"But, ma'am –"

"That's enough, DI Cabbot. I want you to pursue this line of inquiry until I'm satisfied there either is or isn't something to it."

"It'll be too late for Kelly Soames then," Annie muttered under her breath.

"DS Templeton?" said Banks.

Templeton sat up. "Sir?"

"Did you manage to locate Detective Sergeant Enderby?"

Templeton shifted uneasily in his chair. "Er . . . yes, sir, I did." He looked at Superintendent Gervaise while he was speaking.

"What is this?" she asked.

"Well, ma'am," Templeton said, "DCI Banks asked me to track down the detective who investigated the Robin Merchant drowning."

"This is the drug addict who fell into the swimming pool thirty-five years ago?"

"Yes, ma'am, though I'm not certain that he was actually an addict. Not technically speaking."

Superintendent Gervaise sighed theatrically, ran her hand over her layered blonde hair, then looked at Banks. "Very well, DCI Banks. I see you're hell-bent and determined on following this up, so I'll give you the benefit of the doubt. I'll bear with you for the moment and assume there might be something in it. But DI Cabbot sticks with the Soameses. Okay?"

"Fine," said Banks. He turned to Templeton. "Well then, Kev. Where is he?"

Templeton glanced at Superintendent Gervaise again before answering. "Er . . . he's in Whitby, sir."

"That's nice and handy, then, isn't it?" Banks said. "I quite fancy a day at the seaside."

The sun was out again when Banks began his descent from the North York Moors down into Whitby. It was a sight that always stirred him, even in the most gloomy weather, but today the sky was milky blue, and the sun shone on the ruined abbey high on the hill and sparkled like diamonds on the North Sea beyond the dark pincers of the harbour walls.

Retired Detective Inspector Keith Enderby lived in West Cliff, where the houses straggled east off the A174 towards Sandsend. At least his fifties pebble-dash semi had a sea view, even if it was only a few square feet between the houses opposite. Other than that, it was an unremarkable house on an unremarkable estate, Banks thought, as he pulled up behind the grey Mondeo parked at the front. "Mondeo Man." A journalistically contrived representative of a certain kind of middle-class Briton. Was that what Enderby had become?

On the phone, Enderby had indicated that he was keen enough to talk about the Robin Merchant case, and in person he welcomed Banks into his home with a smile and a handshake, introduced his wife, Rita, a small, quiet woman with a halo of pinkish grey hair. Rita offered tea or coffee and Banks went for tea. It came with the requisite plate of chocolate digestives, arrowroots and KitKats, from which Banks was urged to help himself. He did. After a few pleasantries, at a nod from her husband, Rita made herself scarce, muttering something about errands in town, and drove off in the grey Mondeo. "Mondeo Woman," then, Banks thought. Enderby said something about what a wonderful woman she was. Banks agreed. It seemed the polite thing to do.

"Nice place to retire to," Banks said. "How long have you been here?"

"Going on ten years now," Enderby said. "I put in my twenty-five years and a few more besides. Finished up as a DI in South Yorkshire Police, Doncaster. But Rita always dreamed of living by the seaside and we used to come here for our holidays."

"And you?"

"Well, the Costa del Sol would have suited me just fine, but we couldn't afford it. Besides, Rita won't leave the country. Foreigners begin at Calais and all that. She doesn't even have a passport. Can you believe it?"

"You probably wouldn't have liked it there," Banks said. "Too many villains."

"Whitby's all right," said Enderby, "and not short of a villain or two, either. I could do without all those bloody goths, mind you."

Banks knew that Whitby's close association with Bram Stoker's *Dracula* made the place a point of pilgrimage for goths, but as far as he knew, they were harmless enough kids, caused no trouble, and if they wanted to wear black all the time and drink a little of one another's blood now and then, it was fine with him. The sun flashed on the square of sea through the houses opposite. "I appreciate your agreeing to talk to me," Banks said.

"No problem. I just don't know that I can add much you don't already know. It was all in the case files."

"If you're anything like me," Banks said, "you often have a feeling, call it a gut instinct or whatever, that you don't think belongs in the files. Or a personal impression, something interesting but that seems irrelevant to the actual case itself."

"It was a long time ago," Enderby said. "I probably wouldn't remember anything like that now."

"You'd be surprised," said Banks. "It was a high-profile case, I should imagine. Interesting times back then, too. Rubbing shoulders with rock stars and aristos and all that."

"Oh, it was interesting all right. Pink Floyd. The Who. I met them all. More tea?"

Banks held out his cup while Enderby poured. His gold wedding band was embedded deeply in his pudgy finger, surrounded by a tuft of hair. "You'd have been how old then?" Banks asked.

"In 1970? Just turned thirty that May."

That would be about right, Banks guessed. Enderby looked to be in his mid-sixties now, with the comfortable paunch of a man who enjoys his inactivity and a head bereft of even a hint of hair. He made up for the lack with a grey scrub-brush moustache. A delicate pink pattern of broken blood vessels mapped his cheeks and nose, but Banks put it down to blood pressure rather than drink. Enderby didn't talk or act like a boozer, and his breath didn't smell of Trebor Extra Strong mints.

"So what was it like working that case?" Banks asked. "What do you remember most about the Robin Merchant investigation?"

Enderby screwed up his eyes and gazed out of the window. "It must have been about ten o'clock by the time we got to the scene," he said. "It was a beautiful morning, I do remember that. Clear. Warm. Birds singing. And there he was, floating in the pool."

"What was your first impression?"

Enderby thought for a moment, then gave a brief, barking laugh and put his cup down on the saucer. "Do you know what it was?" he said. "You'll never believe this. He was on his back, naked, you know, and I remember thinking he'd got such a little prick for a famous rock star. You know, all the stuff we heard back then about groupies and orgies. The *News of the World* and all that. We assumed they were all hung like horses. It just seemed so incongruous, him floating there all shrivelled, like a shrimp or a seahorse or something. It was the water, of course. No matter how warm the day was, the water was still cold."

"That'll do it every time. Were the others up and around when you arrived?"

"You must be joking. The uniforms were just rousing them. If it hadn't been for Merchant's drowning and our arrival, they'd probably have slept until well into the afternoon. They looked in pretty bad shape, too, some of them. Hungover and worse."

"So who phoned it in?"

"The gardener, when he arrived for work."

"Was he a suspect?"

"Nah, not really."

"Many hangers-on and groupies around?"

"It's hard to say. According to their statements, everyone was a close friend of the band. I mean, no one actually *admitted* to being a groupie or a hanger-on. Most of the guys in the band were just with their regular girlfriends."

"What about Robin Merchant? Was he with anyone that night?"

"There was a girl asleep in his bed," said Enderby.

"Girlfriend?"

"Groupie."

"According to what I've read," Banks said, "the thinking at the time was that Merchant had taken some Mandrax and was wandering around the pool naked when he fell in at the shallow end, hit his head on the bottom and drowned. Is that right?"

"Yes," said Enderby. "That was what it looked like, and that's what the pathologist confirmed. There was also a broken glass on the edge of the pool with Merchant's fingerprints on it. He'd been drinking. Vodka."

"Did you consider other possible scenarios?"

"Such as?"

"That it wasn't accidental."

"You mean somebody pushed him?"

"It would be a natural assumption. You know what suspicious minds we coppers have."

"True enough," Enderby agreed. "I must admit, it crossed my mind, but I soon ruled it out."

"Why?"

"Nobody had any motive."

"Not according to what they *told* you."

"We dug a bit deeper than that. Give us some credit. We might not have had the resources you've got today, but we did our best."

"There was no friction within the band?"

"As far as I know there's always friction in bands. Put a group of people together with egos that big and there has to be. Stands to reason."

Banks laughed. Then he thought of Brian and wondered if the Blue Lamps were due for a split before too long. Brian hadn't said anything, but Banks sensed something different about him, a certain lack of excitement and commitment, perhaps, and his turning up out of the blue like that was unusual. He seemed weary. And what about Emilia? Was she the Yoko Ono figure? Still, if Brian wanted to talk, he would get around to it in his own time; there was no use in pushing him. He'd always been that way. "Anything in particular?" he asked Enderby.

"Let's see. They were all worried about Vic Greaves's drug intake, for a start. His performances were getting more and more erratic, and his behaviour was unreliable. Apparently he'd missed a concert engagement not that long back, and the rest of them were still a bit pissed off at him for leaving them in the lurch."

"Did Greaves have an alibi?"

Enderby scratched the side of his nose. "As a matter of fact, he did," he said. "Two, actually."

"Two?"

Enderby grinned. "Greaves and Merchant were the only two band members who didn't have regular girlfriends. That night, Greaves happened to be in bed with two groupies."

"Lucky devil," said Banks. "I'd never have thought he had it in him." He remembered the bald, bloated figure with the hollow eyes he had seen in Lyndgarth.

"According to them, he didn't," said Enderby. "Apparently he was too far gone to get it up. Bloody waste, if you ask me. They were lovely-looking girls." He smiled at the memory. "Not wearing very much, either, when I interviewed them. That's one of the little things you don't forget in a hurry. Not so little, either, if you catch my drift."

"Could Greaves not have sneaked away for a while during the night? They must have both slept, or passed out, at some time."

"Look, when you get right down to it, any one of them could have done it. At least anyone who could still walk in a straight line. We didn't really set great store by the alibis, as such. For a start, hardly any of them could remember much about the previous evening, or even what time they finally went to bed. They might have been wandering about all night, for all I know, and not even noticed Merchant in the swimming pool."

"So what made you rule out murder so quickly?"

"I told you. No real motive. No evidence that he'd been pushed."

"But Merchant could have got into an argument with someone, gone a bit over the top."

"Oh, he *could* have, yes. But no one says he did, so what are we supposed to do, jump to conclusions and pick someone? Anyone?"

"What about an intruder?"

"Couldn't be ruled out, either. It was easy enough to get into the grounds. But again, there was no evidence of an intruder, and nothing was stolen. Besides, Merchant's injuries were consistent with falling into a swimming pool and drowning, which was what happened. Look, if you ask me, at worst it could have been a bit of stoned and drunken larking around that went wrong. I'm not saying that's what happened, because there's no proof, but if they were all stoned or pissed, which they were, and they started running around the pool playing tag or what have you, and someone tagged Merchant just a bit too hard and he ended up in the pool dead . . . Well, what would you do?"

"First off," said Banks, "I'd try to get him out of there. There was no way I could be sure he was dead. Then I'd probably try artificial respiration, or the kiss of life or whatever it was back then, while someone called an ambulance."

"Aye," said Enderby. "And if you'd had as much drugs in your system as they had, you'd probably have just stood there for half an hour twiddling your thumbs before doing anything, and then the first thing you'd have done is get rid of your stash."

"Did the drugs squad search the premises? There was no mention in the file."

"Between you and me, we searched the place. Oh, we found a bit of marijuana, a few tabs of LSD, some mandies. But nothing hard."

"What happened?"

"We decided, in the light of everything else – like a body to deal with – that we wouldn't bring charges. We just disposed of the stuff. I mean, what were we to do, arrest them all for possession?"

Disposed of? Banks doubted that. Consumed or sold, more likely. But there was no point in opening that can of worms. "Did you get any sense that they'd cooked up a story between them?"

"No. As I said, half of them couldn't even remember the party. It was all pretty fragmented and inconclusive."

"Lord Jessop was present, right?"

"Right. Probably about the most coherent of the lot. That was before he got into the hard stuff."

"And the most influential?"

"I can see where you're going with this. Of course, nobody wanted a scandal. It was bad enough as it was. Maybe that's why we didn't bring drugs charges. There'd been enough of that over the past two or three years with the Stones bust, and it was all beginning to seem pretty ridiculous. Especially after the *Times* ran that editorial about breaking a butterfly on a wheel. Within hours we had them all banging at the door and jumping over the walls. The *News of the World*, *People*, *Daily Mirror*, you name it. So even if someone else had been involved in a bit of horseplay, the thinking went, then it had still been an accident, and there was no point in inviting scandal. As we couldn't *prove* that anyone else had been involved and no one was admitting to it, that was the end of it. Tea's done. Fancy another pot?"

"No, thank you," said Banks. "If there's nothing more you can tell me, I'd better be off."

"Sorry to disappoint you."

"It wasn't disappointing."

"Look, you never did really tell me what it was all about. Remember, we're in the same job, or used to be."

Banks was so used to not giving out any more information than he needed to that he sometimes forgot to say entirely why he was asking about something. "We found a writer by the name of Nick Barber dead. You might have read about it."

"Sounds vaguely familiar," said Enderby. "I try to keep up."

"What you won't have read about is that he was working on a story about the Mad Hatters, on Vic Greaves and the band's early days in particular."

"Interesting," said Enderby. "But I still don't see why you're asking about Robin Merchant's death."

"It was just something Barber said to a girlfriend," Banks said. "He mentioned something about a juicy story with a murder."

"Now you've got me interested," said Enderby. "A murder, you say?"

"That's right. I suppose it was probably just journalistic licence, trying to impress his girlfriend."

"Not necessarily," said Enderby.

"What do you mean?"

"Well, I'm pretty sure that Robin Merchant's death was accidental, but that wasn't the first time I was out at Swainsview Lodge in connection with a suspicious death."

"Really?" said Banks. "Do tell."

Enderby stood up. "Look, the sun's well over the yardarm. How about we head down to my local and I'll tell you over a pint?"

"I'm driving," said Banks.

"That's all right," said Enderby. "You can buy me one and watch me drink it."

"What took you out there?" Banks asked.

"A murder," said Enderby, eyes glittering. "A real one that time."

Saturday, September 20, 1969

"She won't come out of her room," Janet Chadwick said as she sat with her husband eating tea on Saturday evening, football results on the telly. Chadwick was filling in his pools coupon, but it was soon clear that the £2,300,800 jackpot was going to elude him this week, just as it had every other week.

Chadwick ate some toad-in-the-hole after giving it a liberal dip in the gravy. "What's wrong with her now?"

"She won't say. She came dashing in late this afternoon and went straight up to her room. I called to her, knocked on her door, but she wouldn't answer."

"Did you go in?"

"No. She has to be allowed some privacy, Stan. She's sixteen."

"I know. I know. But this is unusual, missing her tea like this. And it's Saturday. Doesn't she usually go out Saturday night?"

"Yes."

"I'll have a word with her after tea."

"Be careful with her, Stan. You know how on edge she seems these days."

Chadwick touched his wife's wrist. "I'll be careful. I'm not really the terrible child-gobbling monster you think I am."

Janet laughed. "I don't think you're a monster. She's just at a difficult age. A father doesn't always understand as much as a mother does."

"I'll tread gently, don't worry."

They finished their tea in silence, and while Janet went to wash the dishes, Chadwick went upstairs to try to talk to Yvonne. He tapped softly at her door but got no answer. He tapped again, a little louder, but all he heard was a muffled "Go away." There wasn't even any music playing. Yvonne must have had her transistor radio turned off. Another unusual sign.

Chadwick reckoned he had two choices: leave Yvonne to her own devices or simply walk in. Janet would favour the former, laissez-faire approach, no doubt, but Chadwick was in a mood to take the bull by the horns. He'd had enough of Yvonne's sneaking around, stopping out all night, her secrets and lies and prima donna behaviour. Now was the time to see what was at the bottom of it. Taking a deep breath, he opened the door and walked in.

The outrage he expected didn't come. The curtains were closed, the lights off, giving the room a dim, twilit appearance. It even disguised the untidy mess of clothes and magazines on the floor and bed. At first, Chadwick couldn't see Yvonne, then he realized she was on her bed, under the eiderdown. When his eyes adjusted, he could also see that she was shaking. Concerned, he perched on the edge of the bed and said softly, "Yvonne. Yvonne, sweetheart. What's wrong? What is it?"

She didn't react at first, and he sat patiently waiting, remembering when she was a little girl and came to him when she had nightmares. "It's all right," he said, "you can tell me. I won't be angry with you. I promise."

Her hand snaked out from under the eiderdown and sought his. He held it. Still she said nothing, then she slowly slid the cover off her face, and he could see even in the weak light that she had been crying. She was still shaking, too.

"What is it, love?" he asked. "What's happened?"

"It was horrible," she said. "*He* was horrible."

Chadwick felt his neck muscles tense. "What? Has somebody done something to you?"

"He's ruined everything."

"What do you mean? You'd better tell me from the start, Yvonne. I want to understand, honestly I do."

Yvonne stared at him, as if trying to come to a decision. He knew he came across as strict and straight and unbending, but he really did want to know what was upsetting her, and not with a view to punishment this time. Whatever she thought, and however difficult it was, he really did love his daughter. One by one, the terrible possibilities crowded in on him. Had she found out she was pregnant? Was that it? Like Linda Lofthouse when she was Yvonne's age? Or had someone assaulted her?

"What is it?" he asked. "Did somebody hurt you?"

Yvonne shook her head. "Not like you think." Then she launched herself into his arms, and he could feel her tears on his neck and hear her talking into his shoulder. "I was so scared, Daddy, the things he was saying. I really thought he was going to do something terrible to me. I know he had a knife somewhere. If I hadn't run away . . ." She collapsed into sobs. Chadwick digested what she had said, trying to keep his fatherly anger at bay, and gently disentangled himself. Yvonne lay back on her pillows and rubbed her eyes with the backs of her hands. She looked like a little girl. Chadwick handed her the box of tissues from the dresser top.

"Start at the beginning," he said. "Slowly."

"I was at Brimleigh Festival, Dad. I want you to know that before I start. I'm sorry for lying."

"I knew that."

"But, Dad? . . . how?"

"Call it a father's instinct." Or *copper's instinct*, he thought. "Go on."

"I've been hanging around with some people. You wouldn't like them. That's why . . . why I didn't tell you. But they're people like me, Dad. We're into the same music and ideas and beliefs about society and stuff. They're different. They're not boring, not like the kids at school. They read poetry and write and play music."

"Students?"

"Some of them."

"So they're older than you?"

"What does age matter?"

"Never mind. Go on."

Yvonne looked a little uncertain now, and Chadwick realized he would have to keep his editorial comments to a bare minimum if he hoped to get the truth from his daughter. "Everything was fine, really it was. And then . . ." She started trembling again, got herself under control and went on. "There's this man called McGarrity. He's older than the others and he acts really weird. He always scared me."

"In what way?"

"He's got this horrible, twisted sort of smile that makes you feel like some sort of insect, and he keeps quoting things, T.S. Eliot, the Bible, other stuff. Sometimes he just paces up and down with his knife."

"What knife?"

"He's got this knife, and he keeps just, you know, tapping it against his palm as he walks."

"What kind of knife is it?"

"A flick knife with a tortoiseshell handle."

"Which palm does he tap it against?"

Yvonne frowned, and Chadwick realized again he would have to be careful. It could wait. "Sorry," he said. "It doesn't matter. Go on."

"Steve says he's just a bit weird because he had electroshock therapy. They say he used to be a great blues harmonica player, but since the electric shocks he can't play anymore. But I don't know . . . he just seems weird to me."

"Is this the man who bothered you?"

"Yes. I went over there this afternoon to see Steve – he's my boyfriend – but he wasn't in and only McGarrity was there. I wanted to go, but he insisted I stay."

"Did he force you?"

"Well, I wouldn't say he forced me, but I was uncomfortable. I was just hoping Steve and the others would get back soon, that's all."

"Was he on drugs?"

Yvonne looked away and nodded.

"Okay. Go on."

"He said some terrible things."

"About what?"

"About the girl who was killed. About those dead people in Los Angeles. About me."

"What did he say about you?"

Yvonne looked down. "He was rude. I don't want to repeat it."

"All right. Stay calm. Did he touch you?"

"He grabbed my arm and he touched my face. He was just so frightening. I was terrified he was going to do something."

Chadwick felt his teeth grinding. "What happened?"

"I waited until he had his back turned to me and I ran away."

"Good girl. Did he come after you?"

"I don't think so. I didn't look."

"Okay. You're doing fine, Yvonne. You're safe now."

"But, Dad, what if he . . ."

"What if he what? Was he at Brimleigh?"

"Yes."

"With you?"

"No, he was wandering around the field."

"Did you see him go into the woods?"

"No. But it was dark most of the time. I wouldn't have seen."

"Where did this happen this afternoon?"

"Just down the road, Springfield Mount. Look, Dad, they're all right, really, the others, Steve. It's just him. There's something wrong with him, I'm sure of it."

"Did he know Linda Lofthouse?"

"Linda? I don't . . . yes, yes, he did."

Chadwick's ears pricked up at the familiarity with which Yvonne mentioned Linda's name. "How do you know? It's all right, Yvonne, you can tell me the truth. I'm not going to be angry with you."

"Promise?"

"Cross my heart and hope to die."

Yvonne smiled. It was an old ritual. "It was at another house, on Bayswater Terrace," she said. "There's three places people, like, gather, to listen to music and stuff. Springfield Mount and Carberry Place are the other two. Anyway, sometime during the summer I was with Steve, and Linda was there. McGarrity too. I mean, they didn't know one another, they weren't close or anything, but he *had* met her."

Chadwick paused a moment to take it all in. Bayswater Terrace. Dennis, Julie and the rest. So Yvonne was part of *that* crowd. *His own daughter.* He held himself in check, remembering he'd promised not to be angry. Besides, the poor girl had been through a trauma, and it had taken a lot for her to open up; the last thing she needed now was a lecture from her father. But it was hard to keep his rage inside. He felt so wound up, so tight, that his chest ached.

"You met Linda, too?" he asked.

"Yes." Tears filled Yvonne's eyes. "Once. We didn't talk much, really. She just said she liked my dress and my hair, and we talked about what a drag school can be. She was so nice, Dad, how could anyone do that to her?"

"I don't know, sweetheart," Chadwick said, stroking his daughter's silky blonde hair. "I don't know."

"Do you think it was him? McGarrity?"

"I don't know that, either, but I'm going to have to have a talk with him."

"Don't be too hard on Steve or the others, Dad. Please. They're all right. Really they are. It's only him, only McGarrity who's weird."

"I understand," said Chadwick. "How do you feel now about getting up and having something to eat?"

"I'm not hungry."

"Well, at least come downstairs and see your mother. She's worried sick about you."

"Okay," said Yvonne. "But give me a few minutes to get changed and wash my face."

"Right you are, sweetheart." Chadwick kissed the top of her head, left the room and headed for the telephone, jaw set hard. Later tonight, someone was going to be very sorry he had ever been born.

14

Annie Cabbot tried to control her temper as she waited to knock and enter Superintendent Gervaise's office after Banks had left for Whitby. It was difficult. She had sensed that Gervaise hadn't liked her from the start and sussed her as another ambitious woman who got where she was the hard way, who was damned if she was going to give any other woman anything less than her worst. So much for female solidarity.

Annie took several deep, calming breaths, the way she did when she was meditating or practising yoga. It didn't work. She knocked anyway and entered even before the slightly puzzled voice called out, "Enter."

"I'd like a word, ma'am," said Annie.

"DI Cabbot. Please, sit down."

Annie sat. She remembered how she had always felt slightly awed and nervous when Detective Superintendent Gristhorpe had called her into this same office, but this time she felt nothing of the kind.

"What can I help you with?"

"You were seriously out of order back there," Annie said. "At the morning briefing."

"I was?" Gervaise feigned surprise. At least Annie believed it was feigned.

"You have no right to make public comments about my private life."

Superintendent Gervaise held a hand up. "Now, let's wait a moment before we go any further. Just exactly what was it I said that has upset you so much?"

"You know damn well what it was. Ma'am."

"We don't seem to be getting off on the right foot here, do we?"

"You said you had no desire to argue sexual mores, *especially* with me."

"These meetings aren't a forum for argument, DI Cabbot, they're called to bring everyone up to date and set the scene for more actions and lines of inquiry. You know that."

"Yet you deliberately insulted me in front of my colleagues."

Superintendent Gervaise regarded her as she might a particularly troublesome schoolgirl. "Well, seeing as we're on the subject," she said, "you do have something of a checkered history with us, don't you?"

Annie said nothing.

"Let me remind you. You'd not been in North Yorkshire five minutes before you were jumping into bed with DCI Banks. And let me also remind you that fraternizing between fellow officers is seriously frowned upon, and liaisons between a DS, as you were then, and a DCI, are particularly fraught with dangers, as I'm sure you found out. He was your superior officer. What were you thinking of?"

Annie felt her heart beating hard in her chest. "My private life is my affair."

"You're not a stupid woman," Superintendent Gervaise went on. "I know that. We all make mistakes, and they're rarely fatal." She paused. "But your last one was, wasn't it? Your last mistake almost cost DCI Banks his life."

"We weren't involved in anything then," Annie said, aware as she spoke of how weak her response sounded.

"I know that." Gervaise shook her head. "DI Cabbot, I'm not entirely certain how you've managed to last here so long, let alone how you were promoted to DI so quickly in the first place. Things must have been very easygoing around here back then. Or perhaps DCI Banks had a certain amount of influence with the ACC?"

Annie felt her heart about to explode at the insult, but a dreadful calm flooded her, disconcerting at first, like a sort of cooling numbness in her blood, a falling away of feeling. Then it warmed a little, transformed into a calm, altered state. *It didn't matter.* Whatever Superintendent Gervaise thought, said or did, *it didn't matter.* Annie cared about her career, but there were some things she just wouldn't take, not for anything, not from anyone, and that knowledge made her feel free. She almost smiled. Gervaise must have sensed some change in the air, because there was a new edge to her voice when she noticed she wasn't getting the desired response from Annie.

"Anyway, in case you haven't noticed it, things have changed around here now. I won't countenance romantic relationships among my officers. They're distracting and sow the seeds for all kinds of mistakes and future difficulties, as you have discovered. And in the future, I would strongly suggest that you think again about continuing your relationship with DCI Banks."

Did Gervaise really believe that Annie and Banks had got back together? Why? Had someone told her? A few moments ago Annie would have leapt out of her seat and throttled Gervaise at such words, but now she took it all in calmly. The superintendent had also known about Banks having a pint in the Cross Keys on the night of the murder. Who had told her about that? Was there a spy in their midst? Annie didn't react.

"DI Cabbot?"

"Sorry," said Annie. "I was miles away."

"That's very irresponsible of you. You come barging in here telling me I'm not doing my job properly, and the minute you realize you're in the wrong, you start daydreaming."

"It wasn't that," Annie said. "Are we finished here?"

"Not until I say we are."

"Ma'am."

"This other business. Kelly Soames."

"It's not other business," said Annie. "It's all connected."

"What do you mean?"

"I defended Kelly Soames's sexual mores, so you attacked mine. It's connected."

"I thought we'd left that behind."

"Look, you want me to subject the poor girl to the ordeal of her father finding out she'd had a sexual relationship with Nick Barber, and I said I'd given her some assurances that wouldn't happen."

"Those assurances weren't yours to give."

"I'm aware of that. Even so, you can hardly attack me for wanting to stand by my word."

"Admirable as that may seem, it's not workable here. This job isn't about saving your conscience and keeping your promises. I want that girl confronted with what happened in the presence of her father, and if you won't do it, I'll find someone who will."

"What is it with you? Are you a sadist or something?"

Gervaise's lips tightened in a nasty smile. "I'm a professional detective just doing her job," she said. "Which is something you should take a little more seriously. Sympathy for victims is all very well, in its place, but remember that Nicholas Barber is the victim here, not Kelly Soames."

"Not yet," said Annie.

"Insubordination will get you nowhere."

"No, but it feels good." Annie stood up to leave. "There's obviously no further point talking to you, so if you're thinking of taking action against me, do it. I don't care. Either shit or get off the pot."

Gervaise's face fell. "What did you say?"

Annie walked towards the door. "You heard me," she said.

"Right," said Superintendent Gervaise. "I want you on statement reading as of now. And send in DS Templeton."

"Yes, ma'am," said Annie, and shut the door softly behind her as she left. *Templeton.* Now that made sense.

Sunday, September 21, 1969

Chadwick went in with the Springfield Mount team because that was the house where Yvonne had been accosted by McGarrity. Two other teams, also with search warrants, carried out simultaneous raids on Bayswater Terrace and Carberry Place. They waited until well after midnight, by which time Yvonne was fast asleep in bed. As any prior announcement of their presence was likely to result in drugs being flushed down the toilet, they were authorized to enter by force.

The streets were deserted, most of the houses in darkness apart from the lonely light of an insomniac here and there, or a student burning the midnight oil; a sheen of rain reflected the amber streetlights on the pavements and tarmac. Directly across from Springfield Mount was a small, triangular park, locked up for the night, wedged between two merging main roads. At the end of the street, across the road, loomed the local grammar school, all in darkness now, with its bell tower and high windows.

The unmarked police car pulled up at the end of the street behind a patrol car. There were five officers altogether: Chadwick, Bradley and three uniforms, one of whom would guard the back. Geoff Broome was leading the Carberry team, and his colleague Martin Young the raid on Bayswater Terrace. They didn't expect any resistance or problems, except perhaps from McGarrity, if he had his knife.

Chadwick could hear music coming from the front room, and candlelight flickered behind the curtains. Good, someone was at home. Surprise was of the essence now. When everyone was in position, Chadwick gave a nod to the uniform with the battering ram, and one smash was enough to break the lock and send the door banging back on its hinges.

As arranged, the two uniformed constables dashed upstairs to secure the upper level and Chadwick and Bradley entered the front room. The officer on guard at the back would take care of the kitchen.

In the living room, Chadwick found three people lying on the floor in advanced stages of intoxication – marijuana, judging by the smell that even two smouldering joss sticks couldn't mask. Candles flickered and dreadful, wailing electric-guitar music came from the record player, a kangaroo with a pain in its testicles, by the sound of it, Chadwick thought.

It didn't look as if their arrival had interrupted any deep conversations, or any conversations at all, for that matter, as they all seemed beyond speech, and one of them could only manage a quick "What the fuck?" before Chadwick announced who he was and told them the police were there to search the premises for drugs and for a knife that may have been used in the committing of a homicide. Bradley switched on the light and turned the music off.

Things didn't look so bad, Chadwick realized with surprise, not what he had expected, just three scruffy long-haired kids lounging around stoned, listening to what passed for music. There was no orgy; nobody was crawling around naked and drooling on the floor or committing outrageous sex acts. Then he saw the LP cover leaning against the wall. It showed a girl with long, wavy red hair and full red lips. She was naked from the belly button up, and she couldn't have been more than eleven or twelve. In her hands, she cradled a chrome model airplane. What kind of perverts was he dealing with? Chadwick wondered. And one of them had been seeing his daughter. This was where Yvonne would have been tonight, had McGarrity not scared her off. This was what she would have been doing. She had been here before, done this, and that set his teeth on edge.

Bradley took their names: Steve Morrison, Todd Crowley and Jacqueline McNeil. They all seemed docile and sheepish enough. Chadwick took Steve aside to a corner of the room and gripped the front of his shirt in his fist. "Whatever comes of this," he hissed, "I want you to stop seeing my daughter. Understand?"

Steve turned pale. "Who? Who am I supposed to be seeing?"

"Her name's Yvonne. Yvonne Chadwick."

"Shit, I didn't know she . . ."

"Just stay away from her. Okay?"

Steve nodded, and Chadwick let him go. "Right," he said, turning to the others. "Where's McGarrity?"

"Dunno," said Todd Crowley. "He was here earlier. Maybe he's upstairs."

"What were you doing?"

"Nothing. Just listening to music."

Chadwick gestured towards the LP cover. "Where did you get that filth?"

"What?"

"The naked child. You realize we could probably prosecute you under the Obscene Publications Act, don't you?"

"That's art, man," Crowley protested. "You can buy it at any record shop. Obscenity's in the eye of the beholder."

There were greasy fish and chip wrappers and newspaper on the floor beside empty bottles of beer. Bradley went over to the ashtray and extracted the remains of a number of hand-rolled cigarettes he identified by their smell as being a mix of tobacco and hash. That in itself was enough to charge them with possession.

What the hell did Yvonne see in this dump? Chadwick wondered. Why did she come here? Was her life at home so bad? Was she so desperate to get away from him and Janet? But there was no point trying to work it out. As Enderby had said, it probably all came down to freedom.

Chadwick heard a brief scuffle and a bang upstairs, followed by a series of loud thumps, each one getting closer. When he went to the foot of the stairs, he saw the two uniformed constables, one without his hat, holding the arms of a man who was struggling to get up.

"He didn't want to come with us, sir," one of the officers said.

It looked as if they had held his arms and dragged him down the stairs backwards, which shouldn't have done much damage to anything except his dignity and maybe his tailbone. Chadwick watched as the unruly black-clad figure with the lank dark hair and pockmarked face got to his feet and dusted himself off, the superior smirk already back in place, if indeed it had ever been gone.

"Well, well, well," he said, "Mr. McGarrity, I assume? I've been wanting a word with you."

Enderby's local, two streets down, was like his house: comfortable and unremarkable. It was a relatively new building, late sixties from its low, squat shape and the large picture windows facing the sea. The advantages, from Banks's point of view, were that it was practically empty at that time in the afternoon, and they sold cask-conditioned Tetley's. One pint wouldn't do him any harm, he decided, as he bought the drinks at the bar and carried them over.

Enderby looked at him. "Thought your resolve might weaken."

"It often does," Banks admitted. "Nice view."

Enderby took a sip of beer. "Mmm."

The window looked out over the glittering North Sea, dotted here and there with fishing boats and trawlers. Whitby was still a thriving fishing town, Banks reminded himself, even if the whaling industry it had grown from was long extinct. Captain Cook had got his seafaring start in Whitby, and his statue stood on top of West Cliff, close to the jawbone of a whale.

"When did this real murder happen?" Banks asked.

"September the year before. 1969. By Christ, Banks, you're taking me on a hell of a trip along memory lane today. I haven't thought about that business in years."

Banks knew all about trips down memory lane, having not so long ago looked into the disappearance of an old school friend whose body was found buried in a field outside Peterborough. Sometimes, as he got older, it seemed as if the past was always overwhelming the present.

"Who was the victim?"

"A woman, young girl, really, called Linda Lofthouse. Lovely girl. Funny, I can still picture her there, half-covered by the sleeping bag. That white dress with the flowers embroidered on the front. She had a flower painted on her face, too. A cornflower. She looked so peaceful. She was dead, of course. Someone had grabbed her from behind and stabbed her so viciously he cut off a piece of her heart." He gave a little shudder. "Someone's just walked over my grave."

"How was Swainsview Lodge involved in all this?"

"I'm getting to that. The murder took place at a rock festival in Brimleigh Glen. The body was found on the field by one of the volunteers cleaning up after it was all over. The evidence showed that she was killed in Brimleigh Woods nearby and then moved. It was only made to look as if she was killed on the field."

"I know Brimleigh Glen," said Banks. He had taken his wife, Sandra, and the children, Brian and Tracy, on picnics there shortly after they had moved to Eastvale. "But I know nothing about any festival."

"Probably before your time here," said Enderby. "First weekend of September 1969. Not so long after Woodstock and the Isle of Wight. It wasn't one of the really big ones. It was overshadowed by the others. And it was also the only one they ever held there."

"Who played?"

"The biggest names at the time were Led Zeppelin, Pink Floyd and Fleetwood Mac. The others? Maybe you remember Family, the Incredible String Band, Roy Harper, Blodwyn Pig, Colosseum, the Liverpool Scene, Edgar Broughton and the rest. The usual late-sixties festival lineup."

Banks knew all those names, even had a number of their CDs, or used to have. He would have to work harder at building up his collection again, instead of just buying new stuff or recent reissues. He needed to make a note whenever he missed something he used to have. "How were the Mad Hatters involved?" he asked.

"They were one of the two local bands to play there, along with Jan Dukes de Grey. The Hatters were just getting big at the time, in late 1969, and it was a pivotal gig for them."

"You've followed their career since then?" said Banks.

Enderby raised his glass. "Of course. I was more into blues back then – still am, really – but I got all their records. I mean, I met them, got a signed album. It was a big thrill. Even if I didn't get to keep it." He smiled at a distant memory.

"Why didn't you get to keep it?"

"DI Chadwick took it for his daughter. Good Lord, Chiller Chadwick. I haven't thought of him in years. What a cold, hard bastard he was to work for. Tough Scot, ex-army, hard as nails. The old school, you know, stickler for detail. Always perfectly turned out. You could see your reflection in his brogues. That sort of thing. I'm afraid I was a bit of a rebel back then. Let my hair grow down to my collar. He didn't like it one bit. Good detective, though. I learned a lot from Chiller Chadwick. And he did apologize about the LP, I'll give him that."

"What happened to him?"

"No idea. Retired, I suppose. Maybe dead now. He was quite a few years older than me. Fought in the war. And he was with West Yorkshire, see. Leeds. They didn't reckon we'd got anyone bright enough up here to solve a murder, and they might have been right at that. Anyway, I heard there was some sort of trouble with his daughter, and it affected his health."

"What sort of trouble?"

"I don't know. She went away to stay with relatives. I never met her. I think perhaps she was a bit of a wild child, though, and he wouldn't stand for that, Chiller wouldn't. You know what some of the kids were like back then, smoking marijuana, dropping acid, sleeping around. Anyway, whatever it was, he kept it under his hat. You should talk to his driver, if he's still around."

"Who's that?"

"Young lad called Bradley. Simon Bradley. He was a DC then, Chiller's driver. But now, who knows? Probably a chief constable."

"Why do you say that?"

"Bit of an arse-licker. They always get ahead, don't they?"

"What was Chadwick's first name?"

"Stanley."

Banks thought that Templeton or Winsome ought to be able to track Simon Bradley down easily enough, and if Leeds was involved, he might be able to enlist the help of DI Ken Blackstone to find out about Chadwick. He offered Enderby another drink, which Enderby accepted. Banks's pint glass, fortunately, was still half-full.

"I take it this murder was solved?" Banks asked when he returned with the drink.

"Oh, yes. We got him, all right."

"So back to how the Mad Hatters and Swainsview Lodge were involved."

"Oh, yes, forgot about that, didn't I? Well, Vic Greaves was the victim's cousin, see, and he'd arranged for her and her friend to get backstage passes for the festival. While she was backstage during Led Zeppelin's performance on the last night, this cousin, Linda Lofthouse, decided to take a walk in the woods by herself. That's where she was killed."

"Any sexual motive?"

"She wasn't raped, if that's what you mean. They did find

some semen on the back of her dress, though, so what he did obviously gave him some sort of thrill. Secretor. Mind you, it was a common enough blood group. A, if I remember correctly, same as the victim's. We didn't have DNA and all that fancy forensic technology back then, so we had to rely on good old-fashioned police work."

"Did you recover the murder weapon?"

"Eventually. Complete with traces of group A blood and the killer's fingerprints."

"Very handy. I suppose he could have argued that it was his own blood. It was *his* knife after all."

"He could have, but he didn't. Our forensics blokes were good. They also found traces of white fibre and a strand of dyed cotton wedged between the blade and the handle. These were eventually linked to the victim's dress. There was no doubt about it. The dye on its own was enough."

"Seems pretty much cut and dried then."

"It was. I told you. Anyway, a week or so later, the Mad Hatters were up at Swainsview rehearsing for a tour, so that was the first time I went there and met them."

"Tell me a little bit more about the personalities involved."

"Well, Vic Greaves was mad as a hatter, no doubt about it. When we tried to talk to him at Swainsview Lodge, he was practically incoherent. You know, he'd keep going, like, 'If you go down to the woods today . . .' Remember 'The Teddy Bears' Picnic'?"

Banks did remember. He had even heard another version of it recently when Vic Greaves said to him, "Vic's gone down to the woods today." Coincidence? He would have to find out. Greaves hadn't been particularly coherent during the rest of their chat in Lyndgarth the other day, either. "Was he on drugs at the time?" Banks asked.

"He was on something, that's for certain. Most of the people around him said he took LSD like it was Smarties. Maybe he did."

"What about the rest of them?"

"The others weren't too bad. Adrian Pritchard, the drummer, was a bit of a wild man, you know, wrecking hotel rooms on tour, getting into fights and that sort of thing, but he settled down. Reg Cooper, of course, well, he was the quiet one. He became one of the best, most respected guitarists in the business. Great songwriter, too, and along with Terry Watson, the rhythm guitarist and lead singer, he pushed the band in a more pop direction. Robin Merchant always seemed the brightest of the bunch to me, though. He was educated, well read, articulate, but a bit weird in his tastes, you know, he was into all that occult stuff – magic, tarot, astrology, Aleister Crowley, Carlos Castaneda – but lots of them were back then."

"What about Chris Adams?"

"Seemed a nice enough bloke both occasions I met him. A bit straighter than the rest, maybe, but still one of the 'beautiful people,' if you catch my drift."

"Did they all take drugs?"

"They all smoked a lot of dope and did acid. Robin Merchant obviously got into mandies in a big way, and later both Reg Cooper and Terry Watson had their problems with heroin and coke, but they're clean now, as far as I know, have been for years. I'm not sure about Chris. I don't think he was as much into it as the rest of them. Probably had to keep his wits about him for all the organizing managers have to do."

"I suppose so," said Banks. "Are you still in touch?"

"Good Lord, no. They wouldn't know me from Adam. The bumbling, awestruck young detective who came around asking bothersome questions? They didn't even remember me from the first time when I went there over Robin Merchant's death. But I tried to keep up with their careers, you know. You do when you've actually met someone as famous as that, don't you? I got to meet Pink Floyd, you know. And The Nice. Roy Harper, too. Now *he* was stoned. They live in Los Angeles these days, most of the Mad Hatters. Except Tania, I think."

"Tania Hutchison? The singer they brought in after Merchant died and Vic Greaves drifted off?"

"Yes. Beautiful girl. Absolutely stunning."

Banks remembered lusting after Tania Hutchison when he'd watched her on *The Old Grey Whistle Test* in the early seventies. Every young male did. "I seem to remember reading that she lives in Oxfordshire, or somewhere like that," Banks said.

"Yes, the proverbial country manor. Well, she can afford it."

"You actually met her? I thought she came on the scene much later, after all that mess with Merchant and Greaves?"

"Sort of. See, she was the manager's girlfriend at the time. Chris Adams. She was with him when we went to investigate Robin Merchant's drowning. They were in bed together at the time. I interviewed her the next morning. She wasn't looking her best, of course, a bit the worse for wear, but she still put the rest to shame."

"So Tania and Chris Adams provided one another with alibis?"

"Yes."

"And you had no reason to disbelieve them?"

"Like I said before, I had no real reason to disbelieve any of them."

"How long had she known Adams and the group?"

"I can't say for certain, but she'd been around for a while before Merchant died," Enderby said. "I know she was at the

Brimleigh Festival with Linda Lofthouse. They were friends. I
reckon that was where Adams met her. She and Linda lived in
London. Notting Hill. Practically flatmates. And they played
and sang together in local clubs. Folk sort of stuff."

"Interesting," said Banks. "I'll have to have a look into this
Linda Lofthouse business."

"Well, it was a murder, but there's no mystery about it."

"Oh, I don't know," said Banks. "And there's still the little
matter of who killed Nick Barber, and why."

Sunday, September 21, 1969
Chadwick could tell right from the start that McGarrity was
not like the others, who had been quickly bound over to
appear before the magistrate first thing Monday morning and
released on police bail. No, McGarrity was another kettle of
fish entirely.

For a start, like Rick Hayes, he was older than the rest.
Probably in his early to mid-thirties, Chadwick estimated. He
also had the unmistakable shiftiness of a habitual criminal
and a pallor that, experience had taught Chadwick, came only
from spending time in prison. There was something sly about
him behind the smirk, and a deadness in his eyes that gave off
danger signals. Just the kind of nutter who likely killed Linda
Lofthouse, Chadwick reckoned. Now all he needed was a confession, and evidence.

They were sitting in a stark, windowless room, redolent of
other men's sweat and fear, the ceiling filmed brownish yellow
from years of cigarette smoke. On the scarred wooden desk
between them sat a battered and smudged green tin ashtray
bearing the Tetley's name and logo. DC Bradley sat in a corner
to the left of, and behind, McGarrity, taking notes. Chadwick
intended to conduct this preliminary interview himself, but if

he met stubborn opposition, he would bring in someone else later to help him chip away at the suspect's resistance. It had worked before and it would work again, he was certain, even with as slippery looking a customer as McGarrity.

"Name?" he asked finally.

"Patrick McGarrity."

"Date of birth?"

"The sixth of January, 1936. I'm Capricorn."

"Good for you. Ever been in prison, Patrick?"

McGarrity just stared at him.

"Not to worry," said Chadwick. "We'll find out one way or another. Do you know why you're here?"

"Because you bastards smashed the door down in the middle of the night and brought me here?"

"Good guess. I suppose you know we found drugs in the house?"

McGarrity shrugged. "Nothing to do with me."

"As a matter of fact," Chadwick went on. "They do have something to do with you. My officers found a significant amount of cannabis resin in the same room where they found you asleep. Over two ounces, in fact. Easily enough to sustain a dealing charge."

"That wasn't mine. It wasn't even my room. I was just crashing there for the night."

"What's your address?"

"I'm a free spirit. I go where I choose."

"No fixed abode, then. Place of employment?"

McGarrity emitted a harsh laugh.

"Unemployed. Do you claim benefits?"

Silence.

"I'll take it that you do, then. Otherwise there might be charges under the vagrancy act."

McGarrity leaned back in his chair and crossed his legs. His clothes looked old and worn, like a tramp's, Chadwick noticed, not like the bright peacock fashions the others favoured. And everything he wore was black, or close to it. "Look," he said, "why don't you just cut the crap and get it over with? If you're going to charge me and put me in a cell, do it."

"All in good time, Patrick. All in good time. Back to the cannabis. Where did it come from?"

"Ask your pig friends. They must have planted it."

"Nobody planted anything. Where did it come from?"

"I don't know."

"Okay. Tell me about this afternoon."

"What about it?"

"What did you do?"

"I don't remember. Not much. Read a book. Went for a walk."

"Do you remember receiving a visitor?"

"Can't say as I do."

"A young woman."

"No."

Chadwick's muscles were aching from keeping the rage inside. He felt like flinging himself across the table and strangling McGarrity with his bare hands. "A woman you terrorized and assaulted?"

"I didn't do any such thing."

"You deny the young woman was in the house?"

"I don't remember seeing anyone."

Chadwick stood up so quickly he knocked over his chair. "I've had enough of this, constable," he said to Bradley. "Take him down and lock him up." He glared at McGarrity for a second before he left and said, "We'll talk again, and the next time it won't be so polite." Outside in the corridor, he leaned against the wall and took several deep breaths. His heart was beating like a steam piston inside his chest, and he could feel his skin burning. Slowly, as he mopped his brow, the rage subsided. He straightened his tie and jacket and walked back to his office.

15

Detective Sergeant Kevin Templeton relished his latest assignment, and even more he relished the fact that Winsome was to accompany him as an observer. Even though he had got nowhere with Winsome, not for lack of trying, he still found her incredibly attractive, and the sight of her thighs under the taut material of her pinstripe trousers still brought him out in a sweat. He'd always thought of himself as a breast man, but Winsome had soon put the lie to that. He tried not to make his glances obvious as she drove out of town and onto the main Lyndgarth road. The farmhouse was at the end of a long, muddy track, and no matter how close to the door they parked, there was no way of avoiding getting their shoes muddy.

"Christ, it bloody stinks here, dunnit?" Templeton moaned.

"It's a farmyard," said Winsome.

"Yeah, I know that. Look, let me do the questioning, right? And you keep a close eye on the father, okay?" Templeton hopped on one leg by the doorway, trying to wipe some of the mud off his best pair of Converse trainers.

"There's a shoe scraper," said Winsome.

"What?"

She pointed. "That thing there with the raised metal edge, by the door. It's for scraping the mud off the undersides of your shoes."

"Well, you live and learn," said Templeton, making a try at the shoe scraper. "Whatever will they think of next?"

"They thought of it a long time ago," said Winsome.

"I know that. I was being sarcastic."

"Yes, sir."

Nearby, a dog was growling and barking fit to kill, but luckily it was chained up to a post.

Templeton shot Winsome a glance. "No need for you to be sarcastic as well. Don't think I didn't catch your tone. Are you okay with the way the super wants us to play it?"

"I'm fine."

Templeton's eyes narrowed. "Am I to take it you don't –"

But before he could finish, the door opened and Calvin Soames stood there. "Police, isn't it?" he said. "What do you want this time?"

"Just come to clear a couple of things up, Mr. Soames," said Templeton, bringing out his best smile and offering his hand. Soames ignored it. "Is your daughter at home?"

Soames grunted.

"All right if we come in?"

"Wipe your feet." And with that he turned back into the gloom and left them to their own devices.

After further wiping their feet on a bristly mat, they followed him into the inner recesses of the house and heard him call out, "Kelly! It's for you."

The girl came downstairs, and her face registered disappointment when she saw Templeton and Winsome standing there in the hallway. "You'd better come through," she said, leading them into the kitchen, which was marginally brighter and smelled of bleach and overripe bananas. A black-and-white cat stirred lazily, jumped off its chair and sidled out of the room.

They all sat on sturdy hard-backed chairs around the table. Calvin Soames muttered something about work and headed out, but Templeton called him back. "This concerns you, too, Mr. Soames," he said. "Please sit down."

Soames let a moment pass, then sat.

"What's this all about?" asked Kelly. "I've told you everything already."

"Well, that's just it, you see," said Templeton. "Being the untrusting detectives that we are, we don't take anything at face value, or on first account. It's like first impressions, see, they can so often be wrong. Any chance of a cup of tea?"

"I'll put the kettle on," said Kelly.

She was definitely fit, Templeton thought, as he watched her move towards the range with just the barest swinging of her hips, encased in tight jeans. Her waist was slender as a wand, and she wore a jet belly piercing, which made a nice contrast to her pale skin. Her blonde hair was tied back, but a few tresses had escaped and framed her pale, oval face. Her breasts moved tantalizingly under the short yellow T-shirt, and Templeton guessed that she wasn't wearing a bra. Lucky bugger, that Barber, Templeton thought. If the last thing on earth he had done was shag Kelly Soames, then it can't have been such a bad way to go. He began to wonder if, perhaps when they'd got this business over and done with, he might be in with a chance himself.

When the tea was served, Winsome took out her notebook and Templeton sat back in his chair. "Right," he said. "Now, you, Mr. Soames, returned back here at about seven o'clock on Friday evening. Am I right?"

"That's right."

"To check if you'd turned off the gas ring?"

"It's sometimes on so low," he answered, "that a puff of air would blow it out. A couple of times I've come home and smelled gas. I thought it best to check, as I don't live far from the Cross Keys."

"About a five-minute drive each way, is that right?"

"About that, aye."

"And you, Miss Soames, you were working at the Cross Keys all evening, right?"

Kelly chewed her thumbnail and nodded.

"How long have you been working there?"

"About two years now. There's not much else to do around here."

"Ever thought of moving to the big city?"

Kelly looked at her father and said, "No."

"Nice place to work, is it, the Cross Keys?"

"It's all right."

"Good spot to meet lads?"

"I don't know what you mean."

"Oh, come on, Kelly. You're a barmaid. You must meet lots of lads, get chatted up a lot, nice-looking girl like you."

She blushed at that, and the ghost of a smile crossed her face, Templeton noticed. Maybe he was in with a chance after all. As Calvin Soames looked on, the frown deepened on his forehead in a series of lines down to the bridge of his nose.

"Do they tell you their troubles?" Templeton went on. "How their wives don't understand them and they're wasted on the jobs they're doing?"

Kelly shrugged. "Sometimes," she said. "When it's quiet."

"What do you do for fun?"

"Dunno. Go out with my mates, I suppose."

"But where do you go? There's not exactly a lot for a young girl to do around here, is there? It can't be very exciting."

"There's Eastvale."

"Oh, yes. I'm sure you enjoy a Saturday night out in Eastvale with the lads, listening to dirty jokes, getting bladdered and puking your guts up with the rest of them around the market cross. No, I mean, a girl like you, there must be something better, something more. Surely?"

"There's dances sometimes, and bands," Kelly said.

"Who do you like?"

"Dunno."

"Come on, you must have a favourite."

She shifted in her chair. "I dunno, really. Keane. Maybe."

"Ah, Keane."

"You know them?"

"I've heard them," said Templeton. "Nick Barber was really into bands, wasn't he?"

Kelly seemed to tense up again. "He said he liked music," she said.

"Didn't he say he could get you into all the best concerts down in London?"

"I don't think so. I've never been to London."

Templeton felt Winsome's gaze boring into the side of his head. Her legs were crossed, and one of them was twitching. She clearly didn't like the way he was drawing the interview out, postponing the moment of glory. But he was enjoying himself. He closed in for the kill.

"Did Nick Barber promise to take you there?"

"No." Kelly shook her head, panic showing on her face. "Why would he do that?"

"Gratitude, perhaps?"

Calvin Soames's face darkened. "What are you saying, man?"

Templeton ignored him. "Well, Kelly?"

"I don't know what you're on about. I only talked to him at the bar when he ordered his drink. He was nice, polite. That's all."

"Oh, come off it, Kelly," said Templeton. "We happen to know that you slept with him on two occasions."

"What —" Calvin Soames tried to get to his feet, but Templeton gently pushed him back down. "Please stay where you are, Mr. Soames."

"What's this all about?" Soames demanded. "What's going on?"

"Wednesday evening and Friday afternoon," Templeton went on. "A bit of afternoon delight. Beats the dentist's any day, I'd say."

Kelly was crying now and her father was fast turning purple with fury. "Is this true, Kelly?" he asked. "Is what he's saying true?"

Kelly buried her face in her hands. "I feel sick," she said between her fingers.

"Is this true?" her father demanded.

"Yes! All right, damn you, yes!" she said, glaring at Templeton. Then she turned to her father. "He fucked me, Daddy. I let him fuck me. I *liked* it."

"You whoring slut!" Soames raised his hand to slap her, but Winsome grabbed it first. "Not a good idea, Mr. Soames," she said.

Templeton looked at Soames. "Are you telling me you didn't already know this, Mr. Soames?" he said.

Soames bared his teeth. "If I'd've known, I'd have . . ."

"You'd have what?" Templeton asked, shoving his face close to Soames's. "Beat up your daughter? Killed Nick Barber?"

"What?"

"You heard me. Is that what you did? You found out what Kelly had been doing, and you waited until she was back working behind the bar, then you made an excuse to leave the pub for a few minutes. You went to see Barber. What happened? Did he laugh at you? Did he tell you how good she was? Or did he say she meant nothing to him, just another shag? Was the bed still warm from their lovemaking? You hit him over the head with a poker. Maybe you didn't mean to kill him. Maybe something just snapped inside you. It happens. But there he was, dead on the floor. Is that how it happened, Calvin? If you tell us now, it'll go better for you. I'm sure a judge and jury will understand a father's righteous anger."

Kelly lurched over to the sink and just made it in time. Winsome held her shoulders as the girl heaved.

"Well?" said Templeton. "Am I right?"

Soames deflated into a sad, defeated old man, all the anger drained out of him. "No," he said, without inflection. "I didn't kill anyone. I had no idea . . ." He looked at Kelly bent over the sink, tears in his eyes. "Not till now. She's no better than her mother was," he added bitterly.

Nobody said anything for a while. Kelly finished vomiting and Winsome poured her a glass of water. They sat down at the table again. Her father wouldn't look at her. Finally, Templeton got to his feet. "Well, Mr. Soames," he said. "If you change your mind, you know where to get in touch with us.

And in the meantime, as they say in the movies, don't leave town." He pointed at Kelly. "Nor you, young lady."

But nobody was looking at him, or paying attention. They were all lost in their own worlds of misery, pain and betrayal That would pass, though, Templeton knew, and he'd see Kelly Soames again under better circumstances, he was certain of it.

Outside at the car, dodging the puddles and mud as best he could, Templeton turned to Winsome, rubbed his hands together and said, "Well, I think that went pretty well. What do you think, Winsome? Do you think he knew?"

Banks had a great deal of information to digest, he thought, as he parked down by the Co-Op store at the inner harbour and walked towards the shops and restaurants of West Cliff. He passed a reconstruction of the yellow and black HMS *Grand Turk*, used in the *Hornblower* TV series, and stood for a moment admiring the sails and rigging. What a hell of a life it must have been at sea back then, he thought. Maybe not so bad if you were an officer, but for the common sailor, the bad, maggot-infested food, the floggings, the terrible wounds of battle, butchery thinly disguised as surgery. Of course, he'd got most of his ideas from *Hornblower* and *Master and Commander*, but they seemed pretty accurate to him, and if they weren't, how would he know?

Thinking back on what Keith Enderby had just told him, he realized he would have been living in Notting Hill at around the same time as Linda Lofthouse and Tania Hutchison. He was sure he would have remembered seeing someone as beautiful as Tania, even though she wasn't famous then, but he couldn't. There were, he remembered, a lot of beautiful young women in colourful clothes around at the time, and he had met his fair share of them.

But Tania and Linda would have moved in very different circles. Banks didn't know anyone in a band, for a start; he paid for all his concert tickets, like everyone else he knew. He also didn't have the musical talent to perform in local clubs, though he often went to listen to those who did. But most of all, perhaps, was that he had always felt like an outsider, had felt somehow merely on the fringes of it all. He never wore his hair too long, couldn't get much beyond wearing a flowered shirt or tie, let alone kaftans and beads, couldn't bring himself to join in the political demonstrations, and most times he found himself involved in any sort of counterculture conversation, he thought it all sounded simplistic, childish and boring.

Banks leaned on the railing and watched the fishing boats bobbing at anchor in the harbour, then walked to a café he remembered that served excellent fish and chips, one thing you could usually rely on in Whitby. He went into the café, which was almost empty, and ordered a pot of tea and jumbo haddock and chips, with bread and butter for chip butties, from a bored young waitress in a black apron and white blouse.

He sat down at the window, which looked out over the harbour to the old part of town, with its 199 steps leading up to the ruined abbey and St. Mary's Church, where the salt wind had robbed the tombstones of their names. A group of young goths, all black clothes, white faces and intricate silver jewellery, walked by the sheds where the fishermen unloaded their boats and sold their catch.

From what Banks had read about them, and the music he had heard, they seemed obsessed with death and suicide, as well as with the undead and the "dark side" in general, but they were passive and pacifist and concerned with social matters, such as racism and war. Banks liked Joy Division, and he had heard them described as the archetypal goth band. On balance, he thought, goths were no weirder than the hippies had been, with their fascination with the occult, poetry and drug-induced enlightenment.

1969 was a period of great transition for Banks. After leaving school with a couple of decent A levels, he was living in a bedsit in Notting Hill and taking a course in business studies in London. He hadn't felt much in common with his fellow students, though, so he had tended to fall in with a crowd from the art college, two of whom lived together in the same building as him, and they formed his real introduction, rather late in the day, to that strange blend of existentialism, communalism, hedonism and narcissism that was his take on late-sixties culture. They shared joints with him and Jem from across the hall, went to concerts and poetry readings, discussed squatters' rights, Vietnam and *Oz* and played "Alice's Restaurant" over and over again.

Banks had no idea what to do with his life. His parents had made it clear that they wanted him to have a crack at a white-collar career, rather than ending up in the brick factory, or the sheet-metal factory like his father, so business studies seemed like a logical step. And he did so much need to escape the stifling provinciality of Peterborough.

He loved the music and had hitchhiked with his first real girlfriend, Kay Summerville, to the Blind Faith concert in Hyde Park the summer of that year, when he was still living at home in Peterborough, and to the Rolling Stones concert in memory of Brian Jones, at which Mick Jagger freed all the caged butterflies that hadn't already died from the heat. He also remembered Dylan at the Isle of Wight, coming on late and singing "She Belongs to Me" and "To Ramona," two of Banks's favourites.

But in Peterborough, he had been fairly isolated from the trendy fashions, causes and ideologies of the times, embarrassingly ignorant of what was really happening out there. For all the hyped-up change and revolution of the decade, it was a salutary lesson to bear in mind that "Strawberry Fields Forever" was kept from reaching number one by Engelbert Humperdinck's "Release Me," and growing up in Peterborough, you could easily see why.

That first college year, he remembered following with horror the saga of the Manson "family," eventually arrested for the murders of Sharon Tate, Leno LaBianca and others. It had all passed into the history books now, of course, but then, as the story unfolded day by day in the newspapers and on television, and as the real horrors came to light, it had a powerful impact, not least because the Manson family seemed a bit like hippies and quoted the Beatles and revolutionary slogans. And then there were the girls, Manson's "love slaves," with strange names like Patricia Krenwinkel, "Squeaky" Fromme and Leslie Van Houten. The way they dressed and wore their hair, they might have been living in Notting Hill. The famous photo of the bearded, staring Manson had given Banks almost as many nightmares as the one of Christine Keeler sitting naked on a chair had prompted wet dreams.

Altamont had taken place in late 1969, too, he remembered, where someone was stabbed by a Hell's Angel during the Stones' performance. There were other things he vaguely remembered – the police charging a house in Piccadilly to evict squatters, rioting in Northern Ireland, stories of women and children murdered by American troops in My Lai, violent anti-war protests, four students shot by the National Guard at Kent State.

Maybe it was hindsight, but things seemed to be taking a turn for the worse back then, falling apart, or perhaps that had been happening for a while, and he had only just noticed because he was there, in the thick of it. He probably wouldn't have noticed the change in political climate if he'd stayed in Peterborough. Perhaps the business career would have worked out if he hadn't got caught up in the tail end of the sixties in Notting Hill. As it was, by the end of his first year, he had lost all interest in cost accounting, industrial psychology and mercantile law.

But he had no memory of hearing about the murder of a girl at a festival in Yorkshire. Back then, the provinces, especially in the north, were of little interest to those at the centre of things, and local police forces worked far more independently of one another than they did today. He wondered if Enderby was right about Linda Lofthouse's murder being the one Nick Barber had referred to. He had been so certain it was Robin Merchant, and he still wasn't ruling that possibility out. But the news about Linda Lofthouse brought a whole new complexion to things, even if her murder had been solved. Was the killer still in jail? If not, could he somehow be involved in Nick Barber's death? The more Banks thought about it, no matter what Catherine Gervaise said, the more he thought he was right, and that Barber had died for digging up the past, which someone wanted to remain buried.

Banks noticed a few clouds drift in from the east as he ate his haddock and chips, and by the time he had finished, it was starting to drizzle. He paid, left a small tip and headed for his car. Before he set off, he phoned Ken Blackstone in Leeds and asked him to find out what he could about Stanley Chadwick and the Linda Lofthouse investigation.

Sunday, September 21, 1969

Steve answered the door late that Sunday afternoon, and when he saw Yvonne standing there, he turned away and walked down the hall. "I never thought I'd see you again," he said. "You've got a bloody nerve showing up here."

Yvonne followed him into the living room. "But, Steve, it wasn't my fault. It was McGarrity. He tried to force himself on me. He's dangerous. You've got to believe me. I didn't know what to do."

Steve turned to face her. "So you went straight to daddy."

"I was upset. I didn't know what I was doing."

"You never told me your father was a pig."

"You never asked. Besides, what does it matter?"

"What does it matter? He violated our space. Him and the others. We got busted. That's what matters. Now we're going to have to go to court tomorrow morning. I'll get a fine at least. And if my parents find out, I'm fucked. They'll stop my allowance. That's all down to you."

"But it wasn't my fault, Steve. I'm sorry, really I am. I didn't know they were going to bust you." Yvonne moved towards him and reached out to touch him.

He jerked away and sat down in the armchair. "Oh, come off it. You must have known damn well we'd be sitting around here smoking a few joints and listening to music. It's not as if you haven't done it with us often enough."

Yvonne knelt at his feet. "But I never sent them here. Honestly. I thought they would just arrest McGarrity, that's all. You know I'd never do anything to get you in trouble."

"Then you're more stupid than I thought you were. Look, I'm sorry, but I don't want you coming around here anymore. Whether you wanted to or not, you've brought nothing but trouble. Who knows who might follow you?"

Yvonne's heart pounded in her chest. She still had one card to play. "McGarrity told me you've been seeing someone else."

Steve laughed. "If only you could hear yourself."

"Is it true?"

"What if I have?"

"I thought we . . . I mean . . . I didn't . . ."

"Oh, Yvonne, for God's sake, grow up. You sound like such a child sometimes. We can both see whoever we want. I thought that was clear from the start."

"But I don't want to see anyone else. I want to see you."

"What you're really saying is that you don't want me to see anyone else. You can't own someone, Yvonne. You can't control their affections."

"But it's true."

Steve turned away. "Well, I don't want to see you. That's just not on anymore."

"But –"

"I mean it. And you won't be welcome at Bayswater Terrace or Carberry Place, either. They got raided as well, in case you didn't know. People got busted, and they're not happy with you. Word gets around, you know. It's still a small scene."

"So what should I have done? Tell me what I should have done."

"You shouldn't have done anything. You should have kept your stupid mouth shut. You should have known bringing the pigs in would only mean trouble for us."

"But he's my *father*. I had to tell someone. I was so upset, Steve, I was shaking like a leaf. McGarrity . . ."

"I've told you before he's harmless."

"That's not the way he seemed to me."

"You were stoned, the way I hear it. Maybe your imagination was running away with you. Maybe you even wanted him to touch you. Maybe you should run away with your imagination instead."

"I don't know what you're talking about."

Steve sighed. "I can't trust you anymore, Yvonne. *We* can't trust you anymore."

"But I love you, Steve."

"No you don't. Don't be stupid. That's not real love you're talking about, that's just romantic schoolgirl crap. It's possessive love, all jealousy and control, all the negative emotions. You're not mature enough to know what real love is."

Yvonne flinched at his words. She felt herself turn cold all over, as if she had been hit by a bucket of water. "And you are?"

He stood up. "This is a fucking waste of time. Look, I'm not arguing with you anymore. Why don't you just go? And don't come back."

"But, Steve —"

Steve pointed to the door and raised his voice. "Just go. And don't send your father and his piggy friends around here again or you might find yourself in serious trouble."

Yvonne got slowly to her feet. She had never known Steve to look or sound so cruel. "What do you mean?" she asked.

"Never mind. Just fuck off."

Yvonne looked at him. He was bristling with anger. There was clearly going to be no more talking to him. Not this afternoon, maybe not ever. Feeling the tears start to burn down her cheeks, she turned away from him abruptly and left.

"It's not so much what he said or did, Guv," said Winsome, "it was the pleasure he took in doing it."

Annie nodded. She was treating Winsome to an after-work drink in the Black Lion, off an alley behind the market square, away from the prying eyes and ears of Western Area Headquarters. Winsome was visibly upset, and Annie wanted to get to the bottom of it. "Kev can be insensitive at times," she said.

"*Insensitive?*" Winsome took a gulp of her vodka and tonic. "*Insensitive?* It was more like bloody sadistic. I'm sorry, Guv, but I'm still shaking. See?"

She stuck her hand out. Annie could see it was trembling slightly. "Calm down," she said. "Another drink? You're not driving, are you?"

"No. I can walk home from here. I'll have the same again, thanks."

Annie went to the bar and got the drinks. There was nobody else in the place except the barmaid and a couple of her friends at the far end. One of them was playing the machines, and the other was sitting down watching over two toddlers, cigarette in one hand, drink in the other. Every time one of the little boys started to cry or make any sort of noise, she told him to shut up. Time after time. Cry. Shut up. Cry. Shut up. There was a tape of old music playing loudly – "House of the Rising Sun," "The Young Ones," "Say a Little Prayer for Me," "I Remember You" – the sort of stuff Banks would remember, competing with the TV blaring out *Murder She Wrote* on one of the Sky channels. But the noise certainly drowned out anything Annie and Winsome were talking about.

Annie was going to get a Britvic orange for herself, as she had to get back to Harkside, but she was still furious after her session with Superintendent Gervaise, feeling far from calm, and she needed another bloody stiff drink herself, so she ordered a large vodka with her orange juice. If she had too much, she'd leave the car and get one of the PCs to drive her home, or get a taxi if the worst came to the worst. It couldn't cost all that much. She had been thinking of moving to Eastvale recently, as it would be convenient for the job, but house prices there had gone through the roof, and she didn't want to give up her little cottage, even though it was now worth nearly twice what she had paid for it.

Winsome thanked Annie for the drink. "That poor girl," she said.

"Look, Winsome, I know how you feel. I feel just as bad. I'm sure Kelly thinks I'm the one who betrayed her trust. But DS Templeton was only doing his job. Superintendent Gervaise had asked him to check the girl's story against her father's, and that was the way he did it. It might seem harsh to you, but it worked, didn't it?"

"I can't believe you're defending them," Winsome said. She took a gulp of vodka, then put the drink down on the table. "You weren't there or you'd know what I'm talking about. No. I'm not working with him again. You can transfer me. Do what you want. But I won't work with that bastard again." She folded her arms.

Annie sipped her drink and sighed. She had been foreseeing problems ever since Kevin Templeton got his promotion. He had passed his sergeant's boards ages ago, but he didn't want to go back to uniform and he didn't want to transfer, so it took a while for this opportunity to come up. Then he nipped a possible serial killer's career in the bud and became the golden boy. Annie had always found him just a bit too full of himself, and she worried what a little power might do to his already skewed personality. And if he thought she didn't notice the way he had practically drooled down the front of her blouse the other day, then he was seriously deluding himself. The thing was, he got the job done, as he had done now. Banks did, too, but he managed to do it without treading on everyone's toes – only the brass's, usually – but Templeton was one of the new breed; he didn't care. And here was Annie defending him when she knew damn well that Winsome, who had also passed her boards with flying colours and didn't want to leave Eastvale, would have been a much better person for the job. Where is positive discrimination when you really need it? she wondered. Obviously not in Yorkshire.

"I shouldn't have made a promise I couldn't possibly keep," Annie said. "The blame's entirely mine. I should have done it myself." She knew that she had deliberately *not* made any such promise to Kelly Soames, but she felt as if she had.

"Pardon me, Guv, but like I said, you weren't there. Listen to me. He enjoyed it. Enjoyed every minute of it. The humiliation. Taunting her. He drew it out to get more pleasure from it. And in the end he didn't even know what he'd done wrong. I don't know if that's the worst part of it all."

"Okay, Winsome, I'll admit DS Templeton has a few problems."

"A few problems? The man's a sadist. And you know what?"

"What?"

Winsome shifted in her chair. "Don't laugh, but there was something . . . sexual about it."

"Sexual?"

"Yes. I can't explain it, but it was like he was getting off on his power over her."

"Are you certain?"

"I don't know. Maybe it was just me, reading things wrongly. It wouldn't be the first time. But there was something really creepy about the whole thing, even when the girl was being sick –"

"Kelly was physically sick?"

"Yes. I thought I'd told you that."

"No. How did it happen?"

"She was just sick."

"What did DS Templeton do?"

"Just carried on as if everything was normal."

"Have you told anyone else what happened?"

"No, Guv. I'd tell Superintendent Gervaise if I thought it would do any good, but she thinks the sun shines out of Kevin Templeton's arse."

"She does, does she?" That didn't surprise Annie. Just the mention of Gervaise made her bristle. The sanctimonious cow, putting Annie on statement reading, a DC's job at best, and making jibes about her private life.

"Anyway," Winsome went on, "I don't have to put up with it. There's nothing in the book says I have to put up with behaviour like that."

"That's true," said Annie. "But life doesn't always go by the book."

"It does when you agree with what the book says."

Annie laughed. "So what do you want to do about it?"

"Dunno," said Winsome. "Nothing I can do, I suppose. 'Cept I don't want to be near the creep anymore, and if he ever tries anything, I'll beat seven shades of shit out of him."

Annie laughed. The phrase sounded odd coming from Winsome, with her Jamaican lilt. "You can't avoid him all the time," she said. "I mean, I can do my best to make sure you're not paired up or anything, but Superintendent Gervaise can overrule that if she wants, and she seems to want to interfere with our jobs a bit more than Detective Superintendent Gristhorpe did."

"I liked Mr. Gristhorpe," said Winsome. "He was old-fashioned, like my father, and he could be a bit frightening sometimes, but he was fair and he didn't play favourites."

Well, Annie thought, that wasn't strictly true. Banks had certainly been a favourite of Gristhorpe's, but in general Winsome was right. There was a difference between having favourites and playing them. Gristhorpe hadn't set out to build a little empire, pick his teams and set people against one another the way it seemed Gervaise was doing. Nor did he interfere in people's private lives. He must have known about her and Banks, but he hadn't said anything, at least not to her. He might have warned Banks off, she supposed, but if he had, it hadn't affected their relationship either on or off the job.

"Well, Gristhorpe's gone and Gervaise is here," said Annie, "and for better or worse, we've got to live with it." She looked at her watch. She still had half her drink left. "Look, I'd better go, Winsome. I'm not over the limit yet, but I will be if I have any more."

"You can stay at mine, if you like." Winsome looked away. "I'm sorry, Guv, I don't mean to be presumptuous. I mean, you being an inspector and all, my boss, but I've got a spare room. It's just that it helps talking about it, that's all. And I don't know about you, but I feel like getting rat-arsed."

Annie thought for a moment. "What the hell," she said, finishing her drink. "I'll get another round."

"No, you stay there. It's my shout."

Annie sat and watched her walk to the bar, a tall, graceful, long-legged Jamaican beauty about whom she knew . . . well, not very much at all. But then she didn't really know very much about anyone, when it came right down to it, she realized, not even Banks. And as she watched, she smiled to herself. Wouldn't it be funny, she thought, if she did stay at Winsome's and Superintendent Gervaise found out. What would the sad cow make of that?

Monday, September 22, 1969

"But we've got no real evidence, Stan," Detective Chief Superintendent McCullen argued on Monday morning. They were in his office and rain spattered the windows, blurring the view.

Chadwick ran his hand over his hair. He'd thought this out in advance, hadn't done anything else but think it over, all night. He didn't want Yvonne involved; that was the main problem. He had seen the bruise McGarrity had caused on her arm, and it was enough to bring assault charges, but once he went that route, he wouldn't be able to do anything for Yvonne. She was upset enough as it was, and he didn't want to drag her through court. If truth be told, he didn't want his name tainted by his daughter's folly, either. He thought he could make a decent case without her, and he laid it out carefully for McCullen.

"First off, he's got form," he said.

McCullen raised an eyebrow. "Oh?"

"The most recent's for possession of a controlled substance, namely LSD. November 1967."

"Only possession?"

"They think he dumped his stash down the toilet when he heard them coming. Unfortunately, he still had two doses in his pocket."

"You said most recent?"

"Yes. The other's a bit more interesting. March 1958."

"How old was he then?"

"Twenty-two."

"And?"

"Assault causing bodily harm. He stabbed a student in the shoulder during a town-and-gown altercation in Oxford, which apparently is where he comes from. Unfortunately the student happened to be the son of a local member of Parliament."

"Ouch," said McCullen, a sly smile touching his lips.

"It didn't help that McGarrity was a Teddy boy as well. Apparently the judge didn't like teds. Threw the book at him. He was a Brasenose man, too, same as the student. Gave McGarrity eighteen months. If the wound had been more serious, and if it hadn't been inflicted defensively during a scuffle – apparently the gown lot were carrying cricket bats, among other weapons – then he'd have got five years or more. Another interesting point," Chadwick went on, "is that the weapon used was a flick knife."

"The same weapon used on the girl?"

"Same *kind* of weapon."

"Go on."

"There's not much more," Chadwick said. "We spent yesterday interviewing the people at the three houses who knew McGarrity. He definitely knew the victim."

"How well?"

"There's no evidence of any sort of relationship, and from what I've found out about Linda Lofthouse, I very much doubt that there was one. But he knew her."

"Anything else?"

"Everyone said he was an odd duck. They often didn't understand what he was talking about, and he had a habit of playing with a flick knife."

"What kind of flick knife?"

"Just a flick knife, with a tortoiseshell handle."

"Why did they put up with him?"

"If you ask me, sir, it's down to drugs. Our lads found five ounces of cannabis resin hidden in the gas meter at Carberry Place. Apparently the lock was broken. We think it belonged to McGarrity."

"Defrauding the gas company, too, I'll bet?"

Chadwick smiled. "Same shilling, again and again. The drugs squad thinks he's a mid-level dealer, buys a few ounces now and then and splits them up into quid deals. Probably what he used the knife for."

"So the kids tolerate him?"

"Yes, sir. He was also at the festival, and according to the people he went with, he spent most of the time roaming the crowd on his own. No one can say where he was when the incident occurred."

McCullen tapped his pipe on the ashtray, then said, "The knife?"

"No sign of it yet, sir."

"Pity."

"Yes. I suppose it might be a coincidence that McGarrity simply lost his knife around the same time a young woman was stabbed with a similar weapon, but we've gone to court with less before."

"Aye. And lost from time to time."

"Well, the judge has bound him over on the dealing charge. No fixed abode, so no bail. He's all ours."

"Then get cracking and build up a murder case if you think you've got one. But don't get tunnel vision here, Stan. Don't forget that other bloke you fancied for it."

"Rick Hayes? We're still looking into him."

"Good. And, Stan?"

"Yes, sir?"

"Find the knife. It would really help."

Some people, Banks realized, never travel very far from where they grow up, and Simon Bradley was one of them. He had, he said, transferred several times during his career, to Suffolk, Cumbria and Nottingham, but he had ended up back in Leeds, and when he had retired in 2000 at the age of fifty-six and at the rank of superintendent, Traffic, he and his wife had settled in a nice detached stone-built house just off Shaw Lane in Headingley. It was, he told Banks, only a stone's throw from where he grew up in more lowly Meanwood. Beyond the high green gate was a well-tended garden that, Bradley said, was his wife's pride and joy. Bradley's pride and joy, it turned out, was a small library of floor-to-ceiling shelves, where he kept his collection of first-edition crime and thriller fiction, primarily Dick Francis, Ian Fleming, Len Deighton, Ruth Rendell, P.D. James and Colin Dexter. It was there that he sat with Banks over coffee and talked about his early days at Brotherton House. Sitting in the peaceful, book-lined room, Banks found it hard to believe that just down the road was Hyde Park, where one of that summer's suicide bombers had lived.

"I was young," Bradley said, "twenty-five in 1969, but I was never really one of that generation." He laughed. "I suppose that would have been difficult, wouldn't it, being a hippie and a copper at the same time? Sort of like being on both sides at once."

"I'm a few years behind you," said Banks, "but I did like the music. Still do."

"Really? Dreadful racket," said Bradley. "I've always been more of a classical man myself: Mozart, Beethoven, Bach."

"I like them, too," said Banks, "but sometimes you can't beat a bit of Jimi Hendrix."

"Each to his own. I suppose I always associated the music too closely with the lifestyle and the things that went on back then," Bradley said with distaste. "A soundtrack for the drugs, long hair, promiscuity. I was something of a young fogey, a *square*, I suppose, and now I've grown up into an old fogey. I went to church every Sunday, kept my hair cut short and believed in waiting until you were married before having sex. Still do, much to my son's chagrin. Very unfashionable."

Bradley was almost ten years older than Banks, and he was in good physical shape. There was no extra flab on him the way there had been on Enderby, and he still had a fine head of hair. He was wearing white trousers and a shirt with a grey V-neck pullover, a bit like a cricketer, Banks thought, or the way cricketers used to look before they became walking multicoloured advertisements for everything from mobile phones to trainers.

"Did you get on well with DI Chadwick?" Banks asked, remembering Enderby's description of "Chiller" as cold and hard.

"After a fashion," said Bradley. "DI Chadwick wasn't an easy man to get close to. He'd had certain . . . experiences . . . during the war, and he tended towards long silences you didn't dare interrupt. He never spoke about it – the war – but you knew it was there, defining him, in a way, as it did many of that generation. But, yes, I suppose I got along with him as well as anyone."

"Do you remember the Linda Lofthouse case?"

"As if it were yesterday. Bound to happen eventually."

"What was?"

"What happened to her. Linda Lofthouse. Bound to. I mean, all those people rolling in the mud on LSD and God knows what. Bound to revert to their primitive natures at some point, weren't they? Strip away that thin but essential veneer of civilization and convention, of obedience and order, and what do you get — the beast within, Mr. Banks, the beast within. Someone was bound to get hurt. Stands to reason. I'm only surprised there wasn't more of it."

"But what do you think it was about Linda Lofthouse that got her killed?"

"At first, when I saw her there in the sleeping bag, you know, with her dress bunched up, I must confess I thought it was probably a sex murder. She had that look about her, you know?"

"What look?"

"A lot of young girls had it then. As if she'd invite you into her sleeping bag as soon as look at you."

"But she was dead."

"Well, yes, of course. I know that." Bradley gave a nervous laugh. "I mean, I'm not a necrophiliac or anything. I'm just telling you the first impression I had of her. Turned out it wasn't a sex crime after all, but some madman. As I said, bound to happen when you encourage deviant behaviour. She'd had an illegitimate baby, you know."

"Linda Lofthouse?"

"Yes. She was on the pill when we found her, like most of them, of course, but obviously not when she was fifteen. Gave it up for adoption in 1967."

"Did anyone find out what became of the child?"

"It didn't concern us. We tracked down the father, a kid called Donald Hughes, garage mechanic, and he gave us a couple of ideas as to the sort of life Linda was leading and where she was living it, but he had an alibi, and he had no motive. He'd moved on. Got a proper job, wanted nothing to do with Linda and her hippie lifestyle. That was why they split up in the first place. If she hadn't been seduced by that corrupt lifestyle, the baby might have grown up with a proper mother and father."

The child's identity might be an issue now, Banks thought. A child born in the late sixties would be in his late thirties now, and if he had discovered what had happened to his birth mother... Nick Barber was thirty-eight, but he was the victim. Banks was confusing too many crimes: Lofthouse, Merchant, Barber. He had to get himself in focus. At least the connection between Barber and Lofthouse was something he could check into and not come away looking too much of a fool if he was wrong.

"What was the motive?"

"We never found out. He was a nutcase."

"That being the technical term for a psychopath back then?"

"It's what we used to call them," Bradley said, "but I suppose psychopath or sociopath – I never did know the difference – would be more politically correct."

"He confessed to the murder?"

"As good as."

"What do you mean?"

"He didn't deny it when faced with the evidence."

"The knife, right?"

"With his fingerprints and Linda Lofthouse's blood on it."

"How did this person – what's his name, by the way?"

"McGarrity. Patrick McGarrity."

"How did this McGarrity first come to your attention?"

"We found out that the victim was known at various houses around the city where students and dropouts lived and sold drugs. McGarrity frequented these same places, was a drug dealer, in fact, which was what we first arrested him for after a raid."

"And then DI Chadwick became suspicious?"

"Well, yes. We heard that McGarrity was a bit of a nutcase, and even the people whose houses he frequented were a bit frightened of him. There was a lot of tolerance for weird types back then, especially if they provided people with drugs, which is why I say I'm surprised these things didn't happen more often. This McGarrity clearly had severe mental problems. Dropped on the head at birth, for all I know. He was older than the rest, for a start, and he also had a criminal record and a history of violence. He had a habit of playing with this flick knife. It used to make people nervous, which was no doubt the effect he wanted. There was also some talk about him terrorizing a young girl. He was a thoroughly unpleasant character."

"Did this other young girl come forward?"

"No. It was just something that came up during questioning. McGarrity denied it. We got him on the other charges, and that gave us all we needed."

"You met him?"

"I sat in on some of the interviews. Look, I don't know why you want to know all this now. There's no doubt he did it."

"I'm not doubting it," said Banks. "I'm just trying to find a reason for Nick Barber's murder."

"Well, it's got nothing to do with McGarrity."

"Nick Barber was writing about the Mad Hatters," Banks went on, "and Vic Greaves was Linda Lofthouse's cousin."

"The one that went bonkers?"

"If you care to put it that way, yes," said Banks.

"How else would you put it? Anyway, I'm afraid I never met them. DI Chadwick did most of the North Riding side of the investigation with a DS Enderby. I do believe they interviewed the band."

"Yes, I've talked to Keith Enderby."

Bradley sniffed. "Bit of a scruff, and not entirely reliable, in my opinion. Rather more like the types we were dealing with, if you know what I mean."

"DS Enderby was a hippie?"

"Well, not as such, but he wore his hair a bit long, and on occasion he wore flowered shirts and ties. I even saw him in sandals once."

"With socks?"

"No."

"Well, thank the Lord for that," said Banks.

"Look, I know you're being sarcastic," said Bradley with a smug smile. "It's okay. But the fact remains that Enderby was a slacker, and he had no respect for the uniform."

Banks could have kicked himself for letting the sarcasm out, but Bradley's holier-than-thou sanctimony was starting to get up his nose. He felt like saying that Enderby had described Bradley as an arse-licker, but he wanted results, not confrontation. Time to hold back and stick to relevant points only, he told himself.

"You say you think this writer was killed because he was working on a story about the Mad Hatters, but do you have any reason for assuming that?" Bradley asked.

"Well," said Banks, "we do know about the story he was working on, that he mentioned to a girlfriend that it might involve a murder, and we know that Vic Greaves now lives very close to the cottage in which Nick Barber was killed. Unfortunately, all Barber's notes were missing, along with his mobile and laptop, so we were unable to find out more. That in itself is also suspicious, though, that his personal effects and notes were taken."

"It's not very much, though, is it? I imagine robbery's as common around your patch as it is everywhere these days."

"We try to keep an open mind," said Banks. "There could be other possibilities. Did you have any other suspects?"

"Yes. There was a fellow called Rick Hayes. He was the festival promoter. He had the freedom of the backstage area, and he couldn't account for himself during the period we think the girl was killed. He was also left-handed, as was McGarrity."

"Those were the only two?"

"Yes."

"So it was the knife that clinched it?" .

"We knew we had the right man – you must have had that feeling at times – but we couldn't prove it at first. We were able to hold him on a drugs charge, and while we were holding him, we turned up the murder weapon."

"How long after you first questioned him?"

"It was October, about two weeks or so."

"Where was it?"

"In one of the houses."

"I assume those places were searched as soon as you had McGarrity in custody?"

"Yes."

"But you didn't turn up the knife then?"

"You have to understand," said Bradley, "there were several people living in each of these houses at any one time. They were terribly unsanitary and overcrowded. People slept on the floors and in all kinds of unlikely combinations. There was all sorts of stuff around. We didn't know what belonged to whom, they were all so casual in their attitudes towards property and ownership."

"So how did you find out in the end?"

"We just kept on looking. Finally, we found it hidden inside a cushion. A couple of the people who lived there said they'd seen McGarrity with such a knife – it had a tortoiseshell handle

– and we were fortunate enough to find his prints on it. He'd wiped the blade, of course, but the lab still found blood and fibre where it joined the handle. The blood matched Linda Lofthouse's type. Simple as that."

"Did the knife match the wounds?"

"According to the pathologist, it could have."

"Only *could* have?"

"He was in court. You know what those barristers are like. Could have been her blood, could have been the knife. A blade consistent with the kind of blade . . . blah blah blah. It was enough for the jury."

"The pathologist didn't try to match the knife with the wound physically, on the body?"

"He couldn't. The body had been buried by then, and even if it had been necessary to exhume it, the flesh would have been too decomposed to give an accurate reproduction. You know that."

"And McGarrity didn't deny killing her?"

"That's right. I was there when DI Chadwick presented him with the evidence, and he just had this strange smile on his face, and he said, 'It looks like you've got me then.'"

"Those were his exact words. 'It looks like you've got me then'?"

Bradley frowned with annoyance. "It was over thirty years ago. I can't promise those were the exact words, but it was something like that. You'll find it in the files and the court transcripts. But he was sneering at us, being sarcastic."

"I'll be looking at the transcripts later," said Banks. "I don't suppose you had anything to do with the investigation into Robin Merchant's death."

"Who?"

"He was another member of the Mad Hatters. He drowned about nine months after the Linda Lofthouse murder."

Bradley shook his head. "No. Sorry."

"Mr. Enderby was able to tell me a bit about it. He was one of the investigating officers. I was just wondering. I understand DI Chadwick had a daughter?"

"Yes. I only ever saw her the once. Pretty young thing. Yvonne, I think she was called."

"Wasn't there some trouble with her?"

"DI Chadwick didn't confide in me about his family life."

Banks felt a faint warning signal. Bradley's answer had come just a split second too soon and sounded a little too pat to be quite believable. The clipped tone also told Banks that he perhaps wasn't being entirely truthful. But why would he lie about Chadwick's daughter? To protect Chadwick's family and reputation, most likely. So if Enderby was right and this Yvonne had been in trouble, or *was* trouble, it might be worth finding out exactly what kind of trouble he was talking about. "Do you know where Yvonne Chadwick is now?" he asked.

"I'm afraid not. Grown up and married, I should imagine."

"What about DI Chadwick?"

"Haven't seen hide nor hair of him for years, not since the trial. I should imagine he's dead by now. I mean, he was in his late forties back then, and he wasn't in the best of health. The trial took its toll. But I transferred to Suffolk in 1971, and I lost touch. No doubt records will be able to tell you. More coffee?"

"Thanks." Banks held his mug out and gazed at the spines of the books. Nice hobby, he thought, collecting first editions. Maybe he'd look into it. Graham Greene, perhaps, or Georges Simenon. There were plenty of those to spend a lifetime or more collecting. "So even after confessing, McGarrity pleaded not guilty?"

"Yes. It was a foolish move. He wanted to conduct his own defence, too, but the judge wasn't having any of it. As it was, he kept getting up in court and interrupting, causing a fuss, making accusations that he'd been framed. I mean, the nerve of him, after he'd as good as admitted it. Things didn't go well for him at all. We got the similar fact evidence about the previous stabbing in. The bailiffs had to remove him from the court at least twice."

"He said he'd been framed?"

"Well, they all do, don't they?"

"Was he more specific about it?"

"No. Couldn't be really, could he, seeing as it was all a pack of lies? Besides, he was gibbering. There's no doubt about it, Patrick McGarrity was guilty as sin."

"Perhaps I should have a chat with him."

"That would be rather difficult," said Bradley. "He's dead. He was stabbed in jail back in 1974. Something to do with drugs."

16

"Is it just me, or do I sense a bit of an atmosphere around here?" Banks asked Annie in the corridor on Thursday morning.

"Atmosphere would be an understatement," said Annie. Her head still hurt, despite the paracetamol she had taken before leaving Winsome's flat that morning. Luckily, she always carried a change of clothes in the boot of her car. Not because she was promiscuous or anything, but because once, years ago, a mere DC, when she had done a similar thing, got drunk and stayed with a friend after a breakup with a boyfriend, someone in the station had noticed and she had been the butt of unfunny sexist jokes for days. And after that, her DS had come on to her in the lift after work one day.

"You look like shit," said Banks.

"Thank you."

"Want to tell me about it?"

Annie looked up and down the corridor to make sure no one was lurking. Great, she thought, she was getting paranoid in her own station now. "Think we can sneak over the road to the Golden Grill without setting too many tongues wagging?"

"Of course," said Banks. He looked as if he was wondering what the hell she was talking about.

The day was overcast and chilly and most of the people window-shopping on Market Street wore sweaters under their windcheaters or anoraks. They passed a couple of serious ramblers, kitted out in all the new, fancy gear, each carrying the two long, pointed sticks, like ski poles. Well, Annie supposed, they might be of some use climbing up Fremlington Edge, but they weren't a lot of use on the cobbled streets of Eastvale.

Their regular waitress greeted them, and soon they were sitting over hot coffee and toasted teacakes, looking through the misted window at the streams of people outside. Annie felt a sudden rush of nausea when she took her first sip of black coffee, but it soon waned. It was always there, though, a low-level sensation in the background.

Annie and Winsome had certainly made a night of it, shared more confidences than Annie could ever have imagined. It made her realize, when she thought about it in the cold hangover dawn, that she didn't really have any friends, anyone to talk to like that, be silly with, do girly things with. She had always thought it was a function of her job, but perhaps it was a function of her personality. Banks was the same, but at least he had his kids. She had her father, Ray, down in St. Ives, of course, but they only saw one another rarely, and it wasn't the same; for all his eccentricities and willingness to act as a friend and confidante, he was still her father.

"So what were you up to last night that's left you looking like death warmed up? Feeling like it, too, by the looks of you."

Annie pulled a face. "You know how I love it when you compliment me."

Banks touched her hand, a shadow of concern passing over his face. "Seriously."

"If you must know, I got pissed with Winsome."

"You did what?"

"I told you."

"But Winsome? I didn't even think she drank."

"Me neither. But it's official now. She can drink me under the table."

"That's no mean feat."

"My point exactly."

"How was it?"

"Well, a bit awkward at first, with the rank thing, but you know I've never held that in very great esteem."

"I know. You respect the person, not the rank."

"Exactly. Anyway, by the end of the evening we'd got beyond that, and we had quite a giggle. It was 'Annie' and 'Winsome' – she hates Winnie. She's got a wicked sense of humour when she lets her hair down, does Winsome."

"What were you talking about?"

"Mind your own business. It was girl talk."

"Men, then."

"Such an ego. What makes you think we'd waste a perfectly good bottle of Marks and Spencer's plonk talking about you lot?"

"That puts me in my place. How was it when you met up at work this morning? A bit embarrassing?"

"Well, it'll be 'Winsome' and 'Guv' in the workplace, but we had a bit of a giggle over it all."

"So what started it?"

Annie felt another wave of nausea. She let it go, the way she did thoughts in meditation, and it seemed to work, at least for the moment. "DS Templeton," she said finally.

"Kev Templeton? Was this about the promotion? Because —"

"No, it wasn't about the promotion. And keep your voice down. Of course Winsome's pissed off about that. Who wouldn't be? We know she was the right person for the job, but we also know the right person doesn't always get the job, even if she is a black female. I know you white males always like to complain when a job goes elsewhere for what you see as political reasons, but it's not always the case, you know."

"So what, then?"

Annie explained how Templeton had behaved with Kelly Soames.

"It sounds a bit harsh," he said when she had finished. "But I don't suppose he was to know the girl would be physically sick."

"He enjoyed it. That was the point," said Annie.

"So Winsome thought?"

"Yes. Look, don't tell me you're going to go all male and start defending the indefensible here, because if you are, I'm off. I'm not in the mood for an all-lads-together rally."

"Christ, Annie, you ought to know me better than that. And there's only one lad here, as far as I can see."

"Well . . . you know what I mean." Annie ran her hand through her tousled hair. "Shit, I'm hungover and I'm having a bad hair day, too."

"Your hair looks fine."

"You don't mean it, but thank you. Anyway, that's the story. Oh, and Superintendent bloody Gervaise had a go at me yesterday in her office."

"What were you doing there?"

"I went to complain about the personal remarks she made about me during the briefing. At the very least, I expected an apology."

"And you got?"

"A bollocking, more personal remarks, and an assignment to statement reading."

"That's steep."

"Very. And she warned me off you."

"What?"

"It's true." Annie looked down into her coffee. "She seems to think we're an item again."

"Where could she possibly have got that idea from?"

"I don't know." Annie paused. "Templeton's in thick with her."

"So?"

Annie leaned forward and rested her hands on the table. "She knew about the pint you had at the Cross Keys that first night, when we went to the scene of Barber's murder. And Templeton was there, too. He knew about that. But this . . . look, tell me if I'm being paranoid, Alan, but don't you think it's a bit suspicious? I think Kev Templeton might be behind it."

"But why would he think we were an item, as you put it?"

"He knows that we were involved before, and we turned up at Moorview Cottage together. We also stayed overnight in London. He's putting two and two together and coming up with five."

Banks looked out of the window, seeming to mull over what Annie had said. "So what's he up to? Ingratiating himself with the new super?"

"It looks that way," said Annie. "Kev's smart, and he's also ambitious. He thinks the rest of us are plods. He's a sergeant already, and he'll pass his inspector's boards first chance he gets, too, but he's also smart enough to know he needs more than good exam results to get ahead in this job. It helps to have recommendations from above. We know our Madame

Gervaise thinks she's cut out for great things, chief constable at the very least, so a bit of coattail riding wouldn't do Templeton any harm. At least that's my guess."

"Sounds right to me," said Banks. "And I don't like what you told me earlier, about the Soames interview. Sometimes we have to do unpleasant things like that – though I believe in this case it could have all been avoided – but we don't have to take pleasure in them."

"Winsome thinks he's a racist, too. She's overheard him make the odd comment about 'darkies' and 'Pakis' when he thinks she's not listening."

"That would hardly make him unique in the force, sadly," said Banks. "Look, I'll have a word with him."

"Fat lot of good that will do."

"Well, we can't go to Superintendent Gervaise, that's for certain. Red Ron would probably listen, but that's too much like telling tales out of school for me. Not my style. No, the way it looks is that if anything's to be done about Kev Templeton, I'll have to do it myself."

"And what exactly might you do?"

"Like I said, I'll have a word, see if I can talk some sense into him. On the other hand, I think it might be even better if I tipped the wink to Gervaise that we're onto him. She'll drop him like the proverbial hot potato. I mean, it's no bloody good having a spy who blows his cover on his first assignment, is it? And gets the wrong end of the stick, into the bargain."

"Good point."

"Look, I have to go to Leeds to see Ken Blackstone later today. Want to come?"

"No, thanks." Annie made a grim face. "Statements to read. And the way I feel today, if I'm doing a menial job, I might even just knock off early, go home and have a long hot bath and an early night."

They paid and left the Golden Grill, then walked across the road to the station in the light drizzle. At the front desk, the PC on reception called Annie over. "Got a message for you, miss," he said. "From Lyndgarth. Local copper's just called in to say all hell's broke loose up at the Soames farm. Old man Soames went berserk, apparently."

"We're on our way," said Annie. She looked at Banks.

"Ken Blackstone can wait," he said. "We'd better put our wellies on."

Annie drove, and Banks tried to find out what he could over his mobile, but coverage was patchy, and in the end he gave up.

"That bastard, Templeton," Annie cursed as she turned onto the Lyndgarth road by the Cross Keys in Fordham, visions of flaying Templeton alive and dipping him in a vat of boiling oil flitting through her mind. "I'll have him for this. He's not getting away with it."

"Calm down, Annie," Banks said. "Let's find out what happened first."

"Whatever it is, he's behind it. It's down to him."

"If that's the case, you might have to join the queue," said Banks.

Annie shot him a puzzled glance. "What do you mean?"

"If you were thinking clearly right now, one of the things that might cross your mind –"

"Oh, don't be so bloody patronizing," Annie snapped. "Get on with it."

"One of the things that might cross your mind is that if something has happened as a direct result of DS Templeton's actions, then the first person to distance herself will be Superintendent Gervaise."

Annie looked at him and turned into the drive of the Soames farm. She could see the patrol car up ahead, parked outside the house. "But she told him to do it," Annie said.

Banks just smiled. "That was when it seemed like a good idea."

Annie pulled up to a sharp halt, sending gobbets of mud flying, and they got out and walked over to the uniformed officer. The door to the farmhouse was open, and Annie could hear the sound of a police radio from inside.

"PC Cotter, sir," said the officer on the door. "My partner, PC Watkins, is inside."

"What happened?" Banks asked.

"It's not entirely clear yet," said Cotter. "But we had a memo from Eastvale Major Crimes asking us to report anything to do with the Soameses."

"We're glad you were so prompt," Annie cut in. "Is anybody hurt?"

Cotter looked at her. "Yes, ma'am," he said. "Young girl. The daughter. She rang the station, and we could hear cursing and things breaking in the background. She was frightened. Told us to come as soon as we could. We came as soon as possible, but by the time we got here . . . Well, you can see for yourselves."

Annie was first inside the farmhouse, and she gave a curt nod to PC Watkins, who was standing in the living room scratching his head at the sight. The room was a wreck. Broken glass littered the floor, one of the chairs had been smashed into the table and splintered, a window was broken and lamps were knocked over. The small bookcase had been pulled away from the wall, and its contents joined the broken glass on the floor.

"The kitchen's just as bad," said PC Watkins, "but that seems to be the extent of the damage. Everything's fine upstairs."

"Where's Soames?" Annie asked.

"We don't know, ma'am. He was gone when we arrived."

"What about his daughter, Kelly?"

"Eastvale General, ma'am. We radioed ahead to A and E."

"How bad is she?"

PC Watkins looked away. "Don't know, ma'am. Hard to say. She looked bad to me." He gestured back into the room. "Lot of blood."

Annie looked again. She hadn't noticed it before, but now she could see dark stains on the carpet and the broken chair leg. *Kelly.* Oh, Jesus Christ.

"Okay," said Banks, stepping forward. "I want you and your partner to organize a search for Calvin Soames. He can't have gone far. Get some help from uniformed branch in Eastvale if you need it."

"Yes, sir."

Banks turned to Annie. "Come on," he said. "There's nothing more we can do here. Let's go pay a visit to Eastvale General."

Annie didn't need asking twice. When they got back in the car, she thumped the steering wheel with both fists and strained to hold back her tears of anger. Her head was still throbbing from the previous night's excess. She felt Banks's hand rest on her shoulder, and her resolve not to cry strengthened. "I'm all right," she said after a few moments, gently shaking him off. "Just needed to let off a bit of steam, that's all. And there was me thinking I'd go home early and have a nice bath."

"You okay to drive?"

"I'm fine. Really." To demonstrate, Annie started the car, set off slowly down the long, bumpy drive and didn't start speeding until she hit the main road.

Tuesday, September 23, 1969

"Yes, what is it?" Chadwick said when Karen stuck her head around his office door. "I told you I didn't want to be disturbed."

"Urgent phone call. Your wife."

Chadwick picked up the phone.

"Darling, I'm so glad you're there," Janet said. "I was worried I wouldn't be able to reach you. I don't know what to do."

Chadwick could sense the alarm in her voice. "What is it?"

"It's Yvonne. The school have rung wanting to know where she is. They said they'd tried to reach me earlier, but I was out shopping. You know what a busybody that headmistress is."

"She's not at school?"

"No. And she's not here, either. I checked her room, just in case."

"Did you notice anything unusual?"

"No. Same mess as ever."

Chadwick had left for the station before his daughter had even woken up that morning. "How did she seem at breakfast?" he asked.

"Quiet."

"But she left for school as usual?"

"So I thought. I mean, she took her satchel and she was wearing her mac. It's not like her, Stan. You know it's not."

"It's probably nothing," Chadwick said, trying to ignore the feeling of fear crawling in the pit of his stomach. McGarrity was in jail, but what if one of the others had decided to take revenge for the drugs squad raids? He had probably been foolish to identify himself to Yvonne's boyfriend, but how else was he supposed to make his point? "Look, I'll come straight home. You stay there in case she turns up."

"Should I call the hospitals?"

"You might as well," said Chadwick. "And have a good look around her room. See if there's anything missing. Clothes and things." At least that would give Janet something to occupy her time until he got there. "I'm on my way. I'll be there as quick as I can."

Eastvale General Infirmary was the biggest hospital for some distance, and as a consequence, the staff there were over-worked and its facilities were strained to the limit. Just down King Street, behind the police station, it was a Victorian pile of stone with high, draughty corridors and large wards with big sash windows, no doubt to let in the winter's chill for the TB patients it used to house.

A and E wasn't terribly busy, as it was only Thursday lunchtime, and they found Kelly Soames easily enough with the help of one of the admissions nurses. The curtains were drawn around her bed, but more, the nurse said, to give her privacy than for any more serious reasons. When they went through and sat by her, Annie was relieved to see, and hear, that most of the damage was superficial. The blood came almost entirely from a head wound, by far the most serious of her cuts and abrasions, but even this had only caused concussion, and her head was swathed in bandages. Her face was bruised, her lip split, and there was a stitched cut over her eye, but other than that, the nurse assured them, there were no broken bones and no internal injuries.

Annie felt an immense relief that didn't diminish her anger against Kevin Templeton and Calvin Soames one bit. It could have been so much worse. She held Kelly's hand and said, "I'm sorry. I didn't know. I honestly didn't know anything like this was going to happen."

Kelly said nothing, just continued to stare at the ceiling.

"Can you tell us what happened?" Banks asked.

"Isn't it obvious?" Kelly said. Her speech was a little slurred from the painkillers she had been given, and from the split lip, but she made herself clear enough.

"I'd rather hear it from you," Banks said.

Annie continued to hold Kelly's hand. "Tell us," she said. "Where is he, Kelly?"

"I don't know," Kelly said. "Honestly. The last thing I remember is feeling like my head was exploding."

"It was a chair leg," Banks said. "Someone hit you with a chair leg. Was it your father?"

"Who else would it be?"

"What happened?"

Kelly took some of the water Annie offered and flinched when the flexi-straw touched the cut on her lip. She put the glass aside and stared at the ceiling as she spoke in a listless voice. "He'd been drinking. Not like usual, just a couple of pints before dinner, but real drinking, like he used to. Whisky. He started at breakfast. I told him not to, but he just ignored me. I caught the bus into Eastvale and did some shopping, and when I got back, he was still drinking. I could tell he was really drunk by then. The bottle was almost empty, and he was red in the face, muttering to himself. I was worried about him. And scared. As soon as I opened my mouth, he went berserk. Asked me who I thought I was to tell him what to do. To be honest, I really thought he believed I was mother, the way he was talking to me. Then he got really abusive. I mean, just shouting at first, not violent or anything. That was when I phoned the local police station. But as soon as he saw me on the phone, that was it. He went mad. He started hitting me, just slapping and pushing at first, then he punched me. After that, he started breaking things, smashing the furniture. It was all I could do to put my hands in front of my face to protect myself."

"He didn't interfere with you in any way?" Annie asked.

"No. No. It wasn't like that at all. He wouldn't do anything like that. But the names he was calling me . . . I won't repeat them. They were the same ones he used to call mother when they fought."

"What happened to your mother?" Annie asked.

"She died in hospital. There was something wrong with her insides – I don't know what it was – and at first the doctors didn't diagnose it in time, then they thought it was something else. When they finally did get around to operating, it was too late. She never woke up. Dad said something about the anaesthetic being wrong, but I don't know. We never got to the bottom of it, and he's never been able to let it go."

"And your father's been overpossessive ever since?"

"He's only got me to take care of him. He can't take care of himself." Kelly sipped some more water and coughed, dribbling it down her chin. Annie took a tissue from the table and wiped it away. "Thanks," said Kelly. "What's going to happen now? Where's Dad? What's going to happen to him?"

"We don't know yet," said Annie, glancing at Banks. "We'll find him, though. Then we'll see."

"I don't want anything to happen to him," Kelly said. "I mean, I know he's done wrong and all, but I don't want anything to happen to him."

Annie held her hand. It was the old, old story, the abused defending her abuser. "We'll see," she said. "We'll see. Just get some rest for now."

Back at the station, Banks found Superintendent Gervaise in her office and told her about Kelly Soames. He also hinted that he knew Templeton had been passing her information and warned her not to put too much trust in its accuracy. It was worth it just to see the expression on her face.

After that, he tried to put Kelly Soames and her problems out of his mind for a while and focus on the Nick Barber investigation again before setting off to visit Ken Blackstone in Leeds. A couple of DCs had read through the boxes of Barber's papers sent up from his London flat and found they consisted entirely of old articles, photographs and business correspondence – none of it relating to his Yorkshire trip. He had clearly brought all his current work with him, and now it was gone. Banks found a Brahms cello sonata on the radio and settled down to have another look through the old *Mojo* magazines that John Butler had given to him in London.

It didn't take him very long to figure out that Nick Barber knew his stuff. In addition to pieces on the Mad Hatters from time to time, there were also articles on Shelagh MacDonald, Jo Ann Kelly, Comus and Bridget St. John. Barber's interest in the Hatters seemed to have started, as Banks had been told, about five years ago, well after his original interest in music, which he seemed to have had since he was a teenager.

Childhood. Now Banks remembered the little frisson of possibility he had experienced when Simon Bradley had talked about Linda Lofthouse's unwanted pregnancy.

It shouldn't be too hard to find out whether he was right, he decided, picking up the phone and looking up the Barbers' number in the case file.

When he got Louise Barber on the phone, Banks told her who he was and said, "I know this is probably an odd question, and it's not meant to be in any way disturbing or upsetting, but was Nick adopted?"

There was a short pause followed by a sob. "Yes," she said. "We adopted him when he was only days old. We raised him as if he were our own, and that's how we always think of him."

"I'm sure you did," said Banks, "Believe me, there's no hint of criticism here. I wouldn't expect it to enter your head at such a time, and from all I've found out, Nick led a healthy and happy life with many advantages he probably wouldn't have had otherwise. It's just that . . . well, did he know? Did you tell him?"

"Yes," said Louise Barber. "We told him a long time ago, as soon as we thought he would be able to absorb it."

"And what did he do?"

"Then? Nothing. He said that as far as he was concerned, we were his parents and that was all there was to it."

"Did he ever get curious about his birth mother?"

"It's funny, but he did, yes."

"When was this?"

"About five or six years ago."

"Any particular reason?"

"He told us he didn't want us to think there was a problem, or that it was anything to do with us, but a friend of his who was also adopted told him it was important to find out. He said something about it making him whole, complete."

"Did he find her?"

"He didn't really talk to us about it much after that. You have to understand, we found it all a bit upsetting, and Nicholas was careful not to hurt us. He told us he found out who she was, but we have no idea if he traced her or met her."

"Do you remember her name? Did he tell you that?"

"Yes. Linda Lofthouse. But that's all I know. We asked him not to talk to us about her again."

"The name is enough," said Banks. "Thank you very much, Mrs. Barber, and I do apologize for bringing up difficult memories."

"I suppose it can't be helped. Surely this can't have anything to do with . . . with what happened to Nicholas?"

"We don't know. Right now, it's just another piece of information to add to the puzzle. Goodbye."

"Goodbye."

Banks hung up and thought. So Nick Barber *was* Linda Lofthouse's son. He must have found out that his mother had been murdered only a couple of years after he was born, and that she was Vic Greaves's cousin, which no doubt fuelled his interest in the Mad Hatters, already present to some extent because of his interest in the music of the period.

But the knowledge raised a number of new questions for Banks. Had Barber accepted the standard version of her murder? Did he believe that Patrick McGarrity had killed his mother? Or had he found out something else? If he had stumbled across something that indicated McGarrity was innocent, or had not acted alone, then he might easily have blundered into a situation without knowing how dangerous it was. But it all depended on whether or not Chadwick had been right about McGarrity. It was time to head for Leeds and have a chat with Ken Blackstone.

Banks made it to Leeds in a little over an hour, coming off New York Road at Eastgate and heading for Millgarth, the Leeds Police Headquarters, at about half past three on Thursday afternoon. Like many things, he supposed, this business could have been conducted over the telephone, but he preferred personal contact, if possible. Somehow, little nuances and vague impressions didn't quite make it over the phone lines.

Ken Blackstone was waiting in his office, a tiny space partitioned off at the end of a room full of busy detectives, nattily dressed as ever in his best Next pinstripe, dazzling white shirt and maroon and grey striped tie, held in place by a silver pin in the shape of a fountain pen. With his wispy grey hair curling over his ears and his gold-framed reading glasses, he looked more like a university professor than a police officer. He and Banks had known one another for years, and Banks thought Ken was the closest he had to a friend, next to Dirty Dick Burgess, but Burgess was in London.

"First off," said Blackstone, "I thought you might like to see this." He slid a photograph across his desk and Banks turned it to face him. It showed the head and shoulders of a man in his early forties, perhaps, neat black hair plastered flat with Brylcreem, hard, angled face, straight nose and square jaw with a slight dimple. But it was the eyes that caught Banks's attention the most. They gave nothing away except, perhaps, for a slight hint of dark shadows in their depths. If eyes were supposed to be the windows to the soul, these were the blackout curtains. This was a hard, haunted, uncompromising man, Banks thought. And a moral one. He didn't know why, and realized he was being a bit fanciful, but he sensed a hint of hard religion in the man's background. Hardly surprising, as there had been plenty of that around in both Scotland and Yorkshire over the years. "Interesting," Banks said, passing it back. "Stanley Chadwick, I assume?"

Blackstone nodded. "Taken on his promotion to detective inspector in October 1965." He glanced at his watch. "Look, it's a bit noisy and stuffy in here. Fancy heading out for a coffee?"

"I'm all coffeed out," said Banks, "But maybe we can have a late lunch? I haven't eaten since this morning."

"Fine with me. I'm not hungry, but I'll join you."

They left Millgarth and walked onto Eastgate. It had turned into a fine day, with that mix of cloud and sun you got so often in Yorkshire, when it wasn't raining, and just chilly enough for a raincoat or light overcoat.

"Did you manage to find out anything?" Banks asked.

"I've done a bit of digging," said Blackstone, "and it looks like pretty solid investigating on the surface of it."

"Only on the surface?"

"I haven't dug *that* deeply yet. And remember, it was essentially a *North* Yorkshire case, so most of the paperwork's up there."

"I've seen it," he said. "I was just wondering about the West Yorkshire angle, and about Chadwick himself."

"DI Chadwick was on loan to the North Yorkshire Constabulary. From what I can glean, he'd had a few successes here since his promotion and was a bit of a golden boy at the time."

"I heard he was tough, and he certainly looks that way."

"I never knew him personally, but I managed to turn up a couple of retired officers who did. He was a hard man, by all accounts, but fair and honest, and he got results. He had a strong Scottish Presbyterian background, but one of his old colleagues told me he thought he'd lost his faith during the war. Hardly bloody surprising when you consider the poor sod saw action in Burma *and* was part of the D-Day invasion."

"Where is he now?"

They waited until the lights changed, then crossed Vicar Lane. "Dead," Blackstone said, finally. "According to our personnel records, Stanley Chadwick died in March 1973."

"So young?" said Banks. "That must have been a hell of a shock for all concerned. He would only have been in his early fifties."

"Apparently, his health had been in decline for a couple of

years," Blackstone said. "He'd had a lot of sick time, and performance-wise there were rumours that he was dragging his feet. He retired due to ill health in late 1972."

"That seems a rather sudden decline," Banks said. "Any speculation as to what it was?"

"Well, it wasn't murder, if that's what you're thinking. He had a history of heart problems, hereditary apparently, which had gone untreated, perhaps even unnoticed, for years. He died in his sleep of a heart attack. But you have to remember, this is just from the files and the memory of a couple of old men I managed to track down. And some of the old information is impossible to locate. We moved here from Brotherton House in 1976, which was well before my time, and inevitably stuff went missing in the move, so your guess is as good as mine as to the rest."

Simon Bradley had told Banks he'd heard Chadwick wasn't in good health, but Banks hadn't realized things were that bad. Could there have been anything suspicious about his death? First Linda Lofthouse, then Robin Merchant, then Stanley Chadwick? Banks couldn't imagine what linked them to one another. Chadwick had investigated the Lofthouse case, but had nothing to do with Merchant's drowning. He had, however, met the Mad Hatters at Swainsview Lodge, and Vic Greaves was Linda Lofthouse's cousin. There had to be something he was missing. Maybe Chadwick's daughter, Yvonne, would help, if he could find her.

They turned down Briggate, a pedestrian precinct. There were plenty of shoppers in evidence, many of them young people, teenage girls pushing prams, the boys with them looking too young and inexperienced to be fathers. Many of the girls looked too young to be mothers, too, but Banks knew damn well they weren't merely helping out their big sisters.

Teenage pregnancies and sexually transmitted diseases were at appallingly high rates.

Because he still had Linda Lofthouse and Nick Barber on his mind, Banks thought back to the sixties, to what the media had dubbed the "sexual revolution." True, the pill had made it possible for women to have sex without fear of pregnancy, but it had also left them with little or no excuse *not* to have sex. In the name of liberation, women were expected to sleep around; they had the freedom to do so, the reasoning went, so they should, and there was subtle and not so subtle cultural and peer pressure on them to do so. After all, the worst anyone could get was crabs or a dose of clap, so sex was relatively fear-free.

But there were plenty of unwanted pregnancies back then, too, Banks remembered, as not all girls were on the pill, or willing to have abortions, certainly in the provinces. Linda Lofthouse had been one of them, and Norma Coulton, just down the street from where Banks lived, was another. Banks remembered the gossip and the dirty looks she got when she walked into the newsagent's. He wondered what had happened to her and her child. At least he knew what had happened to Linda Lofthouse's son; he had met the same fate as his mother.

"Any idea what happened to Chadwick's family?" he asked.

"According to what I could find out, he had a wife called Janet and a daughter called Yvonne. Both survived him, but nobody's kept tabs on them. I don't suppose it would be too difficult to track them down. Pensions or Human Resources might be able to help."

"Do what you can," said Banks. "I appreciate it. And I'll put Winsome on it at our end. She's good at that sort of thing. The daughter may have married, changed her name, of course, but we'll give it a try: electoral rolls, DVLA, PNC and the rest.

Who knows, we might get lucky before we have to resort to more time-consuming methods."

They passed a thin, bearded young man selling the *Big Issue* at the entrance to Thornton's Arcade. Blackstone bought a copy, folded it and slipped it into his inside pocket. Two young policemen passed them, both wearing black helmets and bulletproof vests and carrying Heckler & Koch carbines.

"It's a fact of the times here, I'm afraid," said Blackstone.

Banks nodded. What bothered him most was that the officers only looked about fifteen.

"Sorry I'm not being a lot of help," Blackstone went on.

"Nonsense," said Banks. "You're helping me fill in the picture, and that's all I need right now. I know I'll have to read the files and the trial transcripts soon, but I keep putting it off because those things bore me so much."

"You can do that in my office after we've had a bite to eat. I have to go out. I know what you mean, though. I'd rather curl up with a good Flashman or Sharpe myself." Blackstone stopped at the end of an alley. "Let's try The Ship this time. Whitelock is always too damned crowded these days, and they've changed the menu. It's getting too trendy. And somehow I don't see you sitting out in the Victoria Quarter at the Harvey Nichols café eating a garlic and brie frittata."

"Oh, I don't know," said Banks. "You'd be surprised. I scrub up quite nicely, and I don't mind a bit of foreign grub every now and then. But The Ship sounds fine."

They ordered pints of Tetley's, and Banks chose the giant Yorkshire pudding filled with sausages and gravy and sat down in the dim brass and dark wood interior. Blackstone stuck with his beer.

Banks told Blackstone about their troublesome new superintendent and the fact that Templeton might be bringing in just too many apples for the teacher. Then he chatted about Brian and his new girlfriend, Emilia, turning up, then their food came and they got back to Stanley Chadwick and Linda Lofthouse.

"Do you think I'm tilting at windmills, Ken?" Banks asked.

"It wouldn't be the first time, but I don't have enough to go on to advise you on that score. Usually your windmills turn out to be all too human. Explain your reasoning."

Banks sipped some beer, trying to put his thoughts in order. It was a useful, if difficult, exercise. "There isn't much, really," he said. "Superintendent Gervaise thinks the past is over and the guilty have been punished, but I'm not so sure. It's not that I think Vic Greaves is a killer because he has mental problems. Christ, it might even be Chris Adams, for all I know. He doesn't live that far away. Or even Tania Hutchison. It's not as if Oxfordshire's on the moon, either. I just think that if Nick Barber was as good and as thorough a music journalist as everyone says he was, then he might have struck a nerve, and Vic Greaves is one of the few people he had tried to speak to about the story before his murder. I've also just discovered that Nick was Linda Lofthouse's son, adopted at birth by the Barbers, and that he found out who his birth mother was about five years ago. Barber was a journalist, and I think he simply tried to find out as much about her and her times as he could because he was already interested in the music and the period. One thing he found out was that Vic Greaves was her cousin. Greaves also lived only walking distance away from Barber's rented cottage, and someone saw a figure running near there around the time of the murder. The only things I can find in the past that cast any sort of suspicions on Greaves and the others are the murder of Linda Lofthouse, because she was backstage at the Brimleigh Festival with Tania Hutchison, and she was Greaves's cousin, and the drowning of the Mad Hatters' bassist, Robin Merchant, when Greaves, Adams and Tania Hutchison were all present at Swainsview Lodge. And they're both closed cases."

"Linda Lofthouse's murderer was caught, and Merchant's drowning was ruled death by misadventure, right?"

"Right. And Linda's killer was stabbed in jail, so it's not as if we can ask him to clear anything up for us. Sounds as if he was deranged in the first place."

"But ruling out the angry husband or passing-tramp theory, that's the default line of inquiry?"

"Pretty much so. Chris Adams said Barber had a coke habit, but we can't find any evidence of that. If he did, it obviously wasn't big-time."

"Have you got Barber's phone records yet?"

"We're working on it, but we don't expect too much there."

"Why not?"

"There was no land line at the cottage where he was staying, and he was out of mobile range. If he needed to phone anyone, he'd have had to use the public telephone box, either in Fordham or in Eastvale."

"What about Internet access? You'd think a savvy music journalist would be all wired up for that sort of thing, wouldn't you?"

"Not if he didn't have a phone line, or even wireless access. Blackberry or Bluetooth, or whatever it is."

"Aren't there any Internet cafés in Eastvale?"

Banks glanced at Blackstone, ate another mouthful of sausage and washed it down with a swig of beer. "Good point, Ken. Apart from the library, which is as slow as a horse and cart, there's a computer shop in the market square, Eastvale Computes, and I suppose we could check there. Problem is, the owner's only got two computers available to the public, and I should imagine the histories get wiped pretty often. If Nick Barber used either of them, it'd have been a couple of weeks ago, and all traces would be gone by now. It's still worth a try, though."

"So what next?"

"Well," said Banks, "there are a few more people to talk to, starting with Tania Hutchison and Chadwick's daughter, Yvonne, when we find her, but for the moment, I've got a CD collection with a lot of holes in it, and Borders is beckoning just up Briggate."

Annie got Banks's phone call from Blackstone's office in Leeds late that afternoon and welcomed the break from the dull routine of statement reading. Kelly Soames was still holding her own and would most likely be discharged the following day. They still hadn't found her father.

Before Annie left the squad room, Winsome came up trumps with Nick Barber's mobile service, but the results were disappointing. He had made no calls since arriving at the cottage because he had no coverage there. He could, of course, have used his mobile in Eastvale, but according to the records, he hadn't. If he had been up to anything at all, he had kept it very much to himself. That wouldn't be surprising, Annie thought. She had known a few journalists in her time and had found that they were a secretive lot, on the whole; they had to be, as theirs was very much a first-come, first-served kind of business.

Templeton had just got back from Fordham, and Annie noticed him watching closely as she leaned over Winsome's shoulder to read the notes. She whispered in Winsome's ear, then let her hand rest casually on her shoulder. She could see the prurient curiosity in Templeton's gaze now. Enough rope, she thought. And if he knew that she had stayed at Winsome's the other night, who could guess what wild tales he might take to Superintendent Gervaise? After talking to Banks, Annie's anger had diminished, though she still blamed Templeton for what had happened. She knew there was no point confronting him; he just wouldn't get it. Banks was right. Let him crucify himself; he was already well on his way.

Annie picked up a folder from her desk, plucked her suede jacket from the hanger by the door, said she'd be back in a while and walked down the stairs with a smile on her face.

A cool wind gusted across the market square, and the sky was quickly filling with dirty clouds, like ink spilled on a sheet of paper. Luckily, I don't have far to go, she thought, as she pulled the collar of her jacket around her throat and crossed the busy square. People leaned into the wind as they walked, hair flying, plastic bags from Somerfield's and Boots fluttering as if they were filled with birds. The Darlington bus stood at its stop by the market cross, but nobody seemed to be getting on or off.

Eastvale Computes had been open a couple of years now, and the owner, Barry Gilchrist, was the sort of chap who loved a technical challenge. As a consequence, people came in to chat about their computer problems, and Barry usually ended up solving them for free. Whether he ever sold any computers or not, Annie had no idea, but she doubted it very much, with Aldi, and even Woolworths, offering much lower prices.

Barry was one of these ageless young lads in glasses who looked like Harry Potter. Annie had been in the shop fairly often, and she was on friendly enough terms with him; she had even bought CD-ROMs and printer cartridges from him in an effort to give some support to local business. She got the impression that he rather fancied her, because he got all tongue-tied when he spoke to her and found it hard to look her in the eye. It wasn't offensive, though, like Templeton, and she was surprised to find that she felt more maternal towards him than anything else. She didn't think she was old enough for that sort of thing, but supposed, when she thought about it, that she might, at a pinch, be old enough to be his mother if he were as young as he looked. It was a sobering thought.

"Oh, hello," he said, blushing as he looked up from a monitor behind the counter. "What can I do for you today?"

"It's official business," Annie said, smiling. Judging by the expression that crossed his face and the way he surreptitiously hit a few keystrokes, Annie wondered if he'd been looking at Internet porn. She didn't have him down as that type, but you never could tell, especially with computer geeks. "You might be able to help us," she added.

"Oh, I see." He straightened his glasses. "Well, of course . . . er . . . whatever I can do. Computer problems at the station?"

"Nothing like that. It's Internet access I'm interested in."

"But, I thought . . ."

"Not for me. A customer you might have had maybe a couple of weeks ago."

"Ah. Well, I don't get very many, especially at this time of year. Tourists like it, of course, to check their email, but most of the locals either have their own computers or they're just not interested." Not to be interested, the way Barry Gilchrist said it, sounded infinitely sad.

Annie took a photograph from the folder she had brought and handed it to him. "This man," she said. "We know he was in Eastvale on Wednesday two weeks ago. We were just wondering if he came in here and asked to use your Internet access."

"Yes," said Barry Gilchrist, turning a little pale. "I remember him. The journalist. That's the man who was murdered, isn't it? I saw it on the news."

"What day of the week did he come in?"

"Not Wednesday. I think it was Friday morning."

The day he died, Annie thought. "Did he tell you he was a journalist or did you hear it?"

"He told me. Said he needed a few minutes to do a spot of research, that there was no access where he was staying."

"How long was he on?"

"Only about fifteen minutes. I didn't even bother charging him."

"Now comes the tricky part," said Annie. "I don't suppose there'd still be any traces of where he went online?"

Gilchrist shook his head. "I'm sorry, no. I mean, I said I don't get a lot of customers this time of year, but I do get some, so I have to keep the histories and temporary Internet files clean."

"They say you can never quite get rid of everything on a computer. Do you think our technical unit could get anything if we took them in?"

Gilchrist swallowed. "Took the computers away?"

"Yes. I hardly have to remind you this is a murder investigation, do I?"

"No. And I'm very sorry. He seemed like a nice enough bloke. Said he had wireless access on his laptop, but there were no signals around these parts. I could sympathize with that. It took long enough to get broadband."

"So would they?"

"Sorry, what?"

"If they took the computers apart, would they find anything?"

"Oh, but they don't need to do that," he said.

"Why's that?" Annie asked.

"Because I know the site he visited. One of them, at any rate. The first one."

"Do tell."

"I wasn't spying or anything. I mean, there's no privacy about it, anyway, as you can see. The computers are in a public area. Anyone could walk in and see what site someone was visiting."

"True," said Annie. "So you're saying he was making no efforts to hide his tracks. He didn't erase the history himself, for example?"

"He couldn't do that. That power's limited to the administrator, and that's me. Providing access is one thing, but I don't want people messing with the programs."

"Fair enough. So what was he doing?"

"He was at the Mad Hatters' website. I could tell because it plays a little bit of that hit song of theirs when it starts up. What's it called? 'Love Got in the Way'?"

Annie knew the song. It had been a huge hit about eight years ago. "Are you sure?" she asked.

"Yes. I had to go around the front to check the printer cartridge stock, and I could see it over his shoulder, photos of the band, biographies, discographies, that sort of thing."

Annie knew Banks would be as disappointed as she was with this. What could be more natural for a music journalist writing about the Mad Hatters than to visit their website? "Was that all?"

"I think so. I mean, I heard the music when he first started, and he finished a short while after I'd checked the stock. He could have followed any number of links in between, but if he did, he went back to the main site again." Gilchrist pushed his glasses back up the bridge of his nose with his forefinger. "Does that help?"

Annie smiled at him. "Every little bit helps," she said.

"There's one more thing."

"Yes?"

"Well, he was carrying a paperback book with him, as if he'd been sitting and having a read in a café or something. I saw him writing something in the back of it with a pencil. I couldn't see what it was."

"Interesting," said Annie, remembering the Ian McEwan book Banks had found at Moorview Cottage. He had said something about some pencilled numbers in the back. Maybe she should have a look. She thanked Gilchrist for his time and headed out into the wind.

17

Because of roadworks and poor weather on the M1, it took
Banks almost three hours to drive to Tania Hutchison's
house on Friday morning, and when he got to her village, he
was so thoroughly pissed off with driving that the beautiful
rolling country of the English heartland was lost on him.

He had spent the latter part of Thursday afternoon, and a
good part of the evening, reading over the files on the Linda
Lofthouse investigation and the Patrick McGarrity trial transcripts, all to little avail, so he had not been in the best of moods
when he got up that morning. Brian was still in bed, but Emilia
had been puttering around the place with a smile on her face
and had made him a pot of coffee and some delicious scram-
bled eggs. He was getting used to having her around.

Tania's house, perched on the edge of a tiny village, wasn't
especially large, but it was built of golden Cotswold stone, with
a thatched roof, and it must have cost her a pretty penny. The
thing that surprised Banks most was that he could drive right
up to her front gate; there was no security, no high wall or fence,
merely a privet hedge. He had rung earlier to let her know he
was coming, to get directions, and to make sure she would be
in, but he had told her nothing about the reason for his visit.

Tania greeted him at the door, and though there was no one else present, Banks knew he would have been able to pick her out of a crowd easily. It wasn't that she looked like a rock star or anything, whatever a rock star looked like. She was more petite than he imagined from seeing her on stage and television, and she certainly looked older now, but it wasn't so much the familiarity of her looks as a certain class, a presence. Charisma, Banks supposed. It wasn't something he came across often in his line of work. For a moment, Banks felt absurdly embarrassed, remembering the teenage crush he had had on her. He wondered if she could tell from his behaviour.

Her clothes were of the casual-expensive kind, understated designer jeans and a loose cable-knit sweater; she was barefoot, toenails painted red, and her dark hair, in the past so long and glossy, was now cut short and laced with delicate threads of grey. There were lines around her eyes and mouth, but otherwise her complexion seemed flawless and smooth. She wore little makeup, just enough to accentuate her full lips and her watchful green eyes, and she moved with a certain natural grace as Banks followed her through a broad, arched hallway into a large living room, where a lacquered grand piano stood by the French windows, and the floor was covered with a lush Persian carpet.

The other thing Banks noticed was a heavy glass ashtray, and Tania wasted no time in lighting a cigarette once she had curled up in an armchair and gestured for Banks to sit opposite her. She held the long, tipped cigarette in the V of her index and second fingers and took short, frequent drags. He felt like smoking with her, but he suppressed the urge. There was a fragility and a wariness about her, as well as class and charisma, as if she'd been hurt or betrayed so many times that once more would cause her world to crumble. Her name had been romantically linked with a number of famous rock stars and actors over the years, and with equally famous breakups, but now, Banks had read recently, she lived alone, with her two cats, and she liked it that way. The cats, one marmalade and one tabby, were in evidence, but neither showed much interest in Banks.

As he made himself comfortable, Banks had to remind himself that Tania was a suspect, and he had to put out of his mind the vivid sexual fantasies he had once entertained about her and stop acting like a tongue-tied adolescent. She had been at Brimleigh with Linda Lofthouse and had later been a member of the Mad Hatters. She had also been present at Swainsview Lodge on the night Robin Merchant drowned. She had no motive for either crime, as far as Banks knew, but motives sometimes had a habit of emerging later, once the means and the opportunity were firmly nailed in place.

"You weren't very forthcoming over the telephone, you know," she said, a touch of reproach in her husky voice. Banks could still hear hints of a North American accent, though he knew she had been in England since her student days.

"It's about Nick Barber's murder," he said, watching for a reaction.

"Nick Barber? The writer? Good Lord. I hadn't heard." She turned pale.

"What is it?"

"I spoke to him just a couple of weeks ago. He wanted to talk to me. He was doing a piece on the Mad Hatters."

"Did you agree to talk to him?"

"Yes. Nick was one of the few music journos you could trust not to distort everything. Oh, Christ, this is terrible." She put her hand to her mouth. If she was acting, Banks thought, then she was damned good. But she was a performer by trade, he reminded himself. As if sensing her grief, one of the cats made its way over slowly and, with a scowl at Banks, leaped on to her lap. She stroked it absently and it purred.

"I'm sorry," he said. "I didn't realize you were close, or I would have broken the news a bit more tactfully. I assumed you knew."

"We weren't close," she said. "I just knew him in passing, that's all. I've met him once or twice. And I liked his work. It's a hell of a shock. He was planning to come by and talk to me about my early days with the band."

"When was this?" Banks asked.

"We didn't have a firm date. He phoned two, maybe three weeks ago and said he'd get in touch with me again soon. He never did."

"Did he say anything else?"

"No. He said he was ringing from a public telephone, and his phone card ran out. What happened? Why would anyone murder Nick Barber?"

That explained why they hadn't seen Tania's number on Barber's mobile or land line phone records, Banks thought. "I think it might be something to do with the story he was working on," he said.

"The story? But how could it be?"

"I don't know yet, but we haven't been able to find any other lines of inquiry." Banks told her a little about Barber's movements in Yorkshire, in particular his unsatisfactory meeting with Vic Greaves.

"Poor Vic," she said. "How is he?"

Banks didn't know how to answer that. He'd thought Greaves was clearly off his rocker, if not clinically insane, but he seemed to function well enough, with a little help from Chris Adams, and he was certainly high on Banks's list of suspects. "Same as usual, I suppose," he said, though he didn't know what was usual for Vic Greaves.

"Vic was one of the sensitive ones," Tania said, "much too fragile for the life he led and the risks he took."

"What do you mean?"

Tania stubbed out her cigarette before answering. "There are people in the business whose minds and bodies can take an awful lot of substance abuse – Iggy Pop and Keith Richards come to mind, for example – and there are those who go on the ride with them and fall off. Vic was one who fell off."

"Because he was sensitive?"

She nodded. "Some people could eat acid as if it were candy and have nothing but a good time, like watching their favourite cartoons over and over again. Others saw the devil, the jaws of hell or the four horsemen of the apocalypse and the horrors beyond the grave. Vic was one of the latter. He had Hammer-horror trips, and the visions unhinged him."

"So LSD caused his breakdown?"

"It certainly contributed to it. But I'm not saying something wouldn't have happened anyway. Certainly the emotions and some of the images were in his mind already. Acid merely released them. But maybe he should have kept the cork in the bottle."

"Why did he keep taking it?"

Tania shrugged. "There's really no answer to that. Acid certainly isn't addictive in the way heroin and coke are. Not all his trips were bad. I think maybe he was trying to get through hell to something better. Maybe he thought if he kept on trying, then one day he would find the peace he was looking for."

"But he didn't?"

"You've seen him yourself. You should know."

"Who was he riding with?"

"There wasn't any one particular person. It was meant as a sort of metaphor for the whole scene back then. The doors of perception and all that. Vic was a poet and he loved and wanted all that mystical, decadent glamour. He admired Jim Morrison a lot, even met him at the Isle of Wight." She smiled to herself. "Apparently it didn't go well. The Lizard King was in a bad mood, and he didn't want to know poor Vic, let alone read his poetry. Told him to fuck off. That hurt."

"Too bad," said Banks. "What about the rest of the band's drug intake?"

"None of them was as sensitive as Vic, and none of them did as much acid."

"Robin Merchant?"

"Hardly. I'd have put him down as one of the survivors if it hadn't been for the accident."

"What about Chris Adams?"

"Chris?" A flicker of a smile crossed her face. "Chris was probably the straightest of the lot. Still is."

"Why do you think he takes such good care of Vic Greaves? Guilt?"

"Over what?"

"I don't know," Banks said. "Responsibility for the breakdown, something like that?"

"No," Tania said, shaking her head vigorously. "Far from it. Chris was always trying to get Vic off acid, helping him through bad trips."

"Then why?"

Tania paused. It was quiet outside, and Banks couldn't even hear any birds singing. "If you ask me," she said, "I'd say it was because he loved him. Not in any homosexual sense, you understand – Chris isn't like that, or Vic, for that matter – but as a brother. Don't forget, they grew up together, knew each other as kids on a working-class estate. They shared dreams. If Chris had had any musical talent, he'd have been in the band, but he was the first to admit he couldn't even manage the basic three rock chords, and he certainly couldn't carry even the simplest melody. But he did turn out to have good business sense and vision, and that's what shaped the band after all the tragedies. It was all very well to tune in, turn on, drop out and say whatever, man, but someone had to handle the day-to-day mechanics of making a living, and if someone trustworthy like Chris didn't do it, you could bet your life that there were any number of unscrupulous bastards waiting in the wings ready to exploit someone else's talent."

"Interesting," said Banks. "So in some ways Chris Adams was the driving force behind the Mad Hatters?"

"He held things together, yes. And he helped us with a new direction when both Robin and Vic were gone."

"Was it Chris who invited you to join the band?"

Tania twisted a silver ring on her finger. "Yes. It's no secret. We were going out together at the time. I met him at Brimleigh. I'd seen him a couple of times before, when my friend Linda got me into Mad Hatters events, but we hadn't really talked like we did at Brimleigh. I had a boyfriend then, a student in Paris, but we soon drifted apart, and Chris was in London a lot. He'd phone me and finally I agreed to have dinner with him."

"Brimleigh's something else I want to talk to you about," said Banks. "If you can cast your mind back that far."

Tania gave him an enigmatic smile. "There's nothing wrong with *my* mind," she said. "But if you're going to send me leafing through my back pages, I think we're going to need some coffee, don't you?" She dumped the cat unceremoniously on the floor and headed into the kitchen. The animal hissed at Banks and slunk away. Banks was surprised that Tania had no one to make the coffee for her, no housekeeper or butler, but then Tania Hutchison was full of surprises.

While she was gone, he gazed around the room. There was nothing to distinguish it particularly except a few modernist paintings on the walls, originals by the look of them, and an old stone fireplace that would probably make it very cozy on a winter evening. There was no music playing and no evidence of a stereo or CDs. Nor was there a television.

Tania returned shortly with a cafetière, mugs, milk and sugar on a tray, which she set on the low wicker coffee table. "We'll give it a few minutes, shall we? You do like your coffee strong?"

"Yes," said Banks.

"Excellent." Tania lit another cigarette and leaned back.

"Can we talk about Brimleigh?"

"Naturally. But as I remember it, the man who killed Linda was caught and put in jail."

"That's true," said Banks. "Where he has since died."

"Then . . . ?"

"I just want to get a few things clear, that's all. Did you know the man, Patrick McGarrity?"

"No. I'd met him on a couple of occasions, when I accompanied Linda to her friends' houses in Leeds, but I never spoke with him. He seemed an odious sort of character to me. Pacing around with that silly smile on his face, as if he was enjoying some sort of private joke at everyone else's expense. Gave me the creeps. I suppose they only put up with him because of the drugs."

"You knew about that?"

"That he was a dealer? It was pretty obvious. But he could only have been small-time. Even most dealers had more class than him, and they didn't smell as bad."

"Did you see him at Brimleigh?"

"No, but we were backstage."

"All the time?"

"Unless we went out front to the press enclosure to see the bands, and of course when Linda took her walk in the woods. But we were never with the general audience, no."

"I've read through the files and trial transcripts," said Banks, "and apparently you weren't worried about her?"

"No. We both knew we might go our separate ways. She knew I was heading off to Paris the next day, and she told me she'd probably stay with friends in Leeds, so I had no cause to worry. The very last thing you expected at a festival back then was a murder. This was before Altamont, remember, coming hot on the heels of successes at Woodstock and the Isle of Wight. Everyone was high on rock festivals. The bigger the better."

"I appreciate that," said Banks. "Did you see her talking to anyone in particular?"

"Not really. I mean, we talked to a lot of people. There was a sort of party atmosphere, and I must admit, it was a big thrill to be hanging out with the stars." She gave Banks a coy smile. "I was still an impressionable young girl back then, you know. Anyway, Linda spent a bit of time with the Hatters, but she would, wouldn't she? I mean, it was Vic got us the passes in the first place, and he was her cousin, even if they weren't especially close."

"Did anyone show unusual interest in her?"

"No. People chatted her up, if that's what you mean. Linda was a very attractive girl."

"But she didn't go off with anyone?"

"Not that I knew of." Tania leaned forward and pressed the plunger on the cafetière, then carefully poured two mugs. She added milk and sugar to her own, then offered them to Banks, who declined. "Linda was in a very spiritual phase then, into yoga and meditation, Tibetan Buddhism. She wasn't into drugs, and I don't think she was into men all that much."

"Did you actually see her leave the enclosure?"

"Not as such, no, but she told me she was going for a walk. I was heading to the front to see Led Zeppelin, and she said she needed a bit of space, she'd catch up with me later."

"So where was Linda when you last saw her?"

"Backstage."

"Was she with anyone?"

"A group of people."

"Including?"

"I can't really remember that far back. Some of the Hatters were there."

"Vic Greaves?"

"Vic was around, but he took some acid after the show and . . . who knows where he was. Most people went round the front. It was a real crush in there, I do remember that. People trying to cop a feel in the crowd. I couldn't say for certain who was there and who wasn't."

"So you didn't see Linda head for the woods?"

"No. Look, you're not saying Vic might have done this, are you? Because I don't believe that. Whatever his problems, Vic was always a gentle soul. Still is, only he's a bit disturbed. They caught the killer fair and square. They found his knife with Linda's blood on it. I'd seen McGarrity with that knife myself, at Bayswater Terrace."

"I know," said Banks. "But he maintained at the trial that he was framed, that the knife was planted."

Tania snorted. "He would, wouldn't he? You of all people should know that."

Banks had read all about McGarrity's bumbling efforts at defending himself in court, and he had no doubts that the man had been his own worst enemy. But if Vic Greaves had killed his cousin Linda, it made much more sense of later events, including Nick Barber's murder. Greaves certainly had a violent streak, as he had made evident at the cottage after Banks's visit. Perhaps, Banks thought, Greaves wasn't quite as crazy as he made himself out to be. But he couldn't tell Tania this. She was partisan; she would stick by her friends. He sipped some coffee. It was strong and full of flavour.

"Delicious," he said.

She inclined her head at the compliment. "Blue Mountain. Jamaica."

"Did you know that Linda had an illegitimate child?"

"Yes. She told me she gave him up for adoption. She was only sixteen at the time."

"And that child was Nick Barber?"

"He . . . what? My God! No, I didn't know that. How . . . I mean, that's an incredible coincidence."

"Not really," said Banks. "Plenty of people are adopted. Maybe Nick came by his love of music through Linda's genes. I don't know about that, but the knowledge did give him a particular interest in the Mad Hatters when he found out his birth mother was actually related to one of them. Then, when he found out she had been murdered, I should imagine his journalistic curiosity got him sniffing around that, too."

"You don't think it was anything to do with what happened to him, do you?"

"Only in that it set him on the course that led to his death. He probably wouldn't have been writing that story and found out what he did — if, indeed, that's what happened — if his mother hadn't been Linda Lofthouse. But there again, maybe he would have done it anyway. He was already a Mad Hatters fan. I just find it a curious detail, that's all. You were at Swainsview Lodge the night Robin Merchant died, weren't you?"

"Yes," said Tania. Banks couldn't be certain, but he thought he detected a certain reticence, or tightness, slip into her tone.

"What was he like?"

"Robin? Of all of them, he was probably the brightest and the most intellectual. The weirdest, too."

"What do you mean?"

"He always seemed remote, unreachable, to me. You couldn't touch him. You didn't know where he was, what he was thinking. Yet on the surface he was always friendly and pleasant enough. He was well educated and well read, but musically a bit plodding."

"What was he like with the girls?"

"Oh, they all fancied Robin. He was so pretty with that mass of dark curls and all, but I'm not sure . . . I mean, I don't think he really cared that much for anyone, underneath it all. I didn't know him long, but he never had any sort of relationship during that time. It was all rather mechanical for him. He took what he was offered, then cast them aside. He was more into metaphysical and occult things."

"Black magic?"

"Tarot cards, astrology, eastern philosophy, the Kabbalah, that sort of thing. A lot of people were into it back then."

"As they are again now," said Banks, thinking of Madonna and all the other stars who had discovered the Kabbalah of late, not to mention Scientology, which had also been a powerful presence in the late sixties. If you just wait, everything comes around again.

"I suppose so," Tania said. "Anyway, Robin was usually immersed in some book or other. He didn't say much. As I said,

I didn't really know him. Nobody did. His life outside the band was a mystery to all of us. If he had one."

"Did Linda like him?"

"She said he was cute, yeah, but like I said, she was into other things at the time. Men weren't really high on her list of priorities."

"But she wasn't off them completely?"

"Oh, no. I'm sure she'd have been interested if the right person had come along. She was just tired of the attitude some of the guys had. *Free love.* What they thought it meant was that they could screw any woman they wanted."

"What about relations between Robin and Vic Greaves?"

"Nothing unusual, really. Robin seemed upset sometimes that Vic got more of his songs performed, but Vic was the better songwriter. Robin's lyrics were too arcane, too dark."

"That's all?"

"Yes, as far as I know. It was nothing more serious. Mostly they got along just fine."

"And the rest of the band?"

"Same. There were disagreements, of course, as there always are when groups of people spend too much time cooped up together, but they weren't at each other's throats all the time, if that's what you mean. I'd say, as things go in this business, as a group they were a pretty well-behaved bunch of kids, and I've seen some bad behaviour in my time."

"And after you joined?"

"Everyone treated me with respect. They still do."

"What were the other members like as individuals?"

"Well, Vic was the sensitive poet, and Robin, as I said, the intellectual and the mystic. Reg was the angry one. The working-class boy made good with a bloody great chip on his shoulder. He's over it now, more or less – I think a few million quid might have had a bit to do with that – but it was what drove him back then. Terry was the quiet one. He'd had a rough background. Apparently his father died when he was just a kid, and his mother was really weird. I think she ended up in an institution eventually. He was troubled, but he never really talked about it. He seems to be a bit better adjusted these days. At least he manages to smile and speak a civil word now and then. And Adrian, well, he was the joker, the fun-lover. Still is. Laugh a minute, Adrian."

"And you?"

Tania raised her delicately arched eyebrows. "Me? I'm the enigmatic one."

Banks smiled. "What about your relationship with Chris Adams?"

"It faded over time. It's hard to keep a relationship going, the punishing schedule we had those first two or three years. We were touring or recording constantly. But we're still friends, have been ever since."

"The night Robin Merchant drowned," Banks said, "did you really expect the police to believe that you were all sound asleep in bed?"

She seemed taken aback by the question, but she answered without much hesitation. "They did, didn't they? Death by misadventure."

"But you weren't all asleep *all* the time, were you?" Banks pressed, shooting in the dark, hoping for a hit.

Tania looked at him, her green eyes disconcerting. He could tell she was trying to size him up, figure out what he knew and how he might have found out. "It's a long time ago," she said. "I can't remember."

"Come off it, Tania," Banks said. "Why did you all lie?"

"For God's sake, nobody lied." She shook her head, puffing on her third cigarette. "Oh, what the hell. It was just a lot easier that way. None of us killed Robin. We knew that. Why would we? If we'd said we were all up and about, they'd only have asked more stupid questions, and we were all a bit the worse for wear. We just wanted to be left alone."

"So what really happened?"

"I honestly don't know. I was drunk, if you must know."

"Drugs?"

"Some of the others. I stuck to vodka. Believe it or not, I never did anything else, except for a few tokes once in a while. Anyway, it was a big house. People were all over the place. You couldn't possibly keep track of one another even if you wanted to."

"Were people out by the swimming pool?"

"I don't know. I wasn't. If anybody saw Robin in there, then they knew it was too late to do anything for him."

"So you just left him there until the gardener came the next morning?"

"You're putting words into my mouth. I'm not saying that's what happened. I didn't see him there, and I don't know for a fact that anyone else did."

"But someone *could* have?"

"Of course someone could have, but what use is could have, especially now?"

"And someone could have pushed him in."

"Oh, for Christ's sake. Why would anyone do that?"

"I don't know. Maybe things weren't all as peachy as you say they were."

Tania sat forward. "Look, I've had enough of this. You come into my house and call me a liar to my face . . ."

"I'm not the one calling you a liar. You've already admitted you lied to the police in 1970. Why should I believe you now?"

"Because I'm telling the truth. I can't think of any reason on earth why any of us would have wanted Robin dead."

"I'm just trying to find the connection between then and now."

"Well, maybe there isn't one. Have you thought of that?"

"Yes, I've thought of that. But put yourself in my position. I have one definite murder in September 1969, and though the killer was apparently caught and jailed, there's still room for doubt in my mind. We have another death in June 1970, easily explained as an accident at the time, but now you tell me that people were up and about most of the night, maybe there's some doubt about that, too. And the common factor to all of these: the Mad Hatters. And Nick Barber was going to write their story, specifically Vic Greaves's story, and he made reference to a murder."

Tania drew on her cigarette and thought for a moment. "Look," she said, "I know when you put it like that, it sounds suspicious, but they're all just coincidences. I was at that party when Robin died, and to my recollection there were no arguments. Everyone just had a good time and that was that. We all went off to bed – I was with Chris at the time – but it was hard to sleep, a hot night, and maybe people got the munchies, whatever, and wandered around, went to raid the fridge. I mean, I heard people around the place on and off. Voices. Laughter. Vic was tripping, as usual. Maybe some of the group even swapped partners. It happened."

"You weren't asleep the whole time?"

"Of course not."

"And Chris Adams was with you all night?"

"Yes."

"Come on, Tania."

"Well, I . . . I mean, maybe not every minute of the night."

"So you woke up and he wasn't there?"

"It wasn't like that. For crying out loud, are you trying to blame Chris now? What is it with you?"

"Believe it or not," said Banks, "I'm just trying to get at the truth. Maybe it was a lark. Maybe someone was playing around with Robin beside the pool and he slipped and fell. An accident."

"In that case, why does it matter now? Even if Robin wasn't the only one by the pool at the time, if it was an accident anyway, why does it matter?"

"Because if someone feels threatened by the truth, and if Nick Barber was close to that truth, then . . ." Banks spread his hands.

"Couldn't there be some other explanation?"

"Like what?"

"I don't know. Robbery?"

"Well, Nick's laptop and his mobile were stolen, but that just supports the theory that someone didn't want people to know what he was doing."

"His girlfriend or something, then. A jealous lover. Aren't most people killed by someone they know, someone close to them?"

"True enough," said Banks. "And it's an area we've been looking into, along with a drug connection, but we've had no luck there yet."

"I just don't see how the past could have had anything to do with it. It's over. Judgments were handed down."

"If there's one thing I've learned in all my years as a detective," Banks said, "it's that the past is never over, no matter what has been handed down."

Banks was on his way back from visiting Tania Hutchison when two uniformed constables brought Calvin Soames into Western Area Headquarters in Eastvale. Annie Cabbot had them put him in an empty interview room and let him wait there a while.

"Where did you find him?" she asked one of the PCs.

"Daleside above Helmthorpe, ma'am," he said. "He was hiding in an old shepherd's shelter. Must have been there all night. Fair shivering, he was."

"Is he okay?"

"He seems all right. It might be a good idea to have a doctor check him out, though, just to be on the safe side."

"Thanks," said Annie. "I'll put in a call to Dr. Burns. In the meantime, I think I'll have a little chat with Mr. Soames myself."

Annie called Winsome over and noticed Templeton looking at them anxiously from behind his desk. "What is it, Kev?" she called out. "Sudden attack of conscience? Bit late for that, isn't it?" She immediately regretted her outburst, but it had no effect on Templeton, who just shrugged and got back to his paperwork. Annie could have throttled him, but that way he'd win.

Calvin Soames looked wet, cold and miserable. And old. At least there was some heat in the otherwise bleak interview room, and the constable had had the foresight to give him a grey blanket, which he wore over his shoulders like a robe.

"Well, Calvin," said Annie, after dealing with the preliminaries, and making it clear on the tape that Soames had refused the services of a duty solicitor, "what have you been up to?"

Soames said nothing. He just stared at a fixed point ahead of him, a nerve at the side of his jaw twitching.

"What's wrong?" Annie said. "Cat got your tongue?"

Still Soames said nothing.

Annie leaned back in her chair, hands resting on the desk. "You'll have to talk eventually," she said. "We already know what happened."

"Then you don't need me to tell you, do you?"

"We do need to hear it in your own words."

"I hit her. Something snapped and I hit her. That's all you need to know."

"Why did you hit Kelly?"

"You know what she did."

"She slept with a man she liked. Is that so terrible?"

"That's not what he said."

Annie looked puzzled. "What who said?"

Soames looked at Winsome. "You know who," he said.

"He means Kev Templeton, Guv," Winsome said.

Annie had worked that out for herself. "What did DS Templeton say?" she asked.

"I won't repeat the words he used," Soames said. "Vile, terrible things. Disgusting things."

So Templeton's inflammatory language had set Soames off on his rampage, Annie thought, as if she needed more evidence of his culpability. Even so, she cursed him again under her breath. "What about the drink?"

Soames scratched his head. "I won't say I'm proud of that," he said. "I used to be a hard-drinking man, but I got it under control, down to a couple of pints for the sake of being sociable. I let myself . . ." He stopped and put his head in his hands. Annie wasn't certain what the next words were, but she thought she heard him say "Her mother."

"Mr. Soames," she said gently. "Calvin, would you speak clearly, please?"

Soames wiped his eyes with the backs of his hands. "I said she was just like her mother."

"What was her mother like?"

"A good-for-nothing slut."

"Kelly said she thought you were talking to her as if she were her mother. Is that true?"

"I don't know. I just saw red. I don't know what I was saying. Her mother was younger than me. Pretty. The farm . . . it wasn't her sort of life. She liked the town and the parties and the dances. There were men. More than one. She didn't care whether I knew about them or not. She flaunted it, laughed at me."

"Then she died."

"Yes."

"That must have torn you apart," said Annie.

Soames gave her a sharp glance.

"I mean, she caused you so much pain. But there she was, dying, thanks to medical incompetence. You must have felt for her despite how she hurt you."

"It was God's judgment."

"How did Kelly react to all this?"

"I tried to keep it all from her," he said. "But she's turned out to be just the same."

"That's not true," Annie said. She was aware that the tape was running and she was exceeding her role as interviewer, but she couldn't help it. Let Superintendent Gervaise give her another bollocking, if that was what it came down to. "Just because Kelly slept with someone, it doesn't mean she was a slut or any other of those words men like to call women. You should be talking to your daughter, not beating her with a chair leg."

"I'm not proud of what I did," said Soames. "I'll face the consequences."

"Damn right, you will," said Annie. "And so will Kelly, unfortunately."

"What do you mean?"

"I mean she's lying there in a hospital bed because of you, and do you know what? She's worried about you, about what will happen to you."

"I sinned. I'll take my punishment."

"And what about Kelly?"

"She'll be better off without me."

"Oh, stop feeling sorry for yourself." Annie didn't trust herself to continue the interview. She shoved a statement sheet over to him and stood up. "Look, write down in your own words exactly what happened, what you can remember of it, then DC Jackman here will see that it's typed up for you to sign. In the meantime, the police surgeon will be coming in to look you over, just routine. Anything else you want to say?"

"Kelly? How is she?"

"Recovering," said Annie, her hand on the doorknob. "It's nice of you to ask."

18

As Banks sifted through the files on his desk on Saturday morning, he noticed the extra photocopy he had made of the list of numbers at the back of Nick Barber's book. It reminded him that he hadn't heard back from DC Gavin Rickerd yet, so he picked up the phone. Rickerd answered on the third ring.

"Anything on those numbers I gave you yet?" Banks asked.

"Sorry, sir," said Rickerd. "We've been snowed under. I haven't had a lot of time to work on it."

"Any ideas at all?"

"It might be some kind of code, but without a key it could be very difficult to crack."

"I don't think we have any keys," said Banks.

"Well, sir . . ."

"Look, just keep trying, will you? If I come up with anything that I think might help you, I'll let you know as soon as I can."

"Okay, sir."

"Thanks, Gavin."

As Banks put down the phone, Annie came in to tell him that after fairly exhaustive inquiries made by the Metropolitan Police, there was no evidence to suggest that Nick Barber had been involved with the cocaine business.

"That's interesting," said Banks. "Seeing as it was Chris Adams who suggested we look there."

"A bit of nifty misdirection?"

"Looks like it to me. I want another word with Adams anyway. Maybe I can intimidate him with the old wasting-police-time routine."

"Maybe," said Annie.

"Any news on Kelly Soames?"

"She was discharged from hospital this morning. She's staying with an aunt here in Eastvale for the time being."

"Calvin Soames can't just walk away, Annie, no matter how contrite he is. You know that."

"I know," said Annie. "You don't think I want him to get off scot-free, do you? But it's Kelly I'm concerned about at the moment."

"Kelly's young. She'll get over it. I doubt that any magistrate or jury is going to put Calvin away, should he even see the inside of a courtroom."

"He'll plead guilty. He wants to be punished."

"I'll bet you Kelly won't go into the witness box, and we won't have much of a case without her testimony."

"What's that?" Annie pointed at the list on Banks's desk. He realized that she hadn't been with him when he found it, and he hadn't looked at it since he gave the copy to Rickerd. "Some figures Nick Barber had scribbled in the back of his book."

Annie peered at it. "Of course. The Kelly Soames business put it right out of my mind, but I was meaning to ask you about that. Barry Gilchrist in the computer shop mentioned that he saw Nick Barber writing in the back of a book while he was on the Web. I wonder what it is."

"Does it mean anything to you?" Banks asked.

"No." Annie laughed. "But it does remind me of something."

"Oh? What?"

"Never mind."

"Seriously. It could be important."

"Just something I used to do when I was younger, that's all."

Banks could hardly keep the exasperation out of his voice. "What?"

Annie gave him a look. He could see that she was blushing. "You know," she said. "Ring dates?"

"What dates?"

"For crying out loud." Annie glanced over her shoulder and lowered her voice. She still sounded as if she were shouting at him. "Are you thick or something?"

"I'm trying not to be, but you've lost me."

"My period, idiot. I used to ring the day of the month my period was due. It's something a lot of girls do. I know this isn't exactly the same, not the same time between them, for a start, but it's the same idea."

"Well, pardon me, but not being a girl and not having periods –"

"Don't be sarcastic. Maybe it's family birthdays or lottery numbers or whatever, but it amounts to the same thing. I've told you what you want to know. It reminds *me* of when I used to ring dates on the calendar to mark the start of my period. Okay?"

Banks held his hands up "Okay." he said. "I surrender."

Annie snorted, turned away abruptly and left the room. Still feeling the disturbed air buffeting in her wake, Banks sat and gazed at the numbers.

6, 8, 9, 21, 22, 25
1, 2, 3, 16, 17, 18, 22, 23

10, (12), 13
8, 9, 10, 11, 12, 15, 16, 17, 19, 22, 23, 25, 26, 30
17, 18, (19)
2, 5, 6, 7, 8, 11, 13, 14, 16, 18, (19), 21, 22, 23

Six rows. Many numbers duplicated, and no list going
beyond 30. A calendar of some kind, then? Ringed dates? But
why were they ringed and, perhaps even more to the point,
which months, which year did they refer to? And why were
some days missing? It should be possible to find out, Banks
thought, perhaps with the help of a computer, then realized
that each group was not even necessarily from the same
month, or the same year. They could be strings of days taken
over a period of, say, thirty years. His spirits fell, and he cursed
Nick Barber under his breath for not being more clear with
his notes, realizing that this might be the clue he was looking
for, perhaps the only one Nick had left, and he felt about as far
from understanding it now as he ever had.

Annie had got over her irritation with Banks by mid-
afternoon, when he came poking his head around the squad
room door to tell her that Ken Blackstone had discovered the
whereabouts of Yvonne Chadwick, DI Stanley Chadwick's
daughter, and would she like to accompany him to the interview? She didn't need asking twice. Bugger Superintendent
Gervaise, she thought, grabbing her jacket and briefcase. She
noticed Kev Templeton give her an evil eye as she left the room.
Maybe he was already getting the cold shoulder from Madame
Gervaise, now that what had happened to Kelly Soames had
made the local news.

Banks was quiet as Annie drove the unmarked car she had
signed out of the police garage. She kept snatching sideways

glances at him and realized he was thinking. Well, that was a good sign. She drove on. "I checked the Mad Hatters' website, by the way," she said.

"And?"

"Definite possibilities for the numbers in the back of the book. There are links to other fan sites with tour dates and all sorts of esoteric information. I'll need a lot more time to follow up on it all."

"Maybe when we get back."

"Sounds good."

Yvonne Chadwick, or Reeves, as she was now called, lived on the outskirts of Durham, which wasn't too far up the A1 from Eastvale. The road was busy with lorries, as usual, and on a couple of occasions the inevitable roadworks cancelled out a lane or two and slowed traffic to a crawl. Annie glimpsed Durham Castle high on its hill and followed the directions Banks had written down for her.

The house was a semi with a bay window in a pleasant, leafy neighbourhood where you wouldn't be afraid to let your children play in the street. Yvonne Reeves turned out to be a rather plump, nervous woman of about fifty, who favoured a grey peasant skirt and a shapeless maroon jumper. If she dressed up a bit, Annie thought, she would be much more attractive. She wore her long, greying hair tied back in a ponytail. The interior of the house was clean and tidy. Bookcases lined the walls, mostly philosophy and law, with a sprinkling of literature. The living room was a little cramped, but comfortable once they had wedged themselves into the leather armchairs. There wasn't much natural light, and the room smelled of dark chocolate and old books.

"This is all very intriguing," said Yvonne. Her voice still bore the traces of her Yorkshire roots, though many of the rough edges had been flattened over the years. "But I've no idea at all why you think I might be able to help you. What's it all about?"

"Have you heard about the death of a music journalist called Nick Barber?" Banks asked.

"I think I saw something in the paper," Yvonne said. "Wasn't he murdered somewhere in Yorkshire?"

"Near Lyndgarth," said Banks.

"I still don't understand."

"Nick Barber was working on a story about a group called the Mad Hatters. Do you remember them?"

"Good Lord. Yes, of course I do."

"In September 1969, there was a pop festival in North Yorkshire at Brimleigh Glen. Remember? You would have been about fifteen."

Yvonne clapped her hands together. "Sixteen. I was there! I wasn't supposed to be, but I was. My father was terribly strict. He would never have let me go if I'd told him."

"You might also remember, then, that a young girl was found dead when the festival was over. Her name was Linda Lofthouse."

"Of course I remember. It was my father's case. He solved it."

"Yes. A man called McGarrity."

Annie noticed Yvonne give a little shiver at the name, and an expression of distaste flitted across her features. "Did you know him?" she asked, before the moment was lost.

Yvonne flushed. "McGarrity? How could I?"

She was a poor liar, Annie thought. "I don't know. You just seemed to react to the name, that's all."

"Dad told me about him, of course. He sounded like a terrible person."

"Look, Yvonne," Annie persisted, "I get the feeling there's

a bit more to it than that. I know it was a long time ago, but if you know anything that might help us, then you should let us know."

"How could knowing about back then possibly help you now?"

"Because," said Banks, "we think the cases might be linked. Nick Barber was Linda Lofthouse's son. She gave him up for adoption, but he found out who his mother was and what happened to her. That gave him a special interest in the Mad Hatters and the McGarrity case. We think that Nick had stumbled across something to do with his mother's murder, and that he was killed for it. Which means that we have to look very closely at what happened at Brimleigh and afterwards. Someone who worked on the case with your father let slip that McGarrity had possibly terrorized another girl, but that never came up at the trial, or in the case notes. We also heard that Mr. Chadwick had a bit of trouble with his daughter, that she was perhaps running with a wild crowd, but we couldn't get anything more specific than that. It might be nothing, and I might be wrong, but you are that daughter, and if you do know something, anything at all, please tell us and let us be the judges."

Yvonne said nothing for a few moments. Annie could hear a radio in the back of the house, probably the kitchen – talking, not music. Yvonne chewed on her lip and stared over their heads at one of the bookcases.

"Yvonne," Annie said. "If there's anything we don't know about, you should tell us. It can't possibly harm you. Not now."

"But it was all so long ago," Yvonne said. "God, I was such an idiot. An arrogant, selfish, stupid idiot."

"That would describe quite a lot of sixteen-year-olds," Annie said.

It broke the ice a little, and Yvonne managed a polite laugh. "I suppose so," she said. Then she sighed. "I used to run with a wild crowd, it's true," she said. "Well, not really wild, but different. Hippies, you'd call them. The kind of people my father hated. He'd go on about why he fought the war for lazy, cowardly sods like that. But they were harmless, really. Well, most of them."

"And McGarrity?"

"McGarrity was a sort of hanger-on, older, not really part of the crowd, but they couldn't summon the energy or find a reason to kick him out, so he drifted from place to place, sleeping on floors and in empty beds. Nobody really liked him. He was weird."

"And he had a knife."

"Yes. A flick knife with a tortoiseshell handle. Nasty thing. Of course, he said he lost it, but . . ."

"But the police found it in one of the houses," said Banks. "Your father found it."

"Yes." Yvonne squinted at Banks. "You seem to know plenty about this already."

"It's my job. I read the trial transcripts, but they didn't tell me about the girl he terrorized, the one your father asked him about during the interrogation."

"I suppose not."

"It was you, wasn't it?"

"Me?"

"You knew McGarrity. Something happened. How else could you explain your father's zeal in pursuing him or his reticence to pursue the issue? He abandoned all his other leads and concentrated on McGarrity. Now I'd say that was a little personal, wouldn't you?"

"Okay, I told him," Yvonne said. "McGarrity frightened

me. We were alone together in the front room at Springfield Mount, and he frightened me."

"What did he do?"

"It wasn't so much anything he did, just the way he talked, looked at me, grabbed me."

"He grabbed you?"

"My arm. Just a bruise. And he touched my cheek. It made me cringe. Mostly it was the things he said, though. He wanted to talk about Linda, and when that got him all excited, he started going on about those murders in Los Angeles. We didn't know who did it then – Manson and his family – but we knew the people had been butchered and someone had written PIGGIES on the walls in blood. He found all that exciting. And he said . . . he . . ."

"Go on, Yvonne," Annie urged her.

Yvonne looked at her as she answered. "He said he'd, you know, watched me with my boyfriend, and that now it was going to be his turn."

"So he threatened to rape you?" Annie said.

"That's what I thought. That's what I was scared of."

"Did he have his knife?" Banks asked.

"I didn't see it."

"What did he say about Linda Lofthouse?"

"Just how pretty she was, and how it was sad that she had to die, but that it was an absurd and arbitrary world."

"Is that all?"

"Then he talked about the Manson murders and asked me if I would like to do something like that."

"What happened next?"

"I made a break for it and ran for my life. He was pacing, spouting gibberish."

"And then what?"

"I told my father. He was furious."

"I can understand that," said Banks. "I have a daughter myself, and I'd feel exactly the same way. What happened next?"

"The police raided Springfield Mount and a couple of other hippie pads that night. They gave everyone a hard time, brought some drugs charges against them, but it was McGarrity they really wanted. He'd been at the festival, you see, at Brimleigh, and plenty of people had seen him wandering around near the edge of the woods with his flick knife."

"Did you think he did it?"

"I don't know. I suppose so. I never really questioned it."

"Yet he went on to deny it, said he was framed."

"Yes, but all criminals do that, don't they. That's what my father told me."

"It's pretty common." said Banks.

"So there. Look, what is this all about? He's not due to be released, is he?"

"You need have no worries on that score. He died in prison."

"Oh. Well, I can't say I'm heartbroken."

"What happened after the arrest and everything?"

Yvonne shook her head slowly. "I can't believe what an absolute idiot I was. My father let my boyfriend at Springfield Mount know that he was my father and told him to stay away from me. Steve, his name was. What an awful self-obsessed little prick. But a good-looking one, as I remember."

"I've known one or two like that myself," said Annie.

Banks glanced at her, as if to say, "We'll get back to that later."

"Anyway," Yvonne went on, "It was the usual story. I thought he loved me, but he just wanted me out of the way. It was so embarrassing. You know, it's funny, but the thing I remember most about the room is the Goya print on the wall. *El sueno de la razon produce monstruos. The Sleep of Reason Produces Monsters.* The one of the sleeping man surrounded by owls, bats and cats. It used to scare me and fascinate me at the same time, if you know what I mean."

"Did you go there again after the raid?"

"Yes. The next day. Steve didn't want to know me. None of them did. He spread the word that I was a copper's daughter, and I was ostracized by the lot of them." She snorted. "Nobody wants to share a joint with a copper's daughter."

"What did you do?"

"I was really hurt. I ran away from home. Took all the money I could and went to London. I had one address there, Lizzie, a girl who'd stayed at Springfield Mount once. She was nice and let me sleep on her floor. But it wasn't very clean. There were mice, and they kept trying to get in the sleeping bag, so I had to hold it tight around my neck, and I couldn't really get any sleep." She gave a little shiver. "And there were even more weird people about than there had been in Leeds. I was very depressed, and I started to get frightened of my own shadow. I think Lizzie got really fed up with me. She talked about negative energy and stuff like that. I was feeling lost then, really out of place, like I didn't belong anywhere and nobody loved me. Typical adolescent angst, I can see now, but at the time . . ."

"So what did you do?"

"I went back home." She gave a harsh laugh. "Two weeks. That was the sum of my life's big adventure."

"And how did your parents react?"

"Relief. And anger. I hadn't rung them, you see. That was cruel of me. If my daughter did that, I'd be beside myself, but that's how selfish and how upset I was. My father, being a policeman, always thought the worst. He had visions of me lying dead somewhere. He even told me that at first he thought something had happened to me, and that maybe it had something to do with McGarrity or the others taking revenge on me for shopping them. But he couldn't do anything official because he didn't want people to know. It must have torn him apart. He took his duty as a policeman so seriously."

"Didn't want people to know what?"

"About me and those hippies."

"What was your father like during the investigation and trial?"

"He was working very hard, very long hours. I remember that. And he was very tense, tightly wound. He started getting chest pains, I remember, but it was a long time before he would go to the doctor. We didn't talk much. He was under a lot of strain. I think he was doing it for me. He thought he'd lost me, and he was taking it out on McGarrity and everyone else involved. It wasn't a comfortable time in the house, not for any of us."

"But better than mice in the sleeping bag?" Annie said.

Yvonne smiled. "Yes, better than that. But we were all glad when it was over and McGarrity was convicted. It seemed to take forever, like a big black cloud over our heads. I don't think the trial started until the following April, and it went on for about four weeks. Things were pretty tense. Anyway, in the meantime, I went back to school, got on with my A levels, then I went to university in Hull. This would be the early seventies. There were still a lot of longhairs about, but I kept my distance. I'd learned my lesson. I applied myself to my studies, and in the end I became a schoolteacher and married a university professor. He teaches here, at Durham. We have two children, a boy and a girl, both married now. And that's the story of my life."

"Did you ever hear your father express any doubts about McGarrity's guilt?" Banks asked.

"No. Not that I can remember. It's as if he was on a crusade. I can't imagine what he would have done if McGarrity had got off. It doesn't bear thinking about. As it was, the whole thing ruined his health."

"And your mother?"

"Mum stood by him. She was a brick. She was devastated when he died, of course. We both were. But eventually she remarried and lived quite happily. She died in 1999. We were close right until the end. She only lived a short drive away, and she loved her grandchildren."

"That's nice," said Annie. "We've nearly finished now. The only other thing we want to ask you about is the death of Robin Merchant."

"The Hatters' bass player! God, I was absolutely gutted. Robin was *so* cool. They were one of my favourite bands, back when I used to listen to pop music, and we'd sort of claimed them as our own, too. You know they were from Leeds?"

"Yes," said Annie.

"Anyway, what about him?"

"Did your father say anything about it?"

"I don't think so. Why would he . . . ? Oh, yes. My God, this *is* taking me back. He talked to them during the McGarrity thing, and he got me an LP signed by all of them. I think I've still got it somewhere."

"Must be worth a bob or two now," said Banks.

"Oh, I'd never sell it."

"Still . . . did he say anything?"

"About Robin Merchant? No. Well, it was nothing to do with him, was it? That was the next summer, after McGarrity had been sent to jail, and my dad's heart was starting to show the strain even more. We never really talked about those sorts of things – you know, the music and hippie stuff – not after I came back from London. I mean, I was done with that scene, and my dad was grateful for that, so he didn't go on at me about it anymore. Mostly I threw myself into my A levels."

"Does this mean anything to you?" Banks brought out a photocopy of the ringed numbers from the back page of Nick Barber's book.

Yvonne frowned at it. "I'm afraid not," she said. "I didn't say I was a maths teacher."

"We think it might be dates," Banks explained. "Most likely dates connected with the Mad Hatters' tour schedule or something similar. But we've no idea which months or years."

"Leaves it pretty wide open, doesn't it, then?"

Annie looked at Banks and shrugged. "Well, that," Banks said, "is just about it, unless DI Cabbot has any more questions for you."

"No," said Annie, standing and leaning forward to shake Yvonne's hand. "Thanks for your time."

"You're welcome. I'm only sorry I couldn't be any more help."

"What do you think about what Yvonne told us?" Annie asked Banks over an after-work drink with cheese-and-pickle sandwiches in the Queen's Arms. The bar was half-empty and the pool table, happily, not in use. A couple of late-season tourists sat at the next table poring over Ordnance Survey maps and speaking German.

"I think what she said should make us perhaps just a little more suspicious of Stanley Chadwick and his motives," said Banks.

"Chadwick? What do you mean?"

"If he really thought his daughter had been terrorized and threatened with rape, and he was on a personal crusade ... who knows what he might have done? I try to imagine how I would behave if anything like that ever happened to Tracy, and I tell you, I can really frighten myself. Yvonne told us that McGarrity talked about the dead girl to her, about Linda Lofthouse. Admittedly, she didn't say he'd given her any information only the killer could have known, but we both know that sort of thing mostly just happens on TV. But what he *did* say sounded damn suspicious to me. Imagine how it sounded to her father, at his wits' end trying to catch a killer and worried about his daughter hanging around with hippies. Then he finds out this weirdo who terrorized her had a flick knife and was seen wandering around with it at Brimleigh Festival. Imagine he puts the two together, and suddenly the light goes on. Yvonne told us he didn't really look at anyone else for the crime after that. Rick Hayes went right out of the picture. It was McGarrity all the way, and only McGarrity."

"But the evidence says McGarrity did it."

"No, it doesn't. Everyone knew that McGarrity carried a flick knife with a tortoiseshell handle, including Stanley Chadwick. It wouldn't have been that hard for him to get hold of one just like it. Don't forget, Yvonne says she didn't see the knife when McGarrity terrorized her."

"Because he'd already hidden it."

"Or lost it, as he said."

"I don't believe this," said Annie. "You'd take the word of a convicted killer over a detective inspector with an unimpeachable reputation?"

"I'm just thinking out loud, for God's sake, trying to get a handle on Nick Barber's murder."

"And have you?"

Banks sipped some Black Sheep. "I'm not sure yet. But I do believe that Chadwick *could* have obtained such a knife, tricked McGarrity into handling it, and got access to Linda Lofthouse's clothing and blood samples. It might be a lot tougher now, but not necessarily back then, before PACE. Someone in Chadwick's position would probably have had free run of the place. And I think he might have been driven to do it because of what had happened to his daughter. Remember, this was a man on a mission, convinced he's right but unable to prove it by legitimate means. We've all been there. So in this case, because it's personal, and because of suspicious and disturbing things his daughter has told him about McGarrity that he can't use without bringing her into it and losing all credibility, he goes the extra mile and fabricates the vital bit of evidence he needs. Remember, apart from the knife there's no case; it falls apart. And there's another thing."

"What?"

"Chadwick's health. He was basically a decent, God-fearing, law-abiding copper with a strong Presbyterian background, probably deeply repressed because of his war experiences, and angry with what he saw around him: the disrespect of the young, the hedonism, the drugs."

"Turned psychoanalyst now, have you?"

"You don't need to be a psychoanalyst to know that if Chadwick really did fabricate a case against McGarrity, even for the best of reasons, it would tear a man like him apart. As Yvonne said, he was a dedicated copper. The law and basic human decency meant everything to him. He might have lost his faith during the war, but you can't change your nature that easily."

Annie put her glass to her cheek. "But McGarrity was seen

near the murder scene, he was known to be seriously weird, he had a flick knife, he was left-handed and he had met the victim. Why do you insist on believing that he didn't do it, and that a good copper turned bad?"

"I'm not insisting. I'm just trying it out for size. We'd never prove it now, anyway."

"Except by proving that someone else killed Linda Lofthouse."

"Well, there is that."

"Who do you think?"

"My money's on Vic Greaves."

"Why, because he was mentally unstable?"

"That's part of it, yes. He had a habit of not knowing what he was doing, and he had dark visions on his acid trips. Remember, he took acid that night at Brimleigh, as well as on the night of Robin Merchant's death. It doesn't take a great stretch of the imagination to guess that maybe he heard voices telling him to do things. But Linda Lofthouse was his cousin, so if you work on the theory that most people are killed by someone they know, particularly a family member, it makes even more sense."

"You don't think he killed Robin Merchant, too, do you?"

"It's not beyond the bounds of possibility. Maybe Merchant knew, or guessed?"

"But Greaves had no history of violence at all. Not to mention no motive."

"Okay, I'll give you all that. But it doesn't mean he couldn't have flipped. Drugs do very strange things to people."

"What about Nick Barber?"

"He found out."

"How?"

"I haven't got that far yet."

"Well," said Annie, "I still think Stanley Chadwick got it right and Patrick McGarrity did it."

"Even so, Rick Hayes might be worth another look, too, if we can find him."

"If you insist." Annie finished her Britvic orange. "That's my good deed for the day," she said.

"What are you up to tomorrow?" Banks asked.

"Tomorrow? Browsing websites, most likely. Why?"

"I just thought you might like to take an hour or two off and come out for Sunday lunch with me and meet Emilia."

"Emilia?"

"Brian's girlfriend. Didn't I tell you? She's an actress. Been on telly."

"Really?"

"*Bad Girls*, among others."

"One of my favourites. All right, sounds good."

"Let's just keep our fingers crossed that nothing interrupts us like it did the other night."

For once, it wasn't long after dark when Banks got home, having checked back at the station after his drink with Annie and found things ticking along nicely. Brian and Emilia were out somewhere, which allowed him a few delicious moments alone to listen to a recent CD purchase of Susan Graham singing French songs and enjoy a glass of Roy's Amarone. When Brian and Emilia finally got back, the CD was almost over and the glass of wine half-empty. Banks went into the kitchen to greet them.

"Dad," said Brian, putting packages on the table, "we went to York for the day. We didn't know if you were going to be here, so we picked up Indian take-away. There's plenty if you want to share."

"No," said Banks, trying not to imagine what seismic reactions might occur in his stomach when curry met Amarone. "I'm not really hungry. Thanks. I had a sandwich earlier. How did you enjoy York?"

"Great," said Emilia. "We did all the tourist stuff. You know, toured the Minster, visited Jorvik. We even went to the train museum."

"You took her there?" Banks said to Brian.

"Don't blame me. It was her idea."

"It's true," Emilia said, taking Brian's hand. "I love trains. I had to drag him."

They both laughed. Banks remembered taking Brian to the National Railway Museum, or York Railway Museum as it was then known, on a day trip from London when he was about seven. How he had loved climbing all over the immaculate steam engines and playing at being the driver.

Brian and Emilia ate their curry at the kitchen bench while Banks sat sipping his wine and chatting with them about their day. When they had finished eating, Brian tidied up – an oddity in itself – then said, "Oh, I forgot. I bought you a present, Dad."

"Me?" said Banks. "You shouldn't have."

"It's not much." Brian took an HMV bag from his backpack. "Sorry I haven't had a chance to wrap it properly."

Banks slipped the case out of the plastic bag. It was a DVD. *The Mad Hatters Story*. Judging by the account on the back of the box, it contained footage from every stage of the band's career, including the earliest lineup with Vic Greaves and Robin Merchant. "Should be interesting," Banks said. "Do you want to watch it with me?"

"I wouldn't mind."

"Emilia?"

Emilia took a book out of her shoulder bag, *Reading Lolita in Tehran*. "Not me," she said with a smile. "I'm tired. It's been a long day. I think I'll go to bed and read for a while and leave you boys together." She kissed Brian, then turned to Banks and said, "Good night."

"Good night," Banks said. "Look, before you go, would the two of you like to come out for Sunday lunch with Annie and me tomorrow. If we can get away, that is?"

Brian raised his eyebrows and looked at Emilia, who nodded. "Sure," he said, then added, with the weight of many broken engagements, "*If* you can get away."

"I promise. You are staying a while longer, aren't you?"

"If that's okay," said Brian.

"Of course it is."

"If we're not cramping your style, that is."

Banks felt himself blush. "No. Why should you . . . ? I mean . . ."

Emilia said good night again, smiled and went upstairs. "She seems like a nice girl," he said to Brian when she was out of earshot.

Brian grinned. "She is."

"Is it . . . ?"

"Serious?"

"Well, yes, I suppose that's what I meant."

"Too early to say, but I like her enough that I'd hurt if she left me, as the song says."

"Which song?"

"Ours, idiot. The last single."

"Ouch. I don't buy singles."

"I know that, Dad. I was teasing. And it wasn't even for sale on a CD. You had to download it from iTunes."

"Hey, wait a minute. I know how to do that now. I've got an iPod. I'm not a complete Luddite, you know."

Brian laughed and grabbed a can of lager from the fridge. Banks refilled his glass and the two of them went into the entertainment room.

The DVD started with manager Chris Adams giving a potted history, then segued into a documentary made up of old concert footage and interviews. Banks found it amusing and interesting to see the band members of thirty-five years ago in their bell-bottoms and floppy hats manage to sound pretentious and innocent at the same time as they spoke about "peace and love, man." Vic Greaves, looking wasted as usual in a 1968 interview, went off at a tangent punctuated with long pauses every time the interviewer asked him a question about his songs. There was something icily detached and slightly more cynical about Robin Merchant, and his cool, practical intelligence often provided a welcome antidote to the vapid and meandering musings of the others.

But it was the concert footage that proved most interesting. There was nothing from Brimleigh, unfortunately, except a few stills of the band relaxing with joints backstage, but there were some excellent late-sixties films of the band performing at such diverse places as the Refectory at Leeds University, Bristol's Colston Hall and the Paradiso in Amsterdam. At one of the gigs, an outrageously stoned and enthusiastic emcee yelled in a thick cockney accent, "And now, ladies and gentlemen, let's 'ave a 'uge 'and for the 'ATTERS!"

The music sounded wonderfully fresh, and Vic Greaves's innocent, pastoral lyrics had a haunting and timeless sadness about them, meshing with his delicate, spacey keyboards work and Terry Watson's subtle riffs. Like many bass players, Robin

Merchant just stood and played expressionlessly, but well, and like many drummers, Adrian Pritchard thrashed around at his kit like a maniac. Keith Moon and John Bonham were clearly big influences there.

There was something a bit odd about the lineup, but Banks was only half watching and half talking to Brian, and the next thing he knew, both Vic Greaves and Robin Merchant were gone and the lovely, if rather nervous, Tania Hutchison was making her debut with the band at London's Royal Festival Hall in early 1972. Banks thought about his meeting with her the other day. She was still a good-looking woman, and he might have fancied his chances, but he thought he had alienated her with his probing questions. That seemed to be the story of his life, alienating women he fancied.

The documentary went on to portray the band's upward trajectory until their official retirement in 1994, with clips from the few reunion concerts they had performed since then, along with interviews from an older, chain-smoking, short-haired Tania, and a completely bald, bloated and ill-looking Adrian Pritchard. Reg Cooper and Terry Watson must have declined to be interviewed, because they appeared only in the concert footage.

When the film came to a sequence about disagreements within the band, Banks noticed Brian tense a little. Since the investigation had taken him further into the world of rock than he had ever been before, he had thought a lot about Brian and the life he was living. Not just drugs, but all the trappings and problems that fame brings with it. He thought of the great stars who had destroyed themselves at an early age through self-indulgence or despair: Kurt Cobain, Jimi Hendrix, Tim Buckley, Janis Joplin, Nick Drake, Ian Curtis,

Jim Morrison . . . the list went on. Brian seemed all right, but he was hardly likely to tell his father if he had a drug problem, for example.

"Anything wrong?" Banks asked.

"Wrong? No. Why? What could be wrong?"

"I don't know. It's just that you haven't talked about the band much."

"That's because there's not much to say."

"So things are going fine?"

Brian paused. "Well . . ."

"What is it?"

He turned to face Banks, who turned down the DVD volume a notch or two. "Denny's getting weird, that's all. If it gets much worse, we might have to get rid of him."

Denny, Banks knew, was the band's other guitarist/vocalist, and Brian's songwriting partner.

"Get rid of him?"

"I don't mean kill him. Honestly, Dad, sometimes I wonder about the effect your job has on you."

So do I, Banks thought. But he also thought about killing off disruptive band members – Robin Merchant, for example – and how easy it would have been, just a gentle nudge in the direction of the swimming pool. Vic Greaves had been disruptive, too, but he had made his own voluntary exit. "Weird? How?" he asked.

"Ego, mostly. I mean, he's getting into really off-the-wall musical influences, like acid Celtic punk, and he's trying to import it into our sound. If you challenge him on it, he gets all huffy and goes on about how it's *his* band, how *he* brought us together and all that shit."

"What do the others have to say about him?"

"Everybody's sort of retreated into their own worlds. We're not communicating very well. We're going through the motions. There's no talking to Denny. We can't write together anymore."

"What happens if he goes?"

Brian gestured towards the video. "We get someone else. But we're not going pop."

"You're doing just fine as you are, aren't you?"

"We are. I know. We're selling more and more. People *love* our sound. It's got an edge, but it's accessible, you know. That's the problem. Denny wants to change it, and thinks he's got a right to do so."

"What about your manager?"

"Geoff? Denny keeps sucking up to him."

Banks immediately thought of Kev Templeton. "And how is Geoff dealing with that?"

Brian scratched his chin. "Come to think of it," he said, "he's getting sick of it. I think at first he liked that someone in the band was giving him a lot of attention, not to mention telling tales out of school, but I don't know if you've ever noticed this, it's a weird thing, but eventually people get fed up with their toadies."

From the mouths of babes, Banks thought, as a light bulb went on in his brain. Though Brian was hardly a baby. It was as he had suspected. Templeton was digging his own grave. Nobody needed to do anything. Sometimes the best thing to do is nothing. Annie ought to appreciate that, too, Banks thought, with her interests in Taoism and Zen. "Have drugs got anything to do with it?" he asked.

Brian looked at him. "Drugs? No. If you mean have I ever done any drugs, then the answer's yes. I've smoked dope and taken E. I took speed once, but when I came down I was depressed for a week, so I've never touched it since. Nothing stronger. And as it happens, I still prefer lager. Okay?"

"Okay," said Banks. "It's good of you to be so frank, but I was thinking more about the others."

Brian smiled. "Now I see how you trick confessions out of people. Anyway, the answer's still no. Believe it or not, we're a pretty straight band."

"So what next?" Banks asked.

Brian shrugged. "Dunno. Geoff said we all needed to take a breather, we'd been working so hard in the studio and on tour. When we get back . . . we'll see. Either Denny will have changed his ideas or he won't."

"What do you predict?"

"That he won't."

"And then?"

"He'll have to go."

"Does that worry you?"

"A bit. Not too much, though. I mean, they did all right, didn't they?" The Mad Hatters were performing their jaunty, rocking 1983 number-one hit, "Young at Heart." "The band will survive. It's more the lack of communication that upsets me. I mean, Denny was a mate, and now I can't talk to him."

"Losing friends is always sad," said Banks, aware of how pathetic and pointless that observation was. "It's just one of those things, though. When you first get together with someone it's a great adventure, finding out stuff you've got in common. You know, places you love, music, books. Then the more you get to know them, the more you start to see other things."

"Yeah, like a whingeing, lying, manipulative bastard," said Brian. Then he laughed and shook his empty can. "Want another glass of plonk?" he asked Banks, whose glass was also empty.

"Sure, why not?" said Banks, and he watched the lovely Tania sway in pastel blue diaphanous robes that flowed around her like water while Brian got the drinks.

"There is one thing I'd like to know," he said, after a sip of Amarone. *Plonk*, indeed.

"What's that?" Brian asked.

"Just what the hell does acid Celtic punk sound like?"

19

Annie jotted something down, then turned back to the computer monitor and scrolled. It was Monday morning. On Sunday, most of the team had taken a well-deserved day off, their first since Nick Barber's murder almost two weeks ago. Annie had spent the morning doing household chores, the afternoon on the Mad Hatters' website and the evening enjoying that long bath and the trashy magazines she had been promising herself. At lunchtime, she had gone out with Banks, Brian and Emilia to the Bridge in Grinton. Emilia had been absolutely charming, and Annie had been secretly awestruck to meet an up-and-coming actress. More so than by meeting Banks's rock star son, whom she had met before, though Brian had also, in his way, been charming and far less full of himself than she remembered from previous occasions they had met. He seemed to have matured and become comfortable with his success, no longer the young tearaway with something to prove.

The coffee at her right hand was lukewarm, and she made a face when she took a sip. There was plenty of activity around her in the squad room, but she was still on the Web, oblivious to most of it as she felt herself finally zooming in on the mystery of the numbers in the back of Nick Barber's book.

It wasn't such an esoteric solution after all, she realized with a sense of disappointment. It didn't suddenly make everything clear and solve the case, and it was nothing she wouldn't have expected him to make a note of anyway.

She hadn't found everything she wanted at the official Mad Hatters website, but she had found links there that took her to more obscure fan sites, as Nick Barber must have done in Eastvale Computes. But all the owner had heard was the snatch of song that played when he accessed the official site. Now she negotiated her way through bright orange and red Gothic print, black backgrounds with stylized logos and flashing arrows. All signs that some young Web designer was eager to show off and lacked restraint. Before long, her eyes were starting to buzz, and her eyeballs felt as if they had been massaged with sandpaper.

Once she had the final string jotted down, she printed the whole document, bookmarked the URL and closed the browser. Then she rubbed her eyes and went in search of a fresh cup of coffee, only to find that it was her turn to make a fresh pot. When she finally got back to her desk, it was close to lunchtime and she felt like a break from the office.

"I was just thinking about you," she said, when Banks popped his head around the door and asked her how she was getting on. "I'm feeling cooped up here. Why don't you take me to that new bistro by the castle and we can go over what I've found so far?"

"What?" said Banks. "Lunch together two days in a row? People will talk."

"A working lunch," Annie said.

"Okay. Sounds good to me."

With Templeton's deepening frown following them, Annie picked up her papers and they walked out into the cobbled market square. It was a fine day for the time of year, scrubbed blue sky and just a hint of chill in the wind, and a couple of coachloads of tourists from Teesside were disembarking by the market cross and making a beeline for the nearest pub. The church clock struck twelve as Banks and Annie crossed the square and took the narrow lane that wound up to the castle. The bistro was down a small flight of stone stairs about halfway up the hill. It had only been open about three months and had garnered some good local reviews. Because it was early, only two of the tables were occupied already, and the owner welcomed them, giving them the pick of the rest. They chose a corner table, with their backs to the whitewashed walls. That way nobody would be able to look over their shoulders. Little light got through the half-window, and all you could see were legs and feet walking by, but the muted wall lighting was good enough to read by.

They both decided on sparkling mineral water, partly because Annie rarely drank at lunchtime, and Banks said he was beginning to find that even one glass of wine so early in the day made him drowsy. Banks went for a steak sandwich and frites and Annie chose the cheese omelette and green salad. The food ordered and fizzy water poured, they started to go over the results of her morning's work. Soft music played in the background. Eastvale's idea of Parisian chic: Charles Aznavour, Edith Piaf, a little Françoise Hardy. But it was so quiet as to be unobtrusive. Banks broke off a chunk of baguette, buttered it and looked at Annie's notes.

"Put simply," she said, "it's the Mad Hatters' tour dates from October 1969 to May 1970."

"But that's eight months, and there are only six rows."

"They didn't tour in December or February," Annie said. She showed Banks the printout from the website. "I got this all from a site run by what must be their most devoted fan. The trivia some of these people put out there is amazing. Anyway, it must have been a godsend to a writer like Nick Barber."

"But is it all accurate?"

"I'm sure there are errors," Annie said. "After all, these web-sites are unedited, and it's easy to make a mistake. But on the whole I'd say it's probably pretty close."

"So the Mad Hatters were on tour the sixth, eighth, ninth, twenty-first, twenty-second and twenty-fifth of October? That's how it goes?"

"Yes," said Annie. She handed him the printout. "And these were the places they played."

"The Dome, Brighton; the Locarno Ballroom, Sunderland; the Guildhall, Portsmouth. They got around."

"They certainly did."

"And the ringed dates?"

"Just three of them, as you can see," said Annie. "The twelfth of January, the nineteenth of April and the nineteenth of May. All in 1970."

"Any significance in those two nineteenths?"

"I haven't figured out the significance of any of the ringed dates yet."

"Maybe it was one of his girlfriends' periods?"

Annie gave him a sharp nudge in the ribs. "Don't be rude. Anyway, periods don't come that irregularly. Not usually, at any rate."

"So you did consider it?"

Annie ignored him and prepared to move on just as their food arrived. They took a short pause to arrange papers, plates and knives and forks, then carried on. "The first gap is three months and the second is one."

"Drug scores?"

"Perhaps."

"What about the venues?"

Annie consulted her notes. "On the twelfth of January, they were playing at the Top Rank Suite in Cardiff, on the nineteenth of April, they were at the Dome in Brighton and on the nineteenth of May, they were at the Van Dyke Club in Plymouth."

"You can't get much more diverse than that," said Banks. "Okay. Now we need to find out if there's any significance at all to those dates and places."

The owner came over to see if everything was all right. They assured him it was, and he scooted off. That kind of solicitude wouldn't last long in Yorkshire, Annie thought, finding herself wondering if his French accent was as false as his hairpiece. "I'll enlist Winsome's aid after lunch," she said. "You?"

"I think it's time I paid another visit to Vic Greaves," said Banks. "See if I can get any more sense out of him this time. I was thinking of taking Jenny Fuller along, but she's off on the lecture circuit, and there's no one else around I can really trust for that sort of thing."

"Be careful," said Annie. "Remember what happened to Nick Barber when he got too interested in Greaves."

"Don't worry. I will."

"And good luck," Annie added. "By the sound of him, you'll need it."

Banks cut off a lump of glutinous brown gristle from his steak and put it on the side of his plate. The sight of it made Annie feel vaguely queasy and very glad to be a vegetarian.

"You know," Banks said, "I still can't decide whether Greaves is truly bonkers or just a genuine English eccentric."

"Maybe there isn't much of a difference," Annie said. "Have you thought of that?"

There were plenty of cars parked on Lyndgarth's village green early on Monday afternoon, and several groups of walkers in serious gear had assembled for briefings nearby. Banks found a spot to park near the post office and headed up the lane to Vic Greaves's cottage. He was hoping that the man might be a bit more coherent this time and had a number of questions prepared to jog the ex–keyboards player's memory if he needed to. Since his last visit, he had come to believe that Stanley Chadwick had been seriously misguided about Patrick McGarrity's guilt, for personal reasons, and he now knew that not only had Greaves been Linda Lofthouse's cousin, but that Nick Barber was her son, which meant that Greaves and Barber were also related in some complicated way that Banks couldn't quite figure out. But most important, it meant *connections* between the different cases, and connections always excited Banks.

He walked up the short path and knocked on the door. The front curtains were closed. No answer. He remembered the last time, how it had taken Greaves a while to answer, so he knocked again. When he still got no answer, he walked around to the back, where there was a small cobbled yard and a storage shed. He peeked through the grimy kitchen window and saw that things were in pretty much the same spotless order as they had been when he had first visited Greaves.

Curious, Banks tried the back door. It opened.

He was treading on dangerous ground now, he knew, entering a suspect's premises alone without a search warrant, but he thought that he could justify his actions if he had to. Vic

Greaves was mentally unstable, and Banks feared that he might have come to some harm, or harmed himself in some way. Even so, he hoped he didn't stumble across the one piece of vital evidence that linked Greaves inextricably with Barber's murder, or with Linda Lofthouse's, or he might have a hard time getting it admitted in court. What he would do, he decided, was not touch anything and return with full authorization if he had to.

As he entered, Banks felt a shiver of fear run down his spine. Annie had been right in her warning. If he indicated that he was at all close to the truth, then Greaves might lash out, as Banks thought he had done at Nick Barber. He might already know who was at his door, might be lying in wait, armed and ready to attack. Banks moved cautiously through the dim kitchen. At least all the knives were in their slots in the wooden block where Greaves kept them. Banks stood still in the doorway that led through to the living room and listened. Nothing but the wind whipping the tree branches and the distant sounds of a car starting and a dog barking.

From what he could make out in the pale light that filtered through the curtains, the living room was just as it had been, too, with newspapers and magazines piled everywhere. Banks stood at the bottom of the stairs and called out Greaves's name again. Still no answer.

Tense and alert, he started to walk up the stairs. They creaked as he moved. Every once in a while he would pause, but still he heard nothing. He stood on the upstairs landing and listened again. Nothing. It was a small cottage, and in addition to the toilet and bathroom there were only two bedrooms. Banks checked the first and found it almost as full of newspapers and magazines as the living room. Then he went into the second, which was obviously Greaves's bedroom.

In one corner lay a mattress heaped with sheets and blankets. It reminded Banks of nothing so much as a nest of some kind. Carefully, he poked around with his toe in the bedsheets, but no one was there, either hiding or dead. Though the sheets were piled in an untidy mess, they were clean and smelled of apples. There was nothing else in the room except a wardrobe and a dresser full of old, but clean and neatly folded, clothes and underwear.

After a cursory glance in the toilet and bathroom, which told him nothing, Banks went back downstairs into the living room. It was an ideal opportunity for him to poke around, but it didn't seem as if Greaves had anything worth poking around for. There were no mementoes, no Mad Hatters memorabilia, no photos or keepsakes of any kind. In fact, as far as Banks could tell, the cottage contained nothing but a few basic toiletries, clothes, kitchenware and newspapers.

He started looking at some of the papers on the top of a pile: *Northern Echo* and *Darlington and Stockton Times*, along with the *Yorkshire Evening Post* dating back about three years, as far as he could tell. The magazines covered just about everything from computing, though Greaves had no computer, as far as Banks had seen, to coin collecting, though there were none on the subject of rock music, or music of any kind. Many of the magazines still had free gifts stuck to their covers, and some hadn't even been removed from their cellophane wrapping.

Finding nothing of interest among the papers, Banks headed for the shed in the backyard. It had a padlock, but it was already open, just hanging there loosely on the hasp. Banks opened the door. He expected more newspapers, at the very least, but the shed was empty. It had no particular smell except for soil and wood. Spiders went about their webs in the corners, and one particularly large specimen scuttled across the window. Banks shuddered. He had hated spiders ever since he had found one under his pillow when he was about five.

Banks closed the door behind him and left it as it was. There was one thing, he guessed, that should have been there but wasn't: Vic Greaves's bicycle. So had Greaves gone ride-about, or had he gone somewhere specific?

Banks went back to his car and took out his mobile. The signal was poor, but at least there was one. Chris Adams answered almost immediately.

"Mr. Adams," said Banks. "Where are you?"

"At home. Why?"

"Do you have any idea where Vic Greaves is?"

"I'm not his keeper, you know."

"No, but you're the closest he's got to one."

"Sorry, no. I don't know. Why?"

"I've just been to see him and his bike's not there."

"He does go out from time to time."

"Anywhere in particular?"

"He just rides. I don't know where he goes. Look, are you telling me there's some reason to be worried?"

"Not at all. I'm just trying to find him to ask him a few more questions."

"What about?"

"Things seem to be coming to a head. I think we're almost there."

"You know who killed Nick Barber?"

"Not yet, but I think I'm getting close."

"And Vic knows this?"

"I don't know what he knows. I'll bet he can be remarkably perceptive at times, though."

"You never know with Vic. What goes in, what goes straight through."

"Any idea where he might go?"

"No. I told you. He goes for bike rides from time to time. Helps keep him in shape."

"If you hear from him, please let me know."

"Okay."

"One more thing, Mr. Adams."

"Yes?"

"The night Robin Merchant drowned. Were you up and around at the time?"

"Who told you that?"

"Were you?"

"Of course not. I was fast asleep."

"You and I both know that's a load of bollocks, Mr. Adams, and the police probably knew it even then. They just didn't have any evidence to suggest Robin Merchant might have been murdered, or that his death might have been caused by someone else in some way."

"This is absurd. Is it Tania? Have you been talking to Tania?"

"Why would that make a difference?"

"Because she was pissed. If you've talked to her, she's no doubt told you we were what they call an item at the time. Her drug of choice was alcohol. Vodka mostly. She was probably so drunk she didn't know her arse from her elbows."

"So you weren't up and about?"

"Of course not. Besides, Tania's got it in for me. We haven't exactly been on the best of terms these past few years."

That wasn't exactly what Tania had told him, Banks remembered. Who was lying? "Oh. Why's that?"

"A mixture of business and personal matters. And none of your business, really. Now, look, this connection's getting worse and worse. I'm going to hang up now."

"I'd like to talk to you again. Can you come by the station?"

"I'll be passing nearby on my way to London next week. I'll try to drop in if I have the time."

"Try to make time. And ring first."

"I will if I can remember. Goodbye, Mr. Banks."

As Banks was putting his mobile away, he noticed he had voice mail waiting. Curious, he pressed the button and after the usual introduction heard Annie's voice. "I hope things are going well with Vic Greaves," she said. "Winsome and I seem to be making some progress here, and we'd like to have a chat with you about the possibilities we've raised. Can you come back to the station as soon as you have a moment? It could be important. Cheers."

Well, Banks thought, turning his car towards Eastvale and slipping in an old Roy Harper CD, *Flashes from the Archives of Oblivion*, at least someone was making progress.

Winsome said she didn't need to use the online computer anymore, so they adjourned to the privacy of Banks's office. The market square was busy with tourists and shoppers coming in and out of the narrow streets that radiated from it. The day was warming up, so Banks opened his window about six inches to let in some fresh air. The noise of the cars, snatches of music, laughter and conversations all sounded distant and muffled. A whiff of diesel fumes from the revving coaches drifted in.

"You've been busy, by the looks of it," Banks said as Winsome dropped a pile of paper on his desk.

"Yes, sir," she said. "I've been on the telephone or the Internet over three hours now, and I think you'll find the results very interesting."

"Go ahead."

They sat in a semi-circle around Banks's desk so they could all see. "Well," Winsome began, pulling out the first sheet, "let's start with January 12, 1969. Top Rank Suite, Cardiff."

"What happened there?" Banks asked.

"Nothing. At least not at the Top Rank Suite."

"Where, then?"

"Hold your horses a minute," said Annie. "Let Winsome tell it her own way."

"I spoke with the archivist at one of the big newspapers down there," Winsome went on, "the *South Wales Echo*, and he seemed surprised that somebody else was asking him about that particular date."

"Somebody else?"

"Exactly," Winsome went on. "It seems that Nick Barber did quite a bit of background work *before* he went up to Yorkshire, specifically into the Mad Hatters' tour dates between the Brimleigh Festival and Robin Merchant's death."

"Which makes me wonder why he needed to check the websites at Eastvale Computes and jot what he found down in the back of his book," said Annie.

"John Butler, the editor at *Mojo*, told me that Barber was meticulous about checking his facts," said Banks. "He checked everything at least twice before he went after a story. I should imagine he was getting it right, preparing for another chat with Vic Greaves."

"Makes sense," said Annie. "Go on, Winsome."

"Well, sometimes he had to contact the local papers to see if they kept back issues, but mostly he didn't need to. Most of what he wanted is available at the British Library Newspapers Catalogue, and he could read the papers on microfilm at the library's Newspaper Reading Room. His London phone records, by the way, show quite a few calls to the library, as well as to the local newspapers concerned, in Plymouth, Cardiff and Brighton."

"What did he discover?"

"In the first place," Winsome went on, "I should guess that he was simply looking for reviews of Mad Hatters performances. Maybe a few little quotes from the time to spice up his article. As you said, sir, he was thorough. And it looks as if he was also trying to get a broader context of the times, you know, little local snippets about what was going on that day in Bristol or Plymouth, what was of interest to the people there, that sort of thing. Background."

"Nothing unusual in that, either," Banks said. "He was a music journalist. I imagine he was also scrounging around for any old photos or live bootleg recordings he could find."

"Yes, sir," Winsome said. "Obviously he couldn't research every gig – they played over a hundred towns and cities during that period – but he did cover a fair bit of ground in the reading room. I've spoken to the librarian he dealt with down there, and she was able to give me a list of what he did get around to and fax me prints from the microfilm reader of the newspapers for the three dates in question. She was very helpful. Sounded quite excited to be part of a police investigation. Actually, it was the issues on the days *after* the gigs that interested Barber, of course."

"Because that was when the reviews appeared," said Banks.

"Exactly. Well," Winsome went on, "there's nothing especially interesting in the reviews. Apparently they were in good form that night, even Vic Greaves. It's another item of news that I suspect was more interesting to Nick Barber." She picked a sheet from her pile and turned it on the desk so that Banks could read it. "I'm sorry about the quality, sir," she said, "but it was the best she could do at short notice."

The print was tiny and Banks had to take out his reading glasses. The story was about a young woman called Gwyneth Harris, who was found dead in Bute Park, near the city centre of Cardiff, at six o'clock in the morning of January 13, by an elderly man walking his dog. Gwyneth had apparently been held from behind and stabbed five times in the heart with a blade resembling that of a flick knife. There were no more details.

"Jesus Christ," said Banks. "Linda Lofthouse."

"There's more," said Annie, nodding to Winsome, who slipped out another sheet.

"Monday, April 20, 1970. The *Brighton and Hove Gazette*, the day after the Mad Hatters played at the Dome there. Not very well, apparently. The reviewer mentioned that Greaves in particular seemed barely conscious, and at one point Reg Cooper had to go over to him and direct his fingers to the right keys for the chords. But there's a piece about a young girl called Anita Higgins found dead on a stretch of beach not far from the West Pier."

"Stabbed?" said Banks.

"Yes, sir. This time from the front."

"And I suppose the same thing happened at the third circled gig?"

"*Western Evening Herald*, Wednesday, May 20, 1970, a review of the Mad Hatters gig and an item about Elizabeth Tregowan, aged seventeen, found dead in Hoe Park, Plymouth. This one was strangled."

"So if it was the same person," said Banks, "he was getting bolder, more daring, more personal. The first two he didn't even want to see him, the third he stabbed from the front and the last he strangled. Is that all?"

"Yes, sir," said Winsome. "There may be more, but these are

the only three Nick Barber got around to uncovering. It must have been enough for him."

"It's enough for anyone," said Banks. "If you count Linda Lofthouse at Brimleigh, that's four girls been murdered within close proximity to a Mad Hatters gig. Were any of them at the concerts? Had they any connection with the group?"

"We don't know yet," Annie said. "Winsome thought it best to bring you up to date as soon as possible on this, and we've still got a lot of legwork to do. We need follow-up stories, if any are available, and we need to get onto the local forces, see what they've got in their archives. You know we never give everything out to the newspapers."

"There's one more thing," Winsome said. "It might be of interest, I don't know, but the Mad Hatters were on tour in France most of August 1969."

"So?" said Banks.

"The flick knife," said Winsome. "They're illegal here, but you can get them easily enough in France. And I don't think they had metal detectors all over the place back then."

"Right," said Banks. "Excellent work. So where does this lead us? Before he left for Yorkshire, Nick Barber found out about a trail of bodies after Mad Hatters gigs in the late sixties and early seventies, starting with that of his birth mother. Clearly the local forces at the time had no communication about these killings, which isn't surprising. Even as late as the eighties, lack of inter-force communications botched the Yorkshire Ripper investigation. Stanley Chadwick thought he'd got his man, for good reason, so he had no further interest in the case. He also had problems of his own to deal with. Yvonne. Besides, one of the victims was strangled, not stabbed. Different MO. Even if Chadwick had come across the story, which is unlikely, it wouldn't have meant anything to him.

And who'd be looking at the Mad Hatters as a common denominator?"

"Clearly Nick Barber was," said Annie. "Before his second interview with Vic Greaves, on the day of his murder, Friday, he went to Eastvale Computes in the morning to verify his dates, and he made a note of what he found – what he already knew – in the back of a book he was carrying. We already know from the landlord of the Cross Keys that Barber was in the habit of carrying a book with him when he went for a drink or a meal."

"Lucky for us he was so thorough," said Banks, "seeing as all his other research material was stolen."

"So you think Vic Greaves is the killer?" Annie asked.

"I don't know. When you put it like that, it does sound a bit absurd, doesn't it?"

"Well, somebody killed those girls," Annie argued. "And Vic Greaves was definitely around for each one."

"Why did he stop?" Banks asked.

"We don't know that he did," Annie answered. "Though I'd guess he just became too disorganized to function. Obviously Chris Adams's been shielding him, protecting him."

"You think Adams knows the truth?"

"Probably," Annie said.

"Why would he shield Greaves?"

"They're old friends. Isn't that what you said Tania Hutchison told you? They grew up together."

"What about Robin Merchant?"

"He might have found out."

"So you think Greaves killed him, too?"

"It wouldn't have been difficult. Just a little nudge."

"Trouble is," said Banks, "we're not likely to get much sense out of Greaves."

"At least we can try."

"Yes." Banks stood up and grabbed his jacket. "Great work, Winsome. Carry on with the follow-up. Get all you can from the locals."

"Where are you going?"

"I think I know where Vic Greaves is," said Banks. "I'm going to have a word with him."

"Don't you think you should take backup, sir?" said Winsome. "I mean, if he really is the one, he could be dangerous if you corner him."

"No," said Banks, remembering that Annie had given him the same warning. "That's one thing that'll likely lose him to us for good. He can't handle social interaction, and he's especially afraid of strangers. I can only imagine how he'll react if a few carloads of coppers turn up. At least he's seen me before. I don't think I've got anything to fear from him."

"I hope you're right," said Annie.

So did Banks as he started the Porsche and negotiated his way out of Eastvale towards Lyndgarth. He recalled the fear he had felt searching Greaves's cottage, and it made his mouth dry. People as disturbed as Vic Greaves could sometimes summon up amazing, almost superhuman, strength. At least Banks had told Annie and Winsome where he was going before he set off and asked them to give him a twenty-minute start before they sent in a patrol car as backup. He couldn't be certain that Greaves was where he thought he was, he realized as he crossed the bridge over the Swain and headed for Lyndgarth, but he had a damned good idea.

The estate agent had told him that someone had been seen in the vicinity of Swainsview Lodge, and Greaves had turned uncommunicative at the mention of the place. It must have had very strong associations for him from a particular period of his life, and it would be natural enough for him to gravitate there in times of stress or confusion. Or so Banks hoped as he parked on the bleak daleside, the wind whipping at his face when he opened the car door.

The door through which he had previously entered was securely locked, and Banks was certain nobody could get in that way. An unpaved lane ran down the hill by the side of the lodge to the riverside hamlet of Brayke, and at the top of the lane was a side entrance leading to two large garages, both also locked. A fairly high drystone wall ran down the hill parallel to the lane, but it would be easy enough for anyone to climb, Banks thought, especially in one section, which had lost a few stones. You might not be able to get into the house without breaking a window, he realized, but anyone could gain access to the grounds.

Banks's first clue was a bicycle partially hidden in the ditch and covered with a blue plastic sheet held down by two stones and flapping in the wind. Clearly Greaves couldn't get himself *and* his bicycle over the wall, too.

Convinced that he was right now, Banks hopped the wall and found himself in the garden beyond the swimming pool, where the vast, neglected lawn started its long slope down to the river. He moved up to the edge of the pool, the familiar dark, cracked stone covered with moss and lichens, and the pool itself choked with weeds, littered with broken glass and empty Carlsberg tins.

He called out Vic Greaves's name, but the wind blew it back. There were shadows everywhere, and Banks found himself jumping at each one, a heavy knot at the centre of his chest. He was in the open, he realized, and wished he could be more certain of his assessment that Vic Greaves was harmless.

An empty Coke tin came skittering out of the grass onto the patio and Banks turned, tense, ready to defend himself.

When he reached the side of the pool closest to the house, he thought he could see something sticking out from behind one of the pillars under the upper terrace, close to where the French windows from the studio opened into the courtyard. The area was in the shadows, so it was hard to be sure, but he thought it was the lower half of a leg, with the trousers tucked into the boot. When he got closer, he saw it was actually a bicycle clip.

"Hello, Vic," he said. "Aren't you going to come out?"

After what seemed like a long time, the leg moved and Vic Greaves's shiny bald head appeared from behind the pillar.

"You remember me, don't you, Vic?" Banks said. "There's no need to be afraid. I came to see you at the cottage."

Still Vic didn't respond or move. He just kept looking at Banks.

"Come on out, Vic," Banks said. "I just want to ask you a few questions, that's all."

"Vic's not here," the small voice said finally.

"Yes, he is," said Banks.

Vic held his ground. Banks circled a little, so he could at least get a better view. "All right," he said. "If you want to stay there, stay. I'll talk to you from here, okay?"

The wind was howling in the recess made by the overhanging terrace, but Banks could just about make out Greaves's agreement. He was sitting with his back to the wall, hunched over, arms hugging his knees to his chest.

"I'll do the talking," said Banks, "and you can tell me whether I'm right or wrong. Okay?"

Greaves studied him with serious, narrowed eyes and said nothing.

"It goes back a long time," Banks began. "To 1969, when the Mad Hatters played the Brimleigh Festival. There was a girl backstage called Linda Lofthouse. Your cousin. She got a backstage pass because of you. She was with her best friend, Tania Hutchison, who became a member of the band about a year later. But that's getting ahead. Are you with me so far?"

Greaves still didn't say anything, but Banks could swear he detected a flicker of interest in his expression.

"Cut forward to late on that last night of the festival. Led Zeppelin were playing and Linda needed a little space to clear her head, so she went for a walk in the woods. Someone followed her. Was that you, Vic?"

Greaves shook his head.

"Are you sure?" Banks persisted. "Maybe you were tripping, maybe you didn't know what you were doing, but something happened, didn't it? Something changed that night, something snapped in you, and you killed her. Perhaps you didn't realize what you'd done, perhaps it was like looking down on someone else doing it, but you did it, didn't you, Vic?"

Finally, Greaves found his voice. "No," he said. "No, he's wrong. Vic's a good boy." His words were almost blown into silence by the wind.

"Tell me how I'm wrong, Vic," Banks went on. "Tell me what I'm wrong about. I want to know."

"Can't," said Greaves. "Can't tell."

"Yes, you can. Am I wrong about how it happened? What about Cardiff? What about Brighton? And Plymouth? Were there any others?"

Greaves just shook his head from side to side, muttering something Banks couldn't hear for the wind.

"I'm trying to help you," said Banks, "but I can't help if you don't tell me the truth."

"There is no truth," said Greaves.

"There must be. Who killed those girls? Who killed Nick Barber? Did he find out? Is that why? Did he confront you with the evidence?"

"Why don't you leave him alone?" said a deep voice behind Banks. "You can tell he doesn't know what's going on."

Banks turned and saw Chris Adams standing by the pool, ponytail blowing in the wind, bulbous face red, pot-belly sagging over his jeans. Banks walked over to him. "I think he does," he said. "But seeing as you're here, why don't you tell me? I think you know as much about it as he does."

"It was all over and done with years ago," said Adams.

"You may wish it was, but it isn't. That's what Nick Barber found out about, isn't it? So Vic here killed him."

"No, that's not what happened."

"What about the girl in Cardiff? The one in Plymouth? What about them?"

Adams paled. "You know?"

"It wasn't that hard once we started following in Nick Barber's footsteps. He was thorough, and even his killer didn't manage to obliterate everything he'd found out. Why have you been protecting Vic Greaves all these years?"

"Look at him, Mr. Banks," said Adams. "What would you do? He's my oldest friend. We grew up together, for crying out loud. He's like a baby."

"He's a killer. That means he could kill again. You weren't able to supervise him twenty-four hours a day. I imagine you only came down here because I phoned you and told you things were coming to a head, that I was close to finding out who killed Nick Barber. You guessed where Vic was. He's been here before, hasn't he? And told you about it, too, I'll bet."

"The place does seem to attract him," said Adams, calmly. "But you're wrong about the rest. Vic's no killer."

At first, Banks thought Adams was blowing smoke, but something snagged at his mind, a little thing, and it pulled until it brought a number of other little things tumbling into the open with it. As the wind howled around his head, Banks found himself rearranging the pieces inside and putting them together in a different pattern, one he could have kicked himself for not seeing sooner. He still wasn't sure about everything yet, but it was all starting to add up. Was Greaves left-handed? He tried to remember from their meeting which hand Greaves had been stirring the stew with, but he couldn't.

He was certain of one thing, though: when he was watching the Mad Hatters DVD the previous evening with Brian, he had noticed that Robin Merchant played his bass left-handed, like Paul McCartney. He had simply registered it unconsciously at the time, not really made anything of it, or tried to link it to the case. But now, as he thought about it, he realized that the last killing they knew of was on the nineteenth of May, about a month before Robin Merchant's drowning. Unless there were other, later, incidents that Barber hadn't uncovered, the timing worked. He glanced at his watch. He had been at Swainsview Lodge for only ten minutes.

"Robin Merchant," he said.

"Bravo," said Adams. "Robin Merchant was one sick puppy, as they say. Oh, he was glib and charming enough on the surface, but beyond that it was a case of Jekyll and Hyde. His mind was polluted by all that Aleister Crowley stuff he immersed himself in. Have you heard about Crowley?"

"I know the name," said Banks.

"He was a drug addict and a womanizer, the self-proclaimed

'wickedest man in the world.' The Great Beast. His motto was 'Do what thou wilt shall be the whole of the law.' Robin Merchant took him quite literally. Do you know, Robin even tried to justify his 'sacrifices,' as he called them to me? He had no conscience, even before he got involved in drugs and black magic and all that shit. It just made him worse, made him think he was more godlike, or more devil-like, I should say. But he hid it so well. He got obsessed with those Los Angeles murders, too, the ritualistic elements. He thought he saw some sort of occult significance in them. I don't know if you remember, but they finally caught Manson that October, and Robin started to identify with him and his power trip. He saw himself as some sort of messenger of darkness. He didn't murder rich piggies, though. He murdered beauty and purity. The flower was his signature."

"What happened?"

"Why should I tell you?"

"Because you know I'll find out."

Adams sighed and stared across the pool as if he were staring across forty years of bad history. He reached in his pockets for a cigarette, dipped his head and cupped his hand to light it against the wind. "I saw him," he said finally. "The fifth time, in Winchester. You don't know about that one, do you?"

"No," said Banks.

"That's because I saved her life." Adams spoke without any hint of vanity or self-satisfaction, as if he were stating a mere fact. "I had my suspicions about Robin, and I was about the only one who ever bothered to read the newspapers back then. I saw our reviews, and I read the stories about those girls. At first, I thought nothing of it. It's hard to really believe that the person sitting next to you on the tour bus is a killer. But I should have known. It all kept adding up. Things he said, the way he talked about people. Then I remembered Brimleigh. The first. I still couldn't be certain it was Robin, couldn't accept it, I suppose, but I didn't know where he was at the time.

"Anyway, at Winchester – this would be June, just a week or so before his death – I followed him after the show. There was a girl taking a shortcut through a cemetery, of all places, the fool, and that's where he pounced. I was just behind him. I shouted something. It was dark, and I don't know if he recognized me, but he growled at me like some sort of wild animal, then belted off like nobody's business. The girl was all right. I made sure she got home okay without letting on who I was. I don't know if she reported the incident or not, but I heard nothing more of it. Now the problem became what to do about Robin. I talked to him. He didn't deny it. That's when he gave me all that Aleister Crowley and Charles Manson crap, trying to justify himself and his actions. I couldn't let him go on killing people, but at the same time, a trial, conviction . . . It was unthinkable. I mean, back then, a rock band could get away with most things, but murder . . . especially that kind of murder. We'd have been tarnished forever, especially in the wake of the Manson family trial. We'd never have survived. The band would never have survived. Vic. I couldn't allow that to happen to the others after all the hard years they'd put in. Fortunately, the problem took care of itself."

"No," said Banks. "You killed Robin Merchant. You weren't in bed with Tania Hutchison that night. You went to confront him, here, by the pool. I'm not sure whether you intended to kill him, but you saw something unstoppable in him, and you felt you had no other choice. It worked perfectly. So easy." He glanced over to the terrace. Vic Greaves was still there, apparently listening. "But someone saw you, didn't he, Chris? Vic saw you." Fifteen minutes had now passed since Banks arrived.

"I'm not admitting to killing anybody," said Adams. "You think what you like. You can't prove a thing."

"And you killed Nick Barber," Banks went on. "It was your silver Mercedes the tourist couple and the girl in the youth hostel saw that night. The running figure was just a jogger. It was foolish of me to think that Vic could have done anything like that himself. Everyone was right about him. He might be a bit off in the head, but he's a gentle soul at heart. Vic was upset, and he told you in that roundabout way of his that a music journalist had come around pestering him with questions about the past, about Brimleigh, Linda Lofthouse and the other murders. Cardiff. Brighton. Plymouth. Questions to which only you and Vic knew the answers. The journalist said he was going to come back. He'd left his card. You didn't think Vic could take the strain of another interview. You thought he would soon break down and tell all, given what he'd witnessed all those years ago, so you killed Barber. You couldn't kill Vic, could you, even though he was the one who was carrying the secret, the most obvious victim? Did you know that Linda Lofthouse was Nick Barber's birth mother?"

Adams put his fist to his chest and seemed to stagger back a pace or two as if he had been hit. "My God, no!" he said. "I'm not admitting to anything," he went on. "I talked to Robin, yes, made sure that he knew I knew, and that I was watching him. That's all. The rest was an accident."

"You killed him to make certain. You knew he wouldn't stop, that there would be more victims. And you knew he'd get caught eventually and bring it all tumbling down."

"The world's a safer place without him, and that's a fact. But I'm still not admitting anything. I'm guilty of no crime. There's nothing you can do to me. Anyway, it would have been very easy just to reach out and . . ." Adams reached out his arm to demonstrate and let his hand fall on Banks's shoulder. Then he smiled sadly, ". . . and just give a little push." Almost twenty minutes now. The cavalry would arrive in moments.

But he didn't push. Banks, who had tensed, ready for a struggle, felt the hand relax on his shoulder, and he knew that Adams was about to turn away, that he had reached the end of his resources. Killing Nick Barber and seizing his notes was one thing, but killing a copper in cold blood was quite another.

It all happened at once. Before Banks could move or say anything, he heard footsteps running down the lane, and someone shouted out his name. Then he heard a terrible scream from his left, and a dark, powerful figure came hurtling forward, crashing right into Adams and toppling both of them over into the deep end of the empty pool. The cavalry had arrived, but they were too late.

By the time Annie and Winsome arrived on the scene, the ambulances had been and gone. It was getting dark, and the wind was howling through the trees and the nooks and crannies of Swainsview Lodge fit to wake the dead. The SOCOs had lit the scene with bright arc lamps and were still strutting about in their white boiler suits like spacemen on a mission. There were spatters of blood at the bottom of the pool mixed in with the other detritus. Annie saw Banks standing alone, head bowed, by the poolside and walked over to him, touching him gently on the shoulder. "Okay?" she asked.

"Fine."

"I heard what happened."

"Greaves thought Adams was going to do to me what he saw him do to Robin Merchant all those years ago. Then the uniforms came dashing down the lane and frightened him. It's nobody's fault. I doubt that anyone could have foreseen it and stopped him."

"Wasn't Adams going to push you in?"

"No. He ran out of steam."

"But you think Greaves witnessed Adams push Merchant?"

"I'm certain of it. He was on LSD at the time. That was what sent him over the edge. Can you imagine it? Adams has taken care of him ever since, protected him, as much for his own sake as anything. Persuaded him not to talk, maybe even persuaded him that it happened some other way. Greaves was so confused. He couldn't trust his own judgment. But when he saw Adams rest his hand on my shoulder by the pool . . ."

"It all came back?"

"Something like that, in whatever fragmented and chaotic way Greaves's mind works these days. However it happened, he snapped. He'd been like a coiled spring all those years. Adams protected him from anything that was likely to push him towards his snapping point. But when Barber appeared with his questions about Plymouth, Cardiff and Brighton, it was too much. Greaves had heard Adams's conversation with Merchant at the pool, so somewhere in his messed-up mind he knew about these things, what Merchant had done. But he couldn't confront it. He told Adams, who was terrified that Barber would push too hard and crack the veneer. So he killed him. Barber didn't think he had anything to fear. He knew who Adams was, thought he'd come to talk to him. He was just having a chat, turning away, reaching for his cigarettes, then Adams picked up the poker, seized the moment. Luckily for him, he still had time to gather Barber's stuff before the power cut."

"Can we prove it?"

"I don't know. He's tired of it all, but he wouldn't admit to anything. He's not stupid. You should have seen him down there, crying like a baby, cradling Greaves's head in his lap, even though he must have been in considerable pain himself."

"What's the extent of his injuries?"

"Dislocated shoulder, couple of broken ribs, cuts and bruises, according to the paramedics."

"And Greaves?"

"Landed badly. Broke his neck. Died instantly."

Annie was silent for a moment, staring into the harshly lit swimming pool. "Maybe it's a blessing."

"Maybe," said Banks. "God knows he was a tortured soul."

"What now?"

"We try to get as much evidence as we can on Adams. He's not getting away with this. Not if I can help it. We'll go over the forensics, check and recheck witness statements, interview the entire village again, probe his alibi, the lot. There has to be something there to link him to Barber's murder. Not Merchant's. That's too long ago, and there's no way we'll get him for that now."

"Stefan says he's got some prints and hair from the living room that don't match anyone else's so far."

Banks looked at her, a hint of a smile on his face. "Then I'd say we've got him, wouldn't you? An amateur like Adams would never be able to clean up completely after himself. Besides, when the fact that Greaves is dead sinks in, I think we've also got a better chance of appealing to his conscience. He's got no one to protect anymore."

"What about the Mad Hatters? The past? The reputation? Aren't they supposed to be doing some reunion tour?"

"There's every chance none of it will get out, anyway.

Cardiff. Brighton. Plymouth. Why should it if Adams pleads guilty? Those cases are long over, and the killer died more than thirty-five years ago. Maybe the local forces can put a tick in a box and claim another success in their statistics of crimes solved, but that'll be about as far as it goes."

"Until another Nick Barber comes along."

"Perhaps," said Banks. "But that's none of our business."

"Winsome talked to people in Plymouth and Cardiff, who were able to dig up the old files," Annie said.

"And?"

"In the file, it said that each girl had a flower painted on her cheek. A cornflower."

Banks nodded. "Merchant's signature. Just like Linda Lofthouse."

"They didn't release that to the general public."

"Funny, isn't it?" said Banks. "If they had, we might not be here now." He turned up the collar of his jacket. His teeth were chattering.

"Cold?" Annie said.

"Getting there."

"By the way," she said, "I just saw Kev Templeton come storming out of Superintendent Gervaise's office with a face like a slapped arse."

Banks smiled. "So there is some justice in the world." He glanced at his watch. Seven-thirty. "I'm starving," he said, "and I could do with a stiff drink. How about it?"

"Sure you're up to it?"

Banks gave her an unreadable glance, his features cast into planes of light and shadow by the bright arc lights, his eyes piercing blue. "Let's go," he said, turning away. "I've finished here."

Monday, September 29, 1969

The deserted stretch of canal ran by a scrapyard where the pattering rain echoed on the piles of rusty old metal. Stanley Chadwick walked along the towpath with his raincoat collar turned up. He knew that what he was about to do was wrong, that it went against everything he believed in, but he felt that it was the only way. He couldn't just leave things to chance because, in his experience, chance had no history of supporting the right side without a little help. And he was right; of that he was certain. Proving it was another matter.

Yvonne had been gone almost a week, run away from home. Janet had found some items of her favourite clothes missing, along with an old rucksack they used to carry pop and sandwiches in when they went on family hikes from the Primrose Valley caravan. Chadwick was worried about his daughter, but at least he knew that no immediate harm had come to her. Not that the cities were safe for vulnerable sixteen-year-old girls, but he was certain that she wasn't as foolish as some, and he hoped that she would soon come back. He couldn't make her disappearance official, set the country's police forces looking for her, so he would just have to bide his time and hope she got homesick. It tore at his heart, but he could see no other way. For the moment, he and Janet had told curious friends and neighbours that Yvonne had gone to stay with her aunt in London. She probably *had* gone to London, anyway, Chadwick realized. Most runaways ended up there.

The figure approached from under the Kirkstall Viaduct, as arranged. Jack Skelgate was a small-time fence who rather resembled a ferret, and he had been useful to Chadwick as an informer on many occasions. Chadwick had chosen Skelgate because he had so much on him he could send him away for the next ten years, and if there was one thing that terrified Skelgate more than anything else, it was the idea of prison. Which, Chadwick had often thought, ought to have made him consider another, more honest, occupation, but some people just don't manage to make the connection. They don't get it. That's why the jails are always full. Like so many of the people Chadwick had met and interviewed over the past couple of weeks, Skelgate was as thick as two short planks, but this would play to Chadwick's advantage.

"Miserable bloody day, in'it," said Skelgate, by way of greeting. He was always sniffling, as if he had a permanent cold.

"There was a burglary in Cross Gates the other night," Chadwick said. "Someone drove off with fifty canteens of cutlery. Nice ones. Silver. I wonder if any of them happened to find their way into your hands?"

"Silver cutlery, you say? Can't say as I've seen any of that in quite a while."

"But you'd let me know if you did?"

"Of course I would, Mr. Chadwick."

"We think the Newton gang might be behind it, and you know how interested I am in putting them away."

Skelgate cringed at the words, even though they referred to someone else. "The Newtons, you say. Nasty lot, them."

"They may be planning other raids. If you happen to hear anything, we could come to the usual arrangement."

"I'll keep my ears open, Mr. Chadwick, that I will." Skelgate looked around with his ferrety eyes. Paranoia was another trait of his; he always thought someone was watching or listening in. "Is that all, Mr. Chadwick? Can I go now? Only, I don't want us to be seen together. Those Newtons are a violent bunch. Think nothing of putting a man in hospital for a month, they wouldn't."

"Just keep your eyes and ears open." Chadwick paused, tensing as he realized he was reaching the point of no return. For weeks he had been moving among people who despised everything he valued, and somewhere in the midst of it all, he had become unglued. He knew this, and he also knew there was no going back. All he wanted was for Yvonne to come home and McGarrity to go to jail for the murder of Linda Lofthouse. Then, he hoped, perhaps he might find some peace. But deep down, he also knew that there was every chance peace would elude him forever. His strict religious upbringing told him he would be damning himself to eternal hellfire for what he was about to do. But so be it.

He felt a sudden heaviness in his chest. Not a sharp pain or anything, just a heaviness, the way he always thought the sort of heartbreak that torch singers describe would feel. He had felt it just once before, when he ran out of the landing craft on the morning of June 6, 1944, but that day he had soon forgotten it in the noise and smoke, in dodging the mortar and machine-gun fire. "There is one more thing I'd like you to do for me," he said.

Skelgate clearly didn't like the sound of that. He was practically bobbing up and down on the balls of his feet. "What?" he said. "You know I do what I can for you."

"I want a flick knife." There, he'd said it.

"A flick knife?"

"Yes. With a tortoiseshell handle."

"But why do you want a flick knife?"

Chadwick gave him a hard look. "Can you get me one?"

"Of course," said Skelgate. "Nothing could be easier."

"When?"

"When do you want it?"

"Soon."

"Same place, same time, tomorrow?"

"That'll do fine," said Chadwick. "Be here."

"Don't worry, I will," Skelgate said, then glanced around, saw nothing to worry about and scurried down the towpath. Chadwick stood watching him go and wondered just what it was that had brought him to this godforsaken place on this ungodly mission. Then he turned in the other direction and walked back in the rain to his car.

ACKNOWLEDGEMENTS

I would like to thank Sheila Halladay and Dominick Abel for reading and commenting on early versions of the manuscript, and my editors, Dinah Forbes, Carolyn Marino and Carolyn Mays, for doing such a wonderful job on the final version. The copy editors certainly had their work cut out, too, and came through with flying colours.

They say that if you remember the sixties, you weren't there. I was, so I could hardly rely entirely on memory for the sections of this book that take place in 1969. Jill Bullock, communications coordinator of the Alumni and Development Team at the University of Leeds, proved to be a mine of useful information. Kenneth Lee and Paul Mercs, who were both also there, shared some interesting stories with me, some of which could be repeated in the book. Among the many books I read and DVDs I watched, I would like to single out Jonathon Green's account of the period, *All Dressed Up*, and Murray Lerner's documentary on the 1970 Isle of Wight Festival, *Message to Love*.

A special thanks to Andrew Male, deputy editor of *Mojo*, for interesting conversations and information about some of the more obscure elements of late-sixties music, and for letting me be a fly on the wall in the office. Thanks also, as ever, to Philip Gormley and Claire Stevens.

I also have special thank yous for Dr. Sue, of the Calgary WordFest volunteers; for the doctors, staff and paramedics of Mineral Springs Hospital, Banff; and for Drs. Michael Connelly and Michael Curtis, along with the nurses and staff of the cardiac unit at Foothills Hospital, Calgary, without whom *Piece of My Heart* might have taken on a whole new meaning altogether! Also, thanks for Janet, Randy, Matthew, Jonathan and Megan for a home away from home.

Biserka Livaja

Yorkshire-born Peter Robinson, who now lives in Toronto, is one of the world's top writers of crime fiction and the winner of numerous awards, including the United States' Edgar Award, Britain's Dagger in the Library, France's prestigious Grand Prix de Littérature Policière, Denmark's Palle Rosenkrantz Award, and, several times, Canada's Arthur Ellis Award.

Please visit his website at www.inspectorbanks.com.

VIETNAM: BETWEEN TWO TRUCES

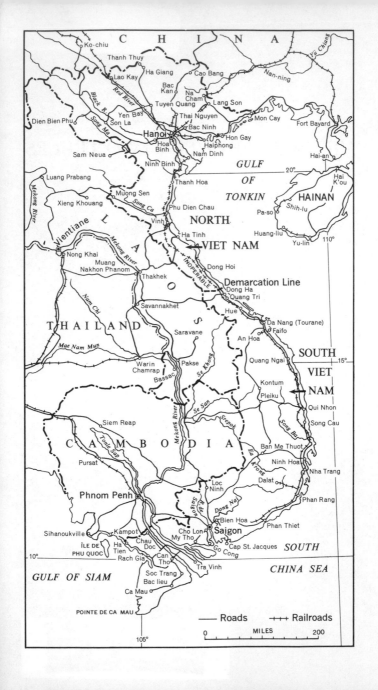

VIETNAM:
BETWEEN
TWO TRUCES

By *Jean Lacouture*

WITH AN INTRODUCTION BY JOSEPH KRAFT

Translated from the French by
KONRAD KELLEN *and* JOEL CARMICHAEL

Vintage Books

A DIVISION OF RANDOM HOUSE

NEW YORK

VINTAGE BOOKS
are published by
Alfred A. Knopf, Inc. AND *Random House, Inc.*

Contents

Introduction

by

JOSEPH KRAFT

High strategic themes, bureaucratic interests, intellectual baggage, and many other kinds of junk have been piled on to the war in Vietnam. It has been called a fatal test of will between communism and freedom. It has been described as the critical battle in the struggle between China and the Soviet Union. On its outcome the future of Southeast Asia is supposed to rest; and so it has also been sometimes described as the critical battle between China and India. At a minimum, claim the Dr. Strangeloves of "sub-limited war," Vietnam poses the question of whether a nuclear power can mobilize the kind of force required to contain guerrilla warfare. And with so much at stake it seems to make sense that the greatest power on earth should send as ambassador to a kind of Asian Ruritania its leading military man and, on two occasions, one of its best-known political figures.

To those who think it does make sense, which seems to include practically everybody in the United States, Jean Lacouture's new book on Vietnam will come as a kind of revelation. He announces his almost revolutionary theme in the opening sentence: "Vietnam," he writes, "lives." His book is about a particular place and a struggle for primacy there. It is, in other words, a political book. It deals with the elements and forces of the conflict, not as if they were apocalyptic and millennial events but as political phenomena. To read La-couture after a dose of the official and even the journalistic literature which we get in this country is to pass from griffins and unicorns to Darwin and Mendel.

For writing a non-mythological political analysis of Viet-nam, Lacouture has the ideal background. As a distinguished correspondent for various journals, including *Le Monde,* he has been to Vietnam repeatedly since he first went there on the staff of General Leclerc in 1945. He has visited both North and South Vietnam several times. He has written on this subject often and at length, notably in a biographical study of Ho Chi Minh and as co-author of a book on the Ge-neva truce of 1954. He knows all the leading figures on all sides from way back. Nor is he a narrow area specialist. The politics of underdeveloped countries, so mysterious to most of us, and so parochial to those who know only a single country, are familiar stuff to him. With his wife, Simone, Lacouture has written the best study to date of Colonel Nasser's Egypt; and one of the best on Morocco since independence. While ob-viously a *pièce d'occasion,* his present book on Vietnam is of the same high quality.

His starting point is the regime of President Ngo Dinh Diem. Just how the United States became connected with Diem has become a matter of controversy. *Ramparts* maga-zine has recently published an account purporting to show that a knot of American Catholic politicos and professional anti-Communists, depending largely upon Francis Cardinal Spellman, promoted our support of the Diem regime. Perhaps. But history has a way of demolishing theories that trace large consequences to little groups of men. Probably the central point is that in 1954, for reasons of domestic politics, the Eisenhower-Dulles regime broke with the policy of moving in concert with Britain and France and tried to establish South Vietnam as a bastion of anti-communist resistance. President Diem was merely the vehicle for that effort.

He had little chance to succeed. Not because, as some say, South Vietnam cannot exist as a separate political entity. In Vietnam, too, it is different in the South. South Vietnam in fact is one of the most richly diversified areas in the world. Its topography includes mountainous areas, peopled by primitive tribes, arid plateaux, and a great alluvial plain. It is a leading producer of rice—a crop requiring the kind of intense personal cultivation that breeds an independent peasantry. The diversity fostered by occupation is further promoted by religious custom: South Vietnam's fourteen million people include large numbers of Catholics, Buddhists, and Confucians, all of whom practice a kind of ancestor worship that places special emphasis on local custom. While political parties in the Western sense have existed in Vietnam only as affiliates of those that had grown up around the old political capital of Hanoi in the North, there remained—and remain—a multitude of local Southern sects (Lacouture likens them to "armed leagues") that mixed banditry with religion. Thanks to a loose provincial reign, the French, as Lacouture points out, had governed this mélange for decades with no greater difficulties than those found in the sleepiest of domestic *départements*—"Herault and Lot et Garonne." Plainly, any Southern regime that was likely to succeed would have to be pluralistic, offering great scope for local differences—and this was especially true for the regime of President Diem, a Catholic aristocrat from the high plains and thus markedly different from the majority of Vietnamese.

But if there was one thing the Diem regime lacked, it was sympathy for pluralism. The ruling family was imbued "with an extra touch of fervor, something of the absolute." The President had an "attachment to the ancient society of Annam—high aristocracy, closed castes, intellectual hierarchies . . . he wanted to revive the old order, the ancient morality,

the respect for the master." His brother and political counselor, Ngo Dinh Nhu, saw in the "strategic hamlets" a re-
creation of the fortified towns of the Middle Ages that he
had studied as a budding Medievalist at the Ecole des Chartes.
Another brother, Ngo Dinh Can, who ruled the Northern
provinces, lived in the old family mansion, dressed in the ancient Vietnamese style, and slept on the floor. Madame Nhu's
war on night life and dancing was thus not a personal aberra-
tion but a true expression of the absolute traditionalism that
typified the regime.

Confronting a diversity of political factions, however,
single-minded dogmatism can prevail only in a climate of
strife—real or contrived. In the beginning the Diem regime
had to fight against the sects and the remnants of French influence. In the course of this struggle President Diem evicted
the former emperor, Bao Dai, and became President "in a
plebiscite as honest as could be expected." But having taken
the sects and the crown, the Diem regime did not know how
to use its victory to develop harmony. "Having won a battle,
it preferred war to peace. . . . In 1955 any opponent was
denounced as a relic of the sects of feudal rebels supported by
colonialism. Beginning in 1956 any opponent was called a
communist." It was in this context that the regime initiated in
1956 a campaign against the Viet Cong—a name manufac-
tured by the regime and supposed to mean Vietnamese communists, but actually embracing a far wider spectrum of political opinion. In the same spirit the Saigon regime, against
the advice of the American Ambassador, publicly abrogated
the clause of the 1954 Geneva Agreements which called for
reunification of Vietnam through free elections—a clause that
Hanoi could certainly not have accepted at the time. But in
the process of fighting the Viet Cong, the regime called forth
the two forces that were to prove its undoing.

One of these was the Army of the Republic of Vietnam, or
Arvin as it came to be called. In connection with Arvin,
it is worth noting one of the intellectual sleights-of-hand com-

mon to Americans who believe it is good for this country to support reactionary governments abroad. After all, they say in the best Montesquieu manner, democracy cannot be exported; the conditions that promote free institutions in the United States do not exist elsewhere, and one should not impose American mores uncritically. True enough. But this is not a stricture that applies to that timid creature, the American liberal. On the contrary, the group that most uncritically projects American ways, that is most ready to overlook and override local custom, and to ignore the tradition of centuries, is the American military. And nothing proves it better than Arvin.

It is an army created in the image of our own. It wears American parade dress and American fatigues. It rides around in jeeps and helicopters and jet planes. It is organized in corps, divisions, and companies, and it has special forces and ranger battalions. It has most of the weaponry available to American forces. It is full of keen young officers, trained at staff schools in the United States, bursting with energy and with clear answers to cloudy questions. What it does not have, of course, is the cultural base of the United States Army. It does not, to be specific, have a strong sense of discipline, nor does it have a tradition that discourages meddling in political affairs. On the contrary, Arvin was called into being by political affairs; and the younger the officers, the more ardently political they tend to be. How could anyone imagine that a force so modern in its outlook, so uninhibited and unrestricted in its background, would for long yield pride of place to a regime as old-fashioned and backward-looking as the Diem government? As Lacouture points out, military plotting against the government got under way as soon as the army was organized. In 1960 and again in 1962 attempted military coups came very close to toppling the regime. Only by fantastic juggling, only by setting unit against unit and commander against commander and by planting spies and rumors everywhere was the regime able to maintain its hold over the army at all. It is typical that on the eve of the coup that succeeded, the regime itself was planning a fake coup to discover which of its generals were loyal. Sooner or later, in short, a military coup would have unseated Diem. As much as anything in history can be, his undoing by his own praetorian guard was inevitable—a consideration to bear in mind when there develops in Washington a hunt for scapegoats who will be charged with having lost Vietnam by causing the downfall of the Diem regime.

The second force brought into being by the absolutism of the regime was the Viet Cong. In keeping with the Geneva accords, almost all the guerrilla forces, and especially their leaders, who had fought for Ho Chi Minh against the French, moved above the 17th Parallel to North Vietnam. There remained, however, in scattered areas of the South, communists loyal to the Hanoi government. Precisely because they were disciplined communists, loyal to the Party line, they did not initiate trouble against the Diem regime. For Hanoi had troubles of its own—first the resettlement; then construction of new industry; and at all times a chronic food shortage and great difficulties with the peasantry. Feeling itself far more vulnerable than the Saigon regime, Hanoi had no desire to give the Diem government an excuse for intervention. For that reason Hanoi protested in only the most perfunctory way when the clause providing for reunification through free elections was unilaterally abrogated by Saigon. For the same reason Hanoi tried repeatedly (and unsuccessfully) to make deals with the Saigon regime, offering to trade its manufactures for foodstuffs. And for exactly the same reason, Hanoi kept the communists in the South under wraps. As one communist quoted by Lacouture said later: "Between 1954 and 1958 we were pacifist opportunists. We hesitated to draw conclusions from the Diemist dictatorship and its excesses."

But as Lacouture shows, other victims of the Diem regime were under no such discipline. Tribal leaders, local notables, independent peasants and smallholders, not to mention intellectuals and professional men in Saigon, found themselves threatened by the militancy of the regime. Many were thrown into prison—for example, the present chief of state, Pham Khac Suu, and one of the more recent premiers, Pham Huy Quat. Others resisted, and inevitably they looked to the communists for support. Thus, local pressure for the communists to start things began to build up. As one Viet Cong leader told Lacouture: "There was pressure at the base. An old peasant said to me: 'If you don't join the fight we're through with you.'" (I have heard very similar explanations in my own talks with Viet Cong officials.) In short, like almost all rebellions, the Viet Cong revolt was not set off by some master planner working from the outside. It was generated basically by local conditions.

The course of events outlined by Lacouture follows this pattern exactly. The formal establishment of the National Liberation Front, or political arm of the Viet Cong, was initiated at a meeting held in the U Minh forest of southeast South Vietnam in March 1960. According to Lacouture, the chief document before the meeting was a letter urging the establishment of the Liberation Front written from a Saigon prison by a non-communist who is now head of the Front, Nguyen Huu Tho. While at least two of those at the March meeting seem to have been communists, most of those on the spot were not. The chief items in the declaration that was then put out were purely local grievances. And it was only after the Front was already in motion, in September 1960, that Hanoi gave it explicit support. As Lacouture puts it: "The leaders in Hanoi did not take this turn [toward backing revolt in the South] except under the express demand and the moral pressure of the local militants."

Once Hanoi had formally supported the Front, there was no backing down. With the United States supporting the Saigon regime there came about the famous build-up of military operations. But how little of the underlying political situation has really been changed by this build-up! The confrontation to be sure has become more dangerous. The American role as backer of the Saigon regime, and especially its army, is now more exposed. So is Hanoi's role as supplier of men and weapons to the Viet Cong. Still, there remains some independence in Saigon—witness, the Buddhists' maneuverings and the government crises that regularly catch American officials by surprise. The National Liberation Front retains a Central Committee that seems to be less than a third communist, and that is, as it always was, especially oriented toward the problems of South Vietnam. While it is true that more communists are to be found on the intermediary levels of the N.L.F., neither Lacouture nor others who know the Viet Cong leaders believe that they are fighting in order to impose a North Vietnamese communist dictatorship on the South. The chief problem remains what it always was: how to find a political means of reconciling the great diversity of interest and opinion in South Vietnam.

Official apologists for present American policy, while acknowledging its dangers, often insist that there is no alternative. This is a little like the peddler selling pills during the Lisbon earthquake, who replied, when asked whether the pills would do any good: "No, but what do you have that's better?" The comparison would be even more apt if the peddler had had a hand in the earthquake. Certainly it is true that the alternatives have been obscured by the resolute refusal of most of the American press to study carefully the politics of the war, including the politics of the Viet Cong. But in fact there remains an alternative well known to all politically alert Vietnamese (though it is difficult to voice because of increasingly harsh American policy). It is the alternative of negotiations between the Saigon government and the Viet Cong. Such talks are an absolute pre-condition to any reconciling of local differences. However difficult to arrange they may now appear, direct discussions with the Viet Cong will sooner or later have to take place if there is to be a settlement in Vietnam. A struggle that began locally—and this is the central point to emerge from Lacouture's book—can best be ended by a settlement of local issues.

I

THE OPEN WOUND

ᔑᔑᔑᔑᔑᔑᔑ

With its strange silhouette of a starved sea horse, its chaotic
history, its ambiguous language, the seeming frailty of its
children, the resignation that seems to emanate from its damp
landscape, and despite the war that has crushed it for almost
twenty years, Vietnam lives. Thirty million people are tied to
the destiny of that ribbon of land attached to the enormous
belly of China like a funny little watch charm, wedged between the chain of the Annamite mountains, the Thai highland, and the Cambodian plateau; thirty million Vietnamese
who, between Lang Son and the Point of Ca Mau, ask for
their bowl of rice or the road to the next village in many quite
different languages.

Vivid, unstable, sensitive, imaginative, passionate, thin but
strong, full of laughter and capable of unlimited attachment,
impulsive and unconcerned, malleable, deceitful, vain, generous, turbulent, most Vietnamese, even the Catholics and the
Buddhists among them, follow a religion of ancestor worship.
What better cement for national unity could there be than
this cult?

Vietnam's colonization—a decentralizing force for reasons of local political necessity—intensified the strictly provincial differences separating the South, where the Mekong and the Bassac are among the richest rice lands in all of Asia, from the Center, which is a simple strip of land yielded by the mountain to the sea, and from the North, which is a circle of mountain ranges rising toward Laos, Burma, and China, surrounding the overpopulated delta of the Red River.

The South was called Cochinchina. This province, wrested two centuries earlier from the declining Khmers by the kings of Hue, was turned by the French conquerors into an opulent French colony, boasting an administration envied by continental Asia, endowed with an ingenious system of representation, agreeable to Europeans, and capable of exporting two million tons of rice annually. And until 1925 it never knew any but the most insignificant political problems.

The Center, cradle of its dynasties and rebellions, whose string of coastal plains extends from Phan Thiet to Vinh, had kept the old name of Annam; the Treaty of 1884, imposing the status of protectorate upon it, had provided internal sovereignty to an "emperor" residing at Hue and complete impunity to the mandarins.

Finally, in the North, there was Tonkin, also a so-called protectorate despite the installation at Hanoi of central services of the Government-General of Indochina, which was an excellent marketplace at the gates of China. It was a cruel land whose five million indefatigable peasants never quite succeeded in wresting a subsistence from the narrow Delta region. This country in the North was often forced to import rice from Cochinchina (the great rice growers in Saigon used to say: "Look at these Tonkin beggars we must feed."), and it exported to the plantations in the South workers recruited by the representatives of the great companies. (This complementary character of the economies of the North and the South is obviously one of the more powerful arguments in favor of Vietnam's unity.)

These three Vietnamese "Kys," divided by French colonization into countries of different standing and welded to Cambodia and Laos, which in their turn depended on Indian Asia
rather than on Chinese Asia, could not but obey the law of
natural attraction. "Indochina," that composite product of
three Vietnamese provinces and the two kingdoms of Khmer
and Lao, was broken up by the war of 1945–1954; and upon
Vietnam, territorially unified in the struggle, an internal frontier was imposed in 1954 that was based on competing ideologies and global strategic imperatives.

While the Vietnamese territories had held together even at
the height of the struggle, national opinion was then split like
a torn flag. The physical partitioning complemented a spiritual division. The role played in this operation by French
politics cannot be denied. Anxious to deprive their adversary,
the communist Viet Minh, of the aid of Vietnamese nationalism, the French, side by side with the old anti-colonial
parties, nurtured and freed forces that eventually eluded their
control and that are now, regardless of their current tactics,
parties of the Vietnam which established itself *against* the
colonial order.

Because Vietnam is a border region between the Western
and the Sino-Soviet worlds, and because the latter knew how
to blend in with local revolts while the former retained its
power to act and its financial influence, the country passed
from colonial tutelage to total war. While India, Burma, and
Indonesia attained independence after a terrible but short
convulsion, Vietnam entered upon a cycle of wars that
threatened to lead it eventually into slavery despite the incredible vitality it demonstrated in the course of the action.

But what has made the solution of the Vietnamese problem
even more difficult than the solution of the Indian or Indo-
nesian crises is the progressive monopolization of nationalist
claims by communist organizations. This does not mean that
the Marxist leaders are not capable of wisdom or moderation;
Ho Chi Minh and his men proved differently when they signed

with France two comparable agreements at Geneva, that of March 6, 1946, and that of July 20, 1956. But as they belong to a radically different world, conforming to particular rules of political morality, and because they were aiming at objectives fundamentally different from those of the opposite side, they could not preserve for long the fiction of an agreement of "coexistence," and they cannot do it in the future except under the pressure of superior necessity dictated by Soviet and Chinese foreign policy.

Negotiating with Ho Chi Minh is different from negotiating with Nehru or Sukarno. The former, regardless of his personal powers, yields not only to the collective, but to innumerable and invisible collectives: the Chinese, Kazakh, Czech, and French as well as the Vietnamese. Facing Mountbatten, Nehru was a free negotiator. To be sure, he depended on Gandhi and the Congress. But what are conservative Hindu bullets compared to the necessities that determine the course of action of an Asian communist leader?

After failing to prevent a colonial war, the French government tried to transform it into a civil war, hoping in this fashion to shift its burdens and responsibilities; but in substituting one conflict for another, France was to discover an endless amount of bitterness and complication. Finally, by permitting the war that had first been colonial and then civil to turn into an international conflict, Paris again hoped to be able to ease its efforts, which had become intolerable. By then, France had been fighting in Indochina for ten years.

Three Wars, Then One More

On March 9, 1945, the Japanese garrisons, stationed for more than four years in Indochina, had thrown themselves upon the French forces, catching them in a trap. Once in command of the colonial administration machinery, they ended in a few hours eighty years of white supremacy. The new occupier immediately proclaimed Vietnamese independence under Japanese colors and persecuted the former masters.

On August 6, 1945, the bomb dropped on Hiroshima extinguished Japanese power in an instant; but if the defeat of the white man in Indochina had seemed to mark the end of an era, of a certain form of civilization, of a certain form of existence and behavior, the sudden collapse of Japan was considered a simple change in the power ratio, a strategic vicissitude.

Nevertheless the colonizers were beaten, the conquerors defeated, and the slate was clean. Which of the Vietnamese revolutionary groups would profit? Better armed, led, and organized, the communists took charge and succeeded. On September 2, 1945, the popular government under Ho Chi Minh proclaimed the Republic at Hanoi, reaffirming the independence and unity of Vietnam, with Saigon and Hue also claiming to be masters of revolutionary groups. Emperor Bao Dai had abdicated on August 25. Everywhere the Viet Minh, emerging from the Sino-Tonkinese highlands, had taken power.

On September 23 a few dozen tattered French soldiers (the last remnants of the Eleventh Regiment of colonial infantry) freed from Japanese prisons seized the public buildings in Saigon that had been occupied during the last days of August by the men of the Committee of Liberation of South Vietnam. The latter considered 1945 to be Year One of the new era. The French, of course, believed that the hour had come to reestablish their sovereignty.

The war in Indochina began.

Or rather, it was the beginning of the first of three wars that have blended one into the other during the last eight years—a colonial expedition, a civil war, and an international conflict, suspended between 1954 and 1959, resumed in 1960 under the pressure of the United States on the one hand and the Asian communists on the other.

The colonial expedition—which began for all practical purpose on September 23, 1945, and officially came to an end on March 8, 1949, with the recognition of Vietnamese independence by France—can itself be divided into three phases. In the course of the first phase, between October 1945 and March 1946, General Leclerc, at the head of some ten thousand soldiers, made efforts to reëstablish French rule. His methods were rough, but not of the kind to dishonor an army and compromise the future. The proof is that on March 6 of the same year General Leclerc signed with Ho Chi Minh, President of the Hanoi government, an agreement yielding to Vietnam its "freedom within the French union," and to France the right to maintain garrisons there for five years.

The second phase of the expedition was a sort of suspension of armed activity, with the French and Vietnamese formally complying with the agreements. But the intention was very clear on each side to interpret these agreements in such a way as to eliminate the other. At Da Lat and Fontainebleau negotiators faced each other without much conviction and with profoundly divergent aims, and sabotage rapidly increased at the local level, particularly after the two paragons of political agreement, Leclerc and Ho Chi Minh, had left for France. The break occurred on December 19, 1946, with the Vietnamese taking the bloody initiative. But French responsibility seems no less great; and communist historians are not the only ones to consider November 20 of the preceding year, when the French navy bombarded Haiphong, as the date of the break.

From then on Ho Chi Minh and his men, having taken refuge in the Tonkinese Middle Region, conducted the war with increasing force and violence, while in France those who had been unable to foresee or prevent these events suddenly saw the abyss opening at their feet. But they could not bring themselves to make the immediate military effort called for by their policy.

· · ·

The war turned into a "civil war" when, two years later, France officially gave the attributes and instruments of independence to Bao Dai and his men, and when, as a result, the Viet Minh came to be considered to be fighting not just for liberty but for another form of independence and government. It was certainly easy for the latter to claim that the independence granted by France was a "trick" in spirit, and was being progressively sabotaged in its application, and that they were not fighting for liberation on the Chinese pattern but simply for a more authentic independence than that which the French parliament had given as a gift to Bao Dai.

The new Vietnam was recognized by more than thirty nations, and that "phantom" state was supplied with all the attributes of legality. The war conducted against it by the majority of the people took on the character of a civil war. But here we should not fall too easily into the trap of looking only at the letter: though theoretically "rebel," the Viet Minh then comprised a majority of patriots and in the eyes of the people—at least until the intervention of Communist China—represented the spirit of resistance against all influence, or rather all imperialism, from abroad.

The internationalization of the war occurred in two ways, and at two different times; it actually began in the first days of 1950, on the occasion of the arrival of Mao Tse-tung's advance units at the Vietnamese frontier, and it developed further on the occasion of General de Lattre de Tassigny's trip to Washington in September 1951. At that time official French quarters defined their new war aims and had them accepted in Washington; these aims had now become a "crusade" against communism, establishing Vietnam as the "barrier in Southeast Asia." From then on France presented itself as the sentinel of the "free world," burdened with the tasks of preventing the "Red tide" from engulfing Southern Asia and of protecting the new independence of Bao's Vietnam.

But in 1954 there was Dien Bien Phu. France could no

longer sustain the war effort without appealing for more men, whom French public opinion refused to dispatch to Asia. On May 7, 1954, the very day of the fall of Dien Bien Phu, there began in Geneva a conference on Indochina, following in the wake of the conference that had been dealing with the final settlement of the Korean war, and assembling nine participants: France, Great Britain, the United States, the Soviet Union, Red China, Cambodia, Laos, the Vietnam of Bao Dai, and the Viet Minh of Ho Chi Minh. For a month the representatives pretended to ignore each other, lost themselves in formalities, and dragged their feet. Suddenly, on June 8, the military delegation of Viet Minh offered to partition Vietnam, accepting control over only about half the territory of which the revolutionary forces were already controlling three quarters. The West had set itself objectives of this kind but had not dared hope to attain them.

For another six weeks debates continued on the demarcation line, the guarantees, and the date of the referendum on the reunification of the two parts of Vietnam. On June 17 Mendès-France, new head of the French government, applied his direct style to the negotiations; he agreed to meet personally with the chief of the Chinese delegation, Chou En-lai, and that of the Viet Minh, Pham Van Dong—which his predecessor, Georges Bidault, had refused to do. During the night of July 20–21 the negotiators arrived at what Mendès-France had fixed as the ultimate limit of trading. This "ultimatum addressed to himself" paid off. The communist delegates did not want to see Mendès-France replaced by another negotiator, and the Soviets even hoped to turn an agreement with him into a new policy of international détente, particularly with regard to Germany.

The principal clauses of the armistice agreement of July 21 concerning Vietnam were: (1) the provisional partitioning of the country at the 17th Parallel, giving the country in the North that was to be controlled by the conquerors of Dien Bien Phu a population of close to fourteen million, as compared to twelve million for the South; (2) the evacuation of French forces from the North during the month of October; (3) a ban on increasing any military matériel in either part of the country; (4) the creation of an International Control Commission composed of Indian, Canadian, and Polish delegates, with the Indian delegates at the head; (5) the organization of elections to assure unification of the country before July 20, 1956. It was further understood that neither of the two parties in Vietnam was authorized to make international military alliances.

It is noteworthy that what has generally come to be called "the Geneva Agreement of 1954" is in fact a series of armistice agreements made by the French army representatives and the Viet Minh delegates, comprising the clauses enumerated above. Nothing else was *signed,* particularly not the final declaration made at the conference. Saigon, which did not hide its disagreement with the final declaration, and Washington, which showed some reserve on that score, therefore had no reason to refuse to apply their signatures to it. They did not consider themselves committed to these texts even though Gen. Bedell Smith, chief of the American delegation, had declared that his country would do nothing to prevent their implementation.

But the Geneva Agreement, which the communist powers accepted more or less as the ground rules for Indochinese affairs, even though they had deviated from their usual practice and had made major concessions by consenting to a territorial withdrawal, was quickly darkened by a double shadow. First there was the shadow that fell across France and the Viet Minh, its negotiating partner at Geneva, which by making known its authority over the North became the framework of the Vietnamese Democratic Republic's regime. That shadow resulted from a letter Mendès-France addressed to the Saigon leaders the day after the negotiations, assuring them that France would not recognize another trustee of Vietnam's sovereignty. This ended any chance of political co-operation between Paris and Hanoi, and rendered hopeless Sainteny's mission to the North Vietnamese government, pushing the latter into an isolation with no outlet except China and the other socialist states.

The second shadow was cast on the day after Geneva: the signing at Manila of the Southeast Asia Collective Defense Treaty, creating SEATO, which welded the United States, Great Britain, France, Australia, New Zealand, Thailand, the Philippines, and Pakistan into a group. This clearly anti-communist coalition could not but alert the Eastern powers, showing them that if the West had arrived at an armistice at Geneva, it still did not understand how to proceed from war to co-operation. Is there a contradiction? This was never admitted by the men on the European side who had been the true builders of these agreements—i.e., Mendès-France, Chauvel, and Eden—but who were constantly denounced with growing bitterness by Moscow and particularly by Peking and Hanoi. The war was over, but the struggle continued by other means, or by means that were different for the time being. Yet it must be recognized that, contrary to persistent legend, the Geneva accords were applied for several years.

The regime that established itself in the South even before the end of the war—Ngo Dinh Diem had been designated by Bao Dai to head the government the same day, June 17, 1954, that Mendès-France was installed by President Coty—insisted, of course, that it did not consider itself bound in any way by the text of July 21. But, unable to survive without the aid of France, which had assumed responsibility for the agreements, or the United States, which refused to contest them, it had to subscribe to them. Diem accepted the provisional continuation of Viet Minh administration in the zones affected by the accords, until their liquidation in 1956, and the installation on his soil of the International Control Commission, even though the latter was comprised of Polish diplomats (Reds!). And Diem took no steps to send his functionaries beyond the

17th Parallel. Reluctantly he acted as legatee and executor of the Geneva Agreements.

But once he felt more solidly established his government increasingly violated the July 21 provisions, particularly by launching a wave of oppression against those in the Viet Minh camp who had participated in war operations, and later by refusing to hold the 1956 referendum on reunification which could not fail to precipitate violent reactions in the North.

I felt it necessary to recapitulate these points, as they are the very links in the chain that led Vietnam from the armistice in 1954 to a new civil war and to the subsequent international conflict of 1965.

II

HOW TO
REVIVE A WAR

1

⟨𝄞𝄞𝄞𝄞𝄞𝄞𝄞⟩

"Diemocracy" Turns Sour

Saigon, December 1959

The first impression was not bad. How could a French visitor
who participated in the first Indochinese war not be captivated
by the courteous reception he was given in Saigon, five years
after Dien Bien Phu? The words he heard and the treatment
he received seemed to go even beyond the exquisite standard
of ordinary Vietnamese politeness. This capital, transformed
by the war into a sort of military supply center in which the
tattered argued with the dilapidated, now looked like an exhibit of "decolonization on the Western pattern": polished,
paved, and adorned with colorful gardens.

The density of the traffic, the hum of engines, and the unchanging elegance of the young women who, heads high,
draped in their charming tunics, had yielded neither to mod-
ernization nor to the invasion of the cinema and its fashions,
all were signs that the living standard at Saigon, if not of all
South Vietnam, was higher than in most Asian countries. The
American aid lavished upon this country was visible at every
step. It showed itself with a certain pride, stimulated the imagination, and had propaganda value.

But, paradoxically, this city that had remained so gay during the worst of the war had taken on in its time of peace and apparent opulence a sluggish air that suited it badly. It is normal for a people who have attained independence to be concerned for their dignity and to try to show it; to exhibit their virtues, but to avoid ostentation. But the heavy atmosphere that one noticed in Saigon beneath the brilliant appearances—did it suggest a certain discontent?

Was the affluence reflected in the appearance of the children and the profusion of vehicles, limited to only certain neighborhoods? Did the all-pervading malaise emanate from other and more remote sources? An enormous portrait several yards high, painted in gaudy colors, was visible on the façades of half a dozen public buildings in the capital: it was the portrait of a man with a round face, a cold gaze, and an austere elegance. The same picture haunted public offices, official buildings, airports. At the beginning of each show at the cinemas the public, asked to "salute the colors," would obediently rise, while this same haunting face, against the background of the Vietnamese flag flying in the wind, appeared on the screen. And the bridge, as well as the great avenue leading to Cholon, was full of large banners with the inscription, among other mysterious symbols: NGO THONG TONG—President Ngo.

In South Vietnam the cult of personality struck an original note. There "collective leadership" was a family council. And if the chief of state was called not by the last syllable of his name, in accordance with Vietnamese practice, but by the first —his patronym—it was perhaps because power resides less in the man than in the family group.

The eminent role played by family relations in Confucian civilizations is well known: no other cult is as important there as ancestor worship. With the Ngo family Catholicism, far from supplanting this primordial religion after two centuries, seemed to have given it even additional fervor, something absolute: the family, the mystical body.

If one considers the circumstances of Diem's accession to power, the methods he employed, the ardor of his religious convictions, his intransigence, his reputation for austerity, one easily sees the master of South Vietnam endowed with the harsh traits of an Asiatic Philip II. But the man was debonair in appearance, bulky, rounded with age like certain ecclesiastics. No matter how lusterless his conversation, five years of power and life in Saigon had instilled the rather jovial manner of the typical Cochinchinese bourgeois into this former seminarian and austere mandarin from the court of Hue.

Yet, despite appearances, Ngo Dinh Diem was animated with an extra touch of fervor, something of the absolute. He had an attachment to the ancient society of Annam—high aristocracy, closed castes, intellectual hierarchies, its cohesive families, its disdain of strangers, its hatred of China.

He wanted to revive the old order, the ancient morality, the respect for the master, the rule of the closed city. But this was beyond his power. The facts were intransigent. This Catholic in the Spanish manner, this puritanical conservative, attached his name to an enterprise that could only defeat him.

This man who at the time of the Indochinese war symbolized the firmest nationalism, even chauvinism, was finally forced to impose upon his country the world's most unrestrainedly technological and most proudly innovating civilization, that of the United States.

These diverse attitudes also expressed themselves with disconcerting clarity within his family, among the five all-powerful brothers, among whom modernism and traditionalism were in constant conflict: there was particularly the conflict between Ngo Dinh Nhu, educated in France, an intellectual trained in the Western world, and Ngo Dinh Can, who called himself uncultured and was proud of it.

The former, who carried only the title "political adviser" and directed the Can Lao ("effort") movement, came from a group whose adherents did not like to identify themselves, in case they had to resume their clandestine struggle against a communist regime; he exercised his influence primarily on Saigon and the South. Though officially the latter was only a delegate of the National Revolutionary Movement of Central Vietnam, he was considered the master of Hue and the provinces close to the North.

This is what Nhu, with his strong, leonine face, and his piercing look and sarcastic smile, said to me:

> We are a reactionary regime, you have been told— are you aware of the fact that we are taking our inspiration from the thinkers of the Western Left, particularly the French? I don't want to name names [he laughed] or compromise anybody. . . . But you must realize that we are basing ourselves on personalism!*

I replied: "This is exactly what you are accused of in certain quarters. . . ."

> You will tell me that not all that we are led to do is in conformity with Mounier's ideal. In political action one is occasionally forced to dirty one's hands. There is a difference between what one wants to do and what one does.

"But could you not . . ."

> Restore freedom, give free speech to the opposition, create conditions of coexistence with communism? First of all, you do not coexist with those who want to exterminate you. Moreover, the opposition is not so badly treated by us. It cannot speak up? Wait a minute. We do not permit ourselves to be incited or destroyed, but these restrictions of liberty we also apply to ourselves. Are you aware of that?

---

* A French doctrine developed by Emmanuel Mounier in the thirties. It is a philosophy of existence akin to Existentialism, but differing from it by its generally Christian orientation.—Trans.

We would not permit ourselves to throw dirt at our adversaries, or trample them down. Look at our newspapers. There you will not find the insults against the opposition that you find in the press of neighboring countries. Is that not liberalism?

No insults? This is playing with words. While Madame Nhu conducted her campaign against "vice" and called all non-classical music "prostitution," Mr. Nhu called every opponent a communist. In a country where Manicheism reigns, what is an "insult"?

I was unable to interview Ngo Dinh Can, master of Hue. Nobody could see Can except his collaborators and those closest to him. Living in the ancient style in his family mansion, dressed in Vietnamese clothing, sleeping on the harsh ground, Diem's youngest brother devoted his life to the struggle against Evil, i.e., communism, and its allies, i.e., all foreigners. The following words are attributed to him: "My hand will never tire of killing communists. . . . Everyone among you should offer the life of *one* Red to your country. As for me, millions. . . ."

The Beginnings of Subversion

When French Foreign Minister Pinay was in Saigon in the fall of 1959, Diem confided to him: "You have your war in Algeria. We, too, have an Algerian war to wage in the South of our country." The Saigon dictator meant to be pleasant, thinking that to share such anguish could bring the two governments closer together.

But the threat to the Vietnamese state was already much more perilous than the Algerian affair was for the French. For three or four months the Southern provinces had been partially under the almost direct administration of what people were beginning to call the Viet Cong, and the Western provinces were heavily contaminated, particularly in the old Hoa-

Hao, where the old militants had more or less risen again from the soil.

The rubber plantation regions in the north of old Cochinchina were also contaminated by nationalist sects, particularly in the area of Tay Ninh, which is the source of Caodaism.*

A few months later, in September 1960, there appeared striking evidence of the opening of the new Front in the highlands zone, a sensitive sector for French authority during the entire Indochinese war. Some very heavy and bloody engagements were taking place in the region of Kontum, inhabited by the Mois.

These mountain tribesmen (like the Berbers in Morocco in an earlier day) had long been considered faithful mountaineers without political convictions, good and dependable peasants. But the South Vietnamese were now discovering, as had the French before them, that these mountaineers were not always easy to lead; they were as impatient with injustice as the people in the plains, if not more so, especially now that they were infiltrated with communist cadres which had long before been implanted in their territory. The Saigon government announced that it had captured infiltrators from the North who had passed not through the small and extremely well guarded frontier at the 17th Parallel, but through Laos, which was already in a state of turmoil.

In a press conference Secretary of State Nguyen Dinh Thuan, speaking to reporters, military attachés, and diplomatic representatives, called the affair of Kontum "grave." For the first time the South Vietnamese government decided to bring the question of its security before the world. In particular, Thuan declared:

This aggression constitutes a new turn in communist action against life and liberty in Southeast Asia and the free world. For the first time since 1954 the enemy has attacked from his bases in the North, with important

* See pp. 99ff.

units, by proceeding via Laotian territory. It follows that the enemy intends to implant himself in the region and from there prepare actions against the South and the coastal zone. . . . The events in Laos are actually staged by the enemy to attack South Vietnam directly from his bases.

Invasion of South Vietnam? Of course not. But the affair showed that subversion all over the country was on the increase, and that the North was beginning to mix in it.

At that very time Ngo Dinh Nhu, speaking to a Paris newspaper correspondent, stated that the authorities in the highland region had established the presence of a North Vietnamese battalion south of the 17th Parallel, and concluded: "The second Indochinese war has begun. . . ."

To give an indication of magnitude—explained by Vietnamese in the opposition, responsible people in this case—it was considered that five thousand irregulars were active throughout Vietnam. This figure does not appear too high. After all, during much of the first Indochinese war it took no more than such a number on the side of the Viet Minh to defy some excellent French troops that were far superior to South Vietnamese units fighting in 1960. Of these five thousand irregulars, according to my Vietnamese informants, hardly more than a quarter were communists; while my informants did not say so, I assumed from what they reported that most of those were officers.

Subversion was not the only danger facing the South Vietnamese regime. The other, more hidden, was almost as grave: graft. Of course, one must not accept at face value the many stories that made the rounds in Saigon, aimed at the rulers of that day, similar to those aimed at the colonial regime in earlier days, and from which only the chief of state was immune. A thousand and one compromising accusations were leveled at various personalities of the regime, to the delight of the blasé Saigon population.

When I discussed the matter of graft with a Chinese who knew a great deal about it and had recently had to endure a "tax withholding" at the hands of a certain functionary, he made this typically Chinese comment: "My dear sir, this is too bad, this interferes with free enterprise. . . ."

Subversion, nepotism, graft: the dangers threatening the regime were clear. But the positive aspects of the situation must also be mentioned. We have already spoken of the administrative successes of the system. Without insisting on the relative efficiency of the governmental machine, we must stress one triumph of Diem's regime: the integration of nearly a million refugees from the North.

However one may judge the reasons that led these hundreds of thousands of men—mostly Christians—to leave their Tonkinese villages and the communist regime of the North to live in the South under a nationalist and Catholic regime, one must appreciate what was done for them in Cochinchina and in the Annam highlands. It will be said, of course, that the credit goes to American money and the activity of the Catholic clergy. Still the Diem state was able to co-ordinate the necessary efforts with great diligence.

As a result the yellow and white flag of the Vatican had been raised beside the yellow and red Vietnam standard over some of the square villages along the Cochinchinese roads and the Mois highlands. In the Da Lat region integration was a success. But the apportionment of certain parcels of land to the refugees from the North provoked considerable discontent on the part of some of the Mois tribes of the region, and swelled the ranks of the underground, which had given the signal for the resumption of the war.

Where Were the Americans?

But where were the Americans? The conspicuous foreigners in Saigon were usually French. In the city streets one could see big old Packards driven by gentlemen in nylon suits, or, at night, the same gentlemen entering cabarets in gaudy sport shirts. But the United States Embassy was installed in a drab building, and either as a matter of policy or because they were uncomfortable in the face of a strange civilization, the employees of U.S.I.S., M.A.A.G., or U.S.O.M. hardly left their dwellings.

What was visible were not the Americans but the credits they were giving. I have spoken of the impression of relative affluence given by the Saigon crowds, and noted the reintegration of almost a million refugees south of the 17th Parallel. Together with the equipment and maintenance of a 250,000-man army of excellent appearance, and the land-repurchasing operation that was one of the elements of the sensible agrarian reform accomplished under the direction of the remarkable American expert Wolf Ladejinsky, these were the most tangible results of American aid then estimated at $200,000,000 a year—which is a great deal for a population of twelve million.

The mere fact that Vietnam was still alive five years after Geneva and showed no sign of immediate collapse, surely justified this enormous effort in the eyes of responsible Americans, even if there was some "leakage" as reported in August 1959 by a reporter of the Scripps-Howard newspaper chain. "Our aid is a shameful scandal," wrote Mr. Colegrave. As a result of these articles a commission of inquiry was hurriedly set up in Washington, and an impressive number of senators went to Saigon.

It is hard to say how independent a country is when 70 per cent of its budgetary deficit is covered by a foreign state which also covers all its military and police expenses. But what must always be taken into account is the great strain inflicted on such an economy by the smallest reduction of foreign assistance. If South Vietnam did not suffer too much in the period of 1959–1960 from a reduction in credits of $25,000,000, it nevertheless faced the risks of a "fading" of American aid, and particularly the substitution of loans for outright gifts.

Was the United States thinking at that time—1960—of revising its attitude with respect to the regime? Shortly before President Kennedy's inauguration several Vietnamese opposition leaders were invited to Washington. They established some important contacts at a time when certain members of Diem's entourage were not being received in Washington. What was even more curious, one of these nationalist Vietnamese opposition leaders was received by Francis Cardinal Spellman, who was playing the role of super-protector of the Diem regime.

Were these prospects casting the shadow of a recession on the Vietnamese economy? There were probably other reasons to be sought for the shortage of money, the dangerous weakness in economic affairs, and the bankruptcies that hit sellers and even manufacturers of luxury and semi-luxury products, such as bicycles, radios, and so on. Naturally the saturation of the market was also responsible, particularly as Vietnam has lived beyond its means for many years.

Reduction of American aid and closer control by Washington, impoverishment of the people of Cholon due to apathy, and a shortage of money due among other things to Chinese capital flowing to Hong Kong and Singapore—all these factors created a difficult situation, forcing responsible top Vietnamese leaders to look for other support.

But the efforts made to obtain aid from France on the occasion of Pinay's visit in November 1959 did not yield the expected results: credits of $20,000,000 might have made it possible to build a cement factory at Ha Tien or some plants on the outskirts of Saigon, but it was not the type of support that the Diem regime was seeking.

One must concede one virtue to Diem: his tranquil audacity that allowed him to take in stride any operation the moment he decided to undertake it. For example, at a time when everybody thought that the Chinese tide was rising inexorably over Southeast Asia, and that, all ideology aside, biological

"Chinization" of that region would be only a question of years or decades, the Vietnamese chief of state decided that he could go against the current and that the time had come to nationalize the Chinese.

It is well known how important in the life of the country the three hundred thousand Chinese of Cholon, Saigon's twin city, had become, not only because they displayed the industrial and commercial genius that is their national heritage, or because they constituted a more compact bloc than émigré Chinese in Bangkok or Djakarta, but also because the colonial regime for reasons of convenience and efficiency had consolidated their power, making them indispensable intermediaries between French and Vietnamese producers and consumers. Transportation, banks, trade, or the distribution of rice were very often controlled by them. It was not surprising that the super-nationalist Diem took some steps to dismantle this economic bastion after the end of the colonial system. But he chose a strange method, forcing every member of the Chinese colony either to adopt Vietnamese nationality or be prevented from participating in the most profitable trades.

After several weeks or months of hesitation, while waiting vainly for word from Taipeh, the people of Cholon gave in. Meanwhile they had lost a number of positions, and several of their rice-processing factories had passed into Vietnamese hands or had been dismantled and sent abroad. Their citadel had been besieged. Armed with Vietnamese passports, the Chinese later tried to reconquer it. But something was destroyed in the process, some equilibrium upset, some dynamism lost, and as a result one of the springs of economic activity in South Vietnam was broken. True, the entire operation should have benefited Vietnamese business. But the losses were greater than the gains.

Looking beyond the economic aspects, what was the likely reaction on the part of these Chinese who were forced to give up their nationality when Chiang Kai-shek failed to come to their aid? After all, Chiang's government should, on general principle, have defended their interests. Did his failure make them turn their eyes toward another power?

But what about reunification? Was there any chance that in the foreseeable future the 17th Parallel, a more vigorous dividing line inside the Vietnamese nation than any frontier in the world, would disappear? The general view in Saigon was that this would be impossible for many years. The Southern authorities in particular stated that since the people in the North were more numerous, reunification would effectively deliver the South to the holocaust of communism.

But the authorities were not content with prognostications and apprehensions. They were taking extreme measures.

The Witch Hunt

In 1954 and 1955 the Diem regime had displayed impressive energy in its struggle with politico-religious sects that threatened it, and had always answered with force all divisive activities aimed at the state, even though these attempts had no serious hope of success. The generals who distinguished themselves in these operations were to attain a different form of notoriety at some other time. Their chief was Duong Van Minh.

But after 1955 and the dismissal of Bao Dai to make room for the "Republic" of Diem, whose accession to the Presidency was based on a plebiscite as orderly as possible in a country barely recovered from the wounds of war and in the process of reunification, the regime did not know how to use its victory to "return" its opponents to its fold, although it had won over the sects and the crown. Having won a battle, it preferred war to peace.

The referendum on the reunification of Vietnam was scheduled by the Geneva Agreements for 1956. The Southern leaders, believing that such an operation could benefit only the North, made every effort to prevent any development in that direction, to discourage any such attempt, and to repress all conceivable initiative that could lead to reunification.

While the Saigon government rebuffed every advance from the North as "subversive"—and, as we shall see, the North did make several advances between 1955 and 1958—it reoriented its aggressive policy and concentrated its blows on a new target. A new enemy was substituted for the sects that seemed to have been crushed: the Viet Cong, or Vietnamese communism. In 1955 every opponent had been denounced as a left-over from the "feudal rebels" supported by colonialism. After 1956 every opponent was called a communist.

A tremendous war machine was then set up against the Viet Cong. At first the struggle was conducted by simple means: concentration camps. After raids on regions reputed to be "rotten," several thousand "Reds" were placed in concentration camps like the one in Phu Loi, about thirty miles from Saigon. In December 1958 a report of poisonings created a scandal; the rumor, taken up noisily by Northern propaganda, was to the effect that of six thousand prisoners more than a thousand had died of poisoning. From Hanoi, Gen. Vo Nguyen Giap denounced these "atrocities" to the International Control Commission. But the Saigon government opposed an inquiry that had been demanded by various international personalities, including several British Labour deputies. It turned out that the number of deaths had been inflated by the opposition; but the attitude of the Southern regime indicated that it definitely had things to hide.*

Was it to give itself a better conscience or to improve its credit abroad that the regime acted in this fashion? On May 6, 1959, Diem gave himself the "legal" arsenal for repression: a law creating special military tribunals which would pronounce judgment within three days after the citation of the accused, sentencing to death

---

* Authorized by Diem to lead the inquiry locally, P. J. Honey, one of the seven or eight outstanding Western specialists on Vietnamese affairs, declared that he could not verify more than twenty deaths at Phu Loi.

anyone who intentionally proclaimed or propagated, by
no matter what means, unfounded news on prices, or
rumors contrary to the truth, or distorting the truth, on
the actual or future economic situation in the country
or outside, likely to provoke economic or financial dis-
turbance in the country . . . anyone who committed or
tried to commit the crime of sabotage or made an attempt against the security of the State or an attempt on
the life or property of the population . . . anyone who
adhered to an organization in order to aid in the preparation or execution of these crimes.

The law also stated that:

Extenuating circumstances will not be allowed the
principal culprit, or the authors or instigators of crimes
falling under the competence of the special military
tribunals. . . .
The special military tribunals will pronounce final
judgment, and no appeal will be possible.
The decisions of the military tribunals will be executed
in accordance with the emergency provisions of the
military penal code.

Thus every person accused of "attempts against the security
of the state" or of being a "co-instigator," or anyone who belonged to an organization in order to help in the preparation
of a crime, or who simply became involved in its commission,
was condemned to death and was executed within three days
without possible appeal. Commenting on this brutal law, the
official journal *Cach Mang Quoc Gie* (*The National Revolution*) wrote:

The law must be broadly applied. . . . There are
crimes that deserve the death penalty . . . for example,
attempts to disturb the economy of the country, to organize strikes, to make demonstrations that damage the
prestige of the nation, to disseminate false news. . . .

To hide a communist, or permit oneself to become involved in anything with a communist, is to risk the death penalty. In connection with the crime there usually is a distant instigator who has only given orders, an immediate instigator and a certain number of those who committed the crime, and all those who have directly or indirectly been of assistance. All must suffer execution. . . .

The courts will not wait for security organs to bring the guilty before them. The court itself must seek out the guilty and their accomplices. The suppression of terrorism must be conducted by the courts themselves. The courts must not only be organs that judge men and apply the law, but organs whose primary task is to exterminate terrorism.

We now have all the means necessary to exterminate the criminals. We have:

— Large armed forces, police units, and a militia;
— Regularly established military tribunals;
— Recently reinforced police forces.

The same paper added that it was not enough to hit the communists.

There are still people in our ranks who must be eliminated. Their crimes equal in gravity those of the communists, and the nation must consider them as traitors. There are still people who have not understood the all-embracing truths of our methods of combat. . . . There also are those who are still indifferent. . . .

2

§§§§§§§

The View from Hanoi

Hanoi, December 1961

What dreams for their country had animated those fierce little fighters who swamped the last fortifications of Dien Bien Phu on May 7, 1954? Under their palm pith helmets their faces seemed thin, and under the green trellises their bodies emaciated. But their heads and hearts had been full of "tomorrows that sing," and they had fought with incredible valor under the orders of a lion-faced, Vo Nguyen Giap, not just for the pride of victory over the white man, but also for a decent life.

Seven years later they had become the cadres of a suffering, divided, tense country which survived only in a state of semi-peace and at the price of sacrifices comparable to guerrilla warfare. After ten years of experience, effort, constantly aborted and renewed plans, foreign aid, and patriotic tension, North Vietnam exercised a growing ascendancy over the South and its neighboring countries but saved itself only by a constant miracle of will power and almost inhuman discipline.

Here was a strange nation that had three births. The first

took place in August of 1945. Ten days after the holocaust at Hiroshima several hundred guerrillas assembled in Southern China by the old communist leader Ho Chi Minh—organized four years earlier in a "patriotic front," the Viet Minh, and gradually infiltrated into Tonkin under orders of the future general Giap—stirred up Hanoi, unleashed a revolution, and proclaimed the independent Republic of Vietnam.

An American mission, led by Commander Patti and later by General Gallagher, offered the protection of the greatest power in the world to these revolutionaries who made no bones about their Marxist orientation. But in Paris, General de Gaulle's government was in no way disposed to recognize this *fait accompli*.

Nevertheless, six months later Ho Chi Minh's Vietnam was born for a second time. General Leclerc had reconquered old Cochinchina and South Annam, forced Chiang Kai-shek's troops to evacuate the area of Tonkin that had been entrusted to them by Roosevelt and Stalin, and led an imposing armada up the coast from Haiphong. Leclerc, politically unsophisticated knight, had understood the intractable force of Vietnamese nationalism and admitted that with France proudly reëstablished in the Far East, it was necessary to treat and recognize the new nation accordingly. This was also the opinion of Sainteny, commissioner of the French Republic for North Indochina. And as Vietnam's leader was sufficiently flexible to adjust his ends to his means, and was ready to put the dignity of his country above his hostility to France, the agreement of March 6, 1946, was concluded, recognizing Vietnam as a free state within the Indochinese Federation and the French Union.

But Leclerc and Sainteny were ahead of their time, at least compared to the men in Saigon, where Admiral d'Argenlieu did not hide his distaste for this compromise with communism; and they were ahead of Paris, where despite the presence of five communists, Bidault's government did not accept unreservedly this first step toward the dismemberment of what had been the Empire—and would have been able to become the French Union.

Because the dangers were not understood, and pressure was exercised, from the Lang Son incident to the bombing of Haiphong, all chances of compromise were ruined, thus leading to the Viet Minh coup of December 1946 at Hanoi.

Close to eight years of war followed. It was a war that compromised French autonomy, killed twenty-five thousand young Frenchmen, introduced bribery into the political mores of the country, stimulated revolutionary fever in Africa, reduced the nation's army, and ended in the greatest military disaster in French colonial history since the eighteenth century. Finally, negotiations courageously conducted with the semi-complicity of Soviet diplomats, anxious at the time to extinguish the fires of international tension in order to smooth the way for peaceful coexistence, allowed France to disengage herself without dishonor at the end of the 1954 Geneva Conference.

This was the third birth of revolutionary Vietnam, which in 1954 assumed as its name the Democratic Republic of Vietnam. But in order to bring the war to an end and reinstate themselves in their capital, the victors of Dien Bien Phu had to permit the partitioning of their country. The final declaration of the Geneva Conference foresaw, of course, that general elections would permit the reunification of Vietnam two years later. And none doubted at the time that this would be to the benefit of the North.

Seven years later, however, Ho Chi Minh and his men were still "parked" in their zone north of the 17th Parallel, which did not produce enough rice for a population whose annual growth exceeded 3 per cent and which, against its national pride, remained largely dependent on the socialist powers, particularly China.

Why did those dynamic people of the North permit themselves to be imprisoned in such a small area, that was in no way justified by the national tradition? It must be remembered that this partition of the country, seemingly so disadvantageous, was clearly proposed first by the Northern general staff, on the occasion of the meeting of the military commission at the Geneva Conference on June 8, 1954. Ho Chi Minh and his lieutenants, practicing once again the policy of a cease fire, as in March 1946, had wanted above all to obtain peace, a final renunciation on the part of France of all colonial thoughts in the back of her mind, the departure of the French army, and possibly some form of economic co-operation with Paris and the West. Yet the Vietnamese communist leaders, on the other hand, had been worried about the extent of the problems concerning Vietnam as a whole, and knowing full well the resistance they would meet when applying socialism to a society where individualism was flourishing—at least in the form of village autonomy—had preferred to proceed in stages.

But there were other factors at work which contributed to changing Ho Chi Minh's policies. The installation of the fanatically anti-communist Ngo family in Saigon, Washington's unreserved support of that dictatorship, and the constant increase of American forces in the Southern zone made it clear to the men in Hanoi that they faced not just a delay with regard to reunification, but a final partitioning, which would imprison them forever in their narrow and meager zone and weld them completely to China; and that moreover a platform was perhaps being established in the South from which some day a military action might be launched against them.

The pitiless "witch hunt" conducted against their comrades in the South, resulting in the latter's pathetic appeals for help to Hanoi leaders, and the economic pressure on them, resulting from the blockade of the undernourished North, led them, after 1959 and five years of honest application of the Geneva Agreements, to intervene progressively in the South in order to press by force for reunification that could not be attained through other means.

.   .   .

I had occasion to visit North Vietnam in November 1961. In February 1946 we had been received at the Gia Lam airport by a starved and tattered band of Chinese "soldiers," or more precisely men from Yunnan Province, for whom the war evidently was a compromise between smuggling and stealing; then, seven years later, a certain Colonel Gardes received the journalists in the midst of a formidable array of transport and bombing planes; in 1961 there was only a glacial silence. Hanoi was a capital in which socialism was being built, but it was a relaxed capital—at least for those who could afford to travel by plane.

On the huge Doumer Bridge, for years a bottleneck for French army operations and so often groaning under the weight of its tanks, nothing could be heard but the soft hum of hundreds of bicycle wheels. North Vietnam, having achieved its independence, thanks to tens of thousands of coolies pushing their bicycles loaded with rice and ammunition across the brush, had become a nation on bicycles. In another day Lenin had defined socialism as "Soviet power plus electricity"; one could say that in Vietnam it was the bicycle plus Uncle Ho.

If the question of reunification preoccupied the Hanoi leaders, it was not so much because of national pride, communist imperialism, or strategic precaution vis-à-vis Washington, but for economic reasons. Before the partitioning of 1954 Vietnam certainly had not always been politically united, and the divisions of the colonial epoch—with Tonkin in the North, Annam in the Center, and Cochinchina in the South—corresponded quite well to the realities of cultural traditions and collective psychology.

But in the economic domain Vietnamese unity took on overriding importance. Tonkin, furnishing unskilled labor and punctual functionaries, ideally complemented Cochinchina, producer of rice, skilled in commercial exchanges, and full of plantations in need of labor. To create two political capitals, Hanoi and Saigon, was partially justified, but to break up Vietnam's economic unity was to attempt the irrational.

Against this attempt the South was able to protect itself after a fashion, thanks to American aid which—no matter how badly it was employed—eventually bore fruit. But in the North the people, hardly over an exhausting war, struggled with heroic and fierce determination against a form of poverty that was aggravated by certain abuses of socialist planning,* and rendered persistent by demographic pressure. But the intense effort in the direction of economic development was not merely an attempt to save these people from famine by giving them bowls of rice. As in every Marxist-Leninist state, industrialization remained the main spring of activity, all the more so as Vietnam was one of the rare examples where the colonizers had initiated industrial production, such as the coal pits of Hon Gai in the Bay of Along and the cotton mill in Nam Dinh. The Geneva accords had permitted a peaceful transfer of these installations to the new authorities, who no longer felt tied by the 1954 text. In any event, Hanoi used this colonial heritage to great benefit.

In November 1961 I was not permitted to visit the steel plant in Thai Nguyen, built after 1960 in Viet Minh's "war capital" in the Tonkin highlands, the first enterprise of this type in Southeast Asia, capable of an annual production of two hundred thousand tons of steel and equipped with presses capable of manufacturing rolled steel for industry. But I was permitted to go to Viet Tri, at the eastern point of the Red

---

* Since the great mistakes of 1956, target adjustments had been brought to bear on the plans for accelerated socialization. In 1956 I personally observed a certain economic slowdown that showed itself in such picturesque ways as the denationalization of hairdressers and sellers of Chinese soup; but more important was the report by René Dumont who, in 1964, on his return from a trip through North Vietnam, stated that the agricultural co-operatives were being reorganized and that the yield per hectare of rice paddy had risen in five years from thirteen to nineteen quintals. This allowed the government to increase individual rice rations by 20 per cent, or from fifteen to twenty kilos per adult per month.

River delta, where an industrial complex had been created out of a small paper factory built in 1939: electrical works, a sugar refinery, a plywood factory, a new paper mill, and so on. The whole was very impressive; one could see many Chinese machines—at least according to the tags on them—and great responsibilities entrusted to young Vietnamese engineers to the exclusion, it seemed, of foreign experts, even socialist experts.

In the great salon of the seat of what was the Government-General of Indochina I met two men clad in the austere high-buttoned jacket that has become the uniform of the Asian revolution. One was old, smiling, with high color and an almost baby face—it was Ho Chi Minh, whom I had known for fifteen years; he was so thin and frail that he seemed able to survive only through sheer zeal. The other, his face swarthy, strongly sculptured as though hammered into a shape by many trials, speaking in abrupt sentences, and with a frequent smile that wrinkled his very high forehead, was Prime Minister Pham Van Dong.

"Uncle Ho," it seemed, was glad to allow the latter (who has been his closest lieutenant for more than thirty years) to answer the visitor's political questions. Ho himself was content to ask questions about Paris, France, and his friends. With some compassion he expressed surprise at General de Gaulle's troubles, the "black shirts," the bombs, and the strikes. He expressed great surprise at the role played by Raoul Salan.

"You know, I knew him very well. We traveled together from Hanoi to Paris in 1946. He was such a careful man, so self-effacing, who never spoke to me of his apartment, his furniture, his position in France after his return. . . . A true bourgeois. . . . And now a resistance fighter!" Ho laughed, spoke for another few moments of his memories, his French friends, of General Leclerc, to whom he was very attached, and the war in Algeria, while drawing on his cigarette with a rather dreamy expression. Then he left, sliding along on his sandals, a friendly smile creasing his face.

When I mentioned to Pham Van Dong that I was struck by the physical vigor and good humor exhibited by Ho, Dong replied: "But you know we are very gay!" Still, gaiety did not seem to me characteristic of the regime or of Hanoi's psychological climate. And now, for two hours, the man who had sat across the table from Mendès-France in Geneva spoke in his turn.

The version of our conversation below, edited by Dong, does not fully reflect the tone of our conversation and the personal and passionate tenor of his statements. In the transcript mere propaganda formulas often take the place of some of the passages in this particularly animated conversation. For example, Dong would interrupt himself, close his eyes, and exclaim: "This is exciting, exciting!" And when I objected to his calling Fidel Castro's communism evolutionary because the Cuban chief seemed too romantic to me, he replied, almost with indignation: "But we communists, particularly we Vietnamese, *are* romantic. . . . Fortunately!"

I asked Dong about the prospects for Vietnamese reunification. He replied:

> If Vietnam is to stay provisionally divided, it is because the implementation of the Geneva Agreements is running into very serious obstacles. The primary obstacle is the policy of intervention and aggression on the part of the American imperialists in South Vietnam who aim at transforming this zone into a "colony of the new type" and an American military base, and to prepare for a new war. As everyone knows, the United States is preparing to bring American troops to South Vietnam. All this represents a great danger for our people and a grave menace to peace in Indochina and in Southeast Asia. These are very grave matters. It is obvious that an end of the policy of intervention and aggression on the part of American

imperialists in South Vietnam is the prime condition for the correct implementation of the Geneva Agreements, the peaceful reunification of Vietnam, and the maintenance of peace in that region of the world.

Diem's administration is another obstacle in the way of the implementation of the Geneva Agreements and peaceful reunification of Vietnam, since his administration is the instrument of American imperialists, has always sabotaged the implementation of the Geneva Agreements, and has rejected all constructive proposals by the government of the Democratic Republic. The cause of Vietnam's reunification and the interest of peace and security in this region require a government in South Vietnam that would declare itself in favor of the correct implementation of the Geneva Agreements and of consultations between the two zones with a view toward the peaceful unification of the country.

For its part, the government of the Democratic Republic is always disposed to enter into negotiations with a government of the South that is similarly disposed. In the course of such negotiations, all problems concerning peaceful reunification of Vietnam can be resolved, above all the problem of the restoration of normal relations between the two zones. Such a government in South Vietnam can only be a government freed of American domination, and a government practicing the kind of national political independence that respects democratic liberties, in short a government with a broad national base.

Dong added to this somewhat conventional presentation a curious detail that illuminated the policy of the North in 1965 and the appeals made in the direction of Paris.

There are, after all, three kinds of people in the South. The friends of the Americans, such as Diem and others: they have already lost their game. The people: they are with us. The intellectuals and the bourgeoisie: they remain very attached to France. Thus, the solution largely depends on an understanding, between you and us, that would permit joining the masses to the intelligentsia and to the middle class in order to establish a democratic rule. Oh, if only Paris would play its role and contribute to peace!

Whether reflecting sentimentality, cleverness, or sincerity, these two hours of conversation, despite the severity of his judgments on French policies, were studded with what is perhaps Dong's attachment to French culture or to the revolutionary instructions he received in France, and also the conviction that in the South of Asia, France has to play a role that in the eyes of Dong, who places France in the camp of those opposed to war, would not make it the inevitable enemy of the Vietnamese revolution.

Regarding the reunification of the two Vietnams, Dong's answers to my questions made me think that the Hanoi leaders were primarily occupied with the consolidation of socialism in their camp. In the same fashion Mao Tse-tung took his time in preparing himself during his retreat at Yenan. This does not prevent the Northern leaders from expressing the judgment that "Diem has now rendered enough service to the anti-American cause" and—even while they are denying it— from undermining with all their power the regime in the South. But the evolution may be very slow.

It should be added that no matter how courteously he received most of my questions, Dong categorically refused to answer some of them and abruptly cut me short when I touched on the relations of the Democratic Republic of Vietnam with Moscow on the one hand and Peking on the other. "These are subjects of discussion among socialists!" he told me rudely.

The North Vietnam situation in this connection was, in fact, particularly uncomfortable. If Ho's heart went out to Moscow because he was a "Khrushchevist," as did those of his closest companions, the "belly" of the regime turns to Peking, for Peking furnishes most of the foreign aid and technicians. The "Chinese" Party is strong inside the Lao Dong, the heir of the Indochinese Communist Party. And China is very close.

President Ho's portrait is flanked almost everywhere by those of "Ko Rut Sop" and "Mao Trach Dong," as the two great brothers are called in Vietnam. At Hanoi, I visited an Albanian exhibit that was primarily a display of Enver Hodja's portraits. But if, when Ho Chi Minh represented his party in Moscow at the Twenty-second Congress of the Soviet Communist Party, articles favorable to Tirana were published in *Nhan-Dan,* organ of the North Vietnamese Communist Party, the commentators have since changed targets and are paying ringing homage to the Soviet Union.

A dangerous course to follow.

Between Peking and Moscow

After 1955 China considered herself responsible for the "Asiatic zone of influence" in the name of international communism. Harrison Salisbury, the *New York Times* correspondent, wrote about it first. The following year events in Hungary and Suez favored the Chinese drive toward Asiatic leadership that had preoccupied the Soviets ever since the spring of 1959.

Beginning in 1960 Chinese expansion in Southeast Asia decidedly worried the Soviet Union, even if the troubles encouraged or sustained by China in Laos and South Vietnam had certain advantages for Moscow. In 1959 the Polish Ambassador to Hanoi confided to his colleague Erickson Brown, Canadian Ambassador and chief of the Canadian delegation to the International Control Commission, that the Soviet Ambassador to North Vietnam had complained of the "aggressive policy conducted by China," which kept creating "annoyance and concern in his government."

In Hanoi the divergencies between the Chinese and other

representatives of the socialist countries revolved perhaps less around ideological factors, shifts in strategy, or national opposition movements than around differences in behavior. The daily living together, side by side, of thousands of Chinese experts and counselors and "European socialists" created a situation in North Vietnam to which those recently decolonized have good reason to attach a great deal of importance. While most of the social advisers and experts of European background stationed in Hanoi or other places in Vietnam often complained to the local authorities about the absence of comfort and the poor dwellings offered them or criticized the bad telephone communications, the Chinese behaved like people accustomed to the traditional conditions of life as lived by the Asiatic masses, as men "poor in spirit." The Vietnamese appreciated that.

On the whole the Chinese behaved cleverly in North Vietnam. They succeeded in attracting sympathy by following a simple policy in order to make people forget the historical past consisting entirely of Vietnam's resistance to China's imperialism.

Vietnamese opinion of the Chinese generally depends on the age of those concerned as well as the social class they belong to. The anti-Chinese sentiment is very active in the countryside. In the towns it was rather strong among intellectuals, and the people resented the fact that a good part of Tonkin's coal and rice from the Delta was sent to China, and that there were not more Chinese products in Hanoi's stores. In their eyes the Chinese remained people to be mistrusted; many thought that they had "only changed masters: yesterday the French, today the Chinese."

But among the small employees and officials firmly controlled by the Party there was an apparently sincere admiration for the "great brother country"; the ill feeling of the past was forgotten.

Those most favorably inclined to the Chinese were the young, who insisted that they understood them "better than

the others," an allusion to the European communists. The
young Vietnamese were impregnated with the idea of Asian
solidarity, more so even than with their fidelity to socialist
alliances. As a result they agreed with the daily statements,
made in each quarter, on the importance of Chinese economic
aid from old resistance fighters for whom the Chinese remained war comrades against colonialism.

Strangely enough the Chinese colony was declining; it was
estimated at about fifty thousand people—of whom almost
half lived in Haiphong—where previously there were eighty
thousand. The colony enjoyed no privilege whatsoever and the
embassy, it is said, never came to its aid; in case of trouble
with local authorities the embassy sided with the latter. As in
the South a "Vietnamization" of the Chinese elements was
undertaken, but here in full agreement with the official representatives of the Chinese government.

Stranger still was a regression with respect to the cultural
position occupied by the Chinese at the time of colonization.
In Chinese schools teachers of Chinese nationality taught exclusively in Chinese, but these schools no longer exist. All
educational establishments provide the regular teaching program of the People's Democratic Republic of North Vietnam,
and teaching of Chinese is limited to a few hours a week.*

Of course, there was in Hanoi a Chinese school, with two
thousand pupils, but it was controlled by the Department of
Education of the Vietnamese People's Republic, though it had
been equipped by the Chinese People's Republic. About sixty
Chinese professors, most of whom were, however, born in
Vietnam, were teaching there. The pupils were all Chinese. It
should also be noted that in 1961 the foreign-language sec-
tions at the University of Hanoi comprised 180 students in
Chinese, as against 220 in Russian and 80 in English. The
"Vietnamese-Chinese Friendship Association" has organized

---

* At the French lycée, which has kept the name of Albert Sarraut, Vietnamese pupils were receiving six hours of French instruction weekly. It is
true, however, that Paris carries the expense.

evening courses attended by more than two thousand people.

Also, the Chinese section in the International Library at Hanoi accounted for half of the books, and French-language publications were more numerous than Russian. Incidentally, one could find there the works of Raymond Aron, though in fewer numbers than those by Louis Aragon.

Thus, Chinese presence in North Vietnam was both considerable and relatively discreet. No matter how favorable the psychological current is to China, it must not be forgotten that the Five Year Plan, the *piatiletka,* begun in 1961, is primarily the work of Soviet experts, with Chinese economists mainly confined to advisory roles.

In 1960, on the other hand, 500 fellowships were granted by the Soviet Union to Vietnamese graduates, for the Petroleum Academy in Baku and the Marine Academy at Odessa, while the Chinese granted only 350 during the same year, and only for the purpose of forming cadres.

Conscious of the psychological errors they have committed, the Soviets in Hanoi make efforts to improve their contacts with their Vietnamese colleagues; Russian engineers have begun to learn Vietnamese and are trying to adjust to the popular psychology.

But one still frequently hears Soviet experts call Chinese technicians "overseers" and the Vietnamese "poor copiers," while the Chinese experts, putting themselves on the level of those with whom they talk, listen to grievances and suggestions, and agree to take them into account and modify their original plans. They know how to hide their technological superiority from their Vietnamese colleagues and give them the impression that it is easy to come to an understanding "between Asiatics."

The given racial facts actually still play a role that is hard to imagine. At receptions in Hanoi, just as in Peking, the "Whites" hardly mix with the "Yellows"; the relationships between Russians and Chinese particularly are obviously cool.

Finally, the Russians are frequently surprised at the attachment on the part of the French for this country: even under present circumstances some Frenchmen maintain relations of human warmth with the Vietnamese such as no Soviet person enjoys.

Even though aid received from China has been by far the most substantial (in 1960–61, it was on the order of $500,000,000, as compared to a total of $200,000,000 in European aid*), the Vietnamese People's Republic continued to turn its eyes toward the Soviet Union. Why? It distinguished between the technological value of the Soviet and Chinese experts; it had, moreover, an unlimited respect and admiration for the Soviet Union, that giant world power and head of the socialist camp. And it had no illusions on the true sentiments animating the Chinese with regard to North Vietnam.

But the doctrinal and personal tendencies of the leaders must also be taken into account. Generally, the role of chief Soviet sympathizer is attributed to Ho Chi Minh himself: "Ho Chu Tich"—"the venerable President Ho." This is so for all sorts of reasons. First of all, in the eyes of this old Bolshevik, who left Paris in 1923 to receive his training in Moscow, the Soviet Union remains the cradle of the revolution, just as it was for Maurice Thorez. Second, because Ho dedicated himself to the revolution at least as much out of national passion as for reasons of social equality, and certainly more so than from doctrinaire attachment, and also because his career bears witness to many responses and decisions where patriotism won out over ideology. There is the particularly extraordinary gesture of 1945, without example in the history of international communism: the dissolution of the Indochinese Communist Party that he had founded, and that he scuttled in order to facilitate union.

By temperament, intellectual inclination, and political choice, the founder of Viet Minh is a "Rightist" among Marxist-Leninists, like Bukharin or Togliatti; everything was

* These figures remained substantially the same until 1964.

bound to lead him to endorse Khrushchev's strategy; by all evidence he is a precursor of Khrushchevism.

Let us not forget either that this Vietnamese nationalist could not but have a certain mistrust of the Chinese. Even though China was now draped in Red and brotherly affection in most ways, it was inexorably the heir of an empire that for centuries had effaced now Vietnam, now Annam from the map of the world. Finally, let us add this: for Ho Chi Minh, a Bolshevik since the earliest days, who was one of the founders of the Comintern, and who even seemed to be the possible leader of Asiatic communism in the years 1925–1928, Mao Tse-tung is not as fabulous a personage as he is in the eyes of almost all Far Eastern revolutionaries. Certainly, Ho credits his Chinese colleague with a great preëminence in matters of strategic invention and doctrinal competence; but he regards him only as one of his peers who has more means at his command rather than more constancy or revolutionary merit.

Apart from the last argument, the same reasons have led Ho Chi Minh's most faithful disciples—such as Prime Minister Pham Van Dong, son of a mandarin, and Gen. Vo Nguyen Giap, or Vice-President Ton Duc Thang, old mutineer of the Black Sea together with André Marty—to follow the old leader on the road shown by Moscow.

Let us give some examples. Before the National Assembly, on December 23, 1959, President Ho Chi Minh praised "the leadership role played by the Soviet Union in the domain of science and peace," without making any reference to China. Similarly, on the celebration of the fifteenth anniversary of the army, the prime minister spoke in the same terms of the Soviet Union, making only brief mention of the military aid granted by China. Again, on January 1, President Ho Chi Minh in his traditional speech, in the presence of the diplomatic corps, praised Premier Khrushchev and the Soviet Union while making no allusion to China.

Until May 1959, however, the talk and speeches and writings were always of the "fraternal socialist camp led by the

Soviet Union, and aided by the Republic of China." During the following twenty months the formula employed was solely "the fraternal socialist camp led by the Soviet Union."

But the partisans of an increasingly close understanding with China, who take inspiration from Chinese methods and strategies, have in their favor the direct support of Peking and they play on the constant pressure the Chinese can exercise in their capacity as a neighbor, and also on the aid in cadres and matériel that China furnishes to the Vietnamese People's Republic.

The principal representative of this tendency is Truong Chinh, former secretary-general of the Lao Dong (Labor Party, the North Vietnamese Communist Party). This son of a mandarin was considered for a long time the best Vietnamese doctrinaire communist, and his pamphlet distributed in 1947 under the title "The Resistance Will Win" was regarded for years as the Bible of the communists. Obsessed, like the Chinese, with the myth of the "great leap forward," he tried in 1955 to put through the agrarian reform at such a pace that eighteen months later North Vietnam was on the brink of a general uprising. Mutinies had already broken out in the region of Vinh. Truong Chinh was relieved of his function as secretary-general of the Party,* and his most famous personal and ideological adversary, General Giap, was charged with pronouncing, in the name of the Party, a terrible self-criticism against "Leftist" excesses.

If, after 1960, Truong Chinh, president of the Permanent Committee of the National Assembly, again emerged as the most important personage of the country next to Ho Chi Minh, it was because he represented the incarnation of the policy of alliance with China and of recourse to Peking's methods. But the more the war in the South continues and with it the policy of austerity, the more American intervention is intensified and the more the authority and the prestige of the doctrinaire and intransigent ideologists grow.

* He was replaced by Ho Chi Minh himself.

This basic aspect of the situation was evident at the Third Congress of the North Vietnamese Communist Party.

The Congress of 1960

From September 5–10, 1960, the Third Congress of the Vietnamese Communist Party took place in Hanoi, in the presence of representatives of the Communist parties of the Soviet Union, China, all other socialist countries, and France, India, Indonesia, Japan, Canada, Italy, and Morocco. The 500,000 members—this is the official figure—of the Vietnamese Communist Party were represented at this Congress by 576 delegates and candidate-delegates.

In the name of the Central Committee, Le Duan, member of the Politbureau, gave the general political report analyzing the situation and outlining the fundamental tasks of the Party, while Le Duc Tho and Nguyen Duy Trinh, also Politbureau members, presented a report on the modifications of the Party statutes and on the directives and tasks of the 1961–1965 Five Year Plan. Others also spoke on ideological tasks, problems of state, the function of democracy, and national defense.

"After ten days of work," said the final communiqué, "the Congress concluded its efforts on the evening of the tenth, after unanimously approving the roads for the building of socialism in the North, and the peaceful reunification of the country."

The Congress also elected a new Central Committee, consisting of forty-three members and twenty-eight applicants, reorganizing the composition of the general staff in Hanoi as follows: president of the Central Committee: Ho Chi Minh; first secretary of the Communist Party: Le Duan; members of the Politbureau: Ho Chi Minh, Le Duan, Truong Chinh, Pham Van Dong, Pham Nung, Vo Nguyen Giap, Le Duc Tho, Nguyen Chi Thanh, Nguyen Duy Trinh,* Le Thanh Nghi, Hoang Van Hoan. Finally, the new secretariat com-

* Named foreign secretary in February 1965.

prised seven members: Le Duan, Pham Hung, Le Duc Tho, Nguyen Chi Thanh, Hoang Anh, To Huu, Le Van Luong.

Despite the climate of the Congress, which was marked by the very favorable reception of the Soviet delegation and the relatively cool reception accorded to the Peking representatives led by the very famous Li Fu Chun, its labors had two principal results: the promotion of Le Duan to the post of secretary-general of the Party, and the emphasis that was placed on the reunification with the South. It was quickly realized, in addition, that the two results were closely interconnected.

The new secretary-general, succeeding Ho Chi Minh in this key post of the Lao Dong, was in effect an old fighter from the South. Though born at Haiphong, Tonkin's great port, he spent several war years in Cochinchina as political commissar of Zone East. His promotion was the symbol of a policy of reunification, and of support for Nam Bo's guerrilla fighters. Finally, the last motion of the Congress placed the accent on the "liberation" of the South from the pro-American dictatorship. Independent of the reception accorded to the Soviet delegates, the Third Congress ended with the triumph of the Chinese theses of permanent revolution and acceleration of the "anti-imperialist" struggle. Diem accounted for much of that: the excesses of a conservative mandarin inscribed themselves objectively in the "line" of a Marxist-Leninist analysis and strategy.

The most important, though tacit, result of the Third Congress was the approval given by the strategists of the North to the creation in the South of a revolutionary organization that was openly to take the lead in the subversion of the Diem regime.

3

𝄞𝄞𝄞𝄞𝄞𝄞𝄞

The Birth of the
National Liberation Front

Except for Lenin's party, revolutionary movements have
rarely announced their existence before going into action:
only when their strength is affirmed do they take on their
name, their form, sometimes even their ideology. Thus, the
National Liberation Front of South Vietnam did not wait to
be known by that name to carry out its first strikes. But once
it was organized, shaped, and named, in December 1960, it
assumed a dimension and efficiency that have continued to
grow.

When at the end of July 1954 the Geneva Armistice Agreements were signed between France and the revolutionary
movements of the three Indochinese nations (Vietnam, Laos,
Cambodia), and Vietnam's division along the 17th Parallel
was decided, the communist cadres that had been operating
in the South accepted for the most part the decisions made
at Geneva and regrouped in Tonkin and North Annam. They
were divided into two groups, one joining the Tonkinese in
"building socialism" under the aegis of Ho Chi Minh, its war-
lord and common inspirer; the other remaining where it was

in order to establish the foundations of the revolutionary movement.

But even the latter, regrouped south of the 17th Parallel into four zones—Quang Ngai, Binh Dinh in the Central region, the Plain of Joncs, and Ca Mau Peninsula in the South—that had been Viet Minh bases and were to become the centers from which the Viet Cong emerged, behaved at first like people who did not want to jeopardize what had been agreed upon at Geneva. Communist discipline played its part, and even though the Viet Minh had been forced to make much greater concessions on July 20 than the guerrillas had anticipated, especially after their victory at Dien Bien Phu, the guarantee given to the agreements by Molotov and Chou En-lai forced the militants to observe them.

Before returning to the North in 1956, however, the Viet Minh cadres had prepared for the future: in the beginning of 1955, after a visit to one of the Southern zones still controlled by the Viet Minh, Joseph Alsop had written in *The New Yorker* of June 25: "I could hardly imagine a Communist government that was also a popular government and almost a democratic government."

But the various national and religious forces that had been only wartime allies for the Vietnamese communists did not consider themselves bound by these agreements and refused to bow before the commitments taken in the name of the guerrillas by the Marxist leaders, or to yield to the authority of the new chief of government in Saigon, Ngo Dinh Diem. Soon the Ngo family's "witch hunting" policy no longer left open to the growing number of its opponents any alternatives other than prison, exile, or the guerrilla forces. Soon future President Suu was in jail, all the former government chiefs were in exile, and many people who wanted primarily to escape the pursuit of Diem's police or Nhu's "Republican Youth" were in the guerrilla forces.

From then on the Saigon authorities called every dissatisfied person a communist or a Viet Cong. In 1959, speaking in

Saigon with the minister of information of that period, Tran
Chan Thanh, I tried to suggest that perhaps certain of the
guerrillas were members of the sects persecuted by the regime,
such as the Caodaists, Hoa-Hao, or Binh-Xuyen. But this
quite intelligent man made every effort to demonstrate to me
that only communists opposed the regime. Since then he himself has become an opponent of the regime, without having
converted to communism.

The Turning Point: 1959–1960

During 1959 the regime's situation in the South changed
decisively. It was then that the only attempt at a democratic
election, made at the request of Washington, proved embarrassing: Dr. Phan Quang Dan, a notorious anti-communist, was triumphantly elected in Saigon over the official
candidate. This choice was later invalidated. At that very
time, as we have seen, new legislation promulgated in
Saigon opened the great period of the "witch hunt": four
persons out of five became suspects and liable to imprison-
ment if not execution. War generally entails extraordinary
legislation; one can say that here extraordinary legislation
entailed war. The Marxist organizations hardly took the first
steps. But, taken by the throat, they counterattacked.

Thus, in the Quang Ngai district, about sixty miles south
of the 17th Parallel in a region controlled by the most violent
anti-communist members of Ngo Dinh Diem's regime—
his older brother, Archbishop Thuc, and his younger brother,
Ngo Dinh Can—a guerrilla force began to operate that was
probably the first sign of the reactivation of communist organisms. In most other cases, at the periphery of the Plain of
Jones or in the Transbassac or in the Ben Cat region north of
the capital, subversive groups fighting the regime had a primarily nationalist or religious orientation.

Probably the actual birth of the National Liberation Front
must be traced back to March 1960. At that time a group of

the old resistance fighters assembled in Zone D (eastern Cochinchina), issued a proclamation calling the prevailing situation "intolerable" for the people as a result of Diem's actions, and called upon patriots to regroup with a view toward ultimate collective action. At the same time a letter by Nguyen Huu Tho, president of the Committee of Peace and therefore incarcerated in the Saigon region, was read to the militants. This letter encouraged his comrades to resistance. No actual signal was given; the principal decisions were made only six months later. But the little Congress of March 1960 was in some ways the "general call" for the creation of the Front, the signal that, coming from the South, was to force the government in the North to assume its responsibility.

The Third Congress of the Lao Dong publicly expressed the intention of the Northern leaders not to disinterest themselves in the affairs of the South. "Liberation of South Vietnam from American imperialism" was then placed on equal footing with the establishment of socialism in the North. But the Hanoi leaders took verbal precautions and stated specifically that the two revolutions ought to follow different strategies, in response to local situations. It must be pointed out that the Hanoi leaders—still careful—did not make this turn except at the specific demand and under the moral pressure of the militants in the South, who criticized their Northern comrades' relative passivity in the face of the repression exercised against them by the Saigon authorities; they expressed their disappointment in the softness with which the Hanoi leaders and their allies in the socialist camp had reacted to the non-observance of the 1956 general elections that had been stipulated by the negotiators in Geneva with a view to reunifying the country.

If the Hanoi Congress of September 1960 marked the beginning of the North Vietnamese entry into the game and of Northern "streamlining" of the rebellion in the South, it was not only because the Congress brought Le Duan to the post of secretary-general, but mainly because the Lao Dong was to authorize the creation in the Southern zone of a genuine revolutionary organization: the National Liberation Front. This organization was to be autonomous, but was evidently going to be tied rather closely to the Lao Dong in order to be able to demand from it aid against the Saigon regime.

At the end of 1960 the latter was to receive a rude shock: on November 11 several units of paratroopers rebelled against the Diem regime, and Diem, his palace encircled, owed his rescue only to the hesitation of the *Putschists*. Superficially the coup of the paratroopers had nothing to do with the activity of the nationalists and pro-communist guerrillas; but the defiance of Diem by his best troops showed to what extent his power was brittle. Some drew the consequences.

Five weeks after the coup, on December 20, 1960, about a hundred persons who had gone underground announced from "somewhere in Nam Bo" the creation of the "National Liberation Front of South Vietnam." If that organization could hardly be identified by the personalities of its leaders, which were kept secret, one could obtain an idea of its orientation from the ten-point program that was soon broadcast over Radio Hanoi.

It was a strange text, a mixture of incitement to social effort that could have come from a religious paternalist regime, and violent denunciations of American policy, which established the tone. The choice of the word "imperialism" and particularly the condemnation of American "monopolies" (which really had little to do with the case) made it sound Marxist. But the "Ten Points of the N.L.F. [National Liberation Front]" also showed a certain moderation and accented the neutrality that was to be established in the South, which was somewhat in contradiction with the intention to do away with the zoning of Vietnam, as the North was not going to declare itself neutral. The text was patently the result of a hasty compromise between Southern democrats desirous of gaining the sympathy of the masses and communist cadres anxious to maintain their contact with the North.

In all, these ten points were reminiscent of the programs disseminated by the Viet Minh in 1941, at a time when the communist leaders, because they found themselves in the territory of a China governed by the Kuomintang and because they wanted to dominate their nationalist companions, practiced a policy of common front that was so subtle and so carefully designed that they gained the support of the American General Gallagher.

Thus was the National Liberation Front of South Vietnam born at the end of December 1960. And at that time the situation developed from obscure combat between a motley crew of dissidents and a neo-fascist system into a regular war between a popular organization with a rather vague ideology controlled by communists and an increasingly military regime controlled by Americans.

But who was the leader of the N.L.F.? He was to appear only one year after the creation of the Front: Nguyen Huu Tho, a Saigon lawyer who had been interned for five years as president of the Saigon-Cholon Committee of Peace, an organization whose communist sympathies were apparently considered criminal by the Ngo family. In December 1961 the Viet Cong network succeeded in organizing Tho's escape. Tho, an intellectual of French culture, was a former student at the law school of Aix-en-Provence; he was a politically uncommitted pacifist until 1952, when he openly advocated for negotiations with the Viet Minh.

Tho was fifty-two at the time, thin, rather tall; his regular face, crossed by deep wrinkles, had a grave, rather gentle look, and his gray hair was bushy and ruffled. He looked like the poet Boris Pasternak rather than a political leader, still less a military one. In his interviews he was not very dogmatic. His thinking was colored by Marxism as was his vocabulary. But one did not receive the impression that he was a cog in a machine. Questions about his attachment to "personalism" (the doctrine locally perverted by the abuse Nhu made of it) provoked an ironic and ambiguous response, never a violent denial. And if he was asked about the dissensions within the Front, he occasionally gave a substantive answer rather than feigning the astonishment customary when such questions are raised.

Bit by bit, the war was to extend and the Front to assume its more or less final form, first with the creation in the South of the People's Revolutionary Party that was to be the "Left Wing" of the N.L.F., then with the establishment in Saigon of a veritable military command, under the direction of General Harkins; finally with the First Congress of the Front in March 1962.

On January 15, 1962, the People's Revolutionary Party was set up; unlike the N.L.F., this did not try to hide its Marxist allegiance. This movement, which came to belong to the revolutionary Front, was soon to appear as the radical branch of the N.L.F. Commenting on this development in a Tass broadcast on January 18, United States Ambassador Frederick Nolting stated that Hanoi's leadership of the N.L.F. could no longer be denied; this was not at all evident, since the communists had been sufficiently well implanted in the South for twenty-five years to set up their own organization.

Did Nolting want to say that a movement of this type would not be created without agreement from the North, that the North was unconcerned about directly compromising Marxism-Leninism in a hapless adventure? Hanoi actually seemed to hold to the strategy of "prior authorization" concerning the initiatives and activities of the revolutionaries in the South. What Ho wanted to maintain was less the leadership than the control. It seems that the formation of the People's Revolutionary Party (P.R.P.) gave him the means better to control the N.L.F. with a genuine nucleus of militants, called "party of the labor and working class," which in effect was a counterpart of the Lao Dong in the South.

It should be noted that the creation of the P.R.P. followed

by several days a very significant exchange of visits: in the first days of January, after a journey to Hanoi by Chinese Marshal Yek Chie Ying, Huynh Van Tam, delegate of the Labor Association for the Liberation of South Vietnam, went to Peking. The decision to create the P.R.P. seems to have been connected with this exchange of visits, just as the creation of the N.L.F. was connected with the Congress of the Lao Dong at Hanoi fifteen months earlier.

Why create, in the heart of this Front, this compromising P.R.P.? Several hypotheses have been offered: (1) Peking forced Hanoi and the revolutionaries in the South to "show their colors," and not to be content to engage in a combat with imprecise ideological foundations and vague objectives; (2) on the contrary, the "Rightists" of Asian socialism wanted to distinguish the moderates from the Front, and by giving them a solid Left Wing of the Laotian Pathet Lao type, permit them to play the "Centrist" role played by Souvanna Phouma in the kingdom to the west.

Americans on the whole seemed to favor the first hypothesis, since they too selected the "hard line" by creating several days later, February 8, 1962, the command of the strategic Vietnam-Thailand sector and entrusting it to a military man of great reputation, Gen. Paul Harkins, former chief of staff at Tokyo. Thus the Pentagon assimilated South Vietnam into the SEATO countries in contradiction to the special stipulations of Geneva. The choice of direct intervention had been made.

In March 1962 the National Liberation Front of South Vietnam held its First Congress. The delegates elected Nguyen Huu Tho president and Professor Nguyen Van Hieu secretary-general. Like these two, most of the members of the Central Committee were moving spirits in the Congress of Peace of the Saigon-Cholon region, founded in 1954, an insignificant pro-Viet Minh organization, none of whose leaders is considered a member of the communist organization proper. Hieu was regarded as pro-Chinese, while most of the others were

regarded as progressives, close to the communists but not indentured to them.

On the other hand one of the five vice-presidents was
automatically a member of the P.R.P., so that if the Central
Committee was to be composed of fifty-five members, the
participants in the Congress of March 1962 decided to make
twenty-three seats available to people who wanted to join the
organization. This attitude of making overtures of at least a
tactical nature was to remain constant with the N.L.F., and
was what kept the Front from setting up a "provisional government," in order not to set the lines too rigidly and to retain
opportunities of enlarging itself by including other "tendencies."

But the most interesting result of the N.L.F. Congress was
the text of its platform, which though clearly revolutionary
with regard to economic and social matters, prescribed a turn
in foreign policy toward a neutrality greatly independent
from the North. It was stated by the Congress, no longer
as in December 1960, that the objective was the reunification
of the two zones and the independence of South Vietnam.
The latter would establish diplomatic relations with all countries, accept aid from states having different political regimes,
and aim at "forming a peace zone, including Laos and Cambodia."

Was this a turn to the Right? It was at least a policy of the
outstretched hand toward all nationalists. In addition, on the
previous January 17 the N.L.F. had launched an appeal to
the "patriotism" of the members of the Diem army. All this
looked as though Hanoi, certain of retaining in the midst of
the N.L.F. a fifth column in the form of the P.R.P., permitted
the Front to play its card of "non-commitment," in order to be
able further to seduce the masses and particularly the Saigon
intellectuals. This was a good strategy, to be sure, and it was
to prove fruitful.

The N.L.F. was to go even further the following July, on
the occasion of the eighth anniversary of the Geneva Agree-

ments, by launching "four proposals for the national good," of which the third was an offer of co-operation with the "parties, sects, and groups representing all political tendencies, social strata, religions, and nationalities of South Vietnam"; and the fourth was a proposition to make "South Vietnam, Laos, and Cambodia a neutral zone with all three states enjoying sovereign rights." The North or reunification were no longer even mentioned, for whatever reason.

But, militarily, the N.L.F. proved itself at once: in January 1963 the battle of Ap Bac, near My Tho, took place, in the course of which a dozen American helicopters were brought down.

4

❦❦❦❦❦❦❦

American Intervention

From "Adviser" to Combatant

While the N.L.F. organized itself and tried to define its doctrine and political strategy, the United States found itself
more involved every day in the wheels of war. In 1959 the
Diem regime had hardened and changed from rigor to frenzy;
in 1960 the N.L.F. had been created with the authorization of
Hanoi, which thus renounced its non-intervention; in 1961
the United States entered the war.

American military men were no strangers to Vietnam.
From before the first Indochinese war they had been there—
in the other camp, to be sure, in the camp of the Viet Minh
that was to become the Viet Cong; men like General Gallagher and Major Patti had hoisted the Stars and Stripes on
the side of Ho Chi Minh and Giap in 1945. Those were the
steps into the clouds of Roosevelt's anti-colonialism.

But very soon these imprudent people had yielded to
"serious" men; in 1950 there came the military missions,
which, on the basis of their experience in the Philippines
and Korea, were to teach guerrilla warfare to French officers.
Of these activities there remained some echoes in *The Ugly*

American, in which a certain Yankee arrived in the midst of the battle for the Tonkin delta to teach Mao Tse-tung's methods—as I can testify from direct observation—to people who had tried to apply such methods for years. Both sides were annoyed that revolution was not made by certain recipes and that if there were any recipes at all, those of revolution could not be applied to counter-revolution. (Even so, ten years later, Henry Cabot Lodge was to declare in Paris that Algeria's parachuting colonels had shown what should be done in South Vietnam.)

In short, before the "French" war came to an end, generals like O'Daniel and Van Fleet made their appearance at the side of Generals de Lattre de Tassigny, Salan, and Navarre, and told them how to apply the lessons of Korea. Then, in the spring of 1954, Paris and Saigon asked the pilots and marines of the U. S. Air Force and U. S. Navy for means to smash Giap's legions. From Hawaii and Manila the navy promised victory at Dien Bien Phu with the help of Operation Vulture. The operation never came off.

But the road was open for some relief after the Geneva accords. To be sure, on July 21, 1954, the Americans, though refusing to confirm the texts signed by France or endorsed by the majority of the conference members, had applauded the solution obtained by Mendès-France with the help of Eden and Molotov. Gen. Bedell Smith, chief of the American delegation, though ill at his hotel, had gone to the Cointrin airport to salute the French premier, who was returning to Paris in a hurry. He kept saying to Mendès-France: "You are a national hero!" And in Washington, President Eisenhower declared: "I have nothing better to offer."

But American diplomacy, operating on several levels, had set up at the same time, i.e., in September, the SEATO pact organization in Manila, and in Saigon had organized France's relief with American troops (after the Diem government had forced France to withdraw its last troops in April 1956). The first phase of this replacement was accomplished in December

1954 after an accord had been signed by General Ely, general commissar of France, and his American opposite number, Lawton Collins. In accordance with their agreement the training of Vietnamese forces was to pass from the French to the Americans. This training was progressively to change into aid in the form of equipment, from equipment to cadres, from cadres to combat support, from combat support to actual replacements.

In any event, between 1956 and 1962 American credits to the army in Vietnam rose rapidly and in 1961 came to $300,-000,000. By 1960 the military mission, the M.A.A.G. (Military Aid and Advisory Group), under General Williams numbered more than four thousand "advisers."

It was in this period, after a time of relative quiet, that decisive changes took place, following the uncovering of scandals connected with American aid to Vietnam. The year 1959 then witnessed the transition of the Saigon regime to total war. In 1960 the N.L.F. was formed. It was also the year of Kennedy's election to the Presidency—an event that could be interpreted in a variety of ways.

Senator Kennedy had declared in 1954:

> I am convinced that American military aid, no matter how extensive, cannot crush an enemy who is everywhere and nowhere, . . . an enemy of the people who at the same time commands the support and sympathy of the entire people. . . . For the United States, to interfere unilaterally and send troops to the most difficult terrain in the world creates a much more complicated situation even than in Korea. . . .

But Kennedy was also the most prominent member of a family, which, like the Ngo clan would listen to the advice of the Catholic hierarchy—which is relatively without influence in American domestic policy—on the subject of such groups as the Tonkin refugees. He was a man who would vacillate between justice and power, as demonstrated by the Bay of

Pigs affair, and not "pull down the American standard" under any circumstances. Generous when he had the choice, he became extremist when American grandeur was being defied; and that was the case in South Vietnam.

From the beginning of 1961 Kennedy wrestled with the most difficult problem facing his administration. He tried to separate the two Indochinese problems, to make peace in Laos while trying to win the war in Vietnam, and he did this to the point of exhaustion. He nevertheless dissassociated himself increasingly from the Ngo regime, until the "brawl" of the summer of 1963, and in September of that year he solemnly denounced at the U.N. the anti-Buddhist policy of the Saigon government. But how can one disassociate a regime from the policy it makes and symbolizes? There, too, Kennedy failed to understand the interconnection, only to arrive three weeks before his death at the bloody expedient of November 1, 1963: the assassination of the Ngos, which his representatives covered up, probably fully aware of what they were doing.

In 1961 that point had not yet been reached. Kennedy was trying to find a way. He was to send three successive missions to Vietnam in search of the truth: in April, Vice-President Johnson; from May to July, Professor Eugene Staley of Stanford Research Institute; and in September, Gen. Maxwell Taylor, the most prestigious of his military advisers, together with the economist Walt Rostow, the most respected of his civilian advisers.

Appearances to the contrary, the second of these missions was the most important. After a stay of six weeks in Saigon, with the help of the Vietnamese economist Vu Quoc Thuc, a law professor at Saigon, and under the direction of Ngo Dinh Nhu, Diem's brother and "political adviser," Staley worked out a war doctrine and an action plan that was to be applied in Vietnam for two years—and more.

The "Staley Plan" is known particularly by the "strategic hamlets" formula it advocated. But the project was much more ambitious; it defined an entire war policy. On the military plane Staley and Thuc recommended placing emphasis on the village militias that would be supplied with modern weapons and on the Garde Nationale, whose effectives would be doubled. They also recommended that the 170,000 men of the regular army be trained in jungle fighting. Moreover, American military advisers were to set up local "Ranger troops" to co-operate with the "Republican Youths" (whose orientation was the same as that of the regime). Finally, the Vietnamese soldiers were to receive some psychological instruction because, according to *Time,* which was regarded by the American army as gospel, "the bad behavior of the soldiers had been one of the principal reasons for the villagers' grievances against the government."

On the social and economic plane the "agro-city" experiment, already tried three years earlier, was to be resumed. There were twenty-six such agro-cities in all, and the plan proposed to boost that figure to over a hundred in the course of a year. Around those agro-cities the strategic hamlets were to be set up, surrounded by bamboo hedges and supplied with guard towers able to receive villagers returning from the fields at night. In this fashion peasants working during the day in the agro-cities could, according to the plan, always find protection in the strategic hamlets at night. The latter, it was calculated, would be able to offer protection and shelter to over eight hundred thousand inhabitants of a rural population of eight million, i.e., for 10 per cent of the population. But Staley's economic program was dependent upon the mobilization of considerable military means.

Charged with the execution of the plan was Sterling J. Cotrell, who, said *Time,* favored the employment in Southeast Asia of "rough and unorthodox methods to stop the communists." This State Department official led the Special Vietnamese Task Force created by President Kennedy after Vice-President Johnson's visit to Saigon. His deputy for military questions was Gen. Edward Lonsdale, the Pentagon's guerrilla expert, who had helped Ramon Magsaysay to crush the Huks in the Philippines and had counseled Diem in 1955 during the battle against the Binh-Xuyen. This general was also well known as one of the originators of American special services in Southeast Asia. One of his subordinates told the South Vietnamese forces: "To defeat the brigands, you must become brigands. . . ."

I shall return later to the application and the results of the Staley Plan of 1961, particularly the strategic hamlets. But as of the following October a new mission from Washington came up with some reservations on these magic formulas. General Taylor himself, aided by Rostow (the man of the "take-off," associated with that of the "flexible response"), objected that such a program could bear fruit and convince the population only if the regime implementing it had more credit with the masses. Therefore a program of relative dem-ocratization was devised to supplement that of Professor Staley's "military economy."

Saigon's reaction was extremely strong. The Taylor report was received with great indignation by Diem and, conse-quently, by the Saigon press: Washington dared to interfere in South Vietnam's political life! What audacity! And the dictator's reply to Ambassador Nolting's suggestion that some popular measures be taken to improve public opinion was to increase taxes.

Washington was not discouraged. And three months later Kennedy made one of the gravest decisions with regard to the war: he appointed in Saigon a commander-in-chief for Viet-nam and Thailand, which meant that he was now deliberately rejecting the earlier hypocrisy and accepting the fact that the time of advisers had passed and that the time of direct inter-vention had arrived.

He appointed a high-ranking commander, Gen. Paul Hark-ins, former chief of the general staff in Tokyo; General Wede, a parachutist of considerable renown, was made his deputy. American effectives rapidly increased from eight thousand to fifteen thousand men, of whom a tenth, then a fifth, and then a quarter were combatants. Special Forces groups were formed at Fort Benning, Georgia; instructed in the Vietnamese language, they were to be charged with creating uneasiness in the Viet Cong zone and—who knows?— also farther to the north.

This trend toward escalation was intensified in June 1962 by the publication of a report of the International Control Commission created by the Geneva Conference of 1954 and composed of Indian, Canadian, and Polish diplomats. The observers—with the Poles dissenting—denounced Hanoi's growing intervention in the conflict in the South, and revealed that supplies and weapons came from the North through Laos. It is true that the same organization also criticized—without the approval of the Canadian member—American intervention, which it considered to be in conflict with the Geneva Agreements. But it was enough for the Americans to have the report in support of their thesis: they cared little that it criticized an action which took liberties with a text they had not signed.

The U.S. war effort kept increasing during all of 1962; the partisans of direct action cited the facilities given to the communists by the agreement on Laos in order to push for a constant reinforcement of military means against the Viet Cong. This trend was not to reverse itself again.

On October 10, 1962, Ngo Dinh Diem, speaking at the Saigon Assembly, declared: "We are no longer face to face with a guerrilla situation, but a genuine war. . . ." Whose fault was it?

Whose fault, indeed? It certainly cannot be claimed that the Hanoi leaders or the leaders of the insurrection in the South were pure pacifists, nor that they were leaders who were concerned only with the defense of the rights of a hard-pressed people. But it must be admitted that the unleashing of the war machine that faced the Ngos from 1962 on had not been the doing of the insurgents.

It was the dictatorship in the South that kindled the fire:

(1) By beginning after 1956, and particularly with the legislation of 1959, the "witch hunt" that, as we have seen, left no choice to those in opposition except prison, exile, or joining the guerrillas;

(2) By categorically and haughtily rejecting all Hanoi overtures for arriving at the unification foreseen in the Geneva Agreements of 1954—whose execution would have benefited the North. In 1955 and 1956 the leaders of the Vietnamese People's Republic made it known in Saigon, on several occasions and through several intermediaries, that they were ready to postpone the plebiscite and to appeal to a foreign arbiter. They received nothing but rebuffs;

(3) By declining all forms of relationship with the North which, in the conviction that Saigon would cut short all attempts at reunification, tried—particularly in 1958—to establish cultural and economic relations between the two zones. Saigon did not even deign to reply to these "Reds";

(4) By provoking American aid, which turned from economic aid in 1954 to military aid in 1956, in direct, evident, and crying contradiction to the 1954 Geneva accords, which Washington had not entirely approved but which its representative had said they did not want to jeopardize;

(5) Finally, by aggravating the "witch hunt" by adding an increasingly discriminatory policy with regard to a religious group that had been insignificant before the Ngos acceded to power, but was to become a determining force in the spring of 1963. What neither military coup nor American pressure had accomplished was made inevitable by several thousand unarmed men: the Buddhists were the primary reason for the fall of a dictatorship resting on a religious minority and plagued by misfortune in war.

III

THE END OF
THE NGOS

1

〰〰〰〰〰〰〰

The Devouring Pyres

One fine day these men with shaven skulls, brown togas, and light umbrellas sprang up in their own country like Martians. An old colonial official, accustomed during a half century to putting Indochina in its place and maintaining the order of Cao Bang in the Plain of Joncs, would have been quite surprised to discover them in such numbers in Saigon in 1963, and to see them pose as arbiters in a national dispute in which they had so far played a minor role.

There had been in the South, of course, "neo-Buddhist" sects—such as the Hoa Hao or the Caodaists—who had borrowed some of the teachings of Buddha, but not more than they had borrowed from Taoism, magic practices, regional folklore, from the powerful tradition of secret Annamite societies, from French literature, Christian teachings, and the Freemasons. The Vietnamese are not irreligious, but they join churches only when the latter are camouflaged as combat groups.

In fact, the ancestor cult dominates all others. In a letter to U. S. Ambassador Frederick Nolting in 1963, protesting

Washington aid to a fanatically Catholic regime that oppressed Buddhism, a group of Vietnamese maintained that their people were and remained people of *Tien Rong*—"Fairies and Dragons"—and specified:

> Our people look back upon four thousand years of history. We have our own religion—that of Ancestors, whose relics are in the temple of King Hung Vuong, first sovereign of the Tien Rong, who was brought up at Phu Tho (North) where for thousands of years the people have commemorated this first ancestor.

The authors of this very significant letter added:

> Even though we have suffered more than a thousand years of domination on the part of the Chinese who tried to assimilate us with the help of Confucianism, we have remained Vietnamese and retained our loyalty to the memory of our ancestor King Hung Vuong. As far as the great religions are concerned, we have three: Confucianism, Buddhism and Taoism. No matter how different these religions may be, our ancestors knew how to assimilate all three of them, and to integrate them into a sort of unique "vision of the world" that entered into the mores and customs of our people. One characteristic of the union of the three religions in Vietnam is the existence of the so-called Pagodas of the Three Religions, seats of the Buddhist cult where homage is also paid to Lao-tse and Confucius.

Seasoned observers had meanwhile revealed, after the end of World War I, that societies for the reëstablishment of Buddhism had been set up in Hanoi, Saigon, and particularly in the Center, at Hue, the region in which Catholicism had not been implanted without suffering or inflicting violence. Circles for Buddhist studies showed a certain vitality there, often encouraged by the colonial administration, which was just as glad to deflect the politically and socially exigent intelligent-sia toward such spiritual pursuits.

But all this was only one of the important components of Vietnamese society. In the neighboring kingdoms—Cambodia, Laos, Thailand—Buddhism was powerful and prosperous. But it existed in a different form, that of the "Small Vehicle" (Hinayana, or rather Theravada—Cult of the Ancients), while Buddhism in Vietnam manifests itself through the "Great Vehicle" (Mahayana).

What are the differences between the two rites? The "Small Vehicle," closely tied to Indian tradition, conforms more to Buddha's original teachings, avoids doctrinal interpretations admitted by the Mahayana, and puts the emphasis primarily upon individual salvation, while the "Great Vehicle," under Chinese influence, speaks of collective salvation.

To these basic differences, which correspond to the two poles of the civilization between which Indochina extends, were added other elements, particularly a veritable Theravada clergy, called the *sangha* (translated as "religious community"), such as was almost unknown until recently among the Mahayanists; hence their relative weakness.

Is this a religion in the true sense of the word? Bonze Sobhita answered the question this way:

> Buddhism properly speaking is not a religion, in the sense that it does not recognize God or soul, and has no dogma. The practice of Buddhism is the search for a conduct that will permit a person to cut short the cycle of rebirths, to destroy desire and, along that road, arrive at Nirvana—which is not annihilation but a state between being and non-being, extinction, appeasement of desires, peace and serenity.
>
> For Buddhism the world itself does not exist: there is no beginning or end: there are only transitory phenomena whose origins are interdependent: all is tied to-

gether by the law of causality. This law of causality is
the result of our actions. Added to our past life, this life
serves our future life. The world is a dynamic world in
a perpetual state of becoming and man is only a succession of psychic states following each other from one
body to the next. Death gives birth to another individual.

Religion or not, Buddhism has taken on in a few years a
considerable place in public life and probably also in public
consciousness, as a result of factors greatly different in importance, but complementing each other.

The first, it seems, was the development of the influence
of the "Small Vehicle" in Vietnam, through the mediation of
monks and teachers from Ceylon, Thailand, and Cambodia.
By developing the influence of a rite making Buddhism the
state religion, which in turn brought forth a clergy whose
members engage in constant action and propaganda, the men
who came from the West gave more force and a stronger
foundation to Vietnamese Buddhism; in fact, several pagodas
on the outskirts of Saigon are now devoted to the Theravada
rite, and the robes of the monks, until now uniformly brown,
tend toward saffron-yellow—the color used in the kingdoms
of the West.

Another factor in the Buddhist revival is the importance,
vitality, and influence taken on by Catholicism in South Vietnam after the Geneva Agreements of 1954, as a result of the
masses of refugees from the North. At that time the number
of Catholics in South Vietnam was estimated at half a million. Now there are a million and a half. Yet it is not so much
the figures that count but rather the style adopted by that
religion since the people from the North arrived—more ardent, more intransigent, with priests who, on the Spanish pattern, are the true community leaders.

This eruption of a flamboyant and passionate Catholicism
gave its religious spirit to a people little impregnated with it
until that time. Previously, people had practiced the ancestor

cult primarily out of religious hunger and the desire to give a spiritual dimension to their existence. In search of a faith, the Vietnamese discovered or rediscovered Buddhism.

Moreover the Diem regime really consigned Buddhism to the Vietnamese sympathy and taste for opposition by its policy if not of persecution at least of discrimination. It cannot be said that Diem cruelly persecuted Buddhists before the crisis of 1963. But his Catholic sectarianism led him to treat the Buddhists as a minor factor and to regard them with such distrust that, by being shown so clearly, ended up by becoming justified. Largely in order to act demonstratively against an unpopular regime, many Vietnamese turned to Buddhism: going in that direction they could be sure to be going against Diem. Finally, another important factor played a role: the growing use of monks by the two antagonists, the communists and the Americans. Rarely in modern history, in fact, did a movement receive stimuli of such a contradictory and peculiar nature, except for Nasserism in 1955–1956.

Buddhism's prestige and neutralist orientation was growing: by 1958 the Venerable Thich Tri Quang had already written in the magazine *Phat-Giao Viet-Nam* (*Vietnamese Buddhism*) that no person or state could mobilize Buddhism for a hot war or cold war, and that Buddhism's place was in *neutral* countries. As a result the leaders of the Extreme Left tried to infiltrate it, while using its pacifism to weaken the anti-communist vigor of a part of the population, and to propagate what the Saigon authorities called "defeatism," while the Americans tried to find a force or a faith capable of opposing communism and bet on the movement pushed forward by the bonzes.

I shall return to the evolution of this strange co-operation between the agents of the United States and the monks; it should be mentioned in passing that it played a decisive role at the moment when Buddhism emerged as the key factor in Vietnamese politics, as the seeming victor over the Diem regime.

The test of strength between the Ngos and the Buddhists began on May 8, 1963: a large mass of people assembled before the government house of the old imperial capital of Hue to protest against Diem's decision to forbid a public ceremony in honor of Buddha's anniversary (while the installation of two bishops in the same region, several weeks earlier, and the anniversary of Monsignor Thuc, Archbishop of Saigon and Diem's older brother, had been met with huge processions).

Had this mass been mobilized by Viet Cong agitators, as the regime claimed? In any event, the military, called in to help, lost their heads and ordered that the crowds be fired at; tear gas thrown at them was badly mishandled, however, so that its acid produced terrible burns. Eight dead were counted, among them three women. Two children had been decapitated by shells.

Mr. Wuhl, a German physician and professor on the faculty at Hue, who had witnessed these horrors, went to Tokyo and then to Europe, where he alerted international public opinion; from then on the Diem regime carried a new mark of shame in addition to those caused by its old mistakes and errors. But Buddhism soon had martyrs that were even more eloquent than the victims of May 8: several weeks later a monk, the Venerable Duc, seventy-seven years old, transformed himself into a living torch to protest against the injustices inflicted upon his co-religionists by the Diem regime.

From June to November 1963 seven more monks were to immolate themselves in this tragic fashion. This incidentally sheds a new light on Buddhism, which has the reputation of being essentially non-violent. How can these frightful actions be reconciled with Buddhist refusal to inflict death?

Sinologists and Indianists have disagreed while trying to discover the significance of these gestures with respect to the Buddhist tradition. Gernet, in *La Revue Asiatique*, recalls that around the fifth century Chinese monks had committed such ritualistic gestures which seemed similar to Christian efforts to attain redemption for others; but Folliozat, a specialist in the tradition of Indian Buddhism, rejects any idea of sacrifice and redemption, and gives two possible interpretations to the voluntary cremations by the bonzes.

According to Folliozat, one may see in these acts primarily an affirmation of eminent dignity and purification. By burning his arm—which is the most traditional gesture—or his body, the initiate, who is "free" or "awakened," freely disposes of what he has come to know to be simple appearance. No longer attached to things, he heroically demonstrates that he understands real values, a deeper order, and in this fashion condemns the attitude of those who persecute his co-religionists.

Folliozat adds that such cremations could also be gestures of protest, condemnation, or vengeance; he states, too, that these acts constitute exploits of an extraordinary psychosomatic technique which, it seems, reduces the sufferings caused by the sacrifice. He insists that in any event these gestures are not in contradiction to Theravada, which has a positive view of such superior manifestations of freedom from matter, and sees their authors as heroes, not because of the gesture itself but because they made themselves worthy of accomplishing it.

Let us hear a Buddhist, Bonze Sobhita, who has already been quoted. He relates that a saint who was a contemporary of Buddha asked: "Why am I alive?" Then he killed himself. Buddha was asked: "Is this wrong?" Buddha replied: "No, he has destroyed all desires, he will not return to earth, he may kill himself." If you have suppressed all desire in yourself through meditation, and you have attained the state of ecstasy, you do not feel death.

The monk continues:

Now there exists in China and in Vietnam another form of suicide that is not known in Ceylon, for example. One might call this the "suicide through combat" or "provoked suicide." To safeguard the equilibrium of the country where you practice your religion, you may give yourself death.

For example, if you feel that the government is not doing its duty or is making trouble, you have the duty to attract attention to that indignity, to make people think, to open the eyes of the military men. For this reason bonzes die of hunger or commit suicide.

A Vietnamese's reaction is the following: if some oppression takes place, the oppressed will commit suicide at his desk: this is a means of attracting the attention of the authorities, as there will have to be an inquiry. According to the bonzes, death is only a natural consequence of the ecstatic state they are in at that moment.

These voluntary martyrs inflicted moral wounds upon the Diem regime that were all the deeper since the comments of his spokesmen, particularly Mrs. Nhu, became more cynical; the authorities were caught up in a cycle of violence that went as far as the sack of the Saigon pagodas at the end of August 1963. Rarely have "moral forces" and those "imponderables," of which Bismarck used to complain that they were uncontrollable, played so powerfully against a regime.

Mrs. Nhu had apparently failed to assess them. But then, she was such a busy woman. She was charming, or rather, she had once been charming, and would have remained so had her look not been so haughty, her smile so acid, her tone so peremptory, her gestures so cutting. True, exercising ten years of power may not enhance the nature of even the best people, particularly if that power is both absolute and semi-secret, and is exercised at the height of a bitter civil war through the double intermediary of a husband who is "political adviser" and a brother-in-law who is dictator.

This little bit of a woman with the round face and the piercing voice, a little too strikingly elegant, transformed herself in ten years from the country's "First Lady"—her husband's two older brothers were an archbishop and a bachelor, respectively—into the state's "First Personality." It was often said of her that she was the true man in the family. But *Time* did not describe the whole situation when it said: "She rules the men who rule the country"; from 1959 until 1963 her authority was exercised more directly than that. The deputies of the Saigon parliament, who listened without visible response to the homilies of the chief of the family and the state, frankly admitted that when minuscule Madame Nhu mounted the rostrum, they felt all the weight of governmental power pressing down on them.

Madame Nhu came from a family of very rich people. Her father, formerly a lawyer at Bac Lieu, a small Cochinchinese town, was "independent" Vietnam's first foreign secretary under the Japanese occupation. This imprudence did not prevent Tran Van Chuong from later becoming the Americans' trusted man in Vietnam, and the new Republic's Ambassador to Washington, until that day in August 1963 when this diplomat, being more subtle than his daughter, disassociated himself publicly from the regime that had violated the Buddhist monks.

In 1943 Tran Le Xuan, age thirteen, married a handsome young man with an earnest expression who attended the Ecole des Chartes and quoted Emmanuel Mounier: Ngo Dinh Nhu, son of the great mandarin Ngo Dinh Kha, younger brother of Monsignor Thuc and a certain Ngo Dinh Diem who had been minister of internal affairs under Bao Dai. It was a union between big business and the nobility represented at the court. Chuong's daughter, born a Buddhist, converted to Catholicism, her husband's religion, and bore him four children.

But ten years after her marriage came Dien Bien Phu: that battle lost by the West was the good fortune of the Ngos. In the ensuing turmoil French and American specialists tried to oppose these Catholic monarchists with their supersensitive nationalism to the rising tide of Vietnamese communism.

The beginnings were difficult and a testing ground for the family group in the face of the Emperor Bao Dai's intrigues, the attacks by the sects, and various foreign pressures. From this confusion there soon emerged the little lady moulded into her silk frock like a dagger in its sheath.

Madame Nhu's political doctrine consisted of four articles of faith: feminism, Catholicism, prudery, anti-communism. She was a passionate feminist, endlessly warring and gesturing at the head of the Solidarity Movement of Vietnamese Women, and recalling at every opportunity that if France had had her Joan of Arc, Vietnam had had two of them: the Trung sisters, who perished tragically more than twenty centuries earlier while battling the Chinese.

Her (doctrinaire) prudery was proverbial; her fight against prostitution was famous. Inevitably such an attitude will attract skepticism and even calumnies. How could such an attractive woman, so occupied with matters of sex, fail to give rise to a legend? And how could such a legend fail to seem like reality itself?

Her anti-communism, visceral as in all the members of her family, in some way sharpened her prudery. When she proposed to parliament a law against taxi-girls and the tango it was, in both cases, in order to conserve energies that were to be entirely devoted to the struggle against Marxism.

Her Catholicism was on the order of that of her brothers-in-law and closer to that of Torquemada than that of John XXIII; she would not have hesitated to light the pyres herself had her enemies not spared her that task by immolating themselves.

A statement she made in August 1963 gave an idea of the Christian charity practiced by this charming person. When a reporter asked her to comment on what was happening at the pagodas, she said: "I would clap hands at seeing another monk barbecue show. . . ."

2

๛๛๛๛๛๛๛

The Day of the Dead

One force, brittle and detested, held South Vietnam together. But that force was made of a will—Diem's; an intelligence—Madame Nhu's; a voice—that of her husband; and a system of influence—that of Monsignor Thuc. Then came the first of November 1963.

The first shots were fired by the parachutists at the Gia Long Palace on Friday, November 1, at 1 P.M. In reality, however, it was the shells fired into the crowds at Hue on the occasion of the Buddhist demonstrations six months earlier, on May 8, 1963, that had precipitated the agony of the Ngo regime.

But there were other reasons for the separation between the Diem regime and the forces that had so far supported it. Even before Washington had decided to suspend its economic aid, Ngo Dinh Nhu—who since the beginning of the year had no longer been content with being the "brains" of the President and had assumed more and more direct powers —had begun to follow a seeming conversion to a more progressive course, both in internal affairs and on the diplomatic plane. Did he think he could return in this fashion to the "personalism" to which he himself referred all the more cynically since actually he must have known to what extent he betrayed the lessons of his teacher, Mounier?

In a press conference of September 7 the "political adviser" made public some bills to reduce expenses for the machinery of state; state employees were to be paid with ration cards and foreign trade was to be nationalized. These prospects, tied to an almost comical increase in the police regime—with Buddhist monks and, in particular, students being secretly arrested—cost this "strong" regime defending the "moral order" the support of the local and foreign trade circles that had so far supported it for lack of any other rampart against communism. This attempt to revive a moribund dictatorship with an injection of "leftism" is reminiscent of the ephemeral Salo Republic, founded by Mussolini after his rescue by Nazi parachutists in 1944. But aside from the fact that the Vietnamese people were no more disposed than the Italians to give a new chance to the dictatorship, even if it were adorned with the trappings of populism, the Americans considered it inopportune to favor the establishment of a socialist regime, even if it was primarily nationalistic.

Another maneuver on Nhu's part, however, aroused the American allies of the Saigon regime even more. After May the "political adviser" had begun some tentative talks with the guerrillas in the South, if not actually with the leadership in the North. Did he feel strong enough to dictate his conditions to the enemy, or did he think he was in such a bad position that only the course of negotiation was left? Strange as it may seem, those who knew Nhu thought it was the former.

But the President's brother, it seems, was primarily intent on using these contacts to blackmail the Americans, all the more so since a declaration by General de Gaulle of August 29 had given a certain "credibility" to a rapprochement between South and North, and had aroused sufficient interest in Vietnamese political circles for Nhu to consider it advantageous to undertake such designs. Thus, at the end of summer, the game began that Washington thought concealed a plot between Paris, Hanoi, and Nhu.

With Nhu's surreptitious help an article by Joseph Alsop was published on September 18 in the *New York Herald Tribune,* sounding the alarm. It quoted facts and proposals by Nhu which tended to prove that with the aid of France's Ambassador in Saigon, Lalouette, and his colleague, the delegate-general at Hanoi, de Buzon, actual negotiations had been opened between the government of Ho Chi Minh and that of Ngo Dinh Diem through the intermediary of the Polish representative at the International Control Commission, Manelli.

If on the French side these assertions were judged too fantastic to merit the least denial, the Polish diplomat, receiving me in his villa in Saigon, explained the true nature of the conversations reported by Alsop. Manelli stressed first of all that he had not been put into contact with Nhu by the French Embassy, and that in the course of the only conversation he had held with the "political adviser," on September 2, no reference of any kind had been made to negotiations. If a contact was, in fact, established between Hanoi and Saigon at that time, it was by the president of the International Control Commission, Goburdhun, an Indian diplomat, who had visited the Presidents of both the North and the South, and had been surprised to hear the former say: "After all, Diem is a patriot after his own fashion." However, Ho talked not to Manelli but to the communist Australian journalist Wilfred Burchett about a possibility of a cease-fire in the South.

The exchanges initiated at the time will bear fruit, perhaps, though in another context. But at the time their content was less important than the publicity given to them by Nhu. He wanted to impress the Americans and show them that he held in his hand trumps other than their protection; but all he accomplished was to exasperate them. On the day following the revelations whispered into Alsop's ear by the "political adviser," the new United States Ambassador, Henry Cabot Lodge, made a number of decisions that seem to have prepared the way for the November 1 coup.

The vise tightened around the Ngo regime, disliked by a population distressed by its arbitrariness and false propaganda and was condemned by international opinion, which, however, looked only at the pyres consuming the monks of Xa Loi. But as long as Washington support had lasted the eviscerated body remained standing in its harness. Now the Diem government suddenly lost its most effective defender, Richardson, the CIA's chief representative in Saigon, who was brusquely relieved of his functions by Lodge; and it saw itself deprived of American credits, as the United States Operations Mission, which gave out the funds, suddenly refused to sign over more.

But it kept Col. Le Van Tung's "special forces" as its praetorian guard, and seemingly also the declared sympathy of Gen. Paul Harkins, commander-in-chief of American forces in Vietnam and Thailand. On October 24, as previously on August 28, the rumor of a coup began to circulate in town. Yet two days later all the army chiefs paraded meekly before Ngo Dinh Diem on the occasion of the anniversary of his ascendency to the Presidency. Was he invulnerable? On October 28, at the end of an official dinner, Nhu said to two foreign correspondents: "What about the coup? The Vietnamese generals haven't got a chance. . . ."

With Col. Le Van Tung's guard the dictator's only protection, the American Embassy told Diem that any financial aid still forthcoming would be stopped unless the "special forces" departed for the rice paddies to fight against the Viet Cong. The Ngos gave in; on October 30 their "SS" left the capital.

Then Admiral Felt, American commander-in-chief in the Pacific, arrived. Obviously it is not known whether he held talks with the junta that had already made its plans, and even less is known about what he said to General Harkins. In any event, on November 1 Admiral Felt and Henry Cabot Lodge presented themselves at the Presidential palace in Saigon a little after 11 A.M. It is said that Diem told them: "There is talk again of a coup by the army. Could it be your little CIA agents who are circulating these rumors?" Did the admiral and the diplomat set their host straight? Those Vietnamese personalities most likely to know say that at 11:30 A.M. the two visitors told Diem that his safety would be assured if he resigned without a fight, and that several telephone conversations between the palace and the American Embassy took place during the afternoon. Resign? To demand his resignation was not to know the little man's indomitable obstinacy or his brother's pride.

When the first shots hit the palace and the guard barracks, Diem and Nhu could no longer ignore the ratio of forces or the help they could expect. Still, they refused to answer the messages of General Minh, president of the revolutionary committee. For seven hours the firing continued; the Gia Long Palace was to show the sorry traces for a year.

Around 9:00 P.M. the shooting ceased. Some emissaries were able to approach the palace and were permitted entry. Was it around 10 P.M. or at dawn the next day that the President and his brother managed to leave the palace in a black Renault? In any event, it seems that the assailants had not really tried to deprive them of a way out.

The fugitives' trail was picked up only the next day at the Church of Saint-François-Xavier in Cholon, Saigon's Chinese twin city, where Diem had been on retreat on several occasions. The brothers participated in the service for the dead, then remained prostrate in an attitude of fervent prayer. Had Nhu been in touch with the general staff? When an armored half-track arrived at the church at 9:20 A.M., the officer emerging from it said to the officiating priest: "We are here to look for them. . . ." Without resistance, Diem and his brother mounted the half-track. A half hour later the radio announced their "suicide."

At this point of the story, so full of gaps and contradictions, our information is mostly confused. Everyone, of course, rejects the story of "suicide," not only because the President was too fervent a Catholic even to think of doing away with himself, but because the bodies, as seen seven hours later by official witnesses, bore no signs at the faces, the temples, or the chests of anything that would have indicated suicide. On Diem's brow were some swellings of the type often caused by blows to the neck, and the only photos taken of the brothers shortly after their deaths show their hands tied behind their backs. These factors also invalidate the "accidental suicide" thesis promulgated five days later by a spokesman of the junta, according to which the prisoners, in the face of a hostile crowd, had tried to seize the weapon from one of their guards, and a shot had gone off during the struggle.

The actual circumstances of the deaths of Diem and his brother matter less than the level on which they were decided. Competent observers in Saigon believe that the two slain masters of the regime were led from the church to general staff headquarters five or six miles away, and that they were ordered by a spokesman of the junta to tell the people over the radio that they had resigned from power. After their refusal (Diem is reported to have said: "I am the chief of the army. I give orders here.") the decision to eliminate them was made. By whom? By one or several officers of the junta? It is a fact that the time between the arrest of the two brothers and the announcement of their deaths could not have left much time for discussion of a sentence, no matter how summary.

The most reasonable hypothesis is that the decision was made by the officer who had been entrusted with this dangerous mission and who had been given *carte blanche*. It seems to be true, in any event, that the news of the President's death caused considerable excitement in the general staff. And the question has arisen whether the armored vehicle that went to collect the two fugitives had been dispatched from Tan Son Nhut by the new masters of the country.

Taken to St. Paul Hospital later in the morning, the two corpses were identified at 4 P.M. by two trustworthy doctors; a relative of the Ngos, Madame Tran Trung Dung, wife of Diem's former secretary of defense who had since broken with the regime, came to claim them. The sisters at the hospital believe that the remains were interred at Hue, where the "founder of the family's power," Ngo Dinh Can, waited until their arrival before taking refuge at the American Consulate, convinced to the last that the whole operation was a trick played by Nhu on the military conspirators. For months the "political adviser" had whispered to those close to him that he had prepared everything to catch the recalcitrant officers sooner or later in their own trap. That had been plan "Bravo I." But it was plan "Bravo II" that was executed.

Two days later, giving in to the crowds that laid siege to his office, the American Consul surrendered Can to the new Saigon masters, who would publicly execute him six months later. Madame Nhu was in the United States, Monsignor Thuc in Rome. The Ngo dictatorship had lasted nine years and five months.

Now that they are dead, can one finally pass a fair judgment on the brothers who held the people of South Vietnam under their rule for almost a decade? After all, it is less a question of two individual destinies than of the regime they inspired, incarnated, and led, of an oligarchical system cut off from the people they claimed to represent, a regime, efficient after a fashion, that survived its political errors but finally, in a sort of suicidal manner, ran up against the moral force of Vietnamese Buddhism.

Ngo Dinh Diem and Ngo Dinh Nhu were the third and fourth sons of the great Catholic mandarin Ngo Dinh Kha. Mandarin and Catholic: those two words would have been sufficient to summarize this strange family regime, this patriarchate—always keeping in mind that Diem's Catholicism was closer to that of Blaise de Montluc than to that of the priests in the Mission of France—if Nhu had not given it the imprint of his strange personality. For the brother and "political adviser" was not only the "gray eminence" behind the dictator, and the husband of a very conspicuous, very intelligent, and very belligerent woman. As everyone knows, he was the true master of South Vietnam.

This former pupil of France's Ecole des Chartes was the family intellectual. In such a narrowly conservative milieu, also weighted down with traditional hierarchies, that alone should have been reason enough for him to remain in the background. Yet his intelligence, which he had permitted for a long time to be overshadowed, finally took the lead—only to turn in a void and lose itself in intrigues, and then harden itself crazily in fanaticism and repression.

Anyone who met Ngo Dinh Nhu fifteen years ago was struck by his warmth and the vivid expression on his face, his leonine beauty, and the force of conviction animating him. At that time he lived in Saigon in a sort of inner exile, confined to the tasks of semi-clandestine librarian. His judgment of the regime then in power—that of Tam— his views of the future, the program he was working on, all indicated that he was a man to whom Vietnam should take recourse. He belonged to a family famous for its caste spirit, its oligarchical inclinations, its attachment to the mandarin system. But could not the revolution that had turned the son of mandarin Pham Van Dong into a communist leader and the prime minister of the North free Nhu from the social ties that held him so tightly?

Nhu had claimed to be an avid reader and a disciple of Mounier, and attached to "personalism." He used the same generous language as other young men in other parts of the world—like Bouabid, Ben Salah, or Rabemananjara—who were equally attached to the emancipation of their countries.

The principal idea of the reigning family, and particularly

of Nhu, was the creation of the strategic hamlets in 1961. To French observers the idea was familiar: in Algeria it had led to the "regroupment camps." The idea was to assemble members of the rural population in fortified or protected enclosures, in order to deprive the rebels of their popular support, to deprive the proverbial revolutionary "fish" of the "water" in which they lived, moved, and fed.* The same causes were expected to produce the same effects—rising hostility on the part of the peasant masses against the "uprisers." But the villages that were remodeled and shaken up in this fashion never played the same role in Algerian society as in that of Vietnam.

By touching the villages Nhu and his friends touched at the very foundations of Vietnamese peasant culture, where the local group, bound in its bamboo collar, had remained the basic unit, the raw material of public life, and even the basis of private life. The village, even more than the individual, was an entity. It was the village that had to pay taxes, and the village that negotiated with the central power. Everything derived from that entity, and all came down to it. It was the expression of that "harmony beneath the heavens" that any society imbued with Confucianism considered essential.

By attacking this unity, Nhu was, strictly speaking, more revolutionary than the Viet Minh, who had never dared touch that cell at its base. But though his "revolution" overturned a society, it brought no solution to the problems facing that society. It was an end in itself, and claimed to play a strategic role only in connection with a purely circumstantial task: the struggle against the guerrillas, who the little people of the Vietnamese countryside saw as dangerous brothers rather than as enemies.

When asked about the origins of the strategic hamlets idea, Nhu replied that it had come to him one day when he was at the Ecole des Chartes, in connection with the description

---

* Mao's description of guerrillas: they must sustain themselves in the surrounding countryside like fish in water.—Trans.

of Medieval French society. This was a strange argument, for a Vietnamese as well as for an historian. And just like the peasant revolutionaries during the reigns of Henry VI and Louis XIV, in Burgundy, several centuries earlier, the Vietnamese in the countryside rejected a certain form of protection.

Being Catholic in Vietnam's tolerant and enlightened society is no problem. But to conduct there a Catholic policy based on combat, a Catholicism soft to the rich, hard to the poor, and rough on the gentle, a Catholicism reduced to an obstinate anti-communist recipe, is to trap oneself in an impossible situation.

As is often the case with Vietnamese questions, one should read in this connection what was written more than twelve years ago in Vietnam by a great sociologist of war, Paul Mus, on the political situation of the Catholics in that country:

> The fact that these Catholics are a small minority—say 10 to 20%—may seem to them, on the religious plane, a challenge and an incentive. . . . But on the patriotic plane, the trial is heavy, as it goes against the instinct of solidarity and national unity, and the challenge is ambiguous. This country is one of those where one can least easily conceive the patriotism of an even well-intentioned minority going against an adverse or silent majority; if, moreover, this minority runs the risk of bottling itself in too much of a religious unity, the claim that its religion comes to it from the outside will place it in a particularly delicate position with respect to a society where it is traditionally inopportune to show oneself to be different, and expose oneself to the kind of anger that is a trait of the national temperament and can express itself politically. The risk is great . . . to win or lose for communism, established as champion of the opposition, the mass of those who feel different from the Catholic element. . . ."

These permanent risks of a Catholic policy, in a Vietnam torn by a civil war, were multiplied by the Ngo family, which crazily blended elements of Christian doctrine with a program and organization of the fascist type like that of the secret Can Lao party, and which tried not only to rule the state with a certain form of Catholicism, but the Church with a clerical state. From this there sprang up the constant conflicts between the "state" hierarchy, personified by Monsignor Thuc, older brother of the President, and the Vatican, represented primarily by the Archbishop of Saigon, Monsignor Binh. And from this conflict arose the dispute between the Catholic minority and the Buddhist majority that was ultimately to be decisive, a dispute that only much later took on the aspect of a religious war; it remained for long confined to a tug-of-war between the politico-military power and the "neo-Buddhist" hierarchy.

But this struggle—which could have taken on the shape of those struggles which led to the revocation of the Edict of Nantes or to the separation of Church and State—was transformed by the "neo-Buddhists" into a matter of persecution and a long and terrible martyrdom; more than the bombs of Trinh Minh The's Caodaists in 1955, and even more than the Viet Cong guerrillas (at least for several months), the pyres the monks had immolated themselves on consumed and destroyed the power of the Ngos, because they managed to transform the growing antipathy against them on the part of international, and primarily American, public opinion into a veritable feeling of horror.

3

〰〰〰〰〰〰〰

A Strange Absence

Saigon, November 1963

A true revolution is visible: trousers grow shorter, caps replace hats, suits are replaced by overalls. At Saigon it was
obvious that something had been happening: the city bore
the marks of combat, and tanks competed with pedicabs. But
the people, who walked around with the curious mixture of
bustle and nonchalance so typical of the Vietnamese, were
more than ever true to form. An arm long stifled in a tourniquet hurts when it is freed. The tourniquet of the Diem
dictatorship was suddenly removed: after the first cries of
joy the longing to move did not seem very strong, and with
their bantering compliance, the people relished the event.

To be sure, the events of All Saints' Day of 1963 left their
traces, but no more so than those of November 1960 or September 1962. The abortive raid by the air force in 1962 deprived Saigon of its extraordinary piece of "rococolonial"
architecture—the Norodom Palace, where thirteen governors-
general had reigned and which, renamed Doc Lap (independence), had sheltered the chief of state until then.

The leaders of Cochinchina used to live three hundred

yards away, in the shadow of the governors-general, in what was the Grandière Palace; they were replaced by the chiefs of Vietnamese governments, who found themselves in the equally oppressive shadow of resident ministers or high commissioners.

After the shots fired on Friday and Saturday, while the two masters of the regime sought their holy refuge, the building was so pricked with bullets and chinked with impacts that it looked like Mirabeau's head. The Paris city hall or the military school, the day after Liberation, were no more defaced by battle than these comic-opera buildings.

All around, tanks stood guard, covered with parachutists asleep or eating, and beyond that martial and tired circle there had established itself that circle of Saigon's marvelous small trade, irrepressible and charming, with merchants of Chinese soup, Coca-Cola, sweets, and papers, and then there was the crowd, with its unconcerned chatter. Before this ghost of the power that had imposed itself on this crowd more than nine years ago, the crowd did not brandish its fists or show any trace of anger: it showed the silent laughter that means so many things in this country, but never what one thinks it means.

Aside from that, Saigon was still the same shaded and musty city, full of alert strollers, svelte girls, and working children. The flower market on what had been the Boulevard Charner was just as beautiful as that in Tunis; on the sidewalks the world's cleverest jacks-of-all-trades, smoking cigarettes and sporting battered felt hats, put something together that might turn into anything from a locomotive to a pedestrian bridge. These small miracles are wrought with laughing patience and frivolous wisdom. The people of Saigon, who for a quarter of a century survived all sorts of horrors, experienced on November 1 a surge of joy. They savored it prudently, because there was talk of a coup that the dictator's friends might yet stage. And were the guns that could still be heard at night from the direction of Tan Son Nhut aimed at the Viet Cong? A people who have received a measure of freedom, but who are not yet freed from war, and who have seen so much, will retain a degree of skepticism and impassivity.

If it is true that nothing is destroyed until it is replaced, it was not obvious to the visitor at Saigon at the end of 1963 that the Ngo dictatorship had finally been abolished. The capital of South Vietnam was a city in which people breathed more freely because they had been freed from a prideful oligarchy that had become more of a police-controlled totalitarianism every day. But it was a city in which one could not find the ruling powers. Here, a void followed the detested regime. Here was a city that seemed to live in a state of prolonged weightlessness, like an astronaut in his capsule. A city in a state of suspended animation.

The fallacious pronunciamentos trumpeted each day by the fallen regime were replaced by an uncertainty that weighed lightly on the people's consciences but was heavy with apprehensions. Where was unfettered South Vietnam going?

"I am making war," said the spokesman for the junta, sincere in his professions of this anti-communist faith which obviously demands the least imagination, particularly from the military. "We are making war," said the Americans, those protectors who were now rid of their headstrong protégés and clearly satisfied with the events of November 1. "They are making war," was the constant claim of members of a government not visible to the naked eye and politicians not yet quite able to adapt themselves to the situation outside their prisons.

But beyond that? In the great humid city, with bustling crowds of sophisticated strollers and graceful girls, there was a strange absence. When an aching tooth is pulled, the relief is great. But while one waits for the dressing to be applied, the sensation of the void can be very disagreeable.

Ngo Dinh Diem was not a great man, and when his statue crashed to the ground, it raised much less dust than that of

Stalin in Budapest. Soon the cloud began to lift before the eyes of the astonished public. As the dust settled, the shape of the new regime emerged more clearly. But it made no great impression. The military were rather pleasant. But what the devil was their program?

In order to show itself different from its predecessor would the regime of November 1 try to cultivate public opinion by staking its fate on freedoms? The press found itself ungagged, and the leading politicians began to emerge from their prisons or retreats. But the most visible freedom was in the area of morals: at a stroke Saigon's night life was revived, and Madame Nhu, in effect, died a little every evening.

And yet no matter how careful the junta of November 1 tried not to break a certain continuity in the public order and administration, it unleashed a process of democratization and restoration of political life that was to press in on it ever after. By turning the key that the dictator and his brother had used to lock up all freedoms, the generals initiated a decompression process that led to significant developments in student and political circles, and was to be a severe test of their intention to contain the "revolution" and turn it into a surgical operation at the upper echelons.

After nine years of political and moral rigor—at least by official rules—Saigon was relaxing, disengaging itself, taking a deep breath: this city in the South had again become truly a Southern city, where politicians released from prison could again take up their positions as popular heroes and where student associations again sprang up. But the gap between the euphoria of the liberated and the authority of the liberators was in danger of causing painful misunderstandings.

The students who, with the monks, had been the prime destroyers of the Diem regime were now trying to enjoy the liberties for which they had fought. From the very first days of November 1963 elections of student representatives to the university council took place at Saigon's university. The fallen regime had banished all organizations of this type; therefore these student elections were a genuine event and the occasion for some rather good-natured demonstrations. In the course of several conversations I found the students less irritated than ironic, less impatient than lucid.

Three thin boys with grave eyes stood before me, law students twenty years old. "Do you think the new regime is too timid or too similar to its predecessor?" No. They thought Vietnam was in a situation in which it could not afford to jump into a political free-for-all. They said: "We deplore the continued presence of some personalities in the new government, but not the fact that priority is being given to unity and stability. The military have rendered us so great a service by ridding us of Diem and his family that we have no right to harass them with demands for faster developments. But if you talk to our fellow students in the arts and sciences, you may hear a different tune. . . ."

An atmosphere of wild celebration reigned at the science faculty, where student elections were taking place to the sounds of a jazz orchestra. Decidedly, the uprising of November 1 was above all an homage to music. My same questions put to young physicists produced much less prudent answers than from the law students, but even they were not violent: "After all, our revolutionaries know the old regime so well that they can correct its mistakes! This provisional arrangement need not last for long."

Undoubtedly these young intellectuals had expected things to be different after the fall of the dictatorship. But, surprisingly, many of them placed the emphasis on anti-communism and accepted the official line, giving anti-communism priority over all other concerns. Clearly, the progressives were holding back.

On November 11, on the Saigon quay, a large, deeply moved crowd received the forty or so political prisoners returning from Poulo Condore, the little island that served for a century as a prison for Vietnamese revolutionaries and was the best Marxist school for the previous generations.

Where we stood, a broken statue showed its laughable stumps: pretending to render homage to the heroic Trung sisters, the statue apparently was actually a portrayal of Madame Nhu and her oldest daughter. On November 2 it was destroyed. On this Friday a table nearby was set with cakes to celebrate the return of those from Poulo Condore, nobody touched the cakes, emotions ran too high. Among the returnees were a considerable number of officers, but a small man attracted all eyes: Dr. Phan Quang Dan, former Saigon deputy, imprisoned on November 11, 1960, who, after nearly two years in prison, had been sentenced in July 1962 by a military tribunal to seven years of forced labor. He seemed less affected by these trials than had been feared, and with a sort of naïveté he expressed his joy at being free and at seeing Diem eliminated. Carried off in triumph, he groped for words: "This is an excellent transition regime for the purpose of preparing for elections six months from now!" And he disappeared, swallowed up by the crowd, before I could talk to him in greater detail.

Despite the verbal endorsement that he had been forced at the time to give the defunct regime, probably under intolerable pressures, Dan kept his friends and a certain prestige. But the Saigon masses anticipated even more impatiently the liberation of former minister Pham Khac Suu, the other leader of the opposition to Diem, who was sentenced at the same trial as Dan to eight years of forced labor. Detained at the Chi Hoa prison, he was not released for a few more days. Receiving me subsequently in his very modest apartment on the road to Cholon, he told me that the idea of neutralizing Vietnam was interesting, even though its form and implications were still very unclear. In the meantime, he said, the regime must be democratized.

The liberation of the prisoners of the Diem regime gave me a chance to verify that torture and ill-treatment had been practiced in the prisons and camps from which they were now

returning. Hundreds of students of both sexes had been subjected to ill-treatment. Many had been forced to drink soapy
water until they had suffered internal damage. At the deten-
tion camp in Le Van Quich forty prisoners at a time were
thrown into a cell in the hot sun. Others had their nails torn
out; still others were blinded; one student died of a crushed
liver.

A British Embassy typist, who had been arrested several
hours before the insurrection, told me how she had been
beaten and tortured at a police post. Another told how she
suffered the well-known ordeal of torture by electrodes.

The political leaders of South Vietnam, anticipating their
colleagues' release, waited in expectation of beginning true
negotiations; that at least is what a man like Tran Van Tuyen,
guiding spirit of the Caravelle group, was saying. Former minister Pham Huy Quat refused to become a member of the
government because the military men, who dominated it,
offered him only "purely technical duties."

While political life everywhere was surging back and teeming, the junta seemed determined to hold on to the idea that
the hour for political activity had not yet come and would not
come so soon.

But while waiting to play their "full roles," the political
personalities were thinking of convoking a "national congress," prepared by former minister Tran Van Tuyen, in order
to define a minimal nucleus of common objectives between the
various factions—without the participation of those principal
leaders who were still resisting abroad. Would South Vietnamese political life emerge from the vain palavers and endless discussions that once opened the road to a civil dictatorship and might now encourage a would-be military dictator?

And the government of Nguyen Ngoc Tho? Just as its chief
had been promoted by the "revolution" of November 1 from
vice-president of Ngo's "Republic" to president of the council
of the new regime, so most of the new officeholders were
former ministerial secretaries now promoted to ministers,

under the control of the military. One must not oversimplify the matter and laugh at this "administrative committee," yet if one wanted to assess the ambitions and powers of this organism on the basis of its decisions, one could not help noticing that the text adopted at the first meeting of the new regime's ministers ruled that it would no longer be necessary to make out medical prescriptions in triplicate.

In fact, there remained hardly any coherent force, group, or organization after the fall of a regime that had systematically destroyed all of them. What about the old nationalist parties created in the North in the thirties, such as the V.N.Q.D.D. or the Dai Viet? They had remained completely Tonkinese, and being merely imports into the South, were composed of exhausted and disappointed politicians.

In the South the notion of the Communist Party—"the Party"—was still very vague. Was that name really appropriate to the circles, small groups, and friendly Trotskyites that were the last remnants of the powerful troops once fired by the eloquence of Ta Thu Tau, who had been assassinated by the Viet Minh in 1945? Could "Communist Party" even have been applied to the three of four socialist groups which —though inspired by men of considerable talent—keep splitting, reuniting, and splitting again over the fundamental question: Must we assume contact, at any price, with the Viet Cong, and deal with them? Actually, only the politico-religious groups gave Southern public life its real color.

For twenty years Caodaism had stimulated newspaper correspondents who, from the smokehouses of Cholon to the sampans in the Bay of Along, were in search of a good slaughter. It is unnecessary to describe here the principles and rites of that humanist religion which, founded by a brilliant man of affairs, is part secret society, part Freemasonry, part spiritual circle (with more than a million adherents). Caodaism, incidentally, knows very well how to render unto Caesar that which is Caesar's; but neither its long collusion with Japan nor its prolonged flirtation with the French damaged its prestige. After having broken with the Viet Minh, "Pope" Pham Con Tac, recalled from exile by Admiral Argenlieu, made Tay Ninh—cradle of the sect—into a miniature Vatican, spreading Caodaist influence into several provinces, affecting a million Cochinchinese and some of the South Annamese population.

The little Caodaist state had its own army, administration, finances, and faith. But it could not resist the central parochial power. Already under Bao Dai's rule, increasing numbers of Caodaist militia men joined the nationalist army. But this sect that had tried so hard to retain its autonomy with respect to the central power had been repressed under the Diem regime. Due to political antagonism, religious divergences, and conflicts of interest, either "Pope" Tac or Archbishop Thuc had had to prevail. Between 1954 and 1956, as a result, Caodaism had partially returned to its illegal status. Eight years later it came back, but weakened. On balance, it remained a force, and an anti-communist force at that, but it was torn by conflicting tendencies.

Hoa-Hao is not a war cry, but the name of a little village in western Cochinchina, where that sect was founded by Huyhn Phu So, one of the strangest people of contemporary Vietnam. A learned Marxist (one of his first companions, Do Ba The, was a Trotskyite leader) and a mystic by temperament, this landowner tried to base his doctrine simultaneously on agrarian socialism, rebellion against the colonial authorities, and the most radical xenophobia. A "Carbonaro" and zealous preacher, he insisted that the landed estates and colonial lands should belong to the little people; he soon came to be called the "mad bonze."

When he was arrested in 1939 by the French police, he already was chief of a group whose two or three apparently ritual murders heralded its expansion. He had already made contact with various Japanese agents; and when, during the war, the Japanese had managed to bring the region under the control of their people, they had snatched Huyhn Phu So away from the French police. In 1945, passing from the Japanese orbit to the Viet Minh, the "mad bonze" finally became one of the members of the revolutionary committee of South Vietnam.

I then had occasion to meet that surprising man. His face—that of a visionary, of arresting beauty and tension—was unforgettable. Eight months later he had been bludgeoned to death, after a meeting of the revolutionary committee. As a result of his execution the sect had resumed its furious hostility against the Viet Minh and its ranks had swelled once more. Violently divided among themselves, the heirs of the "mad bonze"—among them such picturesque characters as Gen. Tran Van Soai, a former chauffeur with a striking mustache, and Ba Cut, an enterprising teacher—prevented the Viet Minh for several months from entering a territory that comprised almost all of western Cochinchina. Ba was executed by Diemists in 1955.

The Hoa-Hao "federation," with seven or eight thousand faithful members, was more important on the economic than on the military plane, for it controlled several rice markets and held the key to commerce between the nationalist and the revolutionary zones, and vacillated between Saigon and the N.L.F., according to the play of various influences.

Despite their feudal, exotic, and anarchic character, the sects remained the only forces in South Vietnam more or less organized, whether among the Buddhists or the Catholics. But, living an artificial existence, these sects and parties were only a mass of conflicting tendencies toward the end of 1963, less and less capable of slowing the expansion of the Viet Cong.

4

❦❦❦❦❦❦❦

Churches and Pagodas

In the face of communism, and pending the revelation of Buddhism's true strategy and distant objectives, Catholicism showed itself, after much hesitation, as the only organized force.

To be sure, it commanded less than a tenth of the population; but the cohesion of these Christians, the strategic importance of the sectors they occupied, the prestige of their leaders, the contacts they maintained in both camps, and the power they exercised at various times inside the nationalist regime made it possible for Vietnamese Catholics to oppose the Marxist-inspired revolution with cadres, a faith, and a way of life.

Until 1948 the Catholics, on the whole, had been rather friendly toward the Viet Minh. In the North the Association of Catholic Youth of Vietnam, led by Nguyen Manh Ha, Ho's minister of economic affairs in 1945–1946, gave the revolutionary movement its enthusiastic support. The anti-colonialism of the Vietnamese Church was at that time stronger than its suspicions of communism, all the more so since Ho Chi Minh was a master politician in that situation.

But a pastoral letter published in Saigon in December 1951 with the signatures of all nationalist zone archbishops (indigenous, Spanish, Irish, and French) condemned communism in such strong terms that it became one of the turning points for the Catholic masses, and particularly the clergy. Moreover, for two years, relations had deteriorated between the Vietnamese authorities and the Catholics under their control.

The most significant episode in this "change of alliances" was the defection from the Viet Minh—and the subsequent union of forces with Bao Dai—of the famous south Tonkinese priests, Le Huu Tu, Bishop of Phat Diem, and Pham Ngoc Chi, Bishop of Bui Chu. Vacillating constantly between unreserved adherence to the nationalist regime and opposition to it, i.e., being in a state of semi-dissidence yet having apparently burned all their bridges with respect to their Viet Minh neighbors, these two leaders of frontier dioceses symbolized the situation of Vietnamese Catholicism: ardently nationalist, tolerating the presence of French forces only where the latter saved it from catastrophe, and constantly reproaching the nationalist government with being too lenient with regard to the foreign "protectors."

Parallel to this rapprochement between Catholicism and nationalism, a similar evolution was taking place in the Viet Minh zone. Was there actual persecution or were there merely the difficulties and pressures that all Christian groups suffer under communism? In any event, Catholics *were* arrested in Thanh Hoa province.

The relations between the Church and the communist powers had entered a critical phase even before Diem's accession to power. In the Baodaist coalition Catholicism had been the least conformist element. Conscious that without it Baodaism would be a motley and soulless mixture, Catholicism had increasingly tried to impose some rather daring views upon it, and to make itself the arbiter—for its own profit— with regard to the internal dissensions in the nationalist grouping.

With the arrival of the Ngos the Catholics had their hour of triumph, but this development must not be overestimated. Many Vietnamese Catholics condemned the Ngos' political Catholicism, this blending of Church and State, and the role of "protector" of the State that Monsignor Thuc, the President's older brother, arrogated for himself. Thuc, toward the end of the Diem regime in 1962, toured the countryside in an armored car; he was called to Rome by the Pope only at the last minute, when the hatred aimed at him in his diocese was on the verge of exploding into horrible violence. (Priests of the Hue region confided to me that in 1964, on the eve of the prelate's departure for Rome, the conspirators had prepared to burn him and his brother Can at the stake.)

In fact, the exodus of seven hundred thousand Catholics from Tonkin and North Annam, which was to arouse the entire Christian world, brought to the South a fanatical mass that was never to become fully integrated. The Catholics in the South wanted only to live in peace around their churches, to say their prayers, and ignore the rest of the country. But the Catholics from the North, installed in the South, blindly followed their priests, who often acted as leaders, particularly the adventurous Father Hoang Quynh who, disregarding the hierarchy of the priests, organized meetings and, setting up organizations without consulting the hierarchy, called upon Christians from the North to fight against Buddhism, communism, colonization, the presence of foreigners— all under the Christian label, but in a spirit that was hardly religious. The hierarchy, itself split, frequently hesitated to intervene against these unhappy and misled exiles.

On the road to Bien Hoa, less than twenty miles from the capital, there was a strange inscription: BUI CHU. Strange, because it was the name of one of two Tonkinese bishops who attained a certain notoriety in 1952 when their pastors, with Msgr. Le Huu Thu at the head, recruited a sort of Vietnamese militia against the Viet Minh. Two years later the people of Bui Chu turned back toward the South, often under dramatic conditions, and with the flag of the Vatican flying over their boats coming down from the North, they asked for asylum in a South that was prosperous and had been armed by Diem against communism.

As a result, surrounded by fortifications turning them into strategic hamlets, some villages filled with refugees from the North formed a sort of belt surrounding Saigon; it was as though the beleaguered regime wanted to fortify its capital with an iron guard composed of those people most hostile to communism and most violently attached to militant Catholicism.

In Vietnam church architecture is not pure. How could the baroque style, here of Spanish origin, become so adulterated? At Phat Diem or Bui Chu the churches, built on the swamplands, still retained something noble or strange. But here, transplanted to richer soil and outside the dramatic climate of the North, they turned into dismal confections. Yet it was hard to laugh at these Christians in black, these thin believers, who crowded around their Tonkin priest with his high sounding words, who, one should hope, would not see Diem's death as the reason for a second exile.

I was unable to learn, in the provincial Catholic communities huddled together in silent reproach, the reactions to the end of the Diem regime. But at Saigon the authorized interpreters of Catholicism did not conceal their view that the fall of Diem produced some confusion in many Christian circles. Still, there were differences among various orientations and geographic sectors.

Those most disturbed and shocked by the ex-President's physical liquidation were certainly the refugees from the North, estimated at 750,000 out of the 1,200,000 Catholics of South Vietnam. Whatever part the Ngo regime had really played in their rescue in 1954, they gave Diem credit for the reception they had received in their distress, and they remained grateful to him. The intolerance and sectarianism of the regime had not displeased this population trained by missionaries who were to some extent Spanish or Irish, and for whom anti-communism had become an article of faith and a reason to go on living.

How far did the Diem regime's preferential treatment of Catholics go? Let us consider this observation by a Jesuit father who, in a very interesting article in the review *Les Etudes,* was trying to prove that Catholics actually received no preferential treatment. To demonstrate the equality of treatment of the two communities, he recalled that a Catholic officer involved in the coup of November 11, 1960, was sentenced to ten years in prison. This shows that the Catholics under Diem were not above the law.

The Christians most affected by the coup of November 1 were those living in Hue. To be sure, not all Catholics in Central Vietnam were unreserved Diemists. A liberal current had formed around Cao Van Luan, rector of the university, who had been removed from his post in June for having tried to defend the Buddhists, and around certain teachers of the Collège de la Providence. This group, obviously without approving the liquidation of the Ngos, considered the fall of that regime a liberation and the end of a burden on Vietnamese Catholicism.

But Ngo Dinh Thuc, Archbishop of Hue and older brother of the President, had turned all his energies in a direction remembered with bitterness: as far as he was concerned Catholicism could survive only in the form of a permanent crusade. Recalling that less than a century ago, under Emperor Minh Mang, twenty-five thousand Catholics had been massacred in this region and that less than twenty years earlier several thousand Christians had fallen victim to the first revolutionary wave of the Viet Minh at Quang Ngai, Thuc kept an entire people in a state of permanent alert, thus precipitating the anxiety that followed the coup.

In the South, in Cochinchina, the Christians coped best with the destruction of the Ngo regime: first because in that region ideas tend to circulate more freely, modernism is likely to develop naturally, and at that time tolerance was on the increase, and also, because the apostolic delegation there had shown its courage by presenting to Diem, on June 16, a pastoral letter full of the spirit of Pope John's encyclical, *Pacem in Terris*. And certain representatives of various orders, such as the Jesuits, and more so the Dominicans, had not hidden their disapproval of the increasingly totalitarian orientation of a regime that was ultimately going to compromise Catholicism. Still, one must not underestimate the feelings aroused in that same circle by Diem's dramatic end, not only because the man remained relatively respected ("A patriot in his way," Ho Chi Minh had said) despite the destruction of his government and the rottenness of his regime, but also because the imputation of his suicide angered the Christians and left them incredulous, and in their eyes added an element of trickery to an act considered unnecessarily cruel.

But just because there was a question of suicide, which nobody believed, a legend arose in some Christian circles that the President was not dead. In an attempt to prove the contrary the junta decided to publish photographs. This meant publicizing an act that was not to the advantage of the victors.

Let us hear what a Belgian priest had to say; his face that of a fighter, his eyes blue in his bright-red face, he was the typical aggressive priest seen in American films:

Who is responsible for that catastrophic situation, the total failure of the Diem regime, the confusion in which our Christianity now finds itself? Who, I ask you? The army? The administration? The Americans? No, the Catholics themselves. Yes, the Catholics, all of them. We triumphed and talked big without ever trying—except at the lowest echelons—to change the course of events, to correct the regime's intolerable abuses. We permitted a total confusion to arise between wealth and Catholicism, the secure bourgeoisie and the hierarchy. That is where we now find ourselves, waiting for Buddhism to take its revenge, which may take a dramatic turn if the Viet Cong succeeds, as it now tries, in infiltrating it. We did not know how to correct or end Diem's power. We must rebuild from the ground up, on the basis of ruins—if the enemy who disposes of four out of five worth-while people in the country leaves us the time to do so.

If Vietnam is not a high point of Christian ethics, Buddhism does not show itself there in any more favorable light. Xa Loi Pagoda, whose name is tied to the burnings and the sacrifices accepted by a community imbued with Buddhist teachings, is a strange piece of architecture, half functional and half ornamental. To be sure, over the door is an impressive inscription from the hand of China's last empress, Tseu Hi, which supposedly says: "THE SEEDS OF THE EAST INUNDATE THE WEST" (an implicit definition of the Mahayana rite, or the "Great Vehicle," which is essentially Chinese and Vietnamese and thus Oriental, as distinguished from Western Buddhism, which is the Hinayana rite). But everywhere else there are only steeples that are too slender and decorations that are too heavy.

I visited Xa Loi Pagoda on the last of a series of prayer days inspired by the recent events. It was devoted to the repose of the "brothers Diem and Nhu": a sign of the very broad outlook on the part of the participants. But as the local authorities had feared that this might be the occasion for "various moves," because not every believer was perhaps capable of such devotion, the crowd had simply been invited to pray for peace in Vietnam. But in what a strange atmosphere: it was like a gay country fair, where the strollers bought sweets and photographs of bonzes incinerating themselves.

At the street level, before the large portraits of seven victims, a speaker talked of the lessons of the holocaust. At the first floor, facing an immense statue of Buddha, the devoted, burning sticks of incense in their hands, prostrated themselves.

I had asked to meet Thich Tri Quang, principal spirit behind the movement at Hue, who had the reputation of being a great orator and the principal figure in South Vietnamese Buddhism. An entirely different man received me—Mai Tho Truyen, secretary-general of the "intersectional committee." In the midst of young monks in plum-colored robes, whose proud looks belied their humble comportment, I met a robust man who exhibited a quiet assurance, a square face, a crew cut, and the gleaming eyes of the big Chinese businessmen of Cholon.

This former Cochinchinese *doc-phu* (assistant prefect) had been a member of Diem's Cabinet in 1954. Then he had published a book on Buddhism in Vietnam. For a year after that, he had been the strategist of the movement that overpowered the Diem regime. Surprisingly broad-minded, he traced the history of "neo-Buddhism," the movement launched over thirty years ago which is at the root of the extraordinary resurgence of that religion in Vietnam's public life.

"In the beginning," he said, "the colonial administration greatly favored our efforts."

"The administration? Why?" From the look he gave me I realized that a Western journalist is a most unsophisticated person when confronted by a specialist in Asian religions.

"Because it was a means of turning to piety those forces that would otherwise have turned to nationalism. But, for our part, we played the game and the new Buddhists have greatly contributed to the national revival."

He spoke eloquently of the Buddhist doctrine, insisting that Buddhism is not only a moral science but leads to metaphysics, and that the notion of God in every religion is a pattern that varies only in breadth and flavor. Still, in view of the teaching of non-violence and compassion, how could the frightening activities of the summer be reconciled with the fundamental rules?

"Buddhism forbids all violence against one's neighbor. It also teaches, as does Stoicism, that man's only struggle should be his struggle with himself. How far does that struggle go? Our monks have pushed it to the extreme limits. Consider that they have made their decision against the advice of the council, and against the advice of our spiritual master, Thich Tinh Kiet. Also consider that if seven of our religious men have sacrificed themselves, more have volunteered. I still have here" —he slapped his pocket—"a list of ten more volunteers who, should the occasion arise . . . ."

Can one say that the Diem regime persecuted Buddhists? "The discrimination was intolerable and humiliating," Truyen replied, without raising his voice. But hadn't Diem offered a large sum for the building of the very pagoda in which we were conversing? Truyen took out a pad and, very much the businessman, quickly wrote on it, "Dollars—zero." Then he continued: "When I asked Diem about it, he replied that the temporal powers should not mix in religious problems. . . . But I took recourse to other means. Since I was in touch with an important personage charged with collecting duty, I learned from him that a minor percentage of revenues from betting was devoted to financing our pagoda." Betting and pyres consuming bonzes all mixed together—no, indeed, nothing is simple.

But is Buddhism ready now to exploit its "victory" over the Ngos, to take its revenge? "Victory?" said Mai Tho Truyen. "What we have won in our struggle against intolerance should not be turned against anybody at all, particularly not against our Christian brethren, most of whom have shown us great sympathy during the period of our trials." But at the popular level, are people equally level-headed? What if some other movement should make its appearance? "We have taken precautions," he said simply. A few days later a monk of whom I asked the same question gave at first the same reply. But he hastened to add: "A man who thinks only of revenge would not be a true Buddhist."

True in 1963. In 1965, as we shall see, things changed.

IV

THE GENERALS' QUADRILLE

1

ଏଏଏଏଏଏଏ

Under the Sign of
the M.A.A.G.

For years Vietnam had permanently played *Waiting for Godot*. Peace? First came the army. Nobody expected the Ngo clan to recognize the existence of the North and admit that the country's future depended on a dialogue between Hanoi and Saigon. But many thought that the army would deliver the country of that troublesome oligarchy and, realizing the vanity of the war, draw the consequences.

It was a strange army, whose brief history had cast it into a role as much political as military. It surfaced on the political plane only on November 11, 1960, when parachute units tried to overthrow the Diem regime; but this was only one episode in a story that had begun in 1950 and had been racked with controversy, abrupt changes, and arbitrary alliances. Its entire creation, its development, its training, and the changes effected in its command, were in fact always marked by negotiations, pressures, and deals that have rendered its climate one of perpetually feverish activity and instability.

Some still remember debates that were precipitated— throughout the entire Indochinese war, and particularly after

the assumption of command by General Lattre in 1951–1952
—by the "yellowfication" of the expeditionary corps, i.e., by
the participation of Vietnamese troops in the war. There were
two conflicting viewpoints: that of the former chief of the
First Army, who wanted to give Vietnamese troops a clear
and official status, heavy armaments, and important assignments, and that of his successor, General Salan, who was
much less convinced of the devotion and loyalty of these units.

Eventually the second position more or less prevailed, with
the chief of the general staff of these units, Gen. Nguyen
Van Hinh, preferring for reasons of efficiency to set up light
formations for combat in the rice paddies with supporting
missions, rather than large units and a general staff and with
its intricate services. From the beginning these discussions had
created an atmosphere of politics and controversy around the
indigenous army. But the considerable efforts of training the
cadres at the interservice school at Da Lat nevertheless eventually provided independent Vietnam with an embryonic army.
This army has perhaps not been given enough credit for having surmounted with considerable fortitude the terrible trial
inflicted on it in July 1954, when the country was partitioned
and it was forced to withdraw from the North, from which
some of its officers hailed.

Subsequently a new struggle ensued, also on the public
plane, that was to weigh heavily on the morale of these
troops: the struggle that broke out between the American and
French general staffs over who would take charge of the
training, equipment, and armament of the young Vietnamese
army. This dispute, which was to affect relations between
Paris and Washington for several months, ended in December
1954 in a compromise agreement between General Ely, then
high commissioner in Indochina, and General Lawton Collins, President Eisenhower's personal representative. But the
South Vietnamese army remained torn by contrary, if not

opposite, influences, and was for a long time to be subject to centripetal forces.

That rivalry had not ended when another crisis began—one less important on the technical plane, but graver from the point of view of morale—concerning the fate of the monarchy. In principle, at least, many officers remained loyal to Bao Dai, because they were natives of Central Vietnam, where Bao's influence remained strong, and because they had sworn an oath to him. Thus they had been hard hit in 1954, when Diem had eliminated the emperor, in 1955, when the Republic was proclaimed, and with the often brutal cashiering of officers who had remained true to the monarchy or Bao Dai personally, such as when the first commander-in-chief, General Hinh, son of the former council president, Nguyen Van Tam, and then his successor, Gen. Nguyen Van Vy, were summarily dismissed. The army was to overcome this new trial, but it remained affected by it for quite some time.

Actually, between purges following changes and psychological controls following spectacular dismissals, the regime did nothing to help its officers forget the crisis. In order to frustrate spies from the North but primarily to prevent the formation of factions, cabals, and insurrectionary movements, the order of battle and the high command of the South Vietnamese army were constantly reshuffled; generals and colonels, it was said jokingly in Saigon, were the only first-class travelers in Vietnam.

Still, this army was not the forgotten and despised force that certain Eastern, and Western, governments assumed from the angry and vengeful treatment it received at the hands of the Diem regime. Distrustful of it, the regime chose to control it by material means, rather than bully it: but where the salaries of the low-ranking officers and noncoms were low, those of the senior officers were quite decent and allowed them to participate with some éclat in public and social life. The organization of social services, equipment, armament, and so on made the Vietnamese army one of the nation's least handicapped organizations.

But the quality of these armed forces, which numbered about 250,000, was due essentially to the efforts made on their behalf by the American military mission. The M.A.A.G. (Military Aid and Advisory Group) in Vietnam was actually a sort of parallel government, equipped with great freedom of action and an annual budget of over $500,000,000. Because of its experience in South Korea experts estimated that the South Vietnamese army had become one of the best in Southeast Asia—although it probably was not the equal of that created by General Giap in the North. The failure of the parachutists to storm the Presidential palace, inhabited by the chief of state and his family, in November 1960, did not prove the army incapable of accomplishing more difficult missions under less complicated conditions.

The efforts made by the Americans clearly gave them very extensive influence. Increasingly worried about the Diem regime, Washington calculated that the army in the South was on its side in any event, and that only with its help could the government be changed or replaced, even if only to put a more efficient adversary than Diem in the path of further progress on the part of the communists.

The recall to the United States at the end of 1960 of the very influential General Williams, one of the staunch protectors of the Diem regime, seemed to herald a change at the top. Everybody began to look in the direction of generals in disgrace or semi-disgrace, such as Nguyen Khanh or Do Cao Tri, who had recently been involved in spectacular reshuffles.

The movement of November 11, 1960, had been encouraged by certain American agencies. Its failure showed, like the Laotian affair, that the various diplomatic, military, economic, and information services maintained in the South by Washington pursued about as many different policies as there were agents.

While the Ngos were guilty of police repression, military

failure, and religious discrimination, the various American services busied themselves in the shadows or semi-shadows, and ever less discreetly, anticipating the great day that was soon to come. The arrival in August 1963 of Henry Cabot Lodge as successor to Ambassador Nolting seemed to presage great changes. Then came November, opening the "coup season" that was to poison all national life, after the people had been freed from the stifling Diem dictatorship.

November 1963, January 1964, August 1964, September 1964, December 1964, January 1965, February 1965—no general trend can be discovered in this pattern.

To sum up the general ideas underlying all these adventures: the first junta was neither totalitarian nor wholly extremist, and it retained some connections with France; General Khanh, who replaced the junta, aimed at dictatorship, and until the end of 1964 he tended to serve only American interests; and the "Young Turks," who at the beginning of 1965 commanded prominent places, were both passionately "revanchist" émigrés from the North and eager young officers bucking for new stars. There was, in other words, a permanent effort to prolong the war with the help of the extremists, even though the February 1965 coup ended with the promotion of a "moderate," Gen. Tran Van Minh.

2

❧❧❧❧❧❧❧

The First Junta Is a Good Junta

Saigon, November 1963

In the humid Saigon autumn one could hardly have failed to remember the torrid summer in Cairo, eleven years earlier, when another junta overthrew another worn-out potentate.

It was said of the "Free Officers" led by General Naguib that they lacked ideology and a class foundation. But no matter how ambiguous their regime appeared at the time, Gamal Abdel Nasser, Gamal Salem, and Khaled Mohieddine had long prepared for their task, within a secret society formed in 1945 by the future *Raïs*. And because they were aware of their ties with the small landed bourgeoisie, they proposed to the Egyptian people a well-conceived agrarian reform. Those who conquered Farouk knew how to identify—by their presence, their gestures, and their simple cordiality—with the common people in Cairo and in the countryside. There was not a day when Naguib was not seen, a pleasant expression on his face and a pipe in his mouth, surrounded by a cohort of laughing men in khaki shirts, inaugurating a children's nursery or presiding over a ceremony of land distribution.

But in Saigon did anyone ever see General Minh and his

comrades, except in photos pasted on the walls of the capital? After a first appeal to the people and some general declarations the overthrowers of Diem—whom the masses awaited, hoped for, wanted to acclaim—locked themselves in the general staff building and made their ideas and intentions known only by statements in the Saigon press or in interviews granted to New York or Paris newspapers. Timidity? Uncertainty? Personal presence is primarily a posture, particularly if it reminds everybody of the end of a hated regime and the chance for freedom, if not peace. Who were these invisible men who sealed the destiny of the Ngos but who would converse only with a few foreign journalists rather than the citizens of Vietnam?

"The only officer missing at that junta," said people in Saigon, "is Gen. Coet Qui Dan"; that was how they stressed what this group owed to its military training and, more generally, to its French education. Education? Some were even of French origin, like Gen. Tran Van Don, who was born in the Gironde; and several others did more than just study in France, having spent a large part of their youth there or having made frequent trips, like Gen. Le Van Kim, who, like Colonel Duc, readily admits to being a Marseillais.

Another trait of this military group was that the military was only a secondary avocation for some of them, and the group also included several men who were only "temporary" soldiers. This was true of General Don, who was studying economics when war broke out in 1939 and he was called to the colors; of General Kim, who trained in Paris to become a movie director (working, it is said, on one of René Clair's films); of General Chieu, who studied medicine at Hanoi; and of Gen. Mai Huu Xuan, who was in the higher echelons of the French police. But General Minh, head man of the junta, was a professional soldier.

Most of the men of the revolutionary committee were also unusual because of their double origin: bourgeois and

Cochinchinese. Just as the fallen regime was composed of some of the great families of the Center—the old aristocratic Annam that was austere and mandarin—the 1963 regime seemed marked with the spirit of the South's landed bourgeoisie, impregnated with the influence of Buddhist sects, tainted with Confucianism and Taoism, and dominated by the cult of ancestors.

Men imbued with the authority of the state, who came from a poor province where the principal occupation was to collect taxes imposed on the rich zones, were thus succeeded by men from opulent regions, where the state is seen primarily as an intruder, a voracious abstraction. Yet the officers of the junta were neither anarchists nor Vietnamese variety of fascist —their military training and their bourgeois attachments prevented that. But they, more than their predecessors, seemed inclined to understand provincial peculiarities, as well as the diversity of interests and subtle play of Southern politics.

Let us add that this junta, hastily formed and not very homogeneous, was made up mostly of men who occupied no positions of command at the time of the coup. It will be objected, of course, that that is exactly why some of these generals rebelled—less because of ambition than because of the damage done to military operations by the Ngos' favoritism, nepotism, and distrust, which eventually deprived the army in combat of some of its best generals. Gen. Ton That Dinh, whom his comrades decided to include in the plot rather than to neutralize, since he commanded the Third Army Corps (that of Saigon), had once been the staunchest supporter of the Diem regime, but had then had only the most stormy relations with that regime, rendering his authority illusory for several weeks.

Observers have been surprised that the conspirators did not include in their organization the chiefs who had led and continued to lead the actual combat operations in the highlands or the rice paddies, Generals Nguyen Khanh or Do Cao Tri, for example. If asked about it, the junta would have said that these officers were consulted, had blessed the undertaking, and were associated with it. But one cannot tell whether General Khanh, for example, whom many had seen for years as the moving spirit behind a new military uprising, did not consider himself somewhat forgotten by the new regime.

And the young colonels did not hesitate to make fun of the junta, that club of general staff officers with too many stars on their shoulders, who were now too safe and too "arrived" either to deserve the appellation "revolutionaries" which they had assumed or to give all they had to the pursuit of the war.

This is a severe judgment. Yet, on the whole, the men at the general staff headquarters at Tan Son Nhut were sympathetic, and even their timidity in the face of the responsibilities they assumed had something touching about it. I have already explained how much Gen. Duong Van Minh was reminiscent of Naguib—his robustness, his simplicity, his apparent objectivity; one might add that at first glance no one like Nasser seemed to stalk the corridors of that general staff.

Four men around "Big Minh," however, asserted their personalities. There was, first of all, Gen. Tran Van Don, former chief of the general staff, and the new minister of defense. With his large face, his attentive look, and his vigorous chin he was an officer renowned for his intelligence, flexibility, and negotiating skill. His colleagues sometimes treated him like a "parlor officer," but they envied the *savoir-faire,* the wide knowledge, and the diversity of his contacts of this talented and ambitious former student of the Ecole de Chartes.

Ton That Dinh was a very different man. Petulant, agitated, loquacious, the minister of the interior was the "loudmouth" of the group. This parachutist liked to wear his camouflage-cloth uniform and parachutist's cap in his office, where he held a sort of permanent press conference. He was, in a way, the Madame Nhu of the new regime. He had that lady's ostentatious daring and striking turn of phrase. Yet he had less of a hold on the new "system" than she had on the old, and he risked becoming somewhat cumbersome to his discreet colleagues once the coup had taken place and his battalions and his audacity no longer were needed.

Some of Ton That Dinh's declarations on the need to suppress the strategic hamlets or on the circumstances of Diem's end ("That man betrayed me!" he said with aplomb) did not go over too well with his fellow officers or—even more serious—with the American Embassy, where he was considered a little "emotional." And students and Buddhists, whose demonstrations he roughly forbade in the course of the summer, did not love him at all.

Gen. Le Van Kim, brother-in-law of General Don, with his pensive eyes, his discreet smile, his soft voice, was even less a "military brute" than the others. The Diem regime held him at arm's length, and only because of his former friendly relations with Nhu did he escape the harsh repressions following the coup of November 11, 1960, whose instigators, it is said, had him in mind for a very high position. Secretary of the junta, entrusted with foreign affairs, he seemed to be a key figure in the new regime. Was he ambitious? He did not seem to be. Likely to play a political role? Probably.

Gen. Pham Xuan Chieu was the group's only Tonkinese and the only man who had been active in politics before entering the army. As a student of medicine in 1945, young Chieu had belonged to the Vietnam Quoc Dan Dang Party (V.N.Q.D.D.), the guiding spirit at the time of the national opposition against the Hanoi regime's Viet Minh. He belonged to what was called the Yen-Bay Group and had to go underground when Ho's friends unleashed their repression against the nationalists. Those early years which he spent as a militant nationalist may make the observer think of Gamal Abdel Nasser, even though this Vietnamese general did not appear to be a man of the Egyptian's stature. Slightly graying, with his sharp eyes and his even voice, he nevertheless gave the impression of being a man who knew where he was going.

And the Colonels?

The personalities of some of the other generals were less visible, particularly those of Gen. Tran Tiem Khiem, who saved Diem during the 1960 coup and seemed to devote himself exclusively to military affairs, to prepare himself all the better for intervening in political affairs; Mai Huu Xuan, former collaborator of Tam at the French police in Saigon, and czar of the new regime's police; and Tran Tu Oai, chief of the "psychological warfare" department, who, of course, became minister of information. Gen. Do Mau, who was in charge of special services during the preceding years and was military attaché in Paris, was the junta's "commissar for political affairs," charged with maintaining with the leaders of political parties those contacts likely to give this mysterious and ambiguous officer some special influence.

The question obviously was: Which colonels are hidden behind these generals? Who, in other words, are the men of tomorrow? Three names of high-ranking officers were often mentioned: Col. Le Van Duc, who seemed to be Gen. Duong Van Minh's right arm and was regarded as being very close to General Kim; Lt. Col. Pham Ngoc Thao, brother of North Vietnam's Ambassador to East Berlin, who was said to have attained exceptional results on the battlefield, but who was abroad at the time of the coup; and Maj. Vuong Van Dong, principal actor in the 1960 coup. After having sought refuge first at Phnom Penh, then in Paris, he had just returned to Saigon. But the South Vietnamese army is rich, and has many colonels.

What did these men have in common? Anti-communism, but of a kind more "functional" and less religious than that of the Ngos; a distaste for a certain form of dictatorship, which led them to promise an ultimate return to democratic liberties (true, there is hardly a military junta anywhere that does not set out by expressing such intentions); and a certain "availability," a certain intellectual curiosity that led a man like General Kim to ask questions rather than make statements.

It may be argued, too, that this primarily Cochinchinese group did not look upon the North with the same intensity as would a clan of émigrés and men who live or have lived at the borders of the Democratic Republic. Such men feel "different" rather than "against." And while nothing predisposed the Cochinchinese military or civilian bourgeois to favor communism's progress in the South, this type of man—sprung from a society of growers and merchants—was better equipped than its predecessors to establish relations with the North on a basis of equality, particularly with regard to trade exchanges. But things had not yet come to that point, and even less to a point where these men might have aimed at Vietnam's reunification within a neutralist framework. A conversation with the chiefs of the junta convinced me that they did not feel ready to take what they regarded as an excessive risk.

Reticent with regard to matters of military and diplomatic strategy, the Saigon officers were even more so in the areas of domestic policies and economic affairs. It may be surprising that they did not sport reformists labels, but they did not make the slightest allusion to agrarian reform, to the most modest nationalization of factories, or to some plan to aid the population. These men could not have been less demagogic. But so much prudence entails the risk of displeasing the masses.

3

⟨⟨⟨⟨⟨⟨⟨⟨

"Big Minh" Speaks

The generals who were victorious over Diem did not move into the ministerial offices or the Presidential palace—which were seriously damaged during the recent upheavals—but instead installed themselves in Saigon's outskirts, in the headquarters near the Tan Son Nhut airport, which had been occupied during the first Indochinese war by the commander-in-chief in Indochina: large buildings without any particular character, with many jeeps, armored vehicles, and agitated messengers. The generals were installed in two chambers on the first floor of the central pavilion, except for Minh, whose top-ranking position allowed him an immense, light office decorated in the national colors.

No matter how immense the room he occupied, General Minh did not seem lost in it. Rarely does one meet a Vietnamese of such stature, a man whose physical presence is so impressive. It is not surprising that American diplomats, military men, and journalists liked him so much: of all well-known Vietnamese he looks most like a baseball player. His large face exudes honesty; those who knew Naguib found it hard not to be reminded by this man of the Cairo revolution's first leader. But the Vietnamese general was much more circumspect than the Egyptian, and did not let himself practice Southern glibness. And he was perfectly satisfied to let his companions present during my visit—Generals Tran Van Don, minister of defense, and Le Van Kim—answer in his stead.

To my first question, on the scope and duration of the mission assumed by the junta on November 1, "Big Minh" gave a direct answer:

A. The struggle against communism. We will confine our activities strictly to South Vietnam. We have not the slightest intention of engaging in reconquest or crusades. We want to be left in peace at home, and to that end we propose to put an end to subversion.

Q. Will you keep the strategic hamlets as bases of the struggle against the Viet Cong?

A. In creating the strategic hamlets, the previous regime had two objectives: to spread the doctrine of communal "personalism," and to give a front to a war without front. Obviously, we reject the first objective, which never had the approval of the Vietnamese people.

Q. By conserving the second, do you not set up a multitude of small Dien Bien Phus?

A. We will follow experience, and of course try to improve matters. We are very impressed with the experiences of the Israeli *kibbutzim* and Malaysia's fortified villages.

Q. Is the junta planning to return all power to the politicians within the near future, and, in the meantime, to permit them to participate in its actions?

A. Let's be serious. The old regime has destroyed all political life. There is not even a party worthy of the name. We feel that political life must be reconstructed, and political structures reëstablished, before we really can call on personalities. Pending elections, we are working at establishing a committee of "wise men" that will bring political knowhow to our work.

Q. Will political leaders exiled to Europe be invited?

A. Why not? Except, of course, for communists and neutralists.

Q. Neutralists, too?

A. In the present situation, such men can only prepare the way for communism. Look at Kong Le in Laos.*

Q. Are your relations with France taking the course you hoped?

A. I'm speaking French to you. So?

Despite the broad smiles that accompanied their answers, General Minh and his companions seemed distrustful and preferred to ask questions in their turn about the meaning given to the word neutrality in Paris. The president of the junta stated that neutrality required a force of arms not yet at the disposal of the Vietnamese state, while his companions insisted that it is impossible to be neutral when under attack, and that a neutral status could not be applied to South Vietnam alone without losing its significance.

I asked General Minh:

Q. But without preparing immediately for reunification, is it not possible to establish between the two Vietnams economic, cultural, and human relations, such as exist between the two Germanys? Do you not believe that rice shipments arriving north of the 17th Parallel would be trumps in the struggle for freedom and a factor in the evolution of the Northern regime toward less rigidity?

A. I am not opposed to gestures of generosity toward undernourished populations. But I think it is impossible

---

* A debatable argument: the Pathet Lao has since denounced this instigator of the neutralist coup as an American ally.

to establish relations with people who are actually making war on us. Let them cease to attack us on our soil, and we can envisage various solutions.

While escorting me out, General Kim, his face tense, suddenly took me by the arm and said: "But this neutralism of which you talk in Paris—what is it, what does it mean? A simple pause before communization? Or a key to the reconciliation of the two Vietnams? General de Gaulle should be more explicit!"

4

♉♉♉♉♉♉♉

Khanh Emerges

Did these words reveal a guileless rejection of war and extremism? Or was it the sympathy for France which these former students at Vietnam's West Point could not hide, despite their distrust of neutralism? Still, the men of November 1 quickly provoked the disappointment of the Americans, particularly of the officers on General Harkins' staff, who soon began to look for candidates and to sound out the malcontents.

Two of these emerged above all the others: Generals Nguyen Khanh and Duong Van Duc. I have talked about the former. The latter already had a "political" history. In March 1960, when the proclamation of the National Liberation Front was about to be announced by the guerrillas in the South, and when the discussions that were to lead to the coup of November 11 were being held in the paratroopers' mess halls, young General Duc suddenly left Vietnam and went to Paris, making it known that he could no longer obey Diem's orders. Duc was to spend three years in Paris, earning a modest living in the restaurant of a political figure, Nguyen Ton Hoan, leader of the old nationalist party, Dai Viet.

Duong Van Duc's quarrel with the Ngo family was primarily because of its absurd military policy, but also because of the manner in which it had suppressed the uprising of the Hoa-Hao, the "neo-Buddhist" sect of Cochinchina's west, where Duc had many friends. The general, brave but rather simple-minded, was manipulated by the leaders of that sect before he was by certain American agencies which exploited his discontent at not having been made the leader of the revolutionary junta in November 1963, although he had been the first to break with the fallen regime.

A dull dissatisfaction was apparent within the first junta. It had not been universally fair: it had forgotten Nguyen Khanh in the North; Duong Van Duc, though he had returned from Paris and now held an important command in the South, still had no power; and it had forgotten the politicians, who, in the opinion of Nguyen Ton Hoan, Duc's old "boss" in Paris (who had also returned to Saigon), should have been given a place by the military, at least the most capable and anti-communist among them.

These various personages alerted Harkins' staff to the "activities" of Gen. Nguyen Van Vy, former army chief of staff —also recently returned from Paris—whom they denounced as a "neutralist" and a man who had established close ties with Le Van Kim. There was talk of a plot, and the rumor was that Don, Kim, and Vy were ready to come to terms with the Viet Cong.

On the night of January 30–31, Generals Kim, Don, Vy, Ton That Dinh, and Mai Huu Xuan were arrested and brought to the headquarters of the parachutists, while airborne units and armored elements took control of the capital; then they were taken to the great headquarters where the former military revolutionary committee had its seat. There they were drawn into a violent discussion by Gen. Nguyen Khanh, who was supported by the majority of his fellow generals. Tran Van Don, Le Van Kim, and Ton That Dinh—minister of defense, chief of the general staff, and minister of the interior—were placed under arrest by forces of the Third Military District, whose commander since the beginning of the month had been Gen. Tran Thien Khiem, key man in this entire affair as in that of November 1, if not with respect to its conception, at least with regard to its execution.

At 11 A.M. the same day General Khanh met Henry Cabot Lodge at the house of a mutual friend, and told him that the aim of the coup was to prevent the "neutralists," supported by a foreign power (that is, France), from taking power.

Several hours later Radio Saigon, silent until that time on the events unfolding since morning, announced in a brief communiqué that General Khanh was assuming the presidency of the Revolutionary Committee.

Besides Khanh, the most important of the new leaders were Tran Thien Khiem, commander of the Third Army Corps; Do Cao Tri, commander of the Second Corps; Nguyen Huu Co, commander of the Fourth Corps; Le Van Nghiem, commander of special forces; Pham Xuan Chieu, former security chief, who had switched camps; Tran Van Minh, former economics commissioner; Nguyen Van Thieu, commander of the Fifth Infantry Division; Lam Van Phat, commander of the Seventh Infantry Division; Do Mau, minister-designate of information; and Duong Van Duc, who, it was said, had personally arrested Don and Kim, and who was to be given the command of the Fourth Corps at Can Tho.

But who was Nguyen Khanh?

With his round face, his large eyes, and his little beard, he looked first of all like a comic-opera figure. But he was by no means just anybody. No matter how modest his origins, no matter how disconcerting the beginnings of his military career (as aide-de-camp to a Viet Minh leader in south Cochinchina, in 1946), he was rapidly promoted at a time when the nationalist Vietnamese army was quite directly controlled by the French general staff, i.e., by people not favorably inclined to the promotion of "resistance-fighter" types. A general at thirty, Nguyen Khanh was regarded by both friends and rivals as one of the four or five best officers of an army that is better than can be gauged by the results it achieved under conditions where even the best troops would have failed. At the head of a division, then an army corps, Khanh cut an honorable figure.

Then came the coup that felled Diem on November 1, 1963. The young general was at his command post at Pleiku, in the Central Highlands, and he little realized that his colleagues had taken power in his absence. He was told about it, at least, and when, several weeks later, it seemed that the chiefs of the first junta were not particularly gifted war leaders, relations became closer between General Harkins, the American commander-in-chief in Saigon, and the young officer whose intelligence and combativeness he appreciated.

We do not know that Ambassador Lodge was happier with the coup of January 30, 1964, that put Khanh in power than Khanh had been with the coup of the preceding November 30.

But the step had been taken. Nguyen Khanh, flanked by Paul Harkins, was in power. Six months later, on the day when the American general left Indochina, a scene took place that spoke volumes about the close ties between the two men: the tall Harkins put his arms around the shoulders of his small colleague, and looking like a father giving final instructions to his son, took a long walk with him at Tan Son Nhut airport.

But the counsel of his American friends was not always good. On August 5, after a strange engagement in the Gulf of Tonkin between two small North Vietnamese torpedo boats and much stronger units of the American Seventh Fleet, Washington decided on a reprisal operation north of the 17th Parallel. This turned out to be an operation strafing military installations in the Hanoi and Vinh regions, which gave the impression to extremists in Saigon that the communist North would now be attacked.

Khanh could not keep his equanimity and he believed that the hour of absolute power had arrived. Secluded in his villa at Cap Saint-Jacques, he composed with the help of two jurists a "constitution" concentrating in his hands all civil and military power, that was promulgated on August 15. Immediately, the people of Saigon objected. Wave after wave of students and Buddhists assembled and marched toward the general's residence.

Surrounded, pressed, called out by a group of students from his residence on August 27, 1964, Khanh was hoisted onto a tank. And there, in response to the shouts of the mass of young people, many of whom were barely thirteen or fourteen years old, he was forced to say things that were hardly popular in military mess halls, especially the following: "Down with military power, down with dictatorships, down with the army!"

Anybody else would have been ridiculed, but not Nguyen Khanh, even though this horrible loss of face forced him to hide for several days in Da Lat. He then talked of resigning. Was he sincere? Did the Americans—who at that time kept saying, "It's Khanh or chaos . . ."—really force him to resume his responsibilities at Saigon? In any event, his "return" to Saigon was tentative enough to rekindle the ambitions of other men, principally the following three: Generals Duong Van Duc, Lam Van Phat, and Nguyen Cao Ky. The first two joined the fray, apparently with little foresight. The third let himself be carried by the wave, and when the moment had come, he knew how to choose the victors' camp and to impose his authority, from the very heights where his planes were flying.

A strange story, that third coup of September 13! Two days before, toward the end of the afternoon, I had been talking with one of Khanh's close collaborators, when the telephone rang: an American colleague wanted to know whether it was true that a "Catholic coup will take place on Sunday." A seemingly preposterous question; but the Vietnamese officer laughed because he had already been apprised of this rumor. The man who had called me even gave the name of the instigator of the alleged coup—Colonel Ton, who had just been relieved of his command of the Seventh Army Corps at My Tho, close to the essential strategic sector of the Plain of Joncs, because of his ties to the Dai Viet party. And a young officer, brilliant, relieved of his prestigious command, harboring ideas different from those of the government, and having tanks at his disposal fifty miles from the capital, does deserve to be taken into account.

Other rumors foresaw hostile actions on the part of General Duc, commander of the Fourth Corps at Can Tho, capital of the Mekong Delta, who—it was then remembered—had been a personal enemy of the four generals eliminated after the previous January 30 coup and who were to be reinstated in the army this same Sunday.

The officer I talked to that evening, who had already been alerted to all this, told me that between Friday night and Sunday morning he had tried to alert all troops around Saigon supposedly loyal to Khanh, but that he had found nothing but fence straddlers. I asked: "And this is the moment Khanh has picked to go to Da Lat and leave the capital?" "Yes, in order to be safe. In Saigon, he felt surrounded by enemies."

The conspirators in the Delta counted on the support or the benevolent neutrality of General Ky, commander of the air force, who favored operations against the North and considered Khanh and Minh to be "soft." He had declared that he would crush any coup within five hours, but from high enough in the sky not to arouse suspicion. As soon as troop movements began from My Tho to Saigon, at dusk on Sunday, Ky's planes constantly flew over them; the troops believed that this was air support, while the air chief actually computed how many troops were on the march and how many had remained loyal. He also seems to have supported Khanh from the beginning of the morning, presumably considering the operation too light and its leader too mediocre, and probably estimating that it was more advantageous to save Khanh than to participate in the fray.

Meanwhile, despite Khanh's appeal issued from Da Lat, the matter remained undecided until evening. Only at 11 P.M., in the course of a meeting in the office of air force chief of staff General Ky, did Khanh (who had returned to Saigon) and Duc (the apparent chief of the rebels), who were soon joined by American Deputy Ambassador Alexis Johnson, and General Moore, and later by General Minh (who was still President), emerge from their clandestine existence in the city and lay down the broad lines of a compromise.

In all, the day had been an illustration of the old Chinese strategy, according to which it is better to use armies to threaten and make a show of oneself than to fight, since soldiers are more valuable alive than dead; the day ended with the promotion of the young chiefs, who had beaten out their elders on this classic terrain and now figured as the arbiters in the army. The colonels were the men of the hour.

The Monday press conference was an amazing spectacle. On the stage of the Vietnamese Air Force Theatre nine men, one after another, read declarations of unity more or less identical with those they had made the night before to tear each other apart. But the names had been scratched out, and the blows were now aimed at shadows. Still, the joint four-point declaration specified that the struggle against the Viet Cong was to be intensified and that religion was not to be mixed up with politics—a swipe at the Buddhists. The theatrical character of the scene was enhanced by the machine guns pointed by the guards at the journalists, apparently to make them take the situation seriously.

Obviously this new patched-up regime was even more

fragile than that of late August, which had put General
Khanh in the saddle. It is no less obvious that Khanh's position as chief of government was saved a second time by Gen.
Maxwell Taylor's providential return at that moment from
the United States. The latter's deputy, Alexis Johnson,
stated that "everything is much better now." Thus, American
policy remained based on General Khanh, despite the new
coup that took place against him. The general, after having
had to accept all the conditions made by the Buddhists at
the end of August, now had to swallow the affront of reconciliation after the challenge of September 13. He seemed to
be a prisoner in a double sense of the word. But whoever
knew his possible successors understood better why the American leaders attached such value to this man of January 30.

This regime of young wolves was to weigh less heavily in
the coming weeks. General Khanh, pressed from the Left by
students and Buddhists, was likely to survive—except for the
fact that he also had American support—only because the
young colonels considered him at their mercy ever since they
tipped the scales in his favor on the morning of September 1.
The mass and youth organizations had taken his measure when
they made him yield on August 27, and they planned to do it
again. Hostage of the military Right, hostage of the political
Left, General Khanh walked a twisting road, more and more
feeble on his two crutches, wedged in by a double opposition.
The Americans no longer tried to hide their confusion and
anger. Khanh's isolation was their isolation, and the army
they coddled for ten years subordinated its strategic tasks to
the settling of half-personal or half-political accounts.

This third coup also provided other lessons: (1.) The air
force played a dominant role in controlling masses of
people, even when the large buildings and key posts were
already occupied; (2.) this air force was itself controlled by
the U. S. Air Force, as it was integrated into it and depended
on it for its fuel, armament, and even ground installations;
(3.) the Americans, in possession of this "absolute" weapon,

continued to bet on General Khanh, but now also through a second man, air force chief General Ky, who was now for them simultaneously transmission belt, control element, and ultimately replacement for Khanh, should he try to play against them.

Thus, that Sunday which had begun as a psychological defeat for the Americans ended up by proving, if not consolidating, their hold on the South Vietnamese politico-military machine. But the question was: Once the names of the fifty-two South Vietnamese army generals were tossed in Uncle Sam's hat, and Ky has been replaced by Vy or by Thi, what would happen?

5

〰〰〰〰〰

Colorful General Ky

The day I went to see General Ky, victor of the coup of September 13, and the rising star of South Vietnam, he was not dressed in the salmon-colored flying suit that prompted the Americans to call him the "colorful" general, but had a silk kerchief artistically tied and slipped into his uniform. With his slight figure, his fine mustache, his slicked-down hair, the thirty-three-year-old general looked at first glance like a daring pilot or a tango dancer. But his look was intelligent, his resolution obvious, his tone polite. He was a man clearly aware of his responsibilities.

Q. Would the coup on Sunday have succeeded without your air force?

A. Yes, at least for a while.

Q. Is it impossible to prevent a similar adventure, or at least cut off the route from My Tho, and prevent access to Saigon to the Seventh Division?

A. From the beginning of the troop movements, my planes flew over the putschists. My men wanted to strafe

them, but I forbade them to kill Vietnamese soldiers un-
aware of the role that their leaders forced them to play.
It was necessary to dissolve the rebellion gently. I am
quite proud to have been able to achieve that.

Q. Are you sincerely in favor of returning power to
the politicians?

A. Of course. It's their job, not ours. We are here to
run the war.

Q. And if, on the occasion of organizing a new state
organism, and then of elections, neutralist or pro-communist elements should come to power?

A. Well, then we would consider it our right to intervene in order to prevent treason.

Q. Are you a Buddhist?

A. Oh, well . . . except for the Catholics, we Vietnamese are not too sure what we are. My parents occasionally went to the pagoda.

Q. Do you approve of the attitude of the Buddhist
hierarchy?

A. I am not a political man, I don't have to answer
that.

Q. Are you from the South?

A. No, from the North.

Q. You have been quoted as favoring military action
against the North. Is that accurate?

A. Absolutely, and some action has already taken
place.

Q. Honestly now, do you consider that wise, and
within the capabilities of the South?

A. My viewpoint is purely strategic. We are being
attacked on our ground. We must reply, else we are lost.

Q. Northern intervention in the South is hard to
prove.

A. Come now! We have found Russian and Chinese
weapons and maps printed in the North. Everybody
knows that this a war between North and South.

Q. But the North claims it isn't—that it is a civil war between Southerners.

A. So? I am from the North, so I could say that I am participating in a civil war between Northerners.

Q. But can you conduct such operations without American agreement and support?"

For the first time in our talk, Ky seemed angry. He remained polite but replied in a passionate tone of voice:

A. Sir, I can order and execute operations at any moment. On our side the time of empty talk has passed. . . .

After that Nguyen Khanh lived on borrowed time. Not only because he was nothing more than the captive of the "Young Turks" and the Americans, or because he was forced to accept the return of a civil government on October 27—with Pham Khac Suu as President of the Republic, and Tran Van Huong as President of the Council—but because his relations with U. S. Ambassador Maxwell Taylor had been deteriorating from day to day.

In the last days of August and the first of September, Khanh, ridiculed by the students and threatened by the Buddhists with the choice between massacre and retreat, had retired to Da Lat without intention of returning; Taylor literally took him by the arm and reinstated him in the Presidential office in Saigon.

The coup of September 13 led to the first break between Khanh and Taylor: the Vietnamese general had been of the opinion that the representative of the United States had not exactly acted as an ally when he let the "Young Turks" arbitrate the dispute instead of giving him alone the means to reëstablish his authority.

Returned to military life, Khanh first took care to rebuild his ties with the unit leaders and staffs which he had somewhat neglected during the past year. He was again seen on the battlefields, and in November he held a press conference near one of the lines of fire. In an effort to rebuild his image as a parachutist with a musketeer's beard, he asserted, with the good-natured demeanor of a big soldier who would rather dirty his boots in the rice paddies than his hands in the ministries at Saigon, that he had no thought of retaking power "unless the situation demands it."

Six weeks later, on September 20, the fourth coup took place, called by its instigators, the "Young Turks," the "partial coup d'état." The operation was essentially directed against the nation's High Council—that organism set up at the end of October and comprising those politicians who, in the eyes of the extremists in the Vietnamese army, had two faults: they refused to retire some of the officers who stood in the way of their promotion, and they had gradually succumbed to the popular pacifism.

Behind the coup the hand of General Khanh was thought to be visible. But the operation was conducted by men who had assumed the role of arbiter in the September conflict, insuring Khanh's appointment in order the better to affirm themselves: Ky, Thi, and Khang, aspiring to advance in rank in return for the great services they had rendered the nation.

Ky's demeanor seems to have been guided by two fixed ideas. The first was his constant intention to carry the war to the North, which in his mind, that of a refugee from Tonkin, assumed the form of an obsession. The second was his fear of appearing to be an American puppet, and of simply executing U.S. air strategy. With him "everything goes," if it affirms his independence of action, and he came eventually to insist that the operation of December 20 was decided, and even executed, without American knowledge. Would he now try to show that he did not need American approval or support to attack bases in the North?

Gen. Nguyen Chanh Thi was one of the leaders of the coup of November 11, 1960, against the regime of the Ngos.

Did he act in self-defense? Those who launched the movement at that time, particularly Commander Dong, have often since stated that this leader had mainly just followed his troops; but the episode remained to his credit, and assured him of a sort of top role in this group of "revolutionaries," with their loud talk and their obvious goals. On September 13 Thi had been in the role of grand inquisitor, announcing that the "umpireship" of the young colonels was primarily aimed at preparing a radical purge of Viet Cong and neutralist elements that had slipped into the army and the administration. Hue had become his fief, and he had first made common cause there with Dr. Quyen's Committee for the Public Weal; but the latter was among the victims of the latest "burning": this public prosecutor hit even at his friends if they seemed to be "neutralists" in any way whatever.

Gen. Le Nguyen Khang, a man from Tonkin like his comrade Ky, never disguised his low opinion of Vietnamese politicians. With the head of a pensive intellectual, he expressed the greatest contempt for those who do not wear uniforms; and the day after the September affair he was overheard to say that no civilian would be able to exercise power in Vietnam.

Aside from organizational motivations that clearly propelled these *nouvelle vague* conspirators—such as rivalry between generations and services, or fear of a counter-purge in the army by Gen. Tran Van Don and the "Da Lat group," defeated on January 30 and recently integrated into the army— the new coup had more serious causes and seemed to have been part of an "extremist" trend.

The coup of December 20 hit Tran Van Huong, head of the government, who had been denounced as an evil man only by the Buddhists, and whom all others had regarded as an old sage without ambition, a man capable of discreet negotiations and efficacious whisperings.

6

❦❦❦❦❦❦❦

Colonel Thao Loses
His Nerve

Thao had opened the way for the operation of January 28, 1965, against the civil authorities, which General Khanh openly supported this time. This was a "return" that could have seemed routine, so simple was it for a military man controlling the armored units and planes stationed in the Saigon sector to install himself in the office of the president of the council. This was the aspect taken on by the return to power of this thirty-eight-year-old general who had publicly been forced to denounce the army's political role, to link himself to the Americans and repress religious movements, and who was suddenly swept upward by a military, pro-Buddhist, anti-American wave.

At that moment the crisis that had been simmering between the top general and the American Embassy broke out in public. Like all U.S. representatives, Maxwell Taylor favored the largest degree of "formal democracy" possible in a war-torn country. And, being a general, he urged all the more effort in promoting a system designed to give a good conscience to the leaders of a nation whose troops were supposed to be defending the people's freedom. Inheriting from his predecessor a general at the head of the Vietnamese government, Taylor tried his best to support him.

But as soon as an apparently legal civilian regime established itself, presided over by Suu—an old leader who was, if not popular, at least respected, and had been one of the most courageous opponents of the Diem regime—General Taylor felt he was on the right track: the United States, in his person, was now defending democracy. And now General Khanh, violating his promises—formulated more specifically in private than in public—destroyed this fragile edifice of legitimacy, using Maxwell Taylor as his intermediary. With obvious sincerity, General Khanh described General Taylor's activities during those last December days: "His attitude concerning my small head exceeded the imagination, *considering that he was an ambassador.*"

The statement is good, but will it not turn against its authors? Is a man really an "ambassador" if he represents a country through whose effort alone, from a distance of ten thousand miles away, the country in which he is representing it can survive? In that sense the 1953 situation of the French representatives was more reasonable, and Lattre's role less thankless than that of his present-day American counterpart.

In other circumstances in other countries, nationalist leaders broke with the United States on the same day that General Khanh denounced American interference in the political affairs of his country; President Nasser made a violent speech against the United States: who would have expected such words from the man who thirteen years before had been the friend and protégé of Jefferson Caffery, and whose position had been saved by Washington during the Suez crisis? But the man in Cairo no longer depended on American good will for his survival. Did the man in Saigon?

Did Gen. Nguyen Khanh, when turning into a haughty defender of Vietnamese independence, think that by knitting

his brow and raising his voice he would get more out of the
United States, as some precedents may have led him to think?
Or did he prepare for a profound political reconversion by
trying to impose himself on the guerrillas and the Buddhist
leaders as a determined patriot? When it was his turn to cry,
"Out with Taylor!"—that slogan which had been inscribed on
placards brandished in February at Saigon by columns of
demonstrators—did General Khanh pose as a true spokesman
of those whose battle in the rice paddies had as its prime objective the expulsion of the Americans from Vietnam?

Clearly, Nguyen Khanh did not have the stature for such
an operation. He was going to be the victim of the sixth coup,
in February 1965, the first staged by a colonel, but a colonel
of exceptional stature. For those who have had contact with
Vietnamese army chiefs, Colonel Thao—whose Catholic first
name is Albert—is one of the two or three most interesting
personalities, and one of the most capable of playing a political role. Member of a great Catholic family of the South,
he had joined the Viet Minh guerrillas in 1946 with his
brother Gaston, then vice-president of the Nam Bao Committee and today president of the Cultural Council of North
Vietnam. Converted to Diemism in 1955 by Msgr. Ngo Dinh
Thuc, Thao underwent long training in the United States
before taking over the command of the most "rotten" province in the Mekong Delta in 1962, where he acquired a reputation of authority and cleverness.

In 1964 he became spokesman for General Khanh. He
turned out to be one of the most intelligent officers of the
nationalist army, and it was whispered that he might be a
connecting link between the two armies to which he had belonged one after the other. But at the same time he did not
hide his attachment to the Catholic hierarchy or to General
Khiem, one of the most reactionary leaders of the Southern
army.

Removed from Saigon in October 1964 by Khanh, who
did not trust his loyalty, Thao was made press attaché at

Washington, where he established contacts with a wide variety of circles, including those of Sen. Barry Goldwater. In December, Thao's friend General Khiem was named Ambassador to Washington: what was being planned by the group that had been broken up by Khanh two months earlier?

On Friday, February 19, a group of officers seized Saigon's radio station and airport. They claimed that their leaders were Col. Pham Ngoc Thao and several of the officers who had tried to lead the coup on September 13, 1964, among them General Phat. The instigators of the coup denounced Khanh's "thirst for power" and called for a civil authority, but one that would be anti-communist and anti-neutralist. General Khiem, South Vietnam's new Ambassador to Washington, approved the coup; and even though Khiem is known to be nostalgic for the old regime, people were surprised to hear Radio Saigon eulogize Diem on Friday night.

After a three-day inspection tour of the troops in the Mekong Delta, General Khanh rallied several generals to his cause. On Saturday morning, troops retook Saigon in his name without firing a shot. The Thao group disintegrated. Was General Khanh again in the saddle? At that point General Thi, arrived from Hue, and declared that Khanh had been removed from the military junta. Arrest warrants were issued for the conspirators of Friday, but the generals that made up the government came out for the removal of General Khahn from the presidency of the army council.

On Sunday morning tank movements were reported near Saigon's airport. Apparently Khanh was trying to make a comeback. But it was learned that he was in Da Lat, where he was initiating telephonic negotiations with Saigon. American officers participated in this. The general soon recognized his defeat and retired from power. The President of the Republic deprived him of his command, and in his stead named Gen. Tran Van Minh, called "Little Minh."

The sixth coup was over. Thao had failed in his effort, despite his support from the Catholics and certain American agencies. But Khanh was removed: he was to become a roving ambassador. The man who had based his career on politics and American agencies had—like the Ngos—paid for his attempt to reëstablish a certain independence from the Americans, or even to prepare, against them, the beginning of a turnaround.

V

KNIFE AND
HELICOPTER

1

❦❦❦❦❦❦❦

Chasing the VC

Saigon, December 1963

General Harkins' spokesman, Commander S., copper-haired, pale, and diligent, described the second war in Vietnam, aided by figures, photos, and lines on the map. His talk conjured up the ghost of another officer who, in 1953 in the office next door, had spoken to us of "our" war (or rather "the war of the Vietnamese against communist subversion, that we are helping them to win"—in American or French, the formula is the same). The officer then was a certain Gardes, who, as a colonel, later attained some degree of celebrity in Algiers.

Between Colonel Gardes and his successor there was that world of difference between the French Expeditionary Corps and the army of American "advisers" which had now been in Saigon for almost three years. The former was a wild armada of more or less romantic conquistadors, swaggering and unconcerned, and pot-bellied refugees from French provincial garrisons. It was followed by a corps of specialists whose behavior was more like that of volunteers rendering technical assistance than of brawling cowboys.

Along the old rue Catinat there is about one night club for

every three buildings—the infrastructure of nocturnal pleasures that was given new life by Diem's defeat. Under Massu or Bollardière, in 1946, as under other French generals seven years later, the soldiers between stretches in the rice paddies lived it up in nocturnal Saigon. In 1963 long lines of soldiers in civilian clothes, resting their elbows gravely on the long bars, patiently drank beer while telling the taxi-dancers about their fiancées in Arkansas or elsewhere, and about the dangerous virtues of their helicopters. Yet on the other side of the Chinese bars an unexpectedly tenacious segregation confined the colored soldiers to the bars on the avenue Trinh Minh The, where they create a somewhat "hotter"—though very decent—atmosphere in the small cabarets still frequented by the robust leaders from Calvi and Toulon.

According to General Harkins' spokesman, by the end of 1963 the new war in Vietnam had brought a corps of guerrillas, with a hard core of about twenty-five thousand plus sixty to eighty thousand irregulars supported by around three hundred thousand "sympathizers," face to face with a nationalist army of four hundred thousand men, including the civil guard and self-defense groups, "advised" by a little more than sixteen thousand American military men (with civilian services estimated at thirty-five hundred persons). These figures were probably reliable, and told us even more when the increase in the number of American effectives since 1961 was compared to that of the guerrillas; in number the increases were strangely parallel. And of course they were on the rise in 1964 and 1965.

The extent to which the American officers emphasized transports, communications, and infrastructure was striking, and it did not seem to square with the idea of a temporary mission in Vietnam, as described in the McNamara-Taylor report of October 1963. The Americans in Saigon did not deny the increase in the number of their forces or in the amount of heavy equipment placed in the hands of the Viet Cong in the course of 1962, nor the progressive increase of Viet Cong units from company size (the famous "chi-doi" of the preceding war) to larger units. Battalions? The Americans did not deny that there were some. In September 1963 nationalist forces encountered a unit of almost a thousand men near Ca Mau.

Can we conclude from this, by applying the pattern of classic revolutionary war, that the Viet Cong had passed from the first phase (conditioning the population) to the second (organized guerrilla warfare) in order to enter the third (the formation of large units) before arriving at the fourth (the "general counter-offensive," like the one announced by General Giap in 1953)? Not yet. But the revolutionary forces constantly increased their hold on very large sectors: Quang Ngai center, the Plain of Joncs, western Cochinchina, Bentré, Ca Mau, and the plantation zone in northern Cochinchina.

From 1954—the year of the Geneva Agreements—to 1959 there was peace in that region. By 1963 it was no longer possible to go to Loc Ninh except by plane or with a heavily armed escort. But toward the east, in the Xuan Loc region, we were able to travel on some Sundays as though going on a picnic near Fontainebleau. We were told that the road was safe, and it was, beyond all expectations.

The rebels were installed in the plantations, and when we traveled through the splendid forest of rubber trees or the high grass in the hills, we felt keenly the presence of the guerrillas. Each of the "planters" told us his story of how things had been taken from him and taxes imposed on him. Some even told us that the guerrillas no longer demanded more ransom, but collected regular taxes apparently calculated on the basis of the taxes which these same people had to pay to the powers in Saigon. The financial operations of the Viet Cong had seemingly attained a sort of codification and "institutionalization." But all this had taken place in a climate of curious secrecy.

For half a day in October 1963, for example, a guerrilla unit blocked the "mandarin" road between Saigon and Hue,

southeast of Phan Thiet, and detoured all vehicles to an immense clearing, where it held a regular meeting, expounding
particularly the ideas held by the South's National Liberation
Front on the change of regime in Saigon, a change the guerrillas considered illusory. The listeners were then permitted
to proceed, after having been relieved of some of their valua-
bles, while the commander of the unit apologized to his
briefly held prisoners. One of these told us of his adventure
and said he was struck by the calm authority of his inter-
locutors, and by the rather belated arrival of government
forces.

But most N.L.F. pressure plainly took other forms. No day
passed without the announcement of an attack on a strategic
hamlet by the guerrillas, nor a week without the fall of one
of these bastions, nor a month in which a large nationalist
unit, officered by American "advisers," was not roughly engaged by the "VCs," who, in the language of the Americans,
replaced the "Viets" of the French war. Strategic Hamlets—
that was the magic formula. Some considered them the beginning of victory; others, the ultimate catastrophe. The only
serious debate on military operation since the end of the Ngo
regime centered around these strategic hamlets. Was it necessary to preserve this "great idea" of the fallen regime even
though with reservations? Or should it have been shunned,
as a poisonous emanation of Nhu's "philosophy"? Nhu had
invented them, in collaboration with the American economist
Eugene Staley, whose 1961 report played such a decisive role,
as we have seen.

In the Go Vap district near Saigon—where the Viet Minh
were so strongly implanted ten years ago that the Viet Cong
now found their bed readymade—was the model hamlet of
Cong-Song, a Vietnamese Petit Trianon. Nowhere did the
buffalo look gentler or the tall, well-balanced coconut trees
more elegant; nowhere were the green landscapes of the rice
paddies more tender or the altars of the ancestors more
charming.

I had seen other refugee villages, also transformed into strategic hamlets, whose fortifications—a simple abutment of earth reinforced with cut-down bamboo trees—had made me think that the technique of Vercingetorix, rather than that of Vauban, was being taught in our Vietnamese schools. This in turn had made me think of the story of an emperor of China. Seeing a peasant raising a small dam around his field, the emperor had asked him: "Do you think you can stop bandits in this fashion?" To which the peasant had replied: "*You* are the one who has to stop the bandits. I defend myself only against the small thieves."

Bandits or small thieves, everybody could get along with everybody else around or inside the model barbed-wire enclosures, so gaily whitewashed that even the most nearsighted of the guerrillas could be sure not to get entangled in them. Even the mines had to be indicated, with (nationalist) flags, and in the center of the reception area, opposite the school where we were being given coconuts, remorseful dissidents were whiling away their days.

But enough irony. Aside from such Hollywood features, these strategic hamlets definitely existed; it was enough to fly over the Mekong Delta or central Cochinchina for several hours to convince oneself of the density, if not the efficiency, of this arrangement. No power conducting the present war in Vietnam could do without this framework. To be sure, the existence of these small hedgehogs did not permit a war of movement. To turn them into shelters, where from dusk to dawn the "legal" population was enclosed in order to isolate the guerrillas, and to leave it at that, meant to prepare just so many small Dien Bien Phus, or another Maginot Line, as an American spokesman has called it.

A war of movement? The American "advisers" were really pushing their allies in that direction, assuming, incidentally, a large part of the risk involved. But could the Army of the Republic of Vietnam (A.R.V.N., pronounced "Arvin") really get down into the rice paddies? These soldiers did not make a bad impression, and many of the young officers deserved their rank. Much serious work had been done since 1950. Yet this army went about in pressed pants, and even though it was genuinely indigenous, did not seem to be brimming over with the desire to dirty its boots in the Vinh Long swamps.

The Vietnamese military leaders admitted, just as did their American colleagues, that it was necessary to "shape up the troops" outside of the bases or the fortified villages. But the Vietnamese were more reserved on one point: General Harkins' staff wanted to increase the number of strategic hamlets to the very maximum—in the beginning of 1964 there were about eight thousand—while General Minh believed that this method should be employed only in zones that had already been more or less recaptured. To establish a strategic hamlet in a contested sector is to risk seeing it fall, or fall again, into the hands of the VC, which would discourage the population by involving it unnecessarily in military action (in the words so often used by our officers, for ten long years, from Phat Diem to Tizi Ouzou).

In brief, this is one of the few areas in which Americans have followed Vietnamese advice; after General Harkins' departure his successor, General Westmoreland, changed course. Moreover, most Vietnamese officers wanted to superimpose the strategic hamlets on existing rural agglomerations as far as possible, in order not to destroy the nation's substructure in the countryside, as Nhu had risked doing in his eagerness to succeed. In this ancient country to jeopardize the village structure by setting up artificial agglomerations is to break the backbone of the country itself, to go against its collective conscience, its beliefs, and its homogeneity at the deepest level; this is true particularly if this system of intensive organization, and close and permanent control—as visualized by Nhu in his attempt at a hasty imitation of his Chinese enemies —destroys the family cell, that other basic fact of Vietnamese society.

"Don't liquidate the strategic hamlets, just remove their political aspects"—with this formula a junta spokesman proposes a solution to the problem. But in an ideological war what weapons has he who does not descend into the political arena? If he who wields power has nothing to propose to those on whom he forces the heavy discipline of the strategic hamlets, such a system must be only a method of sorting out the two segments of the population each night. It would denounce and define the "bad guys," and isolate and protect the "good guys." But today one can apply to the Viet Cong the striking formula of a French officer who said, during the first Indo-Chinese war: "What is a Viet Minh?—A Viet Minh? He is a dead Vietnamese. . . ."

By 1963 it was the Americans' turn to conduct this Sisyphean war in the rice paddies. Perhaps they can do it better than we did, at least to the extent that the struggle now takes its impetus from a reality—Vietnamese nationalism—which France did not know how to nourish in time to make a valuable force of it. Now a Vietnamese state does exist. Whatever its shortcomings, it offers an alternative, at least a provisional alternative.

In an earlier day one could say that a Viet Minh fighter slumbered in every Vietnamese patriot. One cannot say the same of the Viet Cong. The National Liberation Front comprises a good proportion of upright men south of the 17th Parallel (the priest quoted earlier spoke of "four fifths of the Front being good men"), but it does not stand for the nation: it is the party of revolution.

Today one sees that the war only increases the N.L.F.'s numbers and the aid rendered to it, while it impairs the harvests in the South and impoverishes the North, welding it to China.

May 1964

Eleven years ago, on May 7, 1954, the fall of the fortified camp of Dien Bien Phu ushered in the final phase of the liquidation of colonial empires. The assault by General Giap's battalions led to a qualitative change in the history of decolonization, which ceased being one of the possible options of the colonizers, and became an absolute necessity for the colonized. From then on, from Hanoi to Casablanca, there was no longer any choice between maintaining one's position or retreating, but only among various types and rhythms of retreat.

In May 1964 the war in Vietnam was going through a new and possibly decisive acceleration. Perhaps to greet this solemn anniversary? The strategic manual of revolutionary war shows four phases: psychological preparation of the population, organization of the guerrilla force, formation of large units, and the great counter-offensive. Did the leaders of South Vietnam's N.L.F. and their advisers in Hanoi think they had arrived at the fourth stage of their program?

To be sure, one must not attach exaggerated importance to the daring exploit of the Viet Cong frogmen who on May 1, 1964, sank an important unit of the U. S. Navy in the port of Saigon. But for the veterans of the French Expeditionary Corps of 1945, this episode brought back a memory and served as a lesson. When the Viet Minh had announced that its men had sunk the French battleship *Richelieu* at Cap Saint-Jacques, the "exploit" had been greeted everywhere with laughter. By mid-1964 no one laughed.

Perhaps the N.L.F. has not attained the degree of national mobilization—or, perhaps one should say, nationalist mobilization—against the powers in Saigon that the Viet Minh had attained in 1945 against the last forms of colonial power, because in 1964 a great many people regarded such mobilization as Marxist-Leninist measures whose vices were as well known as their virtues. But it must be noted that its technique of combat, its armament, and its strategy have been honed to a fine point and strengthened over the years. If they were losing men every day, they also captured American weapons, which have been supplying the Asian revolution ever since the first defeats of the Kuomintang by Mao during the last engagements at the Point of Ca Mau.

To assess the N.L.F.'s military progress in 1964, one must not look merely at some particular engagement or commando raid or ambush or even at the losses of the nationalists—for example, two thousand men between April 11 and April 18, with two hundred killed—even though the losses registered were double what they were during the corresponding period a year earlier; rather, one must make a more basic observation. Only five months earlier, French and American military observers in Saigon expressed doubts to journalists that Viet Cong units as large as a battalion were in existence, and estimated that the enemy leaders disposed only of company-strength forces, even though they had been able to marshal over a thousand men in a single operation in the south of the Mekong Delta at the end of September.

But subsequent communiqués talked of Viet Cong battalions, and the combined staff of the Plain of Jones and Hanoi considered themselves strong enough to throw powerful units against General Khanh's divisions, which had officers and military support from General Westmoreland's men. This transition to large units had been criticized in 1951, when General Giap had wanted to oppose his first divisions to General Lattre's. He had paid dearly for it, particularly at Vinh Yen. But it marked the turning point of the war: formed as a humble guerrilla force, the People's Army had subsequently prepared the great assaults of 1954.

The indications were that the American and Vietnamese leaders in Saigon were not facing a new Dien Bien Phu. If the political situation in the South Vietnamese capital appeared as chaotic and desperate as ten years before, the military problems were much smaller. If the Southern forces could ward off enemy blows in the Mekong Delta and in Quang Ngai, they no longer would have to cope with that open plain that had plagued Navarre and his predecessors in the Tonkin delta.

Complementing this retrenchment of operations seemed to be an increase of military means, made possible by the Americans, who brought several aircraft carriers to Vietnam, whose planes would be capable of engaging in "carpet bombing," and disposed of infinitely greater fire power per square kilometer than the French command could marshal in 1954.

November 1964

Toward the end of 1945, on the road toward My Tho and the Delta, I had once found myself perched on one of Colonel Massu's armored vehicles. Now the perverse charm of the rice paddies, though it exuded the same insidious and silent hostility, seemed, from an Iroquois helicopter, intensified.

The Iroquois are the best helicopters used by the Americans in Vietnam. Less maneuverable perhaps than the French Alouettes, they are fast and relatively comfortable. Strapped in like a prisoner, I felt as if we were playing a scene from *Dr. Strangelove,* flanked as I was by American warriors in their formidable white helmets that seem borrowed from spacemen.

Warriors, indeed. It is really surprising that after so much reporting on the second war in Vietnam, the legend of the American "advisers" should have been kept alive for so long, to the point that in March 1965 the participation of American pilots and machine-gunners in military operations over the Mekong Delta was greeted as a novelty and even a turning point in the war.

Advisers? The two fellows sitting at my right and my left, as if suspended in the void, with all doors open three thousand feet above the ground, their fingers on the triggers of the heavy machine guns, were indeed combatants. They spent their time flying over the rice paddies, lying in wait for movement in the bamboo forest, at the borders of the villages, and at the sides of the hills which the helicopters pass at close range. "All that moves must be considered as VC," according to the men in the Iroquois.

Whom were they advising, whom were they officering, these hundreds of pilots assembled at the base of Vung Tau, the old Cap Saint-Jacques, in September 1964? Neither on the metal landing strips, nor at the borders of the base, nor in the cafeteria, nor in the general staff offices did I see a single Vietnamese. Those were Americans engaged in war missions, facing an adversary from close quarters who was presumed to be hidden on the sides of the hills, toward Baria.

In the course of high-level, organized operations against the Viet Cong, the Arvin played the "leading role," were the most visible, and suffered the heaviest losses. But in most of the great bases of South Vietnam, from Da Nang to Bien Hoa, and from Tan Son Nhut to Vung Tau, Americans were among them, facing the enemy, and no longer making any distinction between actual combat missions and their tasks of supervision and the technical concerns with which—in principle—they were charged.

Not far from Vung Tau, I was able to observe a curious aspect of this war and the part taken in it by certain Americans, when I saw what was called the "Junk Force." I had been taken in tow by an unbelievable character, a mixture of Popeye and Lyndon Johnson, with the sailor's gait one might encounter in the old port of Marseille, tattoos all over his body, and a tremendous Southern drawl. He was the chief of the "Junk Force."

At the edge of this twenty-first-century war involving the American army there have been some strange operations. This type of primitive guerrilla operation had, I thought, disappeared along with the French Expeditionary Corps, or was at least reserved for the Viet Cong. Not at all. My sailor friend from Alabama actually commanded an incredible armada, composed of a hundred old Chinese junks, more or less battered, but armed with 37-mm. cannon and heavy machine guns, and charged with patrolling the coast between the 10th and the 14th parallels, in order to intercept arms transports to the Viet Cong.

This "Junk Force" consisted of seven to eight hundred fairly young, rather seedy-looking fellows, mostly Viet Cong deserters, whose ingenious chief had asked them to adorn their chests with a formidable tattoo, reading: MAT-CONG— approximate translation: Kill Communists. This phrase was the essence of the philosophy of Popeye, who cared little about the lot of his men in a possible future popular Republic of Vietnam.

One can well imagine the reactions of the dear old U.S. senators, asked to examine the use of funds voted by Congress for the American "advisers" in Vietnam, upon discovering this strange gang chief, knife in hand, fighting among tattered outlaws. Perhaps they will sigh that, after all, at least one unit does not cost the American taxpayer too much.

In a different style, but also side by side with the poor devils stuck in the mud and the traps of the terrain, the men of the Special Forces were engaged in combat. In the June 8, 1964, *U. S. News & World Report,* Robert L. ("Robin") Moore, Jr., a member of the Special Forces in 1963–1964, described that war which was no longer one of helicopter against knife, but of knife against knife. In his interview, Moore stated that men in the American forces ". . . volunteer for Special Forces . . . which make up 6 per cent of the Americans in Vietnam."

    Q. What's the job of Special Forces?
    A. Special Forces do the direct antiguerrilla fighting. They're the ones who are on the ground fighting directly with the Communist Viet Cong.
    Q. Are they really the only ones in direct combat?

A. They are the only Americans who are in daily personal combat with the VC, yes.

Q. Are these the new Marines?

A. They do a different job from the Marines. The Marines are shock troops. The Special Forces are not shock troops. They're not assault troops. They are primarily designed to be dropped into, or put into, an area under enemy control and to take native people, train them, and lead them in guerrilla war, or in an antiguerrilla war.

When asked whether the Vietnamese teams were able, Moore replied:

A. Not usually. That's the trouble. Up until recently, the Vietnamese A teams have just been soldiers with good political connections. . . .

Q. Are these Americans supposed to be fighting, or are they just training the Vietnamese to fight?

A. They're supposed to be training the Vietnamese to fight, but they're in actual combat themselves. . . .

Q. Do we issue [various American weapons] to the Vietnamese, too?

A. They did for a while, and the Vietnamese were losing them to the VC.

According to Moore, the Viet Cong possess a great many captured American arms:

Q. Are most of the VC weapons captured U.S. weapons?

A. I would say certainly many of them are. For every bunch of weapons you capture from the VC, you find maybe 30 per cent were made in the United States. You find a lot of old French weapons—and now you're finding a lot of Chinese copies of Russian weapons. . . .

Q. How many men are going into South Vietnam from the North?

A. It seems to me a never-ending procession.

Q. Is it increasing?

A. It seems to be increasing. We feel it is.

Q. How do they get in there? Do the Communists come in directly across the border between North and South Vietnam, or do they come down through the Ho Chi Minh Trail through Laos?

A. They almost never come in directly across the border between North and South Vietnam—almost never. They come down over the Laotian border, come in through Tayninh Province, generally, where it is believed is the headquarters of the whole VC operation.

Q. Is that all in Laos, or in Cambodia, too?

A. They come through Laos and Cambodia. I was with several Special Forces camps along the border. The VC come down from North Vietnam and just make a little jog through Laos and into South Vietnam.

Q. How about Communist weapons? Is it true that some are shipped by boat into Cambodia, and then sent across?

A. Not necessarily. Intelligence sources feel that the weapons are coming down from China by junk, coming by sea right to the delta region of the Mekong River, coming directly to the VC in South Vietnam. There just isn't much you can do about it.

Moore believed that the land traffic could be stopped without the war being carried to North Vietnam, and that instead of having only 40 Special Forces A teams we should have 100.

A. If we put 40 or 50 Special Forces teams right up to the Laos border—each one 20 or 25 miles from the next—these guys would hold them off, because the VC never go into one of these 25-mile areas dominated by

CHASING THE VC • 167

the Special Forces. They go around them. They would do anything rather than go through a Special Forces area. . . .

Q. So must the U.S. take operational control of Vietnamese Special Forces plus Vietnamese regular forces?

A. Right. Air forces as well as ground forces.

Later Moore says that he believes that the Vietnamese troops will fight, if properly picked and properly led.

Q. Are you convinced that the U.S. can win this war without going into Laos and into North Vietnam?

A. I'm convinced of that. I'm convinced that it's not necessary to bomb North Vietnam. If you bomb North Vietnam, that isn't going to stop those 80,000 Communists in South Vietnam. No matter what you do to North Vietnam, the guerrillas are going to be in the South. And they'll get supplied, one way or another. Red China will supply them.

According to the *Vietnam Diary,* by war correspondent Richard Tregaskis, the American military felt as involved in this war, or almost as involved, as the French were in that of 1945–1954, at least at the junior-officer level. The stories by Tregaskis differ little from those published in French magazines a dozen years ago. One might add that despite the Yankees' good will, the psychological climate between the nationalist fighters and the foreign cadres did not seem to have improved. Tregaskis reported that at the end of a particularly "hot" operation in the Soc Trang region—a bad sector now for twenty years—the American commander called for helicopters to relieve his men. Four machines arrived quickly, and stopped close to a village where the Viet Cong were clearly in control. Americans and Vietnamese crowded in. But the machine boarded by Tregaskis was overloaded and could not take off. Thereupon, "without hesitation, the pilot made one, two, three Vietnamese descend, the engines roared and we took off gently." What became of the "one, two, three Vietnamese" nobody knows.

A little later an American officer confided the following to a journalist:

> One must remember that this is our problem, that if they lose we also lose. But one aspect of our duty is disagreeable: That is to go through a village that has been burned with napalm. . . . As advisers to the infantry, our duty is to report to the U. S. Air Force on the bombings with this incendiary material that burns the flesh and often hits women and children outside military targets. Even if it hits the VC, the result is not very pleasant. I would rather do anything than make inspection tours of these burnt villages. . . .

2

❦❦❦❦❦❦❦

The N.L.F. Uses
Modern Means

In Saigon, on the evenings of the latest coup, the guns continued to sound. But while the generals, in order to obtain a new star for their shoulder or satisfy some personal grudge, used to alert their surprised battalions in the capital, the N.L.F. used to organize itself in the rice paddies. By discrediting adversaries, and immobilizing troops in the streets of Saigon, each such act on the part of the generals was worth to the revolutionaries a regiment, twenty artillery pieces, or ten Northern supply junks.

Of all the various coups, that of November 1, 1963, served the N.L.F. men best. Most of the generals were certainly more closely tied to and more loyal to the Americans than the Ngos had been. But in the popular mind concern with anti-communism was associated with the person of Diem, whose elimination destroyed that image. By inventing the expression My-Diem ("Americano-Diemist"), the Viet Cong themselves created an amalgam they could use to demonstrate that the Americans had suffered a terrible blow by depriving themselves of their compromising but courageous ally.

This was particularly obvious when these new military leaders engaged in the progressive liquidation of the strategic hamlets. And even though experience with strategic hamlets in some sectors had been disappointing, these hamlets had probably been the only strategy that could be marshaled against the N.L.F.'s subversive methods. In short, Henry Cabot Lodge helped the Viet Cong, but they gave him no thanks.

Seven days later, on November 8, 1963, the N.L.F. broadcast six demands over their clandestine radio:

1. Complete and unconditional abolition of the fascist dictatorship of Ngo Dinh Diem.

2. Immediate establishment of a regime with a broad and genuine democratic base.

3. Immediate cessation of American aggression in South Vietnam.

4. Establishment of an independent economic policy, democratic and rational, to raise progressively the standard of living of the population.

5. Immediate cessation of raids and massacres of the N.L.F.'s compatriots.

6. Opening of negotiations between various interested groups in South Vietnam, in order to arrive at a cease-fire and a solution to the great problems of the country.

This text was measured, prudent, and contained only an implicit condemnation of the new regime, in that by demanding the "unconditional" abolition of a dictatorship that to all appearances had been brought down a week earlier, it included that dictatorship's successors in this denunciation.

Two months later the N.L.F. made a clear statement on the operation of November 1. It said the coup had been a result of internal conflicts among its opponents, to wit: the elimination of Diem by the Americans. It continued to call the new Saigon regime a "phantom" regime; but speaking of the military chiefs who had seized power, the N.L.F. declared, with the voice of its own president, Nguyen Huu Tho:

> If it is true that they pursue the high ideal of serving the nation, the men who are now at the head of the army of the Republic will certainly break the chains of the foreigners . . . in order to relieve their patriots from the evils of war. . . . On its part, the Front will do everything in its power to create conditions favorable to a solution of this kind.

At the Second N.L.F. Congress, held somewhere in Cochinchina on January 1, 1964, Nguyen Huu Tho made what can certainly be called an offer to negotiate. It received even less attention because three weeks later the comparatively moderate junta presided over by General Minh was overthrown by General Khanh's more activist group; thus the Front had to continue to battle. And it did, mercilessly.

At this Second Congress the N.L.F.'s leadership was reorganized. The most important change took place in the secretariat-general, which, headed originally by Professor Nguyen Van Hieu, and then by Tran Buu Kiem, president of the Union of Students for Liberation, passed into the hands of Huynh Tan Phat, a Saigon architect who at age forty-seven was already a veteran of the Cochinchinese guerrillas.

How much political importance attached to this change? Hieu was regarded as very favorably inclined toward China: he had been sent to Prague as a delegate of the N.L.F. Tran Buu Kiem was relieved of his function as secretary-general, allegedly because his wife had been arrested in Saigon and he had therefore become vulnerable to blackmail. Huynh Tan Phat was a man of action who had assumed heavy responsibilities during the first war of Indochina, and who had aroused attention as a vigorous trainer of men in a Saigon prison in 1946.

It was also noted that at the end of the Second Congress, the Front had kept Vo Chi Cong as its vice-president in charge of representing the Popular Revolutionary Party, radical wing of the organization, and that it had appointed Tran Nam Trung as co-ordinator of all military operations in the South. In the Central Committee eleven seats had been reserved "for the representatives of political parties, mass organizations, armed forces, and patriotic personalities belonging to the Front." In this way the N.L.F. tried to remain an "overt" organization without claiming a monopoly of all popular patriotic spirit and revolutionary inspiration, as its Algerian counterpart had done in an earlier day.

There were many indications that the Front was not a communist organization, and that communists in it played only a partial role, even though they tried to infiltrate and control a wide array of different forces. Equally clear was the intention on the part of the N.L.F. leaders not to appear as the executors of a policy dictated from the North, or to seem to be satellites of Hanoi. Let me give some examples.

In August 1962 the *Bulletin* of the Liberation Front of South Vietnam published an interview granted to the N.L.F. press agency by Nguyen Huu Tho. When asked a question concerning a conflict between the guerrilla forces and one of the Front's parties, the N.L.F. president did not try to obscure this difference, but simply contented himself with issuing a warning to those who "show their flimsiness by counting on the possibility of dissenters co-operating with imperialist agents." Tho added: "Necessarily, in our vast ranks there are differences and even conflicts."

When his interviewer, quoting from a Cambodian paper, asked whether he was one of those "authentic nationalists who had found it necessary to throw themselves into the arms of the communists because of Diem's brutal policy," the N.L.F. president replied that he would not "object" to being described in this fashion.

During the same period an N.L.F. representative told my colleague Georges Chaffard not far from the Cambodian border: "We have long hoped for aid from the North. But we prefer to settle our affairs among Southerners. The North will not be a decisive element in our struggle. . . . *We have not been fighting for many years only to end up with having one dictatorship replaced by another.* Nobody in our ranks is dependent upon the North."

In Saigon in 1964 a Canadian clergyman who had lived for several months among the Viet Cong declared that according to his personal estimate, only 10 per cent of the N.L.F. were militant communists. Of course, the "common front" strategy that the Marxists-Leninists know how to conduct with such masterful skill does not require a large proportion of communists to assure them of the control of power, provided that the circumstances are favorable to them; we have seen this during the period when some of the popular democracies were established.

To understand better the nature of the N.L.F., one might compare this organization to its predecessor in the whole of Vietnam, i.e., the Viet Minh, in the years 1941 to 1951. In September 1946, after the signing of the agreement between Moutet and Ho Chi Minh, which was the last attempt to pursue the policy of understanding which France and the Vietnamese revolutionaries had begun six months earlier on the initiative of General Leclerc, I had occasion to spend some time in the guerrilla country of Nam Bo (Cochinchina), on the border of the Plain of Joncs, about twenty-five miles from My Tho.

Received there by the Central Committee, I was able to see how very diverse this leading group was, comprising men of Catholic origin, such as Pham Ngoc Thuan; nationalists, such as Nguyen Binh; the principal military leader of the organization, Huynh Phu So; the famous "mad bonze," leader of the Hoa-Hao (who was to be assassinated a month later, probably on Viet Minh orders); a communist, Ung Van Khiem, who later became foreign minister of North Vietnam; and a priest.

Eight years later, at Phnom Penh, I again met the same Pham Ngoc Thuan who had received me in the Plain of Joncs.

He had become Ambassador to East Berlin, and then president of the Committee of Cultural Relations with Foreign Countries; in this capacity he had brought a group of folk dancers to Cambodia. He drew a very interesting parallel between the methods of the Viet Minh in 1946 and those of the N.L.F. in 1964:

> We were very clumsy primitives. We tried to oppose the colonial system and its Vietnamese allies with a "counter-state" with its own administration, currency, and educational system. . . . But our successors, wherever they could, have made a great deal of progress and utilized our experiences and our failures by choosing another way: they make every attempt to infiltrate the state and utilize it. Rather than systematically oppose the existing legal framework, they prefer to use it, in order to substitute another one for it. In simple terms, I would say that in the old days, we were cutting roads to intercept vehicles. They prefer to step into existing automobiles. . . .

But when in March 1965 I listened to a leading personality of the Front defining the overall political and military strategy of the N.L.F., I was struck by the fact that he emphasized much more the political than the military element. But the behavior of the Front will, of course, depend on the power relationships in the various zones, that is—to employ the terminology current among the South Vietnamese guerrillas—whether the Front is dealing with a "liberated" sector, a "contested" sector or a "still occupied" sector. This is what the N.L.F. spokesman said:

> *Occupied sector:* We play it legal, slipping into the legal framework. We launch campaigns for freedom, against repression, for education. We demand schools, and then, as they have none themselves, we furnish teachers, programs, books, and so on.

Contested sector: We play our cards in favor of the young, the children, the women, the aged, in order to paralyze armed action and military brutality. Politization is very rapid, much superior to that in the years 1945 to 1954.

Liberated sector: We apply a prudent policy, without rapid agrarian reform as in 1953, which turned out to be an error. We try to convince patriotic landowners to share their land, preferring to act with them rather than against them.

We work with the co-operatives which are not too strongly oriented in any political direction, but very open and good educational channels, and which will assure us of loyalty at the base when our neutrality provides greater foreign aid for us: U.S. aid must not corrupt us as it did Laos. If that period comes, we must control the commercial channels and the utilization of the economic assistance even if we have a partially bourgeois government at the top.

But what did this leader of the Front think of the Sino-Soviet conflict? He considered it "criminal," at a time when the problem still was to build socialism. He was as critical of the Chinese as he was of the Russians: he condemned the schism rather than the policy of the one or the other. Moreover, he did not hide—we were having this talk in March 1965—his disappointment with the passivity of these two great socialist states in the face of American intervention in North Vietnam.

But it was impossible to learn what the diplomatic objectives of the Front were. Was American withdrawal still the first condition to all negotiations? The Front was very reserved on that subject.

When comparing the "French" war to that conducted by the United States in 1965, the Front leader seemed about to say: "Those were the good days. . . ." But he claimed considerable tactical progress—improvement in armament, strategy, transport, and the replacement of rowboats by motor sampans. He spoke of increased ideological flexibility, fear of leftism, and a better appreciation of the "religious" forces.

The resumption of the war? It dates from 1959. It was impossible to avoid it. There was pressure at the base. Since 1958 we have conducted polls. An old peasant told me: "If you do not enter the struggle, we will turn away from you." We waited too long—we were opportunist-pacifist from 1954 to 1958. We hesitated to draw the consequences from the Diemist dictatorship and its excesses.

But aid from the North is very secondary. All aid coming to us from the outside is contrary to the guerrilla spirit and the popular struggle. Guerrillas don't fight well except with what they have conquered or created. . . .

But we think more of peace than of war, and are preparing for it. We are thinking of the living standard of the population, living democracy, and economic progress without too violent changes. What is needed above all is not to force things but to let them develop and try to co-operate with *all* the sectors of the population.

We must keep all the diversities in mind, such as the differences between the feudal, religious, and nationalist-sectarian region of Annam, and the flexible, bourgeois, liberal region of Cochinchina already modernized by colonialization. . . .

Just as colonialization has played to some extent a modernizing role, the Diem regime, despite its bonds with imperialism, did break up the great rural and semi-feudal bourgeoisie, by imposing what it called its land reform. This hypocritical operation did not at all benefit the people, but at least had the advantage of destroying the large estates. The peasants reaped no advantage from all that, and the super-benefits from the soil then went to the new semi-capitalist, semi-administrative class created by the regime. But the Diem regime, though conservative and reactionary, destroyed the structure of the old agrarian society, without realizing it.

In the cities the Diem regime fostered the establishment of a new bourgeoisie of functionaries and businessmen more reactionary than the old ruling bourgeoisie—that of the pro-French intellectuals. Aside from the repression of the people and the indenturing of the country to the Americans, that was the most harmful action by that regime of sectarian mandarins.

Buddhism? We see in it an aspect of straddling the fence, a sort of elementary neutralism. Buddhism has a nationalist aspect that makes it oppose the Americans. It also has a reactionary aspect that divides it from the Front and prevents it from really joining us. If there are many honest and sincere men among the Buddhists, the movement is also infiltrated with all sorts of foreign agents. . . .

The students? Most often they are of bourgeois origin and tend to behave as such. Most characteristic of that milieu is confusion. Many among them are still under the influence of the Dai Viet. But a profound evolution is visible in their ranks, and can proceed only in a way favorable to our cause. . . .

On the development of N.L.F. strategy, it may be best to consult some passages of a communiqué which drew the military balance sheet of 1964 and was published by Hanoi's information services:

From the tactics of 1963, which consisted of taking the initiative in attacking and routing the enemy's Southern forces in entire sections, the Army of Liberation passed in 1964 to the tactic of conducting an uninterrupted offensive against the enemy, and of destroying a

178 · VIETNAM: BETWEEN TWO TRUCES

great number of his units on battalion and company level, and depriving him of all weapons. . . .

While in 1963 the revolutionary movement of armed struggle and its victories took place primarily in the Center, and west of Nam Bo [Cochinchina], the revolutionary armed forces of the South attacked in 1964 without respite, and won victories throughout the year in all regions, from the demarcation line to the Point of Ca Mau. . . .

Efforts to kill Americans have developed with great vigor and on a large scale in all regions, and particularly in Saigon proper. The actions taken in February 1964 on a basketball field, in the cinemas, particularly in apartments, in front of restaurants, in garrisons; the sabotage against the American aircraft carrier *Card* in the port of Saigon on May 2, 1964; and, more recently, the bombing of the hotel of senior American officers in the very heart of Saigon, proved that the activities of the guerrilla forces have made a step forward, showing more creative and diversified means and causing panic among the aggressors, not only in the provinces but also in the cities of Hue, Da Nang, Saigon, . . . i.e., in the vital centers and places where the aggressor troops are concentrated. In the first ten months of 1964 the number of American aggressors killed or wounded rose to 1,957, almost one and a half times the total number of the entire period from 1961 to 1963.

More striking than these figures (which are propaganda) is the fact that a movement of Marxist inspiration should justify terrorism in the cities as a normal means of action in "guerrilla" operations—which, incidentally, must be distinguished from the activity of the National Army of Liberation.

What kind of men are the South Vietnamese guerrillas? I have already said that they fall into two more or less distinct

categories, the regulars and the irregulars. The former, estimated at around 35,000 men at the beginning of 1965, are
fully and regularly armed, with one automatic weapon per
thirty combatants; the latter—100,000 to 150,000 men?—
are hardly distinguishable from the peasants and are armed
only when operations take place in their sector. The former
usually wear the palm pith helmets made famous by the pictures of the battle of Dien Bien Phu, the latter continue to
wear their black tunics and the flapping pants of the Vietnamese Nha Que.

What has struck every observer in the combat zone or
simply all those who have had contact with Viet Cong prisoners, is the extreme youth of these soldiers. Most of them are
barely twenty years old. Madeleine Riffaud, special correspondent of *Humanité,* with the guerrillas at the end of 1964,
concluded from this that these men therefore could not be
soldiers coming from the North. That may be so, even though
to travel seems to be the privilege of youth, particularly in
wartime.

Another observer of the South Vietnamese guerrillas,
Georges Penchenier, who in 1964 was an "involuntary guest"
of the Viet Cong in north Cochinchina's plantation zone, was
struck by the very firm discipline in the guerrilla ranks, a
discipline reinforced by Marxist-Leninist precepts. He also
noted the strong cadres of these units and the fantastic physical endurance they displayed by marching dozens of miles per
day in the brush in order to deceive their adversary. This excellent observer also reported that when facing the guerrillas,
the nationalist troops often adopted a prudent long-term policy rather than a short-term strategy.

I have before me a little note book taken from a Viet Cong
prisoner in September 1964. It is very clean. This revolutionary soldier is an orderly man. There are thirty pages in *quoc-
ngu* script, the national language (in another day the Viet
Minh guerrillas often wrote their letters in French, but times

have changed). This "breviary of war" is divided into four chapters. All this makes me think that this was a good pupil of the educational courses, which, we know, are frequent, even daily, and are held even in the most dangerous zones. And the meticulous transcription showed that this soldier was also a very good listener.

The first chapter is devoted to the "principles of attacking the enemy." This is the least surprising chapter. Its rules can be found in various publications devoted to "revolutionary war." But I will quote them anyhow, as they are quite revealing.

Our man wrote that the Front fighter should first yield his place to the reconnaisance units, which must be "disguised." He must then engage in a progressive occupation of the terrain, "limiting his personal chances as best he can." He must then wait until the enemy has deeply penetrated into his ranks before firing at a "sure target."

The second chapter is much more significant. It lists the "essential mistakes to be avoided by the revolutionary fighter." The two fundamental errors named there are "militarism" and "mandarinism." While the latter seems to be a target of all N.L.F. instruction, he has some very surprising things to say on the former.

The chapter on "militarism" contains peculiar complaints, which lead us to believe that the "military" must have been taken, in Vietnam as in ancient China, for a sort of low-class highway robber. In its denunciation of "militarism," the general staff of the popular army specifically condemns the "lack of respect for the dead," "thefts and larcenies," "carrying on with the girls," "sharpshooting at birds," and "the throwing of grenades into lakes in order to catch fish"—all complaints grouped under the general heading of "offenses against the public good."

Also regarded as "militarist in spirit" is "lack of frankness toward superiors" and "neglect of the discussion of combat plans by the troops," which is much more revealing and makes us think that the "Bolshevik spirit" of 1917 has maintained itself inside the Vietnamese popular army—a spirit that may be giving its coloration and force to the entire system.

The third chapter is devoted to "political missions during combat." It revolves entirely around the constant preoccupations of a Viet Cong commander: to show to the population that their cause and that of the troops are indissolubly linked, and that the popular army represents "liberty today and peace tomorrow." Three categories of individuals are specifically mentioned here: the growers, the Catholics and Buddhists, and the wounded. The first must be "helped in their labor" when the circumstances allow, and "their property must be respected"; this pertains to requisitioning, which must never be effected without payment or a certificate signed by a responsible man. The second group must be treated in a spirit of respect not only regarding their beliefs but also their property. The Viet Cong fighter is given orders to "reconstruct religious buildings that may have been destroyed in the course of the fighting, either by the enemy or by the forces of liberation." As far as the wounded are concerned, a distinction is to be made between friends and enemies. But it is recommended to take very good care of both categories, to dress their wounds "with pieces of the distributed equipment," and to "lead the wounded to the rear under the best possible condition."

The fourth and last chapter is a long treatise on the principle of "self-criticism," and it is filled with quotations from Lenin and Mao Tse-tung. Quoted at the beginning is this typical sentence: "The constant criticism of his own acts is the most powerful instrument in the hands of the revolutionary fighter." The second sentence is a more characteristic formula, surprisingly reminiscent of the impassive and flowery genius of China's master: "There are only two kinds of people without weaknesses: those in their caskets and those in the bellies of their mothers."

Whatever the true aims of the N.L.F., it is clear that their methods are such as to assure the cohesion of the group, provoke its ardor for battle, and invest its gestures with the striking colors of justice and liberty.

What role does external aid play in the Viet Cong war effort? The White Paper published by the American government on the subject on February 27, the eve of the March bombings of North Vietnam, maintaining the thesis of the "invasion" of the South by the North, is very unconvincing. In an article published at the same time in the *New Republic,* I estimated that this aid was less than 10 per cent of the means received from the Viet Cong. The editors of the magazine, when trying to have the figure confirmed by American officials, were advised by the Pentagon that the deliveries from the North were rather on the order of 15 to 20 per cent, which is in fact likely.

Of course, the claim of communist spokesmen, at Hanoi and elsewhere, that North Vietnam is merely observing the war in the South without reacting, is obviously indefensible. One could even say that it is profoundly unflattering to Ho Chi Minh and his friends; how could a revolutionary state permit the repression of revolutionary compatriots, separated from it only by an artificial demarcation line, by a great foreign power? Such passivity is unimaginable, even where a neighboring foreign state would be concerned. The Soviet Union did not permit the crushing of Republican Spain without reacting, or even of the popular front in France, despite its official "non-intervention." We know the role that was played by Red China in the Korean War. Not to mention Algeria.

In March 1965, during the conference of the Indochinese people at Phnom Penh, the Viet Cong delegation corrected this "line" of the North's non-intervention. When some conferees wanted to obtain a condemnation of "all foreign intervention" in South Vietnam, the spokesmen for the Front said that the aid received from the North, south of the 17th Parallel, was not "foreign," as it was furnished by Vietnamese to Vietnamese. Which is, one must admit, undebatable, and which has the advantage over the preceding claim of giving the truth its due.

But it must be added that the aid given by the North to the South is not easily furnished. Much has been written about what is called in the South the Ho Chi Minh Trail, which, bypassing the barrier dividing the two Vietnams at the 17th Parallel, runs through the Laotian valley from North to South, from the Vinh region to that of Tchepone, ending in Vietnam at the level of the 14th Parallel. There is no question that a steady flow of men and arms passes over it. But it is interesting in this connection to quote the words of one of its "users."

In an interview given to *Le Monde* in September 1964, Dr. Pham Ngoc Thach, minister of health at Hanoi and a former leader of the Communist Party in Cochinchina, recalled that the vagaries of his career had led him to make the North-South journey on foot twice, across the forest and mountains. He said:

> This is an extremely difficult and long road to negotiate with sixty pounds of equipment on one's back. Americans believe that one can easily organize a two-way traffic between the North and the guerrillas of the Front. That makes me laugh. . . . It shows they know nothing of the war in the bush. Besides, the Front does not need men and has no need of officers either.

Still, the problems of arms and ammunitions remain. Certain leaders of the Front admitted at the beginning of 1965 that a problem of ammunition might arise within three or four months if the Americans and their allies were to succeed in completely isolating the theater of operations in the South, be it by the establishment of an effective barrier along the Laotian frontier, be it by stopping the maritime traffic along the

184 · VIETNAM: BETWEEN TWO TRUCES

coast, be it by stopping all forms of arms traffic in centers like Cholon—where, as an American journalist observed in February 1965, no law forbids the sale of firearms.

Concerning arms in general, the spokesmen of the N.L.F. might gladly apply Giap's formula, as stated in his book *War of the People, Army of the People:*

> One must find the source of supplies that go to the Front, and seize the arms of the enemy in order to beat him with his own arms. Our regular troops and our guerrilla formations have in large measure equipped themselves with war booty. The French Expeditionary Corps actually became a transport enterprise specializing in furnishing American weapons to our troops.

Aside from the part played by exaggeration and propaganda, we see here a formula endowed with a sense of humor too rare in communist literature to escape notice. Giap's observation is even more applicable in 1965, when the density of arms per square mile is probably ten times greater than in 1953, and when the nationalist army, less widely officered by the Americans than it was twelve years ago by the French, is more prone to let the matériel entrusted to them slip away.

Obviously, the Viet Cong have benefited by aid from the North and the entire socialist camp, not to speak of aid from arms merchants who hide their nationality. But one probably can say that in 1965 they had attained what one might call an "autonomous war"—much as pilots speak of "autonomous flight"—of several months at least. The bombings of the North begun in February 1965 will perhaps have diplomatic effects. But it seems very unlikely to the great majority of those involved in the second war in Vietnam that these bombings will change the course of the war south of the 17th Parallel in the slightest. In an interview given on March 25, 1965, even Gen. Maxwell Taylor admitted that Viet Cong activity had actually increased since the beginning of the raids on the North.

American spokesmen maintained in March 1965 that certain ultramodern arms of the Viet Cong are of Russian and/or Chinese origin, such as Soviet 7.62-mm. rifles, Chinese bazookas, and other equipment. But the Viet Cong had also been able to seize heavy American machine guns and mortars.

The last balance sheet published by the authorities in Saigon revealed that the Viet Cong find most of their weapons right where they are.

Between January 1 and October 1, 1964, the Viet Cong took nine thousand arms from government troops, i.e., an average of eight hundred per month between January and July, and close to fifteen hundred per month between July and October.

As the fighting was very intense in October and November, the seizure of arms must have remained at the same level during that period. In December the figure exceeded two thousand, in February twenty-five hundred.

Having seized close to twenty thousand arms since January 1, 1964, the N.L.F. lost only seven thousand in the same period. Thus, its "net profit" must be estimated at thirteen thousand arms.

A thousand arms per month? To pursue the war, it is enough for the Viet Cong that the Americans remain within their reach.

3

$$\mathscr{SSSSSSS}$$

The American Temptation: To Change the War

In the beginning of 1965 it was not easier to be an American in Vietnam than it had been to be a Frenchman in Indochina twelve years earlier. Except that the Americans drew upon incomparably larger reserves of power.

Still, they had some very bad moments. Let us take for example the coup of September 13, 1964. It is not pleasant to be taken by surprise by such an event and not even be able to hide that surprise, particularly if one has a certain number of "advisers" inside the seditious division—who did not notice that they were in the process of participating in the overthrow of America's number-one protégé, until the very moment when they approached the suburbs of Saigon.

While it is difficult to define a single policy on the part of such numerous and complicated organisms as the American Embassy's information services, the military services, and the services of the economic experts, one can at least try to discern certain policy aims.

Were those in General Taylor's entourage thinking, in September 1964, of hitting the North in order to create a diversion from the South, i.e., in order to change course? Were they willing to be pushed in this direction by the Southerners, and particularly the pilots of General Ky, who has a reputation for being very impetuous?

American observers in Saigon refused to admit that General Ky's air forces were integrated into the U. S. Air Force. Appearances only, they said, made people believe that the United States had the means of controlling Ky's forces at every moment. They insisted that Southern squadrons were in a position to launch strictly autonomous operations of short duration without their allies even knowing about it, and that these operations might even be quick raids on the North, strafing operations or the dropping of parachutists.

While denying that they had the means to prevent such attacks, the American observers refused to say whether they would welcome them, and insisted that their policy regarding this matter had not yet been set. They obviously preferred to retain their choice of time and means. Despite the reservations and mystery on this point, most of the American representatives seemed to think that such operations would have greater political than strategic implications.

They could hardly fail to notice the rising wave of pacifism that threatened to swamp the war effort sooner or later, or the increasing of anti-American slogans. They did not even seem to find consolation in the fact that the demonstrations of students and Buddhists were giving evidence of anti-French feeling as well.

What is the direction and aim of this deceptive effort, based on quicksand and devouring almost $2,000,000 a day? Let us first hear one of the architects of American strategy in Vietnam, whose views I did not share, but which were significant:

> Given the nature of the problem at hand, we will be here for perhaps twenty years. This Vietnam business does not present itself to us from a geographic angle and does not consist of holding on to a theater of operations

or strategic key positions. There is a permanent problem to be resolved: how can a power commanding a certain range of means reply to a power commanding other means? How can one, with considerable armed force but little political power, contain an adversary who has enormous political force but only modest military power?

This problem poses itself or will pose itself for us, not only in Asia but in Africa and particularly in Latin America. It is here that we must solve it, to some extent through great permanent technological action. We must find the appropriate response, i.e., counter-insurgency, and we have obtained considerable results in this area. But if we should fail, we will draw the tentative conclusion that we must employ much more powerful means within the framework of conventional weapons. No other conclusion appears at the horizon.

But in the course of September 1964, when I heard these "long-term" propositions, a sudden evolution took place in American circles in Saigon, after Gen. Maxwell Taylor's trip to Washington. In military circles, where only a short time before the opinions expressed had been very careful and the principal concern had seemed to center around the maintenance of the status quo—considered none too good, if not actually bad—I heard on September 23 such new and striking proposals that I found myself forced to consider that American policy in Vietnam had changed radically.

This is what, in substance, the Americans said:

We have arrived at a point where the 17th Parallel no longer exists for us. We have had enough of seeing the enemy impose upon us a form of war for which he has practically set up the rules and where we are inferior. In this game of "the knife in the mud" we are necessarily outmaneuvered, and if we respect the frontier of North Vietnam, we cannot give back blow for blow. We are again in the situation we were in at the Yalu River in Korea, and we have had enough of it. Now, we have decided to make the people in the North think. We do not know at all whether the blows we will strike north of the 17th Parallel will immediately change the military situation in the South. But we definitely want to make the people in Hanoi understand that it does not pay to intervene as they have intervened here. From here on they will have to balance the losses they inflict here with the losses they will suffer up there.

The operations we conducted on August 5 against strategic points in the North, losing only two planes and one man in exchange for destroying half of the Northern fleet, have shown us the way. Not all operations will be as profitable; but we will do it again, as the very reason which strongly motivated our response exists permanently. And don't talk to us of reactions abroad or of international opinion. After August 5 we saw how little solidarity there is between the communists and Hanoi. As far as the judgments in the chancelleries and newspapers are concerned, be advised that our admirals are not too terribly concerned with them, and that they will pay less and less attention to them.

We have played the role of dupes long enough. The communists are very strong on the terrain they have selected. Well then, we are stronger in another terrain. They prefer an ambush in the rice paddies, or assassinations; we have our planes and ships, and we are here in order not to lose. Which does not mean that we will pursue only military objectives or consider our operations to be ends in themselves. From here on we will make ourselves feared, that is, respected, as adversaries or as negotiators.

I was struck not only by these words but also by the barely contained tone of violence, which reminded me of statements by the French colonels, whom I knew so well, on the eve of the Suez operation in 1956. All comparisons are risky, and no situation is like another. But, intoxication or truth, this new tone of the responsible Americans made it foreseeable that while the war continued in one area, the Americans envisaged beginning another one elsewhere. Beaten at rugby, they wanted to play football. Change the war? This was already more than a mere temptation.

VI

BLINDMAN'S BUFF

1

𝄞𝄞𝄞𝄞𝄞𝄞𝄞

A People Craving Life

Saigon, September 1964

Between Singapore, where I was coming from, and Saigon there was the striking difference between war and peace. Bristling with barricades and other defenses, streaked with patrols armed to the teeth, gagged, blinded, and immobilized by the curfew, the great Malaysian metropolis resembled a felled giant in those heavy autumn days. Saigon, on the other hand, never seemed more animated, teeming, and carefree.

Less than ten days after the bloody disputes between Buddhists and Catholics at the end of August, the busy nonchalance and the ever present banter had again taken hold of the city. The barbed-wire fences were withdrawn from the Presidential palace, and the armed vehicles put back in their barracks. Censorship was alleviated. Politicians, released from jail, engaged in innumerable little confidential conferences in the open, and the newspapers gave themselves the air of talking almost freely of their government. For a while Saigon seemed like a small island of peace and prosperity. But the flood all around it was rising.

Turning away from the flow of cars, strollers, and customers to ask some questions, I learned that every day the military activities of the Viet Cong were becoming more daring and getting closer to the capital; that it was becoming more and more inadvisable to travel out of town by oneself; that the daily losses of the government troops numerically approached the enemy's; and that if guerrilla pressure had slightly decreased since the beginning of the August crisis, this seemed to be because Hanoi and the N.L.F. thought that it "paid" better to let the regime in the South destroy itself all by itself without unleashing an intervention that might unite the various nationalist elements against the common menace.

From the point of view of psychological warfare—to which the N.L.F. adhered—what victory could be greater than the spectacle Diem's successors offered during the last months to the Vietnamese people? Except for Generals Minh and Khanh, those exercising power in Saigon were completely unknown. The arrest of General Khiem, third triumvir and commander-in-chief of the army, was formally denied soon after by a spokesman of the government, but the denial of the news of Vice-President Oanh's resignation was not at all convincing, and the resignation of two civilian ministers looked like a ridiculous move. It seemed to be a good day for this government when it lost only two of its members!

"To find one's way around in our political situation," I was told by a Vietnamese, "one must be able to orient oneself by the stars, like a navigator." True, stars were what was least lacking in the public life of Vietnam. Did this mean that the Vietnamese people, tired by such games and harassed by the war, were ready for just about anything in order to have the war finally brought to a conclusion?

Two editorials in the Buddhist weekly *Hai Trieu Am* (*The Echo of the Rising Tide*) aroused intense interest. In the first the monks clearly expressed themselves in favor of a cease-fire. In the second the commentator accused the Americans of having fomented troubles between the Catholics and

Buddhists, and insisted that the pursuit of the war was due
to American intervention. This was a thesis of such daring
as to be without precedent here, and possibly indicative of the
results of the end to censorship announced by General Khanh.

The eruption of anti-American sentiments, thus far contained, tied in with a still slow and confused but definite
ripening of the idea of negotiations in the minds of certain
reputedly anti-communist members of the Vietnamese intelligentsia.

I had proof of this in the course of a dinner with six typical
representatives of Saigon's intellectual bourgeoisie—lawyers,
doctors, a journalist, and a diplomat—who had all been at
one point, or will be, ministers, or were members of parties
that had been persecuted or destroyed by communist organizations. Some passages of the conversation deserve to be
quoted, but I will not name the men, who are still regarded
as heretics in the prevailing Saigon climate.

Naturally the conversation was prefaced by the sort of
ritual incantation considered necessary in talks with all
French visitors arriving in Saigon, supposedly of Gaullist
orientation: "Neutralism is diabolical, we will never accept
it." After which the conversation could begin, turning im-
perceptibly to the shame-faced revelation of what "neutralism" so shamelessly describes.

The conversation began with an attempt to define the National Liberation Front, which some considered to be a simple antenna of the Hanoi regime but others regarded as an
autonomous Southern organization, completely dominated by
communists. Others again saw in the N.L.F. a grouping dominated by Marxists during wartime, whose nationalist or liberal elements would however disengage themselves as soon
as the struggle, demanding strict discipline around the most
tightly organized nucleus, had ended. Most of those participating in the conversation seemed rather uninformed about
these differing views, but did not deny that the N.L.F. was
in fact strongly impregnated with the regionalist spirit and

sufficiently concerned with maintaining its freedom of action gained on the field of battle to be seen as a separate force and an autonomous partner in negotiations. All were in agreement that between 80 and 90 per cent of all guerrillas were Southerners, and that there were disagreements between the N.L.F. and Hanoi on the subject of a provisional government for the South, which Hanoi had so far succeeded in preventing from being established.

"But with whom negotiate, with whom establish contact?" A surprising question, not only because it was addressed by a Vietnamese to a stranger, but also because the borderline between legal and guerrilla forces cuts clearly across most Vietnamese families. It may have been in bad taste, but it was inevitable that I should have recalled at that point the precedent of Ngo Dinh Nhu, Hanoi's implacable enemy, who had managed to establish contacts, though not to follow them to a conclusion.

Such conversations would have appeared commonplace had they been held in Paris. In Saigon in 1964 they were almost scandalous and plainly significant. It must be added that they were interlarded with obviously sincere anti-communist protestations, and that they were formulated as questions rather than professions of faith. It must also be added that no matter how anxious for peace or critical of Washington policy my hosts were, they were not unconcernedly looking forward to a possible departure of the American troops. As far as neutrality was concerned, these Vietnamese intellectuals would have liked to have "the thing without the word." Regarding disengagement from Washington, they would have liked to have "the word without the thing."

Enter the Unions

Every hour the South Vietnamese structure was crumbling more. Every shout, every action, widened the cracks in the

wall. Every day another centrifugal force or protest or simple
pacifist foray manifested itself: one day the mountaineers of
Ban Me Thuot would undertake a caveman-type coup against
Saigon's authority, the next day the students would rebel, and
the workers the day after that.

The students were in greater terment than ever, but their
leaders insisted that for the time being they had done enough
for the defense of democracy or the denunciation of militarism, and that they were not in favor of any movement aimed
at keeping the universities closed. Still, they were preparing a
meeting devoted to the establishment of a "national convention," promised by the military for November, a beautiful
subject on which a man can exercise his eloquence and denounce personal power!

But the arrival of the labor unions on the scene was of
greater significance. Repressed by Diem, maintained since
then under iron military rule, trade unions had been almost
forgotten in the last two years despite the importance of their
head office, the Vietnamese Confederation of Labor, the
C.V.T., patterned originally on the French model. Its strange
American-trained leader, Tran Quoc Buu, had had many
heated encounters, with Ngo Dinh Nhu, and with almost three
hundred thousand members the Confederation represented a
considerable force, so much so that its announcement of a
general strike for September 20 seemed a major event. The
cause of, or rather the pretext for the general strike was, of
course, the refusal on the part of the management of a large
textile enterprise on Saigon's periphery to increase salaries
after a long strike. But it was clear that following so closely
on the heels of the September 13 coup, the student demonstrations, and particularly the N.F.L.'s call for a popular rebellion in the cities on September 17, this general strike had
a political aspect, in fact a clearly revolutionary one. The
leaders of the C.V.T., who had often been accused of permitting their head office to be infiltrated by the Viet Cong,

could not start a movement, which would paralyze Saigon, without risking a reaction from the army. They hesitated, and then decided to take the chance.

Thus they brusquely emerged from the strange reserve they had kept for two years. Their show of disciplined strength on September 20—more than the romantic self-immolations of monks or the hysterical demonstrations by students and Catholics—forced the regime to reconsider its policies. A mass, whose roots were deeply anchored in the people of the countryside, was on the move: the depressed proletariat of Saigon's harbor and the outskirts of Cholon. Whatever the actual degree of infiltration by the enemy or the aftereffects left behind by the Diem regime and master-schemer Nhu, for the first time a force arose that could be either a possible replacement for the present regime or a link to the enemy regime or the first pillar of a regime to come. Did it still depend on the generals and their "advisers" which it would be?

The temperature suddenly rose for foreigners in Saigon on that day, and not just figuratively. People who had been lulled to sleep by their air conditioning or electric fans awakened in stifling humidity; the strike of electrical workers had plunged foreign visitors into the same air as the poor people, and the strike at the waterworks reduced us to the discomfort of overdressed coolies. It was the triumph of the climate over money, and the revenge of the underdogs turning the levers in the factories against the white demigods dreaming in front of their air conditioners. The only thing left to do, while sponging oneself off, was to watch this mass led by its dubious leaders.

At the Vietnamese Confederation of Labor, which had ceased calling itself "Christian" even before the fall of the Diem regime, I was received by its secretary-general, Tran Quoc Buu, a day after meeting the secretary for the Saigon-Cholon region, Vo Van Tai. Some accused Buu of having shared Diem's role for too long, while Tai was accused by others of being a crypto-communist. Buu had the cunning frankness and prudence of the old tactician trained for thirty years in the school of Gaston Tessier. Tai, undiplomatic and argumentative, was a fervent advocate of spectacular actions and rapid results.

On Sunday, Tai denounced the management's brutality and methods at the huge Vimitex spinning mill—a management consisting of three Chinese members, of whom one was of Vietnamese nationality, one of American nationality, and one who had retained his Chinese nationality—which had used Khanh's August 7 proclamation of a state of emergency to lock out three quarters of its two thousand workers and had had some transferred to a military training camp. Yet Tai insisted that the strike was purely concerned with labor problems.

When I entered his office on Monday morning, Secretary-General Buu, apparently forgetting the strike he had organized—or had permitted to break out—tried to turn on his fan, but his strikers had rendered the fan useless. Buu smiled and began the conversation by assuring me that the strike would remain entirely concerned with labor problems. I objected that in the eyes of the entire world, considering Saigon's actual climate, it could not but seem to be the opening of the ultimate phase of a Viet Cong uprising.

A. Why? Ever since the proclamation of the state of emergency we have been sworn to complete inactivity. This regime capitulates before any group of children, students for example. Does it take us for babies? If we had wanted to start a truly insurrectional strike, we would have had the chance last Sunday when the failure of the coup created a power vacuum. But we did not take it. Why then are we being accused now of being political?

Q. But four days ago the National Liberation Front

launched an appeal to the urban masses to rise. Your general strike is obviously viewed abroad as the response to this appeal.

A. We have arrived at a point where we must take chances. We are taking this one now with the conviction that for the world of labor we represent the only solution outside of communism. If in a society in which any political club can make itself heard, a democratic labor organization cannot overtly defend the workers, the workers will realize that they have no recourse other than communism. And you know that this debate is not academic here.

Before the Presidential council the labor demonstration showed that Vietnam produced more than just folklorist organizations for ethnographers to study, or demonstrations to be photographed for sneering magazines. The marches and meetings were dignified, and under the heavy rain of the monsoon a discipline and patience more typical of peasants than of workers was apparent.

Early on Monday afternoon a standard spectacle was offered: the Presidential council being besieged by a large mass of people carrying immense posters and setting up a big fair with spices, mineral waters, and Chinese soups. The special aspect on this day was that General Khanh, who had bowed so easily before the pressure of priests of various religions and pupils of various schools, finding himself for once face to face with a real force, refused to capitulate and obtain a compromise. He was absent, or at least he did not show himself.

At the desolate dusk and in the dripping rain this was a strange popular drama: the crowd besieging the Presidential seat made themselves heard through bullhorn-equipped speakers perched on taxis. On the other side of the barricade, behind a strong screen of military units, the minister of labor, Hien—himself a former president of the union that now made its conditions to him—responded through a microphone.

And the crowd played the role of chorus, emphasizing the demands of its representatives and the answers of the "authorities." We saw here, for the first time, an organized mass acting under rational impulses.

In the course of that day, the slogans changed, and the "strictly labor motives" of Monday morning became political. But is it not always that way? One begins arguing over money, and ends up arguing over socio-political structures and principles.

In Saigon all sorts of interpretations were given to that strange and probably very important event. Was it a move by the Viet Cong from the rural terrain to the urban battlefield? If so, it was singularly circumspect, despite some songs that went up in their Red Square. Was it an attempt on the part of non-Marxist unionism to promise hope to the laboring masses? The Khanh regime gave it the opportunity to affirm not its prestige and effectiveness but only its dignity. If it was the first assault on the cities by the Viet Cong, the government was strangely meek about it. If it was a reformist and nationalist counter-effort, the regime was strangely uncomprehending.

In any event, a force came to life, neither marked with Diemism nor indentured to the Viet Cong—a force impressive in its own right. Did it represent a hope for this battered people? It is interesting to see the interpretation given in Hanoi to these events—as in the *Bulletin* of the North Vietnamese Legation in Paris, dated April 1965:

> The workers of the cities and plantations were able to act jointly with the general movement of political struggle, and they found the sympathy of various strata of the population, particularly of the pupils and students, and the overall support of public opinion. The movement also received the support of a part of the regular troops and the police, which made the forces of repression hesitate and enter into negotiations with the workers.

Another fact deserves mention: such a movement is often unleashed spontaneously. Of fifty-six manifestations organized by the workers in September 1964, only four were directed by the unions. The struggles themselves usually begin with simple demands for elementary rights and the application of democratic freedoms, then turn into spreading strikes and lead to the occupation of factories. The use of force by the masses, in order to oppose force, represents progress in the organization of the struggle. By these revolutionary acts the workers have gained the sympathy of various strata of the population in the cities, which increases the political influence of the labor movement among the masses. . . .

The Civilian Spirit, Saigon, November 1964

In September I had left an angry city with boiling streets, where the unions had unleashed a general strike, committees for the public weal had sprung up, and the masses had demanded the resignation of a scared military government. Returning in November, I found a silent and changed city, covered by the storms with a heavy veil of rain; a society slowly melting, fascinated by the destiny it foresaw, which both attracted and frightened it; a country in which the military men, perhaps tired of creating political disorder, seemed for the time resigned to maintain public order; a country surprised to find itself once again governed by civilians. Yet in the wings there was still the thunder of cannon.

The regime, or at least what was left of it by the American protectors and the rebel army, no longer consisted of a half dozen generals devoted to dancing the lancers quadrille, nor the disturbing coming and going of jeeps and tanks from the airport to the barracks: since the end of October and the (theoretical) obliteration of General Khanh, it was a team of elderly gentlemen. There was Suu, white-haired, going to sleep every night in his shanty on the road to Cholon; and

Huong, gray, who replaced his bicycle with a small Renault after becoming prime minister.

While General Ky's planes bombed the immediate periphery of the city around which the vise of the men in black kept getting tighter, Saigon, delivered of the Hue mandarins and the loud-voiced generals, gently turned Cochinchinese once more for a while: little palavers and conferences under the electric fans, small committees and private negotiations that seemed still confined to the nationalist camp, but for how long?

Thus the image of peace slipped between the overly firm phrases of public speeches. That image soon took on the shape of the little white-haired and gossiping gentlemen who trotted from the Gia Long Palace to the old chamber of commerce, the provisional seat of the parliament. It took on shape and outline: in Asia, where written language consists of ideographs, the images orient and speak. Diem was gone, and the pattern of the war—Ho versus Ngo—had disintegrated. With the military leaders pushed into the background, at least for a while, war was no longer the only pattern imposing itself; peace was showing its face, a peace which had changed from a daily dream into an immediate anticipation. In Saigon, wet, chilly, and whispering in the middle of November, one year after the elimination of the brothers Ngo, peace had already installed itself on the altar of the ancestors in the pagodas, if not in the churches.

The war, it seemed, would last for years, but it would no longer be anything but a long accident. Those who wanted to win it, or at least to keep from losing it for a long time, should not have killed Diem, who, obstinately but firmly, incarnated that war, or permitted the military to be obliterated. The era of elderly gentlemen in their civilian suits seemed perhaps to last, and that of the big pronouncements might return. But those one felt would only be interruptions. The transition to politicians in civilian suits would soon dilute the martial symbols and transform the long thirst for peace into a certainty. Obviously, these bourgeois gentlemen, anxious for appeasement, were afraid of a "Red future," and there was much striking evidence for that. But of the two images discernible to the observer, that of peace had a clearer outline than that of revolution.

The regime of Suu and Huong was being heavily buffeted between demands, charges, and denunciations. As a Saigon friend put it, in this climate of feverish stagnation, where the impatient desire for peace was mixed with the general inhibition regarding the only means of obtaining it, "no government that failed to promise the simultaneous abolition of taxes, immediate peace, and exclusive power for all the forces around could be in anybody's good graces."

It is quite true that the Huong Cabinet was quite lusterless, and hardly representative, not much more than a group of pen pushers and bureaucrats whose survival depended largely on two military men, Generals Pham Van Dong, military commander of Saigon-Cholon, and Cao Van Vien, commander of the third army corps; and that this government was hardly more than a living witness of the cry: "This way to peace." How far away peace was seemed unclear, and it was possible that—despite statements made in private by both at the time—neither Suu nor Huong hoped to become the negotiator. But the stage was set, and could not be altogether a *trompe l'oeil.* Among other signs, an article written by Viet Tran in the *Journal d'Extrème-Orient,* demanding a "Vietnamese solution for Vietnamese," was an appeal for a political settlement that the preceding government's censorship would never have passed.

Yet, other forces were lined up against negotiation: the majority of the army officers, not resigned to defeat, much less to retirement; the adherents of "Bac Tien," who advocated the march on the North; the Catholic refugees from the North; and most of the Americans. Only some more or less inchoate groups—intellectuals, Buddhists, unions—were in favor of peace. But if the groups throwing their weight in favor of peace seemed to be barely organized or active, and were apparently leaving their work to be done by the politico-military mechanisms, the forces in favor of the continuation of the war gave the impression of no longer believing in success, but simply in delay only.

Ever since Gen. Maxwell Taylor stated that "every war is terminated by negotiations," from the High Council down to the street in Saigon, only two opinions remained: that of those who wanted to negotiate quickly, before the situation changed still more, and that of those who did not want to negotiate except "from a position of strength," i.e., after a success obtained either in the South (but how?), or at Tchepone, in Laotian territory, or along the Ho Chi Minh Trail, that communication line between the North and the guerrillas of Nam Bo, or in Tonkin itself.

But what was the Front, the N.L.F., the Viet Cong doing? The mystery in which it cloaked itself was very disconcerting when one thought of its effective presence reaching all the way into the capital and every political circle, and the closeness of all personalities involved to the drama of important decisions. What could be gleaned here and there, in one or another Indochinese capital, did however provide some indications with regard to their actual strategy.

Despite the appeal it launched on September 17, 1964, for an uprising in the cities, the Front's first objective apparently was not to seize important positions, but to create a void and simply demonstrate that without its support the exercise of power was not conceivable; then, to open its ranks to a larger range of political trends. It was primarily for this reason that the Front did not set itself up as a clandestine government that would create an accomplished fact and alienate sympathizers. Finally, the aim was to indicate clearly the Front's independence from the North, and its intention to present itself specifically as a Southern force.

When I talked, at Phnom Penh for example, with Hanoi representatives, I found confirmation that the Ho Chi Minh government was very concerned with preserving for its Viet Cong emulators the reputation and appearance of acting on their own and of having no objective other than helping the people of the South. One might even say that this was more than mere appearances.

2

ᎿᎿᎿᎿᎿᎿᎿ

But What Do the
Buddhists Want?

As we have seen, the Buddhists, victors over the Diem regime in November 1963, understood first of all how not to abuse their victory and to beware of a clericalism which they had had to suffer at the hands of the Catholics. When I interviewed Mai The Truyen, secretary-general of the "intersectional" committee and official spokesman of "neo-Buddhism," he assured me that his co-religionists would know how to avoid falling into "triumphalism," and that nothing was less Buddhist than vengeance. But there were the faithful who forgot the spirit of their religion, as many Catholics had done only a short while ago, and who, exceeding their bounds, were seeking to settle accounts.

So much so that in the Buddhist movement some began to exploit the situation and set up a movement for the promotion of Buddhism as the state religion. In the course of the summer clashes took place that were at first sporadic and later more numerous. At the end of August and the beginning of September these clashes multiplied, particularly in the Hue region, that xenophobic province where the memory of Monsignor Thuc still quickened anti-Catholic sentiments. On September 3, 1964, at Qui Nhon and at Duc Loi, villages close to Da Nang, Catholics were persecuted and massacred and some wounded men were slain in their beds. By Buddhists? There is no conclusive evidence. These acts took place in a climate of tension between two communities, but still others may have profited by them.

Several days earlier other bloody upheavals had taken place in the streets of Saigon. The pro-Catholic paper *Xai Dung* was sacked, as was the Christian school Nguyen Ba Tong; the seat of the presumably pro-Buddhist Association of Students was set on fire. Which forces were confronting each other in the name of the two religions?

The majority of the observers reported that the gangs fighting in the streets and outskirts of Saigon and Cholon were composed primarily of young toughs, whose inspiration and objectives seemed to be something less than religious, and that they were hooligans rather than fanatics. But they also played their role in the movement.

Several hundred village Catholics from the Honai region near Saigon were brought to the capital in military trucks, because some American military chiefs and "advisers" had considered it opportune to throw these unconditional anti-communists against the "Buddhist tide," regarded as pacifist, hence neutralist, hence pro-communist. Some non-Catholic military officers were what might be called "politically Catholic": they wanted to use the mass of Catholics that seemed solid to them to fight against communism.

In order to frustrate the encroachments, and later the actual threats of the young Buddhist hierarchy, and with the more or less discreet support of certain officers, a "Central Committee for the Defense of Catholicism" was constituted in the course of the summer, led by a priest, Father Hoang Quinh. This priest was a natural popular leader, on the same pattern as his Buddhist rival, Bonze Tri Quang. Eloquent and daring, he led the crusade against the "Red infidels."

Still, on September 2, 1964, Quinh issued a communiqué defining his attitude toward violence: "Catholics are asking themselves whether, in the face of threats to their existence and property, they have the right to defend themselves and others, without having to fear being accused of seeking a quarrel with the Buddhists. In the course of many conversations with Bonze Thich Tam Chau [one of the three principal leaders of "unified Buddhism"], we have agreed that Buddhists and Catholics never use violence or sabotage public security. But when life or property is at stake, Catholics, like Buddhists, are duty-bound to defend themselves and others, and no one will be accusing them of sowing trouble or violence."

The negotiations mentioned by Father Quinh were to bear fruits other than pious words: an interconfessional committee was soon constituted, at which the representatives of the two religions met on several occasions. On the Catholic side such moderation was due primarily to the influence of Monsignor Binh, Archbishop of Saigon, who, under the Diem regime, had known how to make the disapproval of the hierarchy heard, and of Monsignor Palmas, apostolic vicar. The Archbishop's return from Rome on September 15 marked a détente, and Father Quinh then received very insistent counsels to be patient.

In the beginning of October 1964 the temperature rose again. On the first Friday of the month, at around 11:00 A.M., there was an apparently minor incident that aroused violent excitement in the Christian community: the cross on the cathedral spire in the heart of Saigon exploded with a tremendous noise. This was regarded by some as a violent act, as a "sign" by others: clearly, Buddhist daring was now limitless.

As a result, Hoang Quinh's influence grew again, interfaith contacts were once again interrupted, and the atmosphere of holy war reappeared. The leaders of the Central Committee for the Defense of Catholicism, began to press Monsignors Binh and Palmas to permit their organization to act, arguing that the duty to defend property and persons was now clear.

Still, the Vietnamese Catholics were not the only or even the principal instigators of these troubles. The role of the new Buddhist hierarchy was also important, and on the whole little suited to furthering real coexistence between the South's two principal communities. This was so not only because excesses were committed at the base and by minor members, as was also the case with the Catholics, but also because the doctrine of "neo-Buddhism" was constantly being reshaped and recast by certain leaders of the movement, until it appeared as a doctrine favoring the takeover of power by means that did not reject violence *a priori*. Can violence be the road to non-violence? The history of Christianity has also known examples of this perversion.

But is the word not an insult? Did the Buddhist hierarchy subscribe to everything that was said and done in its name? Did it accept the politicization of its entire movement?

Saigon, October 1964

In order to speak to the Buddhist leaders, it was necessary only a short while ago to go to the Xa Loi Pagoda, scene of the suicides in Diem's day. Today the symbol of the progressive politicization of the Buddhists is the new locality where the venerables receive visitors: in the workers' section on the outskirts of Saigon, not far from the place where the Ngo brothers were assassinated. In the immediate vicinity of the building erected by Madame Nhu for her militants, the bonzes have set themselves up in barracks worthy of the American frontier a century ago or the Foreign Legion in Camerone's time.

By changing over from the irregular and multicolored baroque style of their pagodas to their austere and dilapidated new institute, the Buddhist leaders have crossed a century and given evidence of their desire to "espouse their times."

A marriage of reason, it seems, and a fruitful one, to judge from the meteoric ascent of "neo-Buddhism" in the country's public life.

Thich Quang Do, the spokesman of the association capable of throwing into the streets of Saigon several hundred thousand martyrs, who forced two regimes and three governments to bow before him, was thirty-four years old. He embraced his religion eighteen years ago. Moon-faced, pallid, his skull shaven, his eyes lively, his voice thin, and with a smile ever ready to dissolve into great silent laughter, the Venerable Do was deceptively candid and extremely foxy in his professional naïveté. In France, too, seminarians are specialists in verbal dodges and suave silence, but never in France does the priestly smile take on such efficacy.

Q. From recent editorials in the pro-Buddhist press, can one conclude that the association will definitely enter the political arena?

A. No, certainly not. The Buddhists pursue strictly religious aims. Their only concern is with uplifting their souls in prayer, patience, and compassion.

Q. But if they demand a radical purge of all elements that took part in the Diem regime, does that mean that they consider the militants of Nhu's party (the Can Lao) more dangerous than the Viet Cong?

A. In the immediate situation, yes. To be sure, we are not minimizing the dangers of communism for our faith. But for the short term our security and our cult are more threatened by this small nucleus of Catholic extremists who have resumed their persecutions of our community, particularly in the Center.

Q. When Buddhists demonstrate *en masse* against a regime, Diem's or Khanh's, do they not act as a political group?

A. No, they are simply conscious of the aspirations

of the people; and respect for the people's aspirations demands private and public peace. We know that dictatorship is contrary to the will of the masses, whether it be that of Diem or that which Khanh may be tempted to establish. Therefore, if we act in accord with the aspiration of the people, it is pure coincidence. . . .

My interlocutor's laughter contains no irony except insofar as I infer it, and I would be dense to press him at this point.

Q. But if the dictator is a Buddhist supported by the hierarchy, as in Burma?

A. That changes nothing. If the Buddhist dictator is brutal or cruel, he is a bad Buddhist, and the regime is even worse in our eyes.

Q. In your efforts, you give priority to the struggle against the Can Lao and dictatorship. Do you think you could accommodate yourself to a communist regime? What must we think of precedents that were your community's fate in North Vietnam and in Southern zones under Viet Cong control?

A. All we know is that Buddhist associations have the right to function in the North, and that the cults are theoretically respected in the zones controlled by the Front. But these are only indications which are not, in our eyes, any guarantees.

Q. Your press has just published articles demanding a softening of the war. Is this an appeal to a political solution, and the beginning of your support for a neutralist solution?

Drawing the curtain of laughter over the question, he called it, "too deep," in English, for the Buddhist leaders prefer English to French, a rather surprising phenomenon in a country where the proportion between the two languages is 20 to 1 in favor of French.

A. We have launched an appeal in favor of the reduction of suffering of our poor people, subjected to war for twenty years. This was only an application of our sacred principle of compassion, and we do not dictate any political or diplomatic conduct.

Q. Doesn't your call for a reduction of combat serve the interests of the Viet Cong?

A. No. It is not by stepping up the attacks, but only by conducting popular policies touching the hearts of the people, that one can unite the population around the government.

Q. The last article in your paper violently attacked the Americans. Do you believe that the Americans should leave the country?

A. The Americans have come to Vietnam to defend our liberty. They were animated by true democratic principles; but for several years they have intervened more and more in our national life. This is intolerable and must cease. They must allow Vietnam to stand on its own feet. But as long as the war lasts we need them on our side.

Q. You do not think, then, that their departure would be exactly the means to finish the war?

There his laughter became so great, so silent, and so prolonged that the conversation had to be regarded as terminated. Nothing in the words of the association's official spokesman had betrayed the neutralism, fanaticism, or xenophobia of which the victors over Diem and Khanh were increasingly being accused. If Do wore a mask, it stuck well to his face.

Still, I received a letter from Nguyen An, secretary-general of the overseas association of Buddhists, when in an article I expressed doubts on the political disinterest of the Buddhist hierarchy and drew a parallel between the attitude of some influential monks and the Catholic "triumphalism" on the rampage under the Diem regime. An's letter emphasized the attitude of Buddhists on the occasion of the trial of Dang Si, a Catholic officer sentenced in 1954 for having his soldiers shoot at Buddhist demonstrators in Hue on May 8, 1963:

> We Buddhists can think of no greater leniency—in thought or act—than that expressed in the open letter by Thich Tri Quang, one of the victims threatened by Dang Si's gun on May 8, 1963, in Hue, in which Quang asked for clemency for the accused. If one still questions this gesture of Buddhist compassion, I do not know whether we can believe in anything on this earth.

This was true. But what should one think of the following document, undoubtedly genuine, given out by a witness at the end of a meeting held in mid-September in a pagoda close to Saigon?

Slogans for an Anti-Catholic Campaign

We must accuse the Catholics of having been masters of the Vietnamese nation during the days of the French (eighty years of French domination), and, together with the Americans, during the days of Diem (ten years). The Catholics, supported by French missionaries, "persecuted" the Buddhists.

As far as American aid is concerned, the Catholics are accused in the document of having stolen a great deal of that aid and of having taken much of the national resources to develop their religion.

Measures to be Taken

1. Exercise pressure on the government to forbid all entry of missionaries into Vietnam.

2. Admit Buddhism as state religion.

3. Teach the Buddhist doctrine in schools, even Catholic schools.

4. Impose heavy taxation on real estate in the Catholic community (convents, monasteries).

5. Demand that the government nationalize (French) real estate in Vietnam and distribute it to the people.

6. Request that the Catholic Church sell cheaply the terrains and rice paddies in the hands of its missions.

7. Nationalize Catholic charitable establishments: schools, orphanages, hospitals, and even the small seminaries. Severely criticize American Catholic aid.

8. Demand the suppression of Catholic almonry, for hardly 10 per cent of the people are Catholic.

9. Demand that the military tribunal sentence the old partisans of Diem, the Can Lao.

10. Support a campaign "all for Buddha."

And what should one think of the monks' attitude toward the Huong government from November 1964 to February 1965?

Although the dictatorship of Catholic mandarins had yielded to a military regime with nine of its ten leaders Buddhist, or supposedly Buddhist, it was easy to see that the monks had organized the demonstrations against the Khanh government, particularly after the "coup of Cap Saint-Jacques"—Khanh's August 15 attempt to seize all civilian and military power. This brought about the great wave of mass movements that forced Khanh to retreat at the end of August, and to promise to return all power to the civilians, which he did on October 27, 1964.

However, the attitude of the Buddhist hierarchy then became disturbing. As soon as the High Council, where the Buddhist hierarchy was represented, was instated and had designated Pham Khac Suu as chief of state and Tran Van Huong as chief of government, the great Buddhist machine gradually went into action, and the streets of Saigon began to fill with protesting men in their brown or yellow robes. But if there was a group at all—to the extent that the army or the Americans gave them any freedom of movement— which favored the return to a democracy compatible with the state of war, and the search for political solutions for Vietnam's problems, it was Suu's group. Did they do it timidly? Of course. But who could have been more daring?

Huong's government—he was an old Buddhist like Suu— certainly was neither very skillful nor representative of public opinion, and the Buddhist hierarchy might well have considered itself poorly represented in the High Council by Mai Tho Truyen, one of the rare "laymen" in the community's general staff. But the means put into operation to attain the modest objective then defined by the monks of the Committee for the Propagation of the Faith—a change of government— were comparable to those they had used to kill clerical dictatorship and militarism. Were Suu and Huong, honest politicians, equally pernicious as the integration-bent mandarins or the bellicose generals?

This led to the question of what the real objectives of the Buddhist community were, and whether its aims were the growth of freedom and a return to peace, or an increasing share in the exercise of power—in a word, just plain power. We have seen that a declaration by Huong, demanding that religious movements confine themselves to the religious area, incited the fury of the monks, particularly of Bonze Thich Tam Chau, while for months their spokesmen had insisted that the objectives of the Buddhist community were purely religious.

Where do politics begin? With the definition of an ideology and a creation of an organization to make it prevail. And that was the case here. The ideology worked out by those who might be called "combat Buddhists," who certainly did not represent all the faithful but undoubtedly have been the leaders of the game since the end of 1964, was published at the end of 1964 in a series of articles in the magazine *Hai Trieu Ham* (*The Echo of the Rising Tide*), which was regarded as the official organ of the most ardent Buddhists, and which since then has been suspended several times by order of the hierarchy. The author of the articles was in fact that very well-known monk, Thich Tri Quang, secretary-general of the Committee for the Propagation of the Faith, and the prime mover behind all pacifist, if not anti-American, movements.

In what he has called his "Memoirs," Tri Quang maintained that for many centuries Buddhism was the only national religion in Vietnam; that for a thousand years its leaders occupied the highest posts in the state; and that more recently they fought the colonial regime. Insisting that Buddhism was inspiring 80 per cent of the population, this monk claimed that it was a perfect expression and a reflection of the ideas of the Vietnamese people, and that it completely expressed all their moral and cultural qualities. "The spirit of the people, the soul of the nation, this 'certain something' that has existed since the earliest days in the life of a collective, is indeed part of Buddhism."

Tri Quang considered it "absolutely necessary, in the face of foreign ideologies that have entered and divided our nation," thinking obviously of Catholicism and communism, to create a national spirit of Buddhist orientation. He concluded that Buddhism, in which the soul and aspiration of the Vietnamese people expressed themselves so perfectly, should be recognized as the national religion, as it had been "in the most glorious epochs of Vietnamese history."

Thus one can call the system conceived by Thich Tri Quang "national Buddhism," or a popular religion that wants to become the state's ideology. *Delta,* an excellent Vietnamese students' magazine of Catholic orientation, published in Paris, recently insisted that this doctrine was a perversion of Buddhism, as genuine Buddhism had the advantage of universality and could not be reduced to the role of a national doctrine, all the more so as such ambitions could not be satisfied without appeals to action, which could not possibly be entirely non-violent.

But were Tri Quang and his companions not trying to conquer non-violence with violence? One might have thought so when reading some of their watchwords reminiscent of those which, in 1950, the *Frères musulmans* disseminated in Egypt and with which they too—basing themselves on a religion of compassion—unleashed terror.

The objection will certainly be raised that the majority of Buddhists did not consider themselves in the least affected by this type of campaign. But such currents do not touch the masses any less, and arouse effects not smaller than those provoked by the "great fear of communism" or the Viet Cong slogans.

Just as the discriminations of the preceding regime contributed to radicalizing Buddhism, this form of propaganda evoked anxiety and a desire for revenge among the Catholics, which led to Father Quinh's adventure.

In fact, the dispute between Buddhists and Catholics, limited for a long time to the leading figures of the two religions, tended to spill over into the masses and excite popular passions. This was apparent when, on February 19, 1965, a coup was launched by officers, most of whom were Catholic: in Buddhist circles the reaction was as though the barbarians were about to pounce on the pagodas.

But did this Buddhism, which was so sensitive, exciting, and influential, have any leaders, organization, or precise objectives? Its organization was hazy. It was composed of several superimposed hierarchies: the Clergy's Association; the Committee for the Propagation of the Faith; and other associations vaguely tied together under the presidency of the very ancient Thich Tin Kiet.

But under the aegis of this discreet "pope" men of different types and talents were active, among whom the Venerable (translation of the prefix Thich) Tam Chau, who was officially the number-two man of the hierarchy and—once considered a moderate favorably inclined to the Americans—who on February 20, 1955, took charge of a campaign in favor of "peace above all," which did not suit Washington in the least; Quang Lien, former Yale student and one of Professor Mus's students, who came increasingly to be regarded as the brains of the movement, and founded in January 1965 his committee for non-intervention in South Vietnam, which may turn into a laboratory of neutralism; Ho Giac, trained at Phnom Penh, named chaplain of the army at the end of 1963, who is regarded as the principal representative of the most violently anti-Western trend; and above all Thich Tri Quang, teacher of men, orator, and propagator of that national Buddhism described earlier.

Quang was a fascinating person, reminding me by his wild and abrupt ways of certain of the Near Eastern leaders and also of that strange man Huynh Phu So, who was called the "mad bonze" and thirty years ago founded the "neo-Buddhist" Hoa-Hao sect still very powerful in western Cochinchina, and who was eventually assassinated by the Viet Minh with whom he had apparently co-operated in 1946. However, Tri Quang was a different type of man. He studied at Hue, his native city, the intellectual capital of Vietnam, and among other languages he also learned French. Arrested in 1950 by the French police, he was released soon after.

In 1954, before the palace in Geneva, where the negotiations took place that were to lead to the armistice ending the first Indochinese war, one could see a strange personage fasting under a tent—Tri Quang. Nine years later, in 1963, the fighting bonze had become one of the Diem regime's most ardent critics. The police then pursued him again. He found asylum in the American Embassy. When Henry Cabot Lodge wanted to see him and asked that they talk in private, in French, Tri Quang refused haughtily: he would not, he said, speak with a stranger in "the language of colonialism," thus depriving himself and his followers of a contact essential at the time. This did not prevent the Americans from playing

Buddhism to the hilt, as they considered it an effective barrier against communist ideology.

Did Buddhism really represent a force in the sense generally given to that word? Yes and no. Yes, because with words, sacrifices, and its press it could mobilize hundreds of thousands of people in the streets of Saigon and make them demand any measure from the government that seemed useful to its cause. Also because it could alert international opinion, and it enjoyed various and numerous sympathies in the United States. Finally, because it expressed, less perhaps than Tri Quang claimed but more than other political religious groups, the personality of the Vietnamese peasant—blunt, distrustful of strangers, xenophobic, and passionately eager for peace. As a result, Buddhism was powerful, and likely to play, and to continue to play, a decisive role.

But it was a current rather than a force. It was a magnetic field, where there was lightning and thunder and where "testimonials" found powerful expression. In fact, Vietnamese society remained profoundly Confucian, impregnated with the ideal of order and harmony establishing a permanent equilibrium between the heavens, the sovereign, the people, and nature. Between the heavens and the people, the sovereign is the arbiter—he has received the mandate.

But it happens that this mandate sometimes falls into disuse, particularly as a result of the chief's unworthiness. A period of "interregnum" then begins, with upheavals, strange phenomena, miracles, and the abuses of various forms of magic. The fall of the French colonial system, once recognized as a provisional "mandate of the heavens," opened up one of these periods. Subsequently Diem had been invested in his turn with the role of mediator, but only very briefly, as he quickly became unworthy.

Now Vietnam was indeed in a state of interregnum. As a result Buddhism surged up, imposed itself, not knowing how to establish harmony and authority, but knowing how to profess the faith, illuminate, pronounce messages for the future, and in the present launch appeals for compassion. It was feared and respected, and some threw themselves at it; but it was not obeyed. It was not the heavenly mediator, but a sub-stitute—pending a new "mandate" that would perhaps be as-sumed this time by the "nation" or perhaps by communism.

Provisionally or not, the Buddhist organization pursued the following objectives. It attempted to eliminate from the coun-try influences that perverted the body and soul of the nation and were foreign to it, such as Catholicism or materialism. From the point of urgency—and efficacy—Catholicism was their first target. Fighting it, the Buddhists could, for a while, make common cause with the Viet Cong, who were engaged in driving out the foreigners. At the same time this "common road" could also imply various forms of co-operation with the foreigners—as everybody knew, there were Buddhist groups financed by the American Embassy. But the prime object was nevertheless to get rid of the foreigners.

Sermons pronounced on Saturday nights at the Buddhist Institute in Saigon by Tam Chau or Quang Lien rarely at-tacked the Americans. But Tri Quang and his companions were much less discreet in their sermons, particularly in the Hue region.

They were much more aggressive because in that region the activities of the "committees for the common good," issu-ing from Hue in the beginning of September, had by then made quite a stir in the Center of the country. These commit-tees, inspired primarily by professors at the University of Hue —for example Doctor Quyen, dean of the faculty of medi-cine—associated themselves with Buddhism and campaigned against "all foreign influences." Their official target was France, advocate of neutralism. But the consensus was that their action was more strenuously directed against the United States, and the view was widespread that they were infiltrated by the National Liberation Front. In any event, their propaganda went precisely in the direction of Tri Quang's "national Buddhism." This meant that one could not disregard this current that had now found its political instrument.

We have already alluded to the *Freres musulmans* of Egypt and the Near East. Despite the profound differences between the adherents of a monotheistic, revealed religion and the followers of a system like Buddhism, there were points of contact: the same recruitment of new members from among the peasants and the small merchants in a state of decline, the same thirst for a doctrine both religious and national, the same hope for "social justice" without precise content and on the fringes of Marxism, the same mixture of ambitious wile and pious sincerity among their leaders. And, let us add, the same distrust on the part of both "true" Mussulmans and Buddhists of adventures and violence that can be found in such movements.

Quite a few Americans believed that influential monks were conniving with the Viet Cong, that Thich Tri Quang had once been a Viet Minh militant—like many nationalist leaders— and that his brother was a leader of the Buddhist organization in North Vietnam. In any event, some statements by Tri Quang made it clear that he was among those strongly opposed to American intervention in South Vietnam. But did that mean he was a Viet Cong? Or a xenophobe? Or a patriot?

What seemed to emerge from the various retractions and strategic changes of line by the Buddhist community, like the slogans disseminated not long before in the pagodas of South Vietnam, was that these monks considered themselves the most genuine spokesmen of the nation and particularly of the peasants, and felt that the politico-religious ideology, forged by them on the basis of pacifism, nationalism, and appeals to social justice, gave them the right to claim a place among the official powers. As we have seen, their objective was to have Buddhism proclaimed the state religion, and to make religious leaders the framework or at least the "conscience" of the future South Vietnam.

In that they were opposed to the policy of the National Liberation Front, which was predominantly Marxist. But in the interim they seemed unworried about serving the interest of the guerrillas. And in the short run they seemed not to worry that they were furnishing pretexts for interference to military extremists and the American services supporting them.

To sum up, "national Buddhism" played its card of peace to the hilt, even if, in order to do so, it provisionally had to aid the Front. In times of war the Front has to lead the game. But the Buddhists believed that when peace returned, they could take its place. The Viet Cong was, in their view, the expression of the people's armed revolt against foreigners. Buddhism would be the pacifying agent, and later the true vehicle for the will of the people, after the return of peace.

This was a chance they took. But these political monks had undergone such an extraordinary destiny, they had expected to transform a society based on thought, wisdom, and spirituality into a revolutionary arm and an enormous "pressure group" overnight; and had considered it possible to establish a state religion for their benefit, even against communism. They knew that in the North, Buddhism was just barely tolerated as a cultural enterprise. But they believed that they could brave the storm. The hunger for peace was so strong, in their view, that the people would follow those who would bring peace to them. But would the people then still have a choice?

3

⊛⊛⊛⊛⊛⊛⊛

The Illusions of the
Year of the Serpent

The General Kicks Off

One need not be a chauvinist or conform to Gaullism to see in the declaration by General de Gaulle of August 29, 1963, on the subject of Vietnam, the "kick-off" of a diplomatic game that, incidentally, was to have more interruptions than action.

Actually de Gaulle said nothing very new that day, having been content rather to recall what many knew—that the Vietnamese affair was primarily political, and that as the conflict had been caused largely by the confrontation of foreign powers, only their "non-intervention" could restore peace. He did not even speak of neutralization, but the thought was implicit in his words, and this silence gave birth to a protracted clamor.

After the initial reactions of excitement, interest, or indignation were over, his position slowly gained ground. Particularly after the spring of 1964 the repercussions could be heard, all the more so when on April 24, Robert McNamara, returning from an inspection tour of Vietnamese battlefields, agreed that "no progress could be attained in Vietnam for several months." This was approximately the kind of language that had been used ten years earlier, in February 1954, by French Minister of Defense Pleven, when he returned from his Indochinese mission. Accepting the consequences of the situation, and with his colleagues' accord, Pleven—a member of the Laniel Cabinet—had then tried to make contact with the enemy.

To be sure, the situation that the American leaders had to face in the spring of 1964 was not as grave as the one faced by the French ten years earlier. But one got the impression that the problem was becoming more and more political from day to day, and that the chiefs of state, the diplomats, and the commentators were slowly sketching the great lines of what could become a negotiated settlement, whose key words would be "non-interference by foreigners" and "neutralization."

The most symptomatic manifestations of this development seemed to be an interview accorded by Ho Chi Minh to his friend Wilfred Burchett, the Australian journalist, on April 13, and also a declaration made by the North Vietnamese leader at the end of the very important "special political conference" at Hanoi; a speech by President Johnson on April 27; a speech by Adlai Stevenson before the U.N. Security Council on May 22; and articles published on the same day in *The New York Times* and the *New York Herald Tribune*.

On the occasion of the "special political conference" in Hanoi from March 29 to April 3, 1964, bringing together all North Vietnamese cadres, Ho Chi Minh recalled that if "peaceful" unification of Vietnam should remain Hanoi's objective, it was necessary first to prepare the road for such a new arrangement by the establishment of economic, political, and cultural relations between the two zones. The Vietnamese leader did not set a time limit for such a transitional state of affairs. And it was indeed imaginable that such a provisional two-headed system could lead Vietnam back to a situation such as had followed the Geneva Agreements; stop the ruinous guerrilla activity in the South; and permit Cochin-chinese rice shipments to the North that would put an end to the terrible economic pressure suffered by the Tonkinese.

More than ten years earlier, in November 1953, in an interview with the Swedish paper *Expressen,* Ho had opened the discussion on a political solution of the first Indochinese war, simply by declaring himself ready to explore with France conditions for a cease-fire. This time the Hanoi leader, speaking to Burchett, made two "overtures": a very careful one directed toward Washington, by paying homage to the "American people," just as he had vis-à-vis the "French people" in the days of Henri Martin; the other, more direct, he aimed specifically at France, offering the assurance that "President de Gaulle's suggestion on the neutralization of the part of Southeast Asia including South Vietnam merits serious attention."

This was a curious formula. Its significance was enhanced by the fact that four days earlier, in Tokyo, Georges Pompidou had said very publicly that de Gaulle's propositions were aimed at the whole of Vietnam. The Hanoi leaders were clever enough to have foreseen this point already implicit in General de Gaulle's declaration of August 29, 1963; and no matter how little disposed they might have been to such a solution, they did not seem reluctant to open discussions on that basis.

Signs of American Interest

The declaration made two weeks later by Lyndon Johnson was even more specific. But by stating that Washington would not oppose any settlement permitting South Vietnam to preserve its independence by authorizing it to appeal for its defense to friends of its choice, the President in fact offered to apply to that country the same diplomatic fare that Cambodia had obtained at the end of the Geneva Conference of 1954, after a long struggle with Molotov; Johnson's statement, too, was a formula inspired by that neutrality appearing on the horizon, after various transformations.

Adlai Stevenson's statement received even more attention, since it was made within the framework of the United Nations and in a particularly passionate climate, so heated because of the demands on the part of Republican leaders in favor of military intervention in Vietnam, made in connection with the Presidential election campaign. Stevenson recalled at the United Nations that the United States was in Vietnam only in order to respond to the appeal of a small threatened power, and he let it be understood that once this mission was accomplished, or the appeal revoked, American intervention would cease. Such optimism appearing here and there was further intensified by articles in the two great New York dailies in late May of 1964. Walter Lippmann wrote in the *New York Herald Tribune* on May 21:

> If Gen. de Gaulle is right, as most surely he is, that there can never be a stabilized peace in South Asia unless it is supported by China, then it would be folly on our part not to hope that he will succeed in his diplomatic explorations in Peking. . . .
>
> What is the French hypothesis? It is that the Sino-Soviet conflict is very serious, so serious that it now poses great territorial issues, and therefore that Peking has a strong interest in stabilizing its southern frontier. The real questions are: what is the price of an agreement to stabilize it and what are the guarantees of such an agreement? This is what Gen. de Gaulle has now to find out. . . .
>
> If we analyze the situation fully, we shall conclude . . . that French policy and American are not competitive in Asia but are in fact complementary. This is to say that what Gen. de Gaulle is trying to accomplish is the only conceivable solution of what is certainly an otherwise interminable military conflict. But it is to say also

that what the United States is continuing to do, which is to sustain the resistance of the Saigon government, is necessary to the success of the French action in Peking and Hanoi. It is in this sense that the two policies are complementary. They would become fused into one policy if the Administration adopted as its slogan a modification of Churchill's remark "we arm to parley" and said that "in Viet Nam we fight to parley." . . .

Lippmann concluded that neither government could say that: the United States could not say it without running the risk of undermining what little combat morale there is in Saigon; the French could not say it because they could not simultaneously bless American intervention and negotiate with Peking.

In its turn *The New York Times* of May 24 assured its readers in an editorial that:

The basic goal, as we see it, is implementation of the Geneva accords of 1954 and 1962. This means an end to the subversion supported and supplied by North Vietnam and Communist China in Laos and South Vietnam, reinstatement of the tripartite coalition in Laos and neutralization of all four successor states formed from what was once French Indochina. . . .

While the French government was trying to extend neutralization to all of Southeast Asia, *The New York Times* preferred to apply this solution only to the former territories of Indochina—which seemed more judicious and more within the reach of negotiations for the median term—American public opinion and the American government being what they were.

Lots of People in the Socialist Camp

Did these words and ideas correspond to an actual situation pointing toward an end to the war at the least cost? We have compared McNamara's observations of April 1964 with Pleven's of February 1954. But the problems that they had to solve were not the same, and the reactions of the American leaders cannot have been identical with those of their French predecessors a decade earlier.

While their situation was less dramatic than the French situation in 1954, the problems they faced were even more complex than those for which Bidault and Mendès-France had had to find a solution. The French were faced with a visible and tangible regime, whose chief, Ho Chi Minh, had made it known three months earlier through a Swedish newspaper that he was ready to discuss conditions for a cease-fire. Ten years later the matter was much more complicated.

The war in South Vietnam was being conducted by the guerrillas of the N.L.F. with direct support from Hanoi, with aid from Peking, and with some support from other countries in the socialist camp, including the Soviet Union. That meant a Western government was faced with quite a few negotiators, which was a great problem in a situation where the interest and behavior of its Saigon protégés also had to be taken into account.

On the basis of declarations coming from Hanoi, one could believe oneself to be on the eve of a political maturation comparable to that at the end of 1953. But the complication was that no matter how great a part the Northern regime played in the operations in the rice paddies of the South, or in financing the war effort, the National Liberation Front did not seem disposed to be treated simply as part of Vietnamese communism, and did not miss a single opportunity to affirm its autonomy publicly.

If among the forces of which the Front was composed the Popular Revolutionary Party was clearly tied to Hanoi, other elements of the Front, as we have seen, claimed to be based on nationalism, i.e., Southern particularism. Independently of these internal differences, the N.L.F. wanted to be master of its own decisions, to the extent it was leading the struggle.

During all of 1964 no move on the part of the Front betrayed any desire for a political settlement. When combatants are all steamed up, it is hard to make them listen to other arguments. In April 1964 Nguyen Van Hieu, former secretary-general of the N.L.F., went to Algiers, where the Front's principal diplomatic antenna in that part of the world is installed. From contacts established on this occasion by the leader of the Front, it seemed obvious that he and his comrades were not in a particular hurry to see the fighting come to an end; and that what they were particularly concerned with at the time was to add proof that they were not only capable of exercising military power, but they were politically representative of the South Vietnamese people as well. But how could they attain that? By provoking and aggravating the political vacuum in Saigon. This operation was already well under way.

Neverthelesss, 1965 opened under auspices that were quite favorable for peace. Several weeks earlier, in September 1964, U Thant, Secretary-General of the United Nations, had received word that North Vietnam was disposed to gave favorable consideration to political overtures, particularly if they were to be made by countries like Great Britain and the Soviet Union, co-presidents at the Geneva Conference. While on a "technical" mission in Paris, Dr. Pham Ngoc Thach, minister of public health at Hanoi, had let it be understood in talks with his French friends that a move from Paris would be welcome. Finally, at Phnom Penh, Prince Norodom Sihanouk had called together a Conference of the Indo-Chinese People for February. This had the double advantage of permitting the N.L.F. to emerge from its mysterious status and express itself publicly, and to reëstablish the existence of the Indochinese framework within which the peaceful future of these peoples might take place.

In brief, the "Year of the Serpent"—that had begun five weeks after the Western calendar year—opened under the sign of that animal's wisdom: the preceding years had been those of the cat and the tiger.

And then February 5, 1965, was dawning.

The Missed Rendezvous

It was a sort of planetary rendezvous on the scale of the problem at hand, a world scale. From Moscow, Premier Kosygin, the man of the production plan, the neo-revisionist with the cool head, the man of the channelized revolution, was flying toward North Vietnam. From Washington, Mc-George Bundy, the former Kennedy man and trustee of that President's thoughts underlying the agreements with Moscow in the Laotian compromise, was landing in South Vietnam.

One could hardly imagine that the Soviet prime minister was going to Hanoi in order to preside over the solemn delivery of a few dozen MIGs, or that Mr. Johnson's special adviser was going to Saigon to encourage General Taylor to give battle. A sort of convergence seemed to be beginning.

Everything seemed to indicate that Moscow, six months after having made known its intention to disengage itself completely from the Indochinese sector and even to give up its co-presidency in the permanent body of the Geneva Conference, which it shared with Great Britain, had decided to become active again in Hanoi; to replace the Chinese influence that had progressively taken the place of its own; and to explore the possibilities of a peaceful settlement based on compromise.

It was apparently also an effort to re-create the climate that had made it possible to terminate the first Indochinese war in 1954—an operation in which Molotov had played a decisive role, not without extracting immense concessions from his Viet Minh allies—and also to re-create the climate of the Vienna meeting at which Kennedy and Khrushchev had made public their settlement on Laos that had been in preparation by their diplomats for a long time.

What could motivate Kosygin to undertake this extraordinary and sudden step in Hanoi, where the friends of the Soviets still occupied important posts, but where the friends of the Chinese had seemed to be taking the initiative, particularly after the bombardment of North Vietnamese bases on August 5 of the preceding year?

Surely Kosygin's intention was to convince the North Vietnamese to participate in the March 1 interparty conference at Moscow, and thus to show their independence from Peking. By assuring Hanoi's presence at "their" conference, the Soviets would shake up the Asian bloc, then controlled by the Chinese. But this operation was hazardous—and was not to succeed.

Also, a personage of Kosygin's caliber would not take such a journey to make surveys or overtures, but only to gather already-ripened fruits. As it happened, for four months the Soviets had received various indications that both Hanoi and the guerrillas in South Vietnam had expected Moscow to resume the responsibilities of leadership in the socialist camp.

First there had been the journey to Moscow by Le Duan, secretary-general of the Lao Dong, the North Vietnamese Communist Party. Elected at the Third Congress in November 1960 because of his expertise in Southern problems, on the motion of Ho Chi Minh, pushing hard for a policy of reunification, Le Duan had developed since then in a pro-Chinese direction and along with Truong Chinh had become the leader of that group at Hanoi. But when he visited the Soviet Union, Le Duan had made it clear that the role of the Soviet Union remained important in the minds of the Vietnamese, and that Hanoi would not be satisfied with aid from Peking alone.

On September 24, 1964, a conference for international solidarity with the Vietnamese people opened at Hanoi, where the most firmly pro-Soviet organizations, like the Association of Democratic Jurists, were particularly coddled. Their delegates left, certain of two things: the Hanoi leaders were anxious to arrive at an end of the war, and in the pursuit of that objective they counted on Soviet intervention. Moreover, on December 26, Tass published a notice assuring Vietnam that Moscow was ready to provide increased support.

At the same time the Viet Cong leaders took various measures: they set up in Moscow a representation parallel to that in Peking; they substituted in the secretariat-general the "non-committed" Phat for the pro-Chinese Hieu; and they established increased contacts with such pro-Soviet capitals as Prague and Warsaw.

Kosygin's note book was swelling with interesting information, coming from Washington, concerning the development of American policy. In December there had been a contact—in Prague?—with an American emissary, of which it was only known that it had not been discouraging, as distinguished from the contact that had been made in Warsaw with the Chinese delegate. Contacts had been established in Paris by Anderson, counselor and friend of President Johnson, particularly with General Billotte, that revealed the Americans' desire to learn more about a possible "neutralist" solution. There had also been a request by the American services in Saigon addressed to members of the International Control Commission—Indians, Poles, and Canadians—to explore the N.L.F.'s intentions.

Had William Bundy—brother of McGeorge and Assistant Secretary of State for Far Eastern Affairs, who had been discreetly invited to play a part in the Indochinese theater and who had been asked to suggest an appropriate American move toward a political solution—not spoken of the possibility of a return to the Geneva Agreements? Premier Kosygin could conclude that the overtures had been made and that a determined follow-up was in order.

Then on February 5 came the attack on Pleiku and the American camp in the highlands, causing the U. S. Army to suffer its heaviest losses since the beginning of the war. We must examine the facts before examining their causes and consequences.

A War Act at Ground Level

What happened? An attack like the sinking of the *Lusitania?* The bombardment of a base in peacetime, as at Pearl Harbor? It was an act of war in a time of war. American combatants were attacked and killed by Vietnamese combatants on Vietnamese territory. I am not judging here U.S. policy, or its justification, or the good faith of the G.I.s; I am merely recalling the simple facts. Nine men were killed, and 140 wounded by mortar and machine-gun fire—a grievous but commonplace balance sheet. It was a far cry from the August 4 torpedo-boat attack on the *Maddox,* a dozen miles from the Northern coast. A plain act of guerrilla land warfare, the blow of February 5 was a cruel but "regular" guerrilla action.

It is not really necessary therefore to interpret the events, to look for distant origins and see in it a "coup by Peking," or to attribute it to an effort on the part of Ho Chi Minh to twist Kosygin's arm. One might simply deplore it as a particularly efficient stroke on the part of the N.L.F., who needed neither Peking's advice nor Hanoi's orders to set off a battery of ten heavy mortars close to a U. S. Air Force camp, or to throw some commandos against the base. One is perfectly entitled to assume that the operation was decided at and conducted from Viet Cong headquarters near Tay Ninh, and that it came as a surprise to Giap at Hanoi.

But it took place in such a significant context and at such an important juncture that it was hard to see it as an isolated act. Kosygin's journey—complemented by Bundy's—had opened two perspectives: first, at least a partial substitution of Soviet influence for Chinese at Hanoi; second, the beginning of a dialogue at the summit from which could emerge an agreement that would more or less take into account the aspirations and interests of the guerrillas. Therefore there was reason to believe that the initiative for the action against the Pleiku base may have originated with those threatened by closer Soviet-American collaboration: i.e., either with those who at Hanoi represented most strongly the Chinese line and could not tolerate a switch in the direction of Moscow; or with the fighting men at the base who were little disposed to being deprived of some of the fruits of their victory by an arrangement at the summit, and who believed that such a victory was near.

Only a person who followed the history of decolonialization rather inattentively could fail to recall how consistently the fighters involved in the hardest battles make every effort to delay peaceful solutions. This fascination with suffering has been one of the most consistent phenomena in the history of contemporary revolution. This accounted for a series of Viet Minh provocations during the conference at Fontainebleau in 1946, eventually provoking the bombardment of Haiphong by French guns, which ruined any chance for a settlement; or during the war in Algeria, and particularly on the eve of the Evian meeting, for the massacre at Chenoua, representing guerrilla efforts to stop all peace moves.

All this was easily foreseeable. What might be regarded as surprising in the whole matter was the American reaction. An American colleague told me that when Henry Cabot Lodge heard of the reprisal operations of August 5 against seven bases in North Vietnam, he exclaimed: "These imbeciles are preventing an Asian Yugoslavia from establishing itself here." This seemed to show that Lodge was less simple-minded than some of his previous words had indicated. But on February 6 his mind was less lucid, and he was heard to applaud the reprisals. Yet, the attack on Pleiku had not been anything like the daring foray by the Northern navy against the all powerful Seventh Fleet, but merely a typical guerrilla operation.

Here is where the whole affair begins to make sense. It then reminded me of the conversation with an American diplomat whom I had met the preceding September. When we were speaking about the possibility of escalation and its strategic value, he had considered it perfectly useless, and acknowledged that the Viet Cong war effort depended only to a very small extent on the North. Then he had suddenly exploded, insisting that the Americans would not permit themselves to be pushed around forever or have the enemy impose on them his form of warfare—that of the knife against the helicopter.

I was reminded again of the reactions of the paratroop officers at the time of Sakiet. (It must be remembered, however, that Tunisian aid to the F.L.N. in Algeria was more direct than Hanoi's intervention on behalf of South Vietnam, and, juridically, the position of France in Algeria was stronger in various ways than that of the United States in Vietnam.)

The American reprisal operations could be interpreted on two levels. One was at the level of elementary psychology: "We have had enough!" But it could also have been a premeditated action and part of a general shift in strategy for which McGeorge Bundy's journey would have been the prologue. "Now they can negotiate!" exclaimed a very intelligent Vietnamese on the evening of February 6, when he had learned of the U. S. Air Force operation following the assault on Pleiku.

But on the day after the bombings General Moore allowed himself to be escorted by South Vietnamese air units, led by Gen. Nguyen Cao Ky, the man dedicated to escalation. And President Johnson was already raising the ante by "unleashing" his air force. But the game was much more dangerous when played with General Ky and his companions, who were self-sufficient enough in the air to be able to increase their action against the North from Da Nang, taking their authorization to do so from the precedent of February 6. It was obvious that Hanoi would still be very much less inclined to incursions by the Southerners than suffer reprisals by the Americans. Here was a grave risk. The results were soon to follow.

At Phnom Penh the Neutralists Are Surfacing

On November 9, 1964, in a speech on the occasion of a national Khmer celebration, Prince Norodom Sihanouk launched the idea of a "conference of the Indochinese peoples." A few hours later he told me:

> Rather than enlarge the war as the Americans seem eager to do, why not enlarge peace? Indochina, which is such a perfect synthesis of the civilization from which we have all emerged, would be the best framework for the transfer of the conflict to the political plane, followed by the reconstruction of peace. Indochina is too much of a living reality to be stifled by the memories of colonization. And French culture plays too large a part here not to serve as a factor of unification and development, once the past is forgotten.

In a word, the rendezvous was proposed. Who would attend it? The "progressives," of course, from North Vietnamese and Laotian communists to the N.L.F. But would the others, such as the "bourgeois" neutralists, be accepted? And would the movements of the Extreme Left agree to come in view of the pride they took in their military exploits and the sacrifices they had made? If they participated in the debates, would they recognize the soundness and subtlety of the neutralist concept?

From the beginning of the preparatory conference on February 15 the problem was presented, in fact quite brusquely, by the delegates of the Pathet Lao, the Extreme Left Laotian organization. "We are three countries: Vietnam, Cambodia, and Laos; three delegations will be sufficient . . . or rather four, one for North Vietnam and one for the South—the N.L.F." But the Cambodians who had issued the invitation argued that if they were to invite Tran Van Huu and his neutralist friends from the Committee for Peace and Rebuilding of South Vietnam—whose members were almost all residing in Paris—they would not do so in order to make them cool their heels at the door.

Actually the socialist camp had mounted this attack not in order to exclude "neutralists" of the Huu type, i.e., "bourgeois intellectuals" not politically committed and not involved in the war, but to revenge themselves for the many rebuffs given by the former chief of the Baodaist government of 1950 to N.L.F. offers to meet for discussions (at Algiers and Karlovy-Vary, in 1963–1964), and also in order to test the degree of the support given by Prince Norodom Sihanouk to his "Parisian" guests. As soon as they had convinced themselves of the Cambodian leader's firmness—and they proceeded with enough care to show their anxiety to establish close relations within the Indochinese framework for the postwar period—they permitted Tran Van Huu's delegation to be placed on equal footing with themselves. In this fashion neutralism officially acquired a voice at the conference.

Even so, was it possible to simplify things in this fashion, and attribute the same "line" to all Extreme Left delegations? Yes and no. It seemed that South Vietnam's National Liberation Front differed from the North's Patriotic Front primarily with regard to "style," method, and tone. On the whole the men from Hanoi displayed hard and rigorous attitudes even though a "moderate" led the Northern delegation at the second conference. The men of the South showed a more relaxed and "Southern" comportment, particularly Huynh Tan Phat, new secretary-general of the N.L.F., whose relatively easy tone was in conflict with the rather doctrinaire style of his two companions (who had been his predecessors in the Front's key post), Nguyen Van Hieu and Tran Buu Kiem. This first public performance by several of the principal N.L.F. leaders indicated that by passing from Hieu to Kiem to Phat, the Front had evolved away from dogmatism in the direction of better possibilities of co-operation with the "bour-geois" or "liberal" elements inside the South Vietnamese op-position.

But the differences between the Hanoi delegates and the Front delegates were not just restricted to the tone employed in the debates and hallways. The major idea dominating the conference—to convoke another and much larger interna-tional conference for the political study of the Vietnamese question, on the model of the Geneva Conference of 1954—found them if not divided at least not co-ordinated.

While the men from the North said it was impossible for them to make a statement because their government had not yet taken a stand on the subject (it would have been more correct for them to say that for several months Ho and his government had opposed such a conference, because they were under American bombardment), the Front's representa-tives admitted publicly that "this would be one way of doing things," and that "no means to reëstablish peace should be ex-cluded from the outset." The "prior condition of American departure" was brought up, with more or less conviction. It did not seem to reflect the bedrock of thinking on the part of the communist delegates and their friends.

But in order for the conference not to seem to "solicit" from the Americans a conference on Vietnam and thus to admit that the bombings had been a good way of producing negotia-tions, Tran Van Huu's group suggested the convocation of a conference on Cambodia and Laos that would inevitably lead to the Vietnamese question: in similar fashion the first nego-tiations on Vietnam in 1954 had been begun by way of a dis-cussion on Korea. The North Vietnamese delegation seemed to jump at this suggestion and it paid lively homage to the neutralist leader's cleverness, soon echoed by the Laotians and the Southerners; thus a conference on the subject of the two kingdoms was decided upon, marking the end of the meeting at Phnom Penh, on March 9.

This project, which had been the principal reason for the convocation of the conference by Prince Sihanouk and which aimed at resuscitating the Indochina concept in order to turn it into a framework for negotiations and the peace to come, was the occasion of a very interesting and revealing clash. The spokesmen for the Cambodian leader—particularly Sonn San, the chief of the Sangkum delegation, who led the debates in virtuoso fashion and revealed himself as a diplomat of the first order—proposed the creation of a "permanent secretariat-general" of the organization of Indochinese people. Fearing perhaps to become too involved in this fashion with the "bourgeois" politicians, the delegates from Hanoi did not agree that the liaison organ should be so highly structured, and suggested that there should be a simple "co-ordinating committee."

Sonn San replied that the project which he represented had been decided on by Sihanouk and adopted by his government, and therefore could not be amended. He thereupon proposed to break off the discussion: "Our plan or nothing." After an adjournment the delegates from Hanoi and of the Front approached San to ask him to return once more to the idea of the secretariat-general, and to discuss the matter after all. Little concerned with sparing their pride, the Cambodian diplomat thereupon asked them to approach the Prince himself with their demand. In the end it turned out that Hanoi was anxious to save the Indochinese framework and did not want to alienate the people in Phnom Penh.

Thus the conference of Phnom Penh made it clear first, that there was an Indochinese spirit, whose full impact would be clear only after a return to peace; second, that there was a certain independence and autonomy of action on the part of the Southern National Liberation Front with respect to the North; third, that there was a possibility of co-operation between revolutionary Southerners (the N.L.F.) and the "bourgeois" elements (Huu and his friends). In the hallways and in the course of private conversations all this showed even more clearly than in the public sessions.

But the effort made at Phnom Penh was ruined, at least for the immediate future, by the brusque extension of the war on February 6. Thereafter the key word was no longer "negotiation" but "escalation."

4

𝒮𝒮𝒮𝒮𝒮𝒮𝒮

Some Subjects for Discussion

Discussion? But on what subjects? To what ends? It is easy to see that the interested powers—the nine that met in Geneva in 1954 or the fourteen that met in Geneva in 1962—must meet again. But the short-term aims are more easily discernible than the long-term objectives. The immediate aim would be to cap the results of the two preceding negotiations conducted at Geneva. The results of the first conference were the actual end of the fighting, which is often not clearly remembered; the division of Vietnam into two provisional zones; and the recognition by the Eastern powers of the independence and unity of the kingdoms of Laos and Cambodia, which received not merely the status of neutrality but of unrestricted diplomatic sovereignty. The second conference established Laotian neutrality on the basis of ideological tripartism.

A third conference should try to correct the less propitious effects of the first two. For the time being the division of Vietnam has become so much of a reality that Ho Chi Minh has pleaded in various interviews for the independence of the South—but the conference should foresee the conditions and rhythm of a reunification for the long term and meanwhile should consider a procedure for the establishment of relations between the two zones. It probably should also reëstablish in Saigon a popular front, internationally promoted and guaranteed as in Vientiane, for while at Phnom Penh, Sihanouk does not need to be buttressed from the Left or Right, at Saigon the guerrillas of the N.L.F. do not seem to insist on a power monopoly.

Examining the chances for negotiation, the West should not neglect the advantages that it can derive from the differences in interests and objectives inside the socialist camp. It is clear that the South Vietnamese Liberation Front tries to retain a certain autonomy with regard to Hanoi; that North Vietnam has different ambitions than Peking; that the Chinese are desirous of finding partners in the West; finally, that Moscow would like to stop the Chinese push toward the South. Perhaps not enough attention has been paid to Mikoyan's words in Tokyo, of May 26, 1964, to the effect that Moscow would help Washington find a solution in Indochina.

Some people attribute the resumption of fighting in South Vietnam to the non-application of the Agreements of July 20–21, 1954; for example Couve de Murville did so in his declaration of April 28, 1964, before the National Assembly. Others believe that these accords implied in themselves an inevitable resumption of war, and were never considered by Hanoi or Peking as anything but a very provisional halt in the expansion of communism across Southeast Asia.

In actual fact, these accords applied during a considerable period, permitting a real peace for about five years; from 1954 to 1959 the war had come to an end in Indochina. While it would be difficult to state that the Chinese or North Vietnamese leaders never had other objectives than those agreed upon at Geneva, it must be admitted that the first violations that took place were not theirs. Finally, a new reading of the Agreements of July 1954 and a look at the events since then, show that these agreements were really effective, that they still incorporate elements for a wise solution, and that in the event of negotiation, they could provide useful tools even to those who originally rejected them.

1. The accords were partially applied. Between July 20 and December 31, 1954, it was estimated that more than twenty thousand Vietnamese officers and soldiers left the zone situated south of the 17th Parallel, as the Geneva texts had stipulated.

To be sure, the Geneva Agreements also prohibited the introduction into either zone of "new personnel and matériel." Were these provisions really respected by Hanoi, which demobilized eighty thousand men in 1956–1957, but whose popular army subsequently kept growing, and whose imports from China do not seem to be strictly in the civilian sphere? It is certain, in any event, that the agreements were not respected in the South, where the accords between Generals Ely and Collins, concluded at the end of 1954, transferred a great many of France's military responsibilities to the United States, which did introduce "new personnel" into this region of Vietnam.

It is known that the principal violation of the July 1954 texts was the refusal by the Saigon government to arrange in July 1956 for the general elections stipulated in the final declaration made at the conference—to which Saigon admittedly had not subscribed. That there were no elections had been more Saigon's than Washington's fault, because American Ambassador Reinhardt was considering at the time running the risk of holding a plebiscite at a time when the Northern regime was at its lowest ebb and the Southern regime was riding high.

Was that why Ho Chi Minh and his collaborators, when sounded out by an emissary from Phnom Penh at the end of 1955, had accepted the idea of a postponement of the plebiscite, and had not made its being held on the agreed date a test of the South's sincerity, and why they had been ready to consider a revised procedure for agreement "among Vietnamese" on this point? However this may be, it was the categorical and apparently final refusal on the part of Diem and his regime to consider facing the Communists in general elections that had led the Hanoi leaders to support the subversion in the South, which in turn led to the increase of American intervention and the progressive internationalization of the conflict.

From this episode one can at least conclude that the men in Hanoi are the kind who would be likely to stick to an accord.

2. *Partial application of the 1954 Agreements made one reality emerge: Vietnamese duality.* After the chances of re-unification had been sabotaged and the cycle of war reopened, the most important result of the 1954 Agreements was the division of Vietnam. This is no longer a technical or provisional division as had been originally anticipated, but apparently a permanent division, which has affected the mores and conscience of the people, and from which any future solution must proceed, at least in its first phase.

To be sure, Vietnam was not unified from Lang Son in the North, to the Point of Ca Mau in the South, except for relatively short periods in its history, which is the history of resistance to China. But the 1945 revolution, the long struggle against France, and the attempts on the part of the colonial regime to make division an instrument of rule had provoked a profound and irresistible drive toward unification at the time. All statements by Viet Minh leaders at the time tried to demonstrate the complete unity of the country, and the absurdity of all efforts to set up an independent or even autonomous Cochinchina (Nam Bo). This demand for unity served as basis for all Vietnamese politics, all the more so as the French leaders had been so determined to keep the country divided.

By 1965 everything has changed. While the responsible Viet Minh leaders in the South were only executors of Hanoi's wishes, the leaders of the Liberation Front of South Vietnam today never cease to proclaim their independence and autonomy with regard to the North, and their concern for obtaining a separate future, for the territories south of the 17th Parallel, not indentured in any event to Hanoi's people or system.

It certainly is striking to hear the Southern revolutionaries defend the principle of their autonomy with regard to the North—even if it should be a tactic aimed at sparing the representatives of Cochinchinese or South Annamite particularism for the time being. But it is even more striking to find an acceptance of the political if not historical reality of a South Vietnam among the Hanoi leaders.

Once the idea is accepted at all, it will not apply only to one of the interested parties. The Hanoi spokesmen do not present—or no longer present—the country situated south of the 17th Parallel as a scrap of national territory provisionally torn from the nation's body, but as a reality and the territorial basis of a government that surely is bad, yet could improve, change, and become a perfectly serious partner in reunification negotiations.

Are the men in Hanoi anxious to see this reunification take place soon? Anyone who has had occasion in the last two or three years to talk seriously to one or another among them has reported that neither Ho Chi Minh nor his lieutenants expect to see this take place in the next ten to fifteen years.

To be sure, they feel that this unification would be nothing but an "*Anschluss*" for their benefit. Therefore they do not want to precipitate a reunification that would saddle them with a ruined country in the throes of the convulsions of war. But because they accept delay, why must it be assumed that this delay can work only in their favor?

The war in Vietnam is deplorable, and the American-Diemist policy without Diem is obviously vain and lacking in a serious political basis. But once this has been said, it must be acknowledged that the long, bloody, and blind rear-guard action now taking place does allow South Vietnam to exist, and no matter how badly governed it may be, it remains a partner in the great debate.

If one recalls what the future of South Vietnam was in the minds of those at Geneva who seized it from the victors of Dien Bien Phu, and saw in the whole operation nothing but a delay imposed on communist progress in that region, one must admit that Geneva did produce results unexpected by many of its participants. And what was only a provisional cease-fire, in Ho Chi Minh's mind, has turned into a fundamental political conflict.

This is perhaps the decisive element in the situation, and provides the West a card to play in some general negotiation, which is certainly more of a trump than the card Bidault thought he had in hand the day after Dien Bien Phu.

It will be objected that South Vietnam is thoroughly infiltrated by pro-communist subversion, and that the Western diplomats would have strange allies there. But even without appealing to communist "polycentrism," or entering into the disputes between Hanoi, Peking, Moscow, and the South Vietnamese guerrillas, one probably can say that a recognition of the N.L.F. and its "progressive leadership" would not entail South Vietnam's entry into the Marxist-Leninist bloc. Political life in Saigon would remain marked by a deep-rooted pluralism that would flower even better in peace than in war.

If Vietnam's unity remains the object of all long-term policy, for it alone represents a more profound reality than the actual ideological conflicts, it must be admitted that for the shorter term, i.e., for peace in the peninsula, a dialogue— and then coexistence—between the two Vietnams can be made to reflect the equilibrium of forces and permit the conciliation of present interests.

To the extent that Hanoi, like Peking or Moscow, makes neutralization of the South the object of its diplomacy, it would have to accept a different juridical status for the South, and with it the independent and, one hopes, durable evolution of Southern autonomy.

3. *The negotiations in Geneva made various forms of neutrality emerge, which may serve as models for peace*. It should not be forgotten that the Geneva negotiations, at which Mendès-France had set an ultimatum for midnight of July 20, did not capsize because one of the negotiators prolonged the discussion: Cambodia's spokesman had demanded that his country, for which a status very close to neutrality had been foreseen, ruling out in particular all foreign bases on its territory, should be permitted to appeal for aid to a friendly country in case of "danger" (even though Cambodia's diplomacy has developed in an opposite direction since then, the question at that time was one of possible recourse to United States aid). In the eyes of Molotov and Chou En-lai that formula seemed to open too many opportunities for Washington and its allies; but, tired of war, they ended up by giving in to the little diplomat from Phnom Penh, whose demands were not only accepted, but were extended to Laos at Mendès-France's request.

Wasn't such neutrality, including the right to call in foreign aid in case of "danger"—with the word and the thing obviously left to be defined later—what some American spokesmen have suggested for Vietnam, though only for South Vietnam, and particularly President Johnson on April 7, 1965?

One cannot say that this will be the object of American diplomacy from now on. Nor can one say that Hanoi and Peking would accept such a possibility and that the risk the very G.I.s eliminated by a peace treaty would be recalled to Saigon. But it seems not impossible that the discussion could begin on that basis.

Thus whether or not the dispositions of July 1954 were applied, they retain a political value and provide several ideas for those who are trying or will try to smooth the way for a second Indochinese peace.

Indochina: the name of a lost war can serve as a framework for peace and reconstruction.

Indochina: the word, invented in 1810 by the Danish geographer Malte-Brun, served after 1884 as an original formula applied by those colonizers in search of simplification and centralization who, as good Jacobins, were anxious to give a western bastion—Thai and Khmer—to their Vietnamese possession; to provide Vietnamese cadres for the western territories; to administer the whole region from a common capitol—Hanoi, the intellectual city; and to make the whole region center on a mercantile city—Saigon.

This relatively flexible formula, integrating various types of colonial administrations and regimes, permitted a certain technical development in Vietnam, and the maintenance of some sort of peace in Cambodia and Laos. It adjusted itself to two world wars, and it did not disintegrate until after the successive blows of the Japanese army on March 9, 1945, and the revolutionary nationalist movements emerging from the Vietnamese masses.

Then came the eight year war that, paradoxically, helped to restore the Indochinese concept, though not to redress its structure. In times of war borders are often points of contact, and strategists make better use of them than diplomats. The best proof for that is the Geneva Conference, which, taking the war map as point of departure, established peace in that same Indochinese framework. Negotiations conducted on three rails—the Vietnamese, the Cambodian, and the Laotian—led to compatible if not similar agreements: the Indochinese structure showed itself more receptive to the peacemakers than propitious to the warriors.

But the Geneva settlement rendered one aspect of Indo-

chinese disunity official and durable: the cease-fire border
along the 17th Parallel ideologically isolated the northern
part of Vietnam, permitting an iron curtain to descend across
the old federation.

Subsequently new elements of disunity appeared: the choice
made in 1955 by Cambodia in favor of a neutrality that
placed it in an independent situation with regard to the two
Vietnams; and the progressive neutralization of Laos between
1957 and 1962, under a procedure too different from that
adopted by Phnom Penh for the two kingdoms to constitute
a common zone of development.

What was separated by diplomacy and ideology was again
welded together, for the worse, by war. While Cambodia increasingly feels the repercussions of war—across a frontier
that is irritatingly porous—Laos has again become, as in
1953 to 1954 during the battles of Na Sam and Dien Bien
Phu, a sort of outskirts of the Vietnamese war. No matter
how modest it may be in volume of weapons and men, the
aid given by North Vietnam to the guerrillas in the South
does pass over the Ho Chi Minh Trail, that north-south path
inside Laotian territory from the Lai Chau region to the Atto-
peu region in the south of the kingdom—which thus does not
merely suffer the consequences of the war in Vietnam but
even serves as a subsidiary theater of operations. This in turn
is at the root of the difficulty of all political efforts which try
to make a fundamental distinction between the policies followed on either side of the border, as the American leaders
are trying to do. The growing connection of the two problems will sooner or later lead political men and strategists to
adjust the neutrality practiced in Laos to the war carried on
in Vietnam, or vice versa.

While Washington could, in 1962, subscribe at Geneva to
the multilateral neutralization of Laos and then aggravate at
Saigon the international aspects of the war by designating for
the first time a commander-in-chief no longer charged with
advisory functions but with orders to fight, such contradic-

tory policies will no longer be possible. The problems have lost their local dimensions and have become once again those of Indochina.

This was implicitly recognized in General de Gaulle's declaration of August 29, 1963. Without referring to the old French colonial districting, de Gaulle let it be understood that the future of Vietnam, for which he suggested reunification (before, of course, proposing the actual ways and means of such a policy), could not be disassociated from those of the "neighboring countries." It has become more and more clear that nothing that happens halfway down the Mekong River fails to register in the Delta. And if the source of many attitudes adopted by the Laotian revolutionaries can be found in Hanoi—with the Pathet Lao appearing more and more as a regional office of the Vietnamese Workers Party—the behavior of the Right in Vientiane is teleguided from Saigon.

To seek solutions within the framework of the old Indochinese federation would present a series of advantages. It would first of all free the strictly Vietnamese dispute of some of the passion obscuring it, and spread over a wider area the various ideological confrontations which intensify debates between the groups and personalities which are now irreducibly opposed to each other. It would also provide a sort of provisional stage, a transition to the solution of the Vietnamese affair, the end of which should be reunification, but only after a period of reëstablished normal relations between the two Vietnams. It would be, finally, the recognition of the reality of what this group of states with a common culture actually is—for those living on the East coast and for those who live in the West, where French penetration remains considerable.

It would be contributing also to the growing independence of these states from the strong influences now exercised by Red China and pro-American Thailand. No matter how great the mistrust of the Cambodians and Laotians of Vietnam, almost every leader of these two peoples are still more afraid of Bangkok's imperialism. And there are very few Vietnamese, even those who are ardent communist militants, who want to see their country subject to the Chinese. After all, Vietnam's history until recently has been nothing but a long resistance against China.

Economic motivations, historical reasons, and collective psychology explain Hanoi's interest in the reconstitution of a federated Indochina. In a letter published four years ago in the newspaper *Le Monde,* Professor Paul Mus contrasted what he considered the Chinese target (establishment of a Thai empire composed of a conglomeration of people living along the great rivers, the Mekong and Menam, toward Singapore and the Malaysian straits) with what seemed to be Hanoi's plan, a plan "of a more Marxist than Maoist orthodoxy," envisaging "the formation of a 'transversal unity' that would be economically viable, based on the Indochinese union of the French era. In that framework and on that level, in contrast to the immensity of China, direct attention to Indochina's production base would be possible, and could rapidly become profitable. . . ."

The fact that such a policy would conform to Hanoi's view does not mean, of course, that it is best. But it does not necessarily follow, either, that it is the worst, even for the West. Such a policy has the merit not only of being in the good graces of the power most directly interested in the actual battles now taking place from Vientiane to Saigon, and whose role in the transition from war to armistice will be decisive, but of "by-passing" narrow nationalisms, while giving full consideration to existing economic and cultural imperatives.

The problem, of course, is not to deliver the old federal entity to the power that is strongest by reason of its ideological, political, and military armament. But other than crushing Ho Chi Minh's country under carpet bombing, every solution must take into account North Vietnam's dominance in that region. It does not seem that the quadripartite framework is the least favorable for the channeling and peaceful utilization of this excess of power. Could this framework not permit, better than the confrontation between the two zones, the participation by Vietnam in a statute of neutrality whose first stage would include the reduction of armed forces of the four countries and the transfer of such forces to police units? What would be taken away from Hanoi in the form of immediate power would be returned to it in another form, i.e., by a higher living standard resulting from the resumption of economic relations with the two rice bowls—Cambodia and South Vietnam; by the boost such an arrangement would give to its already vigorous industries; and by the independence that it could regain from China—which is the wish of every Vietnamese patriot, communist or not.

An agreement within such a framework would necessarily include the risk of an ultimate "leap forward" on the part of the dominant power; it is always that way. But it must not be forgotten that this same power, thrown back after its military victory of 1954 upon an overly restricted territory, did respect the Geneva accords for several years, and that it was Saigon's refusal to accede to the reunification of the country that served as pretext for the North to spill over the borders.

Someone who has respected agreements in the past may—just may—respect others, particularly if his intention of doing so is further encouraged by the presence of a persuasive countervailing force.

VII

ESCALATION TOWARD WHAT?

1

𝔖𝔖𝔖𝔖𝔖𝔖𝔖𝔖

The Night of August 4

The evening was not very clear sixty miles off Haiphong on
the North Vietnamese coast: night falls quickly in the Far
East. At 9:52 P.M. on August 4, 1964, the American de-
stroyer *Maddox,* which had seen action two days earlier
against three North Vietnamese torpedo boats, signaled that
she and her sister ship, the *Turner-Joy,* were again under
attack by communist naval units. The *Maddox* also signaled
that none of the torpedoes launched at them had hit home,
and that they had fought a "defensive counterattack." At
10:15 P.M. the two ships signaled that they had sunk one
of the enemy units, but that "the darkness hampered their
action." At midnight the planes of the aircraft carrier *Ticon-
deroga* attacked the North Vietnamese vessels, and sank two.

Twelve hours later—midnight in Washington—Secretary
of Defense Robert McNamara, having become the historian
of the occasion, and filling in the details of a statement made
an hour earlier by President Johnson to the American nation,
announced that reprisal raids on North Vietnam had already
destroyed at least twenty-five enemy torpedo boats and im-

portant fuel-storage facilities. Most observers thought the description of the incident as presented by McNamara to be much less convincing than the version given in Washington of the engagement of August 2 that was barely contested by the communist side.

Many observers remained uncertain for a long time afterward whether the *Maddox* and the *Turner-Joy* had really been attacked early in the night of August 4, in waters which are territorial in the view of the North Vietnamese but located on the high seas in the Western view: wars can begin or spread from such misunderstandings.

Thus the second Vietnamese war was to enter into a new phase: the famous escalation, so often announced since the beginning of the year, had commenced.

Certainly this was not the first time that the 17th Parallel had been crossed. And the Hanoi authorities—experts in the matter—did not fail to recall that many South Vietnamese commando operations, officered or not by Americans, had taken place for three years against the North's territory. In November 1962 I had been told by Ho Chi Minh that there were "imperialist brigands" who had dared to violate the Geneva agreements, and he told me that some of them would be called to account in Hanoi.

Ten days before the first incident in the Gulf of Tonkin, Gen. Nguyen Cao Ky, chief of the South Vietnamese air force, declared publicly that he personally had participated in such missions against the North, which, incidentally, had brought severe criticism by his American colleagues down on his head. And on July 30 as well two Northern coastal islands, Hon Me and Hon Ngu, had been bombarded by South Vietnamese war vessels (and also American vessels, according to Hanoi, which is very debatable). In short, if the Northern leaders knew how to evade the demarcation line at the 17th Parallel in the West in order to bring aid to the guerrillas in the South through Laos, Saigon's allies did not hesitate to outflank it in the East, across the sea, without considering the Northern Republic a "privileged sanctuary," like China in the days of MacArthur.

But the raids of August 4 and 5, which hit seven targets in the Bay of Along at Vinh and caused Hanoi to lose half of its naval force while costing the United States probably no more than three planes and one pilot, changed the nature of the war, just as the establishment of the American strategic command at Saigon in February 1962 had changed it. Washington's engagement, now direct, extended beyond the frontier of an independent country, member of the socialist camp and ally of the Soviet Union and China. The American war effort changed in nature. The conflict became Americanized. The engagement was becoming more difficult.

At that time the strategy of the "graduated response" was defined in several declarations, in conformity with the doctrine made famous by the two men responsible for the affair, McNamara in Washington and General Taylor in Saigon. It could be summed up in three formulas broadcast on August 5 and 6: "We must answer repeated acts of violence against the armed forces of the United States in positive fashion" (Lyndon B. Johnson); "The response will be firm, limited, and will correspond to the importance of the aggression" (Robert McNamara); "All measures will be taken to repulse aggression and prevent further aggression" (Resolution by the United States Congress).

Prevent? Perhaps this little noticed text of the period contained the key to an entire policy that assumed potential and actual risks, and aimed at targets whose choice depended more often on the principle of general reprisals and psychological intimidation than on military considerations. From here on the American leaders believed that all the blows received from a certain but elusive enemy (the Viet Cong) should be returned to a doubtful but clearly visible enemy (North Vietnam).

Graduating the response is fine, but selecting its target properly is another matter. It is stupid to draw a gun in order

to respond to a slap in the face. But it is also stupid to respond with a slap in the face of the neighbor of the man who
has done the hitting. In the following months, American military efforts were to shift from the rice paddies and forests
of the South, where the decisive battles were taking place,
to the installations—first military, then industrial—of the
North. And though aid was reaching the South from the
North, it must be repeated that such aid was not decisive.

What the French general staff in Algiers had tried to ac-
complish against Egypt in 1956—from where, according to
Jacques Soustelle, 60 per cent of the blows struck by the
F.L.N. were launched—the American command was to try
in North Vietnam. These strange strategists, in order to kill
a snake whose head they could not crush, painted its tail red
in order to cut it off—in vain, as everyone knows.

2

∾∾∾∾∾∾∾

It Is Not a Paper Tiger

In September 1964, in Saigon, this was the most pressing problem. One could meet there a growing number of American experts who were persuaded that only reprisals against the North could stop the war effort of the N.L.F.; and such Vietnamese officers as General Ky—whose star was then rising to the greatest heights—maintained that if the conflict in the South was only a civil war among Southerners, he assumed the right for himself, as a Northerner, to start another civil war north of the 17th Parallel. And as his air force men occupied a dominant place among the pretenders to power in Saigon, the risk of escalation grew from day to day.

On September 18 a new incident between American naval units and North Vietnamese units along the Tonkinese coast was reported. Called together by General Khanh for a press conference, we expected him to announce a new operation of reprisal conducted jointly by American and South Vietnamese forces. Instead he spoke only of the relations between Saigon and Phnom Penh. And we learned that Washington had called a halt, and put it very plainly to Nguyen Khanh that he should not mix in the affairs of the Seventh Fleet; that the United States commander would not have his hand forced by his Southern allies, nor permit Saigon to mix in relations between Washington, Hanoi, and Peking. But was this a slowdown in escalation? On the contrary, it was merely an attempt to retain control over operations.

Ten days later it was clear that the American leaders had by no means abandoned their project of "changing the war." In Tokyo, William Bundy, who had become one of the three or four most influential and "energetic" advisers to Mr. Johnson, declared that an "extension of the war might be forced upon the United States by accumulated external pressures."

The talk then in American military circles in Saigon was of the "right of pursuit," so often invoked in Algeria. But this "right," which incidentally is strongly contested by jurists, presupposes that the author of the intervention has been located while trying simultaneously to regain his base and recross the frontier. Which is by no means the case in connection with the combatants infiltrated south of the 17th Parallel. Moreover, for several months the U. S. Air Force did not hesitate to strafe or bomb with napalm columns traversing Laos and believed to be headed for South Vietnam; since June such raids, carried out, incidentally, with the blessing of the Vientiane authorities, had been publicly announced.

On November 1 a new escalation took place: one of the two largest American air bases in Vietnam, at Bien Hoa, fifteen miles from Saigon, was attacked with mortar fire by Viet Cong units, who even managed to infiltrate some commandos. The balance sheet: some twenty U. S. Air Force planes destroyed on the ground (the Viet Cong communiqué claimed fifty-seven) and seven American dead. The affair revealed in particular that the South Vietnamese troops either did poor guard duty when protecting American compounds or actually made common cause with the assailant. The incident was followed by an inevitable reinforcement of American "advisers" with more "advisers," a further Americanization of the battle and a new step on the escalation ladder. Joseph Alsop stated in the *Herald Tribune* that General Taylor had decided to "change the terms of the problem" and retaliate against the North "after each important blow struck by the N.L.F."

On December 24 a Saigon hotel reserved for American officers was bombed; the loss in human life was not heavy, but the challenge was brazen. Was this the moment to meet it? A report addressed by the American Embassy to Washington suggested it, but President Johnson was opposed this time, perhaps in order not to disturb the year-end festivities of the people who had voted for the "President of Peace." But the "possibility of extending the war" was suggested several days later by McGeorge Bundy, special counsel for security matters.

February 1 was the day of the "missed rendezvous" described earlier. McGeorge Bundy, regarded as the best brain in Washington, departed for Saigon. He was to report to the President on General Khanh's personal situation, and how the South would take to possible bombardments from the North. At that same time we learned of Premier Kosygin's sudden departure for Hanoi, with the apparent objective of convincing the North Vietnamese to disassociate themselves from the Chinese and participate in the conference of Communist parties planned for March 1 in Moscow.

Just when the American diplomat was finishing his report and about to take his plane for the United States and the Soviet leader was landing at the Gia Lam airport, an attack on the Holloway Base was reported. That was the Pleiku affair, the most important since that of August 4. The attack gave a decisive impulse to new escalation.

Before McGeorge Bundy had time to give Lyndon Johnson his report, blessing further American support for Khanh and expressing the view that air attacks on the North would have an "exhilarating" effect on the people of the South, the response was unleashed: with bombs and rockets, American and South Vietnamese planes attacked the Dong Hoi region some thirty miles north of the 17th Parallel. Officially, only training camps and fuel-storage tanks were hit. Landing in Saigon after having taken part in one of the raids, Gen. Nguyen Cao Ky declared: "This was the most beautiful day of my life."

But the next day the compound at Qui Nhon, near Hue, where several hundred American military men were billeted, was destroyed by an explosion and some estimates ran to thirty dead. Apparently intimidation had not worked. The planes therefore took off again from Saigon, Bien Hoa, and Da Nang toward the North and again bombed the Dong Hoi sector, but this time nobody went to the trouble of saying that population centers had been spared. The response became a reprisal. And it was then learned that the instructions received by General Taylor upon his departure for Saigon in June, at the end of the very important strategic conference in Honolulu, had also included possible attacks on the Laotian roads, over which aid went to the guerrillas, and the bombing of military installations in North Vietnam.

Decidedly the tiger was not paper, and it howled. *U. S. News & World Report* of February 15 reported that Henry Cabot Lodge, who was to become Special Adviser to the President on Vietnamese affairs, had said that the legal aspect of the problem is the one that matters least and that the United States has the capability of inflicting a great deal of suffering on North Vietnam. And the "shock diplomat" added that he was in favor of taking recourse to that.

3

𝔊𝔊𝔊𝔊𝔊𝔊𝔊

The Ides of March

On February 27 the State Department published a white paper accusing North Vietnam of having launched a regular "war of aggression" against the South, and asking it to choose between peace and "the pursuit of a conflict that will yield increasing destruction for the North."

The argument of the White Paper was not impressive and proofs of Northern intervention were weak, but the American press did not take the trouble to discuss this aspect. From the American viewpoint Moise Tshombe would be within his rights to bombard Cairo, Algiers, or Accra; Antonio Salazar within his to strafe Conakry; Mokhtar Ould Daddah within his to destroy Rabat. The document did not strengthen Washington's politico-juridical position; but it revealed that the American leaders then considered themselves entitled to hit where and when they wanted to. And, after all, they had the means to do so.

Nothing could weaken their determination except the risk of a serious conflict with the great powers of the socialist camp. But what of China? In this period of escalation China was content to fulminate against imperialism. The Soviet Union? Its press was filled with long tirades. All this took place as though Peking and Moscow had only one concern: not to let themselves be outdone by louder accusations in the rival capital. And it seemed as though the American operation, far from reuniting the socialist camp, aggravated the dissensions and made them more poisonous. What better encouragement could the Washington advocates of a permanent extension of the conflict hope for?

The Soviets, balancing peaceful coexistence against the fate of Vietnam, obviously attach more importance to the former than to the latter, and are loath to revise this opinion. But the Chinese? The most common interpretation is that by temporizing, they mean to draw the United States into a trap, force it to swallow the hook and become tied down for a long time in the mud of Asia. The risks are great for Peking. But in the last analysis the price will be still higher for the Americans, and the presence of the "imperialist dragon" at China's portals may ultimately alienate the peoples of Asia from the West and weld the Chinese masses closer together.

Another theory regarding the Chinese attitude points to Moscow and can be summarized as follows: standing aside, the Chinese want to compromise the Soviets by forcing them to admit that they favor appeasement of the West, and coexistence between their own prosperous revisionism and capitalism. But the risk for the Chinese, should the Russians fall in with this, is that escalation will go far enough to lead ultimately to a confrontation of the two great nuclear powers, with full latitude to arbitrate the conflict between them in order to avoid a world war, even to the detriment of the Asians.

This, according to *Jeune Afrique* of April 12, 1965, is approximately what Chou En-lai said to Ahmed Ben Bella when the latter expressed surprise at the obstacles put by Peking in the way of Soviet arms reaching Hanoi. If Moscow installs itself in Vietnam and takes affairs into its own hands, then the matter will be settled like the Cuban affair in 1962 —without those primarily interested having been consulted.

Actually, every one of these arguments can be turned around. And Chinese reserve may simply be the result of the evident insufficiency of its air and naval forces; and of their concern not to give the Americans a pretext to attack their industrial installations, which the U-2s have photographed many times—at least enough for the Americans to know China's infrastructure in sufficient detail to know where to strike in order to make China lose in a few hours all the fruits of ten years of the Chinese revolution's superhuman efforts.

But whatever the reason for the "moderation" or inaction on the part of China and the Soviet Union, the policy encourages the "hawks" against the "doves" in the United States. "You see that the communists give in if one shows determination. We must hit hard, that is the only thing they understand. Why are we waiting to carry this 'good lesson' all the way to China?"

Will this school of thought prevail? In any event, since the beginning of the year the hawks (William Bundy, McNamara, MacNaughton) were clearly dominant in Johnson's entourage while the doves (Vice-President Humphrey, Senate Leader Mike Mansfield, Special Assistant Moyers) were being consulted less and less. For the hawks the problem was not so much to win the war or to hit China, but to make the other side pay very dearly for the coming compromise. They worked out a project, called "December Plan," providing for the systematic bombing of the North so that the United States could offer to stop this bombardment as a major card in negotiations. This is one way of holding a pawn, of selling what one does not have. And as a result the acts of war must multiply.

On March 2 a raid was launched on the North which was not only more massive than preceding raids—160 pursuit and bombing planes participated—but which was also the first that its organizers did not attempt to justify on the grounds of "enemy aggression." The North Vietnamese navy was now regarded as an aggressor *per se,* and therefore permanently culpable. This was perhaps the most significant step in the escalation since August 4: the Americans began to consider themselves entitled to hit the North at their discretion. The North was guilty, because it was communist, because it was a neighbor and accomplice of a people on whose territory armed forces of the United States suffered cruel disappointments, because it did not close its doors to its compatriots from the South who were engaged in combat against the greatest power in the world.

With each blow the hawks showed themselves: on March 10, three thousand marines were sent to Da Nang, formidable shock troops who staged a heroic debarkation on South Vietnamese shores with an incredible luxury of precautions— as though they were not landing in friendly territory. But was there still a "friendly" zone in Vietnam for the Americans?

On March 15 squadrons from the South hit Phu Qui, 180 miles north of the 17th Parallel. The risks were growing—all the more as Saigon discovered the use of phosphorous and napalm bombs. International opinion responded mildly to all that. Strangely enough, it was to react more strongly to the next stage in Saigon's recourse to total war: the use against the Viet Cong of gas of a "temporarily disabling nature"—i.e., against the Vietnamese peasants, for lack of a criterion as to who the Viet Cong are.

On March 22 the general staff at Saigon admitted the use of this most despised if not most reprehensible weapon. Obviously the Americans had by then acquired such a feeling of military superiority that their habitual concern to save their reputation and popularity had completely disappeared. After attaining a certain degree of power, does one lose a sense of balance and concern for one's reputation? If one is so strong, does one need to be esteemed?

After the end of March the American raids on North Vietnam came to be called "armed reconnaisance missions." The pilots were given complete latitude in "selecting" targets that seemed promising. Was the doctrine of graduated response, as followed by McNamara and Taylor, not in danger of getting off the track? The "flexible response" increasingly resembled a spring which, long held back, finally burst with tremendous fury.

On March 29 Ambassador Maxwell Taylor, called back for consultations, landed in Washington. While he waited for an audience with President Johnson that took some time to materialize, a new step on the escalation ladder was reached in Saigon: On March 30 a bomb destroyed the American Embassy in South Vietnam. The toll was heavy. Ambassador Alexis Johnson, deputy to General Taylor, was wounded; eighteen dead, among them two Americans, were lifted from pools of blood and debris strewn all over the busy Ham Nghi boulevard.

When he was finally received by the President, Maxwell Taylor demanded the immediate dispatch of reinforcements (Walter Lippmann wrote at that point that 350,000 men should be sent to Vietnam, which was some step on the accelerator of his own campaign for peace!). But strangely enough the challenge hurled at the United States was not taken up by the proud Texan in the White House: he was just in the process of preparing a speech containing political overtures, which would go poorly with a simultaneous intensification of the war. Meanwhile the American intelligence services reached the conclusion that the operation had been launched against Hanoi's advice.

Certainly, this was the moment for Washington to warn of a new escalation phase: the Chinese Ambassador in Warsaw was warned by his American colleague that reprisals might on occasion be visited on China. But instead the United States took a different tone. While Lyndon Johnson declared on April 1 that "no conference on Vietnam can have any positive results," Washington no longer discouraged U Thant from departing for a reconciliation mission in Asia: this was also the moment when seventeen neutral states—among them the United Arab Republic, Yugoslavia, and Algeria—launched an appeal for conciliation, and British Labour Deputy Warbey revealed, on his return from a trip to Hanoi, that the North Vietnamese leaders were not opposed to unconditional negotiation. At that moment the early departure for Asia by Patrick Gordon Walker, former foreign office chief, was being announced. Prime Minister Harold Wilson had tied his official diplomacy to Washington's, but this did not keep him from undertaking parallel soundings.

Was this the coming calm? A reorientation of the crisis toward the search for a political solution? Had the new American adage, "bomb in order to negotiate," reached its limits? An aerial battle between American F-105s and MIGs claimed by Peking as hers, far from further raising the tension, provoked new hopes, for Washington attempted to play down the affair and abstained from declaring officially that these were machines belonging to Red China. So?

4

❦❦❦❦❦❦❦

Mr. Johnson's Billion

Then, on April 7 in Baltimore, President Johnson presented his peace plan to the world. It can be summarized in four points:

1) Washington will agree to negotiate unconditionally, i.e., without further waiting for the famous "sign" of non-intervention demanded until recently of Hanoi by Secretary of State Rusk.

2) But the United States will not speak directly with the Viet Cong, whom it regards merely as executors of Hanoi.

3) The objective is to obtain the independence of a neutral South Vietnam, which however can appeal to its friends in case of danger.

4) The United States is ready to spend a billion dollars for the economic development of the entire region, including North Vietnam.

An interesting declaration, to be sure, because it did away with the "prior conditions" that had rendered vain all hope of a settlement (Hanoi, claiming non-intervention, could not very well announce the end of its intervention), and accepted the theory of South Vietnam's neutralization and an ultimate reunification of the two zones.

But Mr. Johnson's "overture" had one fundamental flaw: his refusal to negotiate with those who were fighting, i.e., the guerrillas in the South. To be sure, they were entirely free in their actions, but it was also obvious that if kept at arm's length, they could prevent any effort at agreement. Once more, face to face with a four-headed interlocutor—the Soviet Union, China, North Vietnam, and the N.L.F.— the American specialists, strangely, gave privileged treatment to Moscow and Hanoi, to the detriment of those who were probably the most important and the most stubbornly opposed to conciliation: Peking and the N.L.F.

Complementing this strange strategy—consisting as we have said in cutting off the snake's tail, as long as one cannot crush its head—was a curious diplomacy—consisting of throwing water on all the zones where the fire was least violent in an effort to extinguish the conflagration.

The financial offer of a "Marshall Plan for Southeast Asia," was obviously a psychological error: to offer dollars for tomorrow to those whom one bombs today, cannot but arouse reactions of offended dignity. Which was the case.

A tentatively negative response on the part of the communist powers had been anticipated. Peking turned out to be violent and indignant. Hanoi's answer was much more moderate; it contained Prime Minister Pham Van Dong's famous "Four Points." And while the Hanoi leaders stretched out a framework for negotiations, Chou En-lai said in Algeria that he expected China to be bombed, and that he would be glad if it were—for such operations would either weld the socialist camp together again or demonstrate the "treason" of the Soviet Union.

Their anti-Soviet feelings and their pride thus led the Chinese to violate one of the fundamental principles of Mao's policy: to scorn an enemy's strategy, but to respect his tactics. Strategically China is perhaps certain to master the Asian continent in ten to thirty years. But in 1965 tactics required that China not underestimate America's fantastic power, nor step into Washington's net. For if China gets into such a trap, it will find itself doubly trapped, because American strategists know how to play not only poker but chess.

One can see fairly well where escalation leads. Aside from its frenetic and adventurous aspects, the war definitely seems to be shifting from the South Vietnamese ground to the North Vietnamese air, from knife to helicopter.

But beyond that, whether China will be attacked or not, it seems that Mr. Johnson and his men are trying to push the whole matter to a higher plane, to the very summit. They know that they are weak and involved "in a bad business" on the local terrain. But as soon as a dispute is lifted to the global plane, where men talk in terms of ultimate power, Washington resumes its authority, its prestige, and its trump cards that in 1965 are without equal. Lost in the rice paddies and even in the Gulf of Tonkin, American power can redress itself and talk with a loud voice as soon as the dispute is widened and internationalized, and the Cuban situation of 1962 recreated.

One may condemn this strategy of brinkmanship and consider it intolerable that in order to avoid local defeats on a terrain where they operate in violation of an international accord which they endorsed, even though they did not sign it, the Americans thus directly imperil world peace. But the dogmatism of the Asian socialist capitals has also played a part in this situation.

When the Vietnamese people were about to "celebrate" the twentieth anniversary of the war between the French and the Viet Minh, which began in September 1943—a war interrupted only from 1954 to 1959—their distress was greatly increased by massive B-52 attacks on the Mekong Delta, launched by the United States Air Force to crush the Viet Cong.

Saigon and Washington claim that Vietnam's unfortunate peasants are victims of Hanoi's *invasion* led by the communist Viet Cong, and that the peasants are anxious to be delivered from the aggressors by nationalist and American troops. But meantime, waves of B-52s are bombing *them,* although the targets for these planes are supposed to be military objectives. But can anyone who has seen these B-52s in action and witnessed the enormous destructiveness of their huge bombs doubt that this is a terror operation? What could be *less* selective than such methods of warfare as napalm, defoliation, and "temporarily disabling" gas?

The alleged goal is the destruction of the Front's underground installations. But are these found in the Delta, where the river floods the surrounding countryside? In the forests, where the Viet Cong are in sufficient control not to need underground caves? In the villages, where bombs destroy houses before cellars?

Since 1945, when France began the war, and since 1954, when the United States took it over, there has been considerable escalation, of which some steps were more obvious than others: General Harkins' arrival in Vietnam in 1962, the first bombing attacks on the North in February 1965, the Marine landings in July 1965. This blind battering of a whole country and its people forces America's foreign friends to ask if she cannot find better ways to fulfill her responsibilities in Asia.

French observers have been moved to express their views on the Vietnamese conflict partly because they sympathize with the Vietnamese people whose suffering they shared when their country was at war in Vietnam. But most foreign observers have spoken up because in their view the road taken by Washington imperils peaceful coexistence in the short run, and the future of the West and of American democracy, as well as the equilibrium in Asia, in the long run.

The most fallacious of all American arguments is the "falling domino" theory, according to which the loss of Vietnam would result in a chain-reaction, leading to the loss of Cambodia, Thailand, Burma, Malaysia, India, Indonesia, and the Philippines, and would raise doubts in the minds of America's friends all over the world. But the falling domino theory can be countered by pointing out that the American position in most of these countries is very different from their armed grip on Vietnam. From Kuala Lampur to New Delhi, from Rangoon to Manila, the United States' position is based not on force but on friendship and public interest. The war Washington has conducted in South Vietnam ever since the flagrant violations of the 1954 Geneva Agreements (which the North was observing at that time) is entirely different from the sane and equitable relations which the United States maintains with most Asian, African, or Latin American countries—relations which would become even better if the war in Vietnam were to end. Moreover, while the sight of Marines battling at Da Nang may reassure men like Chiang or Tshombe, it drives to despair millions of people—in the West, in the uncommitted nations, and in the socialist world —who place their greatest hopes in peaceful coexistence, which is the key to the liberalization of the totalitarian regimes.

For the United States it is strange to choose the new Syngman Rhees over the hopes of young Poles, Brazilians, Hungarians, or Algerians. Some day Mr. McNamara's magnificent electronic computers should determine how much every square foot of Vietnamese territory occupied by American soldiers or their allies costs the United States in terms of world friendship.

For two major reasons friends of the United States hope that it will promote a political settlement of the war in Vietnam by acting on rather than talking of its desire for an honorable peace. The first reason comes quite naturally to the mind of a Frenchman who has personally experienced the history of decolonization, and who has observed the training and "conditioning" of the men charged with weeding out communism in South Vietnam. Methods from brainwashing to intensive interrogation have been known in Indochina ever since the French war, in Algeria, and wherever else attempts have been made to overcome revolutionary totalitarianism with counter-revolutionary totalitarianism. There is no doubt about the effects of these methods upon their victims, but the effects on those who apply them are equally great. No Frenchman would want to see an enlisted man or officer returning to American shores who has surpassed the Asian communists in the art of remodeling souls. The means employed can vitiate any end, and no executioner can really remain untouched by the tortures he inflicts. These are poisons for which there are few antidotes, and it is to be hoped that American democracy will not be corrupted by citizens who will have learned in Asia how to train men to be like animals.

There are more serious considerations. The methods employed by the United States since July 1965, such as carpet bombings, could enable Washington if not to win the war at least to crush South Vietnam—and the Viet Cong with it. But after the B-52s have finished, what will be left of the Vietnamese people? Thus, in the long run, the American strategists will have done a good job for Peking. For if ever there was a solid, deep-rooted, historic obstacle to Chinese expansionism, it was the Vietnamese nation—this proud people who are communists, non-communists, and anti-communists —which has resisted France and the United States, not merely because they were white and capitalists, but because they were foreigners.

The point is not to play Vietnamese nationalism against China, but to be aware that these forces exist and to permit them to operate. Should the United States decide not to help Vietnam live under a regime of its own choice, should it elect to "destroy in order not to lose," should it continue to prefer dead Vietnamese to Red Vietnamese, China will have won an historic victory.

In another day Mongol emperors sacked and massacred Asian peoples before subjugating them. In Vietnam the first part of the job would then have been done by the Americans. And thus the Chinese would have only to wait for that moment to come, and then play the role of rebuilder and peacemaker. A strange strategy.

It will be said: "Very well. But what do you propose?" One can well understand that a people under bombing attacks does not want to give in. And the American refusal to recognize the N.L.F. as a negotiating partner or to suspend their bombing raids on the North gives Peking and its allies the best escape hatch from all negotiations. But the main thing is not to know who is responsible for the war, but to find means of stopping it—for the benefit of the Vietnamese people.

Such a political settlement of the Vietnamese military conflict cannot depend on the withdrawal of the Americans from the zones they occupy. There can be no Dunkirk in this case without terrible retribution from the Seventh Fleet (it is always useful to take realities into account in political affairs). Nor can a settlement depend on the repression, by force, of the Asiatic revolution, in sectors where abuses by the former ruling classes and Western mistakes have paved its way.

It must take shape on three planes:

1. *Among South Vietnamese,* who are those most concerned, for their soil is being ravaged by the war, and 90 per cent of the fighting in either camp is done by their men. 2. *Between Saigon and Hanoi,* for the peace in the entire country depends on the relations between the two Vietnamese capitals, as well as the nature of the reunification toward which all patriots are quite naturally tending, a reunification that should take place after a delay to be set by them. 3. *Among the great powers,* for the pursuit and intensification of the conflict is

due in part to their intervention—military on the part of the United States, political on the part of China—and the end of the fighting and eventual guarantees for peace depend on their relative impartiality.

1. *The South Vietnamese* must resolve several types of problems by negotiating among themselves. They must give a place in their state structure to a political Left represented in battle by the National Liberation Front; the Front, for that reason alone, might carry the decisive weight in the country's future political development. Whether we deplore this or not, the fact remains that those who have committed themselves and taken risks always carry more weight in the end than the fence straddlers.

But the Front is quite diversified, and the revolutionary Popular Party (the communists) has played such a large role in it that any return to legality must lead to a redistribution of forces on the basis of political tendencies, social class tensions, and religious influences. For this integration to take place within a framework of legality, the South Vietnamese must give themselves institutions capable of expressing the true relationship of forces, and give opportunities to the revolutionaries as well as to the conservatives—which is not exactly what was done by the Diem regime, and which rendered the resort to force inevitable.

It also is the task of the men in the South to define the neutrality that should be the foundation of their country's international relations, and to state specifically what type of foreign assistance would be compatible with such a stance—whether, for example, external intervention in case of violation of its neutrality would be permissible, and on what basis and by whose decisions.

Finally, only in the framework of such non-engagement can the citizens of South Vietnam visualize the reconstitution of an Indochina encompassing the various countries brought together by past colonialization, which remains the best framework for their economic development and diplomatic equilibrium.

2. *Between Saigon and Hanoi* relationships of peaceful co-existence should also be established that would take the place of the present rupture. A plan for normalization could be worked out, including, in the beginning, a reduction of military strength, followed by the reëstablishment of economic exchanges, such as Southern rice against Northern coal, which would put an end to an abnormal situation and probably permit the Northern regime to engage in the more democratic practices that ordinarily accompany a certain raising of the living standard.

Finally, the two governments should progressively undertake consultations with a view to preparing reunification—consultations such as Pham Van Dong proposed in vain to Diem at the end of 1955. But it is known that the men in the North are not in a hurry for that: possibly they would prefer to join only a South first rebuilt and equipped with Western capital.

3. *Co-operation among the great powers* will largely condition that of Southerners among themselves, and of Hanoi with Saigon. However it may be attained, it must include a non-intervention pact that must be the very basis of any peace in Vietnam. The word "neutralization," as it is sometimes used in connection with Vietnam and Indochina or Southeast Asia, is perhaps poorly chosen, because it implies a passivity on the part of the interested peoples. In any event, to reduce the risk process should take its cue from that selected by Cambodia, which was the first to make such a status the aim of its own policy, and only subsequently sought to have it guaranteed by the great powers.

What remains is that the two Vietnams, Cambodia, and Laos should proclaim their joint interest in remaining outside of any military coalition, regardless of its ideological orientation, and that the liquidation of strategic bases and of permanent foreign military forces is a natural objective of all international negotiations on the subject of Indochina.

Perhaps the great powers, even though the interested parties have hardly proposed it to them, could reach an understanding on a guarantee of independence for the Indochinese countries that would go so far as to allow them to appeal to a foreign state in case of "danger"—as Cambodia obtained during the last hours of the Geneva Conference of 1954. Because that formula was proposed by President Johnson, one may well assume that Peking and Hanoi will oppose it. Yet the realities are so strong that they may change their minds. One could well imagine that such an appeal would not be possible except through the intermediary of the International Control Commission, created eleven years ago, whose powers quite naturally would have to be increased again if such a new agreement were to be reached.

It is ultimately the task of the great powers—the United States, China, Great Britain, the Soviet Union, and France— to define the organism of international assistance, which General de Gaulle said recently was desirable, and which should offer its aid to the zone that is to be reconstructed, located between the China Sea, the Mekong River, and the Gulf of Siam, with full utilization of the Mekong River one of the goals of development in that region. It would be useful if the Big Five would also include in such efforts Japan and Australia, whose industry and interests qualify them for the task. Would that transform confrontation into co-operation?

What is necessary, finally, is to return to the Geneva Agreements of 1954, by integrating the N.L.F. into the legal fabric of the South; by avoiding specification of when reunification of the two Vietnams should take place; and by establishing between the two "states"—how can they be called differently now?—normal relations. Once the vanity of escalation and intransigent behavior has been demonstrated, will this be com-

pletely impossible? I agree that such suggestions, written
amidst the loudest clashing of arms in 1965, may seem quite
naïve. The American armada did not debark in 1965 only to
re-embark in 1966. But was it not General Taylor who declared, in September 1964, that "every war is terminated
by negotiation"?

Negotiations are possible, especially since they have already been taken up in rough form by two of the interested
parties, Washington and Hanoi.

Until President Johnson's speech in Baltimore on April 7,
1965, any possible progress was blocked by the "Rusk Doctrine," which rejected all negotiations as long as Hanoi was
not ready to halt its "aggression" against the South. Since
Hanoi was denying—not very convincingly—that it was in-
terfering in the South, this meant going around in circles.

The Baltimore speech removed at least that obstacle and
proclaimed the principle of unconditional negotiation. But
there remained a further obstacle to all serious peace efforts:
the disregard on the part of the United States for the N.L.F.'s
true nature. Interest in peace efforts was increased several
days after Johnson's speech, however, by the announcement
in Hanoi of Dong's Four Points, outlining North Vietnamese
conditions for a settlement. The Four Points can be summarized as follows: 1. Any settlement must be preceded by a
recognition of Vietnam's independence and unity. 2. The
Vietnamese people must be free to decide on conditions for
their reunification. 3. The Vietnamese people must be able
to decide on their own government. 4. Cessation of all foreign intervention is a prerequisite for a return to peace.
Nothing in this declaration was in fundamental conflict with
the American position, announced the day before, unless it
was the assertion in point 3 that the N.L.F. represents the
South Vietnamese people and that its program should constitute Vietnam's ultimate political framework.

American doctrine now began to take an even more favorable turn toward peace. On July 28, during a press confer-

ence, President Johnson hinted that the Viet Cong would be heard in the event of negotiations. On September 1 Senator Mike Mansfield issued a five-point program that was immediately approved by the President (if not by all major officials). The program differed from Dong's Four Points only on the role to be played by the N.L.F. in South Vietnam after the war; but it also strongly emphasized self-determination. Favorable political developments could be expected as a result, particularly since Arthur Goldberg, the new American Ambassador to the United Nations, had clearly been charged by the President to explore peace conditions more actively.

Both sides, however, remained in conflict on the "prior conditions"; the North Vietnamese spokesman joined his Chinese colleagues in maintaining that no negotiations could begin before all American troops had been withdrawn, which Washington would not accept. Meanwhile, in an interview with the Vietnamese expert and historian Philippe Devillers, published in *Le Monde* on August 14, Ho Chi Minh indicated that a political solution would be possible only if the bombing raids against the North ceased "immediately," and if American intervention ended; but he did not add "immediately" to his second condition, which made it appear that for Hanoi the only absolute prior condition was the cessation of bombings. This demand was considered fair even by such good friends of the United States as Canadian Prime Minister Lester Pearson.

While no actual negotiations began, no Washington gesture went unanswered by Hanoi. At least on one occasion Washington ignored a North Vietnamese signal: in May 1965, after the bombings had been suspended for four days by President Johnson at the instigation of Senators J. William Fulbright and Robert Kennedy, a Hanoi representative in an uncommitted capital announced that Dong's Four Points were not "prior conditions" but general principles, which, if accepted, would make the search for a settlement possible. A few hours later, however, the bombings were resumed, before the White House had been advised of the North Vietnamese diplomat's gesture. The opportunity was missed but new perspectives were opened.

Actually, even though any rapprochement between Washington and Hanoi for the purpose of true negotiations is desirable, a more promising path toward a settlement probably lies elsewhere. There are too many misunderstandings between the two capitals, with each basing its attitude on an untruth—Hanoi claims that it is not intervening in the South, and Washington insists that the battle in the South is an invasion, while in reality it is a rebellion which originated locally but which Hanoi has increasingly supplied. The war originated in the South and is being waged and suffered by the South, although with growing participation by the North. The South nevertheless is the seat of the conflagration, and it can be extinguished only there.

As long as the American government is denouncing the North's *military* intervention in the South, why does it want to add a *political* dimension to that intervention? As long as the American government is struggling against the spread of Northern influence in the South, why does it give the North the power to decide on war and peace below the 17th Parallel? It is not up to the North Vietnamese to terminate a war in which they play an important but subordinate part; it is up to the South, not only because it is in line with reality, but also because it is in line with the much desired objective of peace.

Western policy should try neither to build an artificial anti-communist system in Vietnam nor to return to power one of the groups that have been fighting each other for so many years; it should try instead to reëstablish *legitimacy* and permit authority to rest on a popular base. This legitimacy—violated by Diemism, foreign intervention, and a succession of coups—must be reëstablished, first by permitting a resumption of political life, and subsequently by permitting the various revolutionary forces inside the Viet Cong to integrate themselves into such a legal framework.

Various procedures toward this end are possible. The best appears to be an effort to seek a cease-fire with the Viet Cong's military leaders, because that would mean drawing the most appropriate spokesmen into negotiation, without necessitating official recognition of them by Washington or Saigon. Between military leaders in the field such contacts are normal. They would certainly make subsequent political developments possible, whether or not the N.L.F. accepts the cease-fire. This approach would also permit the various parties to circumvent the prior condition that all American troops must leave first, and would enable the Saigon authorities to participate in this phase of the negotiations.

While such talks with the Viet Cong would take place within a military framework, to be gradually extended to encompass political talks as well, the Saigon regime should be democratized to the point where it would permit a new debate between the South's various political and religious forces; the convocation of a national congress to which the N.L.F. would be invited after the end of hostilities; and the establishment of a more representative government than those of the past two years. In this fashion South Vietnam's actual political pattern would be redesigned by the South Vietnamese themselves, and the country's reconstruction could be begun with the help of Front members, who could finally return home.

No political solution, of course, can last unless negotiations include the North, the interested great powers, and Vietnam's neighbors. But peace must be begun in the South, by Southerners, just as the war began there. This does not require permanent partition of Vietnam. Its future must be based on unity and independence. But long traditions, the Geneva Agreements, the war, ten years of a different life and dissimilar political programs all have made the South different from the North.

Pending natural reunification within ten or twenty years, as foreseen by Southern leaders, intelligent policies should encourage the South's separate personality and the establishment of a regime that can discuss conditions for reunification with the North on mutually agreeable terms. This is necessary because by temperament, custom, and recent history the South is more democratic than the North and enjoys a diversity that has often expressed itself by force of arms while being unable to affirm itself in votes. There is a good chance that South Vietnam, under Front pressure, will opt for socialism. But there is also a good chance that socialism there would not be totalitarian as it is in the North.

It must also be remembered that the Front's program clearly favors a Cambodian-Laotian type of neutralism. A Southern regime, as described above, practicing détente and reducing its military establishment, could serve as a good example for the North. Moreover Dong's Four Points are opposed to Vietnam's two zones tying themselves down with military pacts. What is neutrality, if not non-participation in military alliances? In fact the establishment of neutralist regimes in three of the former Indochinese countries would open the road to a military, if not ideological, neutralization of the whole area.

From every point of view, if South Vietnam were given a new chance through a peaceful solution to its present problems, it could do more than merely survive. Its political system would hardly be conservative. But does the United States want to install a new Diem in Saigon, or would it prefer to let the Vietnamese people, at last, choose their own government? If the latter is to be the case, the South's diversity and unique character, which give the Viet Cong its revolutionary drive, will have to find expression outside armed combat. To proscribe and crush these revolutionary forces and drive them North is to start the Diemist adventure all over again. To integrate them and offer them a place corresponding to their social and human importance in tomorrow's state is to respect realities that are neither Chinese nor American but simply Vietnamese.

Index

227, 228, 233, 238, 242, 248, 253, 271, 272, 279, 285
New Republic, 182
New Yorker, The, 52
New York *Herald Tribune,* 83, 225, 227, 263
New York Times, The, 42, 225, 228
New Zealand, 12
Nghi, Le Thanh, 49
Nghiem, General Le Van, 133
Ngo family, 18, 35, 52, 64, 67, 68, 76-80, 81-91, 104, 106, 107, 115, 118, 122, 132; *see also* Can, Ngo Dinh; Diem, Ngo Dinh; Nhu, Ngo Dinh; Nhu, Mme. Ngo Dinh; Thuc, Archbishop Ngo Dinh
Nguyen Ba Tong, 208
Nhan-Dan, 42
Nhu, Ngo Dinh, x, 19-21, 23, 52, 56, 64, 79, 81-84, 85-90, 124, 156, 158, 196, 197
Nhu, Mme. Ngo Dinh (Tran Le Xuan), x, 21, 78-80, 81, 87, 88, 95, 123, 210
Nolting, Frederick, 57, 66, 71, 119
Norodom Palace, Saigon, 92
North Vietnam, viii, xii, 4, 10, 11, 28, 29, 32-50, 57, 67, 68, 102-103, 104, 115, 118, 126, 135, 159, 167, 173, 182-83, 222, 223, 228, 229, 230, 232, 250, 252, 257, 258-59, 261, 264, 265, 269, 271, 272, 284, 285
North Vietnamese Communist Party, 42, 43, 48, 232; Congress of, 3rd, 49-50; *see also* Lao Dong
Nuclear power, vii
Nung, Pham, 49

O'Daniel, General, 62
Oai, Tran Tu, 125
Oanh, Vice-President, 194
Operation Vulture, 62

Pacifism, 187, 222
Pakistan, 12
Pasternak, Boris, 56
Pathet Lao, 237, 251
Patriotic Front of North Vietnam, 238

Patti, Commander, 33, 61
Pearson, Lester, 282
Penchenier, Georges, 179
People's Army of North Vietnam, 161
People's Democratic Republic, *see* North Vietnam
People's Revolutionary Party, *see* Popular Revolutionary Party
Personalism, 20, 56, 82, 88, 128
Petroleum Academy, Baku, 45
Phat, Huynh Tan, 171, 233, 238
Phat, General Lam Van, 133, 135, 148
Phat, Diem, South Vietnam, 105
Phat-Giao Viet-Nam (Vietnamese Buddhism), 75
Philippine Islands, 12, 275
Phnom Penh, Cambodia, 237, 241, 243, 244, 248, 250, 261
Phouma, Prince Souvanna, 58
Phu Loi, South Vietnam, 29
Phu Qui, North Vietnam, 268
Pinay, French Foreign Minister, 21, 26
Plain of Joncs region, 52, 53, 71, 161, 173
Pleiku, attack on, 233, 235, 236, 263
Pleven, René, 225, 229
Police forces, 31, 82
Pompidou, Georges, 226
Popular Revolutionary Party, 57-58, 172, 229, 278
Poulo Condore, 96, 97
Prisoners of the Diem regime, liberation of, 96-98
Prostitution in Saigon, 80

Quang Ngai region, 52, 53, 162
Quat, Pham Huy, xiii, 98
Quinh, Father Hoang, 104, 208-209, 218
Qui Nhon, South Vietnam, 208
Quyen, Dr., 144, 221

Rabemananjara, 88
Radio Saigon, 133, 148
Ramparts magazine, viii
Red River, 4
Red River Delta, 37-38, 43
Reinhardt, Ambassador, 244

ABOUT THE AUTHOR

JEAN LACOUTURE was born in Bordeaux in 1921. He has received degrees in law, in letters, and in political science. He served as press attaché to General Leclerc in Indochina in 1945 and was attaché to the Resident General in Rabat (French Morocco) from 1947 until 1949. From 1950 to 1951 M. Lacouture was Diplomatic Editor for *Combat* and in 1951 he joined the staff of *Le Monde*. He was the Cairo correspondent for *France-Soir* from 1953 until 1956, and subsequently has served *Le Monde* first as head of its overseas bureau and since 1957 as a reporter. In this country he has recently been a contributor to *The New York Review of Books*. M. Lacouture also teaches at L'Institut du Développement Economique et Social.

VINTAGE POLITICAL SCIENCE
AND SOCIAL CRITICISM

VINTAGE HISTORY EUROPEAN

VINTAGE HISTORY—AMERICAN

VINTAGE HISTORY AND CRITICISM OF
LITERATURE, MUSIC, AND ART

A free catalogue of VINTAGE BOOKS *will be sent at your request. Write to* Vintage Books, 457 Madison Avenue, New York, New York 10022.